THE C... GALENOR

WARDWELL

VALLENVOREN

THE SPINE OF

THE NORTHERN ISLES

THE FALKERON CLOISTERS

CAWDER

MARROWGATE

CAIATHOS

BIG DEEP

BLIGHDON

THE TORDELL CLOISTERS

BATHYN

THE SEA OF THE DAWN

EAST TO AIDURRA

N
W   E
S

Brightrun River

BEROGES

PRAISE FOR *A SONG OF ASH AND MOONLIGHT*

"A lush and bewitching gothic romance, where the inner lives of the characters are just as intricately crafted as their sumptuously magical world. I was completely swept away."

— Ava Reid, #1 *New York Times* bestselling author of *A Study in Drowning*

"Claire Legrand at her best! This page-turner of a book will leave you on the edge of your seat, with searing love, furious battles, and twists you'll never see coming."

— Beth Revis, *New York Times* bestselling coauthor of *Night of the Witch*

"*A Song of Ash and Moonlight* sets achingly genuine characters against a stunning world and lush mythos, expertly counterbalanced by a heart-wrenchingly sweet romance. Claire Legrand is a master of sweeping, intricate fantasy."

— Sara Raasch, *New York Times* bestelling coauthor of *Night of the Witch*

"As usual, Legrand leaves her readers breathless and dazed. Her Middlemist world is exquisitely immersive and the pages sparkle with a tender tale of intrigue, romance and extraordinary mythmaking."

— Roshani Chokshi, *New York Times* bestselling author of *The Last Tale of the Flower Bride*

"This is the type of book that stays with you—like an imprint on your heart. Claire Legrand crafts a heart-achingly beautiful story that's captivating, thrilling, gritty, at times spooky, and utterly magical."

— Kate Dramis, *Sunday Times* bestselling
author of *A Curse of Saints*

"Claire Legrand has created A vibrant, ruthless world in which the magically annointed aren't always blessed, and the burden of responsibility carries with it sacrifice and grief. A lush story a reader can fall into and never want to emerge from, where entire worlds exist in the details and the characters are people we want to know and love. A masterful fantasy romance by the talented Legrand."

— Grace Draven, *USA Today* bestselling
author of *Radiance*

A SONG OF ASH AND MOONLIGHT

THE MIDDLEMIST TRILOGY · BOOK TWO

ALSO BY
CLAIRE LEGRAND

The Empirium Trilogy
Furyborn
Kingsbane
Lightbringer

The Middlemist Trilogy
A Crown of Ivy and Glass

A SONG OF ASH AND MOONLIGHT

THE MIDDLEMIST TRILOGY · BOOK TWO

CLAIRE LEGRAND

sourcebooks
casablanca

Copyright © 2024 by Claire Legrand
Cover and internal design © 2024 by Sourcebooks
Jacket design by Stephanie Gafron/Sourcebooks
Cover illustration © Nekro
Map illustration by Travis Hasenour

Published by Sourcebooks Casablanca, an imprint of Sourcebooks
P.O. Box 4410, Naperville, Illinois 60567-4410
(630) 961-3900
sourcebooks.com

Cataloging-in-Publication data is on file with the Library of Congress.

Printed and bound in the United States of America.
MA 10 9 8 7 6 5 4 3 2 1

for all the women who protect their hearts with thorns

PROLOGUE

Farrin opened her eyes to a strange world full of smoke.

She didn't recognize the walls around her, or the ceiling above her, and she didn't understand why the air was so choked and bitter. For a moment, she lay frozen in her cocoon of quilts—yes, these were quilts around her, the ones from her bed: one white with tiny green leaves, one a soft gray like morning in winter, both decorated with her mother's embroidery—and she thought to herself, as she always did when waking from a nightmare, *My name is Farrin Ashbourne. I am eleven years old. I am safe at home, at Ivyhill. My sisters are Mara and Gemma. My parents are Gideon and Philippa. My name is Farrin Ashbourne.*

She pressed a finger to her thigh with each name: *Farrin. Mara. Gemma. Gideon. Philippa.* Five names, five fingers. The familiar recitation cleared her mind. Rooted once again in the waking world, she was finally able to understand that she was not in her bedroom but in her music room on the second floor, lying underneath the piano in a nest of pillows.

The room had been hers since she could remember, and she loved it with every ounce of her being. It boasted soaring ceilings, and little stone birds that perched on the ivied rafters, and huge windows of rippled glass. She liked to push those open on pleasant days and imagine her music drifting across the grounds to greet the earth, the flowers, the tenant farmers in their tidy fields. Long curtains flanked each window—creamy, delicate, fluttery in breezes—and all along the far side of the room, organized neatly on gleaming mahogany shelves, were her collections of sheet music and composer biographies and treatises on bowing technique, and near the windows, on a fancy little pedestal, was a tasseled velvet bed for her kitten, Osmund.

In the middle of the night, Farrin often left her bedroom to creep up to the second floor and make a nest under the piano, which felt secretive and wonderful, as if under the piano was a whole other cozy world to which only she had the key. In her safe, pretty house, in her own safe, private room, in the safe, hidden world under the piano: this was Farrin's favorite place in the whole world.

And it was on fire.

That was the reason for the smoke, and the orange glow at the windows, and the feeling, everywhere, of terrible, encroaching heat.

Ivyhill was on fire.

Panic tore away the lingering fog of sleep, panic like nothing Farrin had ever known. Her heart hammering, horrible coughs seizing her all at once, she scooped up Osmund, who was cowering beside her in the pillows, his black hair standing on end, hissing at something—perhaps at the smoke, or the fire itself. With Osmund cradled to her chest, Farrin ran for the door in bare feet, her braid swinging, and threw it open.

The hallway beyond was black and seething, and the smell of the smoke was terrible—nothing like the sweet, piney scent of wood crackling in the hearth, nothing like the warm breadiness of Mrs. Rathmont's ovens downstairs. It *stung*, lashing at Farrin's throat and nostrils with every breath she sucked into her lungs. She threw an arm over her mouth, eyes watering, Osmund clawing frantically at her nightgown. She could hardly breathe; the smoke was vile, unstoppable, and it was laced with something *else*, something biting and brittle, like the charge of a coming storm.

A chill swept through Farrin, even as she stood there sweating in the sweltering heat. She knew that smell. It was the smell of magic, searing and furious. A spell, she suspected—a spell crafted with wicked intent.

Ivyhill hadn't simply caught fire. No, someone had set fire to it. And Farrin knew only one family equal to such a task, a family with power and resources to rival her own, a family that hated the Ashbournes as much as the Ashbournes hated them.

The House of Bask.

Something crashed downstairs, something huge and groaning that made the floor shake under Farrin's feet. She staggered back into her music room, quaking with fear, coughing so hard it hurt. Tears streamed down her face as she peered down the hallway to the right, then the left. The left, she thought, looked a bit dimmer than the right, which she hoped meant fewer flames. She prayed to Caiathos, god of the earth and all its elements, though something in her heart told her the prayer was useless.

If the Basks had indeed set this fire—if they had found spellcrafters clever enough to break through Ivyhill's protective wards—then the long-dead gods couldn't help her. They were all going to burn. All of them. Mama and Papa. Mara. Gemma. Gilroy. Mrs. Rathmont. Madame Baines. Every maid, every cook.

The Basks wanted only one thing. Farrin had learned this at her father's knee.

The Basks wanted to destroy her family.

She tucked Osmund into her nightgown and pressed his tiny head against her breastbone, hoping the thin fabric would somehow protect him from the smoke. Then she ran left down the hallway, hardly noticing when Osmund lodged his claws in her skin. At the hallway's end stood two staircases. One led upstairs; the other would take her down to the first floor.

Farrin paused, wiped the tears from her eyes. Her hand came away wet and black with smoke. Was the fire upstairs or downstairs? Which way should she go?

She sucked in a breath and tried to yell for her parents, for her sisters, but she couldn't get out a word, only a sort of rasping sound, desperate and frightening. Had the smoke taken away her voice? Would she ever get it back? What if she chose the wrong stairs? Having no voice would then, perhaps, be the least of her problems.

Farrin let out a sob. Her chest drew tight with a primal despair. Was she going to die? She was. Her house was going to kill her.

Osmund had gone still under her nightgown, though Farrin could still feel the frantic beat of his heart under her palm. She gave him a tender squeeze—*it will be all right, precious*—and decided that no, she was *not* going to die. She needed to get Osmund out. He was small and helpless, an innocent, grumpy little fluff goblin, and she was his only chance of salvation.

She squinted upstairs. The air was strange and shimmery with heat. Yes. That way, upstairs. It had to be. The stairs going down to the first floor looked brighter to her blurry eyes, and the air felt hotter. So the fire had begun downstairs.

As she raced up to the third floor, she felt a little twist of hope. If the fire was downstairs, then that meant upstairs could still be safe. Maybe the flames hadn't yet reached that part of the house. She could scuttle through one of the windows in the long hallway that led to the art gallery, then crawl out onto the roof and use the glossy, crisscrossed carpet of her mother's ivy vines to climb down to safety.

But when Farrin reached the top of the stairs, she stopped short and froze.

The long corridor stretching out before her ended in flames. That was the art gallery, there past that roaring mouth of fire. All her parents' sculptures and paintings, all the dimly lit nooks where Mara would sit with her sketch papers and study the play of light on stone faces, the texture of brushstrokes on canvas.

All that beauty, turned to ashes.

Dazed, reeling, Farrin turned to run back downstairs, but just then the whole staircase buckled with a horrible groan, like the house itself had given up. She lurched back with a scream, nearly teetering over the edge into that pit of singed carpet and splintered wood. Below, down the same set of stairs she'd run up only moments before, fresh flames licked up the walls, showing her their tongues.

There was nowhere else to go. Farrin turned left, away from the art gallery and the stairs-that-weren't, and hurried down another hallway so thick with smoke she could barely see her feet. Down this corridor was a series of little parlors and studies meant for guests, and each one had windows, and windows meant fresh air. That was all Farrin could think of as she ran: air, windows, *out*. Those rooms looked out over an inner courtyard, which wasn't ideal, but if she could only stick her head out some window, any window, and *breathe* for a few moments, she would be able to think more clearly and come up with a better plan.

Farrin loved plans. Music was full of them, and once you understood what the composer's plan was—how all the notes fit together and why—the whole of the music became clear to you, laid out in tidy lines and phrases, like bricks set one by one until a house was made. And then it was up to you, the musician, to expand upon that plan laid out before you and make it your own. Fill it with furniture, adorn it with color.

The notes of Merrida Jan-Tokka's *Sonata for an Autumn Morning* raced through Farrin's head: the third movement, joyous and urgent. Leaves spiraling on a brisk breeze, whirlwinds of orange, torrents of gold.

Farrin held on to the notes with her mind and her heart. She had learned that piece when she was five, and she'd performed it for the household staff—her first performance, euphoric, terrifically nerve-racking. A celebration, a perfect night. The house done up in shades of amber and tangerine and gilded scarlet, the windows thrown open to a black chilly sky, stars like snow flurries. Mara, three years old and overcome by the music, hiding her bashful face in Mama's sleeve. Baby Gemma cooing with delight—gold curls and bright blue eyes, already a beauty—and waving her socked feet from her perch in Papa's arms. Papa beaming with pride, so handsome with his broad smile and strong jaw, his golden-brown hair that looked just like Farrin's.

And Mama—Gemma's blue eyes, Mara's brown hair, skin pale as the moon. She had pulled Farrin into her arms afterward, with the house all a-clamor, Gilroy wiping his eyes on his sleeve, Mrs. Rathmont—tearful, ruddy-cheeked—passing around tiny iced cakes, perfect domes of sugar. Everyone elated, everyone's head full of Farrin's music.

Mama had pressed her cool cheek to Farrin's hot one and said quietly in her clear, clean voice, "Your music, little bird, will give the gods new life."

Stumbling down the smoky hallway, pawing at the walls for a doorknob, Jan-Tokka's sonata ringing in her memory, Farrin finally found one of the guest parlors and shoved hard at the door. It barely gave way, swollen and sweating, damp with heat and a crackling, sour magic, and when she tumbled inside, she fell forward onto her hands and knees, and she did not get up.

She *could* not get up. She could only crawl across the rug, and she did so, one-handed, holding poor Osmund to her chest. He was frighteningly still, his heartbeat faint. Could she even still feel it at all? *Yes, he's alive,* she told herself, staring ahead at the far wall, stubbornly clawing her way forward. *He's alive, we're alive, I'm alive.*

Her head hit something solid. The wall. She'd made it. The wall held three windows, and the closest one was maybe two feet above her head.

Gasping, blinking hard, she reached for it. She would push it open. She would pound it to pieces if she had to.

Her hand shook; her arm buckled. She collapsed on the floor and stared at the red-and-blue floral wallpaper. It was peeling away from the wall in jagged strips. Each strip screamed as it unfurled, like the voice of a tiny log creaking in a fire. Woozy, coughing so hard she felt like her chest might burst open, Farrin laid her spinning head on the carpet and cried. Her sobs were weak, her lungs black, each breath harder than the last.

A single charred ivy leaf drifted down from the rafters and fell before her nose, and Farrin grabbed it and held it to her lips. It was a piece of her mother, and it was the last thing she would ever see. She tried to breathe, desperate to find some lingering scent of her mother's perfume or the woodsy tang of her mother's botanical magic, but breathing only made the blackness come faster. Farrin closed her eyes.

Then—a light, flickering and white. It shone even through her closed eyelids, and it was so strange, so clean and bright, that Farrin, trembling on the knife's edge of her young life, found the strength to open her eyes.

A figure knelt beside her. Right there, impossibly, next to the screaming wallpaper. Gangly, graceless, all awkward elbows and long legs. Half boy, half almost-man.

And he was *shining*, a glow radiating from him as if some Anointed artisan had devised a way to paint a living being with starlight. Luminous, a beacon. A shining boy.

Stranger even than the light of him was the mask he wore—made of cloth, Farrin thought, with his nose and mouth covered and the eyes blacked out. Frightening, crude. The mask covered his face entirely, even hiding most of his hair, though Farrin could see a few damp, dark strands escaping the mask.

He reached for her. Pale hand, sweaty and soot-blackened.

"Don't be afraid," he told her. His voice was neither deep nor high, crackling somewhere in between. It was rough but kind, and his dirty hand was steady.

"I know the way out," he said.

Farrin hesitated. The shining boy was bright and lovely, but the world around him was hot, shimmering, terrible. The house was furious; everything shook. The sound of shattering glass exploded far too close, and then came a great sucking noise like all the air in the room being gulped away. At the same moment, the boy lurched forward, knocked Farrin back to the ground, threw his body over hers, and held her there, tucked safely against the wall. Both of them shaking, both of them breathing hard.

When Farrin opened her eyes, she saw a floor glittering with glass. A terrible hopelessness flooded through her. The house was falling apart around them; they would never find a way out. The boy was lying; the boy wasn't even real. She was dying; she was dead.

Just then, Osmund poked his head out of her nightgown and glared up at the shining boy—angry yellow slits for eyes—and he mewed, the plaintive cry he used to announce to the world that he was hungry. The squished, indignant sound gave Farrin strength.

She grabbed on to the shining boy's hand and nodded against his chest.

He squeezed her hand tight, then pressed something to her

mouth—a thick cloth, cool and damp, the most incredible thing Farrin had ever known.

"This will help you breathe," the boy shouted, but Farrin was already gulping down whatever air she could find, leaning hard against the boy as he put his arm around her and hurried her out of the parlor, down the hallway. Which hallway? Which stairs? Farrin didn't know, couldn't follow the path they were taking. The house was a shifting labyrinth, the throat of a beast, and the blessed cloth against her mouth was drying up. Her lungs were choking her again—two black fists, twisting smaller and smaller in her chest. One hand cradling Osmund, the other held tight in the shining boy's hand.

Something crashed overhead. The boy spit out a nasty curse, his hand so tight around hers that it hurt. He darted away, pulling her with him, just as a huge shadow fell out of the sky. A piece of charred ceiling, black and glowing, crowned with seared ivy.

"This way!" the boy shouted, as if Farrin had some choice in the matter. The boy's grip was iron, his strength unending. Flames roared around them, spitting smoke and sparks. Collapsing walls chased them down hallways that seemed never to end.

And through it all, not once did the shining boy flinch. He was like some great eagle, Farrin thought dreamily, colors spinning in her eyes. Orange, gold, throbbing red, blots of black. A great eagle with her held safely under his wing, flying her all the way out to the ocean. No wind could stop him, no storm, no shadow. His eyes were bright and clear, and he knew the way home.

"Farrin!" he screamed from very far away. "Farrin, come on! Keep walking!"

But she couldn't keep walking. Her feet were made of stone, and besides, feet needed lungs to work, and lungs needed air, and there was no longer air to be had.

The world spun around her, lifting her, jostling her. She was running; no, the world was ending, splitting open.

No. The shining boy was running, and she was in his arms.

Her eyes fluttered open, and she saw a cloudy sky slashed in half. White light, cool and soft: the waxing moon. Then orange, shuddering, a whip of rage, heat bleeding into blackness.

Suddenly Farrin was lying flat on her back, smoke behind her eyes, smoke down her throat. The shining boy, leaning over her, smoothed the wet hair back from her face. Then he went very still, held his hand above her mouth for a moment, and let out a shaky sigh of relief.

"You're breathing," he said. "You're going to be all right." He sat back, made a strange sound. Maybe he was laughing? "You're going to be all right," he said again, his crackling, not-quite-a-man voice torn up from the smoke.

Farrin reached for him in confusion, seeing only the faint glow of him, the twin shadows of his strange, blacked-out eyes.

He found her hand and held it. Against the fire, his silhouette was a bewilderment: half shadow, half shine. "Star of my life," he said, pressing a quick kiss to her knuckles. The kiss sent a shock through her tired body. *Star of my life,* she thought. What a pretty thing to say, and odd, since he was the one who shone.

Then the boy's body went rigid beside hers. He released her and stood.

"I have to go," he said. He sounded horribly angry.

Farrin reached for him, tried to protest. He was leaving her? But he couldn't! Where was she? Where was her family? Where was her house? And her piano, and all her music, all the things she loved? If he left her, the fire would come. If he disappeared, so would she.

"I'm so sorry," the boy said, quiet now, gentle, and he touched her face, his hot hand on her hot cheek. "They're coming now. You'll be all right."

And then he was gone. Farrin turned to find his hand, the warm strength of him, and found only wet grass, cold earth. She managed to crack open her eyes, and through the crust of soot and tears, she saw the distant shape of Ivyhill. Her home, afire. Black and misshapen, outlined by a wicked molten pen.

She tucked Osmund under her chin and wept, and then her father was there, frantic, sobbing, pulling her up into his arms so fiercely that she dropped Osmund to the ground. And Gemma was bawling at their father's knee, limp golden curls hanging in ruined ribbons, and there was Mara, ashen but dry-eyed, crouching to catch a disoriented, truly vexed Osmund before he scampered off into the night.

And Mama?

Farrin twisted in her father's arms, heart in her throat, and found her at last—Philippa Ashbourne, her beloved mother, on her knees in the grass not far from them. She cried silent tears as she watched Ivyhill burn, her arms rigid at her sides.

Gemma clung to their father's leg while Mara tried in vain to comfort her. Osmund yowled restlessly in Mara's arms. A few of the servants found them and huddled in frantic conference with their father and the head groundskeeper, Mr. Carbreigh, who was an Anointed elemental. All of them gestured wildly at the distant fire, and, thus distracted, no one else noticed the change that came over Philippa Ashbourne.

But Farrin noticed. Farrin saw the moment when her mother became someone else—*something* else. Farrin saw when Philippa stood and wiped her cheeks, her expression hard and mean and unfamiliar. The fire lit up her whole face, turning her eyes to twin flickering suns. She was incandescent with fury. Farrin could feel it, even half alive as she was. She knew the dips and curves of her mother's body even more intimately than she knew her own, and as the flames roared on, Philippa Ashbourne's body changed right before her eyes.

Every line of wrist and shin and rib became a weapon, every softness hardened to stone. The very air around her seemed to snap to attention as if suddenly shot through with deadly magic, and even though what had happened was a catastrophe, something so big and terrible Farrin's mind couldn't wrap completely around it, Philippa Ashbourne gazed upon the fire and smiled, wide and slow, as if she'd learned a most delicious secret.

And in that moment—so baffled and smoke-poisoned that later she would forget the whole thing entirely—Farrin, for the first time in her life, felt truly, unspeakably afraid of her mother.

CHAPTER 1

E very morning, before the rest of the house woke up, I walked the halls of Ivyhill to make sure it was still standing.

It was my favorite time of day. I never slept well, so finally giving up and getting out of bed after four hours of thin rest was always a relief. And no one was awake yet to ask me questions, to need something of me. The light was dim, the shadows thick. The only sounds were the patient ticking of clocks, the distant bustle of the kitchens, Osmund's velvet paws trotting along at my side.

Ivyhill was its most beautiful just before dawn, and so was my mind.

On my morning walks through the house, I didn't think of my endless lists of tasks, my notebook in my coat pocket, heavy with accounts and letters. Instead I thought of things I would no longer have room for in my mind once the sun rose. I thought of scampering along the hallways with Gemma and Mara when we were small, and how many wonderful hiding places my mother's corridors of vines created. Sometimes—rarely—I thought of my mother herself, and how she had left us, and how completely I loathed her memory, how I longed to tear it out of me by the roots like a weed.

And sometimes, more often than I'd ever admit, I thought of the night of the fire, when I was eleven and Mother was still here and Father still smiled. I thought of the fire, and I thought of *him*: the shining boy. The boy who had saved me. It hurt to think of these things—my sisters, my mother, the fire. It hurt like picking at a scab, feeling the sting, watching it bleed anew.

But for reasons I couldn't explain, thinking of the shining boy sometimes hurt most of all.

I had never forgotten the feeling of his strong hand holding mine, the safety of his arms around me, the kiss of his hand against my forehead.

I have to go, he'd told me. *I'm so sorry*. And I did believe that he was. That voice, which I remembered so clearly: rough with regret, shredded by the same smoke that had nearly killed me. I closed my eyes as I walked down the corridor that led to the guest rooms and let the memory of his voice wash over me. My hands were in fists, holding on to the memory with all my strength.

Where was he now? What would his voice sound like? How would it feel to be held by him now that we were grown?

If, in fact, he actually existed.

I opened my eyes, glaring at the carpet as I stalked down the hallway, despising myself for wasting time on a daydream and furious at the dawn light starting to creep through the windows. Many people prayed in the mornings, to mark the new day; well, so would I.

"I hate you," I whispered to the shadows, to the dead gods. That was my prayer. Either whatever remained of them after the Unmaking had planted the lie of this boy in my mind and let me believe it for thirteen years—the theory held by my skeptical family—or those same god-scraps had brought the shining boy to me, helped him save my scrawny eleven-year-old self, and then torn him away from me before I could even learn his name.

Raging at dead gods about the mystery of my strange childhood savior was far less dangerous than allowing myself to rage at them for the other thing, the unnameable thing in the shape of my mother.

My gorgeous mother with cornflower-blue eyes, hands rough from gardening, and a crease of hidden laughter carved into the left corner of her crooked mouth.

My mother, who had dressed our house in vines not once but twice—once just after she married my father, then again after the fire that had nearly killed us all. The scent of her botanical magic was earthy, floral, loam and lilies and honeycomb and something else, something bright and hot that I could never quite describe.

My mother, who had disappeared one night without explanation or apology, leaving me to pick up the pieces of our shattered household. I was the only one capable of setting aside my grief to do what was necessary, to keep the estate running, to keep Father from destroying himself. Mother would have known that, and she left anyway.

That rage was one I kept buried deep, even on my quiet morning walks. If I let it rise, it would destroy me, and my family could not afford my destruction.

I paused at the turn in the hallway, a staircase before me leading back to the ground floor and the start of my day. I closed my eyes once more, holding on to the memory of the shining boy leaning over me in the wet grass—the warm shield of his body protecting me from the fire's glare, how bravely he'd led me through the flames. I ached with a pain I refused to name. I held myself very still and remembered the rasp of his voice.

The lump in my throat, the ache in my chest, the *longing* I felt pulling at my fingers, as if I could reach out across the years and touch his hand again. Would this feeling of loss and heartbreak, this memory burning forever in my heart, never fade and leave me in peace?

Privately, shamefully, I hoped it never would.

I opened my eyes. The creeping pale sun had reached my toes. It was time to get to work.

I passed the porters standing guard at the front doors, ready to be relieved by the next shift. Tomas, Treska—I told them good morning and made myself smile. A grand, gilt-framed mirror hung on the nearby wall; I ignored it. Mirrors were not my friends. If I looked into this one, I knew what I would see: a skinny, pale woman with golden-brown hair in a severe braid, half-moon shadows under angry brown eyes, dull skin because it had been some time since Gemma had forced me to sit with her stylist, lips cracked because I bit them when I was thinking or worried, and I was always thinking or worried. Whenever I glanced at a mirror or caught my reflection in a window, I looked tired and irritated, because that's what I was. Tired and irritated always, and longing to sleep, and unable to sleep.

So, there was no need to look at the mirror.

Quick footsteps behind me, scurrying across the entrance hall, alerted me to Emry, our newest housemaid, who by the look of things—copper pail of firewood in her hands, clean rag over her shoulder—hadn't yet made it to my bedroom to start the morning fire. She caught me glancing back at her and ground to a halt, eyes wide with panic.

"My lady, good morning," she said breathlessly, with a hurried curtsy. "And my apologies, I overslept the tiniest bit and—"

"Not to worry, Emry," I told her, impressed by how warm and kind my voice sounded when in fact I felt the opposite. "We all oversleep sometimes." Except I never did. "I won't be back upstairs for hours anyway. You can skip my room today."

She curtsied again, gratefully, her eyes shining. She mumbled a thank-you, and I managed to smile at her again, though it dropped as soon as I stepped outside. Truly, I didn't care about the fire, and

I wasn't the slightest bit angry at her. In fact I was glad for her, and envious. I wished my busy mind allowed me to oversleep.

Then, inevitably, as I strode across the pebbled drive, nodding and smiling at every groundskeeper already hard at work on the landscaping, I thought of another person who found it easy to sleep: my youngest sister, Gemma. She wouldn't wake for hours, and when she did, it would be to a warm hearth, full sunlight pouring through the windows, and her maid, Lilianne, coming in cheerfully with a hot breakfast. By then, I would have already finished my morning meeting with Byrn, our head groom, confirmed tonight's supper menu with Mrs. Rathmont, and been halfway through my walk to the tenant farms at the border of our estate.

I knew I shouldn't mind her sleeping in as much as I did. Her lover, Talan, who lived in hiding for his own safety and ours, had come and gone only the day before yesterday, a whirlwind visit that I knew very well was agony for both of them. It had broken my heart to hear her crying after he'd left, though she wouldn't let anyone comfort her, instead shutting herself away in her rooms with only her dog, Una, for company. A few weeks past, Gemma had been the one to break the *ytheliad* curse and rip the Three-Eyed Crown from Talan's head, all while fighting Kilraith's brutal assault. We had all helped her—Mara, the Bask siblings, and I—but Gemma had borne the brunt of it and now sported the glittering scars on her hand to prove it. She deserved some rest. I knew I shouldn't begrudge her that.

And yet, I couldn't help but burn. Resentment squeezed my chest into a fist. I wanted to punch something, but I didn't know how to punch things, and I didn't particularly relish the idea of a broken hand, though the thought *was* tempting. If I had a broken hand, I could lie in bed and heal. Someone else would have to take over my duties.

An absurd fantasy. Gemma couldn't spend all day traipsing about our magic-drenched estate without getting at least a little sick—another thing it was unfair of me to resent her for, especially since she never dared complain about it—and Father…well. Father was another problem entirely.

I turned off the drive and onto the groomed path that led to the stables. Only there did I stop under the guise of adjusting my boot-laces. I needed to wrangle my thoughts into a calmer state. If I started thinking about Father, about the Basks, about punching things and the Three-Eyed Crown and Kilraith—whatever he was, wherever he'd gone—I would never get anything done. I didn't have the luxury of indulging in fear, in anger, in envy. I felt a twinge of love for my sister Mara, who lived far to the north at the Middlemist. As part of the Order of the Rose, she guarded us all against the Old Country and its ancient, wild magic. Mara would understand, if I ever confessed any of this to her; Mara knew what it meant to abandon emotions in favor of duty.

When I stood, my mind was quieter. The morning air held a wel-come, bracing bite. It was early autumn; soon the sunlight would grow scarcer. I could already feel the weight of that bearing down on me, the certainty of darkness. I despised the fall and winter months, every-thing gray and dreary and draped in shadows, each day harder to greet than the last.

Osmund had followed me outside. A rarity—he was solidly a crea-ture of the indoors. But there he was, sitting calmly in the dirt beside my feet, looking up at me with this keen light in his yellow eyes, as if he could hear everything I was thinking and found it all rather pathetic. He let out a grumpy, muted meow. Why had I stopped moving? There was work to be done.

He was right.

There was always work to be done.

◆◇◆

At midday, I returned home from my morning errands to sit for a few minutes and eat lunch—with Father, I hoped, though recently I ate in our family's private dining room alone more often than not, which normally would have been a small blessing. Quiet moments, for me, were rare; I hungered for them.

But Father had been strange of late. Evasive, taciturn. Even short with me, which was rarely the case. I was his favorite daughter, a fact I privately relished.

That afternoon, Father was nowhere to be found. The morning room was empty; the door to his private study upstairs stood open, hiding nothing. And yet I'd seen unfamiliar horses in the stables that morning while meeting with Byrn, and I could have sworn I heard carriage wheels turning on the drive while in the kitchens with Mrs. Rathmont.

As I settled uneasily at the dining room table and opened my notebook to look over the day's remaining tasks, Gilroy, our butler, glided into the room carrying a silver platter of sandwiches.

"Good afternoon, my lady," he said with a little bow. "Cucumber and tomato sandwiches, my lady, and the morning post, which came late, I'm sorry to say. Would you prefer lemonade or mint tea with your lunch?"

Immediately, my mind cleared and my heart leaped into my throat.

The morning post.

"Lemonade, please, Gilroy," I said, barely restraining myself from snatching the stack of letters right out of his hand. Quickly, I sorted through them. An alarmingly thick envelope from our cousin Delia, an Anointed silvertongue who lived on the southern coast and never tired of the sound of her own voice. A booklet of advertisements for various shops in Derryndell, Tullacross, and Summer's Amble, the nearest settlements of note. Notices of payments owed to Mrs.

Rathmont's favorite grocer, Father's tailor, the elemental carpenter who repaired our formal four-horse coach...

Then, at the bottom, two more letters. One bore the rather severe, slanted penmanship with which I had unfortunately grown familiar over the past weeks. It belonged to Ryder Bask, talented Anointed wilder and insufferable ass, son of Lord Alaster Bask. The Basks had for years been my family's greatest enemies, and now? In the wake of everything we had done in the Old Country? After freeing Talan from the curse that bound him to the creature Kilraith, thereby eliminating the evil force behind our families' long feud?

I shoved the letter into my coat pocket. I couldn't handle a missive from Ryder Bask at the moment. The contents would no doubt give me a raging headache: yet another report about increased sightings of Old Country beasts in the northern Mistlands, or an obviously irritated request for us to finally allow him and his horrid sister to visit, or some finicky detail about the speech we were all meant to give at the upcoming royal ball. A speech commemorating a new era of *peace* between the continent's two most powerful families.

Peace. The word sat askance in my mind. Gilroy had gone to the sideboard, his back to me, so I allowed myself to make a quick ugly face at my plate.

Then I ripped open the other letter, the one sealed with a red wax insignia in the shape of a rose. When I tore open the seal, a hot pane of magic cracked open at my touch, allowing me in with a slight shock to my fingertips. A bit of spellwork, no doubt implemented by one of the Order's beguilers to prevent tampering.

Dearest sisters, read the letter in Mara's plain, efficient handwriting, *I miss you both terribly and wish I was writing with better news...*

I pushed my chair back hard and jumped to my feet just as Gilroy approached the table with my glass of lemonade. I knocked into him, sloshing the drink all over his front. He let out a little grunt, and his bushy black eyebrows shot up in dismay, but then I turned to him, holding the letter to my chest like the precious thing it was, and breathed, "It's from Mara."

His face brightened at once, the spilled lemonade forgotten. "Go, my lady," he said, shooing me away with one stained white glove. "I believe Lady Gemma is in the library."

I beamed at him and hurried out of the room, but before I could get even halfway across the entrance hall's gleaming parquet floor, the sound of murmured voices made me turn.

Father was emerging from the corridor on the other side of the hall, accompanied by two people I didn't know: a lean woman with dark brown skin who wore a smart white gown and matching jacket, and a ruddy-faced man, clean shaven, auburn hair curling at his collar. His body sat awkwardly in a brown suit with a dark blue waistcoat, as if he had never worn such garments before. They came out onto the entrance hall floor in pieces: a gloved hand, a polished boot, a crisp hem. Shadows snapped around their bodies, and the air near them wavered as if turned liquid with heat. The sour tang of magic filled the room, making my bile rise and my stomach drop.

It was no wonder I'd not been able to find Father upon returning to the house. He'd made sure I couldn't, that no one could, shutting himself and his companions away behind some sort of spell that hid their voices, their very presence.

Father was no beguiler, deft with spellwork; he was a sentinel, Anointed by the gods with extraordinary strength and speed, unthinkable prowess in combat. One of his guests must have been a beguiler, then, though I couldn't tell which one simply by looking at them. I looked at their faces for a long moment, trying to make sense of it. I didn't know them; how did I not know them? I knew every one of Father's guests, all his friends and enemies, every merchant whose goods he preferred and why.

What was he doing meeting with some beguiler I didn't know?

I hid Mara's letter in my coat pocket, lifted my chin, and strode across the entrance hall to meet them with what I hoped was some kind of smile on my face.

"There you are, Father," I said brightly. "I didn't realize we were entertaining guests today. I'll inform Mrs. Rathmont at once so she can adjust our supper menu."

Father smiled fondly at me, as if I were silly for talking about such things as menus. "No need, dear heart," he said, kissing my cheek. "My friends were just leaving."

I glanced over his shoulder at his *friends*, these strangers whose stony expressions chilled me to the bone. But their gall brought me courage; this was *my* house, not theirs.

"I'm terribly sorry to interrupt, but I really must speak with my father for a moment," I said.

I put a firm hand on Father's arm and guided him across the hall into one of the adjacent anterooms, where the walls were sky-blue velvet and the ceiling was covered in Mother's ivy vines.

"Who are those people?" I demanded in a whisper.

Father looked at me hard and said nothing. The quiet, cold patience of his gaze made something queasy unfurl in my stomach, but he wouldn't cow me as easily as that.

"I don't know them," I went on. "Who are they?"

"Is it a requirement that I introduce to you everyone I bring into my own home?" he said smoothly.

It was meant to make me feel stupid and childish, the sort of question he might have launched at Gemma to discourage her from meddling, but never at me. I'd always been the one to meddle alongside him. I had known the truth of things long before Gemma had figured it out: that the demon who held our family under his control was real, that the path to his lair lay inside the old oak by the fountain, and that there were eighteen greenways scattered across our estate of which Gemma *still* remained unaware.

And now my father was looking at me as if none of that was true, as if every confidence we'd shared, every worry he'd confessed to me, was some figment of a needy daughter's imagination.

"Yes, it *is* a requirement," I replied, unflinching, "because I live here too, and I oversee the daily workings of our house, and I'm not accustomed to having strangers roaming about."

"They were hardly roaming. They were with me."

"Discussing what?"

Father's brow creased. "Really, Farrin, this is tiresome. If I wanted to tell you, I would tell you. Leave me be."

He stepped past me, but I hurried to block his path. I grabbed his sleeve and lowered my voice, trying not to quail at the furious look on his face. Only twice before had my father looked at me this way. Once was several weeks ago on the far side of the oak's hidden greenway, right before he had gone to meet with the demon. The other time was when we'd returned home from Rosewarren, still healing from our trip to the Old Country, and had told Father everything: the demon who had kept us fighting the Basks was Talan, and Talan was now free from his cruel master, Kilraith, and Gemma and Talan were in love, and there was no further need for war. Kilraith was hurt and in hiding somewhere. We could call a truce with the Basks. We could have peace.

And now Father looked at me with seething fury for only the third time in my life. An oil painting of his father's father sat proudly over his shoulder, glaring down at me. Both pairs of eyes, flinty and bright, belonged to sentinels.

I did flinch then. I nearly stepped away from him. For a moment I thought he might strike me, which he had never done before. He'd never even come close. But I sensed the sentinel violence coiling tightly within him. My body's instincts came alive, warning me to run.

Instead I stood firm, terrible scenarios piling high in my mind.

"Tell me you aren't planning something for the queen's ball," I said quietly. "Promise me you'll do nothing."

"Do nothing?" The corner of his mouth went up. He let out a soft puff of laughter. "No, Farrin, that's your special talent. You do nothing. Gemma does nothing. I act."

"Father, the war is over. The Basks—"

"The Basks are still themselves," he spat, shaking off my hand. "That has not changed, and it never will." Then his gaze fell to my coat pocket. I glanced down, saw the corner of Ryder's unopened letter poking out.

My heart sank.

Father's mouth thinned. "Speaking of," he said very quietly, "is that from him? The Bask boy?"

I hated many things about this conversation, none more so than the fact that I had to speak up in defense of a man I despised. Never mind that he'd fought for all of us in the Old Country as fiercely as if we were his own family. He was still a Bask, and I didn't have to like him. I simply had to not kill him.

"His name is Ryder," I said, "and he's hardly a boy. He's twenty-eight years old."

Father raised an eyebrow. "He wants to come here, doesn't he? For a *visit*? He's still on about that?"

"I haven't opened the letter yet."

"You should burn it. It could contain some wicked spellwork. The ink could be poisoned."

"It isn't wartime, Father. Things have changed, and you know it. The queen's ball—"

"The *ball*," he scoffed, and then, quick as lightning, he grabbed my wrist, held me fast. His grip was so ferocious that it shocked the breath out of me. The sentinel anger had awakened in him, gods-given magic that could help him tear a chasm through a battlefield, leaving ruin in his wake.

"No amount of balls, or polite invitations, or gifts sent as peace offerings, or even pretty, freed demons," he said, deadly quiet, "will change the fact that those people are our enemies, and they will take any opportunity they can to hurt us."

I shook my head, tried to protest, but he spoke over me, leaning close. There was a glint in his eyes, like sun flashing on a blade.

"I will *not* let my family be torn apart by the likes of them. Do you think the harmless tricks they've pulled these past few months have satisfied their need for vengeance?"

All at once I remembered that horrible moment at the queen's midsummer ball. My long-lost mother, finally come back to us, had run to my father in the middle of that crowded room, weeping with joy, calling for my sisters and me. Their impossible reunion had cut me in two and left me standing there agape, frozen not with relief but with fury. *Now* she had come back to us. *Now*, after so much damage had been done.

But then the glamour had melted away, revealing Alastrina Bask— crowing, triumphant—and then Ryder Bask, her brother, had stormed through the scandalized crowd to attack my dumbfounded father, to kick and punch him again and again.

"Harmless tricks?" I gasped out, trying in vain to tear away from Father's grip. "You're lying. I saw your face that night. You looked like you'd been shot. In fact, I think you would have preferred that."

He kept on, ignoring me. "Since the curse your mother and I engineered ended, and the forest trapping the Basks at Ravenswood fell, I've been waiting for them to come at us again—*really* come at us, like they did all those years ago. The *fire*, Farrin." He shook his head, and now I saw that the glint in his eyes was angry tears, threatening to spill. "Two daughters safe, one trapped in a house set aflame. No one could find you. And the *smell* of whatever spellwork they'd used to start the fire…bitter, terrible, the sear of poison laced with the stench of rot. I smell it every night in my dreams. Searching the grounds for you while the flames roared on, finding your body at last, smeared with smoke, limp in the grass… No, I will not endure another moment like that. *I will not.*"

I couldn't bear the pain any longer. The bones in my wrist felt like they would snap. "Right now, the greatest danger to all of us is *you*," I said with a little sob. "You're hurting me."

He froze, then looked down at my wrist and let out a soft cry. He released me at once, stumbling away from me. His boot caught on the tasseled rug, and he fell back, knocking against a cushioned bench and then falling hard to the floor.

Without thinking, I went to him, reaching for him with my unhurt arm.

He waved me off, shrinking into himself. A horrible sight, my tall, hale father sitting slumped on the floor. He looked up at me, tears on his cheeks, his face suddenly haggard. I couldn't move; I was mortified.

"Farrin," he whispered. "I'm so sorry. Gods. My darling girl, I'm so, so sorry…I don't know what…"

He fell silent, ran a shaking hand through his hair. He shut his eyes tight, then spat out, his voice thick and shaky, "Damn this magic. Sometimes I feel like it's punishing me. It's as though I don't use it enough for its natural purpose—not enough for its liking, anyway. It gets coiled up tight inside me and snaps loose whenever it wants, like some sort of wild animal. If only I could serve the Mist, as Mara does. Fight a few dozen Olden monsters every month. I'd be docile as a kitten then." He laughed a little, scrubbed a hand across his beard, and then looked up at me. His gaze fell to my wrist. "Farrin, Farrin." He shut his eyes once more, as if the sight of me pained him. "I'm so sorry. I can't be sorry enough, for so many things."

There was much to address in that little speech of his, so much that I felt the words nearly burst from my chest in outrage, but now was not the time. Instead I knelt beside him and touched his arm. He flinched, but I didn't budge.

"This is *good*, Father," I told him. "Peace is *good*. I know it feels like the opposite, but that's only because it's new. Without this feud in our lives, we can become ourselves again. We can simply be a family. We don't have to keep secrets from Gemma. We don't have to plot and scheme, or wait for curses to break, or worry that the allies of our enemy might attack us in their stead. And as far as a healthy use of your sentinel magic is concerned," I added, trying to infuse my voice with a little cheer, "I'm quite sure the Warden would welcome your presence at the Mist. Perhaps training new recruits?"

He shot a grim smile at me. "New recruits? You mean gangly little brats with no awareness of their bodies whatsoever?"

That stung. I remembered the day the Warden had taken Mara from us all too well.

I sat back on my heels. "Mara was one of those gangly little brats, if you'll recall. And she could knock you on your ass even then."

Father's face fell once more—ashamed, I hoped, of his callous remark. Of course, I was used to his thoughtlessness and had been for years. When I was younger, I used to imagine that Mother had literally carved the best bits out of our father to take with her when she left.

Now, at twenty-four, I couldn't be sure that my childhood theory was entirely wrong.

"Of course," Father said softly. "But Mara is special."

She was, even more so than he knew. I thought of how powerful she'd been in the Old Country, every limb a weapon, her strength astonishing. Without her holding on to us in the attic playroom of that evil house, I wasn't sure we could have saved Talan. I wasn't sure we could have saved ourselves.

A little shiver went through me as I remembered the melody I had sung that night, its notes raw in my throat as I'd fought to be heard over the sound of Talan's agonized howls. The horrible smack of Gemma's body once she'd pulled the crown from Talan's head and had gone flying back into the wall. Ryder, scooping her up into his arms, roaring at me to keep singing as we'd all fled.

I swallowed down those memories and said briskly, "And every little Rose is someone else's Mara, so think about that next time before you pass judgment on other people's children."

"Of course," he said quietly, looking thoroughly abashed, which gratified me. I helped him stand, trying not to think too hard about what an old man he seemed in that moment. In the wake of a rush of sentinel magic, especially one that came unbidden, Father sometimes experienced a sudden loss of strength, as if whole years had been sucked out of him. A common enough side effect of magic when it was used improperly, but not one I'd often seen Father endure over the years. He was Anointed. His ancestors had been chosen by the gods themselves to receive a piece of their magic.

And yet here he was, leaning against me as if his legs might fail him, while my wrist throbbed with the echo of his grip.

As I helped him settle on the bench, a horrible tenderness overtook me at the sight of him looking so vulnerable, and yet I was so furious with him, and frightened of him, and *for* him, and for us. Who were those people waiting in the entrance hall? What had they all been discussing? What would the days to come bring, and what would I have to protect us against?

Could two families raised to hate each other ever truly embrace peace?

"I love you, Father," I whispered, and it was true, wrenchingly so. But there were too many questions in my mind all clamoring for attention, and my throat was aching with sadness, and I was angry and tired as ever, and I suddenly couldn't bear to be near him any longer. I had to hope that our conversation had sobered him, that his memory of hurting me would protect us for a time.

What a horrible thing to hope for.

I left him sitting there and went to find my sister. We would read Mara's note together, and I would try to forget that look of rage Father had given me for speaking favorably of peace. I would try to forget how beneath his fury had flashed something even worse.

Disappointment.

CHAPTER 2

Gemma was not in the library but rather in her rooms, surrounded by piles of fabric: silver beadwork, fluffy peach tulle, fringed velvet shawls, some horrifically shiny gold thing dotted with pink silk roses. My baby sister stood in the middle of it all with a furrowed brow. She wore a soft green dress and a white ribbon in her long golden curls, and her arms were full of dresses. With one bare foot, she toed through a pile of satin on the floor.

I stopped dead on the threshold, suddenly remembering the most dreaded item on my list of tasks for the day.

Dress for ball.

These were all for me. I recognized a few of my own gowns in the flouncy chaos, much plainer colors than Gemma's usual—grays and browns, shades of slate blue and dusty rose. Gemma had turned both our wardrobes inside out, determined to dress me as she saw fit for the upcoming ball.

The sight of it all nearly made me turn around and flee, but I already had Mara's letter in hand, and Gemma was quick. She spotted me, let out a yelp, tossed the dresses she carried to the floor, snatched the envelope from my fingers, and tore it open before I could run away.

Defeated, I sank onto the tufted wingback chair by the door and listened to my sister read.

Dearest sisters,

I miss you both terribly and wish I were writing with better news. I'll get right to the point. I'm convinced that the Mist is dying.

Gemma looked up at me, her blue eyes wide with alarm, all her excitement gone. Our gazes locked for a moment, and then she sank onto the edge of her bed and continued to read.

The Warden believes the Mist is simply going through a natural cycle. It has weakened before, she says, and its strength has always returned. As a person might, the Mist—a magical entity itself—likewise endures periods of illness and health, melancholy and cheer. The decline we are experiencing right now is unfortunate but expected, and only temporary. So says the Warden.

However, I think this is something different. Something…else. Mistfires are increasing in frequency and severity, as you already know, and they're far worse than they were even a few weeks ago. Storms have started gathering at the northeastern perimeter of the Mistlands, horrible, fierce ones that do not abate. The sickness I explained to you previously is spreading—more citizens are falling prey to strange visions, awful nightmares, an insidious derangement. I have been keeping a catalog of the afflicted. Their symptoms, their physical appearance, the art and music and poetry they make reflecting their visions. I am keeping careful note of my findings; perhaps soon I will be able to deduce a pattern. Recurring words or images, some reason in the madness.

Meanwhile, my letters to you might become less frequent.

Another unfortunate consequence of the Mist's...sickness, as I suppose I could call it, is a general weakening, as I've said before. But as with the Mistfires, this weakening is getting worse by the day. Passage between realms is no longer limited to the strongest of beings—emissaries, dreamwalkers, fae, and so on—but is becoming possible for ordinary people and for lesser creatures of both realms. Our allies in the Old Country are keeping us as informed as much as they can, and we are fighting hard to limit both deliberate and accidental trespasses, but they are happening more and more, as are kidnappings and illicit trade.

As you can imagine, given the circumstances, the Order is spread thin. My unit is exhausted, and our newest recruits seem more terrified than usual, though I am trying my best to keep their spirits up.

Whether these increasing disturbances are due to our own actions in the Old Country, or to Kilraith's, or are merely coincidence, I can't say. But I think to assume coincidence is shortsighted. And if Kilraith is, in fact, not dead—and I cannot imagine he is—what will happen when he recovers his full strength? When will he attack again? And where, and how?

And what will happen to the Mist when that day comes?

As you can see, my head is a worried muddle of uncertainty, and I don't know what sort of response I expect from you. I'm not sure that there is anything to do right now except keep your eyes and ears open and talk to the people you trust, even when doing so feels impossible.

I think often of your upcoming monthly visit. The thought of home brightens my every morning. I miss you. I love you. Stay safe, and please give my best to the queen at the ball.

Yours always,
Mara

Una had come to me as Gemma read and leaned her lanky fleethound body against my legs. She was now looking up at me with those sad brown eyes of hers, her lips puffing the slightest bit with each breath. For Una, this was a sign of utmost affection. Absently, I scratched the silky spots just behind her tufted white ears and waited for Gemma to speak. I was too tired to utter a word. Mara's words sat inside my stomach like stones.

"She wants us to talk to the Basks," Gemma said slowly. She raised her gaze to mine. "And to the queen. She didn't say it outright, but it's there at the end. *Even when doing so feels impossible. Give my best to the queen.*" Gemma sighed, folded the letter back into its envelope, and flopped back onto her bed in a huff of pale green cotton and golden curls. "She's angry with us."

"She isn't," I said, though I wasn't convinced. "She's very busy."

"She wants you to ask the queen to send aid to Rosewarren for more supplies and weapons. More fortresses along the perimeter too, I suspect."

"I'm not going to put Yvaine in that position," I replied, as I always did when the subject of my friendship with the queen arose.

"And when she says talk to the Basks, she means *really* talk with them—invite them to Ivyhill at last, actually *do* something with them instead of merely exchange letters."

The very thought exhausted me. "Do something like what?"

Gemma sat up, her mouth drawn tight with frustration. "I don't know, but we were all together in the Old Country, and we did an incredible thing there. Maybe we could do more incredible things if we were all in the same space once more. Maybe we could do something to *help* Mara and all the other Roses. They're alone up there—"

"I know very well where the Order is and what they do and how dangerous it is for Mara," I interrupted wearily.

Gemma watched me for a moment. "You can't use Father as an excuse forever."

I resisted the urge to touch my tender wrist. "What are you talking about?"

"Don't try to play dumb. You're bad at it. I'm talking about the fact that in the weeks since we left Rosewarren, we haven't seen the Basks even once. We said we were going to, but we never have, and every time I mention the idea, every time we receive a letter from them, you deflect the whole thing with some excuse about Father's temper or happiness or some other such rot."

"It isn't rot," I protested, though that sounded weak even to my own ears. "Life is easier when he's happy. I know *you* don't care much about his happiness, but some of us *do* care, and have to."

"That's unfair."

"Not really. You've spoken to him perhaps three times over the past month."

Gemma lifted her chin slightly. "I have very little to say to him."

I saw a flash of pain in her eyes, though she'd grown much more adept at hiding it. Softening, though I didn't really *want* to soften, I went to sit beside her, reached for her unscarred hand, hesitated.

Some days, when Gemma's sensitivity to magic was particularly raw, I was afraid to even be in the same room as her, worried that some stray bit of magic would lash off of me and hurt her. I'd hoped, as I knew she had, that our trip to the Old Country and its effect on all our powers would somehow lessen that particular burden for her. But my little sister still hurt unpredictably when magic was near, and it seemed she always would.

"Can I?" I asked quietly, glancing over at her.

In answer, Gemma took my hand in both of hers, her smile lovely and beaming, the gleaming, scarred skin of her left hand—the one that had pulled the Three-Eyed Crown from Talan's brow—just as warm and smooth as the skin of her right. If she did feel pain, she didn't show it, and it broke my heart to see how eager she was for my touch.

"Please," she said, "and thank you."

We sat for a moment in silence, and then, because I couldn't help it, because from my vantage point I could see very clearly how deeply each of them was hurting, I said, "Father is sorry, you know. I know that sounds pathetic and inadequate, but he is."

"For conspiring with our mother to hire an artificer to alter my body from the inside out?" she said, chillingly matter-of-fact. "For mutilating me before I was old enough to understand what was happening, dooming me to unending pain, and then lying to me about it for years? For that, you mean?"

"You know he thought it was for the best."

"I know very well what he thought and how my power frightened him, a grown man—a sentinel, for gods' sake. He can continue to be sorry for the rest of his days." Then Gemma paused, looking down at our hands, and said, harder now, "He hurt you."

I snatched my reddened wrist from her, and then, as if I hadn't already confirmed it, muttered, "He didn't."

"He *did*."

"He didn't mean to."

"He's a fiend," Gemma said, her voice trembling. "I could kill him." Then she laughed, a horribly sad sound. "How can you want to kill someone, and also love them, and also hate them, and also feel sorry for them, all at the same time?" A pause, and then she nudged my leg with her own. "You were born an old lady. Surely you have the answer."

"Alas," I sighed, grateful for the familiar joke, "I have none of the wisdom that comes with old age, but I do have the exhaustion."

"And the fondness for porridge. And the unending grumpiness."

Before I could grumble a retort, Gemma rose and pulled gently on my coat sleeve. "Come, sister, let's forget about everything terrible for a while and find you a beautiful dress—oh! Here, you dropped something... *Oh.*"

Gemma bent to retrieve the letter that had fallen from my pocket, and when she straightened, her pink rose of a mouth formed a perfect pouting frown. *"Farrin."* She held up the envelope. "It's from Ryder."

"Is it?" I said blandly. "That's helpful to know, since I'd forgotten how to read."

"You haven't opened it."

"You are bursting with astute observations today."

Gemma put her hands on her hips. *"Why* haven't you opened it? It could say something important, something about the Mist, some bit of news that their ravens have reported."

"I was going to open it. I just hadn't found the will to do it yet."

"Would you have ever told me about it?"

"Of course," I lied.

My sister was not fooled. Her eyes narrowed. "How many letters have you received from Ryder that you just tossed without opening? *And* without telling me?"

"You know," I said, ignoring the question, "ever since the Vilia abducted you, and you escaped their captivity and broke an ancient curse and all that, you've become much harder to fool, and I'm not sure I'm comfortable with that development."

Gemma grinned, looking quite pleased with herself. "The sex helps with that too."

I blinked at her, stunned. "The what?"

"The *sex*. Gods' honor, every time I lie with Talan, I feel more... myself. Clearheaded, and vivid, vital. It's like he thrusts strength right into me. It's like I ride him to some higher state of being."

A slight shadow of sadness crossed her face. "It's more than that, of course. More than just his body and mine coming together. But they're instruments, you see. Gifts to one another. A form of worship, really. I'm stronger with him. Not only because of him, but because through him, I'm learning more about myself." She looked at me, thoughtful. "And he's extraordinarily good with his tongue. That doesn't hurt."

"Oh, gods help me." I plugged my ears, trying to ignore the flush of heat racing up my body. "I don't want to hear about your and Talan's...activities."

She wrinkled her nose. "Sex, Farrin." With a little skip and a jump, she was right by my ear. "Really *supremely* good sex," she added, and then stepped away to open the envelope, smiling to herself all the while. Girlish, playful, but with a serenity that seemed foreign to me, unreachable.

Rattled, I put my hands on my knees and stared at my fingers, all the parts of me that had loosened during our conversation suddenly clenched up tight. I felt a headache beginning at my temples, a tight knot gathering in my chest. I should have been glad that Gemma was able to mention Talan without despairing; maybe this meant that him being in hiding wouldn't be a constant torment for her.

But all I could feel in that moment was this sudden mire of confusion. Gods, I couldn't even rightly name what I was feeling. Anger? Fear? Mortification? Longing?

"Well, this letter is certainly to the point," I distantly heard Gemma say. "Ryder wants to visit Ivyhill, and bring Alastrina too, of course. He's wondering why you haven't answered—*Farrin*—any of his last *five* letters. Oh, and here's a note from Alastrina." She made a little sound of puzzlement. "She's asking if Illaria has any of her winter scents ready for purchase and if I'll put in a good word for her, persuade Lari to send early samples. *Interesting.* When she wants something, Alastrina can be shockingly cordial. She's practically gushing with compliments for Illaria." Her mouth twisted into a sly smile. "I may have to play matchmaker with those two. What a lovely couple they'd make, don't you think?"

Gemma's words jostled about in my head, rattling me like blows. It was as if some mechanism had switched inside me. Images of Talan and my sister flooded my mind—naked and ecstatic and tender, loving each other—and I couldn't get rid of them, wasn't sure I *wanted* to, and yet I desperately wished them gone.

"We'll see many Basks soon enough at the ball," I managed to reply, hating myself, humiliated. "That will have to satisfy Ryder for now. And perhaps if he put a little more effort into writing all these letters, I'd be more inclined to respond to them."

"He's succinct."

"He's *rude*."

"No-nonsense is what I'd call it. And you aren't exactly a bastion of decorum yourself, dear sister."

"I can write a polite letter that doesn't sound like an order barked at a military subordinate, at least."

Then I felt a gentle touch at my elbow and opened my eyes to find Gemma sitting beside me again, the letter discarded and her brow creased with worry. I hadn't realized I'd closed my eyes. I hadn't realized I'd done it to hold back tears—embarrassing, baffling, bright-hot tears.

"What is it?" Gemma asked softly. "I've said something that upset you. *Really* upset you."

I tried to sound wry and careless. "No, it's only Ryder. One more annoyance to deal with, you know."

"Truly, Farrin. It's more than that. I can see it on your face."

Without answering her, I rose and headed swiftly for the door. I didn't look back even when Gemma called after me. If I did, I would snap at her or say something terrible, something she didn't deserve. She'd done nothing wrong—not that she knew of, anyway, and certainly nothing that would have sent a reasonable person fleeing her rooms in a temper. I would offer her an excuse later, some task I'd neglected to complete, an appointment I'd forgotten.

But right then, I needed the one thing in the world that I knew could soothe this sudden anger boiling inside me and scrub my mind clean.

I needed my piano.

She awaited me in the Green Ballroom, my steadfast love. With the exception of our library and its archives—draped with so many layers of protective ward magic that it would have taken an act of the gods to destroy it—little else had survived the Basks' fire, but my piano had somehow, impossibly, made it through the night intact. Imagine the shock of seeing her—a perfect instrument of rich cherrywood, ornamented with carved wooden vines—standing pristine in a ruin of ashes and embers, wisps of smoke curling all around her. It had taken me days to retune the poor thing, but I'd managed it, and she played as beautifully now as she ever had.

Her survival was the one thing that kept me believing in the gods after everything that had happened to tear my family apart, even if that belief was, at times, hair thin. Something had saved my piano that night, something none of us had ever been able to explain. My mother, insatiably curious, had hired beguilers and elementals and alchemists to assess the piece. Was there any trace of protective magic lingering upon it? Was there something in the wood that repelled fire? Was it not truly a piano but rather something else altered to mimic the appearance of one? No one could ever find a reason it had survived; it was, Father decided at last, a miracle. A gift from the gods.

As a girl, I'd gotten the feeling that my mother had never been satisfied with that answer. This had irked me; couldn't she simply be happy for me, for the marvel of it? Another grievance with her that I held inside me, one of many I clutched in a fist that would never open.

I wasted no time. I closed the doors of the ballroom behind me and hurried to my girl, who stood proud and alone in the middle of the floor, framed by towering green walls and ivory curtains. Alone, but not lonely. She preferred her solitude.

I opened the lid, unveiling the black-and-white keys, every last one of them gleaming and perfect. I slid onto the bench and immediately began to play the first piece that came to mind. I didn't have a name for it; it felt too dear to me to be named, like a thing so precious it was best to avert your eyes from it, to speak of it only in whispers.

It was the piece I'd written about the shining boy, *for* the shining boy, about that horrible night and everything before and after it. How it had felt when he'd found me half dead, shivering beside a decaying wall soaked with malevolent magic, and held me, and told me not to be afraid. How he would look if I were to see him now, grown. How it would feel if his hands—the very same hands that had saved me— were to touch me again.

But the calm that ordinarily fell over me when I disappeared into my music did not come. Instead, with each arpeggio, each crescendo— here, the melody for my sisters and me, fighting futilely against the onslaught of our parents' war; there, the opening notes of the shining boy's theme, hopeful and heroic, coy—the tension inside me wound even tighter.

I was distracted, my thoughts scattered. *Really supremely good sex*, Gemma had said, blissfully unaware, blissfully happy, as I would never be. My piano, alone, not really understood by anyone—a thing to be kept apart, treasured but seldom touched by anyone's hands but my own. The shining boy's sad voice telling me goodbye. My father's iron grip on my wrist, hurting me. Talan pinned to the ground by all of us in that evil house of poison, shouting obscenities at us in a voice that wasn't his own. Mara, alone, overwhelmed, tired, fighting monsters in the shadows of the Mist.

I couldn't bear it, being torn apart from the inside by this confusion of memory, this tumult of too many strange, frightening pains to name. Why had Gemma said anything at all? Why had the letter from Ryder fallen out of my pocket? But she had, and it had, and the nettle of it had stuck in me for some reason I couldn't explain, reawakening every bad thought I'd ever had, making me ache, making me miserable.

A missed note here, an inelegant phrase there. My fingers wouldn't work as they were supposed to, even with all this godly magic coursing through my blood. Was I an Anointed savant, or was I a mere fumbling child?

A volcano of anger erupted inside me. Hot and blazing, head to toe.

I slammed my fists down on the keys with a muted cry, nearly choking on my own frustration. I dashed a hand across my face, swiping at tears.

And then, from behind me, came the sound of one person applauding.

I stood up, whirled around, and saw, standing in the corner of the ballroom next to a voluminous fern, a little tin watering can at her feet, Emry the housemaid.

She was weeping.

"Oh, my lady," she cried, clapping fiercely, "that was *wonderful*. I've not heard you play myself, my lady, not until just now, though of course I've heard the stories, and…oh, I've never heard such music, not once, not ever in my life!"

She stumbled toward me, gibbering about how glorious my music was, how divine, and I could only stare at her, fuming, not really understanding *why* I was fuming but knowing nevertheless that I hated the sight of her. It was as if she'd been reunited with a lost love; her sobs were joyous, giddy.

When she was close enough to touch me, she fell to her knees and touched the hem of my skirt. "Blessed Kerezen, that she should grant to us here in Edyn a gift such as the one you possess, my lady. Such *music*—"

"It was terrible," I said flatly. "I played terribly."

But on she went, praising me. *Food of the gods, drink for the soul, beautiful woman, perfect creature*, and so forth. It was the sort of nonsense I'd heard screamed at me every time I'd performed in front of a crowd.

My mouth turned sour with disgust, with fear. I wanted to run; I wanted *her* to run.

"Get away from me," I told her. I could hear the vitriol in my voice and didn't care; in fact, it brought me a perverse comfort. Through the haze of my anger, I heard a faint noise that I immediately dismissed. Perhaps the house, sighing in aggrieved solidarity.

Emry blinked up at me, sniffling. "My lady?"

"You saw me come in, you saw me sit down at the piano, and you said nothing. You should have made your presence known."

The girl paled. "I'm so sorry, my lady, I didn't know... That is, you startled me when you came in, and then you started to play, and I just couldn't stop you, I *couldn't*—"

"I do not perform my music in front of others, not without strict specifications put in place well in advance."

"Yes, my lady, it's only that—"

"This is my private space," I said sharply. She shrank back from me. A slight pity jolted me; she was new, she was young, I could have looked around the room myself to ensure no one was there. But I couldn't seem to stop talking. "If, when you are in here working, I enter the room, you are to leave at once, as quickly and quietly as possible. And you are to tell no one what you heard here today, or what you saw. Is that understood?"

"Yes, my lady."

"Good. Now, get out."

She froze, gaping at me. She glanced at my hands, then back at the piano. I could see it on her face, a question she was desperate to ask. *Can you keep playing, Farrin? Keep playing, and never stop.*

Every last measure of control I'd been holding on to shattered into pieces.

"*Get out!*" I cried, scaring the life out of the both of us. She scrambled to her feet and ran, tripping twice over her own shoes. With a sob, she bolted out the doors—right past the spot where Gareth stood, watching me, wearing a dusty travel coat, an undone tie of gold, blue, and black hanging loosely around his neck, and a sad, grave expression.

My dearest friend, Gareth Fontaine, and he'd been standing there for how long? How much had he seen?

I found the piano bench and sank down upon it.

"Gareth," I said weakly.

He closed the doors and came to me. The afternoon light glazed his spectacles and messy blond hair with gold. Normally, the sight of him would have lifted my spirits to the sun, but now I could only stare at my feet and blink back tears. Every part of me felt thick and miserable, weighed down by some tacky phantom substance that made it hard to breathe.

Gareth knelt at my feet and turned up my chin with one finger. "Farrin," he said when my eyes met his. "What in the name of the gods was that all about?"

Something about the tone of his voice made me bristle. "I'm not a child, Gareth. Don't talk to me like one."

"I don't know. You yelled at that poor girl like a child might have. A child with an exceptionally bad temper."

Grasping for any weapon I could find, I landed on *change of subject*. "What are you even doing here?"

"I've come to stay until the ball, conduct some research in your family's archives." He cocked one blond eyebrow at me. "About the *ytheliad* curse. Don't you remember?"

I did, at last, thinking of the scrawled reminder in my notebook from weeks ago, buried beneath pages upon pages of reminders, accounts, lists, needs, demands.

"Oh." I sat back against the piano. Thinking of Gareth's work and how I must look to him in that moment made me feel small and raw, utterly ashamed. "Right. I'd forgotten."

And then something reared its head in me, a nasty little monster with thorns on its tongue and a mind of its own.

Its words burst out of me. "I suppose you were too busy bedding barmaids and getting in pissing contests with your colleagues over whose brain is bigger to send me a note reminding me of your visit? But I shouldn't expect you to extend such a common courtesy to me if you can't even find it in you to send a letter to your poor mother."

Silence fell between us like an ax. After a long moment, too horrified to apologize, I dared a look up at Gareth and felt sick. He was smiling, but his eyes, normally so full of mirth, were ice cold.

"You know, Farrin," he said evenly, "bedding barmaids can be a fantastically fun time for all involved. Maybe if you tried it on occasion, you'd actually be pleasant to be around."

We stared at each other, and I saw the regret on his face, and the hurt. He hadn't wanted to say that to me, not really, but I didn't blame him for it. We knew better than perhaps anyone else in the world how to hurt each other, and we'd done it—fast and lethal, like knives thrown by a sure hand.

He broke first, blowing out a soft breath. "Farrin." He rubbed a hand across his brow. "I'm sorry. I shouldn't have said that. Tell me what's happened. You're clearly not yourself today."

But I was. I *was* myself, whatever that meant. This muddled, angry, sad woman was me, and I couldn't bear for her to be in the same room as Gareth for another second.

I found my notebook on the floor, stood shakily, and put my hand on Gareth's sleeve. *I'm sorry.* I squeezed his shoulder; I couldn't yet speak. I hoped he would understand. I fled upstairs, clutching my notebook to my chest.

That night, I tried it. I *tried*, as I hadn't in ages.

Maybe if you bedded a barmaid.

I lay in my bed, naked, sweating—not with desire but with nerves, with exhaustion. I'd been touching myself for nearly an hour, and all I'd earned for my trouble was soreness. My fingers were shriveled and clammy, my cunt dry and tired. *Cunt.* I forced myself to say the word into my pillow, hoping the vulgar shock of it would do something, awaken some latent spellwork buried deep within me. I imagined bedding a barmaid, Gareth, Talan, poor sweet Emry, my stolid lady's maid, Hetty. Even Byrn, our whiskered groom. My mind was a fever of bodies and mouths, hands and whispers, none of it focused, all of it frantic.

But even though every muscle in my body felt wound tight with desperation, the feeling of release everyone went wild about—the feeling I'd read about exhaustively, the feeling I *craved*—remained, as ever, out of reach.

At last I subsided, damp and miserable in my bed, my chest lit up with remnants of the day's anger. I curled into a knot and burned quietly, watching the dying fire in the hearth, listening to Osmund's cat snores at my feet.

Tomorrow I would wake before the dawn, and it would all begin again.

Exhaustion at the thought of enduring such a thing brought me the oblivion that touching myself never did. I fell asleep hoping I would dream of ecstasy, and knowing from experience that I would not.

CHAPTER 3

Normally, when I had occasion to visit the capital city of Fairhaven, it was cause for celebration, for a visit there meant I would see Yvaine Ballantere, queen of our world of Edyn and one of my dearest friends. Between her and Gareth, I was spoiled rotten with friendship, both of them good and kind and beautiful, both with rascally senses of humor and excellent taste in food. But on this particular day in Fairhaven, at the Citadel in the city's center, with everything done up gloriously in blue and charcoal and silver, in green and ivory and gold, I entered the Pearl of the Sea Ballroom feeling cold with dread from head to toe.

Gareth and I had hardly spoken since that day at Ivyhill a week prior. He'd kept mostly to the library, poring through our collections for information about the *ytheliad*—the curse that had bound Talan to the creature Kilraith. Gemma had kept him company, equally curious about the *ytheliad*, I suppose, though I was too busy to ask her about it, or else used that as an excuse to avoid both of them.

And besides Gareth, there was the matter of my father.

Nothing out of the ordinary had happened since the day we had argued; it was as though the two strangers he'd met with had never existed. In fact, he had spent the week leading up to the ball more engaged in the estate than he'd been in some time. He'd visited the tenant farmers, worked alongside Mr. Carbreigh in the gardens, even taken every last one of our horses out for a long ride about the grounds.

Nevertheless, I couldn't shake the feeling that something terrible was about to happen. A kernel of worry turned over and over in my stomach—a small thing, and yet it sent uneasy ripples all through me.

"What's wrong with you?" Gemma whispered at my side. "You look like you're about to be walked over the edge of a cliff."

I glanced at my sister. She, of course, was resplendent, wearing a diaphanous gown the color of pink rose petals, the entire thing overlaid with delicate, diamond-spangled lace. Her golden curls were piled on top of her head. Shimmering peach powder dusted her cheeks, lips, and collarbones. And she wore gloves, of course—intricate lace, with coy ribbons winding up her forearms. She wasn't yet comfortable baring her net of lightning-white scars to the world.

I didn't blame her. Lovely as they were, and as proud of her as I was for what she'd endured to get them, it didn't feel safe to have anyone's eyes upon them but ours.

Nothing felt safe at the moment.

"I feel unhinged," I muttered to her. "Father's been strange all day. Too cheerful. Even *rosy*. There are so many people here. And I hate this dress."

"Rubbish. You look marvelous."

"A subjective assessment that doesn't change my hatred."

Gemma sighed, placed a hand on my lower back, and guided me to a small, curtained anteroom on the ballroom's perimeter. I was so grateful to be led away from the crush of people crowding the dance floor, the feast tables, and the wide veranda with its doors flung open to the evening that I didn't even protest her bossing me around without explanation. Inside the anteroom were two low, tufted benches and, hanging on the wall, a tall mirror in a gilded frame.

I immediately tried to turn away from the thing, but Gemma stopped me, her grip surprisingly firm on my shoulders. "We're going to stand here," she said, "until you can look at yourself and tell me how beautiful you are."

I glanced at the mirror and then away. "Gracious me," I said flatly, "I'm so beautiful. Can I go find Yvaine now?"

Gemma's mouth quirked. "First of all, no, because you're one of the guests of honor and need to show your face for longer than two minutes, and so does she. And second of all, what you did just then most certainly does not count. When I say tell me how beautiful you are, I mean *really* tell me, and believe it. I will accept nothing less." She waved her arm at the mirror. "Even you cannot argue with *this*."

I stared at the floor until Gemma said blithely, "We can stand here all night, you know. It will just be a bit awkward when everyone comes to find us and has to crowd in here for our speech. I suppose you and Ryder and Alastrina and I will have to climb up onto these benches, all pressed together, and—"

"Oh, *fine*," I snapped, and then, reluctantly, looked up at the mirror.

I knew, of course, that Gemma was right. Even looking at myself with cold irritation, I had to admit that the result of her handiwork was impressive and that even underneath all the finery, I was pleasant to look at.

The gown we'd chosen was a compromise. It was from my wardrobe, yes, but from the section I hardly touched and Gemma preferred, comprised of gifts, mostly—from Father, from admirers, from Gemma herself. Not even I could bear to discard such pretty garments. This one was a muted gray blue, plain at first glance, but when you looked harder, you saw that the fabric was fine, rich, iridescent in the light. The neckline dipped too low for my liking, but the way the fabric fell against my upper chest *was* flattering, offset by the ribboned high collar that tied at my throat. *Alluring yet demure*, Gemma had declared upon seeing me in it for the first time, a satisfied sparkle in her eye. There were matching velvet slippers and loose sleeves that gathered at my wrists with rows of delicate gold buttons, each shaped like a swallow in flight. Earlier that afternoon, as we had prepared in the Green House—an airy cottage that sat on the edge of town, a gift to our family from Yvaine—Gemma had plopped me down in front of her stylist, Kerrish, and I couldn't decipher what she'd done to my hair. It shone like satin, and she'd woven pieces of it together in a confusing mass of crisscrosses and tiny braids. My skin glowed; I looked rested, radiant, even happy, my scowl notwithstanding.

"Aren't these the most darling earrings?" Gemma asked quietly, touching the pearls of pale coral that hung from my ears. "They complement the gown so well."

I couldn't answer her. My cheeks were on fire. I hated that she was doing this to me.

And yet only when I'd submitted to my sister's ministrations did I ever feel as pretty as this.

"I'm beautiful," I said thickly.

Gemma's reflection beamed at me. "That's better. And yes, my dear Farrin, you are."

The sound of Father's roaring laughter came to us then, barreling through the ballroom. My stomach dropped. I'd taken my eyes off of him for too long.

I darted over to the curtain to see what the fuss was about, but Father was merely standing beside a feast table, talking with a small crowd of courtiers—Anointed lords and ladies in gowns of Bask blue and sashes of Ashbourne green. Someone had just made a joke; Father was raising a glass in appreciation.

I retreated behind the curtain, feeling faint with relief.

Gemma frowned at me. "You really are worried about Father."

I hesitated, a confession balanced on the tip of my tongue, but then decided against saying anything. Gemma didn't need to know about Father's mysterious guests or the true wrath he'd thrown at me. Someone in our family needed to face the night with no distractions.

"Farrin?" Gemma looked serious, the glow of the party fading from her face. "What's happened?"

"Not a thing," I said quickly. "I don't worry lightly, but I do worry a lot, and nine times out of ten, it's for no reason other than whatever nonsense I've conjured in my head."

Gemma didn't look convinced, but suddenly the curtain swished open, and there was Illaria Farrow, Gemma's dear friend and a low-magic perfumier—one of the most talented in the country, surpassing even her parents. Her warm brown skin glowed from exertion, her shining dark hair hung in coils down her back, and she wore a gown of rich emerald-green satin in support of my family. Her only concession to the Basks was a tiny jewel of dark blue on her left middle finger.

"I just asked the concertmaster to play 'Fair Sword, Fair Lady,'" Illaria said breathlessly, "so if you don't come dance with me right this minute, I'll be positively beside myself."

Then she stopped and looked between us. "What is it? Is it the Basks? Did they do something boorish already? Did they insult you?" She bristled, squaring her shoulders. "I'm not yet drunk enough to punch anyone on your behalf, but I think I could be in roughly ten minutes."

I seized the opportunity and gently pushed Gemma toward her. "Go on, dance. There's no reason for both of us to worry about nothing."

Gemma hesitated, but then the orchestra began playing a new song, a rousing reel that made the crowd send up a cheer.

"If nothing's wrong, then let's *go*," Illaria insisted, grabbing Gemma's hand, and with one last concerned look back at me, Gemma was gone.

I stepped into the shadows, ignoring the mirror behind me, and let myself wallow in the relative quiet for a few seconds before bracing myself and pushing back into the candlelit ballroom. Gemma was right; we were guests of honor and needed to be visible. And if I hid in the anteroom all night, I would neither see Yvaine nor be able to watch over my father.

For what felt like hours I floated about the room, trying not to stay too long in any one place for fear that someone might start talking to me. They would see me and my dress—its blue fabric a respectful nod to the Basks, an acknowledgment of peace—and that would have to be enough until our speech at eleven o'clock forced me to present myself formally to these hundreds of horrible people.

I wondered how many of them had been in this very room the night Alastrina Bask had deceived Father into thinking our mother had returned at last. I wondered how many of them had laughed to see the mighty Gideon Ashbourne made a fool. These terrible thoughts did nothing for my nerves.

I found Father halfway across the ballroom in a fine suit of dark gray and a green vest with delicate ivory embroidery. I began shadowing him as closely as I could without arousing suspicion. He loitered by the feast tables for a time, deep in conversation with Willem Boyde, Ava Gettering, and Janeth Kass—three senior officers in the Upper Army. An elemental, an alchemist, and a beholder; one who could manipulate a natural element, one who could transform one element into another, and one who could see through magical disguises. All of them were Anointed—their magic gifted to their ancestors by the gods—and all had been guests of my father this past summer. I didn't think they would risk any mischief on such a night, in such a crowd.

I dearly hoped I was right.

Father and his company drifted away. I crept after them between the feast tables, nibbling here and there at a pepper-stuffed mushroom, a spicy potato croquette, a date piled high with goat cheese and ham and drizzled with honey. All of it tasted like paper to me. I kept my eyes trained on Father's golden-brown head; Kerrish had wrangled his hair into neat oiled waves. We wove through a maze of antechambers and sitting rooms that abutted the main ballroom, every room choked with feasters, talkers, drinkers, and gamblers, every table laden with dripping wax candles. At some point in the midst of all those roaring, genial shadows, the officers drifted away, and my father was alone. He grabbed a glazed pastry from a servant's offered tray, popped it in his mouth. He was moving more quickly now.

The bells of the Citadel's five clock towers began to chime. Deep, resonant tones bloomed through the air with a supple physicality, as if they were not sounds but breezes, cool and tender, utterly at odds with my rising panic. Flustered, I counted the chimes: ten, eleven.

"Shit," I muttered, feeling sick at the back of my throat. We were meant to begin our speech now—Gemma, Ryder, Alastrina, and I. At Yvaine's request, we would be the ones to speak to the crowd about how hopeful we were now that our families' long feud was over, how eager we were for this new era of peace. Ryder had sent a brusque note about what he and Alastrina intended to say—a letter I had actually deigned to read—and Gemma and I had engineered our own words to echo theirs. The great evils of misunderstanding, prejudice, and distrust slain by a new generation of Ashbournes and Basks. Enemies no longer, but allies. Peace and hope.

It was all utter nonsense, the sort of thing that would please Yvaine, satisfy at least some people's curiosity, and pique the interest of others. *The great evil of misunderstanding?* I could hear the onlookers now, whispering it to each other behind their gloved hands and over the rims of their glasses. *They finally killed that demon, didn't they? How do you suppose they did it?* The legends that already existed about our families would grow wings and take soaring flight. Everyone would look at us with new interest, new respect.

Never mind that we'd done this thing without the help of any of our parents and that the act had nearly killed us all and Talan too. Never mind that the very idea of me standing on a dais beside the Basks was enough to make my own father nearly crush my wrist.

Distantly, I heard a royal herald inviting the crowd to gather at the platform near the grand staircase. "And now," boomed his clarion voice, "we welcome Lord Alaster and Lady Enid of the House of Bask and their children, Lord Ciaran and Lady Alastrina..."

Ciaran. Of course—Ryder's true name, which he hated for reasons I didn't know and didn't care to.

Distracted, desperate, unable to shake the feeling that something terrible was approaching, I followed Father toward the ballroom's eastern veranda, where guests could dine and drink out of doors. Pale curtains tied with green and blue tassels hung at each polished wooden tentpole. The tables were piled high with arrangements of black feathers, sprigs of ivy, tiny glass lights spellcrafted by the royal beguilers to float in the air like fireflies.

Ryder stood there, his back to us and his arm outstretched. He was gently petting the round breast of a fat little sparrow perched on a low-hanging branch. He looked absurd, really, huge and hulking in his finery, the tiny sparrow a mere speck of fluff at his fingers. Alastrina stood at Ryder's side, as pale and dark-haired as her brother, her posture dripping with boredom. Both of them were clad in black and blue, dashes of silver at their waists and hems, feathered epaulets giving them the look of brooding vultures. The herald in the ballroom announced them once more; neither Bask sibling made a move to go to him.

I saw my father stride toward them and raise his arms.

"So, here we all are," he said, his voice booming across the stone veranda, "being feted like any other family would dream of. And yet you two seem as interested in being here as I am."

His voice was light, jovial even. Startled, I watched as if through the haze of a dream. Ryder turned to greet my father, his gaze dark, his smile strained. Beside him, Alastrina bristled with sudden alertness. The crowd nearby tittered, practically salivating, their drinks forgotten. *Here are the Ashbournes and Basks, and they all look ready to pounce!*

And then came a shadow, darting through the floating lights and tinkling glasses. A blurred outline of a man, a flash of silver.

My vision sharpened with horror. The flash was a knife, and the shadow holding it was racing straight toward Ryder.

I ran for him, not thinking anything but *go*. I knocked over a chair, shoved past some faceless spluttering man whose chest glittered with diamonds.

The darting shadow lunged, his blade gleaming—but I got there first, a frightened cry bursting out of me as I leaped in front of Ryder.

Something hard rammed into my stomach, throwing me back against a wall of stone. My fevered mind imagined the knife's blade sinking into my belly, how my blood might spew. In my shock, the world ringing in my ears, I registered only distant echoes and hands firm around my arms, holding me up. My father shouting furiously, the sounds of a fight. The fall of fists, the thud of a body.

"Farrin," said a low voice at my temple, warming my skin. "Farrin, breathe. You're all right."

Shaking, I looked down. The voice was right. There was no knife sticking out of me, no blood. Only a slight tear in my dress, baring a sliver of my stomach, and a pink scrape below my navel from where the blade had hit me. Alastrina bent to retrieve the fallen knife, examined it, then pressed it gently against her thigh. The blade retracted, spring-loaded. A false blade. Harmless.

On the ground near my feet, a pale man with fair hair, dressed all in black, cackled madly. His nose was broken; blood poured down his lips.

"You should see your faces!" he howled, his eyes mad and white. "It was a joke, it was only a joke!"

"Let go of me!" Father was bellowing. "I'll kill him! *I'll kill him!*" He lunged for the man, swinging his deadly fists, his face a murderous red, but ten other men held him back, straining to contain him. Royal guards flooded out of the ballroom to apprehend the man, and beyond them I saw a rush of white and splendid color. It was Yvaine, high queen of Edyn.

My breath caught as I beheld her. No matter how often I looked upon my friend, the sight of her stunned me every time. She was a slight thing, her frame delicate, but her presence was like that of a mountain: fearsome and eternal, unmovable. When the gods had chosen her to be our queen on the day of their Unmaking centuries ago, she had been a simple human girl—a shepherdess, maybe, or a bookkeeper, or a weaver. No one knew; not even I knew. Yvaine would not tell me, and every time the topic arose in conversation, her eyes clouded over, and some distant loneliness came over her.

So I did not ask, and whatever she had been, she was something else now, something more. The gods had shocked her skin and hair white, left a pink star-shaped scar on her brow, and frozen her in a youthful body. Her eyes gave her away. One iris was a deep violet color, the other pale gold. Both crackled with power, years upon years held inside them.

Tonight she wore a long gown of shimmering turquoise—cerulean one moment, emerald the next—a perfect blend of our two families' colors. Girlish sleeves fluttered at her shoulders. Her hair streamed behind her like sea foam, unadorned and unbound.

She paid no mind to the royal guards apprehending the hooting madman and instead came right to me, her swift steps like the fall of rain on glass.

"Farrin," she breathed, and took my hands gently in hers. After a moment, she relaxed, the lines of fear on her face smoothing out. "You're all right. Thank the gods."

Then she glanced behind me, and up, and I turned and realized that the solid wall behind me was the body of Ryder Bask. The voice at my temple, the hands that held me, the chest pressed against my back, holding me up, were his.

I ripped myself away from him. "Don't you—" I stopped myself from scolding him. *Don't you touch me,* I wanted to say, and yet the loss of his presence left me cold. There were far too many people watching us, hundreds of faces crowded at the ballroom windows. I swallowed my indignation, my heart pounding with lingering fear.

Ryder met my gaze with blazing blue eyes. A small, hard smile curved his mouth. "And I thought we were friends, Ashbourne," he said quietly. "Did fighting monsters together do nothing to elevate your opinion of me?"

I didn't answer him, too shaken for words, and turned to find Gemma flying toward us, Illaria just behind her.

"What in the name of the gods," she began. She took in the scene— Ryder, Alastrina, me, the discarded trick knife, Father still yelling in fury, the cackling man being dragged away by the royal guards. Yvaine, standing a little apart from us now, gazed distractedly into the starlit gardens.

The confused expression on Yvaine's face gave me pause. What was she thinking?

Gemma pulled me into her arms and held me fast. "A prank?" she said, angrily. "Some sort of sick joke?"

"One of many we'll have to deal with from now on, I'm sure," Alastrina said, looking around us with barely veiled contempt. Her black hair was slicked back into a tight bun, making her look even more severe and formidable than usual. "Look at them all," she muttered, jerking her chin at the whispering crowd. "That worthless shit of a man, whoever he is, will be famous for the rest of his life. And here we are, being stared at like an exhibition at a museum."

"You do look marvelous though," blurted Illaria, clearly more than a bit tipsy, but Alastrina didn't seem to mind. In fact, her expression brightened, and she took in the sight of Illaria in her gorgeous green dress with obvious delight.

"The famous Illaria Farrow," Alastrina said, with no trace of irony whatsoever. She moved as if to rush over to her, then hesitated, looking *bashful*, of all things, which was not a word I'd ever assigned to Alastrina Bask.

Suddenly, as if he'd swept everyone aside like toys, Father was there in front of me, bigger than anyone watching, bigger than all of us.

"You're unhurt?" he whispered. "Dear heart, he didn't hurt you?"

He cupped my face in his hands and stared down at me. His palms were blazing hot; his body shook with restrained sentinel magic.

I shrank back from him and said nothing. My wrist twinged with phantom pain, and the ground seemed to tilt back and forth under my feet.

"We have a speech to make" was all I could say. My eyes stung at the sight of him standing there, dismayed and bewildered, looking from me to Ryder to the abandoned knife. What if all these people hadn't been here to stop him? Would he have pulverized that man right before my eyes?

I strode across the veranda and into the ballroom, praying I wouldn't fall on my face and gratified to hear Gemma, Ryder, and Alastrina right on my heels. The buzzing crowd parted before us. Distantly, I felt a kiss of cold air against my abdomen and remembered that my dress was torn. If I left to change, I'd never come back.

I kept my fists clenched at my sides, determined not to fiddle with the ripped fabric.

At the dais stood a man and woman, tall and dour, as pale and dark-haired as their children. Both of them stared at me with such scowling confusion that I, still reeling and unsteady, nearly laughed in their faces.

"What happened?" Lord Alaster Bask, patriarch of his house, hissed at Alastrina.

"Later," Alastrina replied quietly, looking around the room with a sharp wariness I felt myself. What if the next blade was real?

"Lord Bask," I said smoothly, curtsying before Alaster, and then before his wife, Enid, who looked at me with eyes as cold and distant as stars. "Lady Bask."

I moved past them to the beguiled receiver hanging from the ceiling, a ball of tightly wound gold mesh that could have fit in the palm of my hand. As I approached, it buzzed quietly with magic, making my lips tingle.

Ryder cut in front of me and wrapped a hand around the receiver. He looked at me hard over his black-feathered sleeve. I noticed with irritated distraction the long dark lashes framing his eyes.

"We can do this later, or another day entirely," he said quietly. "You were just stabbed, Ashbourne."

I pushed past him as politely as I could manage. "I didn't realize a prank as inconsequential as that one could frighten the *fearsome* Ryder Bask."

He glowered at me—I could feel his gaze burning into my shoulder—but I ignored him and began to speak. "Friends old and new, citizens of this continent and of those beyond, we—the children of the Houses of Ashbourne and Bask—thank you for being here tonight. On behalf of my sister, Lady Imogen, and Lord Ryder and Lady Alastrina, and my father, Lord Gideon"—I gestured at my father, who stood uncomfortably halfway up the platform's stairs, seeming distracted, much like the queen had been—"and on behalf of Lord Alaster Bask and Lady Enid Bask, I must tell you how honored we all are that High Queen Yvaine, the gods' own chosen one, has opened her home to us tonight to commemorate the past and celebrate the future."

Remarkable, how the words spilled out of me so easily. The slightly frantic thought occurred to me that perhaps I ought to be stabbed by a trick weapon before every public event. Apparently it did wonders for the nerves.

Then Alastrina stepped forward and began the next section of our address. "As you well know, our two families—Anointed long ago by the gods—have for too many long years been at war. A needless war, its origins lost to the dust of time." She paused, solemn, the look on her face comically reverent. I knew very well how deeply everyone on this stage wished they were somewhere else, *anywhere* else.

"When the gods Anointed our ancestors," she continued, "they intended for their descendants to forever serve the world of Edyn by protecting it, cultivating it, and serving its citizens and its queen..."

"But in that," Ryder said, stepping forward, "we have failed."

And so they went on, and Gemma too. I didn't have to speak again until the end and waited, swaying a little, then suddenly swaying *more* than a little. Everyone's words turned to mush in my head; the sea of faces watching us became a swirl of muddy color.

I blinked hard, trying to clear my vision, but that only made things worse. And then a blazing pain erupted in my abdomen—red hot, violent—and the fiery tendrils of it shot up my arms and down my legs.

I stumbled. A strong hand fell to the small of my back, steadying me, but it did nothing for the sudden rush of sickness surging through me, building fast at the back of my throat. I needed air. I sucked in a breath, then managed another, and a weak third, before

I discovered that I *couldn't* breathe any longer, not more than a thin rasp of air. My throat felt thick and close, and the pain in my stomach kept shooting outward over and over, like the waves of some wicked hot sea.

A faint noise like distant thunder met my ears. Parts of my mind were still working—little corners, diamond-bright and spinning. I saw the gathered crowd applauding us, heard pleased cheers. Someone was helping me walk. The world dipped and darkened, and I fell forward, whacked my shin on a marble ledge.

"What's wrong with her?" came a voice, familiar and frightened and far away. Gemma. Angry voices buzzed behind hers, a backdrop of fury. I heard my father among them.

Something—someone—was rending the fabric of my gown, exposing my midriff to the air, which was agonizingly cold. I would freeze like this, prickling all over; my skin would crack into pieces.

I tried to curl my body against it, instinct making me jerk about and scream. I would fight this cold thing attacking me with my very last breath, and then I would burst into flames, or perhaps my stomach would twist around on itself, wringing me out, turning all my bones to powder.

I cried out, no longer knowing words. The pain was terrible, shooting out my fingernails and eyes and digging into my marrow.

"My gods," someone murmured, and then there were gentle fingers on my stomach, gentle but terrible, like being pierced by true blades, and I looked down to see my bare stomach, my torn dress— and right where the trick blade had stabbed me, where the slight abrasion from the man slamming into me had left a pink mark on my skin, an ugly black bruise had formed, with skinny arms branching out in every direction. They stretched across my skin and disappeared under my dress, tiny dark rivers of evil. I heaved at the sight, clawed at myself. My nails broke skin, tearing open the scrape and drawing blood. A pale steaming liquid seeped out of the wound and dribbled down my dress; seeing it, I was suddenly, violently sick.

There was a confusing clamor all around me. "She's been poisoned," someone cried.

Then another voice, deep and furious, said, "That damned blade must have been laced with something. Bring every healer you can find! And if that man escapes this place before I can get to him, I swear to the gods, I will make every one of you regret it until the end of your days."

The same voice gentled, very close now. "Farrin. Farrin, hold on to me."

I tried to obey. The last thing I saw was a warm white light coming toward me. Someone said tonelessly, "No healer can stop this. The venom is Olden."

Then a hot angry mouth opened inside me, black fire flooding out of its throat, and swallowed me whole.

CHAPTER 4

I came back to myself and found several faces hovering over me: Gemma, Gareth, Alastrina, Illaria. I was lying on the floor, the great ceiling of the Citadel soaring overhead, and my back and head were propped up against something warm and reassuringly solid.

I tried to twist around to see what the thing was, but twisting made my stomach twinge with pain, and all of a sudden everything came flying back to me in bright colors.

I pushed myself upright, gasping, and looked down at my stomach. Someone had draped a pretty violet shawl over me, but underneath that I was half dressed—nearly naked, really. Tears sprang to my eyes, and I clutched the shawl to my throat, covering myself as best I could, and felt around my body with my other hand. I found only normal, unhurt skin, slightly tender, and my poor torn dress.

"What happened?" I croaked, turning, wincing, and I saw that the warm thing propping me up had been Ryder's lap. Beside him, leaning hard against him as if otherwise she might puddle on the floor, was Yvaine. The creamy white of her skin looked sallow, unwell, but her lilac eyes were bright as ever. Her mouth was in a hard, angry line.

Ryder looked at me gravely, quiet fury burning in his gaze. "You were poisoned," he said, "and the queen healed you."

I couldn't think of what to make of that, so I awkwardly gathered the shawl around me—thank the gods it was a generous size—and tried to turn away from all of them, but everywhere I looked was another face. A few royal guards had gathered around us. Their captain, Vara, wore a broad gold sash across her chest.

Then Gareth crouched down next to me and opened his arms, his expression a horrible, frightened thing that made me realize just how close I must have come to dying. I turned gratefully into his embrace and hid myself against him for a moment; after all, he'd seen me naked before at the university baths, and another time, a humiliating moment for both of us, that we hadn't talked about since except in little jokes that never failed to lift our spirits. Gareth loved to laugh.

The thought made my tears spill over. Somewhere behind us, the orchestra played merrily on; the ball had resumed. I realized we were all hidden in an antechamber very near the dais. A pair of guards stood at the door, blocking us from view.

"The trick knife?" I rasped.

"Laced with venom," Gareth replied. "I'd have to study it further to be sure, but based on the effects, I'd guess it was—"

"A fae elixir," Yvaine interrupted softly. "Distilled from the roots of a tree that grew in a lonely wood, where the shadows are restless and every bloom hungers for flesh."

We all stared at her. Alastrina, standing nearby, shifted uneasily and crossed her arms over her chest.

Slowly, the obvious became clear to my muddled mind. Yvaine had *healed* me, Ryder had said. A prickle of awe crept over me, raising goose bumps on my skin.

"You used your magic on me," I whispered, marveling. Then a jolt of panic lanced through me. "Are you all right? You look unwell. The poison, did it hurt you?"

Yvaine smiled from her spot beside Ryder, the sight of her so sweet that two of the guards turned away, visibly overcome.

"It looks worse than it is," she said. "I took the venom from you, and now it lives in me. But it will die soon. Such evil can't survive long inside my body. In fact...ah."

She closed her eyes, cocked her head to the side as if listening to something none of us could hear. Soft pink returned to her cheeks, and she drew in a breath and opened her eyes. She patted Ryder's shoulder and stood, quick and fluid, her hair cascading to the backs of her knees. The mightiest tiny thing that had ever lived.

"Thank you, Lord Ryder," she said briskly. "Your shoulder is most excellently strong."

Ryder blinked, looking suddenly much younger underneath that fearsome black beard, and then stared at his hands, a secret smile pulling at the corners of his mouth.

I knew that smile; I knew what it felt like to receive the queen's love.

"I don't understand this," Alastrina said, her voice tight and impatient. "Some mad citizen obtained a trick knife laced with fae elixir and decided to assassinate an Ashbourne in front of hundreds of people?"

"The blade was meant for me," Ryder corrected her.

I glanced up at him right as he looked at me. Our eyes locked; heat crawled up my cheeks. I couldn't read his face, but I was certain he was thinking the same thing as me. What would it be like now between us? He, the target; me, his savior.

Embarrassed, I turned away.

"A similarly unthinkable situation" came the low, gravelly voice of Lord Alaster Bask, who stood unmoving in his sharp black suit, hands behind his back. "Someone meant to murder my son, here in the Citadel." His gaze slid to Yvaine. "I thought, Your Majesty, that there were protective measures in place here powerful enough to prevent such occurrences."

"A reasonable assumption, my dear," added Lady Enid coolly. She glowered beside him, gorgeous and cold, carved out of porcelain and dipped in ink.

Captain Vara strode forward. "It isn't your place to criticize the queen, my lord, especially in her own home."

Lord Alaster raised an eyebrow. "What a funny thing to say. I would think, as an Anointed subject of the queen, that it is in fact my duty to criticize and question. The gods favored my ancestors too, after all. We were chosen to protect the realm. And if the magic the queen has used to safeguard the heart of our capital is faulty, it is my responsibility to find out why." There was a pause. "I am reminded," he added, "of the incident this past summer, when chimaeric beasts invaded the castle through means that have still not been divulged by the Royal Conclave. There seems to be a pattern emerging."

My blood ran cold as I remembered that day. Five monstrous chimaera had raged through the palace halls. Gareth, Gemma, Talan, and I had tried to flee, only to be waylaid in this very ballroom by one of the beasts—a ferocious, muscled creature with a reptilian aspect, deadly razor claws, a tail like a whip. It had nearly killed me, and would have, had Ryder not thrown himself between us and shot the thing.

The memory reassured me. A life for a life. We were even. I no longer owed him anything. The thought gave me courage to speak.

"You forget to mention the night of the midsummer ball, Lord Alaster," I said, though my throat burned with each word, "when Alastrina assumed a glamour to deceive my father into believing she was my mother. When your son then assaulted my father on the ballroom floor, right there in front of everyone. If there is a failure in the Citadel's ward magic, then your children are guilty of taking advantage of it just as my attacker did tonight."

An uncomfortable silence fell; I could feel Ryder watching me but refused to meet his eyes. Instead I looked to my father, certain he would be grateful for my defense. But he was sitting on a nearby chair, leaning heavily forward, elbows on his knees. And when he raised his gaze to mine, I saw, before he could mask it, a flash of something miserable on his face: guilt and self-loathing and fear. He was utterly shaken.

Understanding pricked me like thorns.

I knew nothing about the cackling madman, but he'd been easily overwhelmed by the royal guard and had done nothing to defend himself. His method of attack had been convoluted, even a little silly. He'd said it himself: *It was only a joke!* This was not a person capable of overpowering the queen's wards on his own.

But an Anointed lord with friends in the Upper Army and a thirst for revenge? That man certainly could have devised a way.

Father must have seen the realization on my face. His own clouded over, went blank; he lifted his chin, ever so slightly defiant, as if daring me to say something.

I felt sick. Of course I wouldn't say anything, not here. And that glint in his eye told me that if I did, he'd be able to deflect the accusation. He wouldn't have done whatever he'd done without a way to avoid being punished for it.

The guards at the door parted to make way for a man wearing fine black robes hemmed with gold and a tasseled velvet hat. His brown skin gleamed, and his beard was neat and white. His name was Thirsk, one of the queen's closest advisers and a member of the Royal Conclave. He went straight to Yvaine and bowed, then bent to whisper something in her ear.

Yvaine nodded, touched his arm, and then looked solemnly at Alaster Bask.

"You are not wrong to express such concern, Lord Alaster," she said. "In fact, the gods would be grateful for it. Such accountability is what they intended. I will sit in conference with you in the morning, hear all of your grievances, and, I hope, set your mind at ease. For now, Thirsk has prepared rooms for you and your party—and yours as well, Lord Gideon—so you can rest and recover in the wake of this alarming incident."

Lady Enid raised her eyebrows and opened her mouth as if to protest, but Yvaine spoke over her, and I felt a slight wave of power push over us, a breeze with a will. Lady Enid fell silent.

"My staff will escort you upstairs for the night when you are ready and attend to your every need," Yvaine continued. "In the meantime, I wonder if your children would remain with me for a moment so I can thank each of them personally for the speech they worked so hard to prepare? They did so at my request, after all."

No one could have argued; the air hummed gently with magic. Nothing too coercive, merely a firm encouragement. It was enough to send Lord Alaster, Lady Enid, and my father docilely into the care of their guard escorts. Only once did Lord Alaster look back, tight-lipped, furious. He knew it was the queen's magic at his back, shepherding him away, but what could he do about it? Nothing, if he didn't want to lose his slight righteous advantage.

Father, on the other hand, left us without even a glance over his shoulder or a word of comfort. He'd be relieved, I knew, to no longer have to look at me and be faced with the enormity of what he'd done, how close he'd come to watching me die.

Gareth gently released me and stood. He and Illaria made to leave us, but Yvaine said smoothly, "Professor Fontaine, if you would remain here, please," which stopped him in his tracks. Illaria glanced at him curiously before the stoic guards led her out of the antechamber. Soon we were alone: Gareth, my sister and I, the Bask siblings, the queen, and her adviser.

It was then that I noticed the sweat on Thirsk's brow, near his hairline.

Yvaine turned to face all of us, her expression suddenly grave and hard. "Come with me, quickly," she said. "There's something you need to see."

The sinkhole swirled like a knot of storm clouds, only instead of roiling across the sky, they churned within a circular chasm cut jaggedly into the floor.

It was as if some great fist had punched through this once-lovely expanse of ivory-and-coral tile, here in the third subbasement of the Citadel, where a forest of marble columns supported the vast ceilings and where artifacts and relics of ages past were stored, some in labeled crates, some displayed on pedestals of jade and pink granite. And what the fist had left behind was a doorway to some other place, a world of storms with inky black clouds. In the mess of darkness, distant lightning flashed; a constant rumble of thunder shook the floor.

Around the sinkhole hummed a ring of magic, invisible but obvious, the sizzle of it like cooking meat. A bitter scent filled the air, and my mouth turned sour and strange, as if I'd put my tongue to an old metal coin. Next to this barrier of magic, forming an adjacent ring, were a dozen tired-looking people, all of them wearing pale robes embroidered with intricate shapes: a language, I thought, but one I couldn't read. Strewn around them were books and scrolls and plates scattered with crumbs. Some of them stood facing the sinkhole with raised hands, murmuring what must have been spellwork. Two rested on velvet pallets.

All twelve of them snapped to attention when they saw us coming.

They smoothed their tunics, scrambled to their feet, hastily tried to hide the abandoned dishes. One of them came to greet us, a squat pale man who smiled at the queen with obvious relief.

"This is Brogan," said Thirsk, the queen's adviser. He patted his brow with a silk handkerchief. "The Royal Conclave appointed him to oversee the reinforcement efforts."

"Your Majesty," said Brogan with a hasty bow, "thank you for coming so quickly. As you can see, there have been several...disturbances today, and...well, we've been pushed back from our previous position by two feet." He pointed to the air above the sinkhole, where a faint circle of blue specks turned slowly in the air, precisely echoing the sinkhole's perimeter. They were small and glinting, like dust motes in sunlight. Within their circle was another, this one bright red, and smaller.

Yvaine stood there for a long moment, very still. My heart thundered as I took in the scene. A ring of shimmering air formed a barrier between the sinkhole and the surrounding space. Dusty piles of shattered floor and broken tiles had been swept into tidy piles.

"A sinkhole of light and shadow," Ryder murmured, a fearsome expression on his face. "Just as the guards said when they released us from your prison that night. *There's a sinkhole*, they told us. *And the chimaera crawled out of it.*" Ryder looked sharply at Yvaine. "And you haven't closed it."

Yvaine's expression was distant, bleak. "I can't," she said quietly. "I've tried."

The room rang with her words as if she'd shouted them. My mouth went dry; I was suddenly, fiercely glad for the strong arm of my sister.

Gemma, holding on to me, said in a small voice, "I don't understand. You are high queen of Edyn. If you can't close this thing, then what—"

"Who made it?" Alastrina snapped, turning away from the sink-hole in disgust.

"I do not know," Yvaine replied, still with that strange, faraway look on her face. "Here is what I do know. The night of my mid-summer ball, I placed Lord Ryder and Lady Alastrina in prison for their assault on Lord Gideon. Weeks later, a sinkhole opened without warning, and chimaera emerged. In a panic, my guards released Ryder and Alastrina in the hopes that their wilding magic would prove effec-tive against the creatures."

"And it did," Alastrina added. Her eyes cut to me. "You're welcome."

"Only you didn't use your magic against *all* of them, did you, Lady Alastrina?" said Brogan, his face flushed. "You saved yourselves and ran. Twenty-two people died that day before we managed to subdue the beasts. Twenty-two. Do you know any of their names?"

Abashed, Alastrina fell silent. Gemma's hand tightened around mine. I was glad; I felt faint. *Twenty-two.* And we had run, all of us, just as the man had said. We'd run to the Old Country and used our power there to save Talan. But if we had stayed at the palace only a little while longer, could we have helped prevent some of that bloodshed?

"Your blame is misplaced, beguiler," Ryder said, hands in fists at his sides. "It took all of my strength and my sister's to turn back just one of the chimaera. And the Ashbournes couldn't have done even that, not before…" He stopped himself. I knew what he'd nearly said: *Not before they went to the Old Country, where something in them was awakened.*

Gemma, rending trees from the earth and tearing the cursed crown from Talan's head.

Mara, impossibly strong, fighting necromancers and demons like a one-woman army.

And me, distracting Kilraith, giving Gemma the time to fight him, using only my voice raised in song.

I swallowed hard. These were not memories I'd allowed myself to consider over the past month since we'd returned home. Thinking of them was like looking at a strange version of myself in a dark mirror, an eerie reflection I did not recognize.

Yvaine went on as if nothing had been said. Her voice was airy and strange. "My advisers tried everything to keep me locked up in my rooms. They wanted to protect me; that is their duty. They exhausted themselves, used all their magic. But I got out, and I slayed the beasts that remained. I closed my fingers into a fist and said a prayer to the goddess Kerezen—ruler of the senses, engineer of all bodies—and I stopped their beastly hearts." She turned to look at me. "But I do not know who sent them, or why, or from where, or *how*. I do not know what this thing before us is, nor do I know where it goes."

I couldn't think of what to say. Yvaine was frightening me. She looked so lost, so young and imploring, her white hair lit up eerily by the blue-and-red light of the floating rings. In this moment, Yvaine seemed less like my friend of many years and more like what I supposed she actually was: high queen of Edyn, chosen by the gods, unfamiliar and untouchable and unknowable. I clung to Gemma's arm.

Gareth crouched a safe distance from the sinkhole. He held his chin in his hand, deep in thought. "You rotate the strains of ward magic daily?"

Brogan bustled over to him. "Yes, Professor. The queen visits every morning and crafts a new design. She teaches us how to bolster it. We do so until she returns the next day." He lowered his voice, looked at Yvaine in awe. "We catalog every variation she devises. The language is entirely new. It does not match the syntax of any recorded spellwork."

"Have any other creatures emerged from it?" Gemma asked.

"No," Yvaine said quietly.

"No," echoed Brogan, "but every few days, the aberration's perimeter expands, despite all our efforts." Nervously, he glanced back at the queen. "If it continues at this rate, we estimate it will engulf the entire Citadel by the end of the year. Perhaps sooner, if the rate of expansion accelerates."

Gareth stood. "Have you consulted the Committee for New and Emerging Magics?"

"No, Professor. We've been instructed to—"

"No one can know," Yvaine murmured, staring at the sinkhole. "They would be so afraid."

Brogan looked helplessly at us. "The queen has forbidden us from working with any other institution to address this issue. We operate alone with her. To prevent a panic, she says."

Thirsk pulled at his collar and cleared his throat. "Yes, and as I've said to you before, Your Majesty, there has been immense pressure from others in the Conclave to do just as Professor Fontaine suggests. The Committee for New and Emerging Magics is a jewel of the university and is headed by the professor himself, as you know. Surely they would be helpful advisers in this crisis."

Yvaine slowly shook her head. "Gareth is important in what's to come. I see that clearly. Not his colleagues. Only him." She looked at me then, and her expression softened. "And the four of you, and your sister in the Order. And Talan—he is part of this too, of course. Oh, Gemma." Yvaine's voice was heavy with sadness. "You must miss him terribly."

Gemma flinched. Now I was the one to grip her hand hard.

Ryder took a step toward the queen. "Your Majesty, why have you brought us here? What are we a part of, exactly?"

Yvaine watched him as she might a beloved child. Her right hand absently played with the air near the ward magic; sparks flashed at her fingers.

"I need your help," she replied. "All of you. I must put every strength, every resource at my disposal, into guarding this place and determining the sinkhole's cause. And"—her gaze flicked over to Brogan—"into ensuring that this secret does not breach these walls. I must remain here. I am strongest in the Citadel, which the gods made for me, which they carved out of stone with their own hands. You, though…"

She looked to each of us in turn. My skin tingled with some ancient instinct.

"You can go anywhere," she murmured, "and everywhere, and you must. I need all of you to be my eyes, ears, and hands out there in the world. Learn what has made this *aberration*, as my advisers are so fond of calling it. This window, this door. What made it, or who, and what other else-things are out there in our world, opening up paths to the unknown?"

At once, I thought of the Middlemist and Mara's recent letter. *The Mist is dying.* Was this sinkhole evidence that its disease was spreading? My mind raced with dire possibilities. More than anything, I wanted to go straight to Mara and wrap both her and Gemma in my arms, never let them go. We could hide away at Ivyhill; I would play my music night and day if it would keep them with me.

"Farrin," said Yvaine on a soft puff of air. *"Farrin."*

The queen's voice pulled me back to myself. Everyone was looking at me; I realized I was trembling, my shoulders tense with anger.

"You *must* work together, all of you, at all costs," Yvaine said after a moment, looking sorry for me. "There are those who may try to stop you from doing so. You must defy them, no matter how dear to you they may be. Even if—"

Suddenly, Yvaine fell silent and went rigid. Her solemn expression cracked open, and before my eyes she became herself again, my friend Yvaine, mighty but human, who knew mortal things like humor and loss and fear. Her face went slack with horror; she ran wildly for the sinkhole, and then, before any of us could stop her, tried to throw herself into it.

The ring of beguilers heaved; a shock of magic rippled through the room with a sharp crack that made my ears buzz. Dimly I heard the beguilers shouting in panic, in pain.

Gemma released me. "Keep working!" she shouted at the beguilers. "Brogan, make them hold!"

Brogan, wide-eyed, muttering an incantation himself, scuttled around to each of the beguilers in turn. He placed his hands on their shoulders, bowed his head, and kissed each of their own, murmuring all the while.

The invisible rope of magic encircling the sinkhole shimmered and darkened. Tongues of power snapped across the room, making our hair stand on end. Yvaine threw herself against the ward magic again and again. She beat at it with her fists, horrible sobs bursting out of her, and then she started shouting in a language I did not know. But at the sound of it, my skin tingled, and my memory flashed to the sad house at the edge of the sea called Farther—the evil echo of Talan's family home, where Kilraith had nearly killed us all.

Whatever the queen was shouting, the language was Olden.

Ryder and Alastrina grabbed her, tried to pull her back from the sinkhole, but she was strong, frantic, and she twisted like a wild animal in their arms. The ring of ward magic echoed her, roaring, thrashing. An arm of it snapped out and whipped across Ryder's cheek, leaving a horrible glowing burn.

"What is she saying?" Gemma called out. "Farrin, do something!"

I'd been too stunned to move, rooted to the floor by absolute terror, but finally rediscovered control of my body and hurried to Yvaine. She was on her knees, Ryder and Alastrina holding her arms. I knelt beside her, feeling numb and useless, hardly able to find my voice.

"Yvaine, I'm here," I managed to say. "It's Farrin. Please look at me."

She shook her head, squeezed her eyes shut, and still the foreign words poured out of her mouth. The room trembled. Out of the corner of my eye, I saw Thirsk run back into the shadows, toward the corridor that had brought us here.

Gareth crouched beside me, shouting to be heard. "She's saying, *They're coming. They awaken.* It's Zelophar, a godly tongue. Found carved into the land in the days after the Unmaking, where the five Cloisters now stand. And in Aidurra and Vauzanne too, on the sides of mountains and the walls of caves. Most scholars agree the gods meant to mark these locations as holy sites, places ripe with power that are important for Edyn's protective infrastructure—"

"Not the time for history lessons, librarian!" Alastrina snarled, sweat dripping down her face from the effort of restraining the queen.

"*They awaken, they awaken.* She's saying it over and over."

"You have to stop this," I shouted to Yvaine. I found some courage and grabbed her hand, though it was so scorching hot I nearly dropped it. I steeled myself and tried to ignore the pain, though it shocked tears from my eyes. "Yvaine, listen to me. You're going to hurt yourself. Look at me, please! Breathe with me. Be with me."

Gareth continued translating, the sinkhole's lightning flashing across his face. "*Make them go to sleep!*" he cried, echoing the queen's screams. "*If they come here, they'll die. Make them go to sleep!*"

Yvaine was hysterical, her sobs so fierce they were making her gag. She clawed at the current of magic nearest her; blood dripped from each fingertip. Not knowing what else to do, I pulled her into my arms and held her, and over her shoulder I met Ryder's gaze. He nodded firmly, the slash of blood on his cheek an alarming bright red. He and Alastrina kept their hold on the queen, gripping her shoulders, her legs.

"Yvaine, Yvaine," I murmured. "It's all right. I've got you. I'm here."

I pressed my cheek against her hair. She was so hot and small in my arms. I cupped the back of her head, chaotic magic battering me head to toe. I thought of Gemma and how agonizing this must be for her; I ached to go to her but instead held on to the queen with all my meager strength. I sang into the buzzing cloud of her hair: no words, just melody. The sweetest tune I could compose, using only the solid, whole notes, full and warm—all the pretty notes, I'd called them as a child, the ones that fill the listener's body with blooming light.

At last, slowly, Yvaine began to relax. Her screams became whispers; her body sagged against mine. She clung to me, her face turned into my neck, and drew a long, deep breath, and was quiet.

Alastrina released her and fell back to the floor, swearing robustly, drenched with sweat. Ryder staggered a little where he crouched and then came over to me. His strong hand at my back was welcome; I wasn't sure my shaking legs would hold up both Yvaine and me, not on their own. I wanted dearly to sit but was afraid any movement would jar Yvaine, set her screaming again.

In the sudden deafening quiet, I heard the faint sounds of a beguiler weeping and another's wheezing breaths.

"What in the name of all the gods just happened?" Gemma whispered somewhere behind me.

"Nothing good," Ryder answered darkly.

Before anyone could say or do anything else, a huge clamor erupted. Bells, some distant and others jarringly near, sent urgent clarion tones echoing through the cold expanse of this vast, ruined room.

Brogan rose shakily to his feet and looked wearily at the corridor that had brought us here—the corridor down which Thirsk had fled.

"If you'll all please leave here at once and take the queen to her rooms," he said, his voice thin and his face newly gaunt, as if keeping the ward magic intact during Yvaine's outburst had knocked years off his life. "It seems that Councilor Thirsk has decided to implement lockdown procedures. Soon the royal guard will flood down here by the dozens, and they cannot see the queen in this state." Then he looked right at me. "I trust you know how best to reach the queen's chambers discreetly?"

I nodded, bristling a little to hear the suggestive tone in his voice.

"Then take her and go, and don't be alarmed if you hear a crackling noise behind you as you depart. We must erect deflective spells to confuse the guard, and it's complicated work." He laughed a little, looking sadly at the sinkhole. It seemed impossible that they would be able to keep this place a secret for much longer. How many guards and advisers and palace staff already knew about it? How many kept their mouths shut only because Yvaine's power told them to? And how many of these exhausted beguilers would soon tire of their endless work and decide to mutiny? Could they even do such a thing? Or did Yvaine have their wills too tightly bound up in her own?

These were questions I didn't want answered. I shifted Yvaine into Ryder's arms, noting with relief how easily he could carry her, and led everyone upstairs.

CHAPTER 5

F or as long as I could remember, my family had visited the Citadel
every month or so as guests of the queen, but it wasn't until I was
twelve years old that I understood this was because Yvaine was lonely.

Ours wasn't the only family she regularly entertained, of course.
She invited the Basks too, and every other Anointed family in the
world, and low-magic families, and families who possessed no magic at
all. Not a day went by when there weren't at least half a dozen families
being hosted at the Citadel, each with their own lavishly appointed
apartments, supper with the queen every day, and unchecked use of
every luxury the Citadel had to offer: the royal baths, the stables full
of gleaming horses, the acres upon acres of royal gardens. You could
spend an entire day wandering the palace grounds and see only a sliver
of their splendor. Then you would stumble to your bed feeling giddy
and blissfully tired, your eyes sore from drinking in every bit of gran-
deur they could find.

But not every family was gifted an entire house of its own, as my
ancestors had been. We called it the Green House, and it was a pretty
cottage on the edge of the city, large enough to hold our family and
any guests who accompanied us. In the center of the cottage was a

gorgeous winter garden, which the queen had commissioned for my mother when I was very small. They were good friends, the two of them, always strolling about the grounds in private conference while my sisters and I romped at their feet. No one understood it. What did the queen of Edyn, the most powerful creature in the world, chosen by the gods, find fascinating about Philippa Ashbourne? My mother was only an elemental from a low-magic family; she had an admittedly keen eye for botanical magic, but that was the extent of her power.

Yvaine loved her, though. As a child I didn't know why; I simply accepted it as the way my world worked. But as I grew older and started paying attention to such things, I noticed that the queen was more relaxed in my mother's presence. She was more like a child, more open and funny, less regal, less frightening. She would sit in the dirt with all of us when Mother started teaching little Gemma about seeds, and she would play our silly card games like Slap the Rat and Jill-in-the-Dale and shriek and laugh just like the rest of us. I grew suspicious and started watching the queen closely; was she seducing my mother? Were they having an affair under my father's nose? I was relentlessly sneaky. I eavesdropped on their conversations when I was supposed to be watching my sisters; after we'd all been put to bed, I crept down the stairs and listened to them chat easily by the fireside over tea and cookies. Sometimes Father would talk with them late into the night; sometimes he would sleep on the couch beside them, snoring; sometimes he would go out, and they would be alone.

But Mother and Yvaine never spoke of anything untoward, and I never caught them in a compromising position. After a long while, I felt satisfied that it wasn't like that between them. And then, when I was twelve years old, I finally understood why Yvaine clung to us so fiercely.

Mother left us in the middle of the night that year. One morning, I woke up to find the house feeling tense and strange, an echo of thunder pulsing in my ears. At first I thought perhaps a nightmare had followed me out of sleep; maybe it was yet another dream about the shining boy and the fire and all that smoke choking my lungs. I picked up a sleepy Osmund, tucked him into my robe, and hurried down the long corridor to my parents' bedroom, but it was empty. The bed linens were mussed; broken glass glittered across the rug.

I stood there feeling sick, staring at the shards of glass, terrified of their wrongness. Osmund poked his head out of my robe and meowed at me unhappily.

And then I heard my father roaring downstairs, and more glass shattering, and doors being slammed open. I raced down to find the source of the noise, thinking someone or something had invaded our home and my father was fighting them. The Basks, maybe, though I knew they were trapped in a forest; my parents had told us all about it, hoping it would comfort us in the wake of the fire. Though they hadn't confessed to hiring the elementals and beguilers who had crafted the cursed forest, I could see it plainly on their faces, and the truth sat like a slimy thing in my chest. I was glad the hated Basks couldn't hurt us, and I took great pleasure in imagining them trying and failing to hack through trees that wouldn't break, but at the same time it frightened me that my parents possessed the capacity for such cruelty. I blamed the Basks for that too; my parents wouldn't need to be cruel if the Basks hadn't forced their hand.

But that morning, the thing making my father crash through the house wasn't the Basks or any sort of invader; it was grief. I watched from the shadows under the entrance hall stairs as he tore through every room, looking for my mother and shouting her name again and again in great booming tones: "Philippa! *Philippa!*" Standing there shivering, Osmund tucked under my chin, I realized that the echo of thunder in my ears hadn't been the remnant of a bad dream. In my sleep, I'd heard the cracked roar of Father's voice calling my mother's name, and the sound had pulled me into an actual, true nightmare, one from which I would never wake. Only a few weeks prior, the Warden had taken Mara from us; now my mother was gone too.

When we visited the Citadel for the first time after that dreadful day, Father refused to stay at the Green House. It held too much of my mother in it; the winter garden was bursting with greenery she had coaxed into brilliant life. Instead, he dumped Gemma and me at the palace and left us to entertain ourselves while he wandered from tavern to tavern. He came home every morning stinking of smoke and drink, and he never woke until late afternoon.

The first time this happened, I was so unspeakably angry for too many reasons to name that I broke my father's rules for the first time in my life. I fled to the Green House and took Gemma with me. She didn't want to go, the poor thing; I think I must have frightened her, silent and furious as I was. But I dragged her there anyway and then sat in the unlit parlor for hours, dry-eyed, Osmund sleeping in my lap, while Gemma wandered the cottage grounds, crying and miserable, little Una anxiously trotting alongside her. Gemma was only eight at the time; it was terrible of me to abandon her to her own despair like that. But I was too mired in my own to care.

And then the queen came, right as the parlor clock chimed the nine o'clock hour. Gemma had fallen asleep in the grass at last, she and Una a pile of blond curls and stained skirts and gleaming white fur just outside the windows. I hadn't moved from my spot all day, as if keeping vigil over the parlor my mother had loved would somehow summon her back to us.

Yvaine joined me in silence, her long white hair tangled and dull, her eyes red from crying. She wore a plain gray gown, and her feet were bare. She sat on the divan opposite me, hands clasped tightly in her lap, and stared at the fire. I watched her for a long time, refusing to speak. In that moment, I hated her; this was our grief, not hers. And anyway, wasn't she high queen of Edyn? If she wanted to, she could find where our mother had gone and bring her home.

But then Yvaine said, very quietly, "I've tried to find her, and I can't. What do you suppose that means?"

I could only blink at her in astonishment. Had she heard my thoughts? Beings who could do such things existed in the Old Country—they were called readers—and perhaps the gods had given the queen that power too, along with all her other ones.

"I know it's terrible of me to be here," she continued. "She's your mother, not mine. I should grant you privacy. But you see, I'm supremely selfish." She looked up at me, and then her face did that extraordinary thing it so often did, when the strange frozen years she had lived melted away, and all that was left was a child not much older than me, looking lost and afraid.

"If I once had a family," she told me, "I don't remember them. Maybe I did. Maybe I was an orphan. I don't know how old I was when the gods chose me. I remember nothing before that, except that I felt very small."

She whispered this in a rush, as if she knew she shouldn't be confessing such things to me but couldn't help herself. "Yours is the only true family I've ever known. I've always thought I should be part of it, which I know is absurd. But when I'm with you and your sisters, and most of all when I was with your mother, I felt not like a queen or some perverse, godly thing. A *creation*."

She spat the word, her eyes glinting with tears. I'd never seen her in such a state. Listening to her, I could hardly breathe.

"When I'm with all of you, I just feel like…a girl. A person. It's such a relief. Next to all of you, my power feels muted. Easier to carry. And now she's gone, and I can't find her. If I try, I can find anyone, anywhere in the world. Did you know that? Thanks to our ever-wise gods"—the words sounded bitter—"I can do most things if I put my mind to them, though sometimes it takes me far too long and I fall prey to exhaustion before I can properly finish. But I can't find her. And I didn't know you were here tonight. I thought the house was empty. And then I came in, and what a surprise to find you and Gemma here. What do you suppose that means?"

"So...you can't read my thoughts?" was the only thing I could think of to say.

Yvaine shook her head and closed her eyes. "No, and it's wonderful. Everything's so quiet here. You're all so quiet."

Part of me wished to argue with her; she'd spent enough time at the Green House to know that when we were all together, my family was anything but quiet. But we weren't all together, not anymore, and perhaps we would never be again.

So I said nothing else; listening to the queen had worn me out. The hot fist of anger I'd held tight in my chest all day melted away without me even realizing it. I watched Yvaine hug her knees to her chest and cry, and I slid into a fitful sleep. When I woke, there was a hot breakfast ready for Gemma and me—crisp waffles piled with fruit and icing sugar, frothy hot cocoa. The day was clear and bright, and the queen was gone.

Years later, as I sat with Yvaine, making sure she slept, I thought of that long-ago night, my eyes burning with exhaustion. It helped Yvaine to fall asleep near me. During each visit to the Citadel, I tried to give her at least one night of that: a peaceful evening in her rooms, just the two of us. She had no other friends, she had once confessed to me—no one she ever brought back to her rooms to simply talk, as people did. So on those nights, we sat by the fire and talked of everything and nothing, with herbal tea and a heaping plate of cookies, just as she and my mother used to enjoy. No official state functions, no harried advisers, no endless documents stacked atop her desk. Sometimes I played music for her, but more often than not, she was asleep before I could make the suggestion.

And tonight, with the palace's lockdown bells ringing in my ears and guards hovering over us every step of the way, Yvaine was asleep in Ryder's arms before we even reached her rooms. I watched him suspiciously as he settled her among the pillows of her bed; would he be overwhelmed by her nearness and try to take advantage of her unconscious state in some way? But he was entirely decent, even reverent, as if it were his own beloved he was tucking in, and when he came to me and said quietly, "Is there anything else I can do?" I could only shake my head and avoid looking at him, clutching my shawl tightly around my body. He'd seen too much of me tonight; I had this awful feeling that he'd been the one to tear open my dress and expose my poisoned skin.

Instead, I went to my sister, who stood anxiously with Gareth in the corridor outside the queen's rooms. I held her to me for a moment.

"Are you all right?" I whispered. "All that chaos must have hurt you."

"A little," she lied with a brave smile. I could see on her pale face, in the shadows under her eyes, how awful it had truly been. "But Gareth's going to find me some bread and cheese, and perhaps more than a little wine. I'll be all right by morning, or well enough, anyway."

I glanced up at Gareth. He was looking at me with a haggard expression, as if at any moment some evil might spring out of the shadows and throw me back to the brink of death. "Farrin, I thought you were…" He lost his voice, cleared his throat, tried again. "I thought I'd lose you without us getting a chance to—"

"Please don't," I said wearily. "I'm fine now. Everything's fine."

"Were you going to say, 'without us getting the chance to declare our undying love for one another'?" Gemma asked blandly.

Gareth and I both made faces at her, though I knew we were both grateful for the distraction. I sent them on their way, and hours later, when I'd changed into a plain nightdress from Yvaine's closet and was about to nod off at last, Yvaine stirred beside me in her bed and whispered, "Thank you, my friend. I feel safer when you're here."

I stroked her hair until she quieted, her breathing even and steady. The tiny silver locket she wore under her gown had slipped out onto the pillow. Carefully, I tucked it back into her bodice. I didn't say what I wanted to: *What does it mean to feel safe?* Gods knew I *should* have felt that way, ensconced in the queen's bedroom, but I only felt restless and tired, heavy with questions. I tried to remember the last time I'd truly felt safe, like there wasn't some awful thing crouching on the edge of my vision, and couldn't find the answer.

I left Yvaine in her bedroom, slipped past the guards at the door, and wandered the royal apartments. There were guards everywhere, at every door and patrolling the hallways, but they didn't bother me or ask me where I was going. They were used to me and I to them. It was nearly five o'clock in the morning, and Yvaine's rooms felt gray and strange, every gleam of glass dulled, every fine fabric brittle under my fingers. It was as if the place itself was holding its breath, waiting nervously for Yvaine to open her eyes and for everything to be as it had once been.

The idea frightened me. What did the rooms know that I didn't?

I couldn't bear to be there any longer. I scribbled a note and gave it to one of the guards so Yvaine would see it first thing. *I've gone to my music room*, it read. *Ring for me when you wake.*

Then I left her rooms and hurried downstairs to a lower floor of the queen's enormous tower, where years ago a suite had been set aside for my use. There was a ballroom, small but lovely, ornamented with mirrored walls and elaborate gilded scrollwork, velvet sofas, tasseled rugs. Beside the ballroom, there was a small chamber holding only a sleeping couch and two walls jammed with books, and outside the ballroom, flowers curtained a stone veranda.

All of it was for me, a private hideaway that the queen had gifted me after the disastrous public concert I'd given at age fourteen. All those people screaming for me, screaming *at* me, rushing the piano to get at me, throwing themselves at me in fits of ecstasy. Ten years later, I still shuddered every time I remembered it, but here I could perform without fear, without an audience.

I sat at the piano in the center of the ballroom—a lovely instrument, petite and glossy white with gold ivy vines painted on its every surface. I opened the lid, tried to ignore the sick feeling in my stomach, the dread quiet in the air now that the lockdown bells had finally stopped ringing, and started to play. I played all the joyful pieces I could think of—a delicate sonata by the Aidurran composer Dakesh Viliaris that had always reminded me of prancing show horses; a fiendishly difficult concerto by the court musician Alessande Bardata, written in celebration of her children, that always left me feeling thunderous and triumphant, my fingers sizzling with power; every rollicking reel the orchestra had performed at the ball. But I could only play a few bars of each before moving on to the next, dissatisfied.

An hour passed, and I pushed back hard from the piano, my shoulders tense and my stomach in knots, and instead tried the pretty green fiddle sitting on its pedestal at the far end of the room. But the strings felt stiff under my fingers, the bow clumsy in my hand, and even when I tried to sing, the notes felt intractable, like they didn't *want* to leave my body. Terrible thoughts rose fast inside me, a confused barrage of images: Yvaine beating against her own magic, trying to tear it down; the stain of poison on my stomach; the cackling, bloody-nosed madman; my defiant, cowardly father.

The more desperately I tried to contain the images, the faster they came, and my voice broke off in the middle of "Willa's Lullaby," one of the sweetest folk songs ever composed, one I'd known my whole life—and yet suddenly I was so angry and muddled that I couldn't remember another note. I stood there, staring at the mirrored wall, frozen with frustration. My reflection was everywhere; I couldn't avoid it.

Maybe if you bedded a barmaid, came Gareth's voice, much meaner in my head than it had actually been that awful day.

With a frustrated cry, I slammed the piano lid closed, barely restrained myself from throwing the fiddle across the room, and burst out onto the veranda. But the perfume of all those flowers was cloying, and I turned away from them so I wouldn't start ripping them off their stems. I raced down the stairs, through the supple shell of ward magic that hugged the queen's tower, and tore into the labyrinth of garden paths just beyond. An astonished guard standing at the entrance said, "My lady? Is everything all right?"

"Trouble sleeping," I responded, my voice ugly and shrill, not convincing whatsoever. I must have looked like a madwoman. "Just need a walk."

I took a few frantic turns, ducking under tree branches and shoving past more godsdamned flowers. I didn't know where I was going; I just knew that if I stopped, I would scream. Another sloppy turn through a bush bursting with pink asters, and I slammed right into the chest of Ryder Bask.

I nearly bounced right off of him—he was solid and tall as a mountain—but he caught my arms before I could fall. I ripped away from him and stumbled back.

"Don't *touch* me," I snarled.

He stepped back, hands raised. "You're the one who ran into *me*, Ashbourne."

I glared at him. "What are you doing out here, anyway? Skulking about like some thief?"

He raised one dark eyebrow. "I'm a guest of the queen, same as you. I couldn't sleep and went to the stables, then took my horse—my *own* horse—for a ride through the game park. And what exactly would I be stealing out here? A mess of twigs?"

He did smell of horse, I belatedly realized, and he wore riding clothes, slightly stained, and his dark hair, most of it gathered into a messy knot, was windswept. I didn't know what to say. An apology for running smack into him seemed appropriate, but the thought made me even angrier. I wanted to storm away from him, but then he would return to his family's apartments, perhaps slightly mystified but otherwise fine, and I would remain decidedly *not* fine.

An imbalance I could not abide.

"Is something wrong with the queen?" he began, but I cut him off with an impatient wave of my hand.

"You never apologized."

He blinked at me, looking annoyed and hawkish in the garden's violet shadows. Dawn was bleeding softly into the sky.

"Apologized for what?" he said.

The nerve of the man. "For deceiving us at the midsummer ball. For making us think my mother had returned. For assaulting my father right there in front of everyone."

"And did you ever apologize for your father beating me senseless at the Bathyn tournament?" he replied quietly. "Or for trapping my family inside a cursed forest for years?"

"And did *you* ever apologize for burning my house down? For nearly *killing* me?" I turned away from him, pushing down hard against a rising sob. "I dream about it every night. I dream about the night I nearly died. And then I wake up and claw through the day and fall asleep and do it again, and again. And not once has anyone from your family apologized."

He was quiet for a moment. "That was a turning point, wasn't it, Ashbourne? That fire made everything worse for all of us."

I whirled on him. "Stop calling me that, like I'm a beetle only worthy of being referred to by official classification. My name is *Farrin*."

He looked horribly unhappy. He clenched his jaw, his gaze burning into me. "Farrin, then," he said. "Farrin."

It sounded as though the simple act of saying my name tore something out of him. I laughed bitterly. "Thank you. That must have been an onerous task, and yet you managed it. Well done." I gestured back at the castle. "And here we all are, meant to be friends now after everything that's happened, and you stand there as if my name on your tongue is the worst thing you've ever tasted. Ridiculous."

"I'm not exactly rejoicing about the situation either, Farrin," he said tightly, "but the queen herself said we must work together. I'm willing to try, though everything in me is screaming not to. Are you willing? *Truly* willing? Or will you spend the whole time yelling at me?"

"I'll yell at you as much as I like," I shot back, so angry I felt dizzy. "I didn't hear Yvaine forbid it."

Ryder fell quiet once more. "Is she all right?" He looked away quickly, scrubbed a hand over his mouth. "She felt like nothing in my arms. I had this terrible feeling she would just fade away. We'd arrive at her rooms and I'd be covered in ash."

The sight of him looking so spooked unsettled me to my seething core. "Clearly she's not all right, but at least for now, she's sleeping."

"And why aren't you?"

"Why do you care, and why should I tell you?"

He shrugged. "I'm a naturally curious man. And since you could have left by now but haven't, I suspect there's a part of you that's bursting to talk. Even to me." He paused, looked hard at me. "You're crying."

"Not because I'm sad," I spat. I was unraveling, and of all people to witness it, it had to be *this* man.

"I didn't say you were sad."

"I'm *angry*."

"That much is obvious."

"And I'm tired," I said, the words coming out of me on a thin breath. "I'm so tired, and I don't see that ever changing. I look into the future, and all I see is more of the same: a house I can barely keep in one piece, strange magic no one understands, the world changing right before our eyes. Some monster out there, licking his wounds and waiting for the right moment to come pouncing back. And *you*." I glared at him through my tears. "You and your terrible sister and your terrible parents, stains on my life that I can't scrub out."

"And music," Ryder added softly. "That too. Yes?"

I scoffed, wiping my face. "Yes. Music I can't even play properly when I'm this upset. And don't you think I'll be upset when Kilraith returns someday? I think I just might be. So when that day comes, I'll be rendered useless, just some sniveling, furious child having a tantrum in a garden, unable to sing even a simple folk tune."

"What about when you calmed the queen only a few hours ago? When nothing else would calm her, your voice did. And when we were all in the Old Country, and your voice stupefied the specters attacking us in the forest? When your voice stunned Kilraith and kept the house from falling down around us as we ran?"

I shook my head, unable to speak. All of those things were true, but the thought of doing any of them again felt too massive to contemplate. I had gone to the Old Country once, and I never wanted to return. In that moment, all I wanted was to sleep. At least my dream of the fire was a familiar thing; if that was all I had to face, I could do it forever.

I sank down onto the ground and sat on the garden's pebbled path. "Please don't talk anymore," I managed after a moment. "Please be quiet."

"All right," Ryder said reasonably, and then stood there with his hands behind his back, looking up at the brightening sky.

After a moment, I snapped at him, "What are you *doing*?"

He lifted his eyebrows, pointed at his mouth.

I could have slapped him, but that would have required standing. "Yes, you can talk."

He bowed sardonically. "Thank you, Lady Farrin. In answer to your question, I was standing here thinking, and I have a suggestion, if you'll permit me to say it."

How had this happened? How was I sitting here in the dirt, being condescended to by Ryder Bask? I glared at him, wishing that my gods-given magic was the power to reduce someone to a crisp using only my eyes.

"Say it, then," I spat, "and without that nasty snobby tone in your voice, and then leave."

"Hit me."

It was the last thing I expected him to say. Dumbfounded, I stared at him. *"What?"*

"I know you want to, and I think it would make you feel better. Stand up and hit me." He leaned down a little and smirked. A lock of dark hair fell over his blue eyes, which sparkled with mischief. "If you can."

It was as if he'd beguiled me. My anger rose up so sudden and swift that I surged to my feet, my tiredness forgotten. I thought of that night at the midsummer ball, how he'd punched and kicked my father, how he and his party had taunted us all with their northern chants, and I made a fist and swung it at him.

He dodged it easily, both his hands still behind his back. He clucked his tongue, shook his head.

"I knew right where you were aiming," he said. "You told me with your eyes, with the way you moved your body. Try again."

I did, still boiling, and swung so hard I nearly fell over. Again he dodged my fist, and I was left swaying a little, blazing with embarrassment.

"Aren't musicians meant to be artful and subtle?" Ryder said. "Whatever that was? The exact opposite. Try again."

"No," I said, fresh tears building behind my eyes. "This is absurd. You're trying to make a fool of me." And I was *letting* him. I'd snatched up his bait without thinking.

"Not trying to make a fool of you. Trying to illustrate a point." Then he stepped a little closer to me, and I held my ground, preparing to try striking him again—but his face, suddenly grave, gave me pause.

"You're right, Farrin," he said quietly. "The world *is* changing. Something is coming. Kilraith, or something worse. The queen is not herself. Her palace is compromised. And in that future of whatever's coming, she has seen all of us. Our siblings. Our friends. You and me. Whether we like it or not, we're going to have to work together. What we did in the Old Country was only the beginning—in more ways than one, I think." He looked at me shrewdly. "You and your sisters…I don't know what power you carry, but I think it's something immense, and I think being there that night, fighting Kilraith, awakened it. I think you think that too."

Speechless, I could only stare at him. My heartbeat roared in my ears.

"And if you'll let me, I can help you," he went on. "I know how to fight. You, clearly, do not."

I bristled, opened my mouth to say something, *anything*, that would kick his legs out from under him a bit. But before I could, he put two calloused fingers against my mouth, exceedingly gentle, and startled me back into silence.

"You worry that you'll lose hold of your power when it matters most," he said, nodding a little. "I understand that fear. So why not broaden your arsenal?"

"You want to teach me how to fight," I said, a little breathless with shock. My lips brushed against his fingers. As if burned, he quickly stepped back from me and nodded sharply.

Disturbed by this entire exchange, I swallowed hard and lifted my chin, fumbling for the upper hand I'd so clearly lost. "And in return?"

"Nothing."

I scoffed. "Well, now I *know* this is some kind of trick."

"Fine. In return, I'll sleep a little better knowing that whatever we're all meant to do in the coming weeks and months, you'll be better prepared for it. Your sisters can uproot trees and slay monsters. I can teach you how to use your body to defend yourself and those you love. You won't be a master warrior by any means, if those punches you just tried are any indication, but you'll be stronger. And therefore so will we."

With great effort, I ignored the smug insult and said, with as much dignity as I could muster, "You make fair points. I'll consider your offer."

He looked at me for another moment, his face illuminated by the growing eastern light. "Good. In the meantime, we should all plan a meeting, a conference of sorts—our families and a few others we trust. Grudges aside, strategy only. The queen wants us to be her eyes, ears, and hands? Then we will. And if the idea of working together offends your honor, as it does mine? Think of the queen, of your sister at the Mist, and swallow your pride, as I will. This is about more than our families and the terrible things we've done to each other, and you know it."

He turned away, made as if to leave, and then stopped and looked back at me over his shoulder. His bearded profile was brutally hand-some; he was no beauty, but the morning sunlight softened him, painting his fierce brow gold.

"And I am sorry, Farrin," he added, his voice gruff, suddenly weighed down. "I'm sorry for it all, and I wish I could undo it. I wish it more than anything."

He stood there, fists clenched, as if struggling with whether or not to say more. Then he straightened and said sharply, "You'll hear from me within the week. Don't ignore me this time."

Then he turned on his heel and strode away, leaving me stunned and overwhelmed, utterly trounced. Absently, I touched my lips, where his fingers had been. I shook myself and hurried up to my rooms.

CHAPTER 6

When we left the capital two days later, Father and I sat alone in our coach, our staff in another, and Gemma rode her gray mare, Zephyr. She refused to sit with our father in a contained space; I envied her ability to so utterly disdain him.

I glanced out the window as we crossed the Godsmouth, the longest river on the continent. Gemma made a splendid picture trotting along the bridge in her sky-blue riding clothes: hose and gleaming boots underneath a ruffled skirt, a smart jacket with ruffled collar, all her curls pinned up beneath a feathered hat. She chatted jovially with Lilianne, her lady's maid, who insisted on riding her own horse just as her lady did, instead of enjoying the comfort of the servants' coach.

Any citizen who caught sight of our caravan would know us at once as the Ashbournes. And if they saw Gemma—riding happily out in the open air, gorgeous and carefree, talking with anyone and everyone—they would be assured that whatever rumors were flying about were just that. The queen ill? The Citadel under attack? Whatever had happened, it couldn't have been *that* serious. Otherwise the Ashbournes would have hurried home using swifter magical means, and Lady

Gemma would certainly not have been out in the open air for all the world to see.

I sat back in my seat and looked across the cabin at Father, who was pretending to read a book. He hadn't turned the page in a half hour.

"So," I began, trying to sound angry and brave, pressing my sweaty palms against the seat cushion, "will you apologize to me now? Will you explain yourself? Or will we pretend that none of this ever happened?"

He surprised me then. He slammed the book closed. "Damn it, Farrin," he muttered, and looked up at me, imploring. "Of course I'm sorry. What do you think it felt like to see you dying on the floor?"

He was bursting; he wanted absolution. And yet I'd been the one to begin this conversation. *I'd* been the victim of his scheming. "I don't know," I replied. "What *did* it feel like?"

"It felt like the night of the fire all over again. It felt like searching the grounds while Ivyhill burned, and not finding you, and not finding you."

I kept my voice cool. "And yet this time, the threat was of your own rash, stupid design. Or did you set the fire yourself too?"

"Of *course* I didn't. Destroy my own home? How could you even suggest—"

"How can you be surprised that I would suggest it?" I sat board straight, fists clenched on my thighs. "You deceived everyone—the queen, the Basks, Gemma, me—and turned what was meant to be an occasion of hope into one of disaster."

"That sinkhole the queen has hidden from us all would have widened just the same that day, even if I'd been the very picture of diplomacy," he said sullenly.

A memory rose of Yvaine, frantically sobbing, throwing herself at her own magic while the beguilers worked desperately to hold it fast.

Yvaine had not divulged that to my father or to the Basks during their long meetings. She had told them about the sinkhole, the efforts to contain it; she had apologized for concealing the truth for so long. She had wanted to mend the breach on her own, she'd told them. In light of the situation at the Middlemist, she had not wanted to burden anyone else with this mystery.

But the madness that had seized her, the things she had shouted—*If they come here, they'll die! Make them go to sleep!*—that, my father still did not know. And never would, I hoped.

"You're deliberately misunderstanding me," I said, struggling for patience. "You're being a child. Worse than a child, because you have the capacity to fully grasp the dynamics of this situation and what an extraordinary ass you're proving yourself to be."

Father leaned forward, bringing his tired face and bloodshot eyes into the sunlight. "What I have done and what I will continue to do," he said quietly, "I do for the protection of my family."

"Father, the war is *over*."

He gave me a tired, grim smile. "This war will never be over."

"You're evil," I said, fighting not to cry. I couldn't contain it any longer; the fear and anger and, worst of all, the wrenching *disappointment* that had been burning in me since the night of the ball was a hot river inside me, flooding its banks.

"You're evil, and you're a fool. This war was never real to begin with. It was the machination of a monster using a string of enslaved demons to toy with us for his own amusement. He fed on the violence our families threw at each other; our hatred sustained him, made him stronger. Made it easier, perhaps, to do whatever he's now trying to do: tearing the world apart, endangering Mara and all the other women and girls who fight at her side. *That's* the legacy you're so desperate to maintain? Kilraith made fools of us all for years and years, and he'll continue to, if you let him. He—and whatever other wicked creatures might be out there, hungering for chaos—will have you blindly throwing punches at the Basks while the world crumbles around you, and they'll be glad of it, because you'll be looking the other way while they destroy everything we hold dear."

I sat back, buzzing with anger and horribly tired. I stared right at my father, who was looking at me as if he'd never seen me before, as if until now he'd dismissed my every worry, every frustration, as mere fits. As if he considered me a daughter who couldn't possibly grasp the truth and would, in the end, see the error of her thinking and obey him, love him, as she'd always done.

"I wish the poison had killed me," I said quietly, not realizing until I uttered the words that this *was* a dreadful wish of mine. The very thought brought me a strange sort of peace. No more notebook of tasks, no more sleepless, miserable nights in my bed, no more exhaustion. "I wish Yvaine had been unable to heal me. Maybe seeing my corpse at your feet would have been enough to make you see reason. Or maybe not." I sighed, closed my eyes, clenched my jaw hard so my mouth wouldn't tremble. "I think you're too far gone for that. I think you're a shadow of the father I once loved."

I heard him shift and wondered if he might try to come sit beside me—to comfort me, maybe, or more likely to try and wheedle me out of the snit I was in, make me see reason. But there was only silence, stillness, and then, I thought, my heart hammering, a muted sound that could have been crying.

I curled my fingers into my skirts and kept my eyes closed. It was better in this place behind my eyelids. Warm and dark, easy to imagine myself far away from everything that hurt.

There were three ways to travel from the southern part of the continent past the Middlemist to the north: greenway, a combination of horse or carriage and ship, and luck.

A person could theoretically cross from the southern half of Gallinor to the north, or the reverse, by simply entering the Mist and somehow surviving the shimmering silver maze of it to emerge on the other side. Certainly people had managed to do so. But it was terribly easy to get lost and very likely that you would starve to death before you found your way out. Olden creatures could slip through the barrier between realms and attack you or eat you, or trick you out of your mind. Or a normal human person, lost in the Mist themself and mad from the loneliness of it, the strangeness of it, its whispers and suggestions, could stumble upon you and mistake you for a chimaera, or a shifter, a fae, and murder you before you could murder them.

These were only some of the stories my sister Mara had told us during her years serving the Order of the Rose, a sisterhood of women and girls bound to patrol the Middlemist and protect Edyn, the human world, from the Old Country, where the gods were born and their magic ran wild.

So, not once, then, had we tried traveling Mistwise. Not even my father was fool enough for that.

Fortunately, being an Anointed family rife with power and business savvy, friends of the queen and the envy of most, had afforded us the kind of wealth that allowed us to hire Anointed wayfarers. These were elemental humans, rare and expensive to work with, whose magic had a narrow but highly useful purpose: instantaneous transportation from one location to another using plant life as a conduit. There were thirty-six greenways that I knew about scattered across Ivyhill, though I'd long suspected that Father kept others secret from me. One of those known to me was located in a hidden lagoon, buried underwater amid ferns and water weeds. An inconvenient location, but that was the point. This greenway led to Ravenswood, the Bask family's estate, and had allowed our family to spy on them for years.

But spying was not our purpose this time; we were visiting

Ravenswood as guests and allies of the family, and our goal was to discuss the safety of the realm. This was not an occasion for sneaking through greenways.

Carriage and ship it was, then, and *gods*, it was tiresome. Two weeks of travel, mostly through mountains—first the Little Grays in the south, and then, after two days traveling by boat through the Gloaming Sea, the taller, meaner Great Grays and their harsh northern winds. By the time we arrived at Ravenswood and I stumbled out of the coach, my legs stiff from our final day of travel, I felt ready to kiss the ground, even horrible and rocky as it was, laced with cold, black northern dirt.

Before I could, Ryder and Alastrina were striding forward to greet us, their parents and the entirety of their household staff arrayed behind them in splendid lines. Everyone, even the kitchen maids, was dressed in black, blue, silver, and rich shades of gray in tribute to the surrounding mountains.

"Lord Gideon," said Ryder, approaching with his hand outstretched. "Welcome to Ravenswood. I hope your journey was swift and uneventful?"

Father glared at Ryder and then at me for making him do this. I glared right back, too tired to feel intimidated by that fearsome scowl of his, and we held there for a moment, neither of us blinking, until finally Father relented with a slight sag of his shoulders and shook Ryder's hand. He looked murderous, his jaw clenched and his eyes burning with a thousand insults.

"Ciaran," Father said in greeting with a hard little smile. He knew just as well as I did that this was not the name Ryder preferred. "Alastrina." He kissed her outstretched hand; I held my breath, certain he would bite off one of her fingers. "Our journey was long but unremarkable," he went on. Curt, stone-faced. "I'm sure everyone in my party would be grateful to be shown to their rooms with all due haste."

Ryder nodded briskly and gestured over his shoulder at a tall, mild-faced man in a sharp black suit who I took to be the family's butler. He clapped his gloved hands together, and the yard burst into activity. Our servants unloaded our coaches; our grooms unhitched our horses; the Basks' aproned kitchen staff scurried back inside to continue preparations for supper while their household staff came to assist ours. As everyone bustled around me, I stood quietly and took it all in. Alastrina stiffly led my tight-lipped father toward Lord Alaster and Lady Enid at the front of the house. Gemma flitted about in her cheerful floral gown, introducing herself to everyone she could find, trying valiantly for cheer.

Gareth came up beside me to gaze up the rocky drive at the house. It was a huge, sprawling structure, all sharp dark towers and broad windows, gray stone walls and black slate roofs, windows bright with candlelight. I imagined it as a monster perched on the mountainside, looking down at us with all the warmth of a carrion bird. Near the house, two other families stood, as finely dressed as our hosts but looking uneasy, like children worried that their parents might start arguing at any moment. I knew them, of course. The Nash family hailed from the southeastern coast, and the Barthel family lived on the Northern Isles. A southern family and a northern one, both Anointed, the Nashes friends of my family and the Barthels friends of the Basks, just as Ryder and I had agreed in our letters—letters my father had refused to read.

"I trust you'll tell me whatever I need to know," he'd told me every time I'd tried to discuss the plans for our trip, falsely warm, not looking at me. We'd hardly spoken since our argument coming home from the ball.

I watched Lord Alaster lead him inside the house, dread churning inside me. Gemma hurried after them, skirts rustling, exclaiming in admiration over the house's architecture. The Barthel and Nash families followed them with some reluctance.

Gareth whistled low and held out his arm to me. "Well. I, for one, expect this to be a *very* entertaining weekend."

I grabbed on to his arm, fiercely grateful he'd come with us. His fathomless brain would be useful in our discussions; his Gareth-ness just might keep me from fleeing this place and running all the way back home.

Ryder strode up to us, looking grim and thoughtful. "Farrin. Professor." Then his eyes met mine. "We should compare notes before supper. Alastrina and Gemma too. And you too, Professor, if you wouldn't mind. An additional clear head would be appreciated, considering the circumstances." He turned and gestured up the drive. "Our staff will show you to your rooms. We'll meet in the west parlor in an hour. Supper is at eight."

Questions crowded my mind. Not once in our correspondence since the ball had we spoken of his offer to teach me to fight, but suddenly, in the midst of this tense, solemn flurry of activity, I wanted nothing more than to try swinging my fist at him again. I imagined what it would feel like to make contact: bone to bone, flesh to flesh.

He glanced at me once more; his blue eyes seemed even brighter here, with the cold northern wind whipping at our faces. He saw my clenched fist, which I hadn't realized I'd closed, and seemed ready to say something. Then he turned and strode toward the house, his dark dress coat swirling in the wind. A raven flew down from the trees to alight upon his shoulder and stared back at us, watching us with unblinking black eyes until they both disappeared inside the house.

That night, we all sat down to supper in the Basks' cavernous dining hall, a grand but cold space with walls of black stone, a gleaming floor of blue tiles, sideboards heaped with food and candles. Gorgeous tapestries of northern mountain scenes hung from iron rods on every wall: a bright blue lake framed by snow and fir trees; white wolves and shaggy reindeer; the goddess Neave soaring through the wintry sky with snow falling from her robes. On one tapestry, a band of fierce northern men rushed at a cloud of silver and gray with their swords raised. Out of the cloud reared monstrous heads, pieces of claws and wings.

The Middlemist.

I looked at that particular image only once before quickly averting my eyes. The sight of it left an uneasy feeling in my throat, like I'd swallowed too large a bite of food. I knew that Ravenswood sat much closer to the Mist than Ivyhill; from the top of their highest tower, Alastrina had said, you could see the Mist running silver across the horizon. But even so, why would any northern men have to fight monsters from the Mist? That was Mara's duty, and the duty of all the other women and girls conscripted into the Order of the Rose.

I reassured myself that it was a symbolic depiction and tried not to think about it further. There was more than enough to face in this room without having to worry about an odd tapestry too.

We—Gemma and I, and Ryder and Alastrina—had just finished telling the other families present about the sinkhole in the queen's palace. In the wake of our words, the room fell into a heavy, fraught silence. I looked around the table, trying to read everyone's expressions, my heart pounding. Talking about the sinkhole had taken me back to that horrible room in the palace; the memory of Yvaine's sobs rang in my ears.

"Hold on a moment," Lady Kaetha Nash said incredulously, pulling me back to myself. She was a formidable woman, tall and elegant, with a rich voice, smooth brown skin, and tremendous skill as a beholder, able to see through lies and disguises based in magic. My family had known hers for years, and Gemma and I had decided to invite her because of her wisdom, her level head, and her wicked sense of humor. But in that moment, she seemed cold, unfamiliar. Quietly furious.

"I must stop you there, Ryder," she went on, "and ensure that I'm not in fact dreaming and have heard you rightly. You're saying that some unknown force has opened a magical sinkhole inside the Citadel, that it's been there for weeks and weeks, that the queen has been keeping this fact a secret and has only just *now* told you about it, and that she has tried to close it and *failed*?"

Lady Kaetha's voice rang through the dining hall. I tried not to flinch at the anger it held, which I had to admit was warranted, reminding myself that it was not a personal insult to Yvaine.

At least, I hoped it wasn't. I hoped this week wouldn't devolve into a long string of bitter tirades condemning the queen for her deception.

"That's right, Lady Kaetha," Ryder replied at once. "The Citadel has been compromised, and we don't know why or how."

Lady Kaetha looked around at all of us; at her wife, Leva, her scowling son, Ewan, and her stricken daughter, Elianor; at the plates of half-eaten food scattered across the huge table of blue-veined marble. Lady Leva shrugged helplessly and put her face in her hands.

I clutched the napkin in my lap and braced myself for whatever came next.

Lady Respa Barthel, pale hands steepled at her lips, drew in a deep breath and let it out slowly. "And you've brought us all here to tell us this why?"

"Because, like ours, your families are Anointed," said Gemma, seated at the other end of the table between Lord Alaster and Ewan Nash. My wonderful sister spoke with a gentle but firm serenity I certainly didn't possess at the moment. "The gods chose our ancestors to help the queen protect the realm. And right now, the realm needs protecting."

"Protecting from what?" said Lady Respa, sounding more than a little irritated. "How can we know how to fight a thing we've not seen?

The queen ought to invite us to the Citadel, allow every Anointed family to set eyes on this aberration for themselves."

Across the table, Lady Leva raised her head and said thoughtfully, "Is it possible this sinkhole could be a simple magical abnormality? A phenomenon that will resolve itself naturally given time?"

"Of course," answered Gareth, "but if that's the case, the question becomes how long that resolution will take and what it will look like."

"And how many people it might kill in the meantime," Lord Alaster said over the rim of his wineglass, his cold blue eyes considering us all without blinking. "Those chimaera that escaped through it this past summer killed twenty-two people. Royal beguilers and royal guards. Loyal subjects of the queen. *Twenty-two*. And yet Her Majesty has not seen fit to explain to her people the real reason for their deaths. She has hidden that reason behind a cloak of secrecy and deception and ordered us to do the same. To lie for her."

I couldn't help but bristle at the tone of his voice. My determination to remain an impartial voice in these discussions vanished in an instant. "Yvaine wanted to avoid a panic," I blurted out, "which for all we know could have drawn countless would-be heroes to the capital, brandishing their magic without thinking. Whatever power feeds the sinkhole is already volatile. At least, Lord Alaster, there have not been more deaths since those tragic twenty-two."

"Not yet," Lady Enid said quietly, sitting at her husband's left hand. At this massive table, without the splendor of the Citadel to make her shine, she looked small and frail, even sad, a delicate shadow of her haler children.

Lord Alaster smiled at me. The unkindness of it sent a chill slithering down my back. "*Yvaine*, is it? Of course the queen's pet would defend her without question."

Father, sitting across from me and two chairs to my left, set his hands flat on the table and glared at his plate, clearly fighting against his rising temper. "You will not speak of my daughter that way," he said, very low, deadly soft. It was the first thing he had uttered since we'd all sat down for supper.

Gemma looked at me frantically. I could have slapped myself for letting the queen's given name slip. I wrestled for control of my anger, threw a hard look at my father. *Don't you dare*, I thought, willing him to somehow hear it, to see my face and calm himself, no matter how awful it felt.

I said hastily, "You're right, Lord Alaster, that I am inclined to defend the queen, but we are not here to argue about my friendship with her or about her wisdom in choosing to keep the sinkhole a secret. That decision lies in the past. What we are concerned with now is what's to come. What does this sinkhole, this breach, mean in the context of the larger world?"

Ruddy-faced Gentar, the genial son of Lady Respa and her husband, Sesar, chewed thoughtfully on his roasted potatoes. "You think that whatever force created the sinkhole could be the same one creating trouble in the Middlemist?"

"We can't be sure without further research," Gareth replied, "but it's a possibility we can't discount. The timing suggests something more than coincidence. I'm going to propose to the queen that a team of scholars from the Committee of New and Emerging Magics join the royal beguilers at the sinkhole. They can study it with fresh eyes, and exchange information with similar scholarly research teams currently stationed in the Middlemist."

Lady Respa raised her eyebrows. "From what you've said, it doesn't sound like the queen will be amenable to such…interference."

Gareth flashed her a charming smile and leaned forward on his elbows, his messy blond hair flopping over his brow. "I am determined to convince her."

"You're that confident in that smile of yours, Professor Fontaine?"

His grin widened. "It has never once let me down."

The Nashes' bashful daughter, Elianor, cleared her throat. Her cheeks flushed pink as she spoke. "Has there been word from Vauzanne about similar occurrences in the Crescent of Storms? Or from Aidurra about the Knotwood? Things like the Mistfires, the increased sightings of Olden trespassers?"

At once I thought of Talan, who was gods knew where at the moment, living in disguise and in hiding, investigating those very questions and never staying in one place long enough for Kilraith to find him—we hoped, we prayed. I glanced quickly at Gemma, aching for her, begging her silently to be brave, but of course she was, beautifully so. There was no trace of heartbreak on her face, nothing that gave away how at every moment she was half out of her mind with worry for Talan's safety. She took a regal sip of her wine, her curls gleaming softly in the dim light. I wished I could have marched around the table and hugged her.

"So far the queen has not informed of us any such communications," Ryder said.

"Though she hasn't exactly been completely forthcoming about other things, has she?" mused Lady Enid, absently rubbing the rim of her largely untouched plate. "Perhaps we can't trust that she isn't keeping that information secret as well."

It wasn't a malicious accusation, simply a matter-of-fact statement, but I felt my hackles rising nevertheless and felt perilously close to making a fool of myself again. I grabbed the hot buttered roll from my plate, tore off a huge hunk of it, and shoved it in my mouth.

Ryder conceded the point with a reluctant nod. "A possibility we have to acknowledge. And part of why we're all here today. We have to—"

"Is the queen ill?"

Another awful silence fell as everyone turned to look at Lord Sesar

Barthel, who, like my father, had said very little since our meal had begun. He was a handsome man, brown-skinned and white-haired, with the stern visage of an exacting teacher.

I glanced quickly at Ryder. We had all agreed not to mention Yvaine's outburst, but now that we were sitting here, it seemed irresponsible to keep that a secret too. Ryder frowned, saying nothing. Alastrina widened her eyes, shook her head ever so slightly at him.

"That silence tells me all I need to know," Lord Sesar said, grim and tired. "What is it? A natural disease? Some sort of magical infection? Is someone trying to kill her?"

Young Elianor looked horrified. "*Can* someone kill her? Is that even possible?"

"We can't say for sure," Gareth replied carefully, "but I imagine it would be extremely difficult."

"But not necessarily impossible," countered Lord Sesar.

Gareth glanced at me, then said reluctantly, "No. Not necessarily."

Gentar leaned forward, earnest and fierce. "But *possibly* impossible. The gods might very well have imbued her with invincible strength when they chose her to be queen. And until proven otherwise, that's what I'm going to believe. She's never done anything but good for us, and if she *is* ill, it's no fault of her own. And she can't be held entirely responsible for poor decisions she might make while not herself, can she? That's why we're all here, isn't it? To help the queen, to be her strength when her own wanes. Right now it seems she *does* need our help. That's all I need to know."

Gentar's mother, Lady Respa, raised her glass. "Hear, hear." More murmurings of agreement rippled down the table.

But then Lord Alaster cleared his throat and said smoothly, "A lovely sentiment, young Gentar, but there's even more to this story than a sinkhole and a mad queen. Isn't there, Ciaran?"

"Lord Alaster," Gemma said reasonably, "the queen is not *mad*, and it's uncharitable to say so."

Alaster waved her silent. "The Barthels and the Nashes, I think, do not yet have all the information they should."

Lady Enid touched her husband's sleeve. "Alaster…"

He ignored her and went on. "My children and their new friends journeyed to the Old Country only a few weeks ago, and there they fought a monster, for lack of a more precise term. A monster who had enslaved a demon and used that demon to foment discord between my family and the Ashbourne family."

Alastrina glared at her father. "I don't know what this has to do with anything. We're here to talk about the sinkhole and the Middlemist, not—"

"But don't you think it's all something of a piece, my dove?" Alaster said, his voice sweet but his eyes hard. "And anyway, our friends ought to know whom, exactly, they're agreeing to work with."

Gentar, his potatoes at last forgotten, looked at Gemma and me with shining eyes. "So it *is* true, the legend about the demon. Did you kill it? And the monster too? What kind of monster was it?"

"No, they didn't kill either of them," Lord Alaster replied. "In fact, they *freed* the demon, if you can believe that. They freed a creature known for deception and bloodlust. And now," he added, his gaze sliding slowly to Gemma, "one of them is fucking it."

Shock washed over everyone like a cold wave. Father slammed his fists against the table and surged to his feet, a slight wave of his sentinel power crackling through the room. Everything—table, chairs, all of us—flew up from the floor an inch or two before slamming back down.

Lord Alaster watched him from the head of the table, expressionless. He raised his glass and took a drink.

"You absolute shit," Father spat at him. Ryder rose, as did Gentar and Lady Kaetha. I tensed, bracing myself for the inevitable, for this whole night to come crashing down around us. We would have to go home at once; we would have to tell the queen we couldn't do it, that we couldn't bring ourselves to cooperate for five minutes, much less long enough to help her.

But then Gemma went to our father and took his hand in hers. He froze and looked down at her gloved fingers, completely stunned, and all the fight seemed to go out of him in an instant. It was the first time Gemma had acknowledged his existence since the revelation of what he and my mother had done to her as a child, how they had hired an artificer to alter her body and stifle her unpredictable power. A horrible softness melted my father's furious expression; I could hardly bear to look at him.

"The demon you speak of is no monster," Gemma said, her head held high, her voice unwavering. She had grown so much, my sister, during these last months. How strange it was to hardly recognize the woman standing before me and yet, at the same time, to see her smiling, innocent child self shining in her face. How marvelous, to know her and yet constantly be meeting her for the first time. "His name is Talan," she said, "and his master was the monster. Talan is just as much a person as you and I and everyone sitting at this table. You will not speak of him otherwise."

Lord Sesar considered her gravely. "And his master? He still lives?"

"We can't be sure," I answered on Gemma's behalf, giving her a moment. "We still know very little about him. But we fought him, and we believe we wounded him, perhaps severely."

Lady Kaetha looked skeptical. "You *believe* you wounded him?"

Gentar sat back down, his eyes still shining eagerly. "How'd you do it, then? What did he look like?"

"We used our gods-given powers," Ryder said, "as we all must in the months to come, in the name of Edyn and in the name of the queen. My wilding magic and my sister's. Farrin's power of song and Mara Ashbourne's sentinel strength."

He paused then, and in the brief beat of silence, Lady Respa looked keenly at Gemma.

"And Lady Imogen?" she said. "What did she do? Being near such a display of magic must have been painful for her."

Lord Alaster let out a soft laugh. "She embraced her demon lover and crooned a lullaby to make him feel better."

Now Alastrina was the one to snap. "Father, for the love of all the gods," she spat, looking fiercely at him, "would you do all of us a kindness and shut your mouth unless you have something useful to say?"

This was perhaps the worst silence of all. Lord Alaster slowly lowered his glass and stared at his daughter, eyes glittering, and I saw the mighty, beautiful Alastrina Bask shrink right before our eyes. She sat back in her seat, pale and speechless, shoulders slightly hunched as if to protect herself from an oncoming blow.

Gemma spoke into the sudden spooked quiet. "I was able to break the curse, Lady Respa. The monster known as Kilraith had woven a wicked glamour around Talan, and I broke through it and dislodged the object that bound them together."

"She also tore entire trees from the ground," said Lord Alaster mildly, still staring down his daughter. "She flung them around like weapons. So my children told me."

I shot an angry look at Ryder, though I had no right to. We'd told our father the same story.

Lady Kaetha was astonished. "But Lady Gemma has no magic."

"It seems she does now. Strange, isn't it? That a woman for whom magic is anathema was able to traipse into the Old Country illegally— with the assistance of a shieldmaiden of the Order, no less—and suddenly bloom into a freak possessing divided magic? The magic of

Kerezen *and* the magic of Caiathos? What other secrets might the Ashbournes be keeping from us, I wonder?"

My father tore his hand from Gemma's grip and took a ferocious step toward Alaster. "You dare to accuse my daughter of misdeeds when she has done nothing but fight evil and free a bound creature from forced servitude? And when your own children were right beside her, helping her, defending her?"

Gemma gaped at him. Now it was her face, shocked and grateful, that I couldn't bear to look at. She reached for Father's hand again with tears in her eyes, and he took it without looking back at her, seething at Lord Alaster like a wild animal defending his young.

Lord Alaster remained unperturbed. "For all I know, she might have influenced my children's minds, forced them to trespass into the Oldenside with her. Maybe her beloved demon has been teaching her his ways."

"Alaster, please stop this," Lady Enid said quietly, gripping the edge of the table hard. "It's difficult enough for us all to sit here and talk about such uncertain things, our friendships so new. What are you trying to prove by riling tempers?"

Lord Alaster whirled on her, his arm raised as if to strike. *"Friendships?"*

I jerked forward in my seat. I heard Lady Leva's alarmed cry, Gentar's indignant shout.

But before any of us could move, Ryder surged forward and grabbed his father's arm. Alaster rose, fighting him, trying to free himself, but Ryder held fast. They struggled in silence for a moment until Ryder seemed satisfied by something I couldn't see. He flung his father free with a grunt of disgust. Lord Alaster resumed his seat and retrieved his fallen napkin as if nothing had happened.

In the shocked silence, Lord Sesar spoke. "It's interesting to me that these events are transpiring all at once," he began, without accusation. He sounded thoughtful, somber. "The sinkhole opening in the Citadel, the chimaera attacking. This...demon...being freed. The monster Kilraith losing his slave, perhaps suffering injury. The Middlemist becoming more dangerous, volatile, violent. A sort of sickness spreading through the Mistlands. Lady Gemma experiencing an onset of powerful and unfamiliar magic. All of this remains unexplained, and yet at the heart of so many of these incidents is an Ashbourne and a Bask."

The unspoken questions hung in the air: *Why you? Why these families? What does it mean? Why has the queen chosen you to rally her people?*

These were questions I couldn't answer. But I tried my best, desperate for any sort of reassurance in the midst of this terrible dinner.

"This is why we've asked you all here," I said, my voice surprisingly steady. "Because we trust you, because you are influential and respected, your blood blessed by the gods, and because no family—not even two families—can unravel this mystery alone."

I looked around at all of them, even Lord Alaster, hoping they would see in my eyes or hear in my voice something true, something inarguable that would strike a chord of understanding in their hearts.

"Whatever is affecting the Middlemist," I said, "whatever created the sinkhole, could also be affecting the queen. She must be protected at all costs. If she falls ill, truly ill, and can no longer reinforce the sinkhole, then the Citadel could fall, and after that the capital. And that disaster, and the Mistfires, and every other new strangeness emerging in our world will only be the beginning. We must find the answers she cannot, allow her the space to heal and protect herself and, therefore, protect her people as best she can."

Those were all the words I could find. Without thinking, I looked to Ryder, a silent plea on my lips.

He did not disappoint me. "And we can't allow old feuds and

bruised egos to interfere with this task," he continued. "Doing so would mean betraying the trust the gods put in our ancestors—and even worse, betraying the trust the people of our country have put in us to keep them safe from what lies beyond the Mist."

I sat back in my chair, my mind whirling. I felt suddenly exhausted. A grave silence filled the room. Alastrina caught my eye and gave me a quick, firm nod. Father quietly took his seat; Gemma stood behind him, her hand on his shoulder, his fingers still holding hers. I clung to the sight of them both and dared to hope that this, at least, was the beginning of something good.

After a moment, Ryder said quietly, "I think it's fair to say that we all have much to consider. I suggest we retire for the night, think on what we've discussed, and resume these conversations at luncheon tomorrow."

I waited at the table until nearly everyone else had left. A strange feeling kept me sitting there, waiting for Lady Enid and Alastrina to leave the room. It was as if seeing them go meant they would be all right, somehow, that the shadows would fold them away into the house and keep them safe.

Lord Alaster noticed me watching them; his cold gaze settled upon me like the feeling of being followed.

I waited a beat, took a drink of water. If he was trying to frighten me as he'd frightened everyone else, it wouldn't work.

I left the room sedately, pausing to examine one of the tapestries, and only began to hurry when I reached the stairs to the guest wing. Once safely in my room, I shut the door and leaned back against it, breathing hard. What a horrible house, so dark and cold and quiet, with its looming black walls and its cruel-eyed master. At least my room was warm. A fire blazed in the hearth, and my bed was piled high with furs to ward off the northern chill. Beside it, on a marble-topped table, sat a small piece of paper, folded in half.

When I opened it, the sight of Ryder's familiar handwriting made my heart jump strangely.

Come to the northern stable yard in the morning, read the note. *I'll be there at eight. It's time to fight.*

CHAPTER 7

When I arrived at the stable yard the next morning, blowing on my fingers to warm them, I found Ryder already there, shirtless and sweating, fighting an invisible enemy with a long wooden staff.

The sight of him stopped me in my tracks. Even when he was fully clothed, his strength was obvious, but without a scrap of fabric on his torso, every line of muscle was startlingly...*present*. Broad shoulders, broad chest, sweat trickling down his abdomen and highlighting every chiseled line. Damp tendrils of his shoulder-length dark hair had fallen loose from their knot and now clung to his neck. He spun and swerved through a series of elaborate movements I couldn't follow. Beyond him, the blanketed horses stuck their heads out of their stalls to watch, their breaths puffing in the cold morning air.

I marched over to the stone wall surrounding the yard before he could catch me staring at him, but whatever advantage I thought that would give me was lost when I blurted out, "Why aren't you wearing clothes?"

He stopped exercising to look at me, then glanced down at his dripping torso. "I got hot," he said simply, "and I wanted to catch you off guard."

Then he rushed at me without warning, leaped over the wall, and swung the staff at my head before I could even think to move. The thing whipped through the air and then stopped right at my nose. Only then, standing there cross-eyed, frozen with fear, did I manage a muted yelp.

Ryder gave me a hard smile. "It seems my ploy worked perhaps a little too well. Do you not know to duck when a weapon comes flying at you?"

Mortified, I opened my mouth, closed it, then finally remembered how to speak. "You surprised me."

"That was the point. Most attackers don't announce their presence before having a go at you." He looked me up and down, frowning. "Why are you wearing that?"

My cheeks grew hot as I imagined how I must look to him: a shivering southern girl wearing a plain work dress, muddy boots, and a fur-trimmed coat so rarely used that the stiff leather creaked when I moved. Wishing fervently that I were anywhere else in the world, I made myself raise my chin and meet his gaze.

"This is what I wear most of the time," I told him. "Well, without the coat. It seemed practical to train in it."

"Fair enough. But we're not fighting today."

I stared at him. "We're not? But your note—"

"You're not ready to jump right into combat training. First I'm going to teach you how to strengthen your body."

"I'm not a weakling. I walk miles almost every day at home."

"I didn't say you were a weakling, did I? And walking isn't fighting."

He jumped back over the wall and strode into the stable while I stood there fuming, staring resolutely at the ground, unable to find even one sufficiently scathing reply and determined not to gawk at his muscled back. In general, I'd cared very little about muscled backs until this morning and didn't appreciate what the sight of his in particular was doing to me.

When Ryder returned, his arms were full of clothes. "These are my sister's work clothes. They'll be a little big on you, but they'll serve for now."

I unlatched the gate set into the wall and joined him, keenly aware of the horses' curious eyes on me. "Do you ever walk through gates like a normal person?"

"Of course. But it's more fun to jump over them."

"Are you a man or an animal?"

He grinned and tossed the clothes at me. I just barely caught them. "I suppose you'll have to wait and find out for yourself, Ashbourne," he said, and then paused, catching himself, and sobered a little. "Farrin," he said, with a little bow. A strange cloud darkened his face; he turned around to tug on a shirt of his own. "Hurry and change. We'll start with a run."

Ryder did his best to kill me. We began with a two-mile run, followed by carrying heavy flat stones the size of serving platters from one end of the stable yard to the other again and again and *again*, followed by punching a painted leather target Ryder held to his chest until I started to see spots.

"You're slowing down," he told me, maddeningly unmoved by the pathetic pummeling of my fists. Even when I missed the target and hit him—which happened more often than it didn't, a circumstance of my inexperience that I couldn't bring myself to be angry about—he was like a tower of stone, not even swaying back on his heels.

Anger blazed up in me, threatening to erupt. My hands hurt, I was sweating right through my borrowed clothes, and I dearly hoped that the horses were the only ones watching us. I shoved Ryder as hard as I could, which was nearly as impactful as a kitten barreling into the side of a bear, and then spun away, breathing so hard my chest burned.

"You're trying to make a fool of me," I gasped out.

"No. I'm trying to show you what you should be doing every day—or at least most days—to strengthen your body."

I wiped the sweat from my drenched brow and started furiously pacing the yard, refusing to look at him. "You could perhaps be a little kinder to start off with."

"You'll only be here a week. We've much ground to cover in that time. I want you to return home with aching muscles and a basic regimen to continue practicing. And you can teach your sister too, once you've started improving."

The thought of Gemma doing this alongside me, witnessing the extent of my disgrace, was too horrifying to contemplate. I pushed against the feeling as hard as I could, but I was too tired to think straight and muttered petulantly, "Why don't we bring her out here now? You can teach us both at once and save me the trouble."

"You'll be a terrible student with her around. Being a captive of the Vilia made her stronger. She'd run circles around you, and you wouldn't be able to focus."

I couldn't stand the matter-of-fact tone of his voice, as if he'd thought through all of this a hundred times and anticipated every single thing I could say.

I marched over to where he stood, putting our equipment away in a large wooden crate. I started to lunge at him, to shove him again, but then stopped, feeling foolish and childish, and lost my footing. He must have heard the imbalance in my footsteps; he turned around to catch me, one hand around each of my wrists, and when I tried to wrench myself free, he held fast. I twisted and fought, but still he had me trapped.

"If you found yourself in this situation during a fight," he said quietly, "how would you get free? How would you fight back?"

I hated him. I hated his godsdamned unruffled teacher's voice, and even more than that I hated how he looked at me, so calm and patient, his eyes like a vivid summer sky.

Inspiration came to me in a flash, and in a fit of rage, I pivoted slightly, put all my weight on my left leg, and slammed my right knee up into his groin.

He did release me then, with a slight pained grunt, and collapsed a little against the crate. But when I turned on my heel to leave him, buzzing with triumph and fury, I heard him laugh out a quiet curse, and he didn't sound angry. He sounded glad.

A strange feeling came over me then, a feeling like lightning on the horizon. A quiet burn in my belly. I fought a smile; I didn't *want* to smile. What was there to smile about? One small victory didn't make up for two hours of humiliation. Feeling hot and edgy with irritation, I hurried up to the house with no plan in mind except to put as much space between me and Ryder Bask as possible.

—◆—

The next few days passed in a blur of activity.

Every day, from the afternoon until late in the evening, our four families met to discuss strategy, scattered around the house in small groups or all gathered around the grand dining table. We debated what other families we could trust with the information we had, which was of course a point of major contention and led to many long arguments. We discussed whether to involve the Upper Army, comprised of magic-wielding soldiers, or perhaps just the Lower Army, whose soldiers used only conventional weapons and no magic. What would be the political consequences of telling one and not the other? There were also the questions of what official petitions needed to be made at the capital and at the university for funding and personnel; how we could make them as discreetly as possible so the Royal Senate wouldn't find us out and bring everything out in the open; and how to coordinate defensive and research efforts with the Order of the Rose.

Every night I went to bed with a raging headache, feeling stuffed to bursting with names and places and ifs and buts. My body was stiff and sore, and my nerves were utterly shot from hours of playing peacemaker between my father and Lord Alaster, the latter of whom seemed determined to provoke Father at every possible moment.

Worst of all, every morning I suffered through training with Ryder until it was time for luncheon. On the fifth morning of working with him, my patience finally snapped.

"Try again," he told me, standing a few paces from me. "And try actually listening this time."

"I *am* listening," I snarled from behind my raised fists. "I'm just not good at this, and no amount of repetition will change that."

"Oh, I don't know," he said mildly. "Let's try anyway. Two."

I blew a strand of hair out of my eyes and punched the leather target marked with a faded number two. I imagined the two was in fact Ryder's face, and my fist landed right where it was supposed to. I felt a small surge of satisfaction—that had been a good one, I thought—but Ryder didn't seem impressed.

"Four," he said.

Angrily, I hit another of the leather targets hanging from the stable rafters, this one bearing the number four.

"Three. One. Three. One. Two. Four. Four."

I obeyed, or at least tried to, but punching the heavy leather bags was hard enough without also having to think about numbers and pivoting my body, for each target hung at a different height and a different distance from me. I had to shift, dart, duck, and stretch, and command my muscles to move as they'd never done before, and I couldn't do any of this quickly enough. I kept forgetting where three was and punching one instead, and four instead of two, and Ryder kept saying the numbers faster and faster, so fast it didn't seem possible that anyone could move that quickly except for Father and Mara, and their sentinel power seemed to me in that moment like the worst kind of cheating.

I felt absurd, stumbling around in the midst of his soft-eyed horses, with Ryder's critical blue gaze on every awkward lunge of my body. I wore one of my own dresses that day—it was true, he'd said, that I needed to feel comfortable fighting in my everyday garments—but the skirts kept getting in the way.

"Aren't you a musician?" Ryder observed. "Farrin Ashbourne, the most talented savant on the continent? Fingers nimble as a squirrel, voice clear as starlight? Isn't that what everyone says?" He raised one sardonic eyebrow. "I wouldn't know, looking at you now. You have no rhythm whatsoever."

I flushed hot with rage and whirled on him, raised my poor throbbing fist to hit him—but then his words truly registered, and I paused, inspiration coming to me in a soft bloom of clarity.

I turned away from him, back to the targets. "Start again," I told him.

He watched me curiously for a moment, then obeyed. "One. Two. Four. Two. Three. One."

This time, I tried something different. This time, I thought of music. When I played my piano, I didn't think of each individual note, nor of the minute movements my fingers and arms and torso had to make in order to strike the correct keys. I thought of the phrasing, how a series of notes flowed and ebbed, how they changed tempo— slow, fast, slowing, now faster—how their dynamics carried them from soft to loud and back again. The theme was the important thing, the overall idea of the piece, the *feeling* the composer and the performer wanted the audience to experience as they listened. When I played my piano, rhythm fed tempo, tempo danced with dynamics, and each note, though precious on its own, was merely a part of the larger whole. When I sang, I was always thinking of the next phrase and where it would take me: the shape of the piece, the flavor of it, its rises and falls. Breathing through and past each peak and valley, working with the natural contour of each string of notes, and allowing them to help me rather than treating them as obstacles to dissect and conquer.

So, this time when I punched, the breath in my lungs became an aria, my feet on the ground worked piano pedals, the pistons of my arms were my fiddle and bow. Instead of agonizing over my body's individual movements, I breathed through every blow and jab, imagining each of them as just another tone in an arpeggio of muscle and breath.

When Ryder finally stopped calling out numbers, my head, arms, and fists were humming with energy—not the same kind of rightness I felt after playing my piano, but a small, stuttering sliver of that. I stepped back, wiped the sweaty hair from my face, and grinned.

Ryder, standing there with his arms crossed over his chest, gave me a small smile right back. "What did you do differently?"

"I'm a musician," I answered archly. "I found my rhythm."

He raised an eyebrow, and his smile grew. "Part of it, anyway. You still missed about half the targets."

"But how was I moving? It was better, wasn't it? Just tell me it was, even if it's a lie. I feel too good right now to receive criticism."

"What an insolent student you are," he said, but he was still smiling as he turned to start unhooking the targets, and the sight warmed me from head to toe, emboldening me.

"When do I get to start fighting *you*?" I asked.

He paused, then turned. I couldn't decipher the look on his face; when his gaze locked with mine, I felt a little shiver of anticipation.

"We could try sparring a little right now," he said slowly, "just for a few minutes, before luncheon."

"Wonderful." I put up my fists and got into position. "Let's do it, then."

He smirked. "So eager to punch me in the face."

"Am I that obvious?"

"To me you are," he said quietly, but before I could think about what he meant by that, he swiveled around and let his fist fly at me. I ducked, felt the air of his punch whoosh past me, and stumbled back on my heels a little, but I caught myself and spun around before he could strike again. I bounced on the balls of my feet, looking at him from behind the wall of my fists. He was wickedly fast and much stronger than me, but I couldn't deliberate forever. I breathed in and out, and then I struck out at his face with my fingers bared. I could claw an eye out, I could rake my nails across his cheeks; these were things he had taught me. But he dodged my blow and punched low; his fist landed squarely on my stomach, and even though I knew he was holding back for my sake, the impact still knocked the wind out of me. He took the opportunity to grab me around my middle and yank me back against him.

At first, stunned, I could only struggle ineffectually in his arms. His chest was a wall at my back, his grip like iron, and my vision was still a little fuzzy from the blow to my stomach.

"Think, Farrin," he said quietly, his breath hot against my ear, his lips grazing my skin. Goose bumps raced down my arms, and before he could do *that* again, my senses returned. I stomped hard on his instep, and he swore and released me. I slipped away and grabbed the wooden staff leaning against the nearby wall; I held the thing with both hands, not entirely sure what do with it, and whirled around to fling it at him.

But he was ready; of course he was ready. He'd grabbed the other fighting staff, and it met mine with a huge crack that hurt my teeth. I pushed hard against his weapon with my own, but I was closer to the wall than I'd realized, and with a single hard push, he had me trapped against it.

Our gazes locked above the cross of our staffs. I was gratified to see that he was breathing hard; he'd won, but I'd made him work for it.

I grinned at him, giddy and exhausted, my head still ringing from our staffs crashing together. And then he did the most remarkable thing. His face softened as he looked down at me, and he reached out with one hand—his other still held his staff against mine, pinning me against the wall—and gently brushed a sweaty strand of hair from my cheek.

"Well done, Farrin," he said quietly.

I stared at him, my heart thundering. I'd never seen Ryder like this, never seen such a tender look on that rough bearded face of his. I didn't understand it, and I didn't understand my own response to it. I was trapped, vulnerable and outmatched, his tall, broad frame looming over me, but I didn't feel unsafe. Far from it. In fact, I found myself leaning toward him, wishing desperately, unthinkably, that he would touch my cheek again. Something about that touch felt familiar; if he did it again, I would lean into it, grab his hand, and hold it against my skin.

"I..." I couldn't think of what to say. I swallowed hard, my mouth suddenly dry. I wet my lips and felt a panicked sort of thrill when I saw his gaze drop to my mouth. "Did I hurt you? You know, when... when I stomped on you?"

"I'll live." He smiled a little, and then something dark and sad fell over his face, and he lowered his staff and turned away from me. He walked back to the hanging targets and resumed putting them away.

The abrupt dismissal galled me for reasons I couldn't explain. I marched over to him. "What was that about?"

"What was what about?" he said flatly, not looking at me.

"The..." I gestured at the wall. "You..."

He turned to look at me straight on, waiting for me to speak. But I didn't know how to put into words how it had felt when he'd touched me, how I hadn't been frightened to be shoved up against the wall by a man who was until recently a sworn enemy, how I had in fact been...

Bristling, mortified by my own realization, I stepped back from him, holding my staff in front of me like a shield, but before either of us could say another word, there was a thunderous roar from outside and a cacophony of flapping wings.

We hurried into the stable yard just as a plume of dark feathers burst up from the expanse of forest between the stables and the mansion. Hundreds of ravens, maybe even thousands, swarmed through the bright autumn sky in obvious confusion. And then, cascading down the mountain from the house, came an urgent clangor of bells.

Ryder turned to find me, his expression fearsome. "Come with me. Stay close."

I hurried up the mountain behind him, my legs like jelly after the hard morning. "What do those bells mean?" I thought of the Citadel going into lockdown, the tapestry of monsters hanging in the Ravenswood dining hall, and a stone of dread dropped into my stomach. "Is it the Mist?"

"Could be," he replied tersely, but he said nothing else, not until we reached the broad stone drive that led up from the forest road to the mansion. A footman came barreling down to greet us.

Ryder stepped a little in front of me, his arm out as if to shield me. "What is it?" he snapped.

"It's Lady Alastrina, my lord," said the footman, eyes wide, face ashen. "She's gone."

At first the word didn't make sense to me, like gibberish uttered by an infant.

"Gone?" Ryder said sharply. "What do you mean? Explain."

The footman shook his head. "We were all gathering for luncheon, my lord, and were about to send for you, but then there was this great darkness that swept fast through the room, and it left everyone cold and confused, and when it was gone, so was Lady Alastrina. She'd vanished."

Ryder stormed past him. "Nonsense. She simply left the room."

"No, my lord," said the footman, jogging alongside him. "She couldn't have. It all happened so quickly—"

"She's elsewhere in the house," Ryder insisted. "She's giving us all a laugh."

But I didn't believe that, and I suspected he didn't either. The cloud of ravens still roiled in disarray above the treetops, calling out to one another—or to Alastrina, I thought, dizzy and cold. They knew she was gone and were trying to find her.

Inside the house, everything was chaos. Lady Enid was running from room to room, calling Alastrina's name and searching every corner for her, shouting at the servants to do the same. Gemma hurried after her, trying in vain to calm her. She threw a helpless look over her shoulder at me, then gestured frantically toward Father, who was huddled in an antechamber off the dining hall along with everyone else.

It was infuriating that one of us had to be watching him at all times, but I gritted my teeth and went to him anyway. He was standing a little behind Lord Alaster, who faced a dark mirror framed with silver filigree. Another man's tearful face stared back at him; the mirror, then, had been spellcrafted by a beguiler, turned into a conduit of communication with another mirror located miles away. I felt begrudgingly impressed; such mirrors were incredibly rare, as the magic required to create them was tremendous and, by all accounts, agonizing to conduct. The man's image was watery and faint, and the pulses of magic coming off the mirror turned the whole room sour, making me think the man was very far away. But the sound of his voice was clear enough, and suddenly I recognized him: Uven Lerrick, a wealthy Anointed wayfarer who lived near Blighdon, on the southeastern coast.

"The same thing happened to us," he was saying. From behind him came the sounds of crying and muffled shouts. "One moment we were all here, and the next, a great rush of shadows washed across the room, and I felt horribly cold, disoriented, my sight gone, my hearing gone. Then the shadows vanished, and my Dornen was no longer here. He just...he *disappeared*, Alaster."

Father's expression was grave. "Two Anointed humans on opposite ends of the continent, both gone in an instant?"

"And in the exact same manner," murmured Gareth. "One I've never heard of before, at that."

"We'll search the grounds for her," said Ryder fiercely. "She'll be here somewhere. Whatever happened is just some minor magical abnormality. The Mist, having a bad day."

"And suddenly abducting people?" said Lady Kaetha, frowning. "One from hundreds of miles away?"

"The Citadel's even farther away than that," Lord Sesar pointed out, "and it's got a sinkhole inside it. What's happening at the Mist is unprecedented in recorded history. None of us can predict what the effects might be."

I touched Ryder's arm before he could stride away. "Wild a raven and send it to Rosewarren," I suggested quickly. "And send one to the queen as well. If anyone else has disappeared, Yvaine or the Warden will know."

Mara, I thought, biting down on the small, dear word. I was too embarrassed to request that Ryder ask after her specifically, but I think he saw it in my face. He found my hand and squeezed it, my small hand held tightly in his own larger, calloused one for a brief second that left me flushed and unsteady. Then he left us, roaring at the servants to search the house, the grounds, the forest. Lord Alaster stayed where he was, staring in shock at the mirror, which had gone dark.

I raced after Ryder but stopped when I saw Gemma sitting on the floor in the receiving hall, holding a sobbing Lady Enid. Gemma's face was gray, drawn. Whatever magic had swept through this house had pulled something from her, but she shook her head at me and said quietly, "I'm all right."

I knelt and quickly hugged her. "Mara," I whispered. "Do you think..."

"Mara's safe," Gemma said firmly. When I pulled back from her, her eyes shone at me like twin blue stars. "She's *safe*. Go. I'll look after Father."

I kissed her forehead and hurried outside. The ravens still circled overhead, casting hundreds of flittering shadows across the ground. Their cries were terrible, hoarse and despairing. I ran into the woods, as everyone else was doing, including each family's servants. I ducked behind a tree before my lady's maid, Hetty, could spot me. I didn't want anyone coming with me and stoking the flames of my rising panic with their own. Shadows sweeping through the house, and in their wake, Alastrina gone? And Dornen too, from so far away, and I hoped no one else, though the sinking feeling in my stomach told me that was a futile thing to wish for.

The pine forest surrounding the Ravenswood estate was vast, the trees tall and ancient. Soon I couldn't hear anyone else shouting for Alastrina; I was alone. I stumbled over ridges and through tangled thickets, looking everywhere for a gleam of shining black hair, a flash of pale skin. I called for Alastrina several times, but as the forest deepened and the trees thickened, every sound grew muffled and strange. Finally I fell quiet; the smothered, flat tone of my own voice was frightening me.

I came to a stop beside a fir tree with a trunk as wide as two broad doors. I leaned against it, reassured by its massiveness, and caught my breath, shivering a little. I looked up at the thick canopy, all those branches laden with needles, swaying and whispering in the mountain air. Very little sunlight managed to break through them, and the air was cool and damp. I looked through the trees for the mansion, but I couldn't see a bit of it, nor of the outbuildings and stables. I could see only trees, and every one of them looked the same. I listened for the ravens; I heard nothing.

Cold feet of fear started climbing up my spine. Running off into a strange forest on my own suddenly seemed like the most foolish thing I could have done. And then, almost as soon as I'd thought that, I felt with absolute certainty that someone was watching me. Everything was so still, the air heavy against my skin. I was not alone.

Frantically I looked around for a weapon, any weapon, and spotted an enormous fallen branch. I heaved it up from the forest floor and spun around clumsily to press my back against the tree. The branch was too heavy to be of any real use to me, but I tried to hold it up anyway, like I thought someone might hold up a spear. My arms shook under the weight of it; I held my breath and listened. Sweat rolled down my back. Then I realized I *did* hear something—a low hum like the buzz of magic, or a distant teeming hive of bees, or maybe a fire roaring in the next room. My mind couldn't quite make sense of it; every time I thought I had pinpointed it, the sound shifted and slipped out of my grasp.

But I knew it was close. Something was making that noise, and it was behind me, beyond the shield of my tree, and it wasn't moving, and I knew—I *knew*, with the instinct of prey—that it was waiting for me.

I couldn't bear to just stand there anymore. I needed to fight; I needed to run. If I stayed where I was, I'd be disappeared, just as Alastrina had been. My heart pounding, white-hot panic tearing through me, I gripped the branch and imagined driving it into flesh and bone. I would do it if I had to. I could kill.

I lunged out from behind the tree and spun around, fumbling with the branch, almost dropping it, a muted cry of terror bursting out of me, and froze.

A creature stared back at me, though I wasn't sure that was the right word. It was made of fire, I thought at first, but then the flames shifted and became feathers in a glorious array of colors: scarlet and gold, sunrise orange and sunset violet, all outlined with shimmering white. It was fire, then feathers, then flames again, and at the heart of this restless conflagration was a white-blue kernel, an agitated shape. First it was a bird, beaked and mighty, a raptor with piercing eyes, its wings rising up as if it was ready to alight upon a mountaintop. Then I blinked, and it was a person, maybe a woman, tall and lissome—*too* tall, unnaturally tall, with the same lightning-hot eyes and feathers falling around her like hair, like an extravagant gown. I blinked once more, and the creature was simply a column of fire, sparks spitting off of it and bouncing harmlessly onto the wet black ground.

For a long moment, our eyes locked—if those were indeed eyes fixed on me, fierce and unblinking, and not an illusion. Then a spark from the creature's wing burst toward me, falling very near my foot. I flinched back from it, my nightmare of that long-ago fire returning to me in a paralyzing rush of fear. When I stepped back, I snapped a twig in two.

The creature flinched and shrank back into itself. Suddenly it was smaller, less terrifying, and it let out an ugly, discordant roar. Was it angry? Was it afraid? I didn't understand the sound, had never heard anything like it: beastly and musical, ancient. I thought I heard a crack of thunder, and the strike of a mallet against a bell, and a great tearing, like an underground seam of the world splitting open.

Then the creature turned and fled, darting off through the trees faster than anything should be able to move. I dropped the branch and took off after it, not knowing what I was doing, not knowing anything except that I couldn't let the creature out of my sight, not until I understood what it was. A word came to me as I tore desperately through the deep forest, following the creature's blazing brilliance. It was the only word I could think of to describe what I was seeing.

Firebird.

CHAPTER 8

I ran after the firebird for as long as I could, tripping over half a dozen tree roots and nearly tumbling down into a few rocky creek beds along the way. The problem was that I couldn't take my eyes off of the creature; the flickering train of its fiery feathers transfixed me, a burst of impossible color in the dark woods. I ran so hard my chest felt like it might split in two, but all my running was for nothing. I dashed through a dense copse of smaller pines, following the creature's trail and reaching desperately through the trees as if that would somehow bring it right to me, and when I burst back out into the greater wood, it was gone. All that remained was a few dwindling embers scattered across the ground and a faint scent of smoke spicing the air.

Breathing hard, blinking away the black spots dancing in front of my eyes, I started to hear faint voices calling to each other and realized I'd run almost all the way back to the house. Its fearsome towers loomed, their windows glaring at me through the trees. I ran for it, my body screaming in protest, and when I reached the stone drive, panting and shaky-legged, unable to speak, everyone there turned to stare at me—house staff, stable hands, Father and Lord Alaster, Gemma and Lady Enid and Gareth, the Nashes and the Barthels.

Ryder strode forward and steadied one strong hand on each of my arms. "What is it? Did you find her? What did you see?"

I gripped his jacket in thanks and said breathlessly, "There was a creature, a fiery thing with wings and long legs. It found me in the woods and then ran, and I chased after it but couldn't catch it."

Gareth hurried over eagerly, sleeves rolled up to his elbows and his hair an utter fright, as if he'd been running both his hands through it. "A fiery creature? Did it appear to be an animal or a human?"

"Both. First a bird, then a person—a woman, I think—then a bird again, and then nothing. Shapeless fire. Pure light."

Ryder glanced over at Gareth, who shook his head. "I've never heard of such a thing," he said. "But there has to be a connection between it and the shadows."

"Or maybe it *is* the shadow," said Gemma, coming over to join us. "If it can shift from bird to woman, maybe it can shift from fire to darkness."

Ryder looked back at me, his eyes bright and furious. I tried to imagine what it must feel like to have your sister torn from you like that, all at once and ruthlessly, by forces you didn't understand, and realized with a blow as mean as a punch that I *did* know what that felt like. I'd felt it the day the Warden took Mara away from us.

I touched Ryder's hand, which still gripped my arm hard, as if I were now the one keeping him on *his* feet. I noticed Gemma and Gareth exchange a glance and made a mental note. The next chance I got, I would robustly disabuse them of whatever ribald notions might be coming to life in those naughty heads of theirs. I merely knew what it meant to lose a sister, that was all, and Ryder had done me a kindness with his lessons over the past few days. Touching him meant nothing more than that.

"Where did you lose it?" Ryder said roughly.

I led them all to the spot, where a handful of embers still glowed in the dirt. Gareth measured each one, examined the singed bark of the nearby trees, and furiously scribbled his observations in a notebook he took from his jacket pocket. Everyone else fanned out through the forest, searching for any further trace of the creature but finding none. By the time we all tromped back to the house, it was evening; stars twinkled in the darkening sky. My cheeks burned with a sort of desperate embarrassment. I hadn't imagined the creature, I *knew* I hadn't, and yet we'd spent hours searching the forest and had found nothing. The silence in the house was sullen and afraid. We gathered around the dining hall table, and tearful servants brought out a cold dinner.

"I'm beginning to question my soundness of mind," I mumbled over a sandwich I couldn't bear to eat.

"We couldn't *all* have imagined the embers and burnt trees," Gemma said firmly.

"Unless that was all part of the same illusion," Gareth pointed out, "designed to distract and confuse us further. Figment sightings are rare by their very nature, but they have happened."

"And with the Middlemist weakening…" Father murmured, rubbing the bridge of his nose as if fending off a headache. I knew the feeling.

Lady Enid looked at Gareth curiously. "Figment sightings?"

"Figments are Olden beings who can create illusions in the minds of their victims," Gareth replied. "No one knows what they really look like, as they disguise their true appearances with what are essentially mirages, but I think they *have* no real appearance. They're ancient entities of an indeterminate magical substance, who have no physical shape we can see other than whatever forms they assume to play tricks on their victims."

I gave Gareth a warning glance; he was starting to sound a little too enthusiastic about Olden arcana, given the situation. He caught my eye and snapped his mouth shut with a sheepish nod.

"An illusion," Lord Alaster said quietly. His gaze lifted to fix coldly on my father. "And is it possible that these *figments* have loyalties that could be bought, should their employer have enough wealth at his disposal?"

Father glared back at him. "What are you implying, Alaster?"

"Hang on," said Gareth quickly, "we don't *know* that figments were involved here. It could have been anything. A team of particularly talented human beguilers, or even a fae, if one got through the Mist—"

"Is this supposed to be comforting, Professor Fontaine?" Lady Kaetha remarked dryly.

"I don't much care if what took my daughter was a figment or a beguiler or simply an ordinary human monster," said Lord Alaster. He rose from his seat, his long face white and pinched beneath his stark beard, and approached my father's chair. "What I want to know is if a guest in my own house has conspired with villainous forces to do the deed. Or hired someone to do it, which is far likelier. Can't get your hands *too* dirty."

At first, Father was just incredulous. He looked around at all of us, then back at Alaster. "You're joking," he said.

"You tried to have my son killed not so very long ago," Alaster replied. "Why would it surprise anyone if you killed my daughter now instead?"

Shock rippled up the table. I felt eyes on me, looking automatically to me for confirmation, but I was too tired and too horrified to do anything but sit there and wait for disaster to come. To my left, Ryder, who'd been standing alone at the hearth, turned to glare at both scowling men.

"This is a waste of time," he said shortly. "Lord Gideon didn't abduct Alastrina, Father. What good would that do him?"

"Gideon Ashbourne," said Lord Alaster very quietly, his eyes glittering, "won't be happy until every last Bask is dead. Isn't that right, Gideon?" He leaned down to look straight at my father. "I don't blame you, really. We're men of war, after all. I myself won't be happy until all three of your daughters' bodies are spread before me, lifeless and cold."

Father lurched to his feet and slammed his whole body into Lord Alaster, his sentinel strength bursting across the room like a blast of heat. Alaster went flying back against the wall, but when he crashed to the ground, blood trickling down his forehead, he looked up with a mean grin on his face. My heart sank; he was an Anointed alchemist, and his specialty was converting elements into raw power. I'd never seen him work magic before; I'd only heard my parents tell of it in revolted tones when I was a child, stories at dinnertime that sent me to sleep with hatred of the Basks brewing in my heart.

But Alaster's alchemical magic was a beautiful sight, or would have been if I hadn't been so frantic. He cupped his palm and dragged it down as if scooping up the air itself, and with a quick murmured spell, it became a white-hot ball of light hovering over his fingers. Another spell, and then he flung it at my father, who dodged it easily; it went flying over his shoulder and crashed into the far wall. Splinters of light went sizzling up to the ceiling and across the floor, making all our hair stand on end.

They kept going, my father with his punches strong as ten men and Alaster grabbing anything he could find—fire from the hearth, the very air around us, the water from our goblets on the table— and turning it to sizzling energy that he threw like Lower Army grenades.

In seconds, the table was in ruins, and everyone was screaming at them to stop, or cowering behind chairs, or preparing to work their own magic. Gentar Barthel was a fair beguiler, Lord Sesar an elemental with an affinity for water, and Lady Leva a healer who could mop up the aftermath. But this was not their house, or their fight, and I sensed their hesitation.

Lady Enid held her head in her hands and sobbed. "Please stop," she said, over and over. "Stop, stop, *stop it*!"

I didn't think before I did it. I was too angry and disgusted with them to think. I stood and began to sing. "Willa's Lullaby"—the folk song I'd been unable to sing in my music room at the Citadel—came to me almost at once. It was a simple melody, tender and lonesome. But in that moment, with all my anger behind it, the song became invective, each word bitten off with a snap.

> "Oh, little star, so bright in the sky,
> oh, big moon, shining up so high,
> can you see the bird's wing?
> Can you hear the bells ring?
> Can you feel my heart sing?
> Oh yes, come down,
> come down, come down.
> There's a world to be seen, oh,
> precious little grimlings.
> There's a life to be lived, oh,
> precious little grimlings.
> Don't you cry for the stars in the sky.
> Don't you cry for the moon so high.
> They can see the bird's wing,
> they can hear the bells ring,
> they can feel our hearts sing.
> Oh yes, come down,
> come down, come down,
> come down, come down."

Brilliant magic coursed through me as I sang, brighter and stronger with each word. When I stopped at last, the silence was deafening, almost physical.

I looked around, blinking back the glittering haze of magic, and saw that my father and Alaster had stopped fighting and now lay prone on the floor, not unconscious but near enough. They stared at the ceiling, their eyes open wide and their mouths moving in an echo of the words I'd sung. Everyone else in the room was either crying, tears streaming down their faces, or smiling insipidly at me—except for Gemma, who was helping Lady Enid back to her seat, and Ryder, who was corralling the servants. They'd gathered at the doors to gawk and weep. Even Gareth dashed a hand across his face, and he'd heard me sing more often than anyone else present.

The sight of their awe exhausted me, and the idea that my power had grown in might and beauty since our journey to the Old Country to save Talan made me feel sick. Now the sound of my music could leave *Gareth* undone? What would be expected of me in the days to come? If there were evils to be fought, would I be forced to sing again and again, even when I didn't want to, reducing everyone I met to a blubbering heap on the floor? And what if, someday, my music rendered its hearers comatose, or even killed them?

I looked at my father and Lord Alaster, glared down at them as coldly as I could manage with so much burning, angry fear roaring through me. "You both disgust me," I said to them, my voice coming out choked and hard. "Grown men acting in such a way, with no sense in your heads and certainly no shame." I took a deep breath; I could feel Gemma watching me, and Ryder too, and suddenly felt so blisteringly sad for us that my throat ached around a sudden fist of tears.

"None of your children asked to be born into your war," I said quietly, "and yet we're the ones doing all the work to end it."

I turned around to leave, afraid to look back at the men on the floor lest I discover that my words had done nothing but fall inert at their feet. Let them clean up their mess on their own, I decided; my bed was calling me, and the smell of the firebird's smoke lingered in my nose. I wanted nothing more than to sleep. But just as I started walking toward the doors, a sudden cry made me turn.

Gentar Barthel was rushing at me, his arms outstretched, a look of anger and desperate need on his face. I knew that look; my music had its hooks in him. I'd seen it before on dozens of faces, hundreds, as the audience swarmed the stage to claim me and my music as their own. I froze at the memory, my body gone cold and stiff, helpless. *Run*, my mind commanded me, but I couldn't obey. I was fourteen years old again, and the world was tearing itself apart right before my eyes.

Then, before Gentar could reach me, Ryder darted between us and launched his fist right at Gentar's face. The man fell back, caught by Gareth before his head could smack the floor.

Ryder stood over him, fists clenched, ready to strike again if need be. His whole body vibrated with anger, his eyes were bright with tears, and when he looked back at me, I saw the telltale signs of wonder on his face. He couldn't quite disguise it quickly enough, though he'd certainly tried.

My song had gotten to him, just as my music did to everyone, everywhere. Ryder Bask was no different than all the rest. I shouldn't have expected anything else; after all, my performance at the Bathyn tournament earlier that summer had propelled him toward the stage like a madman. It wasn't his fault; it was unfair to be disappointed in him.

I swallowed a tired sigh and felt myself pulling inward, my shoulders tensing. Knots burned at every stiff joint.

"We should go to Rosewarren in the morning," I said quietly, to Ryder and Gemma and Gareth. I ignored everyone else. They were the only ones who deserved my attention. "We'll meet with the Warden, tell her what we saw. If anyone knows what a firebird is, it'll be her. And we can meet with her in person about Alastrina, and Dornen, and..." *And anyone else who's been taken*, I thought, not daring to say it. I swallowed hard. "And I think..."

I paused. I hated the words I was about to say, hated what heartache they might awaken in Gemma, but it seemed irresponsible to delay this moment any longer. Guilt flared up inside me; at least three of Ryder's letters had mentioned this very thing, but I'd thrown them away without replying, too frightened by my own memories of that awful night in the Old Country to do what needed to be done.

"I think it's time to examine the Three-Eyed Crown," I said. "It's been hidden at Rosewarren for weeks, but it should be at the university. It should be studied. It may hold the key to"—I waved my hand—"whatever all of this is."

Another word I refused to say: *Kilraith*. But it hung between us nevertheless, giving a dread weight to the air. Were these machinations his doing? Anointed humans vanishing from their homes, the queen's palace compromised...

I met each of their eyes—Ryder, Gemma, Gareth. Ryder nodded curtly at me, his profile largely in shadow. I ached with too many things to name. I hurried upstairs, my boots crunching on shattered plates and ruined supper. That night, I dreamed of fire, but I didn't know if it was Ivyhill that burned, or a bird-woman dashing through a dark wood.

◆◆◆

The Basks had at least one greenway on their property, which led not directly to Rosewarren but rather to Devenmere, one of the little villages dotting the Mist's northern border. From there, we would travel to the nearby Order fortress of Thorngrove, and their greenway would take us to Rosewarren, and to the Warden, and—I hoped—to Mara.

But when we arrived in Devenmere the next morning, we emerged into utter chaos. Fires burned everywhere I looked; the air was thick with smoke, and the sky above us teemed with flocks of birds wheeling about in confusion. There were terrible noises, great piercing shrieks, coming from somewhere, *everywhere*—I couldn't make sense of them.

Ryder took one quick look at it all and then raced toward the biggest fire, maybe one hundred yards away. We followed—Gemma, Gareth, Father, Lord Alaster, Gentar Barthel, Lady Leva, and I. Thank the gods our healer had come; Lady Leva found someone moaning on the ground in a bundle of singed clothes and immediately set to work on them, drawing stoppered vials from the belt she wore around her waist and murmuring spells of healing.

Ryder was talking to a fierce-eyed old woman, her wrinkled face covered in soot and sweat. I walked toward them in a daze, shivering, and loathing the roar and heat of the fire. I searched the inferno for a bird of blue flame. Past the fire loomed a silver wall, seething and shining.

The Middlemist.

"They came all at once, three of them bursting out of the Mist," the old woman shouted. "They killed seven of us before we could even start to fight back. We lit a fire as quick as we could along the Mistline to keep any more from coming out. But our Anointed, our Lords Wynn and Moris, they're gone, Lord Ryder. They disappeared right out of their garden. My own Hari saw them vanish right after a strange shadow swept through the village. And the Order, they haven't come."

Those last words turned me cold, even though the air shimmered with heat. I looked to Gemma just as wood and glass exploded behind us. We whirled to see a huge beast standing in the mess of a ruined cottage: the bulbous head of a lizard, huge muscular shoulders crested with black fur, deadly curling claws on its feet, a bear's hulking furry body, a lion's whipping tail.

A chimaera.

It glared at us with clever yellow eyes, then shook its head viciously from side to side, and I saw with a wrench of absolute horror in my gut that there was a *child* in the creature's jaws, bloody and limp, quite obviously dead.

Arrows flew from three different places: from a man and woman perched on rooftops, using the chimneys as shields, and from Ryder, who'd brought his crossbow and quiver of arrows. Earlier that morning, I'd thought it strange for him to arrive at Rosewarren with an arsenal strapped to his back, but now I understood. He'd suspected something like this might happen, even if he'd hoped it wouldn't.

The arrows flew true, each one slamming into the creature's side with a grotesque thunk, but that only made it angrier. It dropped the poor child into the splintered wood and glass, and then it rounded on us and dragged its claws through the dirt. A flick of its yellow eyes, and I spun around to see another chimaera in the trees, this one slender and wily, feline save for its sharp-toothed goat's head and rattling serpent's tail. It crouched on a branch that sagged under its weight; it would pounce, and so would the other one, the lizard-bear, from the other side. We were trapped. The old woman gave an anguished moan; she expected to die.

Desperation awoke something in me. I found Gemma, and then Ryder, and a strange awareness passed between us, some shared instinct from that night in the Old Country reawakening. We'd fought necromancers and revenants and specters, we'd fought Kilraith in Talan's body, in that evil house by the sea, and we'd won. Even if that victory wouldn't last forever, it had indeed been a victory. We'd fought, and we'd triumphed.

Gemma nodded at me, her sweet blue eyes now grim and hard. Ryder grinned a little and glanced up at the sky full of bewildered birds. And I...

I began to sing.

"Willa's Lullaby" was fresh in my mind. I spat out every word with crystalline precision as Gemma and Ryder flanked me, their backs to me and their magic spilling out of them in ferocious waves.

Gemma flung her arms at the ground, and when she yanked her hands back toward her, a thick web of tree roots sprang up out of the earth, hissing and writhing. The chimaera pounced, both at once, from the cottage and the tree. With an angry cry, Gemma hurled the roots at the shrieking chimaera with the lizard's face, its jaws red from the child's blood. The roots slammed into the beast, knocking it back into the dirt. Gemma stalked toward it, her fingers moving quickly, as if weaving unseen threads through the air. The roots answered her, whipping around and around the monster into a tight net, but even as the roots engulfed it, the chimaera still fought, thrashing. As Gemma's net crushed its body and cracked its bones, its tireless ursine claws slashed through root after root.

With a furious yowl, the other chimaera leaped toward us. The thing was ghastly, unthinkable. A rasping feline roar burst from its mouth; its eyes were mad and white, slitted like those of a goat. The horror of it nearly made me lose my voice. But Ryder didn't hesitate even for a moment. He murmured words in what I thought was Ekkari—the arcane bestial language he and Alastrina had used, weeks ago, to wild the chimaera in the Citadel—and as he spoke, the confused birds wheeling about in the sky fell into formation, suddenly deadly and focused, hundreds moving as one—starlings, crows, sparrows, jays. They flew at the chimaera and swarmed around it, pecking and tearing at it with beaks and claws. The creature roared in fury and swiped at them, batting them away, but more kept coming, a whole sea of birds rising from the distant trees to join their brethren. I glanced at Ryder, wondering if wilding so many animals at once was exhausting him, but though his face was slick with sweat, his expression was ferocious, utterly unafraid. He held his crossbow at the ready, loaded with a thick black arrow.

The chaos gave the villagers time to run away from the fire, the beasts, the Mist, and into the forest to the north. I heard Gentar Barthel shouting at them to hurry, saw Gareth helping children flee a burning cottage right before it collapsed. Father fought a smaller chimaera all on his own, a hissing serpentine beast with a shell of bone protecting its head and chest. He ran at the thing with a roar to match its own and slammed into it with a horrible crack. The blow dazed both of them; the creature writhed on the ground, stuck on its back. Father spat blood and surged to his feet, unsteady. Then a ball of white light zipped past him and hit the stunned chimaera right on its exposed belly. Lord Alaster had thrown it, half hidden behind a collapsed roof, his hand crackling with residual alchemical magic and a triumphant grin on his face.

Father would be furious. Aided in a fight by none other than Alaster Bask? The memory would be a perpetual provocation, and Alaster would never let him forget it. But I refused to succumb to that particular worry. The important thing was that all three chimaera were either dead or nearing it. Gemma was tireless, drawing root after root from the ground and weaving a tight ball of wood around her chimaera attacker. Villagers who had stayed to help kept throwing her branches, even began hacking down trees and tearing up roots themselves to offer to her. The chimaera Father and Alaster had bombarded wasn't moving; brave villagers with cloths tied over their mouths to ward off the smoke were dragging the beast toward the fire. Once Father regained his balance, he waved them off and did it himself, lifting the beast onto his shoulders and single-handedly hurling it into the flames. As its body burned, a horrible stench wafted across Devenmere, rotten and green-smelling, like food left out to spoil.

And Ryder's birds gave him the chance to shoot. He advanced on the confused, mutilated chimaera, which still fought with claws and teeth, dragging down every bird it could. He loosed arrow after arrow into its sleek feline hide until at last the beast lay unmoving in the feather-strewn dirt, seven arrows sticking out of it.

I stopped singing then, feeling a bit foolish for having continued this long. Clearly, none of them had needed my help to fell the chimaera; the villagers had been more of a help than I.

But then from behind me came a skittering sound and a hard, quick clacking as of rattling teeth. I turned and looked up, and up, and my knees wobbled, my legs giving out. I knelt in the dirt before this chimaera, a fourth one that must have somehow gotten through the flames, or gone around them, and now crouched over me, ready to strike. It was a clever thing, its green reptilian eyes focused right on me; it had eight legs like a spider, all of them covered in hard bone and tufts of dark hair, each one ending in a pointed hoof sharp enough to gut me. And its face was indescribable, neither wolf nor snake but something hideously in between. It opened its mouth in utter silence, yellow fangs dripping.

I shook on the ground before it. I couldn't move, couldn't call for the others to help me. All I could do was sing—softly, brokenly, my voice a mere rasp.

"Oh, little star, so bright in the sky,
oh, big moon, shining up so high..."

The creature raised one of its front legs to strike; something viscous and black dripped from its hoof. Desperate, hot and cold all over, I dug deep inside myself and found my voice.

"Can you see the bird's wing?
Can you hear the bells ring?

Can you feel my heart sing?
Oh yes, come down,
come down, come down..."

The familiar lyrics poured out of me on sweet rivers of sound. With the beast's enormous shadow stretching over me, it suddenly felt wrong, even futile, to sing with violence in my voice. "Willa's Lullaby" was a tender song, so I would sing it tenderly. I would sing it with love, as I would have done for one of my sisters, as I *had* done for Gemma in those dark days after Mother left.

"There's a world to be seen, oh,
precious little grimlings.
There's a life to be lived, oh,
precious little grimlings.
Don't you cry for the stars in the sky.
Don't you cry for the moon so high..."

Tears of terror ran unchecked down my cheeks. The creature had frozen and now blinked at me in bewilderment, and I kept going, kept singing even though everything inside me screamed at me to run, to shout for Ryder, for my father. I sang until the chimaera began to sink toward the ground; I sang until its mean glowing eyes started drifting closed.

"They can see the bird's wing,
they can hear the bells ring,
they can feel our hearts sing.
Oh yes, come down,
come down, come down,
come down, come down."

I was running out of both breath and courage, and I began to panic. What would happen if I stopped singing? Would I have to sing for the rest of my life? I began to inch backward, sweat dripping down my body, the flames roaring somewhere in the hazy distance. I kept singing and kept singing, wanting to stop, knowing I *couldn't*, and then my hand landed on a boot, and I nearly cried out with relief. I held on to Ryder's legs as he launched his arrows—four of them in a row, striking right between the creature's closed eyes. The chimaera collapsed, its eight legs splaying out clumsily to all sides; it let out a last putrid breath that made my eyes burn. Blood trickled down its hairy, scaly face. It was still. It was dead.

Faint with relief, I shook there on the ground and listened to the others coming to help. Father couldn't lift the thing by himself and had to shout for Gentar and Alaster, and two other men from the village, and together they staggered to the fire and dumped the beast into the flames. It was only then that I realized how truly gigantic it was, how close I'd come to a gruesome death.

Someone was helping me to my feet, and when I realized it was Ryder, I let out a sob of frantic relief, because I knew then that the danger was gone. Ryder wouldn't let anything happen to me. The beast was dead. I was safe. I clung to him and hid my face in his coat. His hand cradled the back of my head, and I thought I felt his lips in my hair. I closed my eyes for a moment and savored the feeling of him all around me: his strong arms, his head bowing over mine. He was the enemy, and I'd hated him from the moment I'd learned what hate was, and yet in that moment his solid strength was a balm to my wildly beating heart, and I held on to him fiercely as I struggled to catch my breath.

"You're all right, Farrin," he whispered, a note of reverence in his voice. "You did well."

Then I heard a ruckus and glanced past Ryder's arm to see Father and the others rolling the great wooden ball that held Gemma's chimaera toward the fire. Gemma herself was on the ground, her skin gray from the tremendous working of magic, but when I tore away from Ryder to go to her, and drew her into my arms, she shook her head against my chest.

"I'm fine," she whispered, her eyes bright and fierce. "I'll be fine." She gave me a brave smile, and I held her to me as tight as I could.

Gareth came up to us, a dirty child in his arms. The girl was alive but silent, her face hidden in Gareth's collar. Her fingers were like talons in his shoulders.

"I don't understand," he said, clearly shaken. His eyeglasses were fogged over from the heat and smoke. With his free hand, he ripped them off his nose in annoyance and rubbed his face hard. "Why is there a village here, so close to the Mist? Clearly it isn't safe. Living here, with everything that's happening? It's a death sentence. I thought the Senate had long ago passed legislation forbidding *any* settlement within twenty miles of the Mistline, the only exception being Fenwood, for the sake of the Order."

The old woman Ryder had spoken to came over, her expression flinty.

"You've now seen for yourself what so many have tried to keep secret," she said quietly. "We have relocated our village twice, and now we shall have to do it again. The Mist is *moving*. It's growing." She paused, looking suddenly ashen, and then turned and retched into the dirt. "So far we've managed to outrun it," she said, still turned away from us, her voice strained, "but we can't run forever. And now, with our Anointed lords gone, vanished right out from under us? We're defenseless. The only reason I can say even this much to you is, I assume, because the chimaera have disrupted the magic in this area. But soon it will repair itself."

We all stared at her, except for Ryder, who glared stonily at the ground.

"Why wouldn't you be able to say this to us?" Gemma asked the woman, her voice tired and thin. "*What* will repair itself?"

"The Mist is *moving?*" Gareth shook his head. "Dislocating entire villages? Not possible. We would have heard about such a thing. The queen would've sent reinforcements, the Order—"

"The Order? The queen?" The old woman's mouth twisted. "The queen doesn't care about us up here, us poor villages along the Mistline. What do we have to offer her? We're not impressive. We don't throw parties or send tributes. We don't have the coin for long trips south around the Mist, or for greenways—save for the one in our lords' garden, which belongs to the Order and won't let anyone through unless the Order commands it. We're stuck here, running for our lives."

I couldn't stay silent after that. I rose to my feet. "The queen doesn't know about this, I can promise you that. She would have told me if she did."

The old woman looked me over—not cruel, just assessing. "Would she have, my lady?"

I couldn't answer her, unease trickling all through me. An even worse question came to mind: *Could* Yvaine have told me? *Could* she have sent reinforcements? Or was the knowledge of the Mist's moving northern border stuck somewhere inside her mind, trapped by stress or illness, and forgotten?

Father spoke next, his voice solemn, his clothes ruined, blood-splattered. "Why has the Order not come? This is precisely why the Order exists—to protect the people of Edyn from the Mist and from anything that might crawl through it from the Olden realm."

The old woman opened her mouth to reply, then closed it. Her jaw worked as if she were chewing on a word she couldn't say. She threw a furious glance at Ryder. "You were stopping here before going to Rosewarren, my lord?"

He nodded once.

"Then I would make haste and get there before the memory of this day fades from your minds and you no longer have the strength to face her."

"Her?" I asked, though I thought I knew who she meant.

"The Warden," Ryder bit out. "She has—"

He stopped then, exchanged a glance with his father. For once, Alaster didn't look smug or superior, angry or cruel. He simply looked tired, and that terrified me. He tried to speak but seemed to be fighting against something unseen, just as the old woman had, and could only manage a choked sort of sound.

An awful idea began to form in my mind, one so appalling I couldn't look at it straight on.

Ryder broke the silence. "Saska's right." He jerked his head at the old woman. "We should leave now, with the fight still all over us. And…" His mouth twisted; he looked furiously sad. "We should bring the child's body, if the parents will allow it. We should bring every body we can. They might give us the strength to…"

He fell silent then, as if whatever he'd been pushing against to speak had suddenly overwhelmed him.

We began gathering the dead as the flames at the Mistline crackled on. Sobs from the villagers floated through the air like ashes. Ryder led us to the empty house of the missing Lords Wynn and Moris, where the Order's greenway awaited us in a small garden of autumn flowers. A trowel and pail full of weeds sat abandoned among the blooms; a pitcher of cider and two half-empty glasses stood on a nearby table. I turned quickly away from the sight of them; each step I took felt loud and invasive, as though I were treading on bones.

The greenway thrummed quietly in the garden's corner, a dark mouth of ferns and tangled vines. The old woman, Saska, had told us that the greenway permitted passage only when the Order allowed it. I glanced at Ryder, a morbid question on my lips.. "It should allow the dead to pass through unhindered," he answered flatly, his eyes burning with quiet anger.

My stomach turned, the awful idea in my mind solidifying. Was it even possible for the Warden to keep such a secret? To bind people with magic so they couldn't speak about the true state of the Middlemist? The idea seemed ludicrous—I'd never heard of such spellcraft—and yet everything I'd seen made me think it was true. I thought of the tapestry in the Ravenswood dining hall, all those northerners racing toward the Mist to fight monsters, and felt a fresh wave of nausea. How old was that tapestry? How long had this been happening? The unopened letters from Ryder that I'd tossed away so angrily—had he spoken of this in those notes, at least as much as he could? And the northern chants his soldiers had shouted as the royal guard took them from the midsummer ball down to the palace prison—*Ariinya voshte, ariinya voshte!* Had that been a message, some cryptic way to circumvent the Warden's magic and tell everyone present what was happening? And there we had all stood, understanding nothing. And there I'd been at home, throwing Ryder's letters into the fire.

I couldn't look at him as we gathered at the greenway; I burned with shame, and with a desperate hope that the scenario painting itself in my mind was merely a deranged fantasy brought on by the stress of fighting chimaera.

But then an even more horrible question lodged in me, one I couldn't shake. If this was truly the state of things, what did Mara know? What had she kept from us? Or worse, did she know nothing? Had the Warden managed to keep this a secret from her own shieldmaidens, and that was why they hadn't come to help? I glanced at Gemma, at my father, and saw the same questions in their eyes. Gemma looked bleak; my father's face was a mask of angry stone.

Saska and two other women from the village had to peel the quiet, dead-eyed girl from Gareth's arms. She said nothing, but she fought them mightily, kicking with her bloody legs, reaching for Gareth with a desolate look on her face. Wordless protests burbled up from her throat; he had saved her from gods knew what during that battle, and now he was leaving her. How could he leave her? Gareth had to turn away, cover his mouth with his hand.

Once the villagers were gone, it was only us and the dead. I followed my father into the swirl of greening magic, looking back once to see Saska staring after us from the ruin of Devenmere. Beside her, Gareth's girl sobbed, one arm stretched toward us. I turned away with eyes full of tears and let the magic take me.

CHAPTER 9

We arrived at Rosewarren with a passel of Roses from Thorngrove in tow—three girls and two women, all of whom had been horrified to see us arrive at their fortress laden with the Devenmere dead.

The elder of the women, Merta, marched out of the Rosewarren greenway before the magic had even released her properly. A rope of it lashed out at her ankle with a crackling snap, but she paid it no mind. She took us at a brisk pace through the training yards and into the priory, where the dark hallways whispered with Roses watching curiously from the shadows. When we reached what Merta claimed was the Warden's private office, she slammed open the door without knocking, strode to the Warden's desk, and placed the dead child from Devenmere atop it.

The Warden, sitting calmly before a pile of papers, froze and stared. She wore her customary black gown with the squared shoulders and her dark hair pulled back in a tight knot, not a strand out of place. Her pale face seemed to lose what little color it possessed as she stared at the wrapped, bloody bundle. She lowered the paper she held; she placed her hands flat on her lap. I heard Father, Gentar,

Ryder, and Gareth gently lowering the wrapped corpses they carried to the polished tile floor.

"What is this?" Merta snarled at the Warden. She was wiry and fierce, her hair cropped short and her bare brown arms ropy with veins. Furiously she gestured at all of us waiting at the door. "These people have just come from Devenmere, where they say four chimaera attacked. They killed the beasts, but seven villagers are dead, including these, and we're lucky it isn't more."

Merta grabbed the Warden's desk, fuming, as if at any moment she would shred her way through it. "Why did we not know of this? You promised you would stop the old ways. You promised us you would release that binding, at least for *us*, your soldiers. You *promised*."

Shock poured through me like ice. So, there was indeed some great deception here, and at least some of the Roses knew about it. *Not Mara*, I prayed, even though I knew very well that the gods wouldn't listen to me, that they never listened to me. *Not Mara. She didn't know. Please, she didn't know.*

As if she'd heard my prayer, quick footsteps sounded behind me, and I turned to see Mara rushing into the room, her dark hair pulled back into a loose braid, her skin gleaming with sweat, dirt on her cheeks from the training yard. She wore a plain brown tunic and trousers and soft cracked boots, and on her shoulder was a brown, yellow-eyed falcon, small but fierce, with a speckled white belly and a keen, unblinking gaze.

Behind Mara hurried Gemma's friend Nesset, one of the Vilia whom she had helped free from a curse spun by necromancers. I allowed myself a moment of gladness upon seeing her; she was a brusque woman, but ultimately kind, and an excellent trainer to the younger Roses, Mara had said. Tall and muscled, Nesset wore flowers in her thick black hair, and a skintight garment of cloth, hide, and thick vines encased her body like a glove. Though her mottled gray-brown skin had become more brown than gray since breaking free of the Brethaeus's bindings, there was still something of a corpse about her: the green-black tinge to her fingernails, the flower-speckled moss binding the gnarled scars on her neck and arms. She was a revenant, an Olden creature raised from the dead by necromancers, and Gareth had warned us of the very real possibility that, without necromancy to hold it together, her resurrected body would someday fail her. But that day had not yet arrived, and I hoped it never would.

Gemma hurried over to her with an embrace that Nesset fiercely returned, though her stony black eyes were fixed on the dead child. Behind her were two young girls in brown-and-gray training clothes.

My heart seized to look at them; they were as small as Mara had been at ten years old, the year the Warden brought her to Rosewarren. Mara's quick brown eyes took in the entire scene. Her gaze flicked to mine, then to Gemma's. Her mouth thinned, and my stomach sank.

She *did* know.

Mara reached up to the falcon and stroked its breast, whispering something in an unfamiliar language. The only word I recognized was *Freyda*, which I knew to be the falcon's name. Every Rose worked with a familiar like Freyda, an animal born and raised in the Mist and therefore imbued with extraordinary qualities: a long life, preternatural intelligence, an uncanny understanding of language and human behavior. The falcon glared at us all, then flew off of Mara's shoulder and herded the two small girls away, chirping at them in harsh tones they seemed to understand and reluctantly obeyed. Nesset joined them with a scowl, her hands protectively on the girls' shoulders.

"Mara," said the Warden wryly when they had gone, "how wonderful that your family has chosen to visit unannounced yet again. And that they've brought friends as well."

Mara went to each of us, even Ryder, and embraced us one by one. When she came to me, I fought the urge to hold her to me and never let her go. She smelled of dirt and sweat; she was sticky all over from whatever work she'd been doing. She was wonderful.

She stared down the Warden, who looked unimpressed. "What's happened here?" she said, very low. "I heard some of what Merta said. Chimaera in Devenmere? And yet none of us knew of this, and the bells didn't ring to summon us there."

The Warden gave a tired sigh. She touched her temples and said, "Let's adjourn to the parlor and talk. I'll send for tea." Her gaze slid to the child's body on her desk. Something dark flitted across her face, highlighting the fine lines around her mouth and on her brow— the only signs of her age, though even Mara wasn't certain how old she was. "And I'll send for someone to take these bodies back to Devenmere so they can be dealt with properly by their own people. The priory is not a tomb."

"No," I said at once, surprising even myself. Ryder had implied the dead bodies would give us the strength to resist whatever veil of secrecy the Warden had engineered. We would keep them with us. "Where we go, they go."

The Warden stared at me until I very nearly lost my nerve. Then she rose from her desk. "As you wish. Follow me."

Once the tea and cookies had been served by a teenaged Rose in an apron, who stared at all of us with wide eyes, no doubt eager to take gossip back to the kitchens, the Warden began to speak.

"I suppose there's no use in evading your questions," she said evenly. She took a measured sip of tea and looked up at my father. "You saw the chimaera for yourself, Lord Ashbourne. You heard, I'm sure, what the people of Devenmere had to say about what they've endured."

Father ignored his tea, his fists clenched on his knees, and said nothing, didn't even give her a nod. I was glad; the longer we could keep the Warden talking of her own volition, the better.

"The fact is that the state of things here in the Mistlands is far worse than anyone knows, and I've worked hard to keep that truth hidden," the Warden went on. She sat rigidly in her chair, her gaze distant and flat. "One of my duties as Warden of the Mist is to protect the people of Gallinor, yes, but another duty is to prevent needless panic."

"I'd hardly call the people of Devenmere's panic *needless*," Gemma said, her eyes sparking with anger over the rim of her cup. I was pleased to see that some of her color had returned.

Standing to my left near a wall of bookshelves, Mara shifted uneasily from one foot to the other.

"The Order of the Rose has protected the Middlemist since the Unmaking," the Warden responded with awful calmness, "and it will continue to do so without burdening the crown, the Senate, or the people of this continent."

"But we are burdening the people," said Mara quietly. "Aren't we, madam? It's as Merta said. You promised us those days were over."

The Warden's eyelids flickered, not quite a blink. "I lied. I had to."

She stared at Mara for a long moment, but my sister didn't look away. She set her jaw and stared right back. My heart swelled with love for her. Gareth, sitting beside her, seemed quite transfixed by her, as if he'd never seen such a marvelous thing in his life, which didn't surprise me. She was magnificent, lean and strong, self-possessed and unafraid. With a jolt, I remembered that they had never met before, my sister and my best friend. I made a note to give them a proper introduction before we left and stepped softly on Gareth's foot. *Get a hold of yourself*, I said with a look. He hastily averted his eyes from Mara and took a loud sip of tea.

"You *had* to lie?" Merta scoffed, but before she could say more, the Warden silenced her with a single hard look.

"You are out of line, Merta," she said quietly, and only when Merta looked at the floor, angry and abashed, did the Warden continue.

"When the gods created the Mist," she said, "they made certain choices. They chose a woman to serve the people and made her high queen of Edyn. They chose another woman to serve the Mist and named her Warden. She was my ancestor, Llyris, and when the gods chose her, they blessed her with binding magic—unique to the human realm and tremendously powerful. I don't know why they chose her, just as we don't know why they chose the queen. I suppose they must have known Llyris was strong enough to withstand what they would do to her.

"They chose two other women to guard the Knotwood in Aidurra and the Crescent of Storms in Vauzanne. These were Tamina and Mariel, and the gods bound each to the magical rift of her continent, the place where the veil between human and Olden realms was thin. And in doing so, they bound their children, and their children's children, and so on, and with the inexorable compulsions inherent to the binding magic ensured these women had no choice but to have children, to serve the Mist. This magic even prevents them from ending their own lives, thereby ending their service."

A strange look passed over her face then; the corner of her mouth held a sad smile. "Interesting, isn't it? How our gods chose only women to serve them? How they bound them and gave them the power of binding in return, but nothing else? No mercy, no end in sight? And the gods did all of this to compensate for their own failings. They could have made the seal between the Old Country and Edyn complete, and yet they didn't. Was this a mistake? Or was it deliberate? I've never been certain which I think is worse, and now generation after generation has suffered as a consequence."

"A sad story," Ryder said tightly, breaking the awful silence that fell. He loomed at the edge of the room, arms crossed over his chest, brow fierce and furious. "And yet you're using this explanation to justify the secret you've bound us all to keep—this act of binding we too had no choice but to receive."

Suddenly he surged to his feet and rushed at the Warden. He knocked her from her chair and pinned her to the window behind her with his hands at her throat. She looked up at him without fear, as if she'd expected such an assault.

"When my family emerged from the forest that held us trapped," he said quietly, "we found that much had changed in our absence. The Mist had grown—not south, but north. Into lands you perhaps deemed less worthy of protection?"

Father looked away, his expression miserable. I wondered: Would he and Mother have trapped the Basks in that forest, an act of horrible vengeance, even if they'd known the truth? That without the Basks to help protect the north, the people there would be far more vulnerable?

I feared they would have.

The Warden blinked, her face reddening from Ryder's grip. "The Order cannot be everywhere at all times. I must choose how best to use our limited resources."

"And when we discovered what you had done," Ryder went on, "and that the people had been fighting for their lives without you to protect them, without *us* to protect them, we couldn't speak of it, nor write of it. Not to the queen, not to other families in the south. Hardly even to each other. You bound us all to secrecy while we slept. Us and hundreds of others."

The Warden gave him a strained smile. Her eyes were watering. "I did what I had to do. You would have done the same."

"No." He released her, shoving her hard against the window. He turned around, wiped his mouth. He was shaking all over; his voice was thick with sadness. "No, I wouldn't have."

"I don't understand," Gareth said quickly. I could see the gears of his mind turning. "How is such an act possible, binding hundreds of people to secrecy? I've never heard of such spellcraft. I know you're a beguiler, Warden, but—"

"Haven't you been listening, Professor?" The Warden stood with her head held high, red marks on her neck from Ryder's fingers. She didn't touch them. The word *Professor* came out sourly. "My blood is Anointed, just as yours is. Though whereas you were lucky enough to be born a sage, bearing the mind magic of Jaetris and enjoying keen intellect and an unflappable memory, I was born as *this*. I'm not only a beguiler; I'm a binder, one of only three in the world. And someday soon I'll have to find a man to bed me—it won't be difficult; many would do it in a moment out of sheer curiosity—and then I'll bear a daughter, and she'll become the Warden after me. And you ask me why I keep the fact of the Mist's true, ever-changing illness quiet and bear the burden of that secret for our queen?"

Suddenly, watching the Warden's black eyes glitter with that defiant sheen, seeing more emotion on her face than I ever had before in all my years of visiting Mara, I understood perfectly.

"You don't want the Mist to die on your watch," I said quietly. "And you don't want to ask for help from anyone, or tell the queen, because that would mean admitting weakness." I rose to my feet, suddenly so furious that my exhaustion faded in the face of it. "You'll weave secrets and lies to everyone you can, even your own Roses, if it means you'll have more time to repair whatever's gone wrong without anyone knowing the true extent of your failure."

Mara quickly stepped forward. *"Farrin…"*

"It's all right, Mara." The Warden stood behind her chair, considering me thoughtfully. "Your sister is correct. I *don't* want the Mist to die on my watch, and it won't. I'll mend it. I always have, and all my ancestors have, and my daughter's daughters will too. And if I can raise girls every year and send them off to die for this world, and feel my heart break again and again upon finding their slain bodies in the Mist—or worse, never finding them—then the people of the north will have to do the same, or else leave. A freedom I'm not afforded."

Gemma made an incredulous sort of noise. "And what of those who can't leave, for any number of reasons? We could have been helping them relocate all this time, if only you'd let anyone tell the truth about what they were enduring. You're willing to sacrifice the lives of innocent people to protect your own pride?"

The Warden looked sharply at her. "Relocate every northerner to the south, and then any monsters that come sniffing through the Mist for human prey would have to go south instead, dooming everyone on the continent. And what if I *did* tell the queen? What could she do, with her own palace compromised and her mind breaking? Oh." She said it softly, looking at us with mock surprise. "You mean you thought I didn't know? Of course I know. I've known longer than any of you. Yes, even you." She glanced at me with the tiniest of smiles, one that made my whole body blaze with anger. "The Mist was made by the gods, and so was the queen. They are *linked* as much as any two things in our world can be. The Mist is dying, and so is she. So no, I don't bother her with the details of how I protect her country. I simply protect it. And I choose to protect the most people I can, which means bolstering the Mist's southern borders and unfortunately having to abandon some of the northern ones. The south is more populous; the north's people are scattered, and there are far fewer of them. So there you have it."

She sat in her chair once more, hands clasped in her lap, and glared at the floor, her shoulders hunched, her face tired. My mind reeled with everything she'd said; I couldn't think of how to even begin to move through the world after such a revelation. Yvaine wasn't merely sick, she was *dying*? I found a chair and sank into it. I felt like the world had suddenly cracked open under my feet.

After a long moment of fraught silence, the Warden looked up, her ordinary implacable expression restored, and said lightly, "Have I answered all your questions to your satisfaction?"

"In fact, no," said Gareth bluntly. I realized he'd been taking notes this entire time and was now flipping through his notebook eagerly. "I have no fewer than fifteen questions for you—"

But he was cut off by a clamor of noise as Rosewarren's warning bells suddenly began to ring, filling the air both inside the priory and out on the grounds with urgent song. A sharp current of magic darted outward from the Warden in too many directions to follow—seeking out all the Roses on duty, I assumed. The Warden rose from her desk and looked outside, her gaze distant.

"If I have to endure one more eruption of godsdamned *bells*..." Ryder muttered.

"There's been a breach," the Warden said quietly. My skin tingled as I imagined what it must feel like to be connected to the Mist by the ancient binding magic the gods had given her bloodline. What kind of information was this power sending her, and how did it sit in her body? When she looked out at the silver ocean shimmering just beyond the priory's grounds, what did she see?

"Two werewolves coming down from a full-moon turning," the Warden said, "and a furiant, tearing a path through the forest. They're all fleeing...something. They're heading straight for Fenwood."

Fenwood. A chill swept through the room. Fenwood was a village on the southern Mistline, only a few miles from the priory.

"Fleeing something?" Gareth frowned, snapping shut his notebook. "If they're fleeing something, maybe they intend no harm. Maybe they don't even realize where they are. We should investigate—"

"Are you Warden of the Mist," the Warden said coldly, "or are you a professor who lives in a safe tower far from here and knows nothing other than what he's read in books?"

Gareth gaped at her, angry color darkening his cheeks. The Warden muttered something under her breath—spellwords, with another biting current of magic in their wake. Merta sat down heavily on a bench by the window, seething but silent; I suspected that whatever magic working the Warden had just uttered had bound her to her seat.

But Mara...in that moment, with the Warden's spellwork sizzling through the air, Mara became a soldier. She threw Gemma and me one quick look before dashing out of the room. Freyda gave a sharp cry and swooped down to her shoulder from the corridor's rafters. Gareth ran out after her, followed by Ryder and Gentar, and Lord Alaster, and even Lady Leva.

"No, please, don't follow her!" Gemma called out to our companions, but their curiosity was too tremendous, and soon I was racing down the hall to follow them, my heart thundering with new panic. Father, Gemma, and I had witnessed Mara's transformation only once, early this past summer. It had been an accident, one I knew Gemma would forever feel guilty about. This time, maybe I could stop them all—or at least stop Gareth—before they saw Mara in her most vulnerable, most inhuman state.

But Mara was a sentinel, like my father. She was strong and quick, and whatever magic the Warden had woven into her as a child, binding her to the Mist as a shieldmaiden of the Order, made her stronger and quicker. Before she even set foot outside, she began to change: her strides longer, her clothes shredding as her body transformed. Feathers sprouted from her arms; her fingernails elongated into gleaming claws.

Once we were out in the trees, she grabbed weapons from a younger, fierce-eyed Rose standing ready: a quiver of arrows, a spear, a knife belt. She slung it all onto her new body and sprang into the air—part woman, part bird, part indefinable beast. Her limbs were long and muscled and gleaming, silky, as if she were some water creature bursting out of the sea. Scraps of her clothing drifted to the ground like snowflakes as she tore into the air.

I finally caught up with the others, silently cursing both my aching body and Ryder for wearing me out so completely with our training.

"Look away," I snapped at them, panting. "This isn't for our eyes to see."

Ryder, Lady Leva, Gentar, and Lord Alaster all obeyed almost at once, and even Lord Alaster had the grace to look abashed. But Gareth stood there gazing up at the transforming Roses like a child marveling at his first rainbow, his face open and soft with awe.

As she flew, Mara called out to the dozen other Roses hurrying to join her, all of them in various stages of transformation. They grabbed weapons from the young ones and leaped into the air after Mara. She shouted back at them in a trilling sort of language, and they darted into formation behind her—their familiars flying with them or else darting along below on paws and hooves—and then they were gone. The Mist swallowed them whole; a thunderous silence fell over us in their wake.

I grabbed Gareth's arm and spun him around to face me, so furious with him I could barely speak. "I told you not to look at her!"

"I know, but..." He shook his head helplessly, and I was shocked to see that his eyes were bright with unshed tears. He had a small, wondering smile on his face, and he turned back to the Mist, as if the Roses would come bursting back toward us at any moment. "Gods remade, Farrin," he whispered. He wiped his face with his sleeve. "She's magnificent. I've heard the stories, of course, of Roses in battle—fierce and splendid, like something out of Olden tales—but to actually witness it for myself..." He turned back to me, dazed. "Mara. *Mara.* I've never seen a more beautiful woman in my entire life. Will you introduce me when they return?"

I almost slapped him. "Get hold of yourself. What's wrong with you?"

Behind me, Gemma's voice came sharply. "Will you not go with them? Do you never fight alongside the women you've imprisoned?"

I whirled and saw Gemma standing near the Warden with clenched fists, her eyes glittering with everything I felt: pride for Mara, and terror for her, and awful, desolate despair. It was torment to see Mara surrounded by these sisters who were neither Gemma nor me, and to be reminded yet again of how far she was from us, of how unfair it was for these girls to be taken from their families to be raised in this awful, dank place shrouded in the shadows of the Mist.

The Warden towered over Gemma, tall and fearsome in that square-shouldered black gown—but there was a quiet sadness there, too, in the lines of her face. She looked drained, defeated, and I wondered if sending the Roses away to battle took something from her, another freshly cut piece every time.

"My Roses have been well trained," was all she said in reply.

Father, standing in the shadows by the door, turned away and dragged a hand through his hair.

I couldn't bear the awful quiet. If I didn't say something, the cannon of anger in my chest would ignite and shoot someone, most likely Gareth. That moony look on his face made me want to scream.

Instead, I wrangled my thoughts into some kind of order and approached the Warden. Everyone else could stand around feeling whatever they were feeling; I wouldn't allow her to speak first, work some sort of binding magic on us, steer us away from why we were there.

"We've come here for two other reasons, Warden," I said firmly. "One is to report a strange creature I saw in the forest near Ravenswood. A firebird: a creature of flame, with aspects of both woman and bird. Given your experience with all things Olden and the form the Roses take upon going into battle, we thought you might be able to help us identify it and determine whether it was involved in yesterday's abductions of Anointed magicians."

The Warden turned to look at me. "A firebird," she said flatly, as if I'd spoken the strangest word ever conceived.

I resisted the automatic urge to apologize for my description of the creature, refusing to let the Warden cow me. I imagined her face as one of Ryder's faded leather targets, recalled the fluid rhythm of my body as it moved to follow his commands, and felt a welcome surge of calm.

"And we want to take the Three-Eyed Crown to the university for study," I added. "Locked up here at Rosewarren, it's doing no one any good."

"Nor is it doing anyone any *harm*," she pointed out coolly.

I couldn't argue with that, but I pushed my doubt aside and held her cold black gaze nevertheless.

"Very well," she said at last. "You, you, and you." She looked at Gemma, Ryder, and me. "And you, Professor," she added, the corner of her mouth quirking slightly. "You weren't there in the Old Country that night, but I've a feeling you will be someday. I'll take the four of you to see the crown, and we'll discuss terms. The rest of you can wait in the parlor with Merta and finish your tea."

Suddenly Merta was at the door, head slightly bowed. Mutely she guided Father, Lord Alaster, Gentar, and Lady Leva inside. She barely resembled the indignant woman we'd brought with us from Thorngrove. I tried not to think about what that meant, how often Mara might have gotten angry with the Warden only to be bound back into silence the next moment.

The Warden swept past us. "Come with me."

We followed the Warden into depths of Rosewarren I never knew existed—deep, twisting hallways of cold stone that turned back on themselves so many times I gave up hope of remembering the way back. Every now and then the Warden murmured something to her-self, the flames of our beguiled torches flickered, and I felt something in the air give way around us—most likely protective wards, though in my unease I imagined the earth itself shifting under our feet, creating corridors where previously there had been only dense rock.

At last we reached a small, round chamber. It appeared before us so suddenly, so unnaturally, that a chill cascaded down my body. And in the middle of it, sitting on a plinth of stone, was the Three-Eyed Crown.

Gemma went to it at once, crouched beside it, hesitated, then touched the thick silver band and its three embedded yellow jewels. She held it for a moment, then placed it tenderly back on the plinth and walked away from it, her back to us.

"Did you think holding it would summon your lover to you?" the Warden asked mildly. "The thing's inert. Whatever power it once held vanished the moment it was torn from its host."

I couldn't see my sister's face, but I could imagine everything she was feeling—every pang of heartbreak, every stifled nightmare of Kilraith taunting her with the voice and face of the man she loved—and I felt the strangest urge to point at the Warden and yell at Ryder to attack her, as if he were some vicious dog just waiting for my next command.

"Cruel comments like that are unnecessary," I said tightly instead.

The Warden nodded once, her expression unreadable. "I do apologize."

I didn't believe for one moment that she meant it, but I bit my tongue, silently fuming.

"Are you certain it is inert?" asked Gareth. Now he was the one to crouch beside the crown and peer at it, squinting through his glasses.

The Warden raised an eyebrow. "You doubt my assessment, Professor."

"I do. You said it yourself before: You possess binding magic, but no matter how powerful it is, that's only one kind of magic, and it's possible other powers might reveal something yours hasn't." He pulled out his notebook and pen and began scribbling. "I'd like to take some notes, observe the object while it's in an environment it's accustomed to."

"You're speaking of it like it's an animal," Ryder said. It was the first time he'd spoken in so long that the sound of his voice startled me. He glanced over at me, and my cheeks burned.

"I don't think," Gareth said slowly, "that we can discount any possibility when it comes to an object—and a curse—as powerful as this one."

The Warden turned to me. "Tell me more about this firebird."

I did, describing it in as much detail as I could, and when I'd finished, the Warden looked utterly perplexed. "I've never heard of such a creature," she said. "And you were the only one to see it?"

"Yes, but others saw its remains—burned trees, embers in the dirt." Desperate for her to believe me, I added, "I realize it could have been an illusion crafted by a figment, but—"

"Normally a figment's illusions don't leave behind traces for others to find," the Warden said. "I've never heard of an entire group of people hallucinating something like that. Though..." She sighed, a soft breath of sound that seemed to shrink her. "These days, with the Mist as it is and with thirteen Anointed magicians missing—"

"Thirteen?" Gemma turned to stare, looking as astounded as I felt.

"Well." The Warden paused, gave Ryder a quick glance. "Fifteen, including your sister, Lord Ryder, and the boy from Blighdon. By the time your raven reached me, the remaining thirteen had already been reported to me by other means."

"And given all your many years of experience battling Olden forces," Ryder said quietly, every polite word seething, every line of his body radiating tension, "what do you think has happened to them?"

"Impossible to say. Some Olden creatures hunt for sport, others for ransom. And then there's the Mist itself, which is neither benevolent nor malicious. It simply is. Likewise, these abductions could be an act of magic that simply *is*, albeit one we've never encountered before. Which leads me to my next point," the Warden said smoothly, turning to look right at me. "You want to take the crown to the university, try to find information about the curse it once contained. Fine. But in exchange, you must do something for me."

Ryder took a step toward us. "I'd think knowing that we were working to untangle a piece of this great mystery would be enough for you."

"That will be a tremendous comfort, Lord Ryder, to be sure. But I need more than comfort. I need bodies." The Warden took my hand; I flinched, but she held on tight. "The queen loves you. She listens to you, perhaps more than she listens to anyone else. So I need you to use that love for something other than your own enjoyment and privilege and make a request of her—no, a demand." She paused. "The Order's numbers are dwindling. To protect us all, it needs fresh blood, and the ordinary recruiting traditions are insufficient. One daughter only, magical families only…this is not sustainable. We need a mandate. Compulsory and far-reaching."

"What?" I breathed, horrified. "You want Yvaine to ask *all* families to—"

"No. I want *the queen* to *require* service of every family who has a daughter capable of withstanding the binding," the Warden said, her expression as hard and unflinching as her voice. "Every family, regardless of magic, must send their daughters to me—all of them, not just one—and every daughter who passes the trials must be inducted into the Order and bound to service."

Gareth stood, his notebook forgotten.

"You're mad," Gemma said, her eyes flashing. "Not once in the history of Edyn has there been a royal conscription into any army, Lower or Upper or Order."

The Warden glanced at Ryder. "Lord Ryder doesn't think I'm mad. Lord Ryder wishes I'd petitioned the queen for a mandate years ago. If I'd done so, maybe the north wouldn't have had to bear the brunt of the Mist's violence. Maybe his family and all their friends wouldn't have to constantly rush about bringing aid to people I don't have the resources to help myself. Isn't that right?"

Ryder glanced at me, then away. His expression was stony. "It may be the only solution, Farrin. The missing people, the sinkhole..." He trailed off. I heard the word he didn't say: *Alastrina*. And as much as I didn't want to, as much as the realization sat uneasily in my stomach, I understood. If one of my sisters had been taken instead of his, I might not have been so quick to condemn the Warden's request. In fact, I might have scoured the country and brought her new recruits myself.

"And we must begin the process as soon as possible," the Warden added. "The trials take time, and after they've shown us which girls can endure the binding, there's training, which also takes time. And time, I think you'll all agree, is something we don't have much of."

Gemma shook her head, looked at me helplessly. "But what about relocating Upper Army troops to reinforce the Mist, redistributing soldiers who have already volunteered to protect their country?"

"That's been tried before, many times," Gareth answered, frowning at the floor. "Whole army squadrons have become mysteriously ill or been physically *kept* from entering the Mist by some power embedded in the land itself. No fighting force on record has ever been as effective at repelling Olden forces in the Mistlands as the Order of the Rose. Most scholars—myself included—think it's something about the binding magic embedded in the Warden's bloodline, with which the Roses are then imbued during their binding ceremonies. It's like... the Mist *wants* the Order to patrol it. No other army will do."

"The *gods* wanted the Order to patrol the Mist," the Warden countered. Her back straightened proudly. "And the magic they left in the world doesn't take kindly to being defied."

I couldn't believe what I was hearing. "You want to send more children—*everyone*'s children—into battle against something we don't even know the shape of yet?"

"Not only children. Women too. Any girl or woman between the ages of eight and twenty-five. I can't afford to be too selective. And neither can you. And neither," she added, "can the queen."

She looked hard at me. "Remind her of that, would you? And if within a month I've heard nothing from you or the queen, have heard no rumblings of a mandate being drafted in the Royal Senate—or if you try something foolishly heroic like evacuating northerners to the south, when I've already explained to you why doing so endangers far more people than it might save—all of this will tell me you've broken my trust, which means I'll no longer trust you with the crown. I'll retrieve it, and you'll never see it again."

"You have no right to this object," Gemma protested. "It isn't yours. And how are we to trust that *you'll* protect it?"

"I'll remind you that after you trespassed into the Old Country—breaking our queen's laws and using one of my own Roses to do it—*you* brought the crown here, and you were right to do so. This is the safest place in Gallinor, one of the safest in the world, and it is thus because I've made it safe. *That* gives me the right, Lady Imogen."

She looked around at us, appearing both young and old at once, her skin taut but her black eyes ancient, fathomless. I was reminded uncomfortably of Yvaine, how she could shift from mighty to child-like in the span of a moment.

"Some people might think me reckless for allowing this artifact out of Rosewarren and into the hands of people as irresponsible and rash as all of you," the Warden said. "But I do what I must for my country and for my queen, and I need more Roses to do it. So as much as it wounds me to send you crawling to the queen on my behalf, I have no choice. Take the crown, and let's go." She held out her arm, indicating the corridor down which we'd come. "I have a whole list of things to do to keep this country from devolving into chaos and panic now that fifteen of its most powerful citizens have been abducted, and so do you. The sooner we all get to it, the better."

Gareth had come prepared with supplies. He tucked the crown carefully into a soft cloth sack, then into a box that clicked shut with a series of elaborate clasps. He gave the box to Gemma, who held it tight to her chest as if it were the most precious thing in the world—and perhaps it was.

We hurried back up to the world above, and through every inch of those winding dark hallways, my mind whirled with questions, with helpless anger, as the weight of the Warden's gaze pressed like cold fingers against the back of my head.

When we returned to Ivyhill after nearly five weeks away, the first sighting of the familiar vine-wrapped walls sent a feeling of peace pouring into me, like the first spill of light at dawn—but that ended abruptly when Gemma, riding Zephyr a little ahead of our coach, gave a sudden sharp cry.

Terror surged through me, and I sat up straight and looked out the window, fearing the worst—Kilraith had come back, or the firebird, and one or both of them had engulfed my sister in flames—but then I saw Gemma waving at me hastily, dismissing me. Her eyes were shining, and she was fighting a smile that nevertheless beamed out of every part of her, making her light up from the inside as if she were made of fireflies. My heart jumped into my throat. I knew what that look meant, though it happened far too rarely.

She exercised remarkable restraint until we reached the main drive in front of the house. Our staff was waiting to greet us; grooms came trotting up to the carriages to unharness the horses. I watched Gemma give Zephyr to a groom and then walk around the house toward the hedge maze as quickly as she could without making a scene.

I couldn't resist; I had to see the moment of happiness for myself. I turned away from Father's scowl—he knew as well as I did what Gemma's little cry of jubilation had meant—and hurried after Gemma toward the hedge maze, keeping an eye out to make sure no curious servants were following us. Then I hid behind one of our hothouses, around the corner with a hand over my mouth, and saw the moment that Gemma ran into the arms of Talan, who waited for her just inside the hedge maze's entrance. I heard her cry out, heard his low reply. He lifted her into his arms and held her to his chest, and Gemma wrapped her arms around his neck and started kissing him all over— his dark hair, his cheeks, his ears. She was ridiculous and wild, like a puppy who couldn't stop wagging her tail, and Talan threw back his head and laughed. Even from a distance, I could tell he was tired; his shabby clothes wore hundreds of miles on them, and he looked thin, a little gaunt in the face. But with Gemma in his arms, he came alive, just as she had when she'd first spotted him.

I turned away then, letting them have their privacy, but I did go to the Green Ballroom before I went up to my rooms. I threw open the windows and sat at my piano, and I played all my favorite romantic songs, every one of them about love and longing and reunion, every one of them certain to make the listener's heart ache in all the best ways. I played until night fell, hoping that wherever Gemma and Talan were—on the grounds, in the house, shut up safely in her rooms—they could hear my music and were comforted by its power, that the notes helped fold them up into a little cocoon of happiness and blocked out everything else.

Night fell, and I at last went up to my rooms, exhausted but happy. Playing my piano for those long hours had driven the worry out of me, and I didn't know how long that would last, but I was determined to take advantage of it. I snuggled with Osmund, who purred so loudly I felt it in my chest, and then collapsed into bed without even taking off my boots.

When I woke later in the night, cool moonlight spilled across the room, and a slight autumn breeze drifted through the cracked windows, but I was sweating and breathless. The images of the dream I'd just had lingered, following me out of sleep. It had been no nightmare, but a dream of crystalline focus: Ryder pinning me against the wall of his stable, our wooden staffs crossed between our bodies. Only, in my dream, he'd not stepped away after he'd touched my face. Dream Ryder had said, *Well done, Farrin*, just as the true Ryder had that day, but in my dream, he'd then leaned down and kissed me, soft and slow, and his whole body had pressed sweetly into mine—the bulk of him against me, hot and hard and solid, enveloping me, overwhelming me, shielding me. He'd taken our staffs and thrown them aside, and then he'd lifted me into his arms, and I'd felt small in his embrace, tucked away, utterly protected. He'd lowered me gently to the floor, still kissing me, each kiss drawing me up and up toward something bright and hot, something inevitable, and then he'd pressed his leg gently between my thighs, his big hands roaming all over me, teasing me through my clothes, and then—

Suddenly I couldn't bear to just lie there anymore, aching and remembering. I fumbled with the ties of my dress and stockings, cursing myself for not getting properly undressed before sleeping. And when my trembling fingers touched my breasts, my belly, my naked thighs, I cried out at the sheer jolting pleasure of it. I was awkward, to be sure, my fingers clumsy and nervous; my previous attempts had all ended in disaster, after all. But my dream had left me hot and wet between my thighs such as I'd never felt before, and with those images of Ryder held firmly in my mind, I touched myself all over. My hands feathering scattered lines across my belly were his hands, my finger circling between my thighs was his finger. I imagined what it would feel like to kiss him, how the roughness of his beard might rub against my skin, how the strength of him would press me down into the bed, and how intently he might watch me as I writhed beneath him—those bright blue eyes of his, that blazing, quiet intensity.

I thought of the way he'd said my name so gently—*Farrin*—letting the syllables fall from his mouth like rain. How would it feel, I wondered wildly, if he murmured my name against my thighs?

The thought unraveled me. My entire body tensed; a swell of heat came rushing up from my toes, drawing me up into myself, toward an ache deep inside my belly. Then the wave broke, and I let out a soft cry and came apart, pulsing quietly, the world behind my eyelids warm and black and gold. I clamped my thighs tight around my hand and moved against my fingers, chasing the gorgeous pleasure of it until the sensitive ache there told me to stop. When it subsided, my entire body tingling, I lay in the pillows and cried and laughed, my wet fingers trembling against the mattress.

So, that was it. That was what it felt like, or at least something like that. Certainly it was possible to achieve the feeling more skillfully, but I'd done it nevertheless. I'd done it on my own—with assistance from Ryder Bask, of all people.

The thought was absurd and somehow wonderful. I fell asleep half naked atop my bed, feeling wrung out and giddy, wiped clean, and more than a little ridiculous—but for the first time in what felt like years, my sleep was peaceful, long, and free of nightmares.

CHAPTER 10

The next morning, I awoke not knowing quite what to do with myself. There were things to be done, certainly: checking in with the household staff who'd remained at Ivyhill during our absence, visiting our tenant farmers, walking the grounds to assure myself everything was in order. And of course the Warden's deadline loomed large in my mind. We had only a month to propose a national Order draft to the queen, and two weeks had already passed during our travels home.

But after the night I'd had, I felt both rested and restless, and carrying out tasks I'd done a thousand times suddenly felt impossible. I'd slept like the dead, yet it took me thirty minutes to wash and dress when it ordinarily took fifteen. I was fluttery all over, completely distracted, and realized when I got downstairs that I'd forgotten to make my bed. A simple thing, something I'd not once neglected for as long as I could remember, and yet I couldn't bring myself to be irritated.

I glided into the dining room, expecting it to be empty and looking forward to enjoying a solitary breakfast with only my jittery body and provocative thoughts of Ryder for company—but shockingly,

Gemma was already there. She was barefoot in her dressing gown, golden curls spilling everywhere, tapping her toes against the table leg as she scribbled on a piece of paper.

"You're up early," I remarked, a little more testily than was fair. "I expected you to still be in bed with Talan."

Gemma quickly hid whatever she was writing under her napkin and began eating the fruit on her plate with relish. "I woke up thinking about a million things and didn't want to disturb him by rustling about in bed. Poor thing, he's exhausted. We haven't even gotten the chance to talk about where he's been these past few weeks, whether he's learned anything new about Kilraith—"

"What are you writing?"

She blinked up at me, her mouth full of food. "What? I'm eating."

"Gemma, don't lie to me." I sat down in the chair beside her and glanced pointedly at her napkin. "Stealth is not your specialty. I saw you hide whatever that is when I came in."

She hesitated, chewing, then swallowed and relented, withdrawing the sheet of paper. "Fine. But you have to promise not to be angry with me."

"I can't promise that until I know what you've done."

"I haven't *done* anything—"

"And yet you just told me not to be angry with you."

Gemma sighed sharply. "It's just that I know how you'll feel about this and can't imagine talking about it will be productive. But I can see you won't give up, so here it is: I'm writing to Great-Aunt Felicity. I've *been* writing to her since we got home from Rosewarren after fighting Kilraith."

I stared at her. I wasn't sure what I'd expected her to say, but it certainly wasn't that. "You haven't."

"No, you're right. I haven't. I'm lying. I'm writing a novel."

"That *is* a lie. You haven't the discipline to write a novel."

"Not believing me and then insulting me on top of it!"

I snatched the paper from her. My stomach dropped when I saw the salutation. *Dear Auntie Fel…*

"Auntie *Fel?*" I read, incredulous.

"She calls me Gem, I call her Fel." She paused, then added, a note of mirth in her voice, "It's a concept known as nicknaming."

"I know what nicknaming is," I snapped. The giddy, scatterbrained strangeness of my morning vanished in an instant. "I just don't understand why you're talking to her."

"Because she's family."

"By blood, maybe, but not in any way that actually matters." I thrust the paper at her. "We promised each other, you and Mara and me… We promised we wouldn't speak to any of them, not after what they said."

Gemma sighed again, then took my hands gently in hers. "I know we did," she said, "but that was years ago, well before we went to the Old Country. That night, everything changed. You know it did. When we were there, we were stronger than we'd ever been before. We moved differently, we looked different. You saw how Ryder and Alastrina reacted to us."

I did remember, of course. All three of us had glowed from within that night, the Olden air turning our skin and hair unnaturally lustrous and flecking our eyes with gold. While fighting the Brethaeus and the Vilia, Mara had moved so lightning fast that I couldn't keep track of her, darting from tree to ground to attacker like an arrow shot from a bow. Gemma had ripped entire trees from the ground and glamoured herself to hide the glass embedded in her skin, and the wood itself, every tree and piece of brush, had leaned toward us, all of us, drawn to our power like moths to fire.

And I had used my voice as I'd never done before. I'd found a wordless, unfamiliar song in the depths of myself, and I'd sung it in that forest as enemies swarmed us from all sides. My song had sent the specters attacking my sisters into utter chaos, making them scream and writhe and fling themselves to the ground.

And then together, all three of us—Gemma and Mara and I—had fought a monster capable of entrapping a demon.

And we had *won*.

Fae blood, Gemma's Vilia friend Phaidra had declared upon seeing us transformed. *The blood of both Kerezen and Caiathos burns in your veins, just as it did in the veins of the first fae.*

A wild claim, one I hadn't accepted then and wouldn't accept now. Along with the demons, the fae were the most powerful beings in the Old Country, elusive and cunning. The idea that we possessed any of their blood was preposterous. Father was an Anointed sentinel, Mother a low-magic elemental of moderate power with a talent for botanicals. They were human, and so were we, and so were all the generations of our family before us, both on the Ashbourne side and the Wren side. No, there had to be another explanation, perhaps an ordinary aberration in our blood that could exist in any number of Gallinoran citizens. We'd just been unlucky enough—or foolish enough—to venture into the Old Country and see the evidence for ourselves.

"Of course I remember," I muttered.

Gemma was ducking down, trying to get me to look at her, but I refused. I glared at the table and felt petulantly glad to see her half-eaten eggs sitting there, growing cold.

"I wouldn't have written to Auntie Fel if I hadn't a very good reason for it," Gemma said. "I want to know what happened that night in the Old Country, Farrin, and I want to know if it'll happen again, what might set it off. What does it mean, and—considering everything that's happening—can we use it to our advantage in the days to come? Even here in Edyn?"

"And of course Great-Aunt Felicity knows all about such things," I said peevishly, hating the sound of the words even as I said them.

"Of course she doesn't, but she's the person in Mother's family I felt most comfortable reaching out to. I remember her being nice enough when we were little. I remember her smelling like peppermint." Gemma paused. "She's smart and thoughtful, and wickedly funny. I've told her about the panic, about the healer I see to help me with it. She's been so gentle about it, so understanding. You'd like her."

"I'd like her," I repeated flatly. "No, Gemma. I wouldn't. I don't like any of them. Do you remember what they said when Mother left us?"

Gemma had been expecting that one. "I do."

But I had to say it anyway, to remind myself—to remind *her*—of the promise we'd made to each other and why we had made it.

"They said it was Father's fault that Mother left. They stood here in our own home and accused him of hurting her for years, *beating* her, beating *us*, because he couldn't control his temper and couldn't win his war with the Basks. They said he'd been driving her mad, that in her letters to them she'd written about how ill she felt, how she couldn't sleep, how she was hearing *voices*. And from that they drew the worst possible conclusions. When Father asked to see the letters, read her words for himself, they wouldn't show him. Every single one of them insisted the same thing—even your beloved Auntie Fel—and leveled the same awful accusations. They united against us, against *Father*. They tried to take us away from him."

I barely got out those last words, feeling sick to remember those terrible days after Mother left: Mara gone and eight-year-old Gemma constantly wailing. Father vacillating between sleeping the days away and disappearing all night to visit friends and drink himself into oblivion, some days exhausting his body with hours of punishing exercises out on the grounds. The Wrens, Mother's family, had tried every lawful and unlawful means of sneaking Gemma and me out of the house. Some nights, Father had camped out in the entrance hall, fists clenched, eyes trained on the doors. Weapons scattered all around him. Waiting, even eager, for the Wrens to try something.

And then there had been me, twelve years old, watching him from the shadows, too sick and worried to sleep, trying desperately to hold everything together and keep the estate functioning while my world fell apart around me.

"And in light of everything you've learned about the things Father has done," Gemma said, very low, glancing at my wrist, "in light of what he's done to *you*, can you really say their claims were so very outlandish?"

It was as though she'd struck me. Of course I'd had those thoughts myself, but I'd long dismissed them and continued to, even with his mood so black over the past few months. Father hurting Mother, hurting *us*? He'd never done such a thing, had never laid a hand on us in anger. Yet here was Gemma hurling the terrible thoughts back at me, the very fact of what had been done to her as a child reminding me that yes, Father *could* hurt if he thought he had a reason to.

"Father didn't hire that artificer on his own, you know." I didn't want to say it, but I had to. I was desperate to regain some kind of footing in this conversation. "Mother was there too. She could have stopped it, but she didn't. She sat in the room right beside you and let it happen."

Gemma didn't even flinch. "So Father says, now that Mother's not around to dispute his version of the story." She held my gaze for a long time, years of pain swimming in her bright eyes. She sat there proudly, back straight, shoulders squared.

Ashamed, I looked down at my hands.

"Anyway, Auntie Fel has apologized for all of that," Gemma said at last, wearily. "She admits they made unfair, baseless accusations out of grief for Mother and fear for us. And Farrin..." She drew in a breath as if steeling herself. "As I said, I wouldn't have written to Auntie Fel unless I had a very good reason."

Of course I knew the reason. I knew it, and I despised it, and, irrationally, I despised Gemma for having grown into the sort of woman who no longer avoided her problems but instead chose to face them.

I despised myself most of all, anger roiling in my chest like a hot sea, bubbling uselessly, making me feel mighty and dangerous even though I was far from it. In fact, I possessed not even half of my baby sister's nerve.

"You want to ask her questions about us," I muttered. "About Mother."

"Yes."

"About Mother's *powers*, and if she kept something from us, from Father, and why we can do what we did."

"*Yes.*"

"Though I'm not sure I can trust anything you say at the moment, I do sincerely hope you didn't tell her anything about Yvaine, or the sinkhole, or Kilraith—"

"Of course I didn't," Gemma snapped. She looked furious all of a sudden, and I didn't blame her, rightfully so. "Do you really think me that foolish? I'm not a child, Farrin. I'm a woman with as much stake in all of this as you have, and as much responsibility too. Our first letters were just getting to know each other, gaining each other's trust. I've only recently started asking her about the family. I'm making a family tree, I told her. I've grown interested in my lineage, as many people do as they get older."

I scoffed. *I* was being the child, but I couldn't stop myself. "Digging around in hopes of finding *fae blood* somewhere?"

Gemma threw up her hands. "I don't know! I don't know what I'm looking for. But I have to try—I have to do *something*. Whatever the reason for it, I do have powers that seem to be of both Caiathos and Kerezen, which shouldn't be possible. And you and Mara, you changed in the Old Country just as I did. You became stronger versions of yourselves. And we heard the Mist calling to us that night—you, Mara, and me. Not Ryder, not Alastrina, not Phaidra." Gemma's mouth trembled a little at the mention of her late friend. "They didn't hear that voice, that song, telling us where to go, how to cross from Edynside to Oldenside, but we *did* hear it. What does that mean, Farrin?"

I couldn't answer. My head was too full, and my chest hurt, and I itched everywhere in this strange, cold way, as if Gemma's words were beginning to turn me inside out. I'd woken up feeling so different than usual—fidgety and distracted, the whole day unfurling before me with new possibility—and now I could feel myself turning inward again, knotting up from head to toe.

I turned away, waving Gemma silent, but she rose to join me and kept talking.

"We have to do this," she said, "and it would be easier if you would help me." Then she paused. "Do it for Yvaine, if not for me. Without question, we're part of whatever's happening. If we figure out who or what we are—"

"*What* we are?" I stared at her, revolted and furious for too many muddled reasons to count. "And how dare you throw Yvaine at me like a weapon?"

"You're the one choosing to ignore something that could help her," Gemma shot back. "If she really is dying, shouldn't you want to do everything you can to ease her many burdens? I do, and she's not half as dear to me as she is to you." She sighed sharply. "I know it hurt you most of all when Mother left, but—"

I stormed away before she could finish. If I hadn't, I might have said something unforgivably cruel. I hurried out of the house and onto the grounds, which hummed happily with industry—grooms out working the horses, groundskeepers tending to the gardens with both humble shears and elemental magic. Everyone called out to me in greeting; I replied to each of them by name, a false smile plastered across my face, and marched on.

At first, I didn't know where I was going; I just knew I needed to keep moving. If I didn't, the rage boiling inside me might turn into tears, and I couldn't sit around bawling. There was work to be done, a mile-long list of work that I recalled with a cold splash of clarity. Perhaps Gemma could afford to sit and write letters and bed her lover and think about powers and fae blood and what it all meant, but I had an estate to run, one that would crumble around us if I ignored my duties. So I would get to work and put Gemma and Mother and *Auntie Fel* out of my mind. All of those things were in the past, and the past couldn't hurt me. I wouldn't let it.

But telling myself that over and over did nothing to calm me, and by the time I reached the game park, flushing out a startled bevy of quail as I tore through the wetlands in my now-ruined shoes, I knew what I needed. I needed to punch something.

A little jolt shook me as Ryder's scowling face flashed before my eyes. Was the feeling apprehension? A warning of some kind? I didn't care. A chill autumn wind was at my back; the western horizon was dark with an approaching storm, and I was glad to see it. I felt a fierce kinship with its roiling churn, its promise of thunder. I turned toward the lake, where the greenway that led to Ravenswood lay waiting in Father's hidden lagoon.

✦◇✦

When I found Ryder, I was soaking wet and shivering, drenched from my trip through the lagoon-anchored greenway. It had been some time since I'd traveled north using that route, the last trip being one of Father's many efforts to spy on the Basks and prepare us all for the eventual cataclysmic attack that never came. My gown growing stiff and cold around me in the mountain air, my sodden shoes squishing with every step, I trudged through the pines, cursing myself, cursing Gemma, cursing the trees themselves most of all, until I finally saw light ahead and felt a rush of relief that I hadn't gotten lost.

I hurried out of the trees into a clearing beyond and stopped dead.

Ryder was there, sitting on a bench outside one of the Basks' many stables. Torches flickered in the yard, and four blanketed horses had gathered at the fence to nose at Ryder's hair and shoulders. Birds of all sorts hopped about at his feet—cardinals, woodpeckers, ravens.

And Ryder...his head was in his hands, his great hulking body slumped over in utter dejection, and when he looked up at the sound of my footsteps and saw me, he did nothing to hide the devastation on his face, the tear tracks cutting paths across his dirty cheeks and into his beard.

Instead he took in the state of my hair and dress and frowned. "What are you doing here?"

In the face of his obvious despair, the truth seemed absurd and even insulting, but I didn't know what else to say. "I wanted to punch something," I said bluntly.

That made him smile, a soft flash of a grin. "And so you came to see me? I'm touched."

I made to go to him, then hesitated, suddenly keenly aware of how stupid I'd been, tearing over here without any thought of how to explain my sudden appearance.

He seemed to understand. "Not to worry," he said drily, wiping his face on his sleeve. "After I found your sister and Talan snooping about these woods this past spring, Trina and I tracked down your greenway. Cleverly hidden, I'll give your father that. It took us weeks of work to uncover it. The other end lies in water, does it?"

I was fiercely glad that at least for a moment, he wasn't looking at me. Only weeks ago, I wouldn't have felt any shame whatsoever that Ryder knew my family had been spying on his, but now things were different.

I lifted my chin a little and approached him. "Couldn't you find out for yourself?"

"Of course not. It's laced with spellcraft, won't permit a Bask to enter."

"I'm sure the greenways you've built to spy on us are secured in much the same way."

He did look up at me then, with a roguish sort of smile. "Oh no, you won't get me that easily."

I accepted that and apologized with a small nod. "Old habits are difficult to break."

Then I sat beside him, perched gingerly on the bench, and waited for him to speak. He was horribly quiet next to me, the very air around him heavy with grief. I wanted to reach out to him, touch his arm in comfort. An easy enough thing for people like Gemma, or Gareth, or even Yvaine to do. But the idea of touching Ryder not only felt uncomfortable, inexperienced at casual affection as I was, it also felt dangerous, like inching too close to a blazing hearth.

"Is it Alastrina?" I said instead. An old gray gelding snuffled sweetly at my hair.

Ryder nodded, leaning heavily forward on his thighs. "I don't know how to exist without her. For so long, it was just us, trapped here in these trees, in this house. Learning how to live a lonely life cut off from the world, learning how to keep Father happy. And now she's gone, and it's as if half of me has been torn away." He looked down at the birds, clucked his tongue. A raven hopped up into his lap, looking up at him expectantly with clever black eyes.

"I've wilded thirty of them today alone," Ryder went on. "Mother says I'll kill myself wilding so constantly. But I can't possibly stop. Maybe one of them will find her."

He cupped his hands, and the bird stepped into them. He brought the creature up to his face and murmured Ekkari to it, a long string of words. Instructions, I assumed. His wilding magic pulsed gently against me, against all of us gathered—a soft ripple of warmth that made the birds squawk and ruffle their feathers. One of the horses stamped its hoof. Then Ryder lifted his hands into the air, and the raven took off flying. In moments, its dark wings were lost in the trees.

I watched the spot for a long time. Then, carefully, I began to speak. "When the Warden took Mara, she was ten, and I was twelve. I woke up every day praying it had been a dream, that I'd run down the hall and find her safe in her bed. For weeks, I would go check every morning before I did anything else, my heart absolutely pounding, every inch of me aching with hope—only to find my mother there instead, clutching Mara's sheets, crying for her. She wouldn't let the staff wash any of it—her linens, her clothes. Only after Mother left could we finally clean her room. I stopped talking to the gods not long after that. Every now and then a prayer will escape, but only when I'm truly desperate. Those childhood rituals stay with you, even when you would prefer they didn't."

Ryder was very quiet, listening with such intense concentration that I felt a little embarrassed. Somehow I found the courage to look at him and face that hard blue gaze of his.

"I know it's not the same thing," I said, "but I do know what it is to grieve, the kind of grief that hollows you out and leaves you changed forever." I gave him a small, rueful smile. "If I were a woman who prayed with any consistency or sincerity, I'd pray to the gods that you won't have to know this grief you're feeling for very long. But in lieu of that, I'll simply say that if anyone can survive whatever's happening, be it a firebird or Kilraith or just a dying Mist throwing a temper tantrum, it's Alastrina Bask."

Ryder smiled and looked down at his feet. We sat in silence for a moment, and I was ready to rise and say something about the horses, anything to break this strange quiet simmering between us, when suddenly he reached over and took my hands in his, and lifted them to his lips, and kissed my fingers.

He lingered there for a moment, his mouth hot against my skin, his eyes closed tight as if in pain. I couldn't breathe, couldn't move. I could only stare at my small hands wrapped up in his, his dark head bowed over them.

"You act so fierce," he said at last, softly, the words washing over my skin as gently as if he'd drawn a feather across it. "And you are, but..." His voice trailed off. He watched my hands as if trying to decipher a puzzle woven into my palms.

"But?" I prompted, my voice a mere breath.

"That was a kindness, Farrin, what you just said. A kindness I'm not sure I deserve." He released my hands, his brow furrowed, and then looked at me with something like mirth in his eyes. "That's one of the reasons why I like you when all reason and history tells me that I shouldn't. Your tongue is sharp, you're thorny all over, but there's something underneath that, something you don't let people see. A softness. We're alike in that way."

I was too shocked by the direction this conversation was taking to think before I spoke. "You're saying *you* possess a secret softness?"

He frowned at his boots. "I try to. It isn't easy. You make it look easy, though. I don't think other people see it—maybe you don't even see it—but I do. I see what you mean to your family, how much you love them even when they infuriate you, how you'd do anything to protect them even when they may not deserve it." He found an acorn in the dirt, picked it up, tossed it to a passel of squirrels squatting patiently on the roots of a nearby tree. "How safe that must make them feel, your family, to know that kind of love."

At first I couldn't find my words. This was a remarkable moment, and remarkably strange, and I felt ill-equipped to handle it with any sort of delicacy. My heart was beating in my cheeks, my whole body warm and weightless. I was unused to the feeling and wasn't sure I liked it. Flustered, I grabbed for any anchor I could find.

"If this is some sort of strategy to get me to like you," I blurted out, "it's not a very artful one."

It was a terrible thing to say—not enough humor in it to be a joke, and even then, what a bad joke that would have been. I clamped my mouth shut before I could completely wreck our fragile rapport and watched Ryder nod to himself, elbows on his knees, hands clasped before him. The squirrels were fighting over the acorn, chittering furiously at one another. The absurd thought came to me that perhaps a gift from a Bask was something of a trophy for the Ravenswood squirrels.

After a moment of awful silence, Ryder stood, smoothing his tunic. "So," he said lightly, all business now and not looking at me, "you said you wanted to punch something?"

I sat there in a stupor, watching him stride into the stable yard and wanting to scream at myself for ruining whatever it was he'd been trying to say. He retrieved our fighting staffs and the leather targets. The horses trotted after him, whickering happily, and still I couldn't move, nailed to the bench. My fingers burned where his lips had touched them, and my heart raced as if we'd just run a fast mile. I pushed hard against the rise of my tears. A grieving man, worried sick about his sister, had tried to say something extraordinarily kind to me, and I'd bitten it off and spat it back at him as if it meant nothing to me, as if he meant nothing.

I didn't know *what* Ryder Bask meant to me, but it was most certainly not *nothing*.

"Well, come on, then," Ryder called out. He hung the targets from the stable rafters, and when I finally managed to move my shaky legs and join him, a thousand words of awkward apology fighting each other on my tongue, he tossed a staff at me and lunged before I'd even gotten a good grip on it. I flung it up wildly, instinct screaming at me to protect myself. Our weapons locked, and I reeled where I stood, my arms trembling as I pushed my staff up against his.

"You didn't give me time to prepare," I said, glaring at him. "And I said I wanted to *punch* something, not—"

"And will your attacker give you such a choice?" Ryder said, pushing hard against me.

All my regret and shame vanished in an instant. I got a better grip on my staff and pushed back, indignation giving me strength. I was pleased to see him take a step back and steady himself.

He smiled down at me. "Anyway, shoving something feels just as good, doesn't it?"

I scowled and pushed him again, even harder, a sharp, mean thrust that made him stumble back just enough. In that moment of freedom, I managed to step away, reposition myself, and spin the staff around to block his when it came flying back toward me.

"Good," he said, "but try not to give away your next move."

"That one took you by surprise well enough," I said. I blew a strand of hair out of my face and began circling him, my staff raised defensively.

"So you think," he countered with a grin, "but in fact I let you have it as a courtesy."

And then, too fast for me to block him, he whirled around and flung out his staff at my leg. The thing caught me in the back of my knee and sent me crashing to my hands and knees on the floor. The fall jarred me, made my head spin a little. Ryder came up to me, hand outstretched, and said, a little too smugly, "Sorry, Ashbourne, I couldn't resist."

For an instant, I couldn't even see the stable. I saw the hazy red and black of my anger, and I let out a sharp cry and jumped to my feet, reeling, unbalanced, and swung my staff around hard, intending to crack him on the shoulder with it—but he was fast and dodged me. And so it went for an hour, us circling each other and swiping at each other, his staff clipping me nearly every time. Mine mostly hit air, and sometimes the leather targets, but never him, never his broad back or his thick thighs, never his grinning, bearded face.

I swung and struck and darted and spun myself into exhaustion, but I wouldn't give up; I couldn't. As I fought this huge bear of a man I couldn't possibly defeat, my mind whirled frantically, full of distractions. Yvaine, sick in her palace, possibly dying. Mara, fighting monsters in the Mist. Gemma, writing to people I'd sworn to hate for the rest of my life. Father, brooding in his rooms, most likely attempting to drink away all the knowledge we'd learned over the past few weeks. The firebird, and the Warden, and the Three-Eyed Crown, currently on its way to the capital in the care of Gareth. And what would his investigations unearth? And what would Gemma and Great-Aunt Felicity discover as they rooted around in Mother's ancestry? What new problems would soon be mine to solve?

And what in the name of all the gods would I say to Ryder once we were finished sparring?

With my head so full, I couldn't think well enough to aim at anything, and my arms were so wobbly I could barely hold up my staff. I thought I saw Ryder moving in the corner of my vision, and I spun around and let my staff fly—but it only hit one of the targets. It made contact with a deafening *smack*, which I felt all the way up my arms and into my teeth. The feeling was too good; it shook my thoughts loose a bit, hurt my bones enough to distract me from myself. My palms were burning; I'd have blisters in the morning. But I didn't care.

I swung, and I swung, frantic and clumsy, beating the target so hard it began spinning wildly from the rafters.

"Farrin," said Ryder quietly from behind me, and it was then that I realized I was crying, that it was hard to breathe.

Mortified, I tossed the staff away, heard it clatter against the hay-strewn floor. I started to leave, but Ryder stopped me before I could get very far. He came around and barred my way, his hands raised, his posture careful, deferent, and I crashed into him without thinking, curled my fingers into his tunic, and held on as tight as I could. I didn't understand why I was crying, other than the fact that everything, everywhere, was wrong in some way, and I didn't know how to mend any of it.

"I'm sorry," I sobbed, furious with myself. "Here you are, scared to death for your sister, and I'm being absolutely rotten. Rotten person, rotten sparring partner." Angrily, I wiped my face. "I don't *want* to be crying. Gods, what you must think of me."

I tried again to leave him, but Ryder held on to me. "Please don't go," he said quietly into my hair. "You're in no state to go anywhere. Stay here with me. All right? Just for a few minutes."

I leaned my forehead against his chest, too tired to resist his steadiness. "I'm horrified. I'm so embarrassed."

"Don't be. You should have seen me earlier. You witnessed only the tail end of it. I've been a mess for days."

"You're being kind. Thank you, but..." I shook my head and placed my hands flat against him, ready to push him away. "I should go. I'm sorry for saying what I said earlier. Clearly you were wrong. I've no secret softness. I'm thorns through and through. You should stay far away, and I...I should go."

"Please don't."

His voice gentled to something impossibly tender, so at odds with his scruffy face, his stature like a prowling lion, that I couldn't help but look at him. When I did, I lost my breath a little, because he was gazing down at me as if I was dear to him, as if the sight of me crying in his arms was agony. Brow furrowed, eyes soft. He touched the damp strands of hair that clung to my neck; he brushed my cheek with the backs of his fingers. Then he leaned down to press his forehead to mine. He closed his eyes, and his jaw worked as if he was struggling deeply with something.

"Farrin," he said at last, low and rough. "Farrin, Farrin." He smoothed his thumb against my cheek, shook his head a little, and opened his eyes—a sudden shot of fierce blue. "May I kiss you?"

The question was outrageous. That I was even standing here at Ravenswood, that I was holding on to Ryder Bask and letting him hold me, that I was even *considering* his request, was ridiculous enough to warrant serious reflection and a prompt visit to Madam Moreen, our family's healer.

"Why would you want to," I whispered, "after how I've behaved?"

He laughed quietly. "You're too hard on yourself."

I shook my head. I told myself to let go of his shirt, to walk away, but I couldn't make my body obey. "Please let me apologize."

"You've already done that. I accept."

I blew out a frustrated breath. "*Ryder—*"

"Please, Farrin. Will you answer my question?" He touched my face again with the backs of his fingers, his words still lingering in the air—*May I kiss you?*—and I couldn't help myself. I blamed the adrenaline, my exhaustion, my guilt. I blamed how nice it felt to be held, how handsome Ryder looked in the warm lantern light. I leaned into him—the son of my father's enemy, the man I'd sworn from childhood to hate—and I whispered, "Yes."

He gave me a gentle smile, so soft and sweet that it made me ache. He let out a breath—an anxious one, I thought, a little unsteady, as if this huge, fearsome man were nervous to touch me—and then he cupped my face in his hands, leaned down, and kissed me.

I'd been kissed before, but only twice: once by Gareth at sixteen, on the disastrous night when we had decided to try what everyone already thought we were doing, and once at one of Gemma's parties, when I'd angrily downed three glasses of wine in the span of five minutes and then flirted with an Aidurran woman whose name I couldn't even remember. We'd kissed for a very pleasant—albeit hazy—few minutes under the stairs, after which I'd gotten sick all over her very pretty beaded silk slippers. She'd been exceedingly kind about it; she'd found Gilroy, who'd found Hetty, who had taken me to bed, and that was the last I'd seen of her, for which I was grateful. I wasn't sure I could have borne the humiliation of apologizing to her for ruining what was most certainly an expensive pair of shoes.

The experience of kissing Ryder, though, was entirely different. Gareth had been nervous, and so had I; we had both immediately sensed the wrongness of our little experiment but had pressed on anyway. And the Aidurran woman I remembered only in pieces: her hand on my waist, the rose notes of her perfume.

But Ryder held me with a sure strength that I knew would sear itself into my mind forever. At first his kisses were soft, even a little cautious, but his palms were warm on my cheeks, and the feeling of his taller, larger body looming over mine left my knees wobbly: his head bowing low to kiss me, his big hands holding me as gently as if I were one of his wilded birds. I felt enveloped by him, a precious creature being sheltered in the embrace of a mountain. The feeling was so overwhelming, so new and surprising, that I let out a soft cry against his mouth and pressed closer to him, desperate for more.

His arms came around me at once, and mine slid around his neck, and I pressed up against him, my heartbeat like thunder in my ears. He groaned, and the rough, masculine sound was fuel to my fire. Heat flooded my body. I whimpered in frustration, not knowing what I wanted, and I shifted shyly against him, unthinking and clumsy. That unlocked something in him; he easily lifted me into his arms, an exhilarating sensation that scratched at the corner of my mind. Obviously I'd not once in my life been held by Ryder Bask, and yet with his arms around me, his grip strong and steady, my chest pressed to his, I felt a twinge of recognition, of familiarity.

But then our kisses grew deeper, his tongue opening my mouth; his ardor was intoxicating, insistent, and all rational thought disappeared. I curled my fingers into his tunic and clung to him, and let him have me. The shock of it all, the unexpected pleasure, left me breathless. He started kissing my jaw, my neck, and I tilted my head back and held him to me, threaded my fingers through his thick dark hair. We were moving; then we weren't. He'd found a bale of hay to sit on, which for some reason seemed wildly funny to me, but then I was in his lap, his arms holding me tight against him, and I felt him hot and hard between my legs, and then nothing was funny anymore.

I gasped and flinched a little, wholly unused to anything that was happening and feeling suddenly embarrassed and exposed. A sort of panic unfolded in my chest, and even though I loved the feeling of his hair between my fingers, even though the sheer bulk of him beneath me made me ache between my legs, I went stiff. All the beautiful open parts of me that had blossomed in his arms closed up tight.

"Ryder," I whispered. "Wait."

He stopped at once. He pulled back, released my hips, and looked at me in concern, breathing hard, his face flushed. He reached up as if to touch my face and then hesitated.

"What is it?" he said. "Did I hurt you?"

I shook my head, tears of frustration burning behind my eyes. "No, you didn't. You did nothing wrong. I just need...I need to stand up."

He helped me do so, then stood too, then sat back on the bale of hay, obviously and endearingly unsure of himself. He cleared his throat. I tried very hard not to stare at the obvious evidence of his desire.

"Should I leave?" he asked at last. When I didn't answer, his expression of concern softened. "It's all right, Farrin. I can leave right now. I'm sorry if I—"

"No, don't be sorry." I spat the words, then turned away from him and hugged myself. I was so furious and mortified that I couldn't say anything for a moment, and I couldn't leave, and I couldn't face him. I could only stand there and burn, needing him desperately yet afraid of the thing I needed, though I didn't understand why.

"I've never…" I started, then lost my voice. I tried again. "I mean, I'm not…"

Ryder said nothing, waiting for me to say whatever it was I needed to say, only I didn't *know* what I needed to say. All my words were stuck somewhere between my chest and my throat.

"You don't have to explain anything," he said at last, so gently that I had to look at him. I had to make him understand, even if it killed me.

I turned around, my arms still crossed over my chest. "I'm not a virgin," I announced. At first, that was all I could say.

He waited, and waited, and then said patiently, "All right. Thank you for sharing that with me."

The sound of his big gentle voice, and the sight of him sitting there on the bale of hay with his long legs and his beard that needed a trim, gave me a spot of courage. I took two quick steps toward him. I unfolded my arms and held them stiffly at my sides..

"I'm not a virgin, but I've only done this twice. This." I gestured between us. "Whatever this is. And I've done *more* than this only once."

Ryder nodded but said nothing.

"I'm not good with my body," I said quietly. "Gemma is. Gareth is. Other people are. Not me. I don't even like looking at myself in the mirror. Gods." I laughed, feeling slightly hysterical. "I can't believe I'm telling you this."

"You don't have to."

"But I do, because—" I made a frustrated sound; I would *not* allow more tears, not after I'd already embarrassed myself more than enough for one day. I took a breath and blurted out, "Because I want you. It doesn't make any sense, but I do. I thought of you last night, and I… it felt good." My cheeks were burning. I looked very hard at the floor. "And I've never felt that way before. So clearly…" I gestured between us again, laughing a little, because the situation felt so absurd. "Do you understand what I'm trying to say?"

"I do," he said solemnly. "And Farrin…" He breathed in and out slowly. "I'm honored."

My eyes burned. I blinked hard, willing the feeling to pass.

"But you don't have to force yourself to do anything, ever," he went on, "no matter what sorts of handsome bearded men you might like to think of while alone in your bed."

His voice held a smile; I glanced up and saw a slight sparkle in his eyes, and I laughed and covered my face. "Oh gods. I'm sorry. This is…" I waved at him. "You're Ryder Bask, for gods' sake."

"And you're Farrin Ashbourne," he replied. His mischievous smile gentled. "Do you want to punch things some more? Or should I walk you back to your greenway?"

I stood there for a moment, forcing myself to feel all the nervy tendrils of uncertainty shivering throughout my body. In the quiet, with only the snuffling horses nearby, my thoughts began to settle.

"I can walk myself home," I said slowly, "but before I go, would you kiss me again?"

"Are you sure you want me to?"

I nodded, made myself look at him. "I do. I'm sorry for the…" I waved at myself. "I'm sorry."

He rose and came to me, took my face gently in his hands. "Never apologize to me for that."

I let my eyes drift closed, relishing the feeling of him so close to me, the earthy, sweaty scent of him. "Never apologize for what?"

"For knowing your body and yourself," he replied, "and for telling me what you don't want, and what you do."

Then he lowered his mouth to mine and kissed me—unbearably soft, unthinkably sweet, each touch of his lips a tender brush of skin against skin. I melted into him, my eyes still closed, as his lips feathered across my cheeks, my jaw, and down my neck to the hollow of my throat. His hands slid into my hair, so slow and gentle that my skin broke out into goose bumps.

He noticed and laughed gently against my collarbones. "Quite the compliment," he murmured. The soft rumble of his voice left me unable to stand on my own. I leaned into him, and he seemed to sense what I needed in that moment; he drew me to his chest and held me, tucked his head over mine, and with my ear pressed against him, I could hear the wild pounding of his heart and felt a sudden fierce tenderness. I pulled back a little and touched his face, traced the lines of his jaw beneath his beard, marveling at him. He closed his eyes and turned to kiss my palm, my fingers.

"Will you come to Ivyhill tomorrow?" I said quietly, watching him, noticing things I never had: the scar above his left eyebrow, the slightly crooked line of his nose. "You don't have to tell me where your greenways are. I don't care. I'm glad you have them, really. Just come, please. If you want. If you can. Talan is there, and we should talk, all of us. We need to visit the queen as soon as possible."

I wanted to say so much more than that—it felt silly to pretend I didn't—but I couldn't find the courage. It had taken every scrap of bravery I possessed to ask for those last kisses. Instead I mustered up a small smile, hoping he could see in it at least some of what I was feeling—gratitude, and need, and disappointment, and a hard knot of fear, and a secret, wild hope. If he came to Ivyhill, what would happen then? What would it feel like the next time we saw each other?

He searched my face for a moment, then smiled and kissed my forehead. "Of course," he said, his lips against my skin, and I closed my eyes and held on to him for another moment. When he released me, I bit back a cry of protest. Part of me wanted to run away from him and never return; part of me wanted to beg him to take me to the nearest bed so we could try again, and properly.

Instead I took a step back from him, my blood roaring, our fingers still loosely joined. As overwhelmed as I felt, that was the most I could manage. There were so many things to say, and I couldn't untangle any of them. The memory of how it had felt when he held me—that twinge of familiarity, like the faint echo of an old, beloved song—had returned and now sat uncomfortably in my chest. I tried to ignore it; I had more than enough to think about without chasing every stray puzzled thought that flew into my head.

I gave him a small smile. "Tomorrow?" I said quietly.

"Tomorrow," he replied. Then he kissed my hand and turned away, and I hurried into the woods, where the damp air cooled my cheeks and the quiet was a welcome balm to my bewildered, aching heart.

CHAPTER 11

Ryder appeared at Ivyhill's front doors at seven o' clock the next morning, just as I stepped out of them for my daily walk across the grounds. I opened the door, and there he was, frozen, his hand raised to knock. We looked at each other for a long moment, during which I could do very little except stare at him: his crisp black jacket and trousers, the cloth bag slung across his back, his freshly trimmed beard, his dark hair falling to his shoulders in neat waves. And his blue eyes, bright stars improbably shining in the morning light. Heat rose in me like the morning sun. Was it desire? Embarrassment? Nerves? Truly, I couldn't tell the difference and wasn't sure I wanted to.

I had been staring at him for far too long.

"You can come with me," I said briskly, stepping past him, my face flushed, "or you can sit alone in the house until Gemma and Talan wake up, though gods know when that will be."

Ryder dropped his bag inside the doors. "Clothes," he said simply when I raised an eyebrow. "I can leave them there, can't I?"

"Yes, though they might end up in a guest room or get thrown out."

He shrugged, gave a little grunt. "Then I'll buy more."

The carelessness of this remark nettled me, though I easily could have done the same—lost a bag of clothes, bought new ones to replace them. I tried not to think of the ravaged village of Devenmere, of how many clothes the Bask family might have given to other victims of the Mist, while I lived my life at Ivyhill, blissfully unaware and obsessed with my own small problems.

I shook myself, trying to focus my scattered thoughts and forget the sound of Ryder's grunt. What a bear he was. I couldn't believe I had kissed him only the day before.

"Fine," I said. And then again, sharply, "*Fine*," as if trying to convince myself that this was ordinary and good, that I was entirely unbothered by the presence of Ryder Bask. I started storming away.

He followed me easily. "Where are we going?"

"I walk the grounds every morning to ensure everything's in order," I replied.

He grunted again in agreeable assent. "I do the same."

"Well done, you. Would you like some sort of prize?"

"Not particularly. Though a cup of strong, hot coffee wouldn't go unappreciated."

"You'll get your coffee when I do, when the morning's work is done."

"Seems fair."

The complete ease with which he accepted my irritation was in itself supremely irritating. I walked faster, fists clenched, as if it were possible to propel myself through the air by punching it.

"You're angry," he observed after a moment. "I'm sorry I interrupted your morning routine." He stopped walking. "I'll go back to the house and wait."

"Oh gods, please *don't*," I said over my shoulder. "Then I'll just be walking around thinking about how you're sitting on the steps waiting for me like a great black dog. Keep walking."

He caught up with me in a few long strides. "You *are* angry though."

"I'm not angry, I'm just…" I blew out a sharp breath, searching for words that wouldn't come. "I suppose I am angry. But I don't want to think about why I am, and I don't want you to apologize for anything, because you didn't do anything worth apologizing for. Just…thank you for coming, as we agreed. And let's keep walking. All right?"

Out of the corner of my eye, I saw him nod. "All right. But if there's anything—"

"There's not."

"All right." Silence fell for a time. Then he said, "May I make a simple observation?"

"If you must."

"You look very beautiful this morning. The morning light suits you."

I laughed darkly. "I highly doubt that."

"You doubt it? Surely you've seen it for yourself."

"I haven't," I replied. "I don't like looking in mirrors."

He was quiet, then said gently, "I'm sorry. You said that yesterday. I'd forgotten."

The fact that he'd forgotten anything about our time together yesterday when every moment of it, every word of it, had been scorched into my mind like a brand to flesh made me flare up all over in mortification. Of course he didn't remember; moments like that meant nothing to him. He'd had many of them, I was certain. Even during all those years his family was trapped in a forest, Ravenswood was a community of hundreds—the servants, the grooms, the tenant farmers in the little village at the end of the main drive. He would have had years to practice and no lack of willing partners. And here I was, having spent the night twisting and turning in my bed yet again, thinking only of him—his hands on me, his lips on mine, the heat of him, the strength of him, how strangely familiar it felt to be held by him—and all the while aching for something I couldn't find, not even after I'd touched myself and brought myself to shaking completion.

"I wouldn't expect you to remember," I said crisply. "I said many things yesterday and regret most of them."

"Most of them?"

"Telling you to come here, that we need to visit the queen—I don't regret that."

"Ah."

The tone of his voice on that small word was strange, full of something I couldn't read. He said nothing after that, striding in companionable silence beside me and looking out over the Ivyhill grounds while I stewed in absolute misery until we reached the stables, where my stormy feelings grew even fiercer.

Byrn was there, our white-whiskered head groom, already awake and working a horse in the large training paddock with his apprentices. I recognized the horse at once, a black colt with a wicked temper and very little patience for humans. One of the grooms approached him with a lead rope and a simple loop halter that would rest around his neck. They wouldn't even try to put it on him, I knew; they would simply let him smell it and nose it around, get him used to the feel of it against his body. But the colt was having none of it. He watched the groom approach with his head lowered and his ears back, and when the poor boy got close enough, the colt lashed out and snapped at him with his teeth. The boy dropped the bridle and jumped back, and the colt pawed the dirt with one angry hoof.

Byrn, meanwhile, stood to the side, not looking after his apprentice but instead glowering at Ryder and me as we neared the paddock. Some of the other grooms gathered in a watchful knot not far from him. Ryder's face was well known—all the Basks' were—and not once had any of them set foot on our estate so openly. I didn't blame them for being tense; for all they knew, this was some sort of attack and I was actually Lord Alaster wearing a glamoured disguise. Never mind that they all knew we'd recently been to Ravenswood, ostensibly for pleasure. Their whole lives, the Basks had been enemies to us, to them, to their livelihoods.

"What's his name?" Ryder asked me quietly as we reached the paddock fence, his blue eyes fixed on the colt and the furious flick of his tail.

"Jet," I replied, just as softly. "A farmer in Fenwood found him wandering in the woods near the Mist and couldn't find his owner. He managed to get him home, feed him, but every attempt at training him failed. He's aggressive, impossible to work with. Byrn convinced Father to bring him to Ivyhill, take him on as a project. It took five men to wrangle him all the way here. Even our grooms with wilding magic haven't been able to make progress."

Ryder nodded. "I'm not surprised. The Mist got into this one, or else he's seen horrors he can't forget."

I glanced over at him, chilled by the images his words conjured. "Whatever happened to his owner, you mean."

"Possibly."

Ryder put both his hands on the top rail and clucked his tongue. Then he murmured something under his breath, not in Ekkari, but something smoother, gentler—another Olden bestial language, I assumed. The gathered grooms hushed. Even the morning birds went quiet.

Jet turned to stare at him. He tossed his head and snorted, showing us the whites of his eyes. The look on his face was obvious, even to me. *Just try it, stranger.*

But Ryder only smiled, then entered the paddock through the gate nearest us. One of the younger grooms jerked forward, a warning on his lips, but Byrn hushed him with a sharp wave of his hand. He watched closely as Ryder slowly approached Jet, still murmuring quietly, his head lowered and his gaze deferential. He said Jet's name. He held out his hand, a question suspended in the air.

Jet snorted and stamped his hoof, then reared up with an angry cry. I flinched, gripped the fence hard, but Ryder showed no fear. He paused, the cadence of his voice low and calm, songlike. I thought I heard questions now and then in his strange words, to which Jet snorted and whickered in response. Thanks to Ryder's Anointed wilding power, Jet could understand what he was saying, or at least enough of it.

A delicate chill washed over me as Ryder finally reached Jet, still crooning to him with that gentle, low voice. He drew long, slow strokes down the colt's back and under his wild mane that seemed to soothe his anger. He bumped Ryder's arm with his muzzle, then lowered his head, blinking heavily as if overcome with sudden exhaustion or relief, and turned his whole face into Ryder's chest. He let it rest there as Ryder stroked his neck and forehead, and at last the hush that had fallen over the paddock lifted. Birdsong returned, and I felt it was safe to breathe again.

Some of the grooms turned away, wiping their faces. Even Byrn's eyes were bright.

"Impressive, Lord Ryder," he said solemnly. "Can I ask what you said? We've tried Ekkari, and Aavmesh, as you did, and even Griskell and Kezhrati, but he responded to none of the arcane bestial languages, not even when I was the one uttering them."

Ryder glanced at him. "You are an Anointed wilder too?"

Byrn nodded. "And all my apprentices have some wilding magic, though none are Anointed."

"When the Mist touches a living creature, be it beast or human, whether the magic you try is Anointed or low doesn't matter as much as shared experience. Jet has been changed by the Mist. So have I, having lived near it for so long. We understand each other. He doesn't mean you harm. He's just frightened and knows you have not tasted fear as he has."

Then Ryder crooned to Jet again, something that sounded so tender that I had to look away. It was too dear, seeing him like this, with this wild, unkempt horse pressing his face against him, and then there was the incongruity of such gentleness belonging to such a towering, fearsome body. My own body roiled, as did my mind, my questions too muddled and my need too searing to contend with at the moment. I was glad when we left the paddock behind and continued on our walk, though for the remainder of it, I didn't look at Ryder. I couldn't, nor could I speak to him. I was too enmeshed in my own confusion, my own bewildered fantasies. After all, I knew very well what it felt like to be sheltered against the muscled mass of Ryder's body—a feeling of safety and peace, of simple belonging, that I couldn't seem to put out of my mind, no matter how hard I tried.

It was a relief to return to the house, even if that meant shutting ourselves up in Gemma's study to hear what Talan had to say.

Before he even began to speak, I could tell his report would be grave. He was thinner and paler than he had been during his last visit, with shadows under his eyes and a brittle quality to his countenance, as if whatever he'd learned had changed the very essence of him. I tried not to feel irritated that even so, he was still as beautiful as he'd ever been, with the same sculpted cheekbones, the same great dark eyes, the same full lips. Gemma had brought him fresh clothes, and even as exhausted as he clearly was, the simple dark trousers and plain white shirt looked elegant on his tall, slender body, fine enough to be worn to a formal gathering.

"The first thing I'll say," he began, his voice soft and solemn, "is that whatever's happening to the Mist is not unique to Gallinor. The other rifts are changing too. In Vauzanne, the Crescent of Storms is growing. Whatever ancient magic has until now kept its storms separate from the rest of the continent is unraveling, and now those storms are bleeding into the surrounding landscape. And in Aidurra, something similar is happening. The Knotwood is growing beyond its traditional borders, uprooting settlements and consuming ordinary woodlands like weeds overtaking a garden."

He paused, took a breath. The echo of the crown shimmered like faint fingers of lightning across his brow and temples, punctuated by three thumbprint scars in the shape of the crown's three golden jewels. Gemma's left hand echoed these scars, a web of gleaming lines that she hid under neither glamour nor glove while alone with the three of us. Sitting beside him, she reached over to take his pale hand in her scarred one. The sight stirred something in me; irritated, aching, I looked away, focusing instead on the swirling green-and-ivory pattern of the carpet until I managed to find my voice.

"We've learned recently that the Warden has worked binding magic on those living in the Mistlands," I said, "magic that prevents them from sharing the true state of the Mist with others."

Talan nodded. "It seems that the Wardens of the Knotwood and the Crescent have done something similar. The information I learned came in pieces, either through disjointed speculation or from people who clearly wanted to say more but couldn't."

"And have there been Anointed magicians abducted from the other continents as well?" Ryder asked. He stood quietly by the fire, a plate at his elbow on the mantel; his lunch was untouched.

"Yes, at least five in Aidurra, at least seven in Vauzanne. But the numbers could be higher. Since I cannot speak to their Wardens or to the queen, I can't be certain."

"We must go to her at once," Gemma said. I felt her eyes on me and kept my own trained on the floor. "Propose the draft. No, *demand* it."

I did look up at her then, a swift, cutting glare.

"I don't like it any more than you do," she replied before I could protest, "but not only would that add to the Order's numbers, thereby strengthening our defenses at the Mist and offering further protection to the north, it would reassure the people. Their queen is acting. Their queen is unafraid."

"Or it would make them riot in the streets," Ryder said grimly. "I doubt the people of Gallinor want their daughters, mothers, and sisters taken from their beds."

The memory of little Mara, sitting bravely beside the Warden as the black carriage bearing the Order's sigil took her away from us, came with a swift stab to my heart.

Desperate to change the subject, I said sharply, "What about Kilraith?"

A coldness seemed to slither through the room at the mere mention of his name.

"I haven't encountered him," answered Talan after a moment, his voice carefully soft, as if he feared that speaking any louder might summon Kilraith into the room. "Nor have I met any other demons, or any creatures at all, that are bound to his service as I was."

Ryder looked hard at him. "It's not as though his servants wear brands or carry brightly colored banners."

"I would feel it, if someone or something were bound to him. I'd feel it like a chill in winter. His are chains you can never fully be free of. I wear their echoes on my skin."

A beat, and then Talan let out a soft laugh into the uneasy quiet. He scrubbed his hands over his face. "Sorry. That was ominous. But it's true nonetheless. I would recognize a fellow bound servant of Kilraith. I would taste the same magic that once imprisoned me, feel the same weight pulling at the air around me. And in none of my travels thus far have I found anyone like me or picked up any scent of him. He's gone underground since we fought him. Since *you* fought him."

Gemma scooted closer to him, squeezed his hand. "You were

there too, darling. You fought him just as hard as we did, if not harder. Remember, those awful words you uttered were not yours. They were *his*. And without you fighting him from within, we might not have been able to defeat him from without."

Talan turned toward her and pressed his brow to hers. He closed his sad, dark eyes while she kept a close watch over him with her bright blue ones, and I got the sense that he was breathing in the scent of her, letting it cleanse him.

"And there's another thing," Talan said after a moment. He opened his eyes and faced us. "I've found…something. I don't know what it is. A forest in the far north, a place of perhaps twenty square miles, bound by magic I can't penetrate. It's dense and wild, very difficult to find. It's like…" He frowned, thinking. "I think if I were less powerful, or if I had no magic at all, I'd be able to walk right through it and not feel or see anything out of the ordinary. But there *is* something there. A secret forest within an everyday one."

"And your demon blood gives you the power to detect it?" Ryder asked.

My own blood ran cold as a horrible thought occurred to me. "You're thinking Kilraith could be there," I said quietly. "What you felt there is what you described. An echo of his chains on your skin."

Talan nodded, looking grimly resolute. "I could be misinterpreting the feeling, of course, but I can't ignore whatever it is I *did* feel. He could be there, or something else could be. Something that belongs to him."

"The abducted Anointed," Ryder muttered, his eyes glinting in the firelight.

"Or it could be a hidden weapon."

"Or an army," Gemma whispered.

Another silence fell, one rife with dread and unspoken questions, until Talan cleared his throat.

"There's one more thing," he said, rubbing Gemma's fingers

absently with his thumb. "When you travel as much as I've been traveling, when you stop in inns and taverns and sleep on the streets and beg beds from farmers for the night, when you wear a different forgettable face in each town, you hear all sorts of things. Rumors and stories and gossip, most of it nonsense. Tall tales, legends conjured over one too many drinks. But I've made note of things that seem interesting—strange words, or unfamiliar ones. Patterns in different versions of the same story. And there's a particular story that's been growing legs in Gallinor in the weeks since I've been gone. I've caught snippets of it everywhere, from the high streets in Summer's Amble to the humblest seaside villages on the eastern coast."

He drew a breath, lowered his voice. "The word I keep hearing is *Moonhollow*. The story around it is one of a palace surrounded by beautiful gardens, where wine runs through the streets like nectar and the food gives you such vitality that you don't need to sleep. There, you can dance and never grow tired. There, the sun never shines, and the flowers drink only moonlight."

Ryder grunted, waved his hand once in dismissal. "Nonsense tales spun from random pieces of Olden lore, translated by people who don't know what they're talking about. Tales to distract imaginative children and breed lurid fantasies in the minds of bored men. And with everything that's happened, it's no wonder that people are turning to such stories."

"Ordinarily I'd agree with you," Talan said, "but in all my years wandering this world bound to Kilraith's service, I'd never heard this particular tale of this particular place—Moonhollow. And now that we've fought Kilraith and sent him limping off to gods know where..." Talan trailed off.

Gemma finished for him. "Now you're hearing of it everywhere."

"Not everywhere. Not yet. But I'm hearing of it enough to feel uneasy."

I picked at my thumbnail, my mind whirling. "And in Vauzanne and Aidurra? You've heard stories of Moonhollow there too?"

Talan shook his head. "That's the interesting thing. No, I haven't. It's only here, in Gallinor."

"And here in Gallinor stands a forest surrounded by magic that you, a demon, can't penetrate."

"That is no coincidence," Ryder declared.

"No," Gemma agreed, "nor is it a coincidence that Gallinor is where *we* live—Farrin, Mara, and I."

The same thought had occurred to me, but it was too frightening to contemplate. I refused it. I rejected it. I scoffed and rolled my eyes. "Oh, and now we'll start talking about *fae blood*, will we?"

Gemma was defiant. "I'm keeping my mind open to all possibilities. You might try it sometime."

"We must go to the queen," Ryder said, before I could respond. "Tomorrow. You'll tell her everything you've observed, demon, and we'll see how she responds. What she knows, what she doesn't." He paused, noticing Gemma's pointed glare. "*Talan*," he corrected grudgingly.

Gemma nodded. "And we'll assess her health, see for ourselves how she has changed—or how she hasn't—since we were last at the palace."

"You mean *I'll* assess her health," I grumbled. That I was responding to fear and uncertainty with childish petulance didn't paint me in a favorable light, but I couldn't seem to stop myself. "You mean *I'll* spy on my friend and report my observations to you."

"More than your friend, she's the queen," Ryder said bluntly. "And more than her friend, you're an Anointed magician tasked by the gods with protecting your country."

"If the gods really wanted to protect us all so badly, they should've done it themselves," I snapped. "Or done a better job of sealing us off from the Old Country. We're not gods. It isn't fair for us to be tasked with such a thing."

Ryder regarded me with wry amusement. "I didn't hear you complaining about your Anointed duties during peacetime, Ashbourne, nor do I hear you bemoaning the wealth and status afforded to your family."

I rose swiftly, hot with shame. "That was uncalled for."

"As is your fear," he shot back. "You're allowed to be frightened, but you're not allowed to be a coward. You're better than that."

Unnerved by his sudden meanness, so starkly different from the gentleness with which he'd crooned to Jet only hours before, I took two angry steps toward him. "How dare you call me a coward when you're the one who played that awful, craven trick on my father, when you beat him and humiliated him in front of hundreds of people?"

Ryder let out a disappointed hiss. "I've apologized for that, Farrin, and I won't do it again. We were at war. Now we're not. And how dare *you* balk at doing what must be done when your sisters are alive and well, and mine's quite possibly dead somewhere, choking on Mist or gutted by a monster we hardly understand? A monster we only barely managed to defeat *once* and may not be able to beat again?"

I was stunned. There was no other word for it. I felt as if he'd punched me, and worst of all, I couldn't blame him for it. He was right, and looking up at him—his blue eyes hard with anger and grief—I felt sick with self-loathing. They kept talking around me—Ryder and Gemma and Talan—discussing how best to travel to the palace and how we would pay a visit to Gareth at the university beforehand, but I hardly heard them, too furious with myself to pay much attention.

Ryder striding out of the room was the thing that pulled me out of my shock. I'd heard enough to understand that our meeting was over; we would leave for Fairhaven at dawn.

I hurried out of the room and caught up with him at the end of the corridor, where a pretty vine-draped atrium looked out over the entrance hall below. Afternoon sunlight poured through the tall windows, bathing everything in white and gold.

"Ryder, wait," I said desperately, and he did, stopping at the top of the stairs. I didn't think; I rushed over to him and touched his arm, which at the moment felt like a privilege I didn't deserve. I held on to my courage with both hands. I had to make him understand.

"I'm so sorry," I whispered. I stared at his jacket, the silver buttons at his collar. "You're right. I am afraid. But that's no excuse, and you're so worried for Alastrina, and...I wasn't thinking. I'm so sorry. Please believe me."

He took a step toward me, lifted my chin so I had to meet his eyes. "I do believe you," he said quietly. "And thank you. And *I'm* sorry for getting angry."

"At least your anger was righteous. Mine was childish."

"No. You're right to keep reminding me of that day. Trina and I were fools, and it's good to remember it. The more we remember, the less likely we are to do it again." He paused, then gave me a small, rueful smile. "No matter how badly our parents may want us to."

I laughed, so relieved that I felt shaky at the knees. Then Ryder came closer and held me, carefully, giving me time, perhaps, to pull away. But I could think of nothing more awful than pulling away from him, nothing more wonderful than his touch. I closed my eyes, letting myself sink into the strength of him, relishing the solid warmth of his embrace, the impossible sweetness of his head bending over mine. And again came that stitch of familiar feeling in my breast. It felt right, to be enveloped within the shield of his arms. It felt like returning to a place I'd known and missed, terribly.

In this moment of stillness, I was finally able to put a name to the sensation, and my eyes snapped open with sudden shock.

The shining boy. My heart pounding, I summoned his memory:

pale skin, messy dark hair, taller than me, and, it had seemed, a few years older too. And Ryder had pale skin and dark hair, and Ryder was twenty-eight years old to my twenty-four. The shining boy had held me as we dashed out of my burning house. He'd carried me through the flames to safety. And here was Ryder, now, holding me, and only the night before, when he'd lifted me into his arms, I'd felt the same pull of belonging, the same ache.

Then Ryder was kissing my hair and releasing me, and I watched him hurry down the stairs and stride outside—to visit Jet, I assumed, and get his fill of the horses before the morning. I watched him through the stained-glass windows as he marched swiftly across the lawn, which our elemental groundskeepers were magicking a glittering gold in honor of the coming autumn. His coat snapped in the cool breeze; his hair whipped around his face, dark and wild as the animals he so loved.

Absently, I touched my hot cheeks, feathering my fingers across my skin. In Ryder's absence, reason returned to me. I shook myself, leaning hard on the banister. Ryder, the shining boy? Alone on the landing, I nearly burst out laughing. The idea was preposterous. Worse than that, it made me doubt my own sanity. I could hear Gareth's gently teasing voice even now. *Darling, just because you've been held by only two men in your life besides me and your father doesn't mean that those two men are in fact the same man. Especially when one of them might not ever have existed! Don't look at me like that. I believe you, I always have, but we've got to at least acknowledge the possibility that that boy was a hallucination. You were three breaths from death, after all. Come on, now, let's get you to bed. Clearly you need some sleep. I know, I'm being an ass. I don't deserve you, really.*

I rubbed my forehead hard, as if I could physically force my buzzing mind to fall silent, and gazed after Ryder until I felt eyes on me from below. I searched the room, the landings, and froze.

Father was there, halfway up the other set of stairs across the hall. He wore his training clothes and had a towel slung around his neck, and even from where I stood, I could feel the anger radiating off of him as he glared at me. His face was red from exertion and his hair was damp with sweat; he was fully alert, his sentinel power stoked by his exercises, and his eyes flashed. I knew what he would say. Training with Ryder was one thing, though it was hard to tolerate, but being *held* by him? And so tenderly?

I looked right back at him, coolly, though my heart was suddenly racing, and walked away before he could beckon me over. Once I was in my rooms, I shut the door, locked it, and sank slowly to the floor. Osmund trotted over with a chirp, and I welcomed him gladly. I tried not to think about how frightened I was of my own father, or about the sinking fear that he would never accept Ryder, never accept any of them. He would fight peace until the end of his days and die an angry old man. The thought made me terribly sad, terribly angry, and expanded ferociously until I had an awful headache and could think of nothing else. I held Osmund against my chest, pressed my face between his sweet silken ears, and let him purr my weary heart to something like calm.

My calm didn't last. When Gemma, Ryder, Talan, and I arrived in Fairhaven the next morning, I knew at once that something was wrong. We stepped out of the greenway that began in the game park at Ivyhill and ended in one of the city parks abutting the university, and even there among the stately trees and the rolling lawns of gold-tipped autumn grass, the air thrummed with panic.

I saw the smoke first: a long black furl twisting up into the sky from somewhere in the city's central district.

"Is it coming from the Citadel?" Gemma murmured.

No one knew the answer. We glanced at each other. The sight of Talan in disguise beneath a glamour that made him look like a mild-mannered, pale man of fifty, well-dressed and bespectacled, left me uneasy, even though I knew it was for our safety as well as his.

Talan shook his head at my unasked question. "I don't sense Kilraith anywhere nearby."

But I was not reassured, especially when we reached the university. Its buildings of pale brick were as stately as ever, capped with bell towers and clock towers and godly sculptures reaching toward the skies, but its broad, sunny streets were quiet, the air tense. Students and professors and groundskeepers were everywhere in their spotless robes and dirt-smudged coats, huddled in urgently whispering groups or walking quickly, eyes down, expressions grim. They held books in their arms, rakes in their hands; everything was ordinary at first glance. But the undercurrent of unrest was obvious, the air tight and hushed. I kept glancing fearfully at the curl of smoke, as if it were some sky beast that might launch itself at us without warning.

We hurried into the main library and up the stairs to Gareth's office, and we'd barely reached the landing outside his door when it flew open to reveal his assistant, Heldine. She looked as prim and sour as ever, which comforted me; I'd always appreciated how no-nonsense and unpleasant she was, especially since it meant Gareth would never be tempted to flirt with her. I'd held his hand through the aftermath of many a horrible romantic mistake, but breaking the heart of a woman in his employ would be a difficult scandal for me to abide.

"Well, hurry inside, won't you?" Heldine snapped, waving us past her and into Gareth's private study. Bookshelves covered every wall, sagging with the weight of far too many volumes crammed onto them in haphazard piles. As soon as we entered, Gareth jumped up from his desk and ushered us inside.

"All the doors are locked?" he asked Heldine breathlessly.

Instead of looking annoyed at the implication that she hadn't done her job properly—which I fully expected her to do—Heldine only nodded briskly. "Yes, Professor. And I'll put the outer wards back in place at once."

"Good, good. And the—"

"Yes, and the inner wards too."

"Excellent. Thank you, Heldine."

Then Gareth shut the door in her face and spun around to face us. His face lit up with excitement. "Follow me. I've got something marvelous to show you. But I don't keep it in here, of course. You get all sorts of passages commissioned for you once you're a seated professor. It's really *quite* fun, in addition to being practical and necessary."

I grabbed his sleeve before he could dash away. "Hold on a minute," I said, exasperated. "What's going on here? Why is everyone acting so odd? And the smoke—"

Gareth nodded gravely. "Yes, the smoke. Well, that's part of what I want to show you. You see, since the abductions"—he threw a sympathetic look at Ryder and clapped a hand on his back, at which Ryder grunted in wordless appreciation—"there's been a good bit of unrest in the capital, as you might imagine. Nothing too turbulent, not yet, but everyone wants to know what's going on, of course, and what the Upper and Lower Armies are going to do about it, and what the *queen's* going to do about it, and, well..."

Then he looked at me carefully, and I thought I knew what he was going to say. My heart sank.

"She hasn't shown herself, has she?" I said quietly. "She's been locked up in the Citadel?"

Gareth nodded. "Unfortunately, yes, which makes me suspect that whatever sickness ails her has grown worse. Some have gathered at the Citadel gates to protest the silence of the queen and the Senate, the perceived lack of action, and I don't blame them. They've been lighting fires, camping out at the gates, marching along the promenade surrounding the Citadel. Nothing. The gates remain closed, no one knows if the Senate's in session, and the queen hasn't been seen for weeks. But *something's* happening in the Citadel, whether it relates to the sinkhole or the queen or something else entirely, because look at this."

As he spoke, he'd been leading us through a series of quiet brick passages, accessed through a bookshelf behind his desk that swung away from the wall. He ducked at last through a stone archway and flung out his arm dramatically.

There, on a plain wooden table in a cramped stone room, its only companion a single flickering lamp, sat the Three-Eyed Crown.

And it was *moving*.

Talan flinched at the sight. The glamour he'd woven vanished in an instant, revealing his true, ashen face. Gemma grabbed his hand and stepped a little in front of him. Ryder strode right toward the thing and leaned down to inspect it, and I followed him cautiously, transfixed despite my fear—and despite the hook of curiosity that had lodged in me the previous day. I refused to look at Ryder—his broad back, his muscled shoulders, his dark hair. Ryder, the shining boy? I had very nearly convinced myself that it was impossible. The son of my enemy, still young and rash with boyhood, having a heroic change of heart the very night his family tried to murder us? Absurd, laughable. A flowery fantasy pulled out of one of Gemma's romantic novels. And yet vestiges of the idea lingered, annoyingly. I imagined batting them aside like a cloud of gnats and focused my attention back on the crown.

It was as if some mechanism buried within it had activated and pieces of it had unfolded, distorting its shape and exposing its inner workings. It hummed quietly as it moved through a cycle. First the crown's band split open along its carvings into ten different squares. They popped out randomly until the whole circumference was broken into pieces. They remained that way while the great metal shards that thrust up from the band, a parody of royal splendor, sprung outward one by one, expanding, lethal, like a series of traps to catch small animals. The three amber gems embedded in the band spun wildly in their prongs. Then the crown reassembled itself piece by piece until it sat quietly on the table, its familiar horrid self once more. And then, after a moment, the cycle began again.

"Fascinating," Ryder murmured.

"Isn't it?" Gareth was practically bursting. "I don't know what triggered this behavior, but it's been going on for two days. I'm inclined to be grateful. It's much easier to study its inner workings when they're literally presenting themselves for inspection."

Talan approached the crown, stone-faced, deathly pale. "I don't sense Kilraith here. If he were manipulating the crown, I would know." He paused, then shook his head. "It's not pulling at me either. I don't feel drawn to it more than any of you probably do. I can regard it coldly." His expression darkened. "Or coldly enough, anyway."

"No, I agree that whatever force is behind this doesn't seem malevolent," Gareth said. "Nor does it seem benevolent. It just *is*. Some sort of mechanical malfunction."

"It's revolting," Gemma murmured, staring at it with an expression of utter hatred.

I agreed with her sentiment. I took a step back from the awful thing. Its very design, all those sharp edges and grinning carvings, was one of cruelty. "And you say you've been able to study it more easily?"

"Indeed," said Gareth. "When it's fully intact, the crown is difficult to inspect with even the most aggressive uncloaking spellwork—and of course it would, as a defensive measure—but when it opens up, it's far less resistant to examination."

"Spellwork?" I threw him a suspicious look. "But you're no beguiler."

He winced a little. "No, but Heldine is."

Ryder straightened up to glare at Gareth. "You allowed your assistant to see the crown?"

"I was getting nowhere on my own. Or I suppose I was getting *somewhere*, but far too slowly. I'm an Anointed sage. My power is limited to intellect and memory—which," he added, with a roguish sort of grin, "are no small things, mind you."

I pinched the bridge of my nose. *"Gareth."*

"But, my astonishing brain notwithstanding, I can only observe so much without the assistance of other kinds of magic. That's the wonderful thing about working at a university—professors and students with specific talents all collected in one place and books everywhere you look. We learn best by working together, but I *can't* work with my colleagues as I normally would, not on something so sensitive. I can, however, work with Heldine. There's a reason I hired a beguiler as my assistant. The stodgier of my peers thought I was mad. Only sages will do, in their opinion. So many of them are narrow-minded snobs."

"And you trust this person?" Ryder said, a bit of a growl in his voice.

"With my life," Gareth replied at once. "She's a paragon of discretion, and you wouldn't know it by looking at her, but her spellcraft is sharp as daggers."

Ryder grunted. "A clumsy metaphor. If not properly maintained, a dagger can in fact go quite dull."

Gareth waved his hand. "You know what I mean. The point is, she's a vault. She won't tell anyone a thing. And together—my translation of these arcane carvings on the crown's surface, her investigative spellwork—we think we've landed upon something very exciting."

He rifled through a stack of papers on the floor and then, with a flourish, presented a particularly long one, marked from top to bottom with indecipherable scribbles.

We stared at it, bewildered. In the silence, the crown began another cycle, unfolding itself sharply, humming quietly on the table.

"Gareth," Gemma said, clearly annoyed, "that means nothing to us. It's gibberish."

"No," Talan said quietly. "It's not." He took a step toward the paper, then glanced at Gareth. "May I?"

"Of course," Gareth said, handing it to him.

Talan squinted at the paper for a long moment. "I don't understand all of this. Your handwriting's atrocious."

Gareth nodded, sheepish. "It just takes too much time to write neatly, I find."

"And I'm unfamiliar with some of these languages."

"That's the interesting thing," Gareth replied eagerly. "These carvings on the crown, they're words from hundreds of different languages. Arcane, holy, bestial. Some are so obscure I can only guess at their translations because I have no official dictionaries to use as references. But the ones I *can* translate all say essentially the same thing."

"Three," Talan murmured. "They all say *three*."

I felt myself growing impatient. I'd never liked riddles, and suddenly they were everywhere. "What does that mean? Three what? Three jewels on the crown?"

"Three curses?" Gemma mused. "Three different ways of binding servants to Kilraith?"

"Or is it a label?" Ryder said. "There are multiple crowns, and this is the third one?"

Then I saw Gareth's expression, how eager he was to tell us the answer, and my skin turned to ice.

"You think *three* refers to the *ytheliad*," I said quietly. "The curse that bound Talan to Kilraith, the curse powerful enough to transcend the boundary between our world and the Old Country. The curse so dangerous that the gods themselves wanted to destroy all knowledge of it. And it's..."

I trailed off, too horrified by my own theory to voice it aloud.

Gareth did it for me.

"What I believe," he said slowly, "is that this iteration of the *ytheliad* is far larger than a single curse that existed only to bind Talan to Kilraith. The crown served as a magical anchor, as we suspected, allowing Kilraith a dependable servant who could travel from one world to another and carry out his bidding. But I think it was only *one* such anchor, and the *ytheliad* Kilraith has created is vast. A curse with many parts, many functions."

"You think there are multiple anchors," Talan murmured, looking sick, "all of them linked to create a nexus of power for him, all of them scattered gods know where."

"Across this world and the Old Country?" Gemma asked faintly.

"And you think this is only the third of them," Ryder said. His frown was fearsome, his voice grave.

"Three of how many?" I whispered.

Gareth shook his head. "That's what Heldine and I are working to find out, though the images and words she's uncovered through her spellwork are mere fragments, like pieces of glass you'd find after something massive has shattered." He glanced at Gemma's gloved left hand, no doubt thinking of how her whole body had been pocked with glass not so long ago. "When you pick up a piece of glass at the site of a disaster, you don't immediately know how many others there are, how big a thing was broken. It will take time to decipher what she's found and to find more. But..."

"But how *much* time, you can't say," Gemma finished for him.

"No," he agreed, and then looked up at me, and I knew at once what he would say.

I felt so tired it hurt. "But it would take less time if you had access to the royal archives."

"We're going to the queen anyway," he pointed out, "and she *has* given us access before, whether she meant to or not. Remember that book that appeared in my hands the day the chimaera invaded the palace? The book that told us about the *ytheliad*, the book without which I might not have ever known this particular curse *existed*—"

"Yes, yes, I hear you," I snapped, cutting him off.

An expectant silence fell. I knew they were waiting for me to say something, that what happened next depended entirely on me—and knowing that filled me with such a sudden seething anger that I had to stand there for a moment and bite down against a dozen petulant instincts, all of them telling me to run away or refuse to act or insult people who didn't deserve it.

I felt Ryder's eyes on me and remembered his words from the day before. *You're allowed to be frightened, but you're not allowed to be a coward. You're better than that.*

And he was right. I *was* better than that. Or at least I would try to be, no matter how angry it made me that I had to try at all. I was tired of trying so hard to be everything, to do everything. So often, trying felt like climbing a distant northern mountain that never ended.

But if I didn't climb, then what? I'd sit in the freezing snow and let it kill me?

The thought was appealing. I shook myself a little, frightened of my own mind and its capacity to conjure up all manner of dangerous fantasies.

"Well, then," I said briskly, ignoring Ryder with extraordinary effort, "we can't waste any more time. We'll go to the Citadel at once. If they'll let us through the gates, that is."

I turned and left the room, and the others hurried to follow me.

CHAPTER 12

They did not let us into the Citadel.

It was madness there. Hundreds of people were gathered at the northern gates, which stood nearest the university. They shouted for the queen, for the Senate. They grabbed the iron gates and shook them, waved flaming torches, threw rotten food. Those who attempted to scale the great perimeter wall were turned back with almost comical politeness by the guards who stood atop it. And everywhere we looked, the protesters held up portraits of people I assumed were the abducted—children and adults, young and old. Many faces repeated themselves, and some had been hung on the wall above shrines of coins and candles and flowers.

Heart in my throat, I quickly looked over the portraits. There was young Dornen Lerrick, and not far from him were two handsome men—one with pale skin, one with brown—wearing fine robes and beautiful smiles. I wondered if they were Lords Wynn and Moris from the village of Devenmere.

And then, after a few more portraits—a gangly young man, an elderly woman, a grinning, ruddy-cheeked farmer—was Alastrina.

Whoever had commissioned this portrait clearly viewed Alastrina with reverent awe. The portrait had been done in charcoal, all black except for her pale skin and the blue pinpricks of her eyes. Her expression was mischievous, haughty, and her gown and hair were bursting with black feathers.

I looked for Ryder, part of me hoping he hadn't seen it, but of course he had. He stood very near me, staring hard at the portrait with an unreadable expression.

Suddenly all my wild speculation about the shining boy seemed foolish, even outrageous. Ryder was not some phantom of my childhood; he was a man who had lost his sister, a man trying very hard not to let his grief consume him.

I reached for him. "Ryder..."

He grabbed my hand, squeezed it, then released me. "Not right now. This way."

He pushed his way gently through the crowd, clearing a path for us, but when we reached the gates, I felt the pointlessness of what I would say even before I opened my mouth. On the other side stood ten stone-faced guards. One of them recognized me—I saw it flash across her face—but when she whispered something to one of the other guards, the response was a firm shake of his head. The first guard glanced at me with apology, then fell back into line, her expression returning to its previous watchful blandness.

I tried anyway. "Excuse me," I said, shouting to be heard over the clamor, "I'm Farrin Ashbourne, a friend of the queen's. I'd like to see her, please. She's always happy to—"

"We know who are you, Lady Farrin," said the most senior guard, a broad man with dark brown skin and a red sash across his uniform. "But our orders are to let no one through these gates. Not even you."

The specificity of the orders startled me. "You were told to look out for me?"

The guard nodded. "By Lord Thirsk himself. His instructions were clear."

Thirsk, Yvaine's principal adviser. My shock left me speechless.

"However," the guard added, not unkindly, "I'm certain that if you sent the queen a letter, she would be glad to hear from you."

"Yes, I'm sure she would," I said drily before turning away. If Thirsk didn't want me to see Yvaine, I doubted he would allow my letters through either.

We regrouped at the edge of the protesters, not far from Alastrina's portrait and shrine.

"What should we do now?" Ryder asked. He glanced only once at Alastrina's portrait, his shoulders tense, his hands in fists.

"The question is," I said, "has Thirsk decided on his own to keep us out of the Citadel, or has the queen requested it?"

"It is absolutely *not* Yvaine's doing," Gemma said. "It can't be. She loves you, Farrin, and considering everything she said last time we were here about how all of us are important to whatever's happening—"

Suddenly Talan spoke. He wore his glamour again—the mild-mannered, bespectacled man of fifty—and it was as strange as ever to hear his smooth, familiar voice coming out of a stranger's face.

"I can get you inside," he said quietly, "if you can take me somewhere less crowded, where there might be fewer guards."

I met Ryder's eyes at once. "The gardens near my music room," I said. He nodded in agreement. "There's ward magic there," I went on, "but it's designed to admit me, at least. Unless it's been altered, though hopefully Thirsk's influence doesn't reach that far. And with everyone so distracted by the sinkhole, the protests, Yvaine's illness—"

"Maybe the ward magic is unstable enough right now to admit me too," Talan finished, nodding. None of us remarked on the darker side of that hope: if the ward magic was unstable, that would leave the Citadel even more alarmingly vulnerable.

Gemma grabbed Talan's arm. "Wait a moment. What if Kilraith was the one to make the sinkhole? What if its existence gives him a sort of foothold here? You've evaded him thus far, but could using your power so close to a magical aberration of that size draw him to you?"

Talan folded her hand into his and gave her a small smile. "Not if I'm careful and quick." He glanced at me. "Farrin?"

I swallowed my doubts, trying not to meet Gemma's worried gaze. "This way."

◆◇◆

The western gates were far less crowded. Through them, I could see the sprawling gardens that abutted my music room. They were not so grand as those outside the Pearl of the Sea Ballroom; they were smaller, humbler, with far fewer sparkling fountains and elaborately pruned topiaries.

A small crowd of protesters had gathered at the gates, but though they shouted the same complaints as the others—where was the queen, what was she doing to protect us and recover those who were lost?—the mood here felt much less volatile. Ryder and Gemma lingered at the crowd's edge as Talan and I approached the gates. I held my breath, fluttery with apprehension. Talan was one of the greater demons—a descendant of both the goddess Zelphenia and the god Jaetris—and therefore possessed tremendous powers of both the mind and deception. He could disguise himself, sense others' moods and alter them, and convince them that the truth was a lie, that a lie was the truth. I hoped his power wouldn't attract Kilraith to him like a fly to honey.

"Good afternoon," Talan said cheerfully to the five guards keeping watch beyond the gates, his appearance that of the innocuous bespectacled man. "I wonder if you could help me with something?"

Gemma had told me what to expect when Talan used his power, but I still wasn't quite prepared for the sensation of it. The air warmed all at once, as I'd suddenly stepped out of gloomy shade into a bright pool of sunlight. His magic rippled gently through the crowd, subduing both them and the guards, whose stern expressions softened into something more solicitous.

"Of course, sir," said one of the guards, a strapping woman with slightly lined brown skin and cropped white hair. "How can we be of help?"

I hardly listened as Talan spoke. I already knew the lie he would feed the guards: that he hoped to gain access to the royal gardens because they housed a rare type of azalea, which he wanted to study for a book he was writing on botanical oddities of Gallinor. I, his assistant, was there to help him take notes. I kept my head down, too nervous to focus very hard on what he was saying; if there was even a slight flaw in his magic, a single flicker of doubt, one of these guards would surely recognize me.

But soon the guards were grandly ushering us inside with smiling faces and dazed eyes, and the crowd we left behind at the gates waved after us as if bidding beloved family members farewell. I didn't dare turn back to look at Ryder and Gemma. I followed Talan into the gardens, flinching when the gates clicked shut behind us.

A few steps into the gardens, everything grew quiet, the world outside the great stone wall muffled by the profusion of flowering bushes on all sides. Silver birch branches met like arched rafters over our heads. Talan kept up a steady stream of conversation with the guards, complimenting everything from their uniforms to the shine of their swords to the aesthetically pleasing blend of yellow tones in the autumn-touched gardens. I stuck to his side as much as I could without looking ridiculous; I had it in my head that doing this would somehow protect me from being found out, even though I knew quite well that Talan was powerful, talented, and quite practiced at subterfuge. He'd been traveling in disguise for weeks and weeks now, after all, and done it for years before that at Kilraith's behest; this was hardly his first time using deceptive magic.

But every time we encountered a new guard, in that sliver of time between the guard seeing us and Talan soothing their confusion with his lies, I went cold with fear. Would one of the guards we met be Kilraith in disguise? Would Talan not act quickly enough, revealing my identity to these soldiers and ruining the whole charade?

My tension must have been obvious; at one point, Talan put a steadying hand on my back. Distantly, I heard him say, "Ah! There it is."

In my panic, I didn't at first register what that really meant. Talan crouched beside me, inspecting a bright red bloom that might have been an azalea or might not have. "There it is," he said again, loudly. "How odd for a spring bloom to still be alive here in the early days of fall. Tell me, are any of you familiar with the practices of the elemental groundskeepers in charge of tending these gardens? I have many questions for them."

Talan gently set his heel down on my foot, and the slight pain helped me snap back to myself. *There it is.* Those were the words I was meant to be listening for. I looked around wildly, and my heart leaped as I saw through the nearby trees the stone steps that led to my music room's private veranda. Above it rose the great circular base of the queen's tower. We were close enough now for me to run.

I glanced down at Talan, who looked absurd there on the ground, spectacles at the end of his glamoured nose and a flower cradled in his palm. I noticed a bead of sweat on his temple and felt a thrill of fear; a hundred terrible scenarios raced through my mind. He was tired; his magic would soon give way; the ward magic latticed throughout the gardens was killing him.

But Talan gave me a slight firm nod, and a swell of warmth rippled through the air—a fresh surge of his magic, I assumed, reinforcing his hold on the guards.

I turned and fled, racing along the garden paths and up the steps. Layers upon layers of ward magic gave way at my approach, as if I were pushing through invisible fleshy membranes meant to protect something precious from invaders. But I was no invader; this magic knew me to be as much a part of the queen's tower as the stones in its walls.

I burst into my music room, feeling a thrill of equal parts triumph and unease to find the doors unlocked. Once inside, I locked them behind me and leaned against the wall to catch my breath. My mind spun wildly; I needed to think. There would be guards stationed all through the tower, especially if Thirsk and the other advisers were determined to keep Yvaine as sequestered as possible. But years ago, Yvaine had installed a secret bellpull in this music room, hidden behind stacks of sheet music and spelled by a beguiler to reveal itself only to me. The bell on its other end sat in a tiny silver locket that Yvaine always wore hidden underneath her clothes. Wherever she was in the palace, she would hear its chime.

I hurried to the shelves where it was hidden, found the tasseled velvet cord, hesitated. If I rang this, Yvaine would know I was here and come at once. But if they were watching her as closely as I feared they were, and if she was too ill to defy them—

"Farrin?" asked a small, hopeful voice.

I turned and saw a flurry of white hair and peach chiffon just before Yvaine barreled into me. She threw her arms around my neck and buried her face in my hair, and I held her to me for a long moment, feeling shaky with relief. Tears pricked my eyes as I tried to remember the last time we'd been alone and together and well, or well enough. The night of the ball, the night she'd gone mad by the sinkhole, I'd helped her sleep afterward, but there had been guards everywhere, watching us like hawks, and she'd hardly realized where she was, let alone that I was there beside her.

This felt different. This felt dear and familiar.

I pulled back from her a little, hating that I had to, hating all the questions and demands I would soon throw at her. She must have sensed my discomfiture; she looked at me hard and then dropped back down to the floor, light as a feather.

"You're afraid of something," she said. "Come sit. Tell me."

I let her lead me to the sleeping couch tucked into the corner of the room. A stack of books sat beside it, and several half-full cups of cold tea, and a plate or two scattered with crumbs. There were slippers on the rug, quilts draped over the cushions.

"Have you been sleeping here?" I asked.

She sat delicately on the edge of the sofa, looking sheepish. "I hope you don't mind. It's the only place I can find some peace. Thirsk and I worked out a bargain. I can have my privacy here as long as I don't leave. And I haven't, and I won't. Being here, I can almost pretend you're with me." She let out a sad little laugh. "I suppose I should have worked harder to make friends here in the Citadel, friends other than you. But the truth is, most people don't treat me like a person. They treat me like a queen. And that isn't a trustworthy basis for friendship."

I took a breath and sat beside her, choosing my words carefully. Her own felt ruthless, cutting me to pieces before I could even begin. "I have much to talk to you about," I said quietly, "but first, I have to ask you a private question, one that will seem silly on the surface. But it's important to me, and I hope you'll take it seriously."

Yvaine's expression brightened. "I'm intrigued. And I always take you seriously. Ask me."

I forced myself to look straight at her. "You know about the shining boy."

She nodded gravely. "Of course."

I felt a rush of gratitude. She had always accepted my story about him, had not even once tried to dissuade me from holding on to his memory so fiercely.

I said the rest in a rush, stumbling over my words. "Lately I've been spending more time with Ryder Bask, and I wonder...I hate to ask it of you, but I know you have the abilities to read things, to search the world for people, to probe past and future, even if only vaguely. And I never—*never*—want to take advantage of our friendship. But, gods, Yvaine, I know it's absurd, but I've had these strange feelings, these...these *twinges* of something I can't name, and I'm so curious—"

"You're wondering if Ryder was your shining boy," she finished gently.

I nodded, burning with embarrassment. Hearing Yvaine say the words out loud made the question seem all the more ludicrous.

"Darling Farrin." She placed one warm hand on mine and leaned forward to meet my eyes. "Don't you think I would have told you, long ago, if that were the case? I would've easily sensed such a thing, and revealing that truth could have prevented years of strife between your families, perhaps even served as the first step toward peace."

I'd never felt such relief in my life. Yvaine's expression was open, honest, clear; her voice brimmed with compassion. She wouldn't lie to me, not about this.

I closed my eyes, laughed a little. "Thank you. I wouldn't have been able to stop thinking about it if you hadn't..." I bit back the awkward tumble of words; I'd already taken too much of her time for this small, selfish thing. I resolved to put the whole matter out of my mind, at once, and keep it there.

"A very odd weight has been lifted," I said simply. "Thank you."

"You are most welcome," she said, and then, more quietly, she added, "But I think this isn't the only reason you've come to see me."

I shook my head, the euphoric rush of relief fading fast. "No, it isn't. Far from it."

Yvaine looked suddenly very old. Outside, the clouds shifted, and harsh afternoon sunlight fell upon her face. "And none of what you have to say is very good, is it? You feel as gray as I do."

"I won't lie to you—no, none of it is very good. Some of it, maybe all of it, you won't like to hear. But hear it you must."

Yvaine went very still. I saw the last traces of happiness drain from her expression and wished passionately that I could forget all of this, that I could simply sit with her and talk about unimportant things: silly palace gossip, or Gareth's latest romantic catastrophes, or what it felt like to be kissed by Ryder Bask. I could accompany her shockingly off-key singing on the piano, or we could go to the kitchens and raid the pantry, or she could teach me—with limited success, if past attempts were any indication—whatever dance was the latest fashion at court.

But instead, Yvaine nodded and raised her gaze to mine, cool and regal. "Speak, then."

I tried not to be hurt by that voice and instead be glad for it. It would make things easier. We were not friends in that moment, with years of love between us; we were a queen and her subject.

"First," I said, "and I must ask you to be completely honest with me, as we've always been with each other. Are you ill?"

Her answer was unflinching. "Yes."

I swallowed hard. It wasn't a surprise, and yet I still had to fight back tears. "What is the extent of it?"

"I don't know. No one knows. I..." Yvaine's brow furrowed slightly. "Sometimes my powers manifest in surprising ways, without my permission. It's as if for all these years, I've been a tightly capped bottle, and now the glass of my body is starting to crack. Things are getting out that shouldn't. There are whole days that I can't remember. I'll wake up in the strangest places, my advisers frantic because for two, three days they couldn't find me anywhere. And I can't tell them where I've been."

Her voice grew quieter as she spoke. When she finished, she looked up at me, imploring, her white hands tightly clasped in her lap.

I tried not to let the absolute horror I felt show on my face. This was worse than I'd expected. "All right. Thank you for telling me that. And..." I paused, gripping the sofa cushions hard to keep myself from giving her false reassurances—that everything would be fine, that there was no reason to worry. "And your healers, they can't name the affliction?"

Yvaine smiled a little. "They have nothing to compare it to. I'm the only one of my kind, after all."

"But memory loss, unpredictable powers, involuntary use of power—those have to be common symptoms of other illnesses."

"Of course they are." She started counting off points on her fingers. "The degradation of magic due to advanced age. The degradation of the mind due to advanced age. Loss of magic entirely, again, due to advanced age."

I wasn't sure how to phrase my next remark without sounding indelicate. "And I suppose you *are* of advanced age..."

She regarded me with fond amusement. "I both am and am not. I'm ageless, Farrin. I'm a pet of the gods. Hundreds of thousands have lived and died during my lifetime, and hundreds of thousands more will live and die, and still I will be here. *Lifetime* is, for me, an absurd unit of measurement. You know this."

"I know, but...is it *possible* that..." I shook my head, miserable in every way. "Something's wrong with the Middlemist. And with the Crescent of Storms and the Knotwood. And something's wrong with you too. Are these things connected? Is..." And this was a fear none of us—not even Mara in all her grim letters—had yet voiced. "Is our world in danger, Yvaine? Is the end of your life coming? And will that mean the end of Edyn?"

Yvaine's eyelids fluttered. She drew in a sharp breath, hesitated. "There's…there's something wrong with the Middlemist?"

I stared at her, my shock too overwhelming to mask. Terrible fear, colder and greater than any I'd ever known, dropped over me like winter come all at once. She didn't know. No one had told her, none of her advisers—but worse than that, she couldn't sense the truth on her own. She, Yvaine Ballentere, high queen of Edyn, chosen by the gods thousands of years ago to keep us safe.

Suddenly I felt childishly terrified, and hugged myself, and looked down at my feet. The weight of this moment crashed down onto my shoulders with thunderous force, but I wouldn't cry; I refused to cry.

Yvaine touched my hand. I looked up through a glittering sheen of barely restrained tears.

"Tell me everything you know," she said, with the sort of calm patience that reminded me of my mother and hit me with the force of a blow from Ryder's staff. My mother, when our home was complete, content. My mother, before everything had changed and she had left us to endure it alone.

I dashed a hand across my face and obeyed. I told her everything: what Talan had learned in his travels, what Mara had said in her letters—the Mistfires, the sickness spreading through the Mistlands—and everything the Warden had told us too. When I spoke of Devenmere, and of the binding magic the Warden had been using to keep the state of the Mist a secret, Yvaine's expression hardened.

"Llyleth," she muttered angrily, and I realized that this must be the Warden's true name. "That use of power is well beyond her authority. I will send for her at once and speak to her."

"It's more complicated than that," I said. "This binding magic—she didn't work it on Gemma or Gareth or me, and I believe she's released

Ryder from it as well, though I don't know how such a complex work-ing is possible—on such a large scale, yet with such specificity…"

I trailed off, hoping Yvaine would jump in and explain it all to me. But she simply looked at me, waiting.

"What I'm trying to say is this," I went on quickly. "She allowed us to come here, with our knowledge of the truth intact, so that we could make a request of you." *Not a request*, the Warden had said. *A demand*. But I couldn't say that word, couldn't even look Yvaine in the eye.

"She sent you because she thinks I'll be more receptive to her requests if they come from you," Yvaine said gently.

I nodded, staring at my skirts. "She wants you to propose to the Senate a national draft to bolster the Order of the Rose's numbers. And I suppose the other Wardens probably want that as well, on their continents and for their Orders, but I can't be certain. I know only what our Warden requested."

Yvaine was very quiet. "What else did she say?"

I heard the slight dangerous note in her voice and hated that I had caused it, even indirectly. "She told us that if steps toward such a draft haven't been made by the end of next week, she'll confiscate the Three-Eyed Crown from us."

"The Three-Eyed Crown. The cursed object that once lived in Talan d'Astier?"

"Yes. Gareth has it at the university—"

"Don't tell me anything more about it," Yvaine said sharply. She rose and took a few quick steps away. Her back to me, she stared out of the windows at the gardens beyond. "I can't know where it is or what you're doing with it. I don't think it's safe for me to know."

"Because of your illness?"

She nodded. "Because I don't know where I go during these lost days, what I do, and if such an object were to come into my possession,

I'm not sure what I would do with it. I can't be certain I wouldn't do something terrible, though I can't imagine what." She touched her temple, her fingers shaking. "It's not *this* me, here before you, that I'm afraid of. I'm afraid of the me who disappears. The me who started screaming at the sinkhole. I don't even remember what I said that night."

She turned to look at me, her eyes shining, and gave me a sad, soft smile. "I remember your singing, though. I remember you keeping watch over me afterward. I'm grateful for it. I don't think I ever told you that."

I didn't want to say anything more, but I had to, and I hoped she could see how unhappy it made me. "I won't tell you everything, then, about what we're doing, but…Yvaine, I have to tell you *some* things. We're fumbling in the dark, trying to determine what's behind all of this, how everything's connected, how it can be mended or undone, but—"

"You'll have to do so without me," Yvaine said firmly. "At least until I'm well. For now, I must devote myself to keeping this city intact. A bastion of safety, a sanctuary the people of Edyn can turn to for protection."

"But that sanctuary has already been violated, has it not? The sinkhole, the abductions—"

"And don't you think those catastrophes would have been far worse, were it not for me?" Yvaine blew out a sharp breath. "Without my powers reinforcing their efforts, the royal beguilers' spellwork would have failed weeks ago, and the sinkhole would have engulfed the palace by now. Without my presence here in the capital and my power radiating outward from the Citadel, more people could have been abducted. Even sick as I am, I know that. Whatever's happening, whatever dark forces are behind these events, they are being tempered by my very existence. And I cannot be tempted away from staying safe and alive by Three-Eyed Crowns or Mistfires or whatever brave, wild things you're doing to try and find the villains at work in the shadows."

Yvaine came back to me then, stood before me with her arms crossed protectively over her chest. She glared at the carpet, at her bare white feet. "If I could," she muttered, "I would do all of this for you. I would take away the responsibility, the mystery, and bear it on my own, and I would be happy to do it, if it meant you could stay at Ivyhill with your family and your piano and be safe and content. I despise having to ask such things of the one true friend I have."

I stared at her—her bright eyes, her earnest, desperate expression. I'd never seen her so openly frightened, so obviously frustrated by her own limitations. I hadn't ever known her to acknowledge that she *had* limitations. I'd always assumed she had none. I began to understand— really, truly understand—what her words the night of the ball had meant. *I need all of you to be my eyes, ears, and hands out there in the world.*

She must have seen the comprehension dawn on my face. She nodded grimly and sat beside me, took my hands in hers. "Yes, you understand now, as I think you did not before. Maybe you thought I was simply tired that night, or exaggerating the importance of the roles you and your sisters will have to play in what's to come—and these friends you've made, these lovers."

Something strange flickered across her face too quickly for me to read it. I looked away, embarrassed. *Lovers*, she'd said. More than one. There was Talan, and…who else? I thought of Ryder kissing me in the stable, his arms around me, the heat of him under me, my own heat rising fast, my whole body blooming to life.

But surely Yvaine didn't know about that. She was powerful, but she wasn't all-seeing.

"There's…" I began, my voice coming out in a whisper. I was too overwhelmed to think clearly, and suddenly Talan's report from the far north came to mind. "Talan found a forest—"

"*No*, Farrin," Yvaine interrupted. "I can't know anything you're doing, any leads you're following. It's too dangerous—for you, for me, for everyone. You are my knights, and you must ride out across the world in my service. A service I wish I didn't have to ask of you."

She watched my face intently for a moment, her eyes glittering and sad, and then she rose and went to the windows once more, the gauzy peach skirts of her gown drifting after her.

"I will speak to my advisers and my Senate council about the draft," she said at last. "And I will write to Llyleth, apprise her of my actions. The Three-Eyed Crown will stay with you. I promise you that."

And I didn't doubt that; her voice was quiet but resolute. I felt the steel of her from where I sat, the fierce, ancient forces burning inside her tiny body.

I relaxed the slightest bit. At least that one task had been accomplished. I braced myself for the next one.

"There's another thing," I said slowly, "and I'm sorry for asking it of you, for asking any of this—"

"Professor Fontaine wants access to the royal archives." She turned to smile wearily at me. "I can read your face very well, and Gareth is a particularly insistent specimen of academic. I'm sorry, but I cannot allow you or anyone into the archives right now. In fact, even my royal librarians have been banished from them. I can't trust anyone with the knowledge stored there, not even myself. I've stationed a team of beguilers at every access point, whose sole duty is to maintain a constantly rotating schedule of spellwork, ensuring that even I won't be able to enter. So far, they've managed well enough. Though there are those days I can't remember..."

Suddenly her gaze went distant, and a stricken expression fell over her face. She bit her lip, shook her head slightly. And something about the look of her just then—small and ragged, frightened, miles away—left me terribly afraid. I curled my fingers around the edge of the sofa cushions, steeling myself. Ryder's face flashed before my eyes; I wished desperately that he were with me.

"Yvaine?" I managed to say.

"I'm fine," she said, her voice thin. She shook herself a little. "I'm here."

But she sounded unconvinced, and she wavered there for a moment before her eyes glazed over once more. Before me, she changed, her body shifting subtly from familiar to unfamiliar, from very human exhaustion to the quiet, burning vitality of something inhuman and indefinable, something *else*.

"Moon by day," she said, her voice soft as falling snow, "fire by night. Come and dance. Don't try to fight. The beauty of shadows, the garish sunlight. Spin for the watchers, their revels so bright."

A chill tore down my spine. Dancing. Moonlight. Recognition tugged at me. *The word I keep hearing is Moonhollow*, Talan had told us. A story heard across the continent—a legend, a new piece of lore. Scraps of rumor picked up here and there, coming together to make a strange, frightening whole: a palace surrounded by gardens. No sunlight, only that of the moon. Dancing and never growing tired.

"What?" I whispered to Yvaine. I went to her, and though I was afraid to touch her, I held on to her shoulders, desperate for her to start making sense. "Look at me. At *me*, Yvaine, at *me*. Say that again."

Slowly she dragged her gaze up to mine, though it was clear her true attention lay elsewhere. "Moon by day," she repeated, smiling a little, "fire by night. Come and dance. Don't try to fight. The beauty of shadows, the garish sunlight. Spin for the watchers, their revels so bright." Then her soft, dreamy expression shifted into sadness. "No," she said, "not yet."

"Not yet? Not yet what?"

Yvaine slumped under my touch. "They've come for you," she said, rubbing her eyes. Irritation bristled in her voice. "They've found us out."

The next moment, the doors to my music room burst open, admitting Lord Thirsk and three other scowling advisers—Lord Jarvis, Lady Bethan, and Lady Goff, all of whom I knew. Behind them hurried four armor-clad guards.

"Your Majesty," said Thirsk sharply, "though you've indeed honored the terms of our agreement by staying in these rooms, I think you'll agree that entertaining guests, even Lady Farrin, goes decidedly against the many reasons for your confinement."

But Yvaine didn't respond. She stared blankly at Thirsk, and then her gaze hardened, and a mean little smile flickered across her features before she turned away from us to face the windows. Ignoring us, she began to dance—a slow, measured swaying, her hands drifting eloquently through the air to music none of us could hear.

Thirsk dragged a hand over his white beard and jerked his head at the doors.

I stood firm in the center of the room. "I'm not leaving her."

"You will, Lady Farrin," Thirsk snapped, "whether by your own power or that of my guards. Don't make me drag you out of here." He gestured sharply at the queen. "She was well enough today before you arrived. And now look at her. Do you want to upset her even more?"

Gutted, speechless, I couldn't find the strength to argue with him. Whether he was lying or not, the harsh truth was that I didn't know how to help Yvaine out of whatever strange mood she'd fallen into, and perhaps her advisers did. I allowed myself to be ushered out by Thirsk and the guards while the other advisers carefully approached Yvaine. The last thing I heard before the doors closed behind me was Lady Bethan saying, "Your Majesty, perhaps you'd enjoy finishing the rest of this pie? Or shall I send to the kitchens for something fresh?"

Once outside in the corridor, two of the guards resumed their stations at the doors, and the other two, implacable, turned to glare at me. I hardly had time to think of what to say—an apology, a cool defense—before Thirsk rounded on me, his expression more furious than I'd ever seen it.

"You foolish girl," he said quietly. "We've been lenient with you for years. Your family's status, the queen's fondness of you...gods know she has very few joys in this life, and I've been happy to protect this one for her. But are you truly this dense? You saw what happened to her the last time you were here, and now the city's in an uproar and the entire continent is terrified, grieving. Did you really think this was the time to sneak into the castle like some kind of rebellious schoolgirl? I assume the perimeter guards told you the queen wasn't receiving visitors, and yet you considered yourself above such restrictions. The arrogance, Lady Farrin. Did it never occur to you that those safeguards were in place for the sake of the queen's health and that you should respect them?"

"Thirsk..." His reprimand—which, in my misery, I felt I fully deserved—had granted me time to get a good look at the man, and when I did, shock whacked me right in the gut. "What's happened? Are you all right?"

He looked as though he'd aged ten years since I'd last seen him only a few weeks prior—deep lines in his face, his brown skin turned ashen and haggard. His eyes were bloodshot, and his normally immaculate clothes—gold-hemmed black robes, tasseled velvet hat—were rumpled and askew. He blinked at me in astonishment for a moment, and then something in his countenance gave way. I got the horrible feeling I was the first person in quite some time to ask about his well-being.

"My apologies, Lady Farrin," he said, his voice suddenly as dull and tired as his appearance. "You are neither a girl nor a fool. But nevertheless, I'm afraid I'll have to escort you from the Citadel grounds and request that you do not return until Her Majesty's health has improved. I will send you a letter myself when that happens, at which point you are welcome to resume your customary visits. And tell your friends," he added, his expression hardening a little, "that whatever clever magic they possess, they too must honor this request. No, this *order*. An order from the head of the Royal Conclave. Do not make me ask the Senate for an official petition of exile. I don't want to do that. It would upset the queen, and I bear you no ill will. In fact, I'm grateful that you've long been a friend to her. But I *will* go to the Senate if I must. Do you understand me?"

"I'm not dangerous to her," I protested, though even as I said it, I realized I couldn't know that for certain. The thought made it difficult to breathe.

"I don't know what's dangerous and what isn't," he said, "but I do know—as I'm sure you do too, now—that our queen is ill. I know that she needs rest and peace and that often you and your family bring the opposite of that. Late nights and neglect of her duties. Stress and gossip, assassination attempts and public brawls. And I also know that if she gets worse…" He paused, shook his head. His mouth turned down at the corners. "Then gods help us all."

He nodded at the two waiting guards, then turned on his heel and left us, but before he disappeared around the corner, I scrabbled for courage, and for my voice, and found a scrap of each.

"Wait," I called after him. "I have some information you and the other advisers might find useful—"

"Good *day*, Lady Farrin!" he shouted back over his shoulder, his tone brooking no argument. Abashed, utterly defeated, I let the guards escort me away.

CHAPTER 13

After that, we wasted no time. We stopped at Ivyhill only long enough to gather supplies for the journey north, then in the village of Fenwood, in the southern Mistlands, to collect Mara. Even a few miles from Rosewarren, I felt on edge as we waited for her in the village's most popular tavern, even with all of us—Gemma, Ryder, Gareth, Talan, and I—in glamoured disguise. Gemma had used her power to touch each of us, excepting Talan, with the barest hint of a glamour—nothing dramatic, just enough to make our faces uninteresting and unrecognizable. Bland, sleepy patrons in a crowded tavern.

I tried not to worry about how that act of magic might have exhausted Gemma and instead distracted myself with random musings—such as how a town as relatively small as Fenwood could support multiple bustling establishments of drink and revelry—and forced myself *not* to think about my perhaps not irrational fear that at any moment the Warden would come bursting through the doors. She would demand news about the draft, about Yvaine; she would know at once what we'd planned and lock Mara up in the priory, separating her from us forever.

But Mara arrived safely, slipping silently into the tavern along with a cool autumn breeze. She wore the plain brown-and-gray garb typical of the Order of the Rose, and I tensed as I watched her, terrified that some drunken boor would notice her and make a scene, demand information about the abducted, demand to know what the Order was doing to prevent further incidents. But Mara was a Rose, quick and quiet, practiced at subterfuge. There wasn't even a ripple of interest in the room as she crossed it, unremarkable as a shadow.

As agreed upon in our letters, Mara went straight for the innkeeper, who held court with her barkeeps behind a glossy countertop. She paid for a room, obtained a key, and disappeared up the stairs behind one of the inn's housemaids. Not a glance at any of us, not a moment of hesitation. If the innkeeper had her own questions about the abductions, about the Mist, her desire for a customer's money apparently outweighed her curiosity, at least for tonight.

Dizzy with relief, I gulped down a huge swig of my cider. The bubbles sparkling through my body helped me endure the agonizing half hour before I allowed myself to follow Mara upstairs. The inn was huge, boasting dozens of rooms. I passed the locked door to my empty room, my own key tucked away in my pocket, and searched for a room with a brown falcon's feather wedged in the door. When I found it, I felt another giddy rush of relief and swiftly let myself in, catching the feather as it fell.

Gemma was already there, sitting on Mara's bed and happily stroking the speckled white chest of Freyda, Mara's falcon. Freyda's piercing yellow gaze fell sharply upon me, as if to confirm that I was actually me and not some deception of the Mistlands. After a moment, her round eyes drifted shut, and she chirped quietly to herself, in obvious ecstasy from Gemma's ministrations.

Mara came over and drew me into a quick, fierce embrace. I let myself savor the feeling for a few heartbeats—the warm, wiry strength of her, the smell of forest and old books that seemed forever woven into the earth-dark strands of her hair. As Gemma removed my glamour, I pulled back from Mara and met her solemn brown gaze.

"You weren't followed?" I asked.

She shook her head. "My unit covered for me and will continue to, and anyway, the Warden's more than occupied with her duties. I'll have two, maybe three days before she notices I'm gone." She gave me a grim little smile. "Is it wrong of me to hope for constant but minor invasions throughout the weekend to keep her nice and distracted?"

"Not at all," Gemma answered from the bed. "*Minor* is an important word here. The Order can handle *minor*. It's not as though you're wishing disasters upon them."

"Fair enough. I'll keep hoping, then. So." Mara perched on the edge of the bed and fixed me with a grave look. "Tell me what's happened."

I settled on the bed along with them, my chest twisting with too many emotions to name. Being in the same room with both of my sisters was so rare an occurrence as to feel like something out of an Old Country myth. If only we could have used our time together to talk about anything else.

If only I could reach for Mara's hand, and hold on to her, and nestle close to her as easily as Gemma was doing now.

But that was not the way of things. Gemma was the sweet one, who could say and act as she pleased, to whom everything of the body, everything of love, came easily. And I was the one sitting tensely apart from them, rigid as a brittle old twig. I tried not to glare at my sisters, who had done nothing wrong and deserved none of my strange, uncomfortable ire. Instead I looked hard at the worn quilt, bitter longing rankling in my chest as Mara, waiting for me to speak, began absently stroking Gemma's golden hair.

"The Royal Conclave has placed the queen in confinement," I began, and then I told Mara everything. The unrest in the capital,

Gareth's research into the Three-Eyed Crown, what the crown's many carvings meant: *three*, over and over, in dozens of languages. And I told her about being banished from the Citadel, about Yvaine's seclusion in my music rooms and the strange things she had said.

It was here that Mara stopped stroking Gemma's hair and went very still. "What did you say?"

I hesitated, my skin prickling. Mara's posture had changed from thoughtful attention to the bearing of a warrior ready for combat. Freyda fluttered up from the bed, Gemma's caresses forgotten, and darted to the window, where she stood on the sill, glaring out at the world with her keen yellow eyes.

I glanced at Gemma, on whose pretty face realization was slowly dawning.

"I…" I swallowed hard. "Which part?"

"What Yvaine said." Mara inched forward. "The *exact* words, Farrin."

My heart sank, my mouth suddenly dry. This was the first time I'd repeated Yvaine's words out loud; after my ejection from the Citadel, I hadn't told any of the others. It had felt like a betrayal to do so. Yvaine wasn't well; she wasn't herself. Whatever mad ramblings she spouted off while in my company, believing she was safe, believing she could trust me, were not mine to share.

But that lie of omission had run its course. Though I was many things, few of them good, I was no fool. It seemed obvious that, whatever it meant, Yvaine and Talan had been speaking of the same thing, and now I had no choice but to share that terrible revelation.

"Moon by day," I repeated, "fire by night. Come and dance. Don't try to fight. The beauty of shadows, the garish sunlight. Spin for the watchers, their revels so bright."

"That sounds so similar to what Talan told us," Gemma said eagerly. "The stories he's been hearing about the place called Moonhollow. It can't be a coincidence."

Mara glanced sharply at Gemma. "Moonhollow? You're certain that's the word?"

"Oh yes. He says he's been hearing whispers of it everywhere, stories and rumors, but only here in Gallinor. And then there's the forest he found in the far north, surrounded by some sort of powerful ward magic. A barrier he can't penetrate. We didn't want to explain any of this in writing in case our letters were intercepted."

"Ah. That's where we're going, then. To see what this northern forest is hiding." Mara looked back at me, her gaze steady and without judgment, but I nevertheless felt smaller with her attention upon me. "And you haven't told anyone else about what the queen said?"

I shook my head, bristling at the unspoken reproach, even though it was more than warranted. "I didn't plan on keeping it a secret forever. It just felt wrong to come out of the Citadel and immediately spill Yvaine's secrets. She's ill. She *trusts* me."

"Yes, but unfortunately, in these circumstances, she is not simply Yvaine," Mara said gently. "She's the queen. And if we're to have any chance of helping her, we can't keep this kind of information from each other—"

"I know, I know," I snapped. I rose from the bed and strode to the other side of the room. Freyda, still perched on the windowsill, turned to glare at me. Her sharp little bird face was far easier to bear than either of my sisters' pitying expressions. I stared out the window at the black night beyond, blinking hard to clear my vision. Only a few miles from the inn stretched a faint ribbon of silver fog: the Mist's southern border.

"I'm sorry," I said at last. "You're right. Of course you're right. I should've told everyone at once. It's only that..." I blew out an angry breath. "I hate betraying Yvaine, and this feels like a betrayal. She has so few real friends, and here I am reporting on her like a spy."

"And she might actually be glad of that, if she were in her right mind," Gemma pointed out. "She's said it herself: she wants us to help her. And this is helping her, even if the method feels—"

"Wrong," I finished, turning to face my sisters with my arms crossed over my chest. A lump ached in my throat. "It feels wrong."

"It would feel worse to do nothing in the name of protecting her and then watch the world crumble around us," Mara said bluntly.

"Of course I agree," I whispered. "Of course I'll do what I must. I'm sorry."

"There's no need to apologize. We can't look back and rue our mistakes, especially the ones we make out of love. That's one of the first things I learned during Order training. We can only look forward. Anything else is a waste of time, an opportunity for evil to take root. To that end, there's something you need to see."

Mara retrieved a simple canvas bag from a chair in the corner. Out of it she drew a small leather-bound notebook. She opened it and began to read.

"'I dream of gardens that go on forever,'" she said. "'I dream of dancing with bleeding feet, but I feel no pain, and my steps paint the world red as rubies.'"

She turned the page and continued. "'My father disappeared three days ago. I don't think it was like the others, who were taken all at once. I think he meant to go. I found a letter in his desk two days after he left us. *I've been chosen. I must go. Don't worry for me. There I'll be a king. I'll be a pet of the gods' true children.*'"

Mara turned another page. "'I have to find it,'" she read, the words made all the more horrible by the matter-of-fact calm in her voice. "'I have to go to Moonhollow. Don't you understand? They'll paint your body with starlight from head to toe. They'll feed you petals drizzled with honey, every drop squeezed from the bones of the gods. Let me go. Let me go!'"

She closed the notebook. "That last one," she said, "was the testimony of a woman from the village of Cawder, on trial for murdering her brother. She'd been sick for some time, plagued with visions that left her bedridden. They were driving her mad, leaving her unable to work or walk or eat. Her brother, who was tending to her, tried to feed her lunch one day. She attacked him and fled through the village, laughing, covered in his blood, until neighbors managed to apprehend her and bring her to the local arbiter's council."

My heart pounded. I couldn't think of what to say. The words she had read wriggled through my mind, restless and repulsive.

"So it's gotten worse, then," Gemma said solemnly. "Everything you showed me in the caves earlier this summer: the Mistfires, the spreading sickness, the visions…"

Mara nodded. "But as the visions grow in strength and numbers, so does our knowledge of what the people suffering from them are seeing. Moonhollow." She frowned. "And Talan thinks this northern forest could be hiding such a place?"

"He can't be certain, of course, but—"

"But it's worth investigating." Mara tucked the notebook back into her bag. "I've not heard of this forest myself, but the Order seldom sends me that far north of the Mist. And if it's powerful enough magic to keep even a demon from passing its borders…"

"What if Kilraith is there?" I said quietly. None of us had yet said his name, and the moment I did, we fell silent and waited, listening for approaching malevolent footsteps. But the only sounds were that of the bustling tavern downstairs, faintly jovial.

Mara broke the tense quiet. "If he's there, we'll do our best to apprehend him," she said briskly. "The Warden will want to question him. Even if he isn't behind the abductions himself, I suspect he'll know who—or what—is."

I stared at her. "Apprehend him? We barely managed to escape from him during our last encounter."

"We'll kill him if we have to, then. Clearly we're capable of besting him. We'd just have to do it again. And though I'd hate to lose the opportunity to question such a creature, if he's dead, that means one less demon-enslaver in the world. So even if he knows nothing of Moonhollow, if we can't safely transport him back to the priory, I for one will be glad to be rid of him. Anyway, this is merely a fact-finding mission. We'll investigate the forest, try to unearth at least one more piece of this puzzle. We won't necessarily be battling anyone."

"And if we do have to fight, we can, and we will," Gemma added, "just as we did in the Old Country. Our fae blood—"

"Oh, *please* don't start with that right now," I burst out angrily, and my desperate panic must have flared in my voice, because Gemma said nothing else on the subject. She exchanged a pointed glance with Mara; I wondered if *both* my sisters had been secretly corresponding with Aunt Felicity and gods knew who else from our mother's family, trying to find answers to questions I was too frightened to ask.

After a long silence, Mara said simply, "We should sleep now. It's late, and we must leave at dawn."

She was right, of course. Both of my sisters seemed more and more often to be right, as if they'd each grown in ways I hadn't yet managed. The feeling left me mortified, and I yearned for solitude, but I couldn't bear to leave them here without me. I would miss something important, something irreplaceable; the last time we'd been together like this had been just after returning from the Old Country, all of us exhausted and wounded. At least tonight—at least for one more night—we were well. I'd be a fool not to cherish it while I could.

So I lay flat on my back in the bed between them, letting the low sounds of their voices wash over me. Mara told a funny story about a laundry mishap at the priory; Gemma laughed quietly into the darkness. Freyda perched on the headboard above us, a tireless sentry.

Just before drifting off, I reached out to either side of me and touched my sisters' arms, too tired and full of longing to be afraid of my own awkwardness, my own bashful, uncertain way of showing love. Gemma wrapped her smallest finger around mine. Mara folded my entire hand into her own. I fell asleep with an ache in my chest, a small, contented hurt.

The next day, Mara took all of us north through a series of greenways belonging to the Order. At every exit, my whole body tensed, ready to fight or run depending on what greeted us—patrolling Rose or Olden foe—but we passed through each greenway unbothered. Clearly Mara knew which passages to take, and when, so as to evade her fellow shieldmaidens. By the time we reached the northern village of Vallenvoren, which sat tucked into a valley choked with huge pines, I was exhausted from the sheer strain of constant apprehension, though we'd left the Mist behind ages ago.

We stepped out of the last greenway into a tangled thicket overgrown with brambles. Mara hissed in apology and whacked at the mess with her sword.

"Clearly, no one has used this particular greenway in quite some time," she said. "We've been too busy nearer the Mist to maintain our typical northern patrols."

Gareth hurried after her, wielding his own sword—one of several weapons we'd brought with us from Ivyhill along with food, clothes, and healing supplies in case of disaster.

"Here, let me help you," he said, with a gallant sweep of his blade—but it immediately caught in a snarl of thorns, and he had to jerk it free rather clumsily, his face flushing with embarrassment.

Mara glided past him with a look of wry amusement and pointed through the trees at a building's silhouette. It was on the far side of town, perched on a rocky rise. Smoke unfurled from its chimneys, a soft black against the violet evening sky.

"There it is," she said. "The Torch and Thorn. We'll stay there for the night."

"And you've been there before?" said Ryder, pushing his way through the thicket with his bare hands. Thorns caught on his clothes, but he seemed oblivious to their teeth.

"Not for some time, but an old friend of the Order lives in Vallenvoren and has vouched for the new innkeepers in recent correspondence," Mara said. "We'll be safe here for the night. Vallenvoren is quite friendly to the faithful."

Ryder looked unconvinced. "Even *six* faithful all arriving at once?"

"Those making pilgrimages to the Altivar Cloisters usually do so in groups," Mara replied. "The journey north is not an easy one. The closer you get to the Unmade Lands, the harsher the terrain becomes."

"As if warning you to turn around while you still can," Gemma said quietly. She was leaning hard on Talan, her wan skin glistening with sweat after passing through so many greenways.

"Exactly," Mara said, almost cheerfully. "Come on, let's go down. I'm starving."

As we followed her into the valley, I hoped dearly that she was right, that the arrival of five Anointed humans and a demon would arouse no suspicion. But of course we would be disguised, and I did believe Mara that this route was well-traveled by faithful citizens on their way to the Altivar Cloisters, where they would pay homage to the gods. I had never been this far north; the land was harsh and cold, nothing but rocks and pines and mountains as far as the eye could see. The sky was vast and full of stars, and on the horizon twisted bands of brilliant color.

I knew what they were—the Echoes of the Gods, a natural phenomenon left behind after the Unmaking, the day centuries past when the gods had died. The lights had never hurt anyone or shown themselves to be anything but remnants of the gods' death, a sort of beautiful scar upon the world, but the sight of them, of all of this, left me uneasy. I felt exposed and vulnerable, as if phantom eyes were everywhere, watching me bumble down the hill toward the cheery lights of Vallenvoren. When we reached the Torch and Thorn and obtained our three room keys from the innkeeper—a jolly man named George, tall and pale and plump, with soft, friendly eyes and a roaring laugh like a lion—I wanted to run upstairs at once and hide until it was time to leave.

But Mara wouldn't allow it. "We're going to eat and drink together," she said firmly. "We're going to sit here in the dining room and have fun. That's another thing the Warden taught us during training. Being part of the Order isn't just about training with weapons and strengthening your body. It's about being part of a group, fighting as a unit. And the more frequently a unit does ordinary things together, the better they'll fight together."

Gareth nodded a little too eagerly. "I agree. Entirely sound logic."

Ryder grunted his own assent. Then he slapped his palm on the countertop and told the barkeep, "Six pints of the best ale you've got."

As we wove our way through the mass of crowded tables, I felt the cold ripple of Gemma's glamouring magic slide over me, accompanied by the warmth of Talan's demonic power, which brought everyone we passed a jolt of oblivious cheer. Hopefully the combined strength of their abilities would disguise our faces from anyone this far north who might know us, but the sensation was unnerving nevertheless. Then I noticed Gareth hurrying after Mara and recognized the look on his face, even glamoured as it was—one of curiosity, questions, professorial enthusiasm—and suddenly all I could think about was stopping him before he did something stupid.

I grabbed his arm, directing him none too gently to sit beside me and not beside Mara, as he clearly intended to do. He shot me an irritated look as we all took our places around a small table tucked into a corner. Torches in wall brackets and candles in small iron chandeliers that hung from the ceiling cast a soft glow over everything. A strapping barkeep with brown skin and black shoulder-length curls came to deliver our drinks, and as he set them down, I leaned close to Gareth and whispered angrily, "If you don't stop mooning over my sister, I'm going to—"

"I'm not mooning over her," he replied. "It's just that..." He trailed off to gaze across the table at her, watching everything she did—shifting in her chair, raising her cup to her lips—with something like reverence. Apparently her glamoured appearance did nothing to diminish his interest.

Before I could say anything else, Mara caught him staring and lifted one eyebrow. "Just say it, Professor."

That caught Gareth off guard. He blinked at her and awkwardly adjusted his glasses on the bridge of his nose. "I...what?"

"You're fascinated by me—not just me, but my kind. The Roses. The binding magic, how we transform, the mystery of us. I can practically see the wheels of your professor's brain spinning from here. You have questions." Mara took a long drink from her cup, then set it down. "So ask them."

"I..." Gareth recovered quickly, hiding his surprise with a small echo of his familiar dashing smile. "Well. If you insist. You Roses are indeed as canny as everyone says you are."

If Mara was insulted by his attention, she didn't show it. Instead, she looked amused, as if she were humoring a child. "And what exactly have you heard about *us Roses*, Professor?"

"That your physical prowess is unmatched by any other being in Edyn. That the magic binding you to the Mist is woven into your very bones by some dark ritual carried out by the Warden after your trials. That the transformation from woman to beast is agonizing every time."

I was too horrified to speak. Mara sat back in her chair, still with that unruffled look of mirth on her face. Talan cleared his throat as if preparing to interject, but Gemma, still ashen from our journey, hushed him with a kiss to his cheek and whispered words into his hair. Talan's concerned expression softened to one of such affection that I could hardly bear the sight of it. He turned to receive more of Gemma's kisses, one on his brow, the next on his mouth, and even with their plain glamours disguising them, they looked so beautiful there in the corner, so utterly wrapped up in their own tender world, that I had to stare at my hands, my cheeks flaming and my body suddenly all too aware of Ryder's thigh touching mine under the table.

"Woman to *beast*?" Mara was saying to Gareth. "That's how you think it works, then, Professor?"

"If it isn't, please tell me how it does," he said with a sort of oblivious earnestness that might have been endearing had I not been so mortified. "I'm fascinated, truly, and nothing more. I'm a student of the arcana, you see, and you are the closest thing to a being of the Old Country that exists in our world. You are..." He ran a hand through his glamoured brown hair, giving a helpless little laugh. "You're a marvel to me. And please, you can call me Gareth."

"I'd rather not," Mara replied evenly. "If you're going to treat me as a specimen to be examined, then I'll treat you as an examiner and nothing more."

That remark probably would have shamed any other person into silence, but Gareth remained unperturbed. He flashed Mara the same charming grin I'd seen him flash at a hundred other women, which made me want to kick him hard in the shin, but Ryder touched my arm before I could. The press of his hand against my wrist sent a shock of heat jolting through me, as if I'd received a charge of energy from touching metal on a dry winter's day.

"Don't kill him just yet," Ryder murmured, his glamoured gray eyes sparkling. "You would deny a grieving man his entertainment?"

This made me bristle. "And what would Alastrina think of your choice of *entertainment?*"

"Oh, she'd think we were all most decidedly beneath her," he replied at once, "but she's not here, is she?" A shadow passed across his face, and his amused expression closed. He took an aggressive drink from his cup. "So please, let her destroy him, and let me enjoy it."

He softened his words with another touch to my wrist, but as sweet as the sensation was, I suddenly couldn't stand to be there anymore. Gareth and his awful behavior, and Mara tolerating it when he didn't deserve it, and Gemma and Talan holding hands in the corner, their heads bent close together in some kind of lovers' conference—I felt suffocated by all of them and by the lofty raftered room's buzz of noise and laughter. And then there was Ryder: too close to me, so big and warm on the bench beside me that it didn't take much for my mind to start imagining what *we* would look like if we huddled together like Gemma and Talan were doing. Ryder's muscled body looming over my thinner, smaller one; his calloused hands touching my face as Talan was touching Gemma's. What would he whisper in my ear? What would it feel like to be so utterly enraptured by another person that I couldn't be bothered to notice the world around me?

"I'm going to bed," I announced. "I'm tired, and I don't need to be here for this." Indignantly, wearily, I waved at the whole table and clambered out from between Gareth and Ryder, the latter of whom quickly moved to accommodate me. I grabbed the key from Mara, shooting her a look of thanks for not pestering me to stay.

Upstairs, I found the room I was to share with Mara: room eight, clean and tidy, with a huge rickety bed set against the wall and a small hearth crackling warmly in the corner. The bed looked inviting, the chair by the fire cozy, but all I could do was pace across the floor, my body such a snarl of annoyance and longing and confused anger that I had no idea how to begin untangling it.

Then came a quiet knock at the door.

I stormed across the room to fling it open, expecting to see Gareth, come to apologize, or Mara, concerned for me and abruptly tired of Gareth's unforgivable intrusiveness.

But instead, Ryder stood there on the threshold, looking grave and abashed, a thoughtful frown under his fearsome beard. Gemma had released his glamour, and mine too.

"I'm sorry for behaving like that," he told me gruffly. His blue gaze traveled over my face, then fell to the floor. "Forgive me."

"Forgive *you*?" I was momentarily startled enough to find what remained of my tattered wits. "You weren't the one fawning over my sister like some lovestruck boy rather than a grown man who ought to know how to control his selfish impulses."

A corner of Ryder's mouth quirked up. "No, but I dismissed your concerns. I made light of them. And I shouldn't joke about my sister."

"You can joke about whatever you like. I'm certainly not one to tell you, or anyone, how to grieve, how to be afraid."

"Still, it was in poor taste."

I laughed a little. "That's never stopped you before." Immediately I winced. "I'm sorry. That was uncalled for. I really am just tired."

I turned away from him then, resumed my furious pacing.

Ryder observed me for a moment. "You don't look tired. You look like you want to punch something." He paused. "Perhaps you'd like to?"

"No. Yes. *Yes.*" I didn't dare stop pacing; if I did, I wasn't sure what I would say or do. I suspected I would start crying out of sheer bewildered rage, the thought of which was appalling. "Fine. Close the door."

Ryder obeyed, then began clearing the center of the room, deftly sidestepping my warpath. He rolled up the tattered rag rug, pushed it to the side, then assessed the space with a critical eye. "I wonder if we can move the bed," he mused.

The thought of Ryder doing anything near or with the bed I was meant to sleep in made me burn. I altered my path so he couldn't see my face, feeling angrier, more confused, more annoyed with every step. I couldn't put out of my mind the sensation of Ryder's hand on the tender skin of my wrist—such a little touch, not something that would send anyone else I knew spiraling into such a state, and yet it had completely unraveled me. Unbidden, the thought sprang to mind of Ryder kissing me in his stable—his hands lifting me up against him, his lips feathering gentle kisses down my neck.

Remembering the sensation left me feeling shaky, uncertain. My chest drew tight with longing. "My enemies won't make nice and move furniture to make room for me," I snapped. "Leave it."

He grunted in agreement. "Fair enough." I heard him shift, saw him raise his fists out of the corner of my eye. "Now—"

"No. Wait." I paused, staring at the corner, then turned and went to him before I could stop myself. Maybe it was the memory of his kisses driving me to do a mad thing, or maybe I truly *was* just exhausted and therefore vulnerable to ridiculous urges. Whatever the reason, I marched over to him and stopped only inches away. I lifted my arms as if to draw him into an embrace, then put them awkwardly down at my sides. He stood watching me, a question in his eyes, his fists still half raised for a fight.

"Farrin?" he said quietly.

I took a breath, let it out. Made myself look up at him. Told him, my chest aching with sudden, blazing need, "I want you to kiss me."

CHAPTER 14

Ryder lowered his arms, looked warily at me. "Kiss you?" He sounded absolutely baffled.

I started backing away, humiliated. "Unless you don't want to."

"No. I mean, yes." He let out a breathless little laugh. "Farrin." He reached for me, then put his hands at his sides, just as I had done. He looked at the floor between us. "Farrin, I think about kissing you literally every day. I dream of you. I…" His gaze flicked up to meet mine. "*Wanting* you is not the issue. I want you. I want everything about you."

I felt dizzy with him looking at me like that—a hulking mountain of a man with eyes as blue as a summer sky and raven-dark hair that I knew from experience was much softer than it looked. The expression on his face was one of unmistakable yearning, as if he were seeing the sun rise after a long, cold darkness. It softened him, made him look younger.

I found my courage and stepped toward him. "Then kiss me like you did that day," I whispered. "Please, Ryder."

He came to me then, so close I could feel his breath against my lips and just far enough away that my knees went liquid with desperate need. I ached for him to lower his head and touch his mouth to mine.

But instead he said, very low, "Farrin, you're upset. And you told me..." His mouth thinned. He touched his brow to mine, cradled my face so gently in his hands that I let out a soft cry of wanting, a noise I didn't know I could make.

He exhaled shakily. "You told me that you've kissed only two other people, that you've gone to bed with someone only once. And I know you're upset. I know seeing Yvaine was hard for you. I don't want you to..." He looked away, his jaw working. The heat of him was incredible; I found myself leaning into him like a cat into sunshine.

"Gods," he rasped. "Farrin, I don't want you to ask me for this just because you're upset. I don't want to dismiss your desires. You're a grown woman, and you know what you want. But..." He looked back at me, a plea in those fierce blue eyes. "Whatever you ask of me, I'll do it. But I can't bear you realizing later that you regret asking in the first place. Tell me honestly: Is this *truly* what you want?"

The rush of tenderness I felt upon witnessing his conflict, his earnest intensity, left me near tears. I reached for him, my hands trembling as I touched the rough expanse of his beard, the soft skin above it. "I want you to kiss me, Ryder Bask," I whispered. "Kiss me, please. Like you did that day." My heart pounded so hard I could feel it in every part of my body. "That, and...more, please."

I flushed, the sound of my request echoing childishly in my ears, but Ryder only smiled at me and traced my bottom lip with his thumb. I shivered at the sensation and grabbed his jacket with both hands. He kissed my hair, nuzzling it gently.

"What does *more* mean to you?" he murmured, his mouth against my ear.

I closed my eyes, shook my head a little. He kissed my jaw, my neck, my gown's plain stitched collar. I slid my hands up his arms, held him to me.

He paused in his kisses, then pulled back just enough that his lips hovered over my skin. "Farrin," he said roughly. "You have to tell me what you want. *More* to me means…" He laughed again, a soft, gruff sound that sent chills down my whole front and tightened my nipples under my dress, a novel sensation that made my breath catch in my throat.

"*More* means perhaps more than you're ready for," he went on. "And that's perfectly fine, but I need to know. Tell me, or I can't in good conscience kiss you any further."

"I…" I made myself look up at him, meet his hot blue gaze. Gods, his eyes were like twin jewels, brilliant and gorgeous. "I want you to kiss me." I glanced past him, my cheeks burning. "There, on the bed. And…" I bit my lip.

He groaned and touched his brow to mine once more. "And?" he whispered.

"And then I…I don't know. I think I want you to touch me." As I said the words, the heat at the core of me, between my legs, bloomed down my thighs. "I want you to touch me…" I shook my head against him. I laughed, breathless, aching all over. "You know where. Don't make me say it."

And he didn't. Instead, he dropped soft kisses in my hair and gently, slowly, slid one of his hands down my back, around the curve of my waist, and down, down, over the flat plane of my belly, and down even farther, to press his fingers against me, just the slightest sweet pressure through the fabric of my gown.

The pleasure of even that small touch was glorious, sending a rush of blazing heat through my entire body. I cried out and clutched his arm, my head spinning.

"Here?" he whispered, voice and breath and lips against the hollow of my throat. "Is this where you want me to touch you?"

I nodded frantically, found my words. "Yes, there," I gasped out, and the next moment he had swept me up into his arms. Four long strides, to lock the door and take me to the bed, and then he was lowering me down onto it—the pillows below me and Ryder above, his body hovering over mine for a moment before he carefully settled beside me. I turned into him, seeking him with clumsy ardor, and his arms came around me, strong and warm, and he was kissing me just as he had that day in the stable before I'd stopped him—hot, hungry kisses, deep and devouring, as if he were a starving man and I were a feast laid out before him. I was inexpert at kissing, nervous and inelegant, perhaps a little too eager, but as soon as those worries entered my mind, Ryder's kisses drove them out.

He left no inch of me untouched: the soft skin just behind my ears, the line of my jaw, even the turns of my wrists. Just as soon as I thought nothing could feel better than this—his mouth on mine, his kisses on my nape, under my hair—he would move, try something different, something tender and wild and wholly new. He began undoing the buttons at my collar.

"Is this all right?" he whispered.

I could only nod, pressing up against his body, my own an inferno of instinct and need. He worked slowly, lavishing kisses upon each new bit of skin he unveiled before moving on to the next. His teeth lightly grazed my collarbones, and when he reached the button that revealed the first slight swell of my breasts, he let out a low groan, his breath hot on my skin, his hands shaking a little as they cupped my waist. I reached down and placed my hands over his before he could unbutton anything further.

He stilled at once and came back up to find me, breathing as hard as I was. Soft kisses on my chin, across my cheeks, so tender that I had to hold him there against me for a moment and smile into his hair.

"Should I stop?" he asked. "Is this too much?"

"No, please don't. I just…" I glanced down at my opened bodice, the stretch of bare pale skin, and felt a thrill that wasn't entirely terror, nor was it entirely desire. It was something confused and in between, and I tried not to feel embarrassed as I explained. "No more of that, please. I…I don't want to be naked. Not right now."

He nodded, swallowed hard. "Of course." He kissed me, sweet and slow, then found a long tress of golden-brown hair that had come loose from my braid and buried his face in it, breathing in deep. "Is it still all right if I touch you?" he asked, after a moment.

"If you don't, I'll change my mind about not wanting to punch you," I said at once, and he laughed into my hair and said, "All right, love. We'll start slowly. Tell me the moment you want me to stop."

He held himself over me, drawing me up toward his body with languorous kisses, lazy, unhurried, each of which left me feeling drunk and buzzing all the way down to my toes. And then he gently pushed his thigh between my legs, and I latched on to him with a gasp, something ancient and primal within me telling me to move against him. I circled my hips slowly, a little nervously, and each press of his muscled thigh against my core brought a deep thrum of pleasure that left me swooning, panting beneath him on the bed.

"That's it," he said, bending down to kiss my throat. I keened quietly at the touch of his lips, arched up against him. He found my hands clutching desperately at his shoulders, gently unfolded my fingers, and pressed my arms into the pillows, pinning me tenderly beneath him.

The sensation of being trapped by him—the sweet care with which he held his body over mine—made me gasp into his hair as he sucked gently on my neck with lips and tongue. At each point of contact—his hands holding mine, his mouth on my skin, his thigh between my legs—I blazed hotter than any fire.

When he shifted, releasing my hands to drag his fingers down my body, I cried out in protest without meaning to. He paused; he lifted his hands off of me.

"Should I stop?" he asked, his brow furrowing with concern even as I felt the heat of his desire pressing urgently against my thigh.

I could have kissed him; I *did* kiss him, turning up my face to his in silent invitation. "No, don't stop," I murmured against his cheek. "Just…I like it when you're on top of me, when you're all around me, holding me in place," I whispered. "When all I can feel is you. The strength of you next to the smallness of me. I feel…trapped, but in a good way. A safe way."

It was the most embarrassing thing I'd ever said, and yet perhaps the truest, for in its wake came a sense of peace—a sort of clarity, a rightness, as if I'd finally found the words I'd been searching for all my life. Ryder smiled down at me, not in judgment or in jest but with a fondness that made me long even more fiercely for his touch.

He shifted beside me, then said, "Look at me while I do this, Farrin."

His voice was a firm caress, a guiding light in the haze of my desire, and the relief I felt when I heard him tell me what to do, where to look, was overwhelming. Dizzy, smiling with unfettered happiness, I obeyed him, lifting my gaze to meet his. He kissed my arms, from my wrists all the way up to my shoulders, each kiss making me shift and sigh in his embrace. And then he gathered both my hands in one of his and pulled them gently over my head to pin them softly against the pillows.

He kept his gaze upon me the entire time, and though I could hardly bear meeting his eyes, I made myself do it, made myself look right at him even while his other hand—the one not trapping my hands over my head—slid down my body. He took his time, his fingers wandering across my half-clothed torso as I panted beneath him, my hips still circling against his thigh. And then he began lifting my skirts, swirling little circles up my legs—on my knees, my thighs, every trembling bit of skin—until he found the top of my tights and, with a glance up at me first, began slowly tugging them down my legs. I stopped him when they reached my knees.

"I feel safer with them at least partway on," I explained, feeling even in my absolute joy a stab of shame upon making such a request. But Ryder only nodded and kissed me again, long and slow, while his hand slid once again under my rucked-up skirts. My underwear wasn't pretty or elaborate—just plain linen with a simple bow at the top to keep them in place—but when Ryder touched it, gently pushing apart my thighs to draw circles on the sodden fabric, he shuddered beside me and swore quietly into my hair.

"*Fuck,*" he said roughly, and the sound of his voice—so masculine, deep and hungry, completely undone to be touching me—made me cry out a little, a soft, whimpering sob, and arch up against his body. One hand continued to trap mine over my head, while his other hand slipped beneath my underwear, finding me wet and hot and aching. He pressed his hips against mine with a sharp groan and kissed me—hard, desperate—until we both had to pull away to breathe.

"Is that good, Farrin?" he rasped, his thumb circling around me.

I nodded helplessly, shaking under his touch.

"No, no, gods, please, Farrin, *tell* me," he said, looking at me with those blazing blue eyes. "I need to hear you say it."

"It feels good," I gasped out, clinging to him. "Ryder, you feel so good, I…" I shook my head against his cheek, turned my face into the soft black fall of his hair. I was moving shamelessly against him, angling my hips toward him so he would, I hoped, understand what I wanted without me having to ask—and of course he did. With another harsh curse whispered into my hair, he slid a finger inside me.

"Like this?" he asked, his voice strained as he moved against me, in me, his thumb still circling, his hand still pinning me to the bed.

"Yes," I breathed, sobbing a little; the glorious, golden pleasure building inside me was rising fast. *"Yes—"*

And then I could no longer speak, helpless in the throes of it, of Ryder, of my own shaking, humming body. I clung to him for a long time, my heart a jubilant drum, and then began to laugh and cry at once, hiding my face against his chest. It took him a moment to realize that my laughter hid tears; he tensed a little and started to pull away.

"No, please don't go," I whispered. I moved closer, silently rejoicing when he draped a leg over mine, drawing me sweetly against him. There was a question in his eyes; in response I simply smiled, bashful heat crawling up my cheeks.

"Thank you," I told him. "I don't know what else to say right now, don't know how to explain. I'm…soon I think I'll rather lose my nerve."

I could feel it happening already: the awareness of how much of my body was unclothed, the knowledge of that making me tense when only seconds before I'd felt limp and happy, even sultry. Me, Farrin Ashbourne, lying blissfully in the arms of a man—and not just any man, but *Ryder Bask*.

I wiped my face, shut my eyes tight, willed my body to relax, begged my mind to stop its worried nattering.

"You're safe, Farrin" came Ryder's gentle voice. He drew long, lazy lines up and down my back, and then, after a moment, found the quilt at the foot of the bed and drew it up over our bodies. The feeling of being cocooned against him was a delicious one, and soothing, but not even that was enough to quiet my mind. It occurred to me all of a sudden that this didn't seem fair. I'd been selfish. Lovers reciprocated their loving, did they not?

I started to speak, hesitated, tried again. "Ryder. Do you…do you need…or want…"

"Want, certainly. But need? No, Farrin. You owe me nothing. If you *want* to do more, that's one thing, but I don't think you do. Not tonight."

I couldn't bring myself to look up at him. "Not tonight," I agreed quietly. "This was a huge thing for me. I need to…" I couldn't finish, couldn't find the words.

Luckily, I didn't need to. Ryder seemed to understand. He kissed my forehead, my cheeks, my hair. I closed my eyes and reveled in each one. I couldn't imagine ever tiring of his kisses.

Then a thought occurred to me. I plucked nervously at the nearest button on Ryder's jacket.

"I could sing for you," I said quietly. "If you want. I can't give you…" I bit my lip, horribly embarrassed. Suddenly my suggestion seemed silly. "But I can give you a song. A new one, written just for you."

Ryder ducked his head down to look at me. The expression on his face was one of stunned delight.

"You'd do that for me?" he said. "Farrin…" He kissed my fingers, his eyes never leaving mine. "It would be an honor," he said, gravely, "but it isn't necessary."

So he said, but I saw that soft light in his eyes, how overcome he was at the very idea, and felt at once that it *was* necessary—not for him, but for me. To bring him such joy was a kind of victory; if my nerves kept me from lying with him as any other woman would, then I would give him what no other woman could.

Shyly, I opened my arms to him, and once he'd settled against me—carefully, reverently, as if afraid to crush me—I began drawing my fingers through his hair, one long stroke after another, and took a breath, and sang.

It was a simple melody, wordless but sweet, and the notes came to me easily, dropping into my mind like a soft spring rain. Shelter, simple gladness, careful tenderness—these were the feelings I held in my heart as I sang to him, and when I felt the skin on the back of his neck break into goose bumps, I smiled around the notes, sweetening them further. He shuddered in my arms, and I pressed my cheek to the crown of his head, closed my eyes, crooned an aching arpeggio into his hair.

Then a knock came at the door, jarring us from our reverie.

"Occupied!" Ryder barked, sharp and angry, and whoever it was didn't bother us again. I found a vicious delight in imagining it was Gemma, come to say good night and now shocked to realize what had happened in this room to her eldest sister, whom she had always believed to be incapable of such things.

The thought was amusing enough to distract me from the doubt creeping in at the edges of my mind. *Ryder just pities you, that's all. That wasn't* actually *sex; it doesn't count. It was a fluke; you won't manage this again. You're as cold and strange as everyone thinks you are. Keep singing. Maybe that will help ease his disappointment.*

I fought the wicked thoughts hard, sent a silent apology to Mara for taking over our room for the night, and turned into Ryder's body, hiding my face against his chest. He understood the silent request and held me just as I'd hoped he would, kissed my brow, rearranged the quilt to ensure I was properly covered. My unfinished song hung in the air, but Ryder didn't seem to mind. He hummed a little, a deep, satisfied sound. Primal, contented. I smiled into his jacket and let his caresses lull me to sleep.

The next morning, we left Vallenvoren after purchasing horses from a trader who owned several stables along the oft-traveled road north to the Altivar Cloisters. Ryder spoke to each of them before we got underway—four tired geldings and two soft-eyed mares, all of them shaggy and stocky, good mountain horses far more used to this lonesome part of the world than even Ryder was.

I tried not to pay too close attention to him as he went to each of the horses in turn, his deep voice murmuring in some bestial language

I was too distracted to remember the name of. I kept thinking about the night before, images and sensations returning to me in waves—Ryder's hands on me, *in* me, his lips blazing a hot path across my skin, my body twisting in his careful, firm grip.

I turned away from the group, stroked the thick brown mane of the gelding nearest me, whom Ryder had already visited and who now stood with his old ears perked up and his eyes alight with new excitement as he watched Ryder walk through the clearing. I knew the feeling. I touched my lips, smiling to myself. If I closed my eyes, I could feel it all over again: the bed, Ryder's arms, the unthinkable pleasure of coming apart under his touch...

Suddenly Gareth appeared beside me, under the guise of loading the gelding's saddlebags with supplies. But I saw the look on his face and felt all the goodness of the previous night flood out of me on a tide of embarrassment.

"So," he said, grinning, his glamoured eyes sparkling behind his glasses, "I heard there was some excitement last night."

I shot him a withering glare. "I'm surprised you've managed to pay attention to anything besides your dreadful fixation on my sister."

His smile faded. He looked sheepishly at the dirt. "I'm sorry about that. Truly I am. I apologized to Mara too, and to the others. I don't know what came over me." He ran a hand through his hair and glanced over his shoulder, perhaps searching for Mara, then looked back at me with an expression of genuine regret. "Really, Farrin. I'm a scoundrel in many ways, I know, but I'm not a fool, and I have the utmost respect for Mara and for the Order. But I can't help but be fascinated by their existence. They're an impossibility, a marvel in an otherwise mundane world. And the way Mara transformed that day at the priory—fearless, unflinching. The sheer power of her as she called to her sisters and went tearing off into the Mist to face gods knew what..."

"You're not doing much to convince me of your remorse," I remarked drily.

He shook himself a little. "No, you're right. It doesn't matter that they fascinate me. They're people, real people who deserve respect, no matter their extraordinary abilities."

He'd stopped packing the supplies, too distracted by his own nonsense to continue working, I supposed. I couldn't help but roll my eyes at him. He was being sincere enough, but he'd interrupted my daydreaming, and I felt strangely guilty being this close to him with the memory of Ryder's kisses so near. I picked up where he'd left off, shoving wrapped food into the saddlebag.

"The day you actually start showing women respect," I said irritably, "not individual women you actually care about, mind you, like Heldine and me, but all women, no matter who they are—that'll be a day to remember. Or else a sign that I've died and stumbled into a fever dream on the way to Ryndar."

Gareth looked at me curiously, apparently unperturbed by my harsh words. "I haven't heard you speak of Ryndar in quite some time."

Ryndar: the land beyond life and death, where the gods were born. A realm made of pure aelum, the basis of all magical life, and sinaelum, the basis of all life without magic. Otherwise known as the Great Dominion, where many people of Edyn believed they would go after death—to either join the gods in whatever new forms they'd taken, or to return to the worlds of the living as new beings, reborn and remade.

Now I rolled my eyes at myself. "You know, one of the most annoying things about being your friend," I said, "is the fact that every time I even think of something about the arcana, my mind can't help but recite all the relevant facts. It's like you've trained me over the years as you would one of your students."

"You're welcome," he said cheerfully, then watched me work for a moment longer before stopping me with a gentle hand on my arm.

"Did you really go to bed with Ryder?" he asked. His voice was softer now, tender in a way I hadn't heard him speak in a long time.

I made myself look at him, my chin jutting out in defiance even as my cheeks burned. "I don't think that's any of your business."

"It's not," he conceded, "except that you're my friend, and I want you to be careful. I know you're not..." He paused, glanced around, lowered his voice. "I know you're not experienced in such things. Do you have medicine with you to protect yourself from pregnancy? Does he?"

The questions made images flash through my mind—Ryder and me, naked bodies, legs and arms entwined. I shoved the images away hard. They were half formed, anyway; it had been a long time since I'd looked at my naked body, and when I tried to recreate it in my mind, the shape was blurry, formless. What a child I was, unable to stomach even looking at myself in the mirror. The doubts from the previous night crept back into my thoughts. *Ryder just pities you, that's all.*

You're as cold and strange as everyone thinks you are.

"Don't trouble yourself about me," I snapped. "We didn't actually have sex. We did other things, and I sang for him, and it was wonderful. I felt lovely for once, and wanted, and afterward, I fell asleep in his arms, and when I woke up, he was gone, and all of you were still down in the tavern, I suppose, and there was a little plate on the bedside table with a sandwich wrapped in a napkin. It was the sweetest, most wonderful night of my life, but now I'm doubting every moment of it. How stupid he must have thought I was, to not want actual sex and instead just want..."

I waved dismissively at the saddlebag, then resumed fumbling with one of the straps. I couldn't figure out how to buckle the horrible thing and tried three times before giving up and realizing, with quiet horror, that I was crying.

"Hey, hey," Gareth said quietly, coming around to shield me from the others' view. "First of all, sex encompasses many acts of love, not just the one you're thinking of. And secondly, you're not stupid, and I know for a fact that Ryder didn't think that of you."

"For a fact?" I glared at him through my tears. "Have you spoken to him about it? Did you ask Talan to probe him for information?"

"All right, not for a fact, then. But as a man, and as someone who knows you—and who in fact made love with you once upon a time, albeit disastrously—I can assert with great confidence that Ryder Bask does not think you stupid, or undesirable, or disappointing in any way."

Gareth pulled a handkerchief from his pocket and gave it to me. I wiped my face, desperately hoping no one else had noticed my distress. From behind me came the sounds of the others mounting their horses, the clatter of coins as Gemma—glamoured, as we all were— paid the trader.

I couldn't help my next question, though the setting was the furthest thing from appropriate. "When we..." I trailed off, tried again. "When we had sex all those years ago, it wasn't bad because of me, was it?"

"Of course not," Gareth said. He crouched a little and gently lifted my chin to look me in the eyes. "Darling, we've talked about this many times."

"I know, and I need to hear it again. Please?"

"All right, well, no, our sex wasn't bad because of you, or because of me, even. It wasn't even *bad*, really, it just wasn't...it wasn't right, because we don't love each other in that way, though we needed to go that far to realize it. And besides all that, we were terribly young, basically children. But even so, I don't regret it. I only call it disastrous because afterward I was afraid I'd lose you, that we'd ruined the whole thing with two bottles of wine and some truly clumsy, tooth-clacking kisses."

That made me laugh. I wiped my face again, and absently petted the gelding's shaggy head. He turned to whuff at my sleeve, no doubt wondering what all the fuss was about.

"I'm so sorry, Farrin," Gareth said gently. "I started this by asking about Ryder. I didn't mean to upset you. I was only worried. Even so, I should've waited, or at least brought you breakfast or something and asked you about it over hotcakes like a civilized person." He shoved his hands in his pockets and looked away. "I'm really not doing anything right, am I?"

I blew my nose, wadded up the handkerchief, and thrust it back at him. "Not doing anything right on this particular journey, or in life in general?"

He smiled at me, his typical mischievous grin, but I saw the sadness flicker in his glamoured brown eyes before he could hide it, and I sighed and caught his hand.

"Now I'm the one who's sorry," I told him. "I was trying to tease you, and it came out all wrong."

He kissed my hand, chaste and quick. "Well, we're even, then, or at least closer to it. I've still got a ways to go before I can make up for being such an ass last night."

I raised an eyebrow and smiled at him, relieved to resume the old rhythm of our back-and-forth. "I was going to say as much but am feeling strangely merciful."

Gareth looked wistfully at our joined hands. "Remember when being friends was easier?"

That surprised me. The truth was, I'd had the same thought in recent years, but I'd never said it aloud, and I certainly didn't expect Gareth to, especially not hundreds and hundreds of miles away from anything familiar, with the whole cold north spread out before us.

A pang twisted my chest. Suddenly I wanted nothing more than to return to the Torch and Thorn, grab a table, and order hotcakes— just as he'd suggested—and sit with him for hours, and tell him everything, confide in him utterly, as we'd always used to do. Before the return of the Basks, before Talan, before Kilraith. Before these last strange, frightening few months, when Yvaine was well, and Father was his old self—still bitter and paranoid, still wracked with grief, but without the constant thrill of violence simmering just beneath the surface, without the anger boiling ceaselessly in his eyes. When I still felt like I knew how the world worked.

But this was far too much to express on such a morning. Instead I squeezed Gareth's hand and gave him a grim smile. "I remember when a lot of things were easier," I said quietly. "But I still love you all the same."

Gareth's distracted, doleful expression softened. He drew me into his typical oafish hug, and I held on to him and closed my eyes. For a precious moment, the strange world I'd found myself in felt comfortingly familiar.

"Come on, let's go," Mara called from a few paces away. She had chosen one of the mares and was mounted and ready, watching us curiously. "We've a long way to go before nightfall."

Without further delay, we mounted our horses and followed her down the winding gravel road that would take us away from Vallenvoren into the unknown north.

We traveled for two days. Almost immediately after leaving Vallenvoren, we veered off the well-trodden road used by the faithful to reach the Altivar Cloisters and set out into the true wilderness, retracing Talan's previous route through these lands. He led us through pine forests so tall and ancient that it felt irreverent to speak, as if we were treading upon the bones of godly creatures long-dead. The hard earth was black and cold underfoot, the air chilly enough to make our breath puff in the air.

We camped in a large but simple tent sewn of animal hides that Mara had brought from the priory. I slept wrapped in furs and blankets between my sisters, with Talan on Gemma's other side, Ryder's on Mara's, and Gareth beyond him.

But my sleep was restless, and I spent much of each night lying awake, listening to the sound of Ryder's deep breathing—so close to me, but not close enough. And yet I was glad for the distance between us, which made very little sense to me. The contradictions of my own desires left me on edge. We'd spoken hardly since the night at the Torch and Thorn, though not for lack of trying. We stayed close to each other as we wove through the forests, and every few minutes, one of us—mostly Ryder—would try to make conversation, usually about the landscape, or the amusing behavior of the horses, or his interpretation of what a bird was trying to say with its song.

Once, on the second day, during a quiet stretch of travel after we'd stopped to eat lunch, Ryder guided his horse closer to mine, cleared his throat, and said, "The northern light suits you, Farrin."

Immediately a flush of embarrassed delight crept up my body. Gareth, who was just behind me, started whistling cheerily to himself and pushed his horse into a trot, leaving me alone with Ryder. I glared after him, both annoyed by the gesture and glad for the privacy: yet more contradictions, all piling on top of one another. I was beginning to feel as though something was truly wrong with me, that some kernel of madness had burst open the night Ryder had touched me and now nothing would ever make sense again.

"Thank you," I said quietly, not looking at him, staring instead at my horse's mane. I wished suddenly for the illusory mask of Gemma's glamours. "You're very kind."

He grunted a little, a small, frustrated sound. "It's the truth. There's a quickness to you, a sharpness in your eyes and the lines of your body. The way you move. Always thinking deeply about something, about

many things. Too many things, perhaps," he added, his voice softening a little—with worry, I thought, and something like bashfulness.
"Forests are the same way. They teem with life, with secrets. They're
lovely and quick and wild, changing from season to season, from day
to day. They're adaptive. They're steady. They're full of fascinating
incongruities, yet they are completely themselves. "

I laughed a little, overcome. "And I'm all these things to you?"

"That and more." He took a deep breath in, then blew it out. "I've
never felt as content as I do when I'm with you."

I glanced at him at the same moment he looked carefully over
at me. Our eyes locked for one blazing instant, and my whole body
flushed hot. To be looked at in such a way, with such tender fondness,
and to see his fierce Bask brow furrowed with concern, as if the most
important thing in the world to him was determining whether or not
I was happy...I was ill-equipped to handle such a look. Particularly
when, with his eyes upon me, the memories of our night together
took over my every thought.

I shook myself and returned my attention to my horse.

"You're unhappy," he said after a moment. In his gruff voice rang
a note of resigned sadness. "I'm sorry. I've said too much."

"I'm not," I said at once, "and you haven't. And don't be sorry, I
just..."

Freyda, Mara's falcon, swooped down from the trees and over our
heads to dive into the brush. I was glad for the distraction of her
rustling with whatever she'd caught for lunch. It gave me a precious
moment to think.

"I don't know what things are between us now," I said at last. "To
have...done such things with you, and now to be out in the world
as we were before—it feels wrong somehow. It feels like everything
should be different, and it *is*, but it's also strangely the same, and I
don't know how to reconcile that. I don't know how to talk to you,

really, and part of me—the nervous part—doesn't want to, but at the same time, all I want to *do* is talk to you, and…and other things."

I hadn't meant to say so much. My heart pounded with relief, and with fear of how he might respond, both at once. How foolish I must have sounded to him, how inexperienced. But when I dared to look over at him, he was smiling. He was watching the trees ahead of us, riding his horse with the sort of natural ease only an Anointed wilder possessed, and he was smiling—a small thing, half hidden by his dark beard. A spot of sunlight pushed through the trees to illuminate the warm crinkles around his eyes.

"Other things?" he repeated softly, with a sly sideways glance.

I smiled down at my hands, my heart fluttering. "Other things," I said, even softer.

"There will be time for that, and for everything else," he replied. Then he reached out for my hand, and I grabbed on, grateful for the warm anchor of his fingers wrapping around mine. "Right now," he added, "I'm just glad to be with you. Brave Farrin, in the forest light."

Then he raised my hand to his mouth and kissed my fingers, brushed his lips across my knuckles.

After that, we rode in silence once more, but it was simple and sweet, like the quiet right after waking, before the day begins. My worries had, for the moment, been smoothed out by the touch of Ryder's hand, by the warmth of his voice and his gaze, and I found myself wondering if this was what it meant to feel at ease in the world, to feel at ease in one's own body. It was a feeling I was unused to. I closed my eyes and let the forest air wash over me. I breathed carefully, thinly; I didn't want the feeling to fade.

That night, as the late hours crept toward the wee morning ones, I awoke to find Talan crawling out of the tent.

"We're close," he whispered, for we were all awake now. His dark eyes glinted with a faint light, the source of which I couldn't place, and as I sat up, I could feel at once that he was right: we *were* close to something new and strange. The forest beyond us was dead quiet—no night noises of animals, no mountain breeze through the pines. When I ducked out of the tent myself, I was shocked to see snow falling from a sky thick with storms. A low rumble sounded in the distance—thunder, rolling quietly—and every few seconds, a bolt of lightning flashed on the horizon, dimly illuminating the bulbous shapes of the clouds, the spindly treetops.

We swiftly packed up camp in silence. Watchful Freyda sat on a low branch nearby, her crown feathers ruffled and her yellow eyes glaring into the forest beyond, searching for enemies. When Mara whistled low to her, she glided over to perch on my sister's shoulder and chirped quietly into her hair—a strange language of bird and Rose, born of the Mist.

Ryder was listening carefully.

"What's she saying?" I whispered.

"Something about a great wall in the trees. A black place where nothing lives." He glanced at Talan. "Sound familiar?"

"I suppose a bird might describe it that way, yes," Talan replied, the worry in his eyes at odds with the calm silk of his voice. "Beyond the ward magic I can't cross, I can sense only a sort of void. A massive nothingness, or else the ward magic is creating the illusion of size."

"I don't understand," Gemma said nervously. She looked young and pale in the dim storm light, her dark hood drawn up tight over her head. "When we made camp, we didn't feel any of this, and the sky was clear."

"Storms come and go," I pointed out.

"Whatever this place is could have ward magic that isn't entirely stationary," Gareth added, scribbling in a notebook he'd pulled from his coat pocket. Observations, I assumed—the weather, the wind, the sensation of something cold and forbidding in the air. A presence I felt as clearly as if I'd trespassed into a locked room. *Turn around*, it said. *Go no farther.*

Shivering, I wished I could obey and take everyone else with me.

"Ward magic that *moves*?" Gemma said, incredulous.

"To further disguise the thing it's meant to protect," Gareth explained. "If you can't reliably plot the ward magic, you can't know the size or shape or nature of the thing it's hiding."

Mara nodded, listening. "I've certainly encountered such barriers while on patrol in the Mist. Remnants of Olden magic or traps laid by Olden creatures, hoping to catch curious humans."

"That explains why I had such difficulty mapping what I found," Talan said, but before he could say more, a wave of frigid air rippled past us, so icy cold that it was like tiny dagger points raking across my skin. The force of it was physical, a giant, frozen hand pushing me, pushing all of us, back where we came from.

The horses, already uneasy, tossed their heads and pawed at the earth, trying to run, but their leads held them fast to the trees. Ryder went to each of them, murmuring words of comfort, then unfastened their leads and turned them loose. They took off, all their saddlebags still on the ground, full of our supplies.

"I'll find them easily enough when we come back," Ryder said, "but there's no sense in leaving them tied up and terrified. And they'll be useless to ride through something like this."

"Then let's go find this thing, whatever it is," I said tensely. The sight of the horses tearing off into the forest, away from whatever strange magic had crept close as we slept, left me even colder than the whistling air. I clutched a wooden staff Mara had brought from the priory; the familiar weight of it in my hands, so similar to the one I'd used when training with Ryder, was a comfort.

We walked for what felt like hours, Talan making quiet note of every landmark we passed, assuring us that we were on the right path. The cold grew increasingly worse, the snow falling in fast, teeming swirls, and the clouds were so thick that not even the midday sun managed to break through and warm us.

"We'll have to turn back soon," Ryder called out from the rear of our caravan. "We're not equipped for weather much worse than this."

But Mara, at the head of the line, didn't hear him, or else she was ignoring him. She kept pressing on through the snow, her arm up to shield her face. She turned back to us, waved her other arm. It looked like she was saying something, but I couldn't tell what.

"Mara!" Ryder shouted. "We can't hear you!"

Gemma tried next, cupped her hands around her mouth. "*Mara, wait!*"

My stomach sank as the realization set in: something was wrong. Freyda was flapping wildly around Mara's head, pulling at her hair with beak and talons, but soon Mara was lost to the darkness between the swaying, creaking trees. In her absence, Freyda was suddenly beside herself, shrieking a desperate falcon's cry, flying again and again into the shadows only to come shooting back toward us as if flung from a catapult.

Ryder held up his gloved hands and called out to Freyda in Ekkari, the same phrase over and over. He'd be hoarse after this, his voice torn to shreds by the wind. Finally she alighted in his arms, her feathers in complete disarray. He held her close to his chest and shielded her from the snow with his coat, and I felt a rush of relief; at least Freyda was safe, which had to mean *something* good. But a moment later, I heard Talan cry out, and I whirled in a panic to find Gemma running along the path Mara had cut through the snow. Talan tried to hurry after her, followed by Gareth, but they didn't get far. Something—some invisible force—was pushing them back, making them stumble. It looked almost as if they were fighting to wade out into the sea, but roaring, unseen waves kept shoving them to their knees.

And as I watched Gemma's blurred shape disappear into the trees just as Mara's had, an idea came to me—the sort of horrible, sinking-feeling guess that I knew at once was correct. It was as though the idea were a living thing, with claws and muscles and a tenacious will. As soon as the thought formed in my mind, I felt compelled to move—forward, always forward, faster, and faster. The feeling of *turn around*, of *go no farther*, transformed at once into something warmer, sweeter: *Come home. Come to me. Finally. At last, you're here.*

Whatever thing was here—whether a phenomenon of magic or Olden creature or strange moonlit palace where the sun never shone—I knew without a doubt that only my sisters and I could reach it. *Fae blood*, Gemma kept insisting in my mind. I laughed a little, frantic and frightened. The ridiculous idea of fae blood running in my veins seemed suddenly to be the least terrifying explanation.

The next moment, I found myself tromping fast through the snow, following the sloppy footprints my sisters had left behind. I ignored the frustrated shouts of Ryder behind me, Gareth's frightened voice calling my name. There was no song in the air this time, pulling me through the Middlemist toward some unknown destination. I would not emerge on the other side of this and find the woods where we'd fought the Brethaeus, the yellow field, Talan's old house by the sea. No, this was different. This felt...*familiar*. A voice I knew was calling me, and yet not a voice at all, really; it was more a feeling, so distinct and eager that I could hear it welcoming me, even without words.

Squinting against the wind, I pushed forward through the darkness, the looming trees, the whirling snow. I tried to call out for Gemma and Mara, but the roaring storm stole my breath, and I gasped at the cold, gulping for air, groping for some kind of solid anchor in the frigid darkness, until all of a sudden I was...through. A wall of something I couldn't see—some force or power, some shift in the air—gave way at my touch, and all at once the world around me changed: warmth instead of cold, a gentle breeze in place of a gale. When I breathed in, choking on the sudden easy bounty of air, I smelled a cooking fire, the perfume of roses. I heard the drone of honeybees, and my snow-crusted boots trampled tiny yellow wildflowers.

Dazed, I look around, my cheeks still burning from the cold, and was astonished to see the same forest I'd just been in—only these pines were a vivid green, and the forest floor was rife with moss and flowers. New spring growth bloomed everywhere, and above the canopy stretched a sky of cloudless blue.

"Farrin," said a voice—somehow both a jubilant shout from a great distance away and a gentle whisper in my ear.

I blinked, struggling to clear the frost and tears from my eyes, and once I could focus on the figure calling my name, what I saw broke something inside me. I shattered; my heart burst open.

Impossible. It *couldn't* be.

And yet there she was, standing in front of a pretty thatched-roof cottage, my sisters on either side of her, clinging to her, crying and laughing, both of them reduced to the little girls they had once been.

There was only one word to say, and the very shape of it felt wrong in my mouth:

"Mother."

CHAPTER 15

For a few moments, the world moved as it often did in my nightmares of the fire, my dreams of the shining boy: flames all around me, my young legs not strong enough to carry me, the floor shaking underfoot. Each passing second was an agony of confusion. The very air was a mire, pushing against me as I clawed desperately for any door, any window, frantic for a proper breath.

Such was the feeling of watching my mother walk toward me, her arms outstretched and a peaceful smile on her face. She wore a green dress the color of the bright spring buds, plain but fine, and she was barefoot, her feet brown with mud. She carried flowers in her pockets, and on a thin cord around her neck hung a polished black pipe. Beyond her, Gemma sobbed into Mara's sleeve while Mara looked on, silent tears streaking her face.

"Farrin, my dearest heart," Mother said, reaching for me. "Look at you. Look at all of you. Such lovely women you've become."

Her hand touched my sleeve. The sensation jerked me out of my stupor. I took three quick steps back, out of her grasp.

"What is this?" I said, my voice coming out hoarse, my throat tight with anger. "Who are you?"

My mother's smile melted into something even kinder, even gentler, as if I were the child I'd once been, come to her for comfort after scraping my knee. "Farrin, it's me," she said, trying once more to reach for me. "It's your mother."

This time I shoved her hard. My own force surprised me; I stumbled back, nearly fell. "I have no mother," I snapped. "She died years ago."

Her brow furrowed slightly. A shadow fell over her face. She lowered her hand and stepped back. "Clearly I didn't die."

"You might as well have. In fact, it would've been better if you had. Instead, you *left* us. Or she did. What are you, some Olden creature? A figment guarding Moonhollow, sent to confuse us, lull us into inattention?"

"Moonhollow?" Her head tilted to the side, inquisitive. "What's Moonhollow?"

I whirled around, scanning the trees that encircled the little cottage. I couldn't look at this person anymore; her face was too familiar, pale and oval-shaped, as Mara's was, but softer, rounder. And her eyes were the same blue as Gemma's, and her hair was long and dark brown, also like Mara's, and even the way she stood upon the earth was the same. She took up the same amount of space in the world as I remembered, moved with the same easy grace.

And her mouth was thin, a little pinched, her brows sharp and angry even when her face was at rest.

Pieces of my own face, staring back at me.

My bile rose. I marched toward the trees, away from the thing wearing the perfect mask of my mother's face. "Gareth? Talan? *Ryder!*"

"If you're calling for the men in the forest," she said from behind me, "they can't hear you. Nothing can enter Wardwell, or hear or sense anything of Wardwell, unless I wish it."

"Wardwell?" Gemma asked, wiping her face. "Is that what this place is called?"

"It is. My own private sanctuary."

"Stop crying," I snapped at Gemma. "Both of you, stop crying. Don't you see that this is some kind of trick?"

Mara blew out a long, shaky breath. "I don't think it's a trick, Farrin."

"How do you know?"

"I don't, but—" She gestured helplessly. "Look at her."

"I'm looking, and all I see is the same face Alastrina Bask wore when she came to the midsummer ball and humiliated us."

The creature's eyebrows rose. "Alastrina Bask? That's a story I'd like to hear. But I promise you, I wear no glamour. This is no trick."

And suddenly, the bubble of anger rising inside me burst. I still wore the fighting staff; it rested against my back, held in place by a padded leather strap slung across my torso, over my coat. I reached around and tore it loose, then rushed at this false creature, this evil lie. I ignored the cries of my sisters; not even Mara was fast enough to stop me, turned slow by her own dazed joy.

I raised my staff high and swung it hard at the creature's head. If she was a figment, some being sent to trick us, a mechanism created by Kilraith or Moonhollow or whatever terrible place this Wardwell *really* was—then she would defend herself. She would fight back. Her mother-skin would peel away to reveal the monster beneath.

But she did nothing. She didn't even dodge the staff as it came flying at her. She stood there and let it come. It thwacked her hard on her temple; she let out a sharp cry and crumpled to the ground, then lay there among the flowers in a stunned heap.

Mara was on me before I could strike again; she grabbed the staff, easily overpowering me, and tossed it away. Then she seized my arms and pulled them behind me, securing me against her front while I struggled uselessly to break free.

"What's *wrong* with you?" Gemma cried. She knelt at the felled creature's side, helped her turn over, and gasped when she saw the damage I'd done.

I saw it too: her temple was split open, blood spilling onto the ground. And her jaw, I realized with a sick twist in my stomach, was no longer where it should be, as if the force of my blow had knocked it half out of her skull.

"Oh gods," Gemma whispered, hovering over her. She tore off her own coat and pressed it to the bright red gash. "Here, lie still. Let me just hold this here, stanch the blood—"

But the creature gently shook her off. "It's all right," she croaked, her voice thick with pain. "Just give me a moment."

Then she slowly sat up—not with extraordinary effort, more like stretching out one's limbs after a long night of sleep. She touched her temple and lightly drew her hand down her body, her fingers trailing thin streaks of blood across skin and gown. A cold, clear sort of feeling washed over me, as if I'd plunged into a glacial lake faster than any human could move and then been thrown back out. She was working some kind of magic, but it was swifter than any I'd ever felt, a quicksilver ripple through the air, and it hurt my teeth, left every hair on my body standing on end. And then, as we watched, her mangled jaw cracked back into place. The wound on her temple closed. She shook her head and shoulders, as if to make sure everything was back where it belonged, then rose, looking much wearier than she had before I'd bludgeoned her.

Gemma scrambled to her feet and hurried over to join us, staring at the creature in horror. Mara's grip on my arms loosened. Her body tensed behind me, ready to fight. "What are you?" she said, her voice newly flat and hard.

"I wasn't lying to you," the woman said quietly. The serene expression she'd worn upon our arrival was gone, something grave and old and tired in its place. "I am Philippa Ashbourne. I am your mother, and I..." Her voice broke a little. She shook her head, let out a single soft laugh.

I stepped forward, trembling, my hands in fists. I glanced at the fighting staff, lying abandoned in a patch of clover. It wasn't too far; if I was quick enough, I might be able to grab it before she attacked us.

"But?" I prompted.

"But," she agreed, "I am also more than that." Then she lifted her gaze to meet mine, and then Mara's, and then Gemma's, one at a time, before coming back to look straight at me. She gave me a sad smile. A bird passed overhead, singing cheerfully, and as its tiny shadow passed over the woman's face, her blue eyes—Gemma's eyes—flashed a subtle but unmistakable amber.

A chill dropped over me.

"I am Kerezen," she said, and as she spoke the words, her voice became deeper, more sonorous, as if it were echoing through a long tunnel of stone. "Goddess of the senses. Mother of all bodies, singer of all songs, maker of bone and blood." She paused, then glanced beyond us at the trees. When she blinked, another cold ripple of the magic I'd felt before shot past us—a crackling jolt of power, so quick I wondered if I'd imagined it.

Truly, I wondered if I was imagining all of this—this place, this impossible woman standing before us. My body felt hot and cold in waves my heartbeat roared in my ears, a drum of disbelief.

"There, I've let them in," she said. "The others, your men. They will arrive soon." She looked at us with resigned exhaustion on her face, as if muted, frozen shock was not the reaction she'd been hoping for. She gestured back at the cottage. Her voice was smaller now, her eyes an ordinary blue. "Come. Let's go sit and wait for them. As you might imagine, there is much to discuss."

◆

When Ryder, Gareth, and Talan arrived, they were stiff with snow and ice, and frantic to find us. Freyda, chirping angrily, flew like a shot arrow to Mara's shoulder and started tugging irritably at her braid. Talan rushed straight for Gemma and drew her tenderly into his arms, his eyes squeezed shut as if in pain. He murmured something into her hair; she held his cold face in her hands and told him something in response, something sweet and low I couldn't hear. The next moment, Gareth was upon me, his hug so fierce it knocked the wind out of me.

"Thank the gods, Farrin," he breathed, his voice thin with relief. "We called and called after you, and our voices bounced back to us. It was like screaming at a wall of rock in the canyons back home."

I held on to him for a moment and looked over his shoulder at Ryder. He stood a little apart from us, snow dusting his hair and beard, his eyes blazing an angry blue. Gently, I detached myself from Gareth and went to him. He didn't reach for me, as I assumed he would. The air around him snapped as if it contained unseen fire, and the sight of him looming there, glaring at our surroundings with enraged skepticism, filled me with a strange comfort. He looked like he wanted to tear down the cottage with his bare hands, and yet I knew how gentle those hands could be.

I touched his sleeve. "Ryder..."

"You're not hurt?" He finally looked at me. He cupped my cheek, his fingers cold and gentle. His gaze searched my face, my body, as if checking for wounds. I saw the fear in his eyes. "You disappeared into the trees. The darkness took you so suddenly."

I shook my head, leaned closer to him. "I'm not hurt. In fact," I added, offering him a little smile, "just before you arrived, I pummeled the shit out of her." I jerked my head at the woman gliding about the cottage's main room, offering hot tea that no one would touch.

Ryder's fearsome expression softened; he took a deep breath in and out, some of the tension leaving his shoulders. He returned my smile. "Farrin of the forest light," he said quietly. "Stronger than she looks."

Warmth blossomed through my body. I closed my eyes and allowed myself to feel the mountainous presence of him, so near and angry—a shield and sword both at once, ready to strike, ready to protect me.

Then I stepped back and opened my eyes, feeling calmer. I lightly squeezed his fingers; our eyes locked, a silent conversation passing between us. We were safe for now; he would kill anyone who made it otherwise.

"Please, sit," said the woman pretending to be my mother— pretending to be a *god*. She sat in a fine wingback chair by the dark hearth, as serene and unbothered as Yvaine holding court. She'd lit her pipe and now puffed on it for a moment, considering Ryder, Gareth, and Talan in turn.

Her gaze slid to Gemma. "You trust these men?"

Gemma, dry-eyed now, her expression stony, replied, "More than we trust you."

The woman nodded once. "I understand that, and I understand your anger. But allow yourself to believe for a moment that what I've told you is true. Think about what that means." She looked at Mara, then at me. I hated the feeling of her eyes upon me: my mother's eyes, and yet there was a mighty weight to her presence, cold and foreign.

The sheer absurdity of what she was asking us to consider made me want to laugh. She was my mother, and she was also a god. My mind couldn't wrap itself all the way around such a preposterous idea. And yet, as I said the words to myself—my mother, a god; a god, my mother—a slow bloom of comprehension, of acceptance, began to unfurl in my stomach. It was the feeling of a horrible truth settling inside me, making itself inexorably known.

"Now," said the woman after a moment. She seemed satisfied by my discomfiture. "I ask you again: Do you trust these men?"

"Yes," Gemma said at once, lifting her chin a little. Beside her, Talan's eyes shone with love.

Mara glanced at them, then at Gareth, who sat tensely on a pretty footstool that was too small and delicate for his long, lanky body. He looked grave; though he'd not brought out his notebook, his quick green eyes darted around the room, observing every detail. The power of his mind—the mind of an Anointed sage—would allow him to remember everything. Another small comfort.

Mara's brow furrowed as she watched him; her mouth twisted. But she relented. "Yes," she replied.

All eyes were on me, but I could look only at Ryder, brooding watchfully not far from me, arms crossed over his chest. He was the only one who hadn't taken a chair. Fierce and hawkish as he looked, he nevertheless gave me a small smile. My body lit up quietly in response, and I found it easier to breathe.

"Yes," I whispered.

"Well, then." The woman in the chair took a contemplative puff of her pipe. "Let me say this, before I begin. My daughters trust you. This is no small thing. And I know the importance of allies. It is unnatural for anyone to walk through the world in solitude, especially creatures as fragile and short-lived as humans. But if any of you men reveal what is said here today, rest assured that I will find you and avenge the breaking of my daughters' trust. And the punishment will not be swift."

She said it very simply, in easy conversation, and yet the threat was clear and physical; the room trembled with it, as if the very structure of the world we'd found ourselves in were absorbing her words, holding them fast until they were needed again. The air took on the brutal bite of winter.

An instant later, warmth returned. The woman relaxed into the velvet brocade of her chair, took another puff of her pipe, and set it down on a glass tray on the table beside her.

"As I just told my daughters," she began, "I am Philippa Ashbourne, their mother. But I am also more than that. I am a human woman, yes, and I was born to human parents, and I possess the low human power of elemental magic, with a talent for botanicals, just as I always have. I am Philippa Ashbourne, once Philippa Wren. But...I am also Kerezen, goddess of the senses." She paused, the air heavy with the weight of her words. "I understand that this may be difficult for you to believe."

I burst out laughing, suddenly near tears. My body couldn't decide how to respond. "That is a terrific understatement."

"You lie," Ryder said bluntly. "The gods are dead."

"We were. Well, I was dead, that is. I can't speak for the others. If they live now, if they have been reborn in human bodies, as I have, that knowledge is beyond me. I can't hear them or feel them. The bonds that connected us in our godly lives were broken in the Unmaking and have yet to be reforged." A flicker of sadness moved across her face. "I suppose it's possible," she added quietly, "that the others are still dead. It's possible I am alone."

"Wait, wait, wait just a moment," said Gareth, leaning forward eagerly. He took off his glasses and rubbed his face. He opened his mouth as if to speak, then closed it. He rubbed his face again; he dragged both hands shakily through his hair.

The woman regarded him with quiet amusement. "Even I, goddess of the senses and not of the mind, can hear the whir of your many questions, Professor Fontaine. You may ask them, if you can find your voice."

Gareth nodded a few times, swallowing hard. "All right." He set his glasses back on his nose. "First question, then—"

"Is that why you left us?"

Gemma's quiet voice cut across the room, silencing us all. She sat on a midnight-blue divan beside Talan, who took her hand. She grabbed on to him, held on tight.

The woman, Philippa—I refused to call her *Mother* or *Kerezen*, even in my own mind—lowered her head in a single sad nod. "I left when it became clear to me that something was wrong. I first became conscious of the signs when you were born, my darling. The last of my daughters, remarkable right from the start, though I know that extraordinary nature has been more a burden to you than a blessing."

I was already losing my patience; the swift blow of Gemma's question had cut me to the quick, destroying the fragile calm Ryder's strength had brought me.

"Speak plainly," I snapped. "Not in riddles or pretty language. We deserve an explanation. A proper, simple attempt to convince us you're not lying. Because right now, I'm just wishing I could hit you again."

Philippa raised her eyebrows, her eyes sparkling a little. "Ah, but if you did, though it would hurt me, as it did the first time, my wounds would soon heal, as you saw with your own eyes." Then her smile faded. "You're right though. I should get on with it. It is difficult to explain such a complicated story. But I shall try."

She took a breath, closed her eyes, then opened them. Shock startled the anger right out of me; her blue eyes were now fully changed—a lambent gold, like Freyda's.

"I was born Philippa Wren, but when I emerged from my mother's womb, a kernel of greater life ignited deep inside me, unknown to me. I don't know why I chose this body, this particular woman, to bring me back into the world. I was dead for so long, and then I wasn't." She shrugged. "Not even we gods know the whys of our choices."

Suddenly, my frustrated comment about Ryndar from two days

before seemed eerily prescient. Gareth must have thought the same; his eyes cut to mine.

"Ryndar sent you back," he suggested. "The Great Dominion."

"The land beyond life and death." Philippa nodded thoughtfully. "Perhaps. There are certainly forces more powerful than even I was at the apex of my godly glory. But whatever the reason, back I came. At first I didn't understand what I truly was. I was simply Philippa Wren. I grew up in Gallinor's southern heartlands, as had every generation of my family before me. In my blood ran the magic of Caiathos, god of the earth. I was an elemental, blessed with low magic. I could manipulate plants and flowers. I could coax life into dried-out husks of leaves and stems, urge them to grow faster. My power was limited but sweet. And when I was grown, I met Gideon Ashbourne, and he, mighty Anointed sentinel that he was, thought me sweet too."

A distant smile played at her lips. "We had daughters. One a savant with a voice clear and brilliant as starlight." She glanced at me, the affection on her face soft, terrible. I made myself glare back at her, my heart thundering painfully.

"One," she went on, turning to Mara, who sat on a plain bench by the door, hands clasped tightly in her lap, "a sentinel like her father, with strength and agility we both knew would someday surpass his. And one"—she looked at Gemma, her expression stricken—"with abilities neither of her parents understood. Unpredictable and frightening, or so I thought at the time. The power of glamours *and* the power of elemental magic, warring for dominance in one little girl's body. An impossibility. But my mind was still fully human then. I didn't understand what was happening to either of us. Forgive me, Gemma. An impossible ask, I know. What we did to you—hiring that artificer, requesting that he alter you, stifle your power, sew you up tight—it was what we thought best at the time, but now I see it for the evil act it truly was."

The sadness in her voice, the regret, was painful to hear, sincere enough to make my eyes burn with emotion. But I didn't trust it, and the stricken look on Gemma's face stoked a sudden raging fire in my chest. I stood, ready to fly at Philippa even though I had no weapons in hand.

"How dare you mention that right now," I said quietly. "How dare you try to make us pity you—"

"It's all right, Farrin." Gemma's voice cut me off, a quick slash of steel. "It's my body she's talking about. If I wish for her to stop, I'll ask her to."

Abashed, I returned to my seat. I put my hands flat on my thighs, feeling wild and helpless, my anger churning fast with nowhere to go. Without thinking, I looked to Ryder. He nodded once, his gaze steady. *Breathe, Farrin*, his grave expression seemed to say. *I'm here. I understand.*

I did breathe, holding for a beat after each inhale, each exhale. A sliver of calm returned to me. I wiped my sweaty palms on my dress.

"What I didn't know then," Philippa continued, "was that the things I was experiencing—the sleepless nights, the voices whispering to me of strange songs, beautiful other worlds—was my godly self, the twin life within me, stretching her limbs. Growing, taking her first breaths. My human body had been born with a god-seed inside it, resurrected after centuries of darkness. And now that seed was opening." She looked once more to Gemma; her next words were heavy with regret. "That is why, daughter, your power is twofold—power of the senses, power of the elements. You can weave glamours. You can tear trees from the earth. When you were small, you choked on flowers. You are a creature of conflict because when I birthed you, I too was in conflict of the deepest kind, though I didn't yet understand why."

"And Farrin and I..." Mara said, after a moment. "Our abilities are less conflicted because when we were born, you were more woman than god."

Philippa nodded, smiling warmly. Mara's astute observation had pleased her. "And when Gemma was born, I was becoming more god than woman. Though it would be years before I understood that, and years more before I understood that I must leave you. To protect you. To protect myself, and everyone else too."

I scoffed at that. My mind struggled with too many emotions, too many unthinkable questions. I couldn't even look at Mara; that she was so calmly putting together the pieces of this woman's wild tale felt like a betrayal of the worst kind.

"You left us to *protect* us?" I spat. "Parents don't protect their children by abandoning them to grief and confusion. You insult us by saying otherwise."

But Philippa seemed unbothered by the anger in my voice and continued her story. "Sitting beside Gemma while the artificer changed her body was the first great blow to my heart. I'd thought it was the right thing to do, and yet as my daughter screamed and twisted under his magic, I knew I'd been wrong, that Gideon had too. But it was too late, and that knowledge shattered a piece of my human heart, making room for the godly one to take its place. Then," she said, looking at me, "there was the fire."

I stiffened; my mouth went dry. Ryder shifted where he stood, his shoulders square with ready anger.

"My home was destroyed by our enemies," Philippa said. "All that beauty, the safety of those halls and rooms, every sprig of greenery coaxed to life by my fingers: gone. And my daughter, my eldest, my songbird, was nearly taken by the flames. There was a whole hour, Farrin, when we thought you had died. Searching the black grounds, the acrid smell of smoke—that was the second blow to my heart. I was two-thirds a god after that, and only one-third a human woman."

I went cold, remembering that night. So many moments of those long dark hours had been seared into my mind, shaping me—the screaming wallpaper peeling away from the walls, the shining boy leaning over me in the damp grass—and then, abruptly, even memories I'd buried resurfaced: my mother on her knees in the grass, staring at Ivyhill in grief and fury as it burned. I remembered the wicked smile she'd worn, how her whole body had blazed as if some ageless fire had been lit within it.

A pit opened in my stomach. I wanted desperately not to believe her, and yet it made a sudden, perfect sense. That night, my mother had changed; a piece of her had died, and a piece of a god had found new life. I'd seen it with my own eyes, though neither of us had truly known what was happening.

Philippa's gaze hardened, slid over to Ryder. She looked him up and down appraisingly. "Trapping the Basks in their forest was a balm to my grief, helped soothe my anger. How foolish I was, and Gideon too. How childish. But you and your parents and your sister—Alaster, Enid, Alastrina—you were all the same. Held in thrall like worms on a hook, just as we were."

She glanced at Talan, and a flash of confused pity crossed her face. "Poor demon," she said quietly. "Something terrible was done to you too, was it not?"

I shivered. That cutting stare, calm and still, fixed on Talan as if Philippa could peel away the layers of his very self to discover everything he had ever known.

Shadows of memory darkened Talan's face. "Something terrible," he agreed, his fingers tightening around Gemma's. "But Gemma saved me. And so did Mara, and Farrin. All of them did."

Philippa beamed at us, a light from within making her skin glow. "Of course they did. My daughters, brave and strong, just as I always knew they would be—"

"Your story," I snapped, interrupting her.

She blinked once and said, "Of course. Well, those were the first two blows, each unmaking me and remaking me at once. And then the third, perhaps the worst of all." Her sad gaze moved to Mara. "My little Mara was taken from me."

"From all of us," I corrected. "You weren't the only one to suffer when the Warden took her."

"I concede that. But the blow of that grief—the third great one I had borne in only a small handful of years—it completed my Remaking, you see. I was no longer Philippa Ashbourne, not entirely. I was something else, something more. That day, watching Mara borne away in the Warden's carriage, the tide of my self turned. I was more god than woman, more Kerezen than Philippa. Though I could not yet put the feeling into words, I knew the truth. I felt it in my marrow. My anger was volcanic. One daughter mutilated, another nearly killed, the last taken from me. If I had stayed, I would have hurt someone. I know it." Her voice was low, thick, her amber gaze distant. "Gods are selfish beings in the way that beasts are selfish, concerned only with their own survival, the thriving of their domain, the marvel of their own strength, the safety of their young. If you'd seen me during my first life, creating and destroying with no regard for the consequences..."

Philippa shook her head wryly. I got the sickening sense that she was *amused* by whatever horrific memories she held.

"But humans are not this way," she said, "and there was enough of Philippa left in me to realize that what I was feeling—this great uncoiling inside me—was dangerous. I contained powers I did not understand. I couldn't remain at Ivyhill, or anywhere else that people lived. I had to explore myself, to learn what it meant to be a god—and to do that, I had no choice but to leave everything behind. My children, my husband, my home. And so I fled. I lived in solitude for years, and with my strange twin powers—human and god, elemental and physical—I built this place, and I named it Wardwell."

She gazed around the cottage's main room, a lofty, airy space with greenery draped over every rafter. "Here, I am safe from myself, and so is everyone else. This is no longer a world made for gods, and yet here I am living in it. So I exist as I must, in solitude. My daily prayer is that enough of Philippa remains alive in me that I am content to stay here, tucked securely away. The day I become fully a god, leaving my mortal shell behind...this day is one I dread, and I hope it never comes. I hope to live forever in this strange peace I've constructed, a god in a human shell."

She laughed quietly and held up her left hand, marveling at it. "I wish you could experience even a moment of how it feels to live like this, a vessel of mere flesh and sinew that contains godly amounts of power. To be two selves at once. To have memories of pushing babies from my body and also to remember crafting the first ancient humans with my own hands. Scooping up earth and water, mixing it with my let blood, sifting through the Olden realm for sinaelum and using it to weave a lattice, holding all the fragile pieces together. The first humans: limbs and scalps, breakable bones and pulsing hearts."

"Stop it," I whispered. I was shaking, revolted. Hearing such words coming from my mother's mouth—from *my* mouth, mirrored on her face—made me feel sick. Philippa looked at me, serenely curious, perhaps waiting for me to say more, but then Gareth spoke. He hadn't heard me; he was bursting with the same question that was turning over and over in my own mind. I could see it on his face, in his dazed, ashen expression.

"Does this mean," he began, very quietly, "that Farrin and Gemma and Mara are all..."

In the end, he couldn't say it. I could hardly *think* it; the very word felt monstrous.

"Gods themselves?" Philippa finished, with a quirk of her eyebrow. "No. There's too much of their father in them for that. But it is not only Gideon Ashbourne's blood pumping through their bodies. It is mine too. Philippa's, and Kerezen's." She retrieved her pipe from its glass tray, puffed on it, blew out a curl of white smoke. As if all of this were nothing, mere frothy gossip after a dinner among friends. "They are both mortal and not," she said simply around her pipe. "Humans and gods. *Demigods* is the word." She tilted her head, considering Gemma with fond amusement. I hated the expression, wanted to wipe it from her face with another jaw-cracking blow.

"Fae blood indeed," she murmured. "Not a bad guess, Gemmy, but not the correct one."

The use of Gemma's nickname was the final blow. I couldn't stand to be in that room for another second. I surged up from my seat and stormed toward the door. Mara moved to stop me, then relented. I burst outside into the world of green spring beyond the cottage. I didn't stop to think where I was going, nor to consider if the magic boundaries of Wardwell would expand to accommodate me. I simply ran, tearing across the clover-soft lawn, through the vegetable garden beside the cottage, across the wildflower-strewn fields beyond. I ran as fast as my shaking body could take me. Tall grasses whipped past me; lazy bumblebees bumped drunkenly into my legs. The air smelled fresh and green, every petal and blade of grass sugared with nectar. I smelled honeysuckle, roses, jasmine. The sweetness made me want to cry; I let out an angry, gasping sob, ducked under a low branch, and hurried into the woods.

The shade of the pines towering overhead was a relief. The air was cool, less cloying. My side cramped; my lungs and legs burned. And still I ran, until suddenly I couldn't. I stumbled down a slight rocky slope, tripped over a jutting stone, let out a sharp cry of surprise.

But I didn't hit the ground. Ryder caught me before I could. He was breathing hard, though not as hard as I was. He held my arms, steadying me. He'd run after me into these strange spring woods.

I glared up at him, sweaty and on edge, my heart still pounding. I'd never seen anything as beautiful as his frowning, bearded face.

"You caught me," I said, panting hard. I shoved at him a little, and he let me go. But I didn't *want* him to let me go. I went back to him, fisted my hands in his coat. "How did you catch me? How are you not even *sweating*?"

He raised one dark eyebrow. "Farrin, love, you're not that fast a runner."

And that made me laugh, though tears were not far behind. I relished the feeling of him lovingly tucking a strand of damp hair behind my ear, and then the relief of him being there—the sensation of his warm body under my hands, holding me up—pushed me over the edge of my anger into pure overwhelmed release. I hid my face in his chest and cried, and he asked of me no explanation, no apology. He simply held me, one hand cupping the back of my head, his cheek pressed against my crown. In his deep, gruff voice he told me again and again, "I'm here, Farrin. I'm here with you. I'm not going anywhere. Feel me, love."

He pressed my palm flat against his chest, right over his pounding heart. "I'm right here." He kissed my hair, rocked me slowly against him. "Farrin, Farrin." His voice was like a strange, rough song, a lullaby under the trees. "Farrin in the forest light," he said, a tender smile in his voice.

I clung to him as the pines whispered around us. A cool breeze kissed my skin, and I pulled back at last to look up at him, a hundred clumsy words of love on my tongue—but Ryder wasn't looking down at me, as I'd imagined. He was staring past me, into the woods. His whole body tensed against mine.

"Stay very calm," he said quietly, "and don't move."

But I'd already turned to see what he was seeing, fear bolting through me like lightning, and what I saw staring back at me—at us—was a blazing, familiar figure peeking out from behind a tree. White-gold flames, sparking wings, two eyes of cold blue fire.

My breath caught. *The firebird.*

CHAPTER 16

Ryder slowly reached for his crossbow, which he still wore across his back on a leather strap slung around his torso. I shouldn't have been surprised that he still carried his weapons, though he'd long ago discarded his winter coat and now wore his shirtsleeves rolled up to his elbows. He took a thick black arrow from the quiver at his hip, nocked it. All the while his eyes remained trained on the firebird. Its flames shimmered and snapped as it crouched there behind the tree, apparently frozen in place—with fascination? With fear?

Or with the focused attention of a predator on the hunt?

I tried to swallow, but my mouth had gone dry. I made myself speak. "Who are you? What do you want?"

"Farrin, don't," Ryder muttered under his breath.

The firebird's form shifted every time I blinked: a woman, tall and alien, bright as snow gleaming under the sun. Then, a bird, or something *like* a bird—beaked and winged, with long, slender arms ending in talons of crackling fire. Whether it couldn't maintain a single form or simply chose not to, the effect was mesmerizing. My eyes glazed over, like I'd been staring too long at a hearth fire. I started moving toward the creature without meaning to.

Ryder snapped at me—"Farrin, *don't*"—but he didn't dare lower his crossbow and arrow, so I kept going, even as he roared at me with increasing panic. Only a few steps more and I would reach the firebird's tree. I put out my hand, palm up. I crouched a little, as if approaching Osmund when he'd gotten spooked by something.

The firebird cocked its head, considering me. A spray of scarlet plumage burst from its head, shedding embers that scattered across the mossy ground. It let out a soft cry—the jangle of gold coins, the trickle of water down smooth black rocks—and reached for me with a long arm of fire. Somehow, even with the memory of that long-ago fire etched into my every bone, I was not afraid of the creature's flames. Soon those flames became feathers, a thousand shades of gold and orange, scarlet and violet, and each one gleamed as if silkspun. I reached for its brilliant talons, every curved tip glowing like a tiny blazing sun. Heat gathered under my hand; a distant, distracted part of my mind screamed at me in warning, but that was easy to ignore in the face of such beauty.

A crash, a curse, and suddenly Ryder's arm was around me, pulling me back against him, out of the firebird's reach. We stumbled back together, as if a cord connecting me with this fiery creature had suddenly snapped. The force of it was so strong that I felt Ryder lose his grip on me, and I fell to my hands and knees in the dirt.

And then, with a sharp, angry cry that stabbed my skull, the firebird lunged, a column of fire so quick and hot that the gale of it blowing past me pulled tears from my eyes. I turned to follow it with a scream in my throat, but it was too fast for me, too brilliant, its wings and talons outstretched, and before I could warn Ryder, before he could move out of its path, the firebird's flames engulfed him.

Immediately, his screams filled the crackling hot air.

The sound of his agony made me wild. I shot to my feet and ran for the fire without thinking. What would I do with it? Spray it with water I didn't have? Would the firebird even respond to such things as normal flames would have? I didn't know, I couldn't think. Ryder's screams were awful, each animal cry shattering my heart. Suddenly I was back at Ivyhill, trapped in smoke and flame, but this time Ryder was the one trapped in the firestorm, and I was my parents—powerless to stop disaster from unfolding right before my eyes.

"Stop it!" I cried, uselessly. I could barely hear my own voice over the roar of the firebird, and if it heard what I said, it gave no sign of it. It simply stared at me from within its sea of flames: two brilliant blue eyes, unblinking, unfeeling.

I tried once more to run straight at it. In the Ravenswood forest, the creature had seemed skittish, fearful. At the mere sight of me, it had flown as if in terror. Maybe, I thought, I could frighten it away, spook it, like a horse that would bolt at the slightest strange sound. But the sheer heat of the firebird threw me back before I could take three strides, and I landed hard on my backside. I thought wildly of Gemma, of Talan, of Philippa—or Kerezen, or whoever she was, *whatever* she was—but by the time I fetched them, it would be too late. Already, it was too late. I could no longer hear Ryder screaming.

I crawled as close to the fire as the heat would allow, great heaving sobs tearing out of me. The ground was wet, steaming. My hands sank into black mud.

"Please let him go," I whispered, a pathetic heap in the dirt, but the firebird remained unmoved, the only sign it had heard me a slight ripple of light that raced across its face like the flit of a stray sunbeam.

It was the first time I'd seen anything like an expression on its inhuman face, and some instinct told that expression was...*annoyance*.

The realization snapped me out of my frantic fear, clearing my desperate mind just enough to think, *Oh.*

Of course.

In my panic for Ryder, I'd forgotten all about the greatest weapon I possessed: my voice.

An avalanche of despair crashed down on me. If I had acted faster, if I had remembered sooner the power of my music, perhaps I could have saved him.

So when I began to sing, it was with bright, sharp anger, hot enough to rival the flames that had taken Ryder from me. From the huge library of music that lived in my mind, I pulled a chant of battle written decades ago, when for a brief time the continents of Gallinor and Vauzanne had been at war over a newly discovered chain of fertile islands. I hardly registered the words as they formed on my tongue; I knew only my grief, my desolate fury, which grew with each ragged note, each spat syllable. But the firebird seemed unaffected by me. It observed me with those blaze-bright eyes for such a long moment that I began to feel truly afraid. I had fought specters with my voice, I had fought Kilraith, but it seemed this creature was impervious to whatever power I held.

Then, suddenly, it shot up into the canopy with a stifled cry of pain. And where it had stood, within a charred ring of earth, was Ryder, dazed but unburnt.

He stared at me, and then his knees buckled and he fell, and I was there beside him in an instant, moving faster than I ever had in my life. He was nearly unconscious, and the bulk of his body was too heavy for me to hold up properly, but I tried with all my might. I pressed my face against his hair and swallowed hard against the sobs bursting to escape me. Then I inspected him—his hair, his arms, his dear face. I touched his beard, held his cheeks.

"Ryder," I choked out, "say something, please."

"I'm all right," he rasped. He raised his sweaty, scorching-hot hand to touch mine and let out a rough cough. "It was just...very hot in there."

I laughed through my tears and grabbed on to him, kissed his wonderful unhurt fingers. Then my wits returned, and I looked up with a jolt to find the firebird, smaller and paler than it had been, hovering a few paces from us.

Fiercely I drew Ryder to me and glared at the horrible thing. But before I could even consider what to do next, a fist-sized spot of pale light began to glow on what I thought must be the firebird's face, beneath its lapis eyes.

"You understand now," it croaked, in the same common tongue I used. The sound was a strange one, a combination of a shrill avian cry and a broken human voice, neither male nor female. Bizarrely, the creature seemed to wince as it spoke, as if offended by the tone of its own voice.

"You understand," it continued, falteringly, "what must be done."

My shock rendered me mute for a moment. I felt Ryder shifting slightly beside me; I knew with certainty that he was reaching for his crossbow.

"I understand nothing of what just happened," I managed to say, "except that you attacked my friend without provocation."

"And you were frightened of her, and cowed by her fire," the creature continued, cocking its head—a human head crowned with flames, tresses snapping like ropes of molten gold, then a bird's head, sleek with shining feathers. The shape of it was always shifting, always transforming. "At first you did not remember the weapon you carry. At first you knew only grief and terror. In war, there is no room for grief or terror. You understand now. You must practice this. You have let it sit idle for too long. She had to remind you."

I shook my head in frustration. "I don't understand you. You speak in riddles. Who are you? *What* are you?"

"Ankaret." The firebird's voice softened around the word. The syllables came haltingly. "Her name is...Ankaret."

"Ankaret," I repeated, trying out the unfamiliar word. My blood roared in my ears. I wanted desperately to run, but if we moved, would it—*she*—strike us down?

Before either of us could utter another word, Ryder shot to his feet. He was lightning fast, even after what had just happened, and furious; the arrow of his crossbow flew true and hit the firebird's right wing.

She shrieked and flailed, all human voice stripped from her—only bird now, only beast. One of Ryder's thick black arrows pinned her to a mammoth tree just behind her. Her light had dimmed; her form flitted frantically from human to bird to pale fire, and back again.

Ryder strode toward her, his expression murderous, and nocked another arrow.

I scrambled to my feet and raced over to put myself between them. "Wait! Ryder, wait."

He swore and spun away, lowering his bow. "Gods, Farrin. Wait? For what? For her to trap me in fire again? For her to actually burn one of us next time?"

He was right; my common sense told me that. But something else gave me pause, a strange idea that had started turning in me at the sound of the creature speaking. And her cries were terrible, shredded with pain.

"She can speak," I insisted desperately. "We can talk to her."

He looked at me as if I'd lost my mind, and maybe he was right. "I have nothing to say to her except goodbye," he ground out.

"Let me try something first," I said, still with my hands up, placating him.

"Farrin—"

"Please, trust me. Let me try this."

He glared at the creature. "If it hurts you..." he began, his voice tight and miserable.

"Then you can loose all your arrows at it. But first I *must* try this. Do you trust me?"

He finally lowered his crossbow to his side. He nodded once. "Of course I trust you," he said, in a rough whisper.

I gave him a quick smile, my heart racing, hoping fervently that I wasn't making a terrible mistake. Then I swallowed hard and turned to the creature. She writhed in pain upon a bed of thorns, sprawled across the tree's roots. She had taken on a more solid form, as if the arrow in her wing, pinning her to the physical world, had eroded whatever Olden power she possessed. Her dim fire flickered quietly: flame, feather, flame once more.

I approached her slowly, crouched so I could meet her unblinking eyes. Each was a brilliant blue jewel wreathed with white fire.

Then, my palms sweating, my skin cold with fear, I began to sing.

It was a folk song from Big Deep, the great region of canyons and rivers on Gallinor's eastern coast where Gareth's ancestral home stood. He'd first sung it to me on that night long ago in his bed—rather badly, every word slurred with wine. We hadn't yet undressed, hadn't even kissed, but I'd sensed nonetheless that something new and momentous was about to happen, and so I recalled every word, every lilting note, with tenderness.

As I sang, the firebird began to calm, and so did I. This song couldn't have been more different from the song of anger I'd launched at her only moments before. My voice rose up from my chest on an unbroken rush of supple air. Each note felt round and full in my throat; the melody fell like a tumble of smooth stones through their river. By the time the last note faded, the firebird had ceased her struggling. Her former effulgent glory was gentle but steady—fresh candlelight flickering on a bedside table. She stared at me with an expression I couldn't read. How was one to read a face made of fire?

I hesitated, and then, ignoring Ryder's gruff, tearful plea, reached out to touch the feather nearest me: thick, long, glossy red as a polished ruby, each silken fiber glowing softly with light. Warmth flooded my hand, raced up to tickle the back of my throat, but it wasn't scalding or even unpleasant. In its wake, I felt more alert, more clearheaded, as if I'd just scrubbed myself clean in a hot bath.

I gave her a tight smile. "All right, then. You said your name is Ankaret. Mine is Farrin. That's Ryder."

The firebird's eyes cut to Ryder. *Ankaret*'s eyes. White-hot. Angry, maybe, or afraid. "She wasn't going to kill you," she said mournfully, her voice a multitude of eerie tones—not quite human, not quite animal. "Please, let her go."

Ryder came to stand over us. I was glad to see he had yet to raise his bow again. "Can you not *burn* yourself free?" he asked caustically.

Ankaret shook her head, dislodging a soft shower of sparks. "The arrow has broken her wing. She cannot burn with real strength, not like this."

The sadness in her words made me ache, but I kept my own voice cool. "You said you weren't going to kill him. Why, then? Why did you make me think you were?"

"In war, there is no room for grief or terror." She looked right at me as she said it, her bird's head tilting sharply. Each word bent under the weight of some great emotion I could not name. "You need to understand. War is coming. In your blood is old power, and you cannot be afraid to use it."

Philippa's story from the cottage slithered back into my mind. *Demigods is the word.* Cold slipped down my arms.

"Old power?" I repeated.

Beside me, Ryder shifted uneasily.

Ankaret continued as if she hadn't heard me. "You must use it even when you are afraid. You must use it even when you are angry. You must keep it always sharp, always ready. Do you understand? What she did was not to hurt you but to show you."

I thought I was indeed beginning to understand. I glanced up at

Ryder, then back at her. "At first I didn't remember the weapon I carry," I murmured, repeating her earlier words. "At first I knew only grief and terror."

"And more of that will come," she said forlornly, beginning to struggle once more against the arrow's hold. "And she will show you again and again, if she must. You must understand. You cannot be afraid."

It was unthinkably strange to speak with a creature whose eyes I could not read: no pupils, no irises. Simple glowing discs, flat yet fathomless.

"Afraid of what?" Ryder said, his voice snapping with impatience. "Of Kilraith? Do you know him?" He knelt beside me and looked closely at Ankaret. "Are you a messenger of his? Are you his enemy? This isn't the first time we've seen you. You've been following us, spying on us. Why?"

"She is not following," Ankaret protested. "She is..."

Then her voice trailed off, and suddenly I *could* read her shifting face of fire. The flames gathered and snapped. Her great blue eyes shrank to bright pinpricks. Fear. She was afraid.

"She must go. Please." She wriggled in vain, sparks flying from the tips of her trapped wings. "Someone is calling her, and she must go."

"Who's calling you?" Ryder demanded.

"Whoever it is, they can't find you here," I said, though I didn't quite believe my own assurance. Philippa seemed to think Wardwell's protective magic couldn't be breached, and yet here was Ankaret.

"It isn't that, it isn't just finding." Ankaret shook her head. Her free wing snapped bright with frustration. "Mercy, please. Let her go, and she will grant you a gift. Let her go, and she will answer a single question with what time she has. And she will see you again, she promises."

I exchanged a glance with Ryder.

"Is that promise meant to be reassuring?" he asked, incredulous.

"What kind of question, Ankaret?" I asked slowly.

"Anything," she replied. She wrenched her body hard against the arrow and cried out softly in pain. I watched in horrified wonder as bright teardrops of fire streaked down her cheeks, snaking into the white-gold feathers of her breast. "If she knows the answer, she will tell you. If she does not know the answer, she will find it."

I looked again at Ryder; he was staring hard at Ankaret, his expression suddenly not angry but closed, guarded.

"And that is the gift?" he asked quietly.

"No. No, the gift is this," said Ankaret, and as she spoke, she plucked from her pinned wing a single feather of fire, long as my forearm and thin as my wrist, with a downy tuft at its base, where the silver barb began. The barb itself was thick and bloody, freshly wrenched from…skin? Muscle? She held it out to me, her blazing arm shaking as if from exhaustion. As the feather rested in the flaming white cup of her palm, its snapping firelight soon faded to a rich hue of scarlet and violet, reminding me of a brilliant sunset horizon.

"It will not hurt you," she cooed, in her warped dove's voice, and when I looked into her eyes, though I could not read them, I felt the certainty of that promise. This feather would not hurt me.

I plucked it from her hand before Ryder could stop me. It weighed nothing, of course, and yet the air around it seemed to bend and shift, as if drawn to its slight form. I hesitated, then stroked its length; it was like water in my fingers, a ribbon of finest satin.

"Keep this with you always," said Ankaret. "Someday you will need her. Use this to call her. She will hear you, wherever she is."

I cradled the feather against my chest, feeling suddenly, fiercely protective of it.

"And in exchange, we free you?" Ryder asked.

"And in exchange for the freeing, an answer for you as well," Ankaret reminded him. "Ask now, if you must. She will tell you before you free her, if she must. An act of trust. A promise."

Ryder looked hard at her for another moment, then stood and walked a few paces away. "Farrin," he called quietly.

I joined him, still holding the feather. "What do we ask her?"

"I don't like this. How are we to know this feather is truly just a feather? What if it's some kind of trick? And if we ask her anything we *really* want to know—"

"She could use it against us, or give that information to anyone she chooses," I finished, realizing the truth with a sinking feeling. "The enemies we know, the enemies we don't." All of our questions—about the Mist, Yvaine, the abductions, Kilraith—the very topics themselves were too sensitive to speak of beyond our small trusted numbers.

"And even if she never told a single creature, living or dead or Olden," Ryder continued, "she could still burn us to a crisp the moment she's able to fully burn again."

"Your sister lives."

Ryder and I froze. I recovered first, turning back to stare at Ankaret. "What did you say?"

Her color paled further. She was shrinking in size, like a dying fire. "Your sister, Alastrina." She was looking not at me but at Ryder. "You love her so. She knows this. She sees it in you. And she must tell you that your sister lives. She lives, but she isn't safe."

There was real pity in her voice, and when Ryder hurried toward her, she did not flinch, merely stared up at him with her round unblinking eyes.

He knelt before her, heedless of the thorns and fire. "How do you know this?"

"She does not know," she said mournfully. "And yet she knows much. She sees it in her dreams, and her dreams are only fire and light. Your sister lives, but she is not safe. She hardly sleeps. When she does, she dreams of games in dark hallways. Hide-and-go-seek. Quiet cupboards, everything black and safe. A cave in a house in a wood." She went quiet for a moment, then shook her head and let out a sharp, strained cry. "She tries to see more but cannot! This is all she knows, Ryder Bask of the north. Please, let her go. *Please*."

Ryder turned away abruptly, dragged shaking hands across his face. His expression was horrified, his color suddenly ashen. Looking at him, I felt cold. What Ankaret had said was nonsense to my ears, but clearly something in her words had struck home.

"Please?" Ankaret begged, her voice small, her crackling body now the size of an ordinary human girl. "Please, let her go."

"Do it," Ryder said hoarsely, his back to us both.

I was glad to. With both hands, I yanked the arrow from the tree, and once Ankaret was free, she did not fly away. She unfurled her glorious wings to a span of perhaps thirty feet and once more bloomed into a bird woman, at least twelve feet tall, and yet she did not burn us. In fact, she seemed jubilant. She stretched her beautiful body of fire up into the trees, taller and taller, then dropped down to our height again. Her feathers rippled and fluttered, a sea of red and gold.

"Thank you for your mercy," she said, her voice stronger, less frightened. "She will not forget it. Now, ask her your question, and she will answer if she can."

Ryder glanced over at me, his eyes bright. I could feel a despair radiating from him like the working of acrid magic. He couldn't speak. He looked lost, and young—a boy without his sister.

So, I was the one to speak. "What is the city called Moonhollow?" I asked.

Immediately I deplored my choice. Out of all the questions teeming in my mind, this one seemed suddenly the least important. I could have phrased it more precisely; I could have insisted Ryder give me his opinion before we decided what to say. *What are you, truly? Why are you following us? Where is Kilraith? Where is Alastrina?*

But the words had been spoken, and Ankaret drew her wings close to her body, becoming a single column of fire.

"Moonhollow," she repeated. My stomach sank when I heard the regret in her voice. "This is a word she does not know. This is a word she has never heard, not in any wood, not on any mountain. But..."

And then she surged toward me, too close, too bright. I flinched back from her overwhelming warmth, and she shrank away. She bowed her head—an apology, I thought. A tendril of feather-fire lingered in the air near me, as if suspended in water. The sight of it seemed somehow wistful.

"Do not worry, Farrin of the forest light," she said, "and Ryder, raven-wild. This city called Moonhollow—she will find it. A promise is a promise. She will find it, and she will tell you. Watch for her, and be always sharp, always ready. Do not fear your blood's old power, Farrin of the gods. You will need it. It is a friend."

Then, a quick flicker of heat past me, a circle of light whipping around Ryder, and she was gone. No trace of her remained in the woods—no embers, no singed trees.

We stood in silence, and at last my courage faded and my wobbly knees gave out. I sank slowly to the ground and sat there in the moss, staring at the feather in my hands.

Ryder knelt beside me. I couldn't look at him.

"I'm sorry," I whispered. "I should have asked about Alastrina. I should have—"

"No, it was a good question," Ryder said at once. "The mystery of Moonhollow, whatever it is, connects all the other ones. At least it seems to. You did well."

I nodded, then said quietly, "Farrin of the gods. That's what she called me." I looked up at Ryder, imploring. "She knew. Somehow she knew."

"Or," he said, his expression grim, "this is all some test of your mother's, some twisted game."

"Maybe, but..." I shook my head. "I don't think so, and I don't think you do either. The things she said about Alastrina—games in dark hallways, quiet cupboards." I hesitated, hating the images the words evoked. "Those things meant something to you."

Ryder nodded, staring at the ground, his gaze like daggers. He said nothing else, though his jaw worked as if he was fighting mightily for words he could not find.

I touched his arm, and almost at once he grabbed my hand and held it with something like desperation.

"We can't tell Philippa about her," I said, after a moment. "About Ankaret, I mean."

"She might already know. Her ward magic might have alerted her to Ankaret's presence."

"If she asks, we'll tell her. There'll be no point in lying then. But I want to see what she'll say when we return. If this is all some game of hers, maybe she'll drop coy hints, pleased with herself. Or she'll smell Ankaret on us and recognize the scent, give us information. Until then, though..."

He nodded. "We won't say anything. Not yet."

"Not *ever*," I added firmly. "That woman can't be trusted, and neither can her home or anything she's touched. We'll tell the others, but not here. And meanwhile, we'll observe her, see if she gives anything away."

I stood, not allowing him the chance to argue, keeping my expression as fearless as I could manage, though in the crash of nerves following Ankaret's departure, a hundred different questions boiled in my mind. *War is coming*, Ankaret had said. But when? And had I lost my senses to even for a moment give weight to the broken riddles of a creature I did not understand?

I tucked the feather into my coat and started walking back the way we had come, Ryder following behind me. With every stride, I wondered if my new treasure would dissolve in my hands, or if we would step back into the sunlight of the Wardwell fields and forget all we'd seen. But the feather remained, a press of warm silk in my coat, and when I closed my eyes, Ankaret's unblinking gaze stared back at me, seared into my eyelids like the glare of twin white-blue suns.

The others were still talking in the cottage's main room when Ryder and I returned.

They fell silent as we walked in. I couldn't bear to look at any of them, and I certainly didn't want to talk any further about gods and demigods, and mothers who weren't entirely mothers. The walk back to the cottage had utterly drained me; I couldn't even bring myself to observe Philippa for signs that she recognized the traces of Ankaret's flames, or a telltale twinkle in her eye that would tell me this had been some terrible game of her design. Ryder was paying better attention than I was, I hoped. I had only the capacity to stay upright.

Philippa seemed to sense my exhaustion. She watched me quietly from her chair, the air around her hazy with pipe smoke. "Upstairs and on the left is a room you can use. The bed is clean and comfortable."

I didn't even acknowledge her. Gareth stood as if to join me, but someone stopped him—Ryder, probably—and I walked past them all and up the stairs. Alone in the little wood-paneled room, I took off my coat, tucked Ankaret's feather into my bodice, and curled up on the bed, which looked very much like my bed at home: plain white linens, crisply made. I pressed my palm against the place where the feather lay and let its warmth soothe me to sleep.

When I awoke, it was night, and the house was quiet. I saw a shape across the room: Ryder, his bulk crammed onto the too-small sofa by the window, a quilt of green patchwork covering only his legs. Even in sleep, he was frowning. I was tempted to go to him, press a kiss to his brow, but I instead rose and left the room as quietly as I could. The upper floor contained three other rooms, all with closed doors, and for a moment I stood in the dark hallway, considering retreating to my bed. But I was stiff and dirty, I needed to stretch, and my growling stomach could no longer be ignored.

I crept downstairs, hardly breathing, hoping no step would creak, but my stealth was for naught. Philippa was in the kitchen, sitting alone at a small table of polished wood with elaborately carved legs, each adorned with leafy wooden vines. It was far too fine a thing to decorate a plain cottage in the middle of nowhere. The very sight of it enraged me; any hope I had of getting back to some kind of peaceful sleep was gone.

I started to leave, but of course she'd already heard me.

"You can come and eat something," she said. She held a steaming cup of tea in her hands and stared over its rim at nothing in particular: the shadowed wall, a clock softly ticking. "There's bread and cheese, fruit, honey. I won't bother you."

To leave seemed childishly stubborn; to stay felt like a concession. In the end, I obeyed my stomach. I gathered a plate of food and stood at a window eating it. Minutes passed in uncomfortable silence, and as I ate, I considered all that had happened. Ankaret's feather seemed to pulse against my skin, as if it contained its own heartbeat. The warmth of it gave me courage; the food gave me clarity. And suddenly it seemed unimportant to examine Philippa for some sign that she knew Ankaret. If she did, so be it. A more important mission had presented itself to me, one that made me sick to consider.

I sat at the table and clasped my hands atop it. I looked at my fingers, not at her. "Come back with us. We need your help. If you are who and what you say you are, that is."

"The others have already told me what's happening," Philippa said quietly, "and though it disturbs me very much—a dying Mist, a dying queen—I cannot leave Wardwell, Farrin. I'm sorry."

She sounded sad, extraordinarily tired. I could feel her looking at me, and for a moment, a lonely part of me—perhaps a part untouched by anger, even after all these years—imagined that we were simply a mother and her daughter, unable to sleep, enjoying a quiet conversation over midnight tea.

I ripped myself from the foolish reverie and dared to look across the table at her. "You *can't* leave Wardwell? Or you won't?"

"It's more complicated than that simple distinction."

"It isn't. Something is deeply wrong in our world. A monster is roaming free, perhaps the force behind it all. You claim to be a god reborn. And yet you'll sit here and do nothing?"

"A god reborn, yes," she replied wearily, "and yet even after years alone, learning how to exist in my human body, I am a mere shadow of what I once was. My power is still a child who has only just learned how to walk. And none of you can tell me who or what Kilraith is, nor the true extent of his power. What you do know is that he bound a demon to his service for years, and that this demon was the last one of many. A demon—one of the strongest Olden beings we ever created. This Kilraith possessed his mind and body, nearly defeated all of you fighting him at once, and managed this when he was not even in his true form. It was him, yes, but diluted through his possession of Talan. His real self was likely hundreds, maybe thousands, of miles away. Perhaps he was not even in the Old Country that night. And this is the sort of power he can wield? One that can transcend the boundary between the realms?"

She fell silent, as if waiting for me to answer the question. But I couldn't, of course; I could say nothing. My heart raced as I listened to her, this creature speaking godly words with my mother's voice. For they *were* godly—every sentence shivered against my skin with the weight of ages.

"Gareth told me of this curse, this *ytheliad*," she went on. She shook her head, her mouth thin. "I don't doubt that we created such an abomination when we were young and stupid, drunk for millennia on our own power. But I remember nothing of it now, nothing that can help you. Whatever knowledge I hold of it is buried deep within me, perhaps lost forever, or else it might take years for me to uncover it. And what would this monster do, I wonder, this Kilraith, if he discovered there was a resurrected god in Edyn? A god who is still remembering how to be a god? Would he try to bind me as he did Talan? Or would he kill me outright? I would rather be dead than bound. But from what the others told me, I do not think he would kill me. I think he would want to use me."

She closed her eyes, set down her cup. "Poor Talan," she said quietly. "The things he has seen, the things he was made to do…those wounds will never heal."

I bristled at the hopelessness in her voice. "You underestimate the strength of his love for Gemma, and hers for him. Whatever wounds they live with—some of which you yourself inflicted—they will learn from each other how to heal. They already are."

Philippa opened her eyes and looked at me. "You speak of love with such conviction. It warms me to hear it. My little bird, with her song of starlight."

Her expression was soft with affection, and the sight of it revolted me. A woman and a god; my mother and yet not. The contradictions were too many and too overwhelming: my mother's voice, my mother's body, Kerezen's words of portent, her ability to heal a shattered physical form. Wardwell, hidden from everyone and everything except for us, her daughters, because our human bodies carried, as hers did, the blood of a god. Her ward magic had admitted us easily, had called to us in that northern forest.

And Ankaret? How did she fit into this puzzle? The ward magic of my mother's secret home had either allowed her passage, or she was powerful enough to override it.

The feather, pressed against my torso, suddenly felt like a brand on my skin.

I shoved back from the table and stood. "Don't look at me like that. I am not your little bird."

She smiled, her eyes glazed with memory. "Do you remember the first concert you gave at Ivyhill? I do. Merrida Jan-Tokka's *Sonata for an Autumn Morning*. What a gorgeous piece of music, though no one had ever played it as beautifully as you. And do you remember what I said to you afterward?"

Of course I did, though I hadn't thought of it since arriving at Wardwell. It was one of many memories of my happy childhood that I had tried in vain to forget, for every recollection brought with it a twist of pain.

"Your music, little bird..." Philippa whispered, remembering.

"Will give the gods new life," I finished. A chill swept lightly across my skin. "Did...did I..."

Philippa laughed. "Did you resurrect me? No, darling, though don't you see? Even then, before the great changes began in me, part of me knew exactly who and what I was. And therefore part of me knew who and what you and your sisters were too: daughters of a goddess and a very human, very frustrating man."

That last remark left me burning with fresh anger. "Don't speak of him," I whispered. "Don't you dare speak of him. You don't know what your leaving did to him. You can't imagine."

It was as if she'd not heard me. She leaned across the table, her hands open to me, as if hoping I'd take the opportunity to grab on. "Stay here with me, my Farrin," she said. "Convince the others that they must too. My Mara, my little Gemmy. If anyone can persuade them to stay, it's you."

"Absolutely not."

"It's safer here, don't you see? Whatever's going on out there in the world, it hasn't touched Wardwell. It hasn't touched me. Here, I can protect you. We can learn about your powers, all of us together. I can teach you what I've learned. In this sanctuary, we can truly become ourselves."

"I couldn't possibly—"

"Remember what you saw yesterday?" she interrupted. "Remember how you struck me, my strong, angry girl? Perhaps a human would have died from such a blow to the head, but I didn't. I healed myself in an instant, right before your eyes. You saw it. Imagine being able to protect yourselves in such a way. It's in you somewhere, all of you, latent but alive. You are the daughters of Kerezen and therefore demigods of the body, of the senses. Fighting and creating glamours and making music—these things you can already do. But there is more buried in your power, and I can help you find it."

Her words shook me; they seemed to me cousins of Ankaret's earlier warnings. *War is coming*, she had said. *Do not fear your blood's old power, Farrin of the gods.* And yet I could see no guile on Philippa's face, nothing that told me she had even the slightest idea what had happened to Ryder and me in the forest. My heart sank. Only then did I realize that part of me had been hoping the whole thing *had* been some sort of game, some outrageous deception designed by Philippa as a punishment for breaking her jaw.

"You already spoke to the others, it seems, and they gave you their answer," I said sharply, biting off each word as if my very teeth and tongue could conquer the fear roiling inside me. "Well, that's my answer too. You may be able to stay here and ignore a world that needs you, but we cannot."

I felt lightheaded with rage, tempted to pull the feather out of my dress and summon Ankaret to me right then and there, if such a thing were truly possible. *Burn this woman*, I would tell her. *She is hateful, she is evil. Reduce her to ashes so I never have to hear her voice again.*

Blinking back tears, I stepped away from the table. "We're leaving in the morning. I trust that with all your many mighty powers, you'll be able to devise a way to speak to us, or come to us, if you ever change your mind and decide to be useful. But I suspect you won't. I think you're too selfish to do anything you don't want to do, even for the sake of those you love, much less to help innocent strangers. If the other gods are like you, I sincerely hope they're still dead."

With that, I turned and left her.

Ryder was awake when I returned to my room. He still lay on that ridiculous small couch, pretending to sleep, but I could hear the truth in his breathing.

"Ryder," I said, crying. It was all I could say. I was so angry I could hardly breathe; my chest ached with too many memories, too many fears all fighting for air. He came to me at once, joined me in the bed. He held me close to him, his hands gentle in my hair, and we slept, the feather pressed between us, thrumming its strange, quiet heat against my skin.

CHAPTER 17

We returned to Ivyhill over the next few days, an excruciating journey south through forest and greenway. Ryder found the horses not far from where we'd left them, grazing contentedly in a scrubby mountain meadow, and we rode them back to Vallenvoren. I traveled in a sort of numbness, punctuated on occasion by seething jolts of anger. Philippa could have made our journey home shorter, easier—of this I was certain, as certain as I had reluctantly become of her godliness. I couldn't stop thinking about her broken jaw snapping back into place, the horrific sound of it like a great branch breaking.

But she sent us from Wardwell without aid—a punishment, I assumed, for refusing to stay. As my sisters and I walked through the slippery curtain of the ward magic—Mara silent and grave, Gemma crying quietly, the men following shortly afterward—the disturbing thought occurred to me that Philippa could have forced us to stay. I supposed I should be grateful for her mercy, but instead I felt only resentment.

When at last we arrived at Ivyhill, we were without Mara, who had returned to Rosewarren. I hoped her absence had gone unnoticed by the harried Warden; to me, the loss of Mara after days spent in her company stuck in my throat, an ache that wouldn't budge. I couldn't imagine not knowing where she was every moment of every day, if we were ever lucky enough to once again live in the same place. But then, I loved Mara. What did the Warden feel for her Roses? Surely not love, or at least not the same kind. An instinctive possessiveness of the chicks in her care, perhaps. I didn't think the Warden was capable of actual affection.

We'd all spoken on the way home, in those strange quiet days in the northern forest before we'd reached Vallenvoren, and Ryder and I had told the others of Ankaret. Gareth was eager to return to the university and his research—of Ankaret, of the concept of godly resurrection, of the *ytheliad* and the Three-Eyed Crown. Gemma would go with him—eager, I think, to avoid Ivyhill and its memories in the wake of so much time spent with our mother—and Talan would return to his travels, now searching for rumors that might point to the existence of other gods come back to life.

Demigods. The word haunted me with every step I took, every breath I drew. What did it mean, for the blood of a god and the blood of a human to live in one being? Had such a thing ever happened before? Were there other demigods elsewhere in the world, born of humans and gods in human shells? Gods who were only just now awakening, as Philippa was?

The weight of my innumerable questions pressed down on my shoulders, making them ache. They would need to be answered, but who could we trust with such information? The Warden? Yvaine? Gareth's many books?

I told myself that nothing could be done until I'd slept. From the steps of Ivyhill, our weapons and supplies heaped at my feet, I watched the others in the violet-tinged evening light. A chill breeze gusted across the drive, rustling the manicured lawn edged with golden autumn blooms. Gemma and Talan were saying a tearful goodbye at the mouth of the hedge maze. I was glad I couldn't hear them; I didn't think my brittle heart could bear the added weight of their sadness.

One of Ryder's wilded ravens, tired and homesick, had found us on our journey south. It was one of the many he'd sent off in search of Alastrina, but it had brought him nothing—no news, no leads. I wouldn't soon forget the sound of its mournful cries. Now Ryder was speaking to the creature, preparing it for a new mission: to be Talan's companion, to guard and guide him as he roamed the world listening for gods. He held the raven in his cupped hands as if it were a treasure. I couldn't hear his voice from where I stood, but I could imagine it— low and gentle, the rhythm of whatever bestial language he used like a cool wind rushing through dark trees.

Then I heard a quiet cough behind me—Gareth, clearing his throat. I turned to see him standing awkwardly in the entrance hall beside Gilroy, who worried his hands together. His bushy black eyebrows were furrowed in obvious distress. My stomach sank to see him in such a state. I knew before he said a word what it must have meant: something was wrong with my father.

I hurried to them, but before I could utter a word, a door opened to my left, and a column of firelight spilled across the floor. Father stood in silhouette at the threshold of the morning room, posture slumped, shirt untucked, hair in greasy disarray.

"You're back," he slurred, his voice hoarse as if from disuse. "I wasn't sure you would return."

Gareth touched my arm, but I shook him off. I could handle my father.

I joined him in the morning room, shutting the door quietly behind us. The air reeked of drink. Empty glasses stood on tables and lay strewn across the floor. That our staff hadn't collected them told me Father hadn't allowed them in, perhaps not for days. I could picture it clearly—he'd call for them, ask for a drink, and make them leave it outside. Once they were gone, he'd push open the door just enough to retrieve the glass, then shut it again.

I knew the ritual. I'd seen it many times over the years since our mother had left.

As I watched him stumble to his chair by the crackling hearth, my heart twisted, warring with itself. I saw him clearly—how pathetic he looked, and how embarrassing, how unworthy of any of us. And yet I loved him still. I had spent years loving him through every mess he'd made, every danger he'd put us in; I didn't know how to stop.

But for the first time, I found myself wishing I could.

He fell heavily into his chair, gestured at the one across from him. "Sit, then, and tell me: Have you fucked the Bask boy yet?"

The words were meant to shock me, and they did; meant to infuriate me, and they certainly did that. But greater than my shock and anger was a wrenching pity. The sight of him brooding drunkenly before me compared to the memory of Philippa, clear-eyed and mighty, luxuriating in her isolated paradise—the contrast was stark, even humiliating. What would she think of him, if she saw him now? I felt fiercely glad that she'd insisted on staying at Wardwell.

I didn't sit; I stood behind the other chair, keeping it between us.

"Have you eaten today?" I asked him.

He glared at me, bleary-eyed. "I asked you a question."

"And I refuse to answer it." I kept my voice calm. "It's good to see you. I missed you while we were gone."

He laughed. "There's no need to lie. You've never been good at it, anyway."

He was right. I wore everything I felt on my face, though I'd always tried my best to hide it with a scowl, a forbidding glare. Such looks were considered off-putting, especially on a woman—a ridiculous opinion held by much of high society that I'd always used to my advantage.

Still, I tried again. "How is Ivyhill? Has Byrn made any progress with Jet?"

"Answer my question, Farrin."

I clutched the back of the chair. My palms felt clammy. "I'll send for supper. I'm sure Mrs. Rathmont can easily warm something for you—"

He surged to his feet with such sudden violence that it shocked the breath out of me. "Answer my question, Farrin!" he roared, and then he flung his drink at the fire. The glass shattered against the mantel; pieces of it went flying across the carpet.

A deafening silence fell. He glared at the fire, breathing hard. I couldn't move. I held on to the chair, a cold, sick feeling crawling slowly down my body. My heart raced with rabbit panic. I wanted to run; I'd shove the chair at him if I had to. Two thoughts occurred to me, one after the other: that I was a fool for having taken off my fighting staff, and that it was awful—and horribly sad—that I had to worry about such a thing in my own home.

Father stared at the mess he'd made as if he couldn't believe what had just happened. Then he looked over at me in horror.

"Gods..." he whispered. His shocked expression crumpled. "Farrin, I'm sorry..."

A moment later, the door to the morning room swung open so hard it hit the wall. Ryder stroke in, looking murderous; beyond him stood Gareth and Gilroy, and our wide-eyed housemaid Emry, carrying tea and sandwiches on a tray.

Ryder came to me at once. He didn't look at Father; he looked only at me.

"Farrin?" he said quietly. I knew he was angry, could feel the seething heat of it matching my own. But his voice was soft, his gaze on my face steady and calm. *I'm here, Farrin. I'm here with you. Farrin of the forest light.*

With his eyes on me, I could almost believe we were back in Wardwell's quiet wood, before Ankaret came, when it was only his arms around me and his strength holding me up, bolstering me, reminding me to breathe.

And suddenly I decided not to be there anymore. Not in that room, not in any room containing my father. Let him clean himself up, I decided. Let him clean up his mess and come apologize to me later, when he was sober and remorseful. Only then would I speak to him, and not a moment before.

My decision left me feeling lightheaded, like I'd stood up too quickly from a chair. I blinked back my tears, my chest aching with sadness and anger and a sort of disgusted, tired clarity. I looked up at Ryder and gave him a brave smile.

"Let's eat something," I told him. I held out my hand, and he took it gently in his own, his eyes soft on me. "I'm starving. And look, Emry's brought sandwiches. We'll eat in the dining room."

I walked away with my hand in his, shut the door to the morning room behind us, and didn't look back even once.

The next morning, Gemma and Gareth left for the capital at dawn. Neither of them wanted to be at Ivyhill for a moment longer than they had to. Our dinner the previous night had been a sober affair in the wake of Father's tantrum, and no doubt Gemma saw echoes of Talan wherever she went.

While Ryder worked with Jet at the stables, I busied myself with an endless list of tasks for most of the morning, determined not to think of either of my parents. Father had locked himself in his rooms upstairs, for which I was grateful. At least now the staff could clean the morning room. This was the single thought that ran coldly through my head on a loop, like a depressing prayer. *At least now the staff can clean the morning room.*

Then, at lunch, a letter came bearing the seal of the queen. I opened it with shaking fingers, expecting the worst: an edict of exile, a letter from Thirsk telling me that Yvaine's illness had gotten much worse.

But the letter held only Yvaine's familiar looping handwriting.

Dearest Farrin,

I'm writing this with Thirsk hovering irritably over my shoulder. In fact, he just let out a grunt of disapproval. But the important thing is, I'm feeling much better, and given that, I've been able to explain to Thirsk and my other advisers how furious I am with them for turning you away from the Citadel. I've shown them the error of their ways. You are always welcome here, and in fact I've drawn up an official letter, signed by all members of the Royal Conclave, that grants you and your sisters and your friends admission to the Citadel whenever you wish it. No guard will turn you away. Thirsk has reluctantly agreed that I am of soundest mind, and therefore neither he nor anyone else can in good conscience protest my decision. I hope this letter brings you some comfort. I've missed you.

And because I've missed you so terribly, I'm throwing a party the day after next to celebrate your return. You will come to my party, won't you? And do bring Gemma with you, and Ryder too. His quick thinking the night of your poisoning saved your life, and therefore he is dear to me. And I suspect you would be glad to have him with you. What a fearsome beast of a man he is, and yet he held you so tenderly that night as you came back from the brink of death. I certainly

*understand the attraction. Bring him, then, so I might get a
closer look at him and officially grant my approval.*

Yours,
Yvaine

I read the letter with my heart in my throat, relieved and amused
and yet feeling the faintest twinge of unease. I hurried out to the stables and thrust the letter at Ryder before I could think better of it. I
waited for him to read it, and when he was finished, his eyes lifted
to meet mine, and a delicate thrill of nerves skipped down my back.
Words from the letter had stuck in me, fluttering frantically in my
chest like pinned butterflies. *Attraction. Approval.* As if Yvaine had
looked at us and decided something that we ourselves had not yet put
into plain words.

But I shook those thoughts away as best I could. The more important thing was the letter's tone—a little arch, a little unbalanced. A
slight thing, and yet it worried me. *I've shown them the error of their
ways*, she'd written. *I am of soundest mind.* Brief, almost casual decla-
rations woven through a letter that on its surface seemed innocuous
enough. And yet reading it had left me feeling discomfited in more
ways than one.

"We'll go, of course," I said. "Unless you'd rather return to
Ravenswood? I'd thought you might, after being gone for so long."

Ryder's laughter was dark and quiet. He handed the letter back to
me. "No. I don't want to go home. There's nothing for me there. I've
left behind instructions for our staff, for our tenants. They know what
villages to monitor, how to distribute aid when necessary. And Father,
for all his faults, has never neglected those particular duties, so…" He
paused, his expression shuttered. "No. There's nothing for me there."

I sensed he wanted to say more—Alastrina's name hung unspoken between us, lonely and dear—but instead he turned back to Jet in silence, his shoulders high and tense, a shroud of sadness enveloping him. I hesitated; perhaps it was too bold a thing to do. But then I thought of Gemma rushing at Talan whenever she first saw him after he had been gone, showing him her unabashed, untempered joy. What a beautiful thing it must be, I thought, to receive love like that, to be able to *give* such love.

So I went to him before he had the chance to turn around. I wrapped my arms around him and held him close, burying my face in the warm, broad stretch of his back. I closed my eyes and through the press of our bodies tried to send him everything I felt, everything I wanted him to feel: *I don't know why your home makes you so sad, but I'm sorry it does. Wherever Alastrina is, your love for her will give her strength. I wish I could take your sadness from you, and your anger, so that you might know peace. Thank you for the way you looked at me in the morning room last night, telling me without words that I was safe, that I was brave. Thank you. Thank you.*

Ryder's hands came up to hold mine, pressed them softly against his chest. Beneath my fingertips drummed his racing heartbeat, matching my own.

◆◇◆

The day of Yvaine's party, Ryder and I traveled to Fairhaven using the greenway that for generations had connected my family's home to the capital. This was not an occasion for pageantry, but rather for speed; both of us were tense and uncertain. What would we find at the Citadel? We would say nothing of Philippa, nor of Wardwell; knowledge of a resurrected god was our burden to bear and not Yvaine's, not with her sickness, and the sinkhole roaring quietly in the Citadel, and the country still grieving its lost. But would she sense the truth nevertheless, and if so, what would she do with it?

The city was quiet, yet its streets felt restless to me, as if behind closed doors and windows roiled storms I could not see. Portraits of those lost still papered the Citadel walls, but no protesters gathered there, and only bedraggled petals skipped across the ground where before there had been piles of flowers. The city was tired; its exhaustion was heavy in the air.

On the western horizon, a true storm gathered over the choppy gray waters of the Bay of the Gods. The churning sky was green and purple, the line of the storm's approaching front a startling blue gray against the autumn trees, which gleamed red and gold. *Like Ankaret*, I thought, then quickly put the thought out of my mind, lest the mere act of thinking of her could summon her to me. I hadn't dared to leave her feather at Ivyhill; if it could truly bring her to our aid at any moment, with all her snapping fire, I'd be a fool to ever travel without it. And yet suddenly it felt careless to have come to the Citadel with such an item tucked into my dress. Would Yvaine sense its presence at once, demand an explanation? I had to hope that the feather would protect itself, remain quiet and hidden unless I decided to use it.

Guards ushered us into the Citadel and escorted us to the queen's tower without issue. No advisers came to intercept us, bearing sobering news—the queen was in fact quite ill and could not be seen; the queen was dead; the queen had disappeared, abducted by whatever phantom evil roamed the land. The cavernous marble halls were eerily quiet; our footsteps, and the clanking ones of the guards escorting us, echoed like thunder in a lonely canyon.

But then we arrived at the tower, and the doors swung open as we turned the corner, as if Yvaine had been standing on the other side, waiting for us. Her receiving rooms were a riot of color. Brilliant purple silks hung from the rafters; luxurious velvet cushions of midnight blue and periwinkle lay scattered across the gleaming floors. There were revelers everywhere, most of whom I recognized: fluttering courtiers and gregarious merchants' children, some of Yvaine's favorite servants from the palace. Ostensibly this party was to celebrate my return to the Citadel, but no one looked up upon our arrival; they kept on with their singing and dancing, their drunken lolling by the windows thrown open to the evening. There was a giddy thrill in the air, a tremble in even the most jovial voices. *The queen is not ill, she is well, and we are here in her tower as favored guests. There is nothing to fear. Everything is fine and good. Can you believe it?*

"Darling Farrin," Yvaine said. She gathered me to her in a whirl of white hair and ruffles of lilac chiffon, her breath sweet with wine. Her fingers were like claws, digging desperately into my flesh through the thin fabric of my plain gray gown. "I can't tell you how happy I am to see you. Thirsk has apologized a hundred times for sending you away, but I'm not sure I'll ever forgive him."

I held her, noting with alarm how thin she felt in my arms, and how hot, as if she burned with fever. Each word she spoke was breathless and nervy.

I pulled back from her a little, searched her face. I saw the shadows under her eyes, her chapped pink lips. "How are you? Have you been sleeping?"

She dismissed my concern with a wave and looked past me at Ryder. She smiled to behold him looming there at the doors—bearded and scowling at all the merriment around him, looking deeply uncomfortable even though, in his blue-and-black finery, he was as grandly dressed as any guest of the queen.

"Lord Ryder," said Yvaine, extending her hand. "I'm so glad you came too."

There was no reason not to believe her—she had asked for him in her invitation, after all—yet I heard a slight edge in her voice. She watched Ryder with curiosity, her eyes sparkling, as he bowed his head to kiss her offered white fingers, each one heavy with pearlescent jewels.

"Your Majesty," he intoned. "You honor me with your invitation. It is…" He hesitated, glanced around. His implacable expression gave nothing away. "It is a marvelous party, to be sure."

Yvaine burst out laughing. "Oh, Ryder. There's no need to lie. It's awful here—everyone's far too loud, and they've made a mess of my rooms. But Thirsk is funny like that. All my advisers are. They seem to think a party is less of a danger to me than an Ashbourne on her own. Isn't that odd?" When her eyes cut to mine, their hard glitter softened. "So, a party it is, if that's what I must do to see my friend. I do hope Gemma will join us too, and Gareth as well, if they can bear to pull themselves away from their books."

Then, before I could reply to any of this, Yvaine grabbed my hand and pulled me into the room, past the crackling hearth and the tables piled high with plates and goblets, the fiddlers in the corner, the dancers spinning beside them. There was laughter everywhere, and someone was playing a jolly reel on a piano in an adjoining chamber. Yvaine's guests called out to us in greeting as we passed; I gave them only the barest distracted replies. I was too focused on Yvaine. She darted through the room like a newborn lamb, her gait unsteady. Her hand was sweaty around mine, her grip hard. I glanced back once at Ryder, who was following us, and saw in his thoughtful frown that he was thinking the same thing: something was wrong. Yvaine was not as well as her letter had said. My stomach dipped, unsettled; I wondered what exactly she'd said to her advisers—what she'd done—to make them relent and allow my return.

She led us to a corner of the room adorned with cushions and blankets, lit by a crystal chandelier that spun slowly, casting soft fragments of light across the floor. She sat on a tasseled burgundy chair, grabbed a flute of sparkling wine from a passing servant's tray, and knocked it back in one gulp.

I reached for her in alarm, words of caution on my lips, but she started talking before I could say a word.

"So, tell me, my gallant champions, my eyes and ears," she said, looking back and forth between us, "what is the latest news from out there in the world? What evil forces have you rooted out and conquered in my name?"

Flummoxed, I at first said nothing. A hundred different answers came to mind—resurrected gods, Ankaret, Wardwell tucked away in the northern forest, Gemma and Mara and me, all demigods—but I dared not voice any of them.

Ryder spoke first. "This is hardly the place to discuss such matters, Your Majesty. With so many people about—"

"No, of course, you're right." Yvaine waved her hand, silencing him. She watched two dancers whirl by, something pensive on her face. They were drunk and laughing; they knocked over a small table and sent glasses crashing to the floor, which made them laugh harder.

The sound made me flinch; I thought of Father locked in his rooms at home, the glass flying against the mantel, his roar of fury.

Yvaine jumped to her feet and reached for me, her eyes shining. "Dance with me," she said abruptly. "Won't you, Farrin?"

Quite lost for words, I glanced at Ryder, who looked deeply unhappy, and let Yvaine pull me to my feet with a flutter of fear in my chest. We whirled about the room, and those gathered cheered us on, raising their glasses to us, urging the fiddlers to play faster, and faster. The musicians were competent enough, though their instruments could have used a good tuning, but I didn't have time to ponder that for long. Yvaine didn't allow it. I could hardly keep up with her; she was so light in my arms I thought she might fly away with every step. The changes in her made me feel sick at heart—how thin she was, how her every movement was frantic, edgy. At last, the song finished, and we returned to our little corner. Yvaine grabbed another drink and flopped down onto a luxurious emerald-green cushion. Panting, grinning, skin damp with perspiration, she looked up at me, then at Ryder.

"Now you," she said, gesturing at us. She shot Ryder a playful smile, but her fingers trembled. "I know you want to. Dance, and show me how good you look together."

I wanted desperately to do anything else; Yvaine's snappish voice belied her indulgent smile. But what were we to do? Our queen had commanded us to dance.

Ryder stood, and so did I. I couldn't look at him; in his direct blue gaze, I knew I would see all my discomfort, all my worries, reflected back at me, and I wasn't sure I could bear that. What was happening here? Yvaine was even less herself than she had been the last time I'd seen her, when she'd murmured those strange words: *Moon by day, fire by night. Come and dance. Don't try to fight. The beauty of shadows, the garish sunlight. Spin for the watchers, their revels so bright.*

Moonhollow. The word danced through my mind on slippery heels. The fiddles were playing a slower song now, a little melancholy. I clung to Ryder as we danced, letting him lead me with his easy strength. He was a surprisingly graceful dancer, sure-footed and confident. His hand at my waist was firm, and the heat of him was intoxicating—not fevered and strange like Yvaine's, but steady, comforting, like a lit hearth in winter. When we finished dancing, I squeezed his hand gratefully. Moving with him had cleared my mind.

We returned to Yvaine, who sat regarding us over the rim of her goblet. Her expression was troubled, wistful; her eyes no longer held that hard gleam. Then she nodded to herself, as if something had been confirmed for her, and said to Ryder, "Tell me about Ravenswood." Her voice was grave now, almost solemn. "I've been there before, but it's been many years."

Ryder looked surprised. He glanced at me, then back at Yvaine.

"It's…cold. Not as far north as some other places, but high enough in the mountains that the wind often cuts you. The mansion has forty-two rooms, and everything is made of black stone. We have five stables, and our forests stretch for miles—"

"No, no. Not the house. Tell me about your life at Ravenswood. Your…" Yvaine hesitated, and I saw a glimmer of her normal, steady self, a flash of pity and kindness. "Your sister, Alastrina. You grew up together in those halls. You were close. You always have been."

At the mention of his sister, Ryder's expression closed. "Alastrina," he repeated flatly. "You want to know about Alastrina."

Yvaine looked away, took a sip of her wine. "They've been coming to the Senate hall every day," she said quietly. "The families of those who were taken. They tell me everything about the lost, trying to make me love them as they do, I suppose. They don't understand that of course I already do. The whole world is my home, every creature my child."

She took another sip, and her voice hushed even further, her gaze distant and flat. "They plead with me to do something, and every time I must deflect them without frightening them. I can't tell them how I search and search for the taken, stretching my power as much as I dare, and yet find nothing. I can't tell them about the sinkhole, about my illness. What would they think? They would be even more afraid, and there are already rumors enough." She touched her temple, her fingers unsteady.

"More recently," she went on, "these people have been making petitions to my councils, because Thirsk and the others, the Royal Conclave, haven't let me attend their sessions. They fear the distress of these people will distress *me*. And of course it will. It *does*, and it should. I went to the Senate hall today, despite their protests. I told them I would banish them from Gallinor if they tried to stop me. They believed me. I think I sounded very fearsome when I said that.

I knocked Lady Bethan off her feet with only my voice. I didn't mean to. She cried for hours afterward."

The matter-of-fact way she said it made my blood run cold. Yvaine was usually careful to disguise her might from us all. It was a kindness, I'd always thought, a way to make us feel safe in the presence of something unthinkable—a human chosen by the gods to be a queen. But tonight she seemed almost relieved to speak of such things so candidly. Her words were tired, blunt.

She looked up at Ryder, silently imploring. "But no one has come to speak for Alastrina—not yet, anyway. So I want to hear it from you, if you'll grant me that gift. Tell me about her, and about you."

Ryder sat in silence for a moment, his mouth thin. Then a cold ripple of power swept over us—a power of compulsion, urging us wordlessly forward. Yvaine didn't look ashamed; she fixed Ryder with an even, unblinking look.

He spoke then, reluctantly, which made me think the nudge she'd given him was only a small one. Yet still I felt sick to see it happen, to hear his rough voice and know he had no choice but to use it.

"There isn't much to tell," he began. "It's a simple story. My father is a cruel man. He always has been. Like Lord Gideon"—he glanced at me, a slight apology in his eyes—"he was ruled for years by Kilraith's will, by the machinations of every demon he held in his thrall. And so was his father before him, and his father before that. When you are raised in a house of violence, it is all too easy to become violent yourself."

Ryder drew in a shaky breath. "My father's moods were capricious. I woke every morning not knowing if it would be a day of terror or of peace. If a blizzard came, would that be enough to send him raging? If he slew a big enough stag while on a hunt with his men, would that buy us a few hours of quiet? Mother took the brunt of his anger, when it came. When we were little, Trina and I were too frightened to fight for her. We quickly found all the best places to hide—every cupboard, every dark corner, every loose floorboard. This was how I learned to be quiet, to move with stealth. Trina made it a game. The worst days were when Father sent his men to search the house for us while he roared at them from downstairs to hurry up, to not be so stumbling and stupid. *Just be very quiet*, she told me on those days, both of us crammed into a kitchen pantry full of pots and pans, or a wardrobe behind our dead grandmother's dresses. *Be very quiet, and they won't be able to find us. Not here. Not ever.*"

Listening to him, I could hardly breathe, my chest knotting up with breathless sadness. I had known none of this. Had my parents known, and walled up Ravenswood in that cursed forest for years even so? My stomach dropped to think of Ryder and Alastrina and poor Lady Enid trapped in a house they couldn't escape, locked up with a father and husband who was more terror than man. It was suddenly, heartbreakingly clear to me why Ryder had chosen not to use the name his father had given him.

"She protected me," Ryder said, quieter now. "She was afraid too, of course she was, but she didn't let me see it. I was her little brother. Protecting me was more important than being afraid. Later…"

He paused, swallowing hard. I wanted to spare him this revelation, to yell at Yvaine to stop it, to free him, but I couldn't speak, and I wondered with a spark of fury if she'd done that too. If she'd known I would protest and had seen to it that I couldn't.

I couldn't look at her, too angry to bear the sight of her. Instead I looked at Ryder, right at him, only at him: his dark beard, his bright eyes, the little scar above his eyebrow, his hands in fists on his thighs. My heart was in my throat, every inch of me bursting with a tenderness so fierce it made me dizzy. I knew what it was to live like a shadow in your own house, to not know when you woke what the day would bring—a father lost in his own despair or a father who remembered to eat, to change his clothes, to love you as he should.

"Later," Ryder began again, "as we got older, it became more difficult to hide, but it also became easier to fight him. Alastrina and I befriended every animal in the forest; there was little else to do. And we made them hate him, and he grew afraid of them, would sometimes lock himself up in his rooms for fear that some forest cat would come for his throat when he wasn't looking. And we were tempted to make that happen. The deaths we imagined for him, each more gruesome than the last. But Mother..."

He shook his head, shut his eyes. "She forbade us from it. She's an Anointed beguiler, and her talent is narrow but powerful: persuasion. Every time we neared the brink, hungry to kill him at last, she would turn her magic on us—some spell, some clever working of language—and convince us it was folly to turn on him. He was the lord of the house. He'd given us life. She *loved* him." He spat the words. "Incredible, what sorts of lies a mind will conjure up just to survive."

He fell silent then, and after a moment the slight pressure in the air disappeared. Yvaine had released us. She leaned back into her cushions, her face carefully blank. She looked between us, reading us. I hoped she could see how angry I was, how utterly the whole strange evening had unnerved me. I grabbed Ryder's hand and held it fiercely. He sat slumped in his chair beside me, spent from the telling, and I hoped that the grip of my hand would bring him some small comfort, some scrap of strength.

Yvaine's gaze fell to our joined hands. I thought she would say something; her pale brow furrowed as if she were thinking something over very hard. But then the oblivious dancing crowd near us parted, and a harried-looking adviser bustled over—Lady Goff, with her smooth brown skin and her head of dark braids. She shot me a watchful sort of look, then bent and whispered something to Yvaine that I couldn't hear.

Yvaine listened, nodded, then rose sedately from her cushion, the folds of her lilac skirt cascading into place around her. "I'm sorry to leave so suddenly, but I am needed downstairs," she said, not quite looking at either of us. She cautiously put her hand on Ryder's shoulder. "Thank you, Lord Ryder, for sharing that with me. I hope you..."

She hesitated, then looked at me beseechingly. "I envy you," she said quietly. "I envy you both. Hold on to each other. And you're... you're welcome, of course, to stay here as long as you wish."

I couldn't make sense of it—how scattered she was, how obviously, horribly sad. I thought she might be ashamed of what she'd forced Ryder to do and gave her a pointed look—*apologize, now*—but she said nothing and instead let herself be led away. I dug my fingernails into my palms as I watched her go, dangerously close to jumping up and making some sort of scene, demanding she make amends in front of everyone. Never mind her too-thin shoulders, bared by the ruffled gown; never mind the way she leaned on Lady Goff as they hurried out of the room. Using her power to protect her people was one thing; brandishing it to force a grieving man to recount his sad family history was quite another. The next time I saw her, I would tell her as much. No champagne, no advisers. She would apologize and mean it, or I would leave the Citadel and never return.

In her wake, we sat in exhausted silence. I let Ryder have a few moments of peace before I turned to him, feeling bold and brave, and said, "My rooms are nearby. They'll be ready for me, and no one will disturb us. Would you like to go there with me?"

The relief on his face made my heart swell. I wanted to wrap him up in a blanket and protect him from the world—this big burly man with a boy's broken heart.

He took my hand. "Please, Farrin."

—◆—

My rooms were quiet and clean—the fire crackling, the bed turned down, a plate of sandwiches and a pitcher of lemon water on the table by the bathing room. I fussed about nevertheless, tidying blankets that didn't need tidying, straightening rugs that were perfectly straight. In the private haven of my rooms, with a breeze fluttering the curtains and no noise to distract me from my thoughts, my courage from before seemed foolish and slight. Ryder's body took up too much space in the room, turned it unfamiliar. It was not altogether an unpleasant feeling; in fact, it thrilled me. I trembled with anticipation, feeling on the edge of something I couldn't name.

I poured myself a glass of water and then one for Ryder. I gave it to him, shaking a little, not looking at him. What did I expect to happen here? I should go into the bathing room, use that as an excuse. I needed a bath, he could make himself comfortable on the sofa, and I would see him in the morning.

"Farrin, please don't worry." He set the glass on the table, then did the same with mine. "I expect nothing. Just being here with you is all I need to be content."

He took my hands in his, so gentle I wanted to cry. All of it made me want to cry—Yvaine's strangeness, Ryder's horrible story. The image of him hiding in a cupboard with Alastrina, their fingers over their lips. *Let's count to one hundred and see just how quiet we can be.* Most of all, I wanted to cry because being so near Ryder was like standing on the edge of a cliff, the wind at my back and my toes curling in the dirt. I was going to fall, and the idea both frightened and exhilarated me. What sort of madwoman wanted to fling herself off a cliff into the unknown?

I put my arms around him, drawing him to me. "I'm so sorry," I whispered, which seemed far too pale a thing to say. So I touched his chest and reached up on my toes to kiss him. I decided I would press all my pity and tenderness, all my understanding, right into him. My touch, unpracticed and halting as it was, would tell him what my words were too small to encompass. My heart pounded hard in my ears, in my wrists, at the back of my throat. I pulsed with need and nerves, with a fear of what this could be, of what *we* could be. But then his lips were in my hair, his hands sliding gently down my back, and though I still trembled, I felt stronger, less afraid. Always, when he was near, I felt less afraid.

He led me to the bed, helped settle me among its feather pillows, its blankets of soft linen, and I drew him down to me, shaking all over, breathless with joy and wanting. The gentle firelight warmed his face, softening the faint lines that years of grief, fear, and anger had carved into his skin.

I wound my fingers into his dark hair and held him to me, kissed him until my head spun. The weight of him above me, the muscles of his back under my hands, sparked in me a feeling of simple, vivid joy. He drew his fingers lightly down my arms, making them prickle with goose bumps, and then circled his thumbs over my breasts, my ribs, my waist, learning with unending, focused patience every dip and curve. My gown was plain but fine, a gauzy gray, and through its silk I could easily feel the careful heat of his hands, every warm caress.

Then he moved lower down my body, dropping kisses on each pleat of my dress along the way, and began sliding his hands up my legs, under my skirts. I ached for his touch—my thighs were damp and trembling—and yet suddenly a fist of nerves seized me, and I went rigid, felt my heart began to race in a different way. Not with wanting, but with doubt.

With a gentle touch to his shoulders, I stopped him. I whispered, "Wait." He moved his hands away at once and came back to me. He pressed his brow to mine, breathing hard, a question on his face. Those eyes of his were soft and warm on my face, his lashes thick and dark.

The old fear had come back to me—my body, its frightening nakedness, how for so many years it had remained closed to me, stubbornly quiet. What would Ryder see if I bared myself to him completely? I couldn't answer that question. I'd spent so many years ignoring myself, tired and angry, every now and then futilely trying for release, that even now, as desperately as my body ached for his touch, I felt the familiar terror of the unknown. What did I look like under these clothes? Only Gareth could truly say, and it had been years since that night, and he didn't love me, and I didn't love him. Not like that. Not like this.

"Is it all right with you if we keep our clothes on?" I whispered. I closed my eyes, humiliated. What a question. He would think me a child, a cold fish. I couldn't look at him.

But then I felt him kiss me—my brow, the tip of my nose, the sharp curve of my chin—and I opened my eyes and saw him smiling down at me, tender and dear. No judgment on his face, no confusion.

"Of course," he said gently. He brushed my cheek with his thumb. I was crying; he dried my tears. "Farrin, look at me."

I obeyed, because I loved looking at him. I obeyed, because being told what to do, having the choice made for me, unwound some tight coil of fear within me. I was nervous, and still he wanted me. I was uncertain; he would be certain for both of us.

"You're beautiful," he told me, his gaze locked on mine. "Every day, every moment. Everything you wear, everything you don't. Every time I look at you, every moment I'm apart from you and have to imagine your face instead." He drew in a breath, let it out. He cradled my face in his hands, his eyes storm-bright. "Farrin, you're the most beautiful woman I've ever known. In the forest light, in the candle-light. Star of my life. You're perfect. I know you don't believe it, but someday you will. I swear it, you will. I'll make sure of it."

Chills raced up and down my body. *Star of my life.* A peculiar thing to say, but lovely, and also familiar in a way my fevered mind, fogged with desire, couldn't place. And then the thought was gone, bolting cheerfully away, because Ryder was lowering his mouth to mine and kissing me, and with that kiss, the last of my fear dissolved. I whispered my assent: "Yes, Ryder," I told him, feeling suddenly light as air and brave as I ever had. I wanted this; I wanted him. And I knew that at any moment I could say *stop*, and he would at once, without question. This most of all was the thing that helped me find my courage.

So I gave myself up to him, let him guide us both toward the cliff's edge. The thrill of it was astonishing—his kisses licking up and down my body like slow-burning fire; his hands holding mine, pinning me to the bed as he knew I loved; his palms sliding my skirts up my legs just enough, rolling down my tights just enough. He kissed my thighs, reached under my gown and drew light circles across my trembling belly. I whimpered something, some wordless plea, and the sound elicited from him a sharp, desperate groan. Quickly he undid his belt and loosened his trousers. Then, his mouth on my breasts through the thin bodice of my dress, the hard heat of him pressing inside me. His size matched the might of his muscles, and for a moment I gripped his shoulders in shock, stilling him.

He held himself over me, his arms shaking, and I breathed for a moment, eyes closed, until I was able to relax a bit. I nodded and said, "Please, it's all right now." I looked up at him with a smile, panting a little, shifting to accommodate him. "Really," I reassured him. "It's all right. I'm all right." Because, incredibly, I was. I laughed a little from the sheer joy of it; I arched up into him, wrapped my arms around him. His beard prickled my cheek, and I relished the feeling, rubbing against the soft bristle of it as a cat might.

And then he kissed me, so sweet and soft that I couldn't contain my happiness. I cried out against his mouth, a sob sticking in my throat. He began to move, his hips pressing slowly into mine, filling me, pushing with unhurried insistence against the glorious ache between my legs, and it was that—the care with which he claimed me, the incongruous gentleness of all that hard muscle—that began to unravel me. He slid one of his hands down my body to cup my backside and lift me slightly higher, an angle that brought him deeper inside me, and I cried out, overwhelmed, delighted, and when inspiration came, I didn't shy away from it. I tugged on his belt, which hung loosely at his hips, and whispered, "Tie my hands, Ryder. Tie them to the bed."

I made myself look up at him through the heat of my embarrassment, refusing to hide my face. I wanted to be completely under his control: my hands pinned, my hips cupped in his palms. Trapped beneath him, held immobile by his belt and by the force of him, the rhythm of him. I wanted this with a sudden clarity that left me giddy.

He blew out a sharp curse, then said my name—"Farrin, *gods*"— and went to work. He slid the belt free of his trousers with a swift snap, then used it—gently, such unbearable gentleness—to bind my wrists to the headboard. I tested its strength, tried to tug free, and couldn't. He was hard as steel against my thigh, hot and wet from our union, and I shuddered, feeling delicious, feeling delirious.

"Is it all right?" Ryder asked, his hands still hovering near mine. "I'll undo it in an instant, if you wish. Just say the word—"

"No, leave it," I breathed. The sensation of abandon, of giving myself up to him, left me dizzy, triumphant. This—yes, *this* is what I wanted. I didn't know what would come next, and it didn't matter; Ryder would choose for me, for us, and while in his arms I would always be safe.

I arched up a little, begging him silently to come back to me, and when he did—a swift, smooth thrust that made us both cry out—it was like coming home to a haven I'd never known. His breath came in hard bursts against my neck as we moved together; his voice broke on my name, and the sound of him so overcome, the feeling of my arms held in place, of his broad, muscled weight pressing me against the bed, shielding me from everything that could hurt me, left me undone.

A great wave of pleasure was building inside me, drawing me up into myself, into him—the sure grip of his hands, my name hoarse on his lips. I knew he was being gentle for me; I could feel the restraint in his body, how desperately he wanted more—more of this, more of me. Harder, faster. I ached to imagine it, my mind wild with a hundred fantasies all blurring together.

Our rhythm grew erratic and frantic, a thrilling respite for my metered, musical mind, and when we fell over the edge at last—one right after the other—I wasn't afraid. There was nothing to be afraid of, because he was with me. As I came apart beneath him, my vision went soft and dark, tinged with gold. Almost at once he reached up to tug the belt loose, freed my hands, whispered hoarsely to me, "Hold on to me, Farrin. Please, hold on to me," and I did, clinging to him as he shuddered in my arms.

"You're safe," I told him, without thinking. I knew only that it felt like the right thing to say. I threaded my fingers in his hair, kissed his rough cheek. "I've got you."

And as I held him, determined that he should feel in the fierce press of my arms all the kindness he'd been denied as a child, I decided that next time—*next time!*—I would like to try loving him with my tights all the way off. With my naked legs so freed, I could wrap them around him, pull him even closer to me, urge him deeper.

The obvious revelation made my cheeks burn, but I was too happy to be embarrassed for long. I laughed into Ryder's hair, flushed and damp beneath my rumpled dress. I turned my face up to his, felt him smile against my cheek—easy, open, his own laughter rumbling happy and deep between us—and let him kiss me.

CHAPTER 18

In the morning, I awoke sore and happy, and when I turned to find Ryder sleeping beside me, I had to stare at him, watching him breathe in and out, to convince myself that the night we'd passed together was real.

After a moment, he startled awake, but as soon as he saw me and remembered himself, he relaxed. He held out his arms, and I was glad to go to him, to burrow against the mountain of his body. I pressed my face to his chest and breathed in his scent: sweat and warm skin, a hint of wine, the sharp, sweet scent of our passion.

"Was I snoring?" he asked. I shivered to hear his voice, hoarse with sleep.

"You were not," I told him, "but your mouth was hanging open a bit."

He laughed. "What a sight to wake up to."

"In fact, if I've ever in my life woken up feeling so at peace in the world, I don't remember it."

I spoke the honest words into his shirt, part of me hoping the fabric would muffle my voice and he wouldn't hear me. But of course he did hear me and shifted us both so he could look at me, his blue eyes soft under that fierce dark brow.

"You honor me by saying such a thing," he said quietly. His gaze traveled over my face, and he shook his head in wonder. "What a vision you are in this bed."

I felt bashful at his attention, tried to dismiss it. "With my hair a mess, like a lion's mane, and my dress bunched up everywhere?"

"Yes, all of that," he replied, and when he drew me to him for a kiss, I felt lissome in his arms, a precious creature who deserved such affection and wouldn't ever be foolish enough to run from it. Such a new feeling—to know I was desired, to feel worthy of it. Lion-haired, trembling in my gray silk, I pulled Ryder close, and we moved together, quiet and slow, everything golden in the morning light.

Later, after we bathed and changed our clothes, we went downstairs to the queen's dining hall. A messenger had delivered a note: Yvaine requested our company at a private luncheon.

I approached the dining hall with trepidation. What would we find there? Had Yvaine come back to the party from her errand and been hurt to find us gone? Giddy as I was, the taste of Ryder's kisses lingering on my tongue, I still entered the room with a flutter of nerves in my throat, readying all kinds of excuses. We were tired, we'd had too much wine, the raucous noise of her guests had given me a headache.

Yvaine, however, wasn't there. Instead, Gemma and Gareth sat at the table, Gareth in a tie and a gray morning suit, Gemma wearing a pretty gown of sea-foam green with a slight sheen of copper to every fold.

I startled to see them and paused in the doorway. "Where's Yvaine?" I blurted out.

"We aren't sure," Gemma said, looking at me and then at Ryder with a pleased, assessing gaze that made me bristle. "We received a message at the university this morning telling us we were missed at last night's party and inviting us to luncheon, and came at once. That's all we know."

I nodded and said nothing, taking a seat across from Gareth. I didn't dare look at him. A servant in a violet tunic came over and offered me a bowl of cut fruit. I took it and began to eat at once.

Gareth cleared his throat. "So. How *was* the party, anyway?"

"Abysmal," Ryder muttered, "as all parties are."

"But the night wasn't a complete loss, I hope?"

Ryder tore a hunk from a hot buttered roll and began to eat with relish, a fearsome glare of warning his only answer.

Wisely, Gareth quieted, but he did touch his foot to mine under the table, and when I looked up at him, his expression was kind, not a teasing glance to be found. I felt a rush of gratitude and tapped his foot in answer. *Thank you.*

Then the doors opened, and Yvaine glided into the room. She looked fresh and calm at first glance—her hair done up in an elaborate knot of white braids, her gown a soft sky blue—but as she came closer, I saw the shadows under her eyes, even deeper than they had been the previous night, and a patch of skin on her lip that bled, freshly chewed. A sheen of sweat shone on her brow. She took her seat at the head of the table with a magnanimous smile, looking around at all of us while servants bustled about with platters and tongs, piling our plates high. Once they were finished, she dismissed them, and we five were alone with our crystal and silver.

"I'm so glad you could all join me for lunch," Yvaine said cheerfully. Her eyes darted over to me, not quite meeting my gaze. She made no move to touch her food.

Gareth dabbed the corner of his mouth. "Yes, thank you for inviting us, Lady Queen, and our apologies that we couldn't attend the party last night. We were quite caught up in our research, and before we knew it, the evening had gotten away from us."

"Research?" Yvaine asked mildly. "Remind me, what sort of research are you conducting?"

"We're reading everything we can about necromancy, Your Majesty," Gemma answered, watching the queen carefully. "We're hoping to unearth spellwork that might reinforce the body of my friend Nesset, who now lives at Rosewarren."

It was their cover story, and an entirely reasonable one, yet Gemma's words hung strangely in the air, as if not even the dining room itself was willing to believe what she had said. Yvaine stilled for an instant, her smile frozen. Then she grabbed a fork and speared a melon cube, popping it in her mouth. She looked ill, chewing it. It seemed to take great effort for her to swallow.

"Of course," she replied. "I remember now. Forgive me for needing the reminder. It's just that…well, you know how hard I've worked in recent months to watch over the city, given the…" She trailed off, frowning, and set down her fork.

"Given the sinkhole?" Ryder prompted.

Yvaine nodded. "Yes, the sinkhole. I've been concentrating so hard on reinforcing the beguilers' work and monitoring the city's borders, that it sometimes feels as if that is the entire world, and everything beyond is an illusion."

Absently, she traced the rim of her plate with one white finger.

"And is that…working?" Gareth said carefully. "All is well downstairs?"

The word made me sit up straight. *Downstairs.* Last night, Lady Goff had retrieved Yvaine from the party, and Yvaine had said, *I'm needed downstairs.*

And I'd been so distracted by everything—the party, her behavior, Ryder's nearness—that I hadn't even thought about what that meant.

"Yes," Yvaine whispered, "everything's quite in order. My beguilers are tireless. The sinkhole hasn't budged in three days." She looked up at me, smiling. "Isn't that wonderful, Farrin?"

I felt everyone's eyes upon me and struggled for what to say. "It is, Yvaine, and impressive. You've appointed your beguilers well. But…"

I hesitated. Now that we were alone with her, a thousand questions sat ready in my mouth, and yet I couldn't forget Yvaine's warning from two weeks prior: *I can't know anything you're doing, any leads you're following. It's too dangerous—for you, for me, for everyone.*

"You want to know about the draft," she said wearily, misinterpreting my silence. "The Senate is working out the language as we speak. They're being quite slow about it, and I can't blame them. Who wants to tell everyone in the country that they must send all their daughters to war against an evil they don't understand?"

"When will it take effect?" Gemma asked quietly. She was thinking of Mara, as I was.

Yvaine looked suddenly irritable. "I don't know. When they've finished, I suppose. Why do you all look so worried? Has Llyleth grown impatient and come after the Three-Eyed Crown? I warned her to do no such thing. I told her quite plainly, looked at her with my own eyes and watched her quake to hear my voice."

Llyleth. The Warden. I couldn't bring myself to feel sorry for the awful woman, and yet it wasn't like Yvaine to speak so callously of making someone cower, just as she'd bragged last night about making Lady Bethan weep.

"No, the crown is safe," Gareth began, before a slight jab from Gemma made him fall silent.

Yvaine leaned forward eagerly. "And you've been studying it, have you? Both of you? What have you found?"

I cleared my throat delicately. "Yvaine, you told me it wasn't wise to share such things with you—"

She shot me a ferocious glare. "I remember very well what I told you. But do not think that just because I love you, I will tolerate your interruptions."

Her words stunned us into silence. Breathing hard, her eyes glittering, she returned her attention to Gareth. Her mouth trembled as if she were fighting back tears.

"Tell me what you've found," she said, her voice low, and as she spoke, the air grew heavy around me, thick and cold, and I felt pinned to my chair, bound to it with invisible chains. I could see by the others' expressions, the way they went rigid, that it was the same for them.

"Tell me," she repeated, looking at Gareth. Her eyes flashed—one violet, one gold. Against her wan, slick skin, the pink scar on her brow looked angry and red, barely healed. "What have you found?"

Gareth looked suddenly green with nausea. I could see him fighting not to speak, but in the face of Yvaine's power he had no choice. The words came out of him roughly, as if tugged from the deep on a fisherman's line.

"While I was gone," he began, "Heldine continued our work. She is a beguiler with a particular talent for investigative spells." He drew in a ragged breath. "Her spellwork revealed colors, sounds, all of it gibberish," he continued. "What can a flash of blue tell you, or the shriek of a bird? But then I came back from—" *Wardwell*. He'd almost said it, his lips forming the word, but then he hesitated, swallowed. The tendons on his neck stood out from the strain of fighting Yvaine's magic. "When I came back, I brought Gemma with me."

"My power of working glamours has helped to unveil more of the crown's secrets," Gemma continued. Her eyes were closed; her fingers gripped the edge of the table, white-knuckled. "Just as I was able to that night in Talan's house. I saw beyond his flesh and bone to the crown beneath. I saw the truth in the lie and unraveled it."

She turned away, tight-lipped.

"And what truth did you see?" Yvaine persisted.

The pressure in the air grew colder, heavier. Beside me, Ryder let out a low grunt of pain.

"It's begun to bleed shadows," Gareth burst out, panicked. "Like furls of smoke from a dying ember. And Heldine and Gemma, they've managed to uncover in its shadows...shapes. Words. A flake of gold, a rod of metal. And I've translated the words. The shadows...they *whisper*."

Ordinarily, Gareth would've been elated to share such remarkable news—his eyes lit up behind his glasses, his blond hair a mess from having dragged his hands through it a hundred times. But now he looked terrified, as if each word being pulled from him was another glimpse of an approaching disaster.

"What do they whisper?" Yvaine said eagerly.

The sight of her—fervent and hungry, so clearly not herself—gave me the strength to push against the cold hand on my chest. Unbidden, an image of Ankaret flashed into my mind.

Do not fear your old power, Farrin of the gods.

You must use it even when you are angry.

You must use it even when you are afraid.

I began to hum quietly, a patchwork tune.

"Tell me what they whisper!" Yvaine shouted. "What do you see in these shadows?"

"An egg, a goblet..." Gareth trailed off.

"A key," said Gemma, her eyes full of tears. "A black lake under a full moon."

I couldn't bear seeing my sister's quiet distress. I forced open my mouth, urged my hum into a song. There were no words, and I didn't recognize the melody. It was new, a song composed out of my own desperation. At first my voice was thin, pressed flat by the queen's will. But then my thoughts went to Philippa: her portentous words, her broken body healing itself, the maddening calm of her voice as she sat smoking in her chair, telling us all those impossible things. *Demigods is the word.*

The memory gave me an angry burst of strength. My song grew, and my voice poured forth, a supple river of sound. Each wordless note made me feel mightier. I was a torrent, a storm surging toward the shore.

Yvaine's head snapped toward me, her eyes flashing, but when she tried to rise from her chair, the wave of my song pushed her back down. Baffled, she gasped for air. Her magic shot out in all directions, diverted from its course.

I stood, my legs shaking; I took a step forward, held my arms out to her. I gentled my voice. *It's all right. It's me, Yvaine. I'm here. Don't be frightened.*

But as she struggled there, confused and furious, groping through the fog of my song, a stray piece of her baffled magic lashed out wildly and caught me in the throat. It was like being struck by a bolt of icy air whistling down from the Unmade Lands in the farthest north.

The cold stole my breath. I lost hold of my song and staggered, stumbling into the table. Our uneaten lunch rattled. Five glasses of sparkling lemonade tipped over all at once; the tablecloth bled pink.

And when I tried to sing again, it wasn't music I found but a question, one of many I ached to ask but didn't dare to, one of the many secrets I had, until that moment, successfully kept from Yvaine. But even in its disarray, her magic was tenacious, willful. It found my question and tore it from my throat.

"What do you know about demigods?" I croaked.

Yvaine, reeling in her chair, grew suddenly very still. My song had muddled her; now she was fully awake, her eyes a bright fury of violet and gold. Shadows ripped across her face, contorting the sweet lines of her jaw, the delicate sweep of her brows.

"What do you know?" she whispered, her voice low and rasping. A horror. "What have you seen?"

I didn't know how to answer, couldn't even turn to the others and ask for help. I shook my head, tried to back away. But Yvaine was fast. She shouted, "What have you seen?" with such desolation that it sounded like agony, inexplicable heartbreak. She flew at me and tackled me to the floor. She shook me, knocking my head against the tile. I was too shocked to breathe, to speak. The impact rang in my ears, drowning out everything but Yvaine's furious screams.

"Tell me!" she said, tears streaming down her face, and yet that face was contorted in anger, in fear, and I couldn't decipher its ugliness. But whatever she wanted of me, she was desperate for it. "What have you seen?" she cried. "You lie, you're a liar! It's impossible!"

All the magic she'd used to compel the others was now rushing right at me, pinning me to the floor, flattening me. The weight of it would crush my bones. I began to gag, choking on my own bile. In a flash of hope, I remembered Ankaret's feather; I'd tucked it into my dress before coming to the dining hall, and now it flared hotly against my skin. *Use me*, it seemed to say. *Call for help*. But I was trapped under Yvaine and couldn't move my arms to grab it.

Vaguely, I saw Ryder and Gareth trying to pull Yvaine off of me. Ryder had something in his hands, a vase or a pitcher. He brought it crashing down upon Yvaine's shoulders, but that did nothing to deter her. She snarled over her shoulder at them and kept clawing at me, screaming at me. Other blurry shapes crowded into the room: advisers, guards, servants. Yvaine jerked her head at them and sent them all skidding away across the floor.

And then there was Gemma. Even as blackness crowded my vision, I could see her. Resplendent in her green gown, its copper patina gleaming, she flung her arms toward the far wall and then ripped them back toward us. Trees burst into the room, an explosion of autumn gold that shattered every window. Gnarled branches and great black roots snaked across the floor. I saw them out of the corner of my eye, reached desperately for them. They belonged to my sister; my sister would save me. I was beginning to fade. I saw my arm, streaked with my own blood.

Then the trees were upon us, guided by Gemma's sure hand. The roots grabbed Yvaine, tore her off of me, flung her across the room. I heard the sick crack of bone when she hit the wall, then screams of horror—her advisers, the terrified servants.

But all I knew in that moment was Gemma. She came to me and held me on the floor, cradling my bleeding body against hers. Her golden hair fell all around me, and the fabric of her dress was blessedly smooth and cool. I let her hold me, let my eyes fall closed.

"I've got you," she told me, her voice thick with tears. "My brave Farrin. You're all right. I'm here."

As she whispered comforts to me, it occurred to me that I was extraordinarily lucky. I had Gemma, I had Gareth, I had Ryder. They were all here, and they had fought for me. I opened my eyes, though the pain of my body was beginning to bloom like fire—all the places Yvaine had clawed at me, the bones she'd smashed against the floor—and through the haze of that pain, I saw Ryder looming nearby, shielding Gemma and me from the rest of the room. I heard Gareth talking to the panicked advisers, trying to explain. The idea made me want to laugh; how could any of this possibly be explained?

Then, without warning, the room shook. Ryder stumbled, nearly losing his footing. Someone screamed; a wave of shouts crested sharply. Gemma gasped, and when I turned in her arms, I saw Yvaine tearing across the room, knocking aside quaking servants, even Thirsk in his black robes. She raced out the door with a sharp, frightened cry, and I called after her, my voice breaking.

"Farrin, you can't," Gemma said, trying to keep me still, but I fought her, my head reeling with pain.

"Something's wrong downstairs," I gasped out. "The room

shaking...that's where she's going. We *have* to follow her. If the sink-hole...if she..." I couldn't finish. There were too many terrible scenarios to imagine. I looked up, reaching for him with desperation. "Ryder?"

At once, he scooped me up into his arms. Then we were out the door, Gemma and Gareth right on our heels. A crowd surged around us. Servants ran for safety; Lady Goff shouted commands at the guards. Lord Thirsk's panicked voice boomed distantly, giving an order to sound the lockdown alarms.

The path downstairs was strewn with bodies—guards, palace staff, anyone else who'd tried to stop Yvaine. Frightened as I was, my whole body throbbing with pain, I clung to Ryder and murmured a quick prayer to Kerezen, goddess of the senses and the body. In my exhaustion, those childhood teachings broke through all my determination to forget them. *Let them live*, I prayed. *Please let her not have killed anyone. She is not herself. Protect her.* I wouldn't remember until later that I'd been praying to my mother.

At last we reached the third subbasement of the Citadel, where the sinkhole raged. The inky churn of it, cut into the floor and raging like storm clouds, flashed blue and white and the vivid violet of Yvaine's left eye. Yvaine herself stood at the perimeter, arms stretched toward the high ceiling. The sinkhole's wind whipped her sky-blue skirts around her legs, tore her hair from its pins. She was working some great power; the air rippled with it, swirling, a violent heat mirage that distorted all shapes, all colors.

Guards flooded the cavernous stone room, their swords raised and their weapons trained on Yvaine—gilded crossbows, gleaming Lower Army rifles. Thirsk, hobbling after them, held a bloody cloth to his head and shouted at them to hold their fire. Then he hunched over and retched. Gemma ran past him and knocked a cowering servant out of the way just before a section of the ceiling came crashing down.

My heart thundered like the quaking room around us. I searched for the royal beguilers and found them scattered about, dazed but alive. Yvaine had thrown them back; she was keeping them away with a shimmering wall of her own magic, which rippled past her like a river. Brogan, the beguiler who'd been appointed to oversee the sinkhole's maintenance, crawled toward her, cradling a broken arm to his chest. Tears glistened on his cheeks. He shouted for Yvaine—I saw his mouth move—but I couldn't hear his words. Gareth hurried to him, helped him stand.

I pressed my lips to Ryder's ear. "Let me down," I told him, and he did at once, though he stood just behind me, holding me up. Together we staggered toward Yvaine, struggling to keep our balance as the floor pitched under our feet. A great wind whirled through the room with the sinkhole as its eye. With Ryder's hands on my waist, steadying me, I reached for Yvaine, screaming my throat raw. I didn't know what I could do to help her, nor did I care that she had hurt me. The thing that had beaten me hadn't been her. A single word spun wildly through my mind: *Kilraith. Kilraith.* Somehow he'd breached the Citadel. He'd sunk his claws into the queen. I fumbled at my bodice; I would use Ankaret's feather. Surely there couldn't be a better time.

But before I could do that, before we could reach Yvaine, everything exploded. A dark wave of shadows rushed out from the sinkhole, cold as death. The shadows flooded the room, obscuring my vision, stopping up my lungs; for a moment, I was a child back at Ivyhill, lost in a world of smoke, certain I would die.

Then a great burst of light erupted, clearing the room of all darkness and enveloping the sinkhole entirely. I screamed in terror, "No, *Yvaine!*" But a sucking silence swallowed my voice, and then a deafening boom ripped through the room—a hundred thunderclaps all at once. Ryder and I dropped to our knees, and he threw his body over mine, shielding me.

Silence fell. The world was dark; a distant clamor of bells began far above us. The Citadel had locked its doors, reinforced its wards.

For a few frantic heartbeats, I allowed myself to huddle under the heavy shelter of Ryder's body—his arms around me, his breath short and hard in my hair—and then I lifted my head and made myself look.

The sinkhole was gone. In its place, a jagged seam glimmered across the floor, faintly smoking. The sight of it reminded me of the scars on Talan's brow, on Gemma's left hand. Remnants of the Three-Eyed Crown.

And Yvaine… My stomach dropped when I found her. She was a smoking heap on the ground, her clothes torn, her skin blistered and bloody. She was *charred*.

I scrambled away from Ryder, shoving him off when he tried to stop me. I sobbed her name, ignoring the scrape of my battered hands and knees along the floor. No pain was worse than this: my friend, my queen, ravaged and still. Not moving. Not breathing.

I tried to sing—that would help her, that would bring her back—but my throat burned, and I could only rasp out a few ragged notes. But it must have been enough. As I wept, fumbling for some kind of song—any song, *anything;* I was a demigod, Philippa had said, so *where* was my god-liness, why wasn't it coming to help me?—Yvaine began to stir. At first I thought I was imagining it, but then she reached up for me with one red hand and opened her eyes—violet and gold, clouded with pain.

"Farrin?" she whispered. "You're still here."

I laughed through my tears and dashed a hand across my face. "Yes, I'm here, but you mustn't speak, all right? You're…Yvaine, you're quite hurt."

Yvaine shook her head slowly against the stone floor, a faint smile on her lips. "He will not touch you again," she said. Her voice was stronger than the rest of her, a blade glinting in the darkness. "I prom-ise you, Farrin, I won't allow it. I'll kill him if he tries."

My blood ran cold. "Who? If who tries?" I made myself say the hated word. "Kilraith? Was he here just now?"

Yvaine's eyes fluttered shut.

"Was that him in the dining room?" I choked out. "Was he inside you?"

"Just like Talan," came a faint whisper from Gemma. She sat stunned on the floor, not far from me.

We shouldn't have come. The realization was like a boot to the gut. All our work with the crown, our journey to Wardwell—we'd brought some invisible evil into the Citadel. Kilraith had been shadowing us, and now he'd followed us here. We should've listened to Thirsk, I thought wildly; we should've let Yvaine be. The feather pulsed frantically against the sweaty skin of my torso, its rhythm reflecting my own wild alarm. But what could a firebird do to help a woman who'd already been burned?

"Oh gods, Yvaine, I'm sorry," I whispered, and then I heard her draw in a wheezing, thin breath, and my whole body flooded with white-hot terror. "Yvaine? Please, stay with me. Yvaine!" I shouted for Thirsk, for the guards, for anyone. "Send for healers, now!" I screamed, but they were already there, six of them bustling over to us in their white robes, their faces grim and drawn. They lifted Yvaine's body onto a canvas stretcher, and though I tried to go with them, I could barely stand and instead fell back, furious and desperate, into Ryder's arms. I watched them carry her away, and it was then that I began to understand that something *else* was deeply wrong.

The royal beguilers were huddled together in frantic conference beside a pile of smoking rubble. Some were weeping; others, stricken, wandered about the room, calling out, "Brogan? Brogan!"

Brogan—the head beguiler, who'd been working for months to keep the Citadel safe from the sinkhole's inexorable expansion.

One of the beguilers wept into her hands. "He's gone," she said. "They took him!"

They? At first the word didn't make sense to me. Then I remembered the shadows. Clarity smashed into me like a falling rock. I remembered the message of Uven Lerrick in the Basks' beguiled mirror, that day at Ravenswood when Alastrina had disappeared. *One moment we were all here, and the next, a great rush of shadows washed across the room, and I felt horribly cold, utterly disoriented, my sight gone, my hearing gone. Then the shadows vanished, and my Dornen was no longer here.*

He just...he disappeared.

Just then, Gemma let out a strange noise, a strangled gasp of horror. "Gareth?" she whispered.

I whirled to find him, heart in my throat. I looked wildly around the room for a familiar blond head, a lanky frame in a gray suit. He'd come downstairs with us. I'd seen him only moments ago. He had been helping Brogan—

With a lurch of fear, I realized the truth without even having to search the room. Gareth could have been injured by falling debris, I reasoned; he could have been knocked off his feet in the chaos and now lay unconscious in the dark somewhere.

But even as the thoughts came to me, I knew them for lies. I couldn't pretend away the sudden emptiness in the room, the obvious void at my side.

Gareth—my brilliant, infuriating, dearest friend—was gone.

CHAPTER 19

We went looking for him at once, but hours of tearing through the Citadel calling his name, searching every room, peering into every dark corner, yielded nothing. Everywhere we went, servants wailed through the halls, calling after their friends and sisters and lovers, now gone. Advisers and senators, councilors and archivists, the royal beguilers, the royal cooks, the royal astronomers—all of them were bereft, tumbling through the marble halls like lost children. Everyone had lost someone—or knew someone who had lost someone—during that brief instant when shadows had snapped through the Citadel, before Yvaine had closed the sinkhole and driven them away. The air in every corridor was sour with terror.

At last, I could walk no longer. Ryder, who'd been beside himself—trying to no avail to get me to stop and rest—noticed me fading the moment before I whispered, "I can't."

My shaking knees gave out, and he was there before I could fall, as he always seemed to be. Gratefully I leaned into him and closed my eyes, trusting him to lead me to a place I could sit. *Gareth, Gareth.* I whispered his name into Ryder's sleeve, as if that would somehow call him to me, though it was shatteringly clear that he was gone, that dozens were gone. Dozens from this palace alone. Then the pain I'd been fighting off reared its head and said, *No more.*

Blackness rose up to claim me, and when I next opened my eyes, I was in my rooms, on a velvet sofa by the windows. Gemma sat beside me, cleaning the dried blood from my skin, her hair drawn up into a messy bun and her expression troubled.

I soon understood why. "Lord Ryder, we *must* do this," came an angry voice from somewhere in the room. I turned, ignoring Gemma's murmur of caution, and saw Ryder and Thirsk by the door. Ryder loomed; Thirsk bristled. His head was bandaged, his white beard singed. He saw me staring and hurried over, looking relieved.

"Lady Farrin," he said, "I'm glad to see you awake."

I cut him off. "Yvaine? Is she well? Is she—"

His expression softened the slightest bit. "The queen is alive. But her wounds are grave. She has told us she will heal, but it will take days."

I sank back into the couch, squeezed my eyes shut. She was alive, she was alive—a joy I would hold fiercely to my heart.

Thirsk cleared his throat. "I've come to tell you that we must enact the draft at once. The Citadel is in an uproar, the city even worse. In the queen's absence, I must use my authority as her speaker and issue an order to the Senate. They must institute the draft immediately—no more fussing over language and niceties—and dispatch soldiers from both armies to enforce it."

His words washed over me like waves, dashing me against the rocks of my own pain. I struggled to sit up. "Absolutely not, Thirsk. We cannot ask that sacrifice of anyone right now, not when we don't yet know the true reach of what's happened."

Past Thirsk, Ryder's expression turned relieved. I felt a quiet thrum of pleasure; he and I were in agreement.

But Thirsk stood firm. "Lady Farrin," he said coolly, "I hope you know I am here as a courtesy, not to ask permission. In the event that the queen is incapacitated—as she is now—I have the authority to act in her name. And in her name, I must do this. The country can sit and wait for action no longer."

"Rash action is worse than no action at all. We must think of the days ahead—not just today, when everyone is frightened and grieving."

A distant explosion drew our attention to the windows. Gemma helped me limp over to look outside, and what I saw left my skin crawling. Illuminated by the moon, the city was chaos; crowds flooded through the streets far below us and past the Citadel walls. Scattered flames burned, and protesters gathered once more at the palace gates. Distant rifle fire popped; I hoped it came from desperate citizens and not from the guards who'd taken oaths at the queen's feet to protect them. A low drone of unrest rose up through the air to meet my ears: desolate screams, angry shouts. It was like an anthill disturbed, all its glittering inhabitants spilling out in confused disarray. Through it all, the bells of the Citadel chimed—not in warning now but in sorrow. Low, deep chimes, each separated by a few seconds. A death knell.

"You see, Lady Farrin?" Thirsk said quietly. He'd come to join me at the windows. "The people demand action."

Part of me understood what he meant and thought his judgment necessary. But I knew Yvaine would disagree, and the thought of her lying unconscious on a healer's cot while such decisions were made without her made my stomach turn over. It was procedure, I knew; a hundred contingencies had been meticulously engineered over generations to prepare for a hundred different catastrophes. But the thought of Upper Army soldiers dragging so many women and girls from their homes and bringing them to the Warden for trials and training—tomorrow, perhaps, if Thirsk had his way—that was a horror I could not abide. Not now, not after what had happened. In one horrible day, everything had changed.

"What I see is fear and chaos," I said, "both of which an immediate draft will heighten. The city is tinder, and a draft will set it fully ablaze."

I drew in a deep breath and turned to face him; Gemma held on to my arm, helping me remain on my feet. "We need time," I told him, "and information. How many were taken, and from where? Did this abduction follow the same patterns as the first? Are all the taken Anointed, like the first time, or do some possess low magic, or no magic at all? What is the state of our armies, both Upper and Lower?"

Ryder, standing beyond Thirsk, nodded thoughtfully. "They will need to reconfigure their ranks, redistribute personnel to account for any losses."

I agreed. "Information, Thirsk, is what we need most of all."

Thirsk listened closely to us both. I saw his shoulders sag a little and knew we had won the argument. Perhaps part of him had been hoping we would.

"And what of the Warden?" he asked. "She will not take kindly to this delay."

"Let us deal with the Warden," Gemma replied, her voice hard. "She won't bother you, Thirsk, not after we've spoken to her."

Thirsk turned away and was quiet for a long time. "The queen trusts you," he said at last, "and though she hasn't told me every-thing, she's told me enough." He turned to look at me, his expression solemn. "I know she deems you important—all of you, and your sister at Rosewarren, and the demon named Talan, and..." He paused, a quiet beat of sympathy. "And the librarian."

"Gareth," I whispered, my heart twisting. Gently, Gemma's fin-gers squeezed mine.

Thirsk nodded, then took a long, slow breath. "Therefore I will heed your guidance in this moment, though you'd be foolish to think I will always do so. I am not a cruel man. I do not relish the idea of tearing families apart." He dragged a tired hand across his face. "I will send out soldiers to survey the land, gather information, catalog our losses. But in two weeks' time, if the queen has not yet recovered, I will enact the draft in her stead."

Ryder shifted. "And if she is well?"

"I don't imagine I'll have trouble convincing her to agree with me," Thirsk answered wearily, "not after what's happened here today." Then he gave me one last look—searching, worried—and left us three alone.

Gemma helped me back to the sofa. "We'll go to Rosewarren, then?" she said. "Speak to the Warden, try to calm her? She'll be furious about the delay."

I nodded, wincing as I settled. Everywhere Yvaine had scratched me stung as if I'd been lashed with nettles. "And we'll offer help as we can."

"We're not trained Roses," Gemma said doubtfully.

"But we're demigods, it seems, whatever that means. We can tear up forests and sing down queens. That has to count for something."

Ryder looked entirely unconvinced by my wry humor. "You're in no condition to help anyone, Farrin. Gemma can go to Rosewarren. You should rest."

"I can't possibly do that, not now. With Gareth gone, and…" I choked on my own sudden despair, shaking my head. Alastrina, and now Gareth, and so many countless others. "I'd go mad sitting at home, waiting. I have to do something. Besides, the royal healers will send me off with their best tonics and salves. I'll be good as new before you know it." I offered him a small smile. "And I'll rest when I can," I added quietly.

His mouth quirked, though in his eyes I saw true naked fear and freshly uprooted grief. "Promise me, Farrin."

I reached for his hand, and he took it gently. "I promise," I told him.

Gemma had already begun packing up my things, rustling about the room in her shining skirts. "Before we leave," she said briskly, "I'll go to Heldine and tell her what's happened. She should hear it from one of us."

Ryder looked over at her. "Will she be able to keep working? Those things you saw in the crown's shadows—we need to know more about them. An egg, a goblet, a key. A lake under a moon. What are these objects, and where? What are they made of? Are they other anchors of the *ytheliad*?"

"Or are they simply nonsense images?" I mused. "Scattered memories of places the crown has been? A three-eyed crown is unique. An egg, a goblet…there are millions of those."

"Oh, Heldine will continue working, all right," Gemma said, "especially now. The trick will be to convince her to stop and eat every now and then. It's a wonder she and Gareth are still standing, what with all their awful habits…" Abruptly, she stopped speaking. *Still standing*. Gods, I hoped he was, wherever he was.

"And you?" I glanced up at Ryder. "Will you come with us to Rosewarren?"

He shook his head, looking miserable. "I must go home. I've been gone for a long time, and my mother…" He hesitated, and in the silence I read a thousand sad things. It hurt my heart to imagine those dark halls—everything made of black stone, the cupboards and closets still shrouded with the memories of Ryder's childhood's darkest days. I put both my hands around his, pressing what little strength I had into his skin. He circled his thumb over my wrist and stood a little straighter.

"I need to see my mother," he finished roughly. "And the north needs me. I'll travel among the villages there, help as I can. Seeing my face, knowing I'm alive and well, will reassure them. It will be chaos, much as it is here, given everything that's just happened, and the Mist's borders constantly shifting…" He shook his head once more.

"I'll have to hope that whatever's just happened hasn't sent a new wave of monsters crawling out of the woodwork."

"We'll meet at Ivyhill in one week, then?" said Gemma. My bag was packed, sitting ready on the bed. She stood at the mirror, shook out her hair, efficiently tied it back into a neater bun. "Perhaps we'll have heard from Talan by that time, though I don't know what I hope he'll tell us. Gods resurrected, gods still dead—at this point, I'm not sure which would be better. I only hope..." She bit her lip; I watched her reflection waver. "I only hope that Kilraith coming to the Citadel doesn't mean he's out there hunting Talan too."

"He'll be all right, Gemma," Ryder said. "A lesser creature would've broken during so many years in Kilraith's service. Besides, he isn't alone. He's got one of my birds with him now."

Gemma smiled at him in the mirror, her eyes bright. "And a Bask raven makes a fierce companion, does it?"

"You're damn right it does."

I looked up at him, a sudden rush of love warming me, distracting me from all my aches and bruises, and from the prick of nerves I felt as I remembered Philippa's eager words. *Fighting and creating glamours and making music—these things you can already do. But there is more buried in your power, and I can help you find it—*

Was I wrong to have left her? If we'd stayed at Wardwell, started learning from her as she'd proposed instead of coming to the Citadel, would none of this have happened? Would Gareth and all the others still be here? Would Yvaine have stayed unhurt, untouched by Kilraith?

I swallowed hard against these questions, ones I couldn't answer. An image came to my mind of Kilraith as a great wolf, trailing after us with sharp, tireless eyes, never quite catching us but nevertheless bringing chaos wherever he went. Wherever *we* went.

But what was done was done. Wasting time worrying over the past would do nothing but hinder the future.

"One week, then," I said softly, offering Ryder a brave smile.

He nodded at me, brought my fingers to his lips and kissed them. In his eyes, I read the same sadness I felt. A week apart, and the whole country a mess, and all I wanted was to crawl back into that bed we'd vacated only this morning. But our world needed us—whatever we were, whatever secrets our godly blood held—and the north needed Ryder.

"One week," he replied.

When Gemma and I emerged from our family's greenway hidden on the grounds of Rosewarren, we heard the protesters before we saw them: a muffled roar, constant but rippling, as if we were underwater listening to people howl on the shore.

Gemma leaned hard on me, winded from the passage through the greenway. "What is that?" she murmured. She looked behind us at the watery silver fog streaming through the trees—the southern border of the Middlemist.

But the noise was coming from the other direction. We hurried around the priory's great walls of red-and-black brick to its front doors, and from there we looked down the rolling green lawn at the crowd gathered along its edge. Dozens, perhaps hundreds, of people swarmed the iron gates of the priory. But some sort of ward magic blocked their passage, obscured their figures. I couldn't see faces or even distinct bodies, just a blur of colors and shapes that emitted a distant roar of muddied sound. Faceless figures crawled up the wall that surrounded the priory's grounds and tried to jump to the other side; they battered at the gates with sledgehammers; they tossed stones and torches. But everything that touched the priory's ward magic—every stone and torch, every body—was flung back, stunned and harmless, until someone in the crowd dared to try again.

My stomach turned as I watched them. Even through the ward magic, I could feel their fear scrambling up the sloped lawn, nipping at our ankles. Could they see us standing here, blurred and frozen, doing nothing to help them?

"Do you think she said anything at all to them before shutting herself away behind the ward magic?" Gemma muttered.

"I doubt she so much as posted a notice," I replied. "'Yes, we know there've been more abductions. We're doing the best we can. Please come back later.'"

Gareth's name turned painfully in my chest. *Abductions*. Such a clinical word for such a horrible thing.

Grimly, Gemma raised her hand to knock on the priory doors— but before she could, one of them swung open just enough to reveal Mara on the other side. The sight of her stunned me. She looked deathly pale and haggard, with deep shadows under her brown eyes that reminded me unsettlingly of Yvaine. She wore her hair slicked back in a tight bun and was dressed in Order garb of dark brown and charcoal gray: a long, square-shouldered jacket, knee-high leather boots. Worse even than the shadows under her eyes was that, with her hair pulled back and her shoulders high and sharp in that coat, she looked eerily like the Warden.

"Come in, quickly," she whispered, and we obeyed at once. She shut the door behind us, pulled us into an alcove off the entrance hall, and gestured for us to be quiet. I listened past the pounding of my heart for the Warden's steps gliding across the stone floor, but only silence met my ears. After a moment, Mara seemed satisfied.

"This way," she said quietly. "I need your help with something."

"Wait—" Gemma began.

Mara shook her head. "No time."

I hurried around her, blocking her path. "Mara, *wait*."

She could have evaded me or pushed me aside, of course, but

instead she only said, rather impatiently, "I had Cira beguile our family's greenway with a spell that notifies me whenever it's used. That's how I knew you were here. And I'm sure I look terrible to your eyes, but I assure you I'm quite well. And most importantly, will you *please* come with me without further delay? Later we can talk about whatever it is you came to talk about. But right now, I need your help." She paused, her urgent expression hardening into something cold and careful. "*Everyone* needs your help."

I exchanged a worried look with Gemma but said nothing more, instead stepping aside and letting Mara lead us through the priory. The dimly lit hallways buzzed with activity. Older Roses, fearsome and focused, strode off to what I assumed were various assignments. Younger Roses trotted after them, arms full of gear and weapons. From all corners came the distant, industrious clamor of weapons being sharpened, horses neighing out on the grounds, voices of girls and women shouting to each other. *Throw it up here, quick, now, grab another one from the armory!*

Every now and then as Mara led us quickly through the twisting corridors, their walls decorated with murals of Roses in combat, I felt curious eyes upon us, but no one stopped our progress. Perhaps by now they'd heard of what we'd done in Devenmere, or else they were so focused on their own duties that they couldn't be bothered to stop and question us. And besides, we were with Mara.

Yet the longer we followed her, the more uneasy I became. She led us through a series of carpeted corridors, then out across one of the stone training yards, which bustled with horses and weapons and Roses in their browns and grays. We hurried after her to a small outbuilding a fair distance away from the priory, where we could hear nothing but our own footsteps—not the noise of the Roses readying for patrol or the crowd of people yelling in vain at the gates. Stately pines flanked the building, whispering ominously in the silvery wind.

Once we were inside with the door shut behind us, everything grew still. The air was close and damp and smelled sour, like unwashed bodies.

Mara grabbed a torch from the wall. The flames cast harsh shapes across her skin, made the fresh slash on her face look doubly gruesome. "This way," she said quietly, and we obeyed, though my body screamed at me to run and never come back to this place. Its stone staircases and winding corridors led us down into the earth, and the deeper we went, the fouler the air smelled. It felt like we were entering a tomb.

"Mara, are you taking us to the caves?" Gemma said at last, her voice a mere whisper.

"Quiet," Mara snapped, and then she seemed to feel sorry for it and said more gently, "No. Not the caves. Something else."

We reached a heavy wooden door reinforced with huge iron brackets, and after a slight hesitation, Mara pricked her finger with a needle she took from her pocket and pressed her bloody skin to the door's flat brass latch. A slight ripple of magic swept past us, raising the hair on my arms, and then the door swung open, revealing a small chamber sunk into the ground a good twenty feet, the only access a narrow set of stone steps.

And in the middle of the room—bound by a dozen chains anchored to the stone wall, the stone ceiling, the stone floor—was a harpy.

At first my mind couldn't make sense of what I was seeing. After years of hearing Olden children's tales and Gareth's incessant lectures, I could identify the creature immediately, but I'd never seen one in the flesh. At first my mind refused to accept its existence. She was enormous, twice as tall as Mara, with a broad torso, a hunched back, and wings that would have filled the room if they hadn't been strapped cruelly to her body. She was, as were all of her kind, part bird, part woman. A startling combination, and much more jarring, more weathered, than the Roses' sleek feathered bodies when they transformed. Her neck was ringed with pale flesh mottled with scabs, and she had a hooked nose, a wide mouth stuffed with fangs, and two round yellow eyes sunken deep into a gaunt skull. A wild mane of brown-and-gray hair crested her head before transitioning into feathers. She crouched within her chains on naked muscled legs tipped with huge black talons. I was glad that at least we could not see her bare torso.

But we could see enough. The wounds on her legs, the festering sores on her neck were fresh, glistening. She had been beaten.

I froze in horror, staring down at her.

Gemma, just behind me, whispered faintly, "Mara, what is this?"

Mara shut the chamber's door and started down the stairs. "This is Nerys. My unit caught her yesterday, just before we started receiving word about the latest abductions. She was feeling bold, I suppose, knowing what was to happen. Because she did know." Mara stopped in front of Nerys, nearly nose to nose with the massive creature, whose head hung low, her eyes closed. Mara's own eyes glittered. "She attacked some of us coming home from a night in Fenwood, caught us by surprise. She got Cira worst of all. She'll live, but barely. The rest of us managed to get her here, secure her."

The harpy, Nerys, stirred at the sound of Mara's voice. She raised her head, a movement both graceful and grotesque. Such fluid motion, and yet there was that grinning mouth of fangs, those sunken eyes. Eyes, I noticed, that didn't quite meet my sister's.

"Ah, you're back," Nerys rasped—the voice of an old woman, with something glottal rattling wetly underneath. "How I've missed you."

Mara's hand twitched at her side, drawing my gaze to the spiked club leaning against the chamber wall. My bile rose, and Gemma drew in a sharp breath. Had those wounds on Nerys been inflicted by my sister's hand? If we weren't here, would Mara have... I could hardly form the thought.

"Nerys has been resistant to most of our normal methods of extraction," Mara continued coolly. "She's old and strong. But not as strong as me."

The harpy barked out a harsh laugh that rapidly dissolved into a horrific cough. She hocked up a wad of phlegm and spat it, but her aim was poor. It went at least a foot wide of Mara and splatted harmlessly on the floor.

"Fool girl," growled Nerys. "Strong? If we met on equal terms, without these chains binding me to your floor, I would tear you to ribbons."

"I'm not sure that you would, or that you even could. You see," Mara went on, raising her voice, "there's something about me that Nerys can't seem to resist. When she looks at me—looks right at me—she starts to talk. Most of it's nonsense, but every now and then, she'll let slip an immensely useful nugget of information. Like the location of not just one underground market hub facilitating illegal trade between Edyn and the Old Country, but *three* such hubs: Yennore, Tenevis, and Irethe, they are called. Their locations, what sort of trade passes through them, what Olden safeguards keep them cloaked from us—and all of this in a day. No, Nerys," Mara said, a little quieter now, "I think that if we met out there in the world, I could just look at you and tell you to lie down in the dirt, harmless as a fat cat, and you would obey me."

My growing panic wedged itself into my throat like a knife; I could no longer keep quiet. "I don't understand. How did you do this? *Why* are you doing this?"

The harpy's head jerked against her chains. She couldn't move enough to look at me, but her eyes darted about, searching. "Who's there?" she called out, fresh terror in her voice. "Who did you bring here?"

"Oh, them?" Mara said. "Those are my sisters. I thought you might want to meet them. Farrin, Gemma?" She turned back to look at us, and when she met my eyes, her expression faltered just the slightest bit. A hesitation, a flinch.

The sight warmed my cold bones. There was my sister, there in that flicker of uncertainty. Whoever this other person was—this woman with the hard voice and the glittering dark eyes—she hadn't yet taken over the Mara I knew, not completely.

"No, no, no..." Nerys's wings strained against her bindings. "No more of you, *no more...*"

"Come down here and join us," Mara said. When neither Gemma nor I moved, she whirled on us, blew out a frustrated breath. "Now. *Please.* We don't have a lot of time. We don't know when the next people might be taken, and the Warden—"

Mara stopped, seemed to collect herself. She lifted her chin and looked hard at us. "You want to help our country, the people in it? Alastrina? Gareth?" Her eyes cut to mine. I thought I saw a flicker of something sad cross that cold expression on her face. "Yes, I know he's been taken, and I'm sorry, Farrin. Now, come here and do something about it. I know neither of you is a coward, nor are you useless. So prove it. Help me."

I started down the stairs on watery legs, Gemma just behind me. "I don't understand," I said again. It seemed the safest thing to say. Perhaps if I got her talking, it would buy us all some time, stop Mara from doing whatever this was, shake some sense into her, shake Gareth's name and dear face from my mind so I could *think*. If I could only touch Mara's hand, remind her of herself, this would end. "Tell me how you're able to persuade such a creature to tell you anything, much less such specific, valuable information—"

"Because of who we are," Gemma whispered, cutting me off. She grabbed my hand, held me back. "Isn't that right, Mara? Because of..."

Mara glared at us. "Yes," she said. "Because of who we are. She looks at me, and she can't help herself. We are the flame, and she is the moth. *Because of who we are.*"

She said it carefully, not divulging anything too particular. But I knew precisely what she meant. *Demigods.* My mouth went dry as Philippa's voice ran through my mind in a relentless loop. *Fighting and creating glamours and making music—these things you can already do. But there is more buried in your power, and I can help to find it—*

But Kerezen was god of the senses and the body. The power of persuasion seemed more like a trick of the mind—the god Jaetris's domain.

Then Gemma exhaled shakily. "Sirens," she whispered. "Succubi, incubi. Even…" She glanced back at me. "Your voice, Farrin."

An icy curtain of dread dropped through me. Of course. There were other means of persuasion besides powers of the mind. Many Olden creatures crafted by Kerezen's hand—the fae, the sirens, the succubi and incubi—held powers of the senses, powers of beauty, allure, music, seduction. And then there was me, a mere human savant who could nevertheless bring listeners to their knees and stun monsters like Kilraith—like Ankaret—using only the power of my voice.

Thanks to Philippa, such powers of persuasion lay in our blood. And here was Mara, abusing it without fully understanding it. *We should have stayed at Wardwell,* I thought, my stomach churning. We should have let Philippa teach us. We weren't safe. Danger was inherent to our very blood.

Desperate, I hurried toward Mara. I would pull her away from this, make her look at *me*, not at this poor creature tormented by her very presence. I would be quick; I wouldn't look at Nerys, wouldn't give whatever power I held the chance to snare her.

But merely being near the harpy, it seemed, was enough. Nerys strained mightily against her chains and managed to shift just the slightest amount—enough to look at me, and at Gemma a step behind me.

She let out a low, awestruck groan. Her putrid breath puffed into my face. "Three of you," she whispered, "all at once? Gods help me. What are you? Who are you?"

I couldn't help but look at her. I shouldn't have; there was no need to. And yet I think part of me was curious to see what would happen, to confirm that this was real. Could my simple presence, combined with my sisters', muddle a mighty Olden beast?

The harpy's yellow eyes—round and small as river stones, dull as old brass—darted helplessly about the room but always, always, came back to us: Mara, then me, then Gemma. The sight of us didn't render her completely helpless; she still struggled against her bindings and clawed at the floor, her massive body vibrating with anger.

And yet she gaped at us, struck with confused dread, and then Mara spoke, her voice stony. "Tell me who you work for."

The harpy squeezed her lipless mouth shut. Her skin bulged over her profusion of yellow fangs.

Mara pressed on. "I know you work for someone. Harpies are self-ish and solitary, concerned with their own welfare above all else. They don't attack humans out in the open like you did, not unless they've a very good reason. So what is it? *Who* is it?"

Finally, keening quietly, rocking herself as best she could despite her chains, Nerys began to speak. "I work for He Who Is All," she rasped. She spoke falteringly, fighting against every word. "I came to Edyn in search for new children for His city."

"Whose city?" Mara said sharply.

"He Who Is All," Nerys spat.

"And what city is this? Where is it?"

The harpy croaked out a pained sound; I couldn't be sure if it was a laugh or a sob. She closed her eyes, their faint yellow glow disappearing behind lids of wrinkled skin.

"The splendor of its revels," she said, "the palace in the green, the towers in the night."

"What *city*?" Mara insisted.

Gemma hurried over, put herself between the harpy and Mara. "Stop this," she hissed. "You're hurting her."

"And do you think all the people who've been taken, who are being kept by *He Who Is All*, aren't hurting?" Mara snapped.

I turned blindly for the stairs, tears in my eyes. *Gareth. Alastrina.* I felt sick, like the worst kind of coward. Once again, we were in a place we shouldn't be. Once again, we had brought only ruin and pain.

"We're leaving," I bit out, turning toward the stairs. "Gemma—"

But then I stopped, for at the top of the stairs stood the Warden— not a hair out of place, her square-shouldered black gown pristine. She held her hands clasped behind her back and surveyed the scene dispassionately.

"Tell me more about the revels," the Warden commanded, her cold, clear voice booming through the small chamber.

The harpy shivered in her chains, sucked in a rattling breath. "They are like nothing that has ever been or will ever be. Oldens in the finest robes, Oldens in jewels, feasting and drinking. Flowers in the streets, honey in the goblets, fae in gowns of moonlight, vampyrs who've nothing to fear, for there is no sun in this city. There are only shadows made by the cool white moon. And humans...there they become the animals they truly are, pathetic dregs of weak-minded gods."

"You're lying," Mara said, her voice hard. But I saw the slight twinge of surprise on her face. "Fae and vampyrs are proud and tribal. They keep to themselves. They wouldn't ever deign to live in the same place."

The harpy laughed deep in her throat. "You think you know so much about the Old Country, little Rose. But you have not seen its grandest city, and you should pray that you never do."

"The city called Moonhollow?" the Warden asked mildly.

Nerys lifted her head, folds of skin peeling open to reveal her eyes once more. She looked longingly at Gemma, who had turned away to hide her face. "No," the harpy growled. *"Mhorghast."*

The Warden started gliding down the stairs. I scrambled out of her way, blurted, "Stop, please," but whatever power I possessed that held the harpy in its tormented thrall seemed to have no effect on the Warden. She walked on, unhurried, untroubled.

"What an interesting word, *Mhorghast*," she said smoothly. "Is that the true name of this city, then?"

The harpy glared at her. Drool dripped from her fangs. Her naked legs shook. *"Mhorghast.* You say it improperly. You dare to misname it."

"Mmm." The Warden crossed to a small table in the corner, upon which stood a series of stoppered bottles, each filled with a sickeningly bright liquid: yellow, green, red. There was a gun there too, though not like any I'd seen Lower Army soldiers carry. Not as long as a rifle, but much thinner than one—a simple, sleek design. And beside it, an array of feathered silver needles.

"And does Mhorghast have other names?" the Warden asked.

"It needs no other names!" Nerys roared, fighting hard against her chains.

The Warden opened the bottle of bright green liquid and dipped one of the feathered needles into it. "You don't seem to be listening to me," she said. "I've heard that some people call this city Moonhollow."

The harpy spat. *"Moonhollow.* Your languages are as pitiful as you are."

I couldn't bear to listen to this exchange any longer. I didn't know what the Warden was doing with that needle, those bottles, that gun, but I knew I couldn't let her succeed. I ran back down the stairs, opened my mouth, drew a breath—I would sing Nerys into compliance, I would end all of this with a few well-chosen notes—but then

Mara was on me, holding me back, a hand clamped over my mouth. I fought her hard, remembering everything Ryder had taught me—an elbow to her gut, a heel smashing into her instep. But Mara was a Rose and a sentinel. She grunted in pain but didn't release me.

"Mara!" Gemma shouted, disbelieving. She pounded uselessly on Mara's arm. *"Mara!"* Under my feet, the room began to tremble, as if the roots pushing against these underground walls were waking up, eager to obey Gemma's commands.

Nerys struggled as I did, and even trapped as she was, she was a sight to behold, her feathered muscles bulging under their chains, her great claws carving furrows into the stone floor.

"Leave us," the Warden said, loading one of the feathered needles into the gun with a practiced, chilling snap.

Mara seized Gemma with her free hand and dragged us both up the stairs, out of the room, through the winding corridors that led us back up to the priory grounds. As we stumbled through the dark, pulled by Mara's inimitable sentinel strength, I heard the harpy begin to scream, an awful blend of avian shrieks and agonized human cries. Mara shut the door on the sound, and suddenly we were back outside with the whispering pines, and the air that shimmered silver.

As soon as I found my footing, I rounded on Mara. "How dare you," I said, struggling to catch my breath. "You knew of our power's influence and didn't tell us. The moment we stepped in that room, we made Nerys our victim without even knowing it!"

Mara stood a little apart from us, not looking at either of us, her posture rigid. "I had to do it. When I realized the influence I had on her and then not long after, the two of you showed up... The Warden's conventional torture was taking too long. This will get us answers more quickly. She won't suffer as much."

Gemma scoffed, incredulous. She flung out her hand toward the door. "That certainly sounded like suffering to me!"

"We brought much of her knowledge to the surface," Mara said, still not looking at us. "The Warden won't have to work as long now to get everything she wants. The procedure will be more…efficient. What we did is a mercy."

"And then what will the Warden do?" I shot back at her. "Once she's wrung all the information she can out of this poor creature?"

Mara lifted her troubled gaze to mine at last. She said nothing, but I saw the answer plain as day on her face.

My heart sank. "Mara, how could you?" I whispered.

"You don't know what it's like," she began.

"What, torturing someone for information?" Gemma asked sharply, spots of angry color in her pale cheeks. "Being used for my power? Well, thanks to you, now I know what *both* those things are like."

"You had no right to bring us to Nerys," I told her. There was a distant ringing in my ears, some faraway bell of shock. I couldn't silence it.

"I know," Mara said, a note of bitterness in her voice. "But I chose to do it anyway. And do you know why?" She lifted her head high, no longer shrinking with shame. "Because the Middlemist isn't the only thing that's dying. My sisters are dying too. Every day, more and more Olden creatures break through the barrier between realms, bringing terror with them wherever they go. Hunting humans, invading villages, trading goods, bodies, blood, bones. A fae elixir for a child. The murder of an enemy in exchange for a pledge of subservience. Humans are disappearing, some wandering off into the Mist of their own accord, plagued by a sickness no one understands. Others vanish without warning, whisked away by shadows in the space of a blink. And nothing we do helps, and no one is helping *us*."

She shook her head miserably, turned away to stare at the Mist's roiling border. "You have no right to criticize our methods, not from the safety of Ivyhill, not when you don't have to wonder every night when you go to sleep if you'll wake up to find that one of your sisters has been killed."

"But we do wonder that, Mara," I said quietly. "Every day, when Gilroy brings me the post, I feel the same jolt of fear and hope the same desperate hope."

Still with her back to us, Mara hugged herself, bowed her head. She said nothing, and the Mist slithered quietly on through the distant trees.

The next moment, the door opened, and the Warden came out to join us. I heard no more screams as she emerged; the air was ominously silent. I had to exercise tremendous restraint to keep from knocking her to the ground right then and there. Her expression was serene, her dress spotless. She looked curiously at Gemma, then at me. I saw the question in her eyes: *How did you get her to talk with no elixirs at your disposal, no spellwork, no empathic power?* Maybe she wondered if Talan had taught us a thing or two about influencing others' minds.

I approached her before she could ask a thing. Anger and grief steeled my spine. For once in my life, I wasn't cowed by the sight of the Warden's calm black eyes.

"We've come from the Citadel," I told her sharply. *From which Gareth was taken,* I wanted to say, the words desolate on my tongue. "The queen closed the sinkhole in the palace and was gravely injured in doing so. I believe that had she not succeeded, many more people would have disappeared. The Royal Conclave is sending out teams to determine how many were abducted and from where. The Upper and Lower Armies are regrouping, and the Senate will postpone issuing the new draft for another two weeks while the queen heals and her advisers take stock, determine how best to address the citizenry."

I took a breath. Only then did my courage waver slightly. "The Three-Eyed Crown will remain in the capital during this time for continued study. You will do nothing to bring it back here to the priory."

The Warden lifted her eyebrows, looking slightly amused. But before she could say anything, I added, "I think you'll consider this a fair exchange for the service we just rendered you with the harpy."

I felt sick to say the words. *The harpy.* Her name was Nerys.

And yet Mara was right. We didn't know what it was like to live up here, to serve the Order of the Rose. And when I tried to imagine myself in her place—fighting monsters every day, watching villages fall apart before my very eyes—I couldn't predict what I would do, how strong I would be. Would I be so quick to balk at such tactics then? Or would I too come to accept them as a necessary evil of war?

I didn't know the answer to that question, couldn't even fully wrap my mind around the complexities of it. Instead I held my ground, staring at the Warden until she finally relented with a nod.

"A fair exchange indeed," she replied, still amused. The condescending note in her voice made me want to scream.

I watched her glide back to the priory. Her tracks carved a faint line through the dew-soaked grounds, the slick carpet of pine needles. The grass, the trees, every bit of green here near the Mist was always wet. Mara had said in one of her earliest letters home that she thought this was because the Middlemist was lonely, that it missed the gods who had made it and cried its grief upon the world every day.

And what did the Mist think now, I wondered, with the daughters of a god so near? Had it always recognized, from the first moment Mara set foot in the priory, the true power lying dormant in her blood?

"Is that what you came here to do?" Mara asked hollowly, still not looking at either of us. "Tell the Warden about the queen, the draft?"

"Yes," I answered sharply, just as Gemma said, "Yes, but—"

"But *what*?" Mara sounded tired.

"I think..." Gemma paused, glanced at me. "I think we should all return to Wardwell. Not forever," she added hastily, "but...for a few days, at least. We know very little about what Mother—Kerezen—can actually do in her current form. We should let her teach us, apply her strategies to our own powers. Think of what we could learn, how we might be useful to the queen—"

"Absolutely not," I interrupted.

Mara's expression was unreadable, her gaze distant. "I can't leave right now, Gemma. The Order needs me. Maybe when things become a little calmer..."

Gemma threw an exasperated look my way. "But Farrin, don't you think it's wise to learn more about—"

"No, I don't," I said, cutting her off. The specters of my disastrous childhood concert, the echoes of the audience's desperate cries, whispered meanly in my memory. *Farrin, marry me. Farrin, I need you!* "Whatever we just did down there? I don't want to know a thing about it. I want it to stay deep down inside me and wither away. I certainly don't want Philippa to make it stronger. What I *do* want is to go home. Our presence there will reassure everyone—the staff, our tenants, the nearby towns. We headed straight from the capital to Rosewarren. We didn't even stop for a moment to check in at the house. I should have insisted on it." The fresh guilt of this threatened to smother me. "Has Lilianne been taken? Has Gilroy? Byrn? Mrs. Seffwyck?"

Gemma blanched at my sharp tone. I was glad. Anything to knock Philippa out of her head.

"Anyway, that's where we belong," I said, "not running away to play at magic with a god too afraid to show her face when her people need her."

Mara looked keenly at me. "Are you talking about a god leaving her people or a mother leaving her children?"

For a moment, I was too stunned to reply. Then came a fresh wave of anger. "If we can't criticize you for the atrocities you and your *sisters* commit here," I said, very low, my voice thin as a blade, "then you have no right to criticize us for what we endured when you were already well and gone. You know what it's like to be taken away, I'll grant you that. But you don't know what it's like to be *left*."

And I did leave her then. I left both of them. *See this, Mara?* I thought. *Feel that pang in your chest? That frustration, that anger? Imagine that, but a thousand times more painful. Imagine living for years and years with that storm raging inside you, and no end in sight, no relief.*

I didn't know if Gemma would follow me, and I didn't care. I marched across the priory grounds, ignoring the chaos of the training yards, the Roses riding off into the Mist with their familiars scampering or flying alongside them. I could think of only one thing: *home.* That was where I was needed. That was where I could be of use. Not torturing harpies or appeasing cowardly mothers who scarcely deserved the title. *Philippa.* I said her name until the word *mother* disappeared from my mind. *Philippa. Philippa.* She was nothing more than that.

I reached our family's greenway, hidden behind its curtain of beguiled, chiming snow-blossoms. A cardinal darted out of the blooms at my approach, brilliant red against the white petals. The sight of its feathers reminded me suddenly of Ankaret, and I realized with a hot prickle of shame that I wore her feather tucked into my dress, as had become my habit. Its presence was warm against my skin, a comfort I'd quickly grown used to. And yet I hadn't thought to use it to call for help. Ankaret could have freed Nerys, could have reduced the Warden's weapons to ashes.

As I pushed past the tinkling snow-blossoms, Ankaret's bizarre, inhuman voice cooed in my memory. *Someday you will need her. Use this to call her. She will hear you, wherever she is.*

My head was heavy with all the things I could have done and all the things I shouldn't have. I sent a bitter prayer to the gods—*Keep Gareth safe*—and let the greenway's magic carry me home.

Chapter 20

When I arrived at Ivyhill, I felt as if months had passed since I'd last set foot in the house, though it had been only three days. The moment I stepped into the entrance hall, the tight knots in my chest unraveled. I listened to the afternoon sounds I knew so well: the autumn breeze rustling across the golden lawn, the distant whickering of the horses being worked in their paddocks, the faint clatter of tea being set in the dining room.

This was where I belonged. Not Rosewarren, not the Citadel, not Wardwell. Here. Ivyhill.

Gilroy came out of the dining room just as I started across the entrance hall. At the sight of me, his stern countenance melted into one of stark relief. He set down his tray and hurried toward me, hesitated, then screwed up his face in defiance and pulled me into a fierce hug.

This was not the sort of thing Gilroy ever did, but I was glad for it. His stocky body was warm, his suit immaculately pressed. I held on to him, dizzy with my own relief. He, at least, had not been taken.

"My lady, it's good to see your face," he said gruffly. He pulled away and cleared his throat, tugging sharply on his waistcoat. "We've heard some of the news from Lord Gideon, but...with you and Lady Imogen gone..."

He fell silent, clearly overwhelmed. The more emotional Gilroy became, the more his bushy black eyebrows turned down, as if a fearsome frown would help him remain unflappable when nothing else could.

"I'm well, and so are Gemma and Mara, whom we've just seen up at the priory. Gemma will be here shortly. She had some things to attend to." Or would she disappear to Wardwell? I didn't think so, despite all her grand ideas. Talan would come here if he needed help, and so here Gemma would stay.

The thought brought me a fierce, almost smug satisfaction. I should have been ashamed of the feeling, but I was too tired for further shame, my body still aching from Yvaine's attack and my heart heavy. I took Gilroy's white-gloved hands in mine.

"Tell me, Gilroy," I said. "You've heard of what's happened. Are you..." I swallowed. I would not think of Gareth, I *could* not, not now, not until I'd taken stock of my home. "Are you all here and safe?"

"No one's been taken from Ivyhill," came the answer from behind me. Father was descending the stairs. I noticed with relief that he looked clean and groomed; he wore a fresh suit. He looked sober, even solemn. He came to the bottom of the stairs and couldn't quite meet my eyes. I wonder if he'd seen me embrace Gilroy, and when I tried to remember the last time I'd embraced *him*, I realized with a twinge of dismay that I couldn't. I fought against the guilty feeling; if we no longer embraced as we once had, if indeed we hardly saw each other, it was his fault, not mine.

"As soon as I heard what had happened," Father went on quietly, "I took a count of everyone. All our staff, all our tenants, all *their* staff. Ivyhill hasn't been touched."

A wave of relief swept through me. "And Derryndell?" The nearest town.

Father's expression darkened. "Four were taken from Derryndell. Two children, a young woman, a man of seventy. None of them Anointed. The woman is a low-magic oracle with a fortune-telling shop in the center of town. Neither children nor the man possess any magic at all."

My heart sank. So this time was different. This time, the Anointed weren't the only targets.

"What does it mean, my lady?" Gilroy said, his voice grave.

They were both looking at me, eager for an answer. I'd just been to the Citadel and Rosewarren; surely I came with news.

But all I could do was tell them a half truth. "I don't know."

What I didn't tell them was what we'd learned from Nerys—that there was a place called both Mhorghast and Moonhollow. A city where the sun never shone, ruled by He Who Is All, where Olden beings held revels and tormented humans. What had Nerys said? *And humans...there they become the animals they truly are. Pathetic dregs of weak-minded gods.*

Imagining what that could mean, picturing Gareth trapped in such a horror, my knees nearly buckled under me. Father must have seen my distress before I managed to mask my expression; he moved toward me, then hesitated. I couldn't look at him, couldn't bear his disappointment, his shame, all his feelings that had been mine to tend to for far too long. And I worried that if he looked into my eyes for too long, he would read things I didn't want him to see—Philippa's face, and Mara's, cruel and cold as she regarded the harpy in her chains.

Instead I asked Gilroy to have tea sent up to my rooms and then left them both for the grounds. I would walk for what remained of the daylight and hope that the air of Ivyhill would scrub my mind clean.

It didn't.

That night, I couldn't sleep, my mind fevered, my body restless. Moonhollow. Mhorghast. Yvaine. Nerys. Philippa. The shapes forming in the Three-Eyed Crown's shadows, pulled into being by Heldine's spellwork and Gemma's glamours: an egg, a goblet, a key, a black lake under a full moon. Ryder's hands, Ryder's mouth, Ryder's body and warmth and strength, his voice cracking against my neck as he moved in me. A whirl of images, memories, questions. I stretched my arm across my bed and closed my eyes, trying to imagine Ryder's weight next to me, the slash of his beard in the sputtering candlelight, the deep rhythm of his breathing as he slept and dreamed.

Osmund jumped up onto the bed with a chirruping meow, interpreting my outstretched arm as an invitation. I lifted him onto my stomach, let him purr and knead for a good half hour, then decided I'd go mad if I stayed in bed a moment longer. I kissed his head between his silken black ears, left him staring at me grumpily from the pillows, and went downstairs to the library in my dressing gown. If I couldn't sleep, I would work. Our family's archives were among the best in the country. Gareth was far from the only scholar to regularly visit our collections. I would read everything I could about the gods. I would search the reference catalog for any mention of significant goblets, keys, eggs. I would make a list of every lake in Gallinor, in Aidurra, in Vauzanne, and make note of any folktales, legends, and customs born on their shores. I was no scholar, but I could read, and I could use a reference catalog. I could do *something*.

But Gemma was already there, Una curled up at her feet. She sat at a candlelit table in the library's heart, books and maps spread out around her. A silver kettle of fresh coffee steamed at her elbow. She was barefoot and distracted, chewing on her pen. The book she was reading was bigger than her entire torso. She was rapt, squinting at it. She drew the candelabra closer, then scribbled something on the piece of paper at her elbow.

My heart ached to see her there. She hadn't gone to Wardwell, as I'd suspected she wouldn't, but she hadn't come to tell me that herself. *I'm home, Farrin. I'm safe. I thought you'd want to know. And you're right. Whatever Philippa may be able to teach us? I don't want it.*

I should have never even considered that she would leave home in such a way. I stayed in the shadows for a moment, watching her, all the words I wanted to say held tight behind my teeth. I could sit with her, read along with her. We could take notes together, maybe even begin to whisper our questions and fears aloud. What did it mean, to be a demigod? We believed Philippa, didn't we? Could we teach ourselves without involving her at all? Explore our powers together with Mara and let Philippa rot up at her precious Wardwell?

But I knew that wouldn't happen. Instead I'd snap at Gemma, say something nasty about Philippa, bristle at anything and everything. I'd disrupt Gemma's peace simply by being there; all my seething thoughts would seep out and infect her. And she already had so much to bear—Talan, her panic, her pain—without me around to make it worse.

Una was watching me with her great dark eyes, though she hadn't yet lifted her head. I sent her silent thanks for her discretion and left them. I wandered the quiet house like a specter might haunt her place of death—untethered, agitated.

Morning came, and with it at least one decision, a pinprick of light in a roiling black storm. I couldn't wait five more days to see him again. No, I needed him now.

I needed Ryder.

—◆—

I used the lagoon's hidden greenway and emerged shivering and wet in the forest of Ravenswood, cursing my past self for not planning ahead. I could have left fresh clothes tucked away in a thicket somewhere for just such an occasion. I could have done that; I should be dry and calm. I could have, I should be.

The words rattled through my head as if pulled on a noisy chain. A chain as noisy and cruel as those that had bound Nerys in her chamber? Or those that perhaps held Gareth in whatever prison he now found himself in?

I shook myself, wrestling for calm I knew would not come, and marched on through the forest for an hour, then two. The sky rumbled. It was only midmorning, yet everything was dark. Black clouds roiled overhead, tinged with green. Distant lightning flashed. The air was acrid and stark, as if shot through with the ice of angry magic. Some foul energy prickled at me, raising the hair on my arms. I felt as though I were being watched, like the storm cloaked a hundred seeking eyes. My exhaustion was making me imagine things; a storm was simply a storm, I told myself, even knowing it was a lie. Nothing was simply itself in these northern lands, with the Mist spreading ever outward.

Finally, I reached the stables where I'd trained with Ryder, just as fat, cold drops of rain began to fall. I held my breath, searching the yard, the surrounding trees. My muscles ached; my heart ached. Was he here? Was he up at the house? Had he gone to a village somewhere in the Mistlands?

Then a flicker of movement caught my eye, and I saw him. He was leading two horses into the stables, perhaps after having worked them in the yard. They followed him eagerly, like ducklings trotting after their mother, and once they were inside, Ryder began shutting the stables' doors and windows, closing out the storm. At the final door, he shot a look up at the clouds, then began to shut himself into the stable. So, he would not be going back up to the house. I was glad; I didn't want to set foot in that place.

I found my courage and hurried over to him before he could fasten the door. He saw me slipping through the gate and waited for me, then closed the stable door once I was inside, where everything was warm and strewn with clean hay, the air sweet with oats and horses. I turned to him, my mind racing as I tried to figure out how best to explain myself. *I couldn't sleep last night. I'm so angry at everything—the world, my parents, myself—that I can't concentrate on anything but that.*

I've missed you.

Before I could speak, his arms came around me, and I melted into his embrace.

"I've missed you," he said, his voice deep and rumbling.

I smiled against his chest, dizzy with gratitude. "After only two days?"

"In fact, I started missing you the moment we parted." He put his hand in my hair, then let out a soft, irritated grunt. "Farrin, you're icy cold. Come here, love."

He took my hand gently, and I followed him without question down a quiet hallway, past tidy rooms of stored tack and stacked sacks of feed. At the end of it stood a small room with a stove, a chair, a chest of drawers, a bed. A metal rod with clothes hung upon it spanned the room on one side. There was a faded blue rug on the floor and a messy stack of books on a small bedside table of polished walnut.

I froze on the threshold, tears pricking my eyes as I took in the room. It was the humblest, coziest, sweetest space I'd ever seen, and a fist of sadness squeezed my heart as I realized what it meant.

"Did you come here when you were younger?" I whispered. "To get out of the house?"

"I did," he answered simply. "Father never liked the smell of horses, so I knew he wouldn't come here. Trina had—*has*—her own room at the other end."

He practically growled the word *has*. Then he brought me clothes:

a soft flannel shirt, linen trousers, a pair of thick woolen socks. He stood there frowning at them, then at me. "These will be far too big for you, of course."

I took them gratefully, held them to my chest. "They're perfect."

Our eyes met, and I felt suddenly bashful of my tangled hair and muddy clothes. But Ryder's expression held no judgment, his gaze so soft that my cheeks burned to behold him. He came to me with a towel, kissed my forehead, and said quietly, "Take your time. I'll be just down the hall." He closed the door behind him.

In the quiet, the stove crackling softly, I peeled off my sodden clothes and hung them as best I could by the fire, grateful that this room held no mirrors. If it had, I wasn't sure I could have done so much as take off my boots. The clothes Ryder had given me were soft and clean, and they smelled like him. I stood for a moment and closed my eyes, feeling enveloped in him through his clothes—his touch, his scent, the warmth of him. I combed the snarls out of my wet hair and weaved it into a loose braid, listening to the thunder rumbling quietly, the steady rain driving against the roof. The storm was fully here, and I was glad. The sound of it was strangely comforting, like the familiar industrious hum of Ivyhill. I took a steadying breath, opened the door, and padded down the hallway in my sock feet.

I found him in one of the tack rooms, folding the horses' blankets. Of course he hadn't been able to just sit still and wait for me. He looked up at my approach and froze, then set down the blanket he was holding and sat on a nearby bench with a sharp exhale, something like a laugh. He dragged a hand through his dark hair, which he wore loose to his shoulders.

"I wasn't at all prepared for that," he said with a rueful smile. His blue eyes shone in the lamplight. "You look so beautiful right now that I think you should forego ever wearing your fine dresses again and instead simply raid my wardrobe. From now on, it's trousers and flannel work shirts for you, my beauty, and huge socks especially."

With his delighted gaze upon me, I felt warm down to my toes, and newly bold. I turned around as Gemma might to model one of Kerrish's new gowns. "It's the newest style. Clothes so big you're practically swimming in them."

He laughed, his expression soft and dear. "The next royal ball should be interesting. Everyone will be tripping over their hems." Then he leaned back against the wall and regarded me. "You came here, I think, because you missed me as much as I missed you. But there's something else, isn't there?"

Now I was the one to laugh ruefully. "There are many things. Too many. My mind is full of questions and doubts and..." I sighed, shook my head. "And *anger*. Anger at so many things I can't begin to untangle them. It all sits right here." I tapped my throat. "A burning, an ache I can't dislodge. And when I'm with you..."

I hesitated, my courage faltering. I could say it, but I couldn't look at him when I did. "When I'm with you, that ache is easier to bear."

He was quiet for a moment, then said, "I understand that, both the anger and the relief. The peace that comes when I'm with you. All your anger, your mighty shields, and underneath you're still soft as a kitten, Farrin." I heard a smile in his voice. "You inspire me. Did you know that?"

I made myself look at him then, drinking in the sight of him. This bear of a man, sitting patiently before me with his diamond eyes and his dark beard, the folds of his plain gray shirt falling around his broad torso as finely as any royal silk.

"Would you like to talk about any of it?" he asked.

I shook my head, my mouth suddenly dry, my heart racing.

"What would you like to do, then?" His deep voice was velvet soft.

"I want to make love with you," I said quickly, the words spilling out of me. "I want to…I want to see you. And I want you to see me, all of me. I want to feel…" I paused, flushing.

"You want to feel safe," he finished quietly.

I nodded. "Yes, I want all of those things, I do, desperately, but… it will be difficult for me. So I'm telling you now, before I lose my words. I want this. I want you. All of you. But I don't want to make the decisions—what to do next, how to move—because I'll end up talking myself out of everything. So can you do that, please? Can you…" I hesitated, lifted my gaze to his. "Can you take charge of things completely? I think it will help me if you do."

"Farrin." He held out his arms to me. "Come here."

I obeyed, grateful for even that small direction. I climbed into his lap and nestled against him, sighing happily when his arms slid around me. He held me there, stroking my back; I could feel his heart pounding against mine, the quickening of his breaths. Rain drummed against the roof, sheets of it pulsing in the wind.

Ryder pulled back and looked up at me, stroking my cheek with his thumb. "I can do all of that for you," he said, "for us, but you must promise me something. If at any point you feel hesitation or discomfort and want to stop, you have to tell me. You know yourself. You know the difference between being brave and being needlessly self-punishing."

I laughed a little, shaky in his lap. "I'm not sure that I do. But I will tell you. I promise. I might tell you too much."

He shook his head, traced his fingers along my jawline. "There's no such thing. I'll stop whenever you want me to. We can stop right now if you want."

"No," I whispered, trembling at his touch. "Don't stop."

He nuzzled my cheek, kissed the hollow of my throat. I leaned into him, letting my eyes flutter shut as I reveled in the strength of his hands at my neck and hips, holding me to him. His lips blazed a slow, sweet path past the collar of my shirt. *His* shirt. Remembering that made me squirm, my hips shifting. He let out a sharp hiss.

"Do that again," he said, very low.

I obeyed, rolling my hips against his. Even through our clothes, I could feel the hard heat of his desire between my legs. The slight pressure—hard against soft—sent a thrill of pleasure blooming through me. I let out a breathy laugh, bore down on him again and again, seeking more of that, more of *him*. His hands were on my hips, helping me move, determining our rhythm. He kissed my neck, my collarbones, nudged the shirt aside. It was so loose on me that it slipped easily off my shoulder, baring my skin. The shock of cold air made me shiver, but not for long.

"Hold on to me," he whispered, and I slid my arms around his neck and let him carry me back down the hallway to his room. The light was soft, the air warm from the stove. He set me on my feet beside the bed and drew me up against him for a long, slow kiss. He cradled my head in his hands, and I stretched up to meet him, my skin prickling everywhere he touched me.

"I have an idea," he murmured against my mouth. A kiss, and then another, my lips tingling from the soft scratch of his beard. When he pulled away, I swayed closer, bereft.

"But wait," I protested. My words came out a little slurred; I was already drunk on his kisses, and I needed more of them. I curled my fingers into his shirt and tugged on it gently, whimpering a little.

He smiled, tucked a strand of hair behind my ear, rewarded my pleading with a kiss. He drew my lower lip gently between his teeth, and I shuddered at the feeling, new to me and scorching.

"Do you trust me?" he asked me, his brow pressed to mine, and though months ago I'd have answered such a question with laughter, suspicion, hatred—now, when I leaned into his touch with my eyes half closed, I felt only certainty, a slow-blooming calm.

"I trust you," I whispered, smiling up at him. He drew me against him, kissed my hair, my temples, and held me for a moment with a sort of fierceness, as if convincing himself that this was real, that I was real. And then he began.

Slowly, Ryder slid the shirt off my shoulders, as far as it would go without him undoing any buttons. The fabric gliding against my skin—the way the sleeves fell down my arms, trapping them gently against my torso—brought me an unexpected prickle of desire. And then Ryder fisted his hand in the voluminous fabric hanging off my back, tightening the shirt even further around my arms, and used it to tug me harder against him.

The shock of pleasure was incredible and made me cry out, a sound I couldn't contain. Being trapped by him, his arms like hot iron around me, not knowing what he would do next—and yet knowing all the while that one word from me would end it, that every moment, every second, he was listening to me and reading me, that if I lost my voice he would help me find it—the unfamiliar duality was over-whelming. He was stronger, laughably so, and yet his every kiss, his every touch skimming down my arms felt reverent, like a prayer said with his body. He was the mountain, intractable and mighty, but I was the god who could undo him with a wave of my hand.

I let my eyes drift shut as he lowered his head to my bared shoul-ders. He kissed every exposed inch of skin, followed each kiss with a smooth, slow glide of his hand. A stroke, a caress, and then another, his fingers feather soft and teasing. And then he murmured hoarsely against the fabric pulled taut across my breasts, "Farrin, turn around."

My stomach tightened at the sound of his voice; my knees went wobbly. I hesitated, looked up at him.

"Should I stop?" he whispered.

His eyes were soft, a tender blue. Marvelous, how those eyes could change, like daggers of ice when he was angry or sweet as bluebells when he was happy. I touched his face, traced the line of his dark brow.

"Don't stop," I told him, and then I turned around, facing the stove, and I held my breath, waiting for what I knew would come— what I dreaded, what I hoped for.

His hands settled first on my shoulders—huge and warm, like the weight of a favorite blanket. He kissed my braid, then my neck, and then he reached around me and found the buttons of my shirt. *His* shirt—every time I remembered that was like a new, thrilling discovery. I was wearing Ryder's shirt, and now he was unbuttoning it, slowly, carefully. With each button, his fingers brushed against my breasts, then my navel, then the trembling skin below it. I closed my eyes, my body tightening under his touch. I swayed back into the heat of him; my body knew what it wanted, even with its pounding heart and fluttery nerves. He slid the sleeves off of my arms, let the fabric fall to the floor.

I squeezed my eyes shut, forcing myself to feel the air on my bared skin and not recoil from it. My mind began to race. What did my back look like? I certainly didn't know. Was I still beautiful to him? The trousers he'd lent me were comically large; even with the waistband rolled over twice, I hardly dared to move for fear they would fall. Suddenly this seemed not endearing but childish. My feet were sweating in my borrowed socks. Tears pricked my eyes.

Then Ryder's arms came around me once more, this time to find my hands. I'd balled them into nervous fists, and he gently unfolded them, twined my fingers with his for a moment, kissed the dip between my shoulder blades. He then released me and brought his hands to my shoulders, started gently kneading my tense muscles. The steady press of his thumbs, the soft drag of his fingers down my spine, was the best thing I'd ever felt. I reached back and grabbed on to his shirt, steadying myself.

He laughed quietly. "I thought you would like this. Gods." His breath was hot on the tender skin behind my ear. "Your skin is unfairly soft. I could do nothing but touch your back for the rest of my life and be happy."

I let out a soft puff of laughter, shivering anew with each caress of his hands. "Now you're just flattering me."

"No, I'm simply speaking the truth." He circled his hands around my waist, his fingers spanning the trembling skin of my belly. He pressed his thumbs into the dip of my lower back, making slow circles, each one unspooling me. I felt limp under his touch and leaned my head back against his chest, not thinking of how that might expose me until I heard his indrawn breath.

He slid his hands up my belly, cupped my breasts, circled his thumbs around my nipples. I arched into him and cried out softly. I reached back for his head, grabbed at his hair. I didn't know what I wanted, but I knew I wanted him closer.

Gently, he released me and helped me stand upright. "No, not yet," he said, a smile in his voice. "First it's your turn." I heard him move a little and felt the cold of his absence against my back. "You can turn around. I'm not looking."

I hesitated, then obeyed. He was standing with his back to me, his arms at his sides. Even so, my skin prickled with goose bumps; he could turn around at any moment and see more of my body than whatever flashes of it I'd nervously glanced at over the years. But with the memory of his hands on me, the echo of his lips on my skin, that possibility didn't seem so terrifying.

And yet my heart still thundered as I went to him and began unbuttoning his shirt, as he had unbuttoned mine. At first I felt a little silly doing it; I fumbled to find each button, much clumsier than he had been. But then I began to notice how rigidly he held himself, how his breath came quiet and quick, the heat of him radiating under my palms as if he were the sole source of warmth in this room, of light, of life. The state of him, all tense anticipation and quiet yearning, emboldened me; I found my courage and finished.

His shirt fell to the floor, and the sight of his naked back took my breath away. He was all muscle and taut skin, every line of his body one of beauty and power. But what shook me most of all was the faint web of scars crisscrossing his skin—silvery and thin, quite old. He could've easily gotten rid of such scars; the Basks could certainly afford the finest salves and the best healers in the north. But Ryder had kept them, and I thought I understood why.

"Your father's work?" I said, quiet anger in my voice.

He nodded, fists at his sides.

"And you kept them so that every now and then he might see them and remember?"

He nodded again. "To remind him. And to remind myself."

I stood on tiptoe and pressed a kiss to each scar. My touch seemed to calm him; his shoulders loosened and his fists unclenched. Tenderness such as I'd never known ached in my chest. I wrapped my arms fully around him, pressed my bare skin against his. His hands came up to seize mine. I felt his heartbeat under my fingers.

"I'm turning around now," he said, and I nodded against his back, my heart pounding fast, and when we faced each other fully, a soft-ness came over his face. His eyes shone. There was no other word for it: he was marveling at me.

"Farrin in the stove light," he said, a smile playing at his lips. He shook his head. "You're exquisite, love. If I were the savant and you the wilder, I'd write a thousand songs about you."

That made me laugh, relieved and delighted and perilously near tears. "A thousand? That seems excessive."

I began to cross my arms over myself without really thinking about it. I wasn't used to being naked for longer than it took to bathe or dress, and though I still wore my trousers and socks, I might as well have been completely bare for how exposed I felt.

"No, Farrin." He came to me and lowered my arms, firm but gentle. He turned my face up to his, kissed my cheeks, the corners of my mouth. "You trust me, don't you?"

"Yes," I whispered, letting my eyes fall closed, letting my arms hang loose. "Yes."

"Then help me undress."

I did, my fingers shaking, and when he stood completely naked before me, I burned at the sight of him: his obvious strength, the grace in even his smallest movements. I felt some of my nerves melt away. I knew that body, even though I hadn't seen it properly until now. I knew the tenderness of his hands, the weight of his muscles, how it felt to be filled by him.

He let out a low groan and came to me, cradled my head in his hands, and kissed me deeply, his tongue opening my mouth, his hands sliding into my hair. I stretched as tall as I could, then slipped my arms around his neck. I felt his hard length between us, pressing against my stomach, and whimpered into his kiss.

"When you look at me like that," he murmured against my lips, "it makes me forget all the bad, and I can think of only the good."

I nuzzled his cheek. "When I look at you like what?"

"Like you want what I want."

I shivered as his hands slid down my back. He tugged at my pants, fumbling at the knot I'd tied in the drawstring so they had a chance of staying on.

I laughed a little, reveling in his obvious, earnest desire. "And what do you want?"

"To love you, Farrin," he whispered, dropping a kiss in my hair. "All I want is to love you."

His words opened something in me—a door I hadn't known was

there, a door that had been locked all my life. To be safe in the arms of such a man, to be loved for everything I was, to feel the rightness of my angry, lonely heart meeting another. I held him fiercely to me. I wanted more of him but couldn't find the right words to say so. "Ryder," I begged, with only that single, gasped word.

He seemed to understand. He grabbed the fabric of my trousers in both hands and shoved them down past my hips. They slid down my legs to pool on the floor, and then his hands were on me, cupping my backside, pulling me close.

"Gods, you're..." He buried his face in my neck, kissed me hard, sucked on my skin. "Beautiful Farrin. You're exquisite, love. A sunrise in my arms." He laughed ruefully. "Soon you'll have me writing poetry in your honor."

My whole body warmed at his words. I pressed myself toward him, let him gather me up against his body. The glide of skin on skin took my breath away; it hadn't been like this with Gareth, nor in any of my scattered, clumsy fantasies. I felt like a mere bird in his hands, light as air but sheltered against all wind and storms, all enemies. My many worries were gone; the weight strapped to my shoulders had lifted.

He guided me toward the bed, which boasted a fine blue quilt, a blanket of gray cashmere, and two pillows stuffed with down. It was a bed in a room in a stable, but he was a Bask, after all. I sank luxuriously into the fine fabric and reached for him, ready to welcome him into my arms, but he wasn't there. He knelt at the foot of the bed and peeled off my socks, the last bit of clothing I wore. My cheeks burned as he kissed the arches of my feet, the turns of my calves. I had no idea what I looked like from such an angle; a quick swoop of doubt winged its dark way through my heart.

"Ryder—" I began, ready to stop him, flushed from head to toe with embarrassment and wanting, so frustrated I could cry.

But then his hands slid up my legs, and he was kissing my thighs, parting them gently, and with my name on his lips, he sank down and put his mouth on me—right there between my legs, on the softest, hottest part of me.

I arched up against him with a gasp. My hands flew to his head, grabbed his hair. I'd never felt such a thing: his tongue stroking me, his lips lightly sucking on my skin. *Ecstasy*. That was the word. With his every touch, my pleasure crested higher and higher, white-hot and aching.

He paused to look up at me. The sight of him there, settled happily between my thighs, was its own kind of magic. My legs were jelly, my stomach tight and trembling. I laughed shakily, sinking back into the pillows.

"Should I stop?" he murmured against my skin.

"Gods, no," I burst out, making us both laugh. Then he buried his head between my thighs again, and I was no longer laughing. I had no lover to compare him to—Gareth had not done such a thing, perhaps hadn't known to do it or *how* to do it; we'd been so young—but Ryder's skill was obvious even to me. He flicked his tongue lightly, sucked at my tender skin, kissed the damp crease of my thigh. I grabbed fistfuls of the quilt, twisting hard under his mouth. He reached up for my wrists and firmly pinned them to the bed, stilling me. The weight of him holding me down, the sureness of his kisses—I could hardly breathe, every inch of my body pulled tight. Then, with one more hard press of his tongue, I shattered.

Pleasure rushed through me in hot waves, each golden crash unwinding all the tension of my body. The world was soft and dark, pulling me into a delirious haze—until I felt Ryder moving up my body, his skin hot against mine. We were both sweating, both breathing hard. Everywhere he touched me was too much, a lightning bolt of sensation that bordered on pain, but I craved it even so and twisted against him, pleading with only my body, my breath. I felt him between my thighs, let my legs fall open to welcome him. He grabbed them, hooked them roughly around his hips.

"Like this," he said, his voice hoarse, desperate. When he kissed me, I could taste myself on his tongue. "I want to feel your legs around me. Understand?"

I nodded, breathless, my blood roaring. To be handled by him with such certainty, such quick masculine strength, nearly made me come apart again. I teetered on the edge of pleasure, ravenous for it, murmuring nonsense, practically begging. Almost there, he was *almost there*. I let out a soft frustrated cry, shifted my hips underneath his.

He went still above me, his weight heavy and hot and fitting perfectly against me. He fisted one hand in my hair, gently pulled my head back to bare my neck, and nibbled lightly at my skin. So held by him, I couldn't move, and I didn't want to. I wanted to live forever in the sturdy nest of his arms, in the gorgeous freedom of this surrender.

"Should I stop?" he whispered. He lifted his head, and our gazes locked. My legs trembled around his hips.

I shook my head. "Don't stop."

And he obeyed.

CHAPTER 21

I woke with a chill of warning on my neck. Something was near.

I lay still in Ryder's arms, listening. The room was quiet, soft. Our clothes lay scattered across the floor. The fire in the stove had burned down to embers. Was the feeling merely a remnant of a dream?

Ryder's arms tightened around me. He was awake too. Even in my watchfulness, I couldn't help delighting in how sweetly we fit together. I was naked, and so was he. Our tired bodies were curled around each other, cocooned under the blankets—him flat on his back on the pillows, me tucked against his side. His arms were warm around me, one hand cradling my head protectively against his chest.

I silently cursed whatever had woken us. How dare it disturb such a perfect peace?

Then I noticed a glint of light in the room's corner, where I'd hung my sodden clothes to dry. Ankaret's feather gleamed in the pocket of my jacket. Each of the feather's fibers—scarlet, gilt tangerine, rich violet—glowed with its own inner light and stood alert, trembling, as if awakened by a static charge.

Ryder noticed it the same moment I did. "Ankaret?" he murmured. "Maybe she's close."

"Or something else is, and the feather is frightened of it."

"Stay here." Ryder brushed a kiss across my forehead and released me, rolling out of bed with a lion's grace. I watched him dress for a moment, admiring the lines of his body in the dim light, and then rose and put on my plain slate-blue dress, my tights, my boots. Quickly, my fingers shaking, I tucked the feather into my bodice. I could have sworn it curled happily against my skin.

Before Ryder could protest, I said, "Whatever it is, I'm hardly defenseless. You've taught me a few things, and besides that, I have my voice. My old power, remember? Ankaret said I shouldn't be afraid of it, and she was right. I can help."

He looked unhappy about it but nodded sharply, opened a drawer in the bedside table, unfolded a piece of velvet cloth, and withdrew from it four polished knives. He slid two into hidden sheaths in his boots, gripped a third serrated blade in his right hand, and handed me the fourth—an elegant dagger with a smooth obsidian haft. I followed him out, creeping quietly down the hallway just behind him.

Out among the stalls, the horses were restless, tossing their heads and prancing uneasily, snorting out warnings. A soft word from Ryder soothed them, but they were still alert, their ears pricked, their gleaming bodies poised and ready. I shivered to imagine what they could do at Ryder's command—charge any enemy, kick an attacker's chest in, tear off ears and fingers.

I wondered if they had done such things to Lord Alaster, ordered to violence by little Ryder or little Alastrina. I wondered what Lord Alaster had done later as punishment.

Pushing those dark thoughts out of my mind, I kept to the shadows as Ryder patrolled the main broad hallway, where we'd punched our leather targets what felt like ages ago. I breathed deeply, readying my voice. I would sing down the entire forest if anything tried to hurt him.

At the far end of the hallway, he paused at the door for a moment before flinging it open, knives at the ready.

Out in the woods beyond the stable yards paced Ankaret, a dazzling figure of feathers and flame. And before either of us could move to greet her, she flung two bursts of fire right at us.

We were ready and dodged the fire easily, but it landed squarely on the stable wall, and suddenly the horses were shrieking in terror. The flames spread fast, even though everything was storm-soaked.

"Go!" I shouted at Ryder. "Help them!"

Then I ran for Ankaret, dodging more knots of flying fire that raced past me, singed my dress, and struck the stable again and again. As I ran, I sang—another of the Gallinoran battle chants from the War of the Isles—and though my heart raced with fear, my voice came out strong. As I sang, I thought only one thing, a single word: *Stop.* I let the familiar notes bring the thought into sharp focus. *Stop.* Into my voice I imbued images of a doused flame, a fresh downpour snuffing out the stable fire, the faint hiss of steam.

Distantly, I noticed that the fire bursts wheeling through the air were growing dimmer, smaller. They no longer reached the stable, instead plopping harmlessly to the drenched earth. And by the time I reached Ankaret—livid with anger, buzzing with power—her glorious firebird form had shrunk to a mere peacock-size chick in the moss.

I stood over her, trying to catch my breath. "Can you stop the fire?" I snapped. I gestured back at the stable, where the flames were climbing high and Ryder was frantically throwing pails of trough water.

Ankaret looked up at me with those strange unblinking eyes, bright as stars. As before, I could not read her expression, but when she spoke, her strange multi-tonal voice sounded pleased.

"Farrin of the gods, Farrin of the old power," she said, her face a knot of fire, her mouth a snapping disc of bright light. "You did well just then."

I did not allow myself to savor the strange delight that blossomed inside me at her words. I flung out my arm sharply at the stable. "Stop the fire, Ankaret. Now. You've proven your point."

She obeyed with a slight sweep of her left wing. In an instant, the flames vanished, and the stable stood unburnt, undamaged. Ryder froze mid-stride, water sloshing from the pail in his hands. He whipped around to glare at Ankaret, murder on his face.

She rose on long legs of fresh fire and began to pace. The flames swept her along like a dancer across a stage. "She is sorry," she began, her voice troubled, crackling. "She doesn't want to do these things, to frighten you. Either of you. But she must prepare you. Do you understand?"

I nodded, watching her pace. Eerie, and beautiful, to see her flitting back and forth, quick and restless now, obviously perturbed. Her feathers stood on end, a brilliant conflagration falling around her body like a gown sewn of flames. With each movement, she shifted into a new shape. First, a fiery outline of a woman, then, in a flash, a fearsome crimson bird. The ground sizzled beneath her; each darting footstep dried the leaves she trod upon, but nothing burned.

"I understand," I said, "but the horses don't. Next time, don't terrorize innocent bystanders in the name of helping me."

Perhaps that was too bold of me, but Ankaret was seemingly too preoccupied to care. Her footsteps drew sparks along the ground, and she shook her head, muttering to herself.

I hesitated, then placed a hand on my stomach, as if to remind us both that there had been an exchange between us—a pledge of duty, if not outright friendship. The feather pulsed beneath my dress, warming my palm. "Why have you come here?"

"Because she can go where she likes," Ankaret snapped in response. She seemed to speak more easily now, as if she had been diligently practicing human speech since our last meeting. "And here is where she would like to be just now."

Ryder, glaring, came up beside me. Ankaret's white-blue gaze flew to him. "Apologies, Ryder of the House of Bask. I am glad to see you both."

Ryder gave her a hard smile. "I'm not. I don't trust you."

She tossed her head with a harsh laugh, throwing off sparks. "Has she given you reason not to trust her?"

"Well, you did pretend to burn me, and you just scared my horses into a panic, and beyond that, you are a mystery whose origins and motivations remain unclear to me. Anyone would distrust such a creature."

Ankaret paused in her pacing and fixed her blazing eyes on me. "Farrin trusts me," she said. "I see it on her face."

I felt Ryder glance at me, but I kept my eyes on Ankaret. "I think that if you wanted to hurt us, you would have done it long ago. You would have let your fire burn true and killed Ryder. I think," I added slowly, "that you could someday be a friend, and I hope I'm not wrong." I tried and failed to read some sort of expression in the flames, a face I could understand. "What have you come to tell us? Or did you simply come to test me again?"

She resumed her pacing, the air between us shimmering with heat. Curls of steam drifted up from her feet.

"You asked her, what is Moonhollow?" she said, her voice harder now, a little angry. "And she said she would find out for you, since you released her from your arrow, sparing her life and her dignity. And she did find some things. She asked and she watched, she pulled it from tongues and plucked it from the air. Moonhollow, here in your world. Mhorghast, in theirs."

I remembered Nerys's words. *Moonhollow. Your languages are as pitiful as you are.*

"Their language," I said. "You mean an Olden language? Is that where Moonhollow is, then? In the Old Country?"

Ankaret nodded, her feathers fluttering. "It is a city and it is a palace, hidden in Olden lands, and there are gardens that stretch for miles, all of it ruled by a great storm. The storm lives in the walls, and sometimes in the sky. The storm is not like others. It has a will, and a hunger. It does not simply storm; it seeks. It has many arms, and they travel far."

My mind raced as I listened to her, trying to tuck away her every word so I would remember it later. The sky overhead, thick with its own waning storm, seemed newly ominous. Ryder was tense beside me, held as rapt as I was.

"There are many beings there," Ankaret continued, speaking faster and faster, as if she would soon run out of breath. "Blood eaters and glittering tricksters, old winds with mischief in their eyes. Beasts made of many other beasts. Lady Winter and Lord Summer, and the forest folk with their smiles and charms. Some go, some stay. There is music that never stops and a moon that never sets."

I deciphered the riddles, each one making my stomach twist in fear. *Blood eaters.* Vampyrs. *Beast made of many other beasts.* Chimaera. *Forest folk.* Fae. Mara had said the Olden races were isolationists, loath to cohabitate. But first Nerys and now Ankaret had said otherwise. I tried not to linger on how disturbing it was that my sister, soldier of the Mist, possessed outdated knowledge.

"And are there humans as well?" Ryder said tightly.

Ankaret paused. Her light sputtered. "Yes. Taken humans are there in chains and cages, on tables and stages. They are not themselves. They are made to do things they don't want to do."

Ryder let out a breath, turned away in despair.

I ached to touch him but instead took a step forward. I would remain calm, clearheaded, for both of us. For Alastrina. For Gareth. I would not grieve for them now, not yet.

"Where is this place?" I asked. "How do we get there?"

Ankaret cocked her head. "You do not wish to go to this place."

"I do. My friends are there. Many people of my country are there. They are in chains, you said, in cages. They are prisoners, and we must free them."

A white light rippled sharply across her body. "You should not go. You are needed here."

"Do you have no pity for the humans held prisoner there?" Ryder spat. His blue eyes blazed almost as brightly as hers.

She watched him, uncowed. "Of course she pities them. She is no monster, like the storm that rules such an awful place."

"The storm that sometimes lives in the walls and sometimes in the sky?" I said slowly.

She looked to me sharply. "That is what she said."

"Does the storm have other names? I have heard of a being named He Who Is All. Could they be the same?"

"She has heard this name too," Ankaret replied. "In the winds and in the whispers. They call him storm, they call him He Who Is All, they call him…"

She trailed off, her light flickering once more. The brilliant column of her body seemed to shrink, as did the flaming blue pinpricks of her eyes.

"Do they also call him Kilraith?" I whispered.

The woods went deadly quiet, the only noises the rain dripping from the trees and Ankaret's crackling heat.

Her answer came thinly, a mere quiver of sound. "She hates that word."

A chill skipped down my arms. I would take that as a yes.

Ryder spun back around. "Well, where is it, then? Tell us or leave. And do it plainly, not in riddles."

In an instant, Ankaret stretched to her full incandescent height. A crest of fresh red feathers poured down her body like a waterfall. Her face was bright as the sun.

"You dare to make such demands of her?" she roared, her voice suddenly a torrent of rage. Behind us in the stables, the horses shrieked, terrified anew. She grew and grew, her wings spanning a hundred feet, the white-blue core of her body stretching half as tall as the nearby pines.

"She is Ankaret!" she howled. "Old as the mountains and vast as the sky. She saw the making of the world and will see its unmaking. And here you stand, Ryder of the House of Bask, speaking to her as though she is one of your horses, a simple beast who falls prey to your magic as a tree does to an ax. Presumptuous. Foolish!"

My mouth went dry, my eyes burning from the furious heat of her. All at once I was back in Ivyhill all those long years ago, with the house crashing down around me, the sweltering air pressing my lungs flat. I reached for Ryder, pulled at his arm, tried to find my voice.

"Ryder," I croaked. I coughed, searched my frantic mind for a song, *any* song.

But Ryder wouldn't move—not for me, and not for her. Unflinching, he stared up into Ankaret's inferno, and when he spoke, his deep voice boomed, easily heard above the spit and roar of flames.

"Will you burn down the forest now, and all the life inside it?" he called out. "And here we thought you could be a friend. We hoped we could trust you, but I suppose we cannot."

Ankaret's wings beat three times, thunderous claps that sent showers of sparks raining down upon the wet black ground. But Ryder stood firm.

"You remind me of my father," he said, his eyes reflecting the glint of Ankaret's fire. "He too has no control over his temper. He often uses his anger to hurt innocents, even children. Is that what you do as well, Ankaret of the ages?"

For a moment longer, she glared down at him with her lightning eyes, and I felt certain with each beat of her wings that *this* hot rush of air would send us flying to our deaths, that *this* one would hurl a wall of flames at us, reducing us to ash. I held on tight to Ryder, hid my face in his arm.

Even with my eyes closed, I knew the moment she decided to calm. The light burning through my eyelids paled; the roar of fire quieted. I dared to peer past the angry tower of Ryder's body. Ankaret shrank to her former size—taller than us, taller than any human, but herself again, at least the self I knew. I let out a shaky breath of relief.

"Trust," Ankaret said quietly, as if musing to herself. Her gaze flicked to mine. The bright white flames of her beak sprang open and then slammed shut. "You hoped you could *trust* her."

"Indeed we did," Ryder replied. "Were we wrong to do so?"

A shudder went through her; she shook out her feathers like a bird might after a bath. "Such a mouth on you. Such insolence cannot be borne. But she has a question now: Can *you* be trusted, Ryder Bask?"

"Of course I can," he spat. "We're talking about you, not me. Don't lead us down another road of riddles."

She stood very still, considering us both. "You want her to tell you the way to Moonhollow, do you not?"

"Yes." I thought Ryder might snap in two with sheer impatience. His arm under my palms was like a hammer, poised to strike.

Ankaret drew herself up into a quiet column of light. Her feathers gleamed as if freshly polished. "She will tell you where it is if you tell a truth to this woman whose love you think you deserve. A truth you have kept inside you for far too long. A truth she has the right to know. Refuse, and I will leave and take all knowings of Moonhollow with me."

With those words, with Ankaret's eyes trained on him as if they were in silent, private conversation, something in Ryder changed. The tension bled from his body; his shoulders seemed to sag. He said nothing.

I looked back and forth between them. "What truth? What is she talking about?"

"How do you know?" he said dully.

"She doesn't know all, but she can find what she wants to," Ankaret replied. I thought I heard a twinge of regret in her voice. "She listens and asks, she reads and seeks. She cannot hold all things in her thoughts, but some things she will never let go, once she uncovers them."

"That doesn't really answer my question," Ryder muttered.

"Then you are not listening."

It was as if I were no longer there. They glared at each other, the man and the firebird. I looked angrily at each of them, willing them to look at me.

"*What truth?*" I asked again.

"Do we have a bargain?" Ankaret asked, still ignoring me. "A fair one, she thinks. You would be a fool not to take it."

"Of course we have a bargain," Ryder said sharply. "And after you've fulfilled your side of it, I hope you'll return to whatever ancient pit you crawled out of."

Ankaret's flames didn't so much as ripple at his furious tone. "It is best, Ryder of the House of Bask," she said solemnly, "that this should happen. It is a kindness. Would you never have told her on your own? A coward does not deserve such a love." Then she seemed to soften a little. The brilliant snap of her fire dimmed to something cooler, more bearable. "Here. Poor heartbroken boy, frightened and alone. I see him inside you, that child. We will do it together."

Ryder didn't answer, looking miserably at the ground, and Ankaret turned her full attention to me. "When you were small," she said, "a child of eleven, you nearly died. A nefarious plot, one of many your families dreamed up for one another. For who else besides your mortal enemies would have been so bold as to burn down the House of Ashbourne?"

My blood ran cold at her words, more with shock than anything. The last thing I'd expected her to say was *this*. I braced myself against the inevitable rush of memories: the smoke, the fire, Osmund clinging to my chest, the certainty drumming through my mind that I would die.

"You tell me something I already know," I said coolly. "You speak to me of a fire while standing there blazing with flames yourself, looking hungry and unkind. Do you mean to frighten me? To reopen old wounds?"

The stars of her eyes disappeared into the fiery swirl of her face before reappearing—smaller, paler.

"No," she said, her tone uncanny, multipronged, but gentle. "She means to tell you the truth."

With that, she looked at Ryder, who looked so tensely despairing that I could hardly stand to look at him.

"Ryder of the House of Bask?" Ankaret said.

After a long moment, his jaw working, Ryder said quietly, "A boy saved you that night, Farrin."

"The shining boy, you call him," Ankaret added. "And he did shine, for he wore spellwork meant to persuade you to run. A spell to coax you beyond your fear. And he wore a mask to hide his face from you. For if you'd seen it, you would not have trusted him."

"You would have seen an enemy," Ryder said. Still he would not look at me. "You would have run away and died. The mask was necessary. The spellwork too."

My heart pounded, each of their words falling through me like a clap of thunder. "What?" I whispered. "What are you saying?"

"He is telling you a truth you should know," Ankaret replied. Her brilliant eyes were fixed on me. Her scarlet feathers gleamed in the light of her own fire. "He should have done it long ago but has been too afraid."

Her eyes cut past me, and I turned to follow her gaze, my whole body tingling with slow-blooming shock. Ryder stood still and silent. He finally looked at me without defiance or shame, with only a sort of tired acceptance. He was expecting a blow; it seemed he would welcome it.

Every moment I'd spent considering the impossible—Ryder, the shining boy; the shining boy, Ryder—unfurled anew inside me. My mind whirled with memory as I recalled the shining boy's pale skin, the dark hair curling out from under the crude mask with the blacked-out eyes, his voice—rough, but kind—his strength and courage. Once we were outside and safe, he'd held my hand. He'd kissed my knuckles. *Star of my life*, he'd whispered, and then he'd heard my family coming, and he'd gotten angry. *I have to go. I'm so sorry. They're coming now. You'll be all right.*

With Ankaret's words ringing in my ears, each piece of the memory rearranged itself and fell into its rightful place. I could no longer deny the truth I'd long convinced myself was laughable, that even Yvaine in all her kindness had implied was far-fetched. My sight, at last, was clear, my understanding horribly complete. Suddenly I recalled what Ryder had said that night in the Citadel, when I'd asked him to kiss me, to bind my wrists, to claim my body with his. *Star of my life*, he had murmured to me, and I'd thought the words familiar, but out of my mind with pleasure, comforted by Yvaine's promise— *Don't you think I would have told you, long ago, if that were the case?*— I'd forgotten to care. I'd *decided* not to care.

But Yvaine wasn't well, and I was the worst kind of fool for accepting her reassurance so easily, for ignoring my own instincts, all because I was desperate for the affection of a man.

I felt sick and cold, as if I'd woken up from a restless night of sleep to remember something I'd forgotten to do the day before, something that had slipped through the cracks despite my lists and routines, something that would disappoint someone or anger Father or make a servant's life more difficult. Something avoidable if only I'd been sharper, more disciplined. Except this feeling was a thousand times worse than that. Tears gathered behind my eyes.

If Ryder had kept *this* from me—the truth of this pivotal moment in my life—what else had he decided not to tell me?

"It was you," I whispered, staring at him. "You're the shining boy."

For one desperate moment, I hoped they were lying, that I was wrong and Yvaine was right, that this was some cruel game Ankaret was playing with us for an unknowable Olden reason.

But my hope died quickly. Ryder nodded, solemn. Resigned. Surrendering.

"It was me," he answered quietly.

I laughed a little, a harsh breath of disbelief. "I don't understand. You wore spellwork? You came to find me? But it was your family who—"

"No, it was my father and my father alone." Each of his words fell heavily, as if it came at a dear cost. "Mother tried to talk him out of it, but he wouldn't listen. It was time to end this, he said. It was time to show you whose family was truly the mightiest. It was time to show the Man With the Three-Eyed Crown," he added, his voice darkening with anger, "which family was truly deserving of all his many splendid promises."

Everything was becoming clear too quickly. I felt like I was kicking hard to keep my head above water. "And the spellwork you wore, the spell that made you shine..." I found the answer before I even asked the question. Was there no end to how foolish I could feel? "Of course. Your mother—a beguiler with a talent for persuasion. That was her doing."

He nodded. "When I came to her, pleading with her to change Father's mind, she said she couldn't, that she had tried. Her eye was black, her lip swollen. She'd tried, and he'd beaten her, nearly pounded the life out of her. But she could do this one thing. She could grant me a spell that would help me do *something*, save *someone*, anyone I could find."

He drew in a deep breath, his fists clenching. "And of course I went to find you. I was fifteen and stupid. I didn't care about the others, I'm sorry to say. Your sisters, your staff—maybe I would have helped them if I'd come upon someone and felt I had the time. But all I could think of was finding you. I waited until Father left, then took the greenway. He and the elementals he'd hired worked quickly. By the time I arrived at Ivyhill, the house already burned."

"Wait," I said, cutting him off. The world around us had shrunk to him and me, and the faint glow of Ankaret in the corner of my eye. "Why did you care about finding me? We hated each other, all of us did. Why didn't you just stay at home and let everyone burn?"

That made him look away once more. His mouth twisted. "Father often sent me on reconnaissance missions. I surveyed your estate, used your animals to gather information. I skulked around and observed. At first I felt proud to do it. Father hadn't picked Alastrina for this— he'd picked me. I hated him, and he hated me, but maybe this would change something. Maybe he would be proud of me at last; maybe this would end the war. And without the war, perhaps his tempers would fade, and I wouldn't have to be afraid anymore, and neither would Trina or Mother. But then one day, I came to Ivyhill and heard you singing."

He paused, took a breath. His gaze lifted back to mine. He looked miserable, his resigned calm shattered. "I'd never heard anything so beautiful," he whispered. "I knew you were a savant, that your talent was music, but I'd never witnessed it for myself until that day, and it…" He put a fist to his chest, clearly struggling for words. "It unlocked something in me, Farrin. It was like the ringing of some bell forged by the gods, chiming all the fear and anger out of me, and for the first time in my life, I understood that the Ashbournes were not just faceless foes to strike at however we could. You were people, like my sister and me, like my mother. People who had been blessed by the gods, just as we had."

He shook his head. "It shouldn't have taken me so long to reach that conclusion, but as I said, I was fifteen and stupid, raised in a house of anger and violence and plots. I'd seen you and your sisters before, of course—at the Citadel, at the parties both our families attended, all of us prowling around like wolves, plotting how best to attack. But as I listened to you that day—you were singing something new, I think, learning the notes; every now and then, you faltered and started again—as I listened to you, I truly saw you for the first time. I understood what we were doing—really understood it—as I never had before. We were trying to destroy each other. It seemed suddenly like the worst thing I could imagine, for the world to no longer have you in it, for such a voice to be struck silent."

I took a step back from him, from Ankaret, toward the black forest soaked with rain. My voice cracked all the way through. "How many times did you sneak around my house, listening to my music without my knowledge, without my permission?"

"Only when Father forced me to, I swear it," he said fiercely. "I wouldn't have kept coming if I'd had any choice, even if it meant giving up the chance to hear your voice again. I wanted to stop; I wanted it all to stop. Don't you see? Hearing you sing was a revelation. We can't choose when and how such epiphanies come. But that was mine, and from that day on, everything changed. Everything except Father." He took a step toward me, imploring. "You've seen him for yourself, Farrin. You know how he is. I've told you what it was like for us—"

"Yes, you've told me many things, and now I question all of

them." I hated how brittle and fragile my voice sounded, but most of all I hated having to wonder if any of what had passed between us was true. A memory resurfaced of the Bathyn tournament, months ago.

"The tournament," I whispered. "The song I played, I wrote it for you. For the shining boy. And you were sitting there listening to it, and you rushed the stage, yelling things in some northern tongue…"

"Talan and I have talked about that," Ryder said. "I'm so sorry for that day. He and Gemma were looking for ways to humiliate Trina and me in front of everyone, and he sensed my feelings for you without really knowing what he was sensing, and he brought them to the surface, and I—"

"And you couldn't control yourself," I said flatly. "You ran at the stage, scaring the life out of me."

"I wouldn't have hurt you," he whispered. "Even though I wasn't myself, stirred to madness by Talan's influence, I wouldn't have hurt you. I would *never* hurt you."

"But you *have* hurt me," I shot back, a sob stuck in the back of my throat. "We've become friends, and we've…" I gestured at the stable. "We've *loved* each other, Ryder, and all this time, you've known things I haven't. You've kept this secret from me when I've bared all of myself to you, everything I am, everything I feel. I *trusted* you," I said hoarsely, "and now that trust has been destroyed. What else are you keeping from me?"

"Nothing, Farrin, I swear to you," Ryder said, his voice thick with emotion I didn't want to hear.

Cruelest of all, it occurred to me with vicious suddenness that I had come here and spent hours in the bed of a liar when I could have used that time to search for Gareth. What a selfish, senseless woman I was.

I could no longer contain my furious tears. My mind was spiraling to all sorts of horrible places, most of which were completely irrational—products of my wounded pride, my embarrassment—and yet I could do nothing to stop it. When Ryder stepped toward me as if to comfort me, I stumbled away, flung out my arm at him to ward him off. "Don't touch me. Don't come near me."

He froze at once, his entire countenance crumbling. "Farrin, I'm so sorry. I should have told you the moment we started becoming friends."

"Yes, you should have, but you didn't." I took two more steps back from him. "And I've been mooning over you all this time without understanding the true imbalance between us. You knew the truth, and I knew only a lie. What a fool you must have thought me. How smug you must have felt, knowing that you'd finally gotten your prize after all these years."

"No," he said in horror. "Absolutely not."

"Then why didn't you tell me?"

"Because by the time I realized that I should have, it was long past the right moment. For all those years, trapped in my house behind that cursed forest of your parents' design, one of the only things that brought me solace was thinking of you, and your music, and the hope that by saving you that night, I'd helped you find the peaceful life you deserved. Every night, I went to sleep hoping I'd wake up to find the forest still there, still trapping us. I prayed that the curse would never fade. As long as were trapped, there was no war. As long as we were trapped, you were safe. But the curse *did* fade, and everything returned to what it had been before: more fighting, more hatred. You know what it's been like. Your father has his own temper."

"Don't speak of him," I whispered.

"And then there was the midsummer ball, and the chimaera attack in the Citadel, and fighting Kilraith in the Old Country. It all happened so quickly, and suddenly we were part of each other's lives in a way I'd never imagined. We were even becoming friends. And then...*gods*..."

His voice fractured. He looked away, dragged a hand across his mouth. Even in my anger, my heart ached for him; he was desolate, hopeless.

"I fell in love with you," he said quietly. He looked up at me, his eyes blazing and bright. "I *am* in love with you. In truth, I think I've loved you for years, ever since I first heard you sing, even before I dared to say it out loud. And every moment I've been with you these past few months has been a happiness I've never known, a dream become real, a peace I've never dared to imagine for myself. And I've been godsdamned *terrified* to lose it, to lose *you*. Ankaret is right. I have been a coward."

His gaze flicked to her, then back to me. "But I have not for a single moment *ever* thought you a fool. Not for even a fleeting second have I felt proud or smug or pleased with myself for keeping this secret from you. *I've* been the fool, too in love with you to think straight. Too afraid to lose you to do the right thing. You're right, I should have told you that very first day when we started training together. I should have told you, and I'm sorry I didn't. I'm so sorry, Farrin. If I could go back and do it over again, I would."

I did believe he was sorry. I'd never seen such raw devastation on his face, such miserable, biting shame. But no matter how insistently the rational part of my mind warned me to take a breath, to put space between us until my shock had faded, I couldn't think of anything but how angry I was, how humiliated. I'd been lovestruck, lovesick, distracted by my anger at Father and my unending collection of worries.

And then, as if flung at me like a spear from a merciless attacker, the night we'd spent together at the inn in Vallenvoren came roaring back to me, bathed in a new, garish light. One of the most beautiful nights I'd ever known, and now my stomach turned to think of it.

"But can you be sure of what you're saying?" I whispered. "You say you've loved me for years, ever since you first heard me sing."

Saying it aloud felt as if someone had clamped their fingers around my throat. "How can you know that you truly love *me*, then, and not just my music? How can you know that you're not like everyone else? And how can I *ever* believe that you're not just trying to worm your way inside my heart so you can keep my music close to you, like a hoarder of treasure?"

Ryder opened his mouth to speak, but I hurried on before he could. "That night in Vallenvoren," I said, "when you touched me, and then I sang to you. I gave that song to you out of love, and I convinced myself that doing so was a triumph. I wasn't brave enough to let you fuck me, but I'd sing to you, and that was something no other woman could give you."

Looking back at the moment made me feel unclean, as if I'd given away a part of myself under false pretenses. I drew in a ragged breath, dashed a hand across my face.

"Maybe that's what you wanted all along," I whispered. "My music. Maybe that's what you've really wanted ever since you heard me sing all those years ago. And you took me to bed *hoping* I'd freeze with nerves, hoping I'd feel guilty and embarrassed and sing for you instead."

The words were awful, cruel, and even as I uttered them I didn't believe them. It was my fear talking; it was the ecstatic mob from that long-ago concert ripping me to pieces. Ryder wasn't like that; Ryder thought I was brave, that I was strong, a devoted sister, a patient daughter. I was so much more to him than a pretty voice. At the tournament, he'd been a victim of Gemma and Talan's scheming. He would never hurt me, *never*.

But I was lost in the mire of my dread, all the worst things I'd ever thought about myself bubbling up to drown me. The words had been said, and I couldn't find the strength to take them back.

It was as though I'd struck him. He slumped a little, his eyes bright with tears, and then he came toward me, his hands out, beseeching. "Farrin, I swear to you—"

Quickly I stepped away. "I trusted you. I *exposed* myself to you. And for what?" I put a hand to my throat; I felt like I would be sick. "So I could follow you around for the rest of my days, oblivious, like putty in your hands?" I spat the words. Anger was my only defense, my last gulp of air. "You love my power. It's had its hooks in you since the day you first heard me sing. And that's what you love, not me. Not *me*."

I turned away from him before he could reply, my whole body burning with tears I fought to contain, and went to Ankaret. As I looked up at her unreadable face, her overwhelming heat licked at my fingertips, but I was too furious to be afraid.

"Where is Moonhollow?" I demanded. "He told me the truth, as you requested. Now give us the information we need. Or are you as much a liar as he is?"

Ankaret's flames were a subdued yellow glow, her eyes wide and pale. "All the storms that now live belong to him," she said quietly. "Follow them to the place where they are born, and you will find his city."

Another riddle. I couldn't even find the will to be angry at her for that, and anyway, her answer seemed genuine. This was the best she could do. I simply nodded, her words held tight in my mind, and left both her and Ryder. Each step away from him was like tearing off a piece of my own skin, but I pushed onward, my chest aching, and neither of them came after me. I was glad; I was *grateful*. I headed straight into the woods, toward the distant greenway to the hidden lagoon.

It was dark at Ivyhill, the smell of rain in the air. The sky teemed with the same rumbling storm clouds that had churned in the north. I couldn't bring myself to care. I walked in a daze, drenched and shivering, so lost in my own unhappiness that I didn't see the raven flying toward me until he was right in my face, flapping wildly.

I jumped back with a yelp, and the poor thing fell to the ground. He had expended the last of his energy flying toward me, and when I realized what I was seeing—one of Ryder's wilded ravens; it *had* to be—I knelt and lifted him carefully. His tiny heart pounded hard and fast, and one of his wings was broken. How he'd managed to fly at all, I didn't know. Winded as he clearly was, he still flapped out of my hands and then away toward the hedge maze—half flying with one wing, half hopping on tired legs.

I followed him into the maze, readying myself for whatever I would find. The raven was most likely Ryder's, but it also could have been a trap. I forced my breathing even, tried to slow my racing heart; if I was going to sing for defense, I needed calm, I needed air.

But singing wasn't necessary, because now I saw what the raven was leading me to. He hopped toward a heap on the ground, clicking with his great curved beak, letting out strange rasping cries that sounded eerily like the word *help*.

The heap groaned, struggling to turn over, and a beautiful pale face came into view, framed by dark hair. His neck and arm gleamed black with blood.

My stomach dropped. *Talan.*

I hurried to crouch on the ground beside him, the raven hopping pitifully at my elbow. *Help, help.*

"Talan, hold still." When I touched his coat, my hands came away wet. "Oh gods. What happened? Please, don't move. I'll get Gemma, Madam Moreen."

But before I could rise, he caught my arm, holding me back. In the dim light, the tendons in his neck strained with the awful effort it cost him to stay conscious The crown's scars glittered faintly on his forehead.

"I found it," he whispered, a small smile playing on his lips. "I found Moonhollow."

CHAPTER 22

I ran to the house, woke Gemma, and quickly told her what I'd found. If she wondered why I'd been walking about the grounds in the middle of the night, she didn't ask. She ran at once to fetch Gilroy and Madam Moreen.

Father must have heard me clattering through the house in a panic. He came out of his room with clothes thrown on over his sleep shirt—a coat, trousers, boots. His appearance caught me off guard; he looked rested and clean. His brown eyes—*my* eyes—were clear and sharp.

Hope fluttered in my chest as I beheld him. He looked so much himself, so different from the drunken, staggering man who'd yelled at me in the morning room and thrown his glass. But I pushed hard against the feeling, kept my face composed. As much as I wanted to—as much as I loved him, even with all his faults—I could no longer trust him.

In that moment, with the memory of Ryder's despairing face so freshly seared into my heart, it felt like I couldn't trust anyone, perhaps most of all myself.

"Talan?" Father asked quietly.

I nodded, joining him as he strode down the hallway. "He's badly hurt. Gemma went for Madam Moreen. I can only hope that will be enough. I didn't get a good look at his wounds."

"Madam Moreen is one of the finest Anointed healers I've ever known. She will save him, whatever his wounds." Father spoke with such confidence and moved with such fluid grace as we hurried downstairs that the eager child's heart inside me leaped with happiness. Father knew what to do; Father would make everything right. But the woman I'd become was skeptical. Fleetingly, I wondered if I would always feel torn between these two parts of myself. Would I always be a creature of conflict, of contradiction?

"What did he say?" Father asked. "Did he bring news?"

"He says he found Moonhollow," I told him, with some hesitation. "That was all he said before falling unconscious."

Father nodded. He seemed utterly unsurprised, so Gemma must have told him some of what we had learned from Yvaine and from the harpy, Nerys. I wasn't sure if I should be glad or angry.

"If it's true, then we'll have to move quickly," he said. "Something could have followed him here. The way to Moonhollow could shift or change before we have the chance to go there ourselves."

"Talan wouldn't have come here unless he was sure there would be no danger to us," I insisted.

"We can't be sure of that. Even demons can lose their reason when badly hurt."

At the bottom of the stairs, Father stopped me with a hand on my arm. Though his grip was gentle, I flinched at the contact nevertheless. At once, he let go and stepped away. He didn't quite look at me, but I saw the remorse on his face. My two selves still warred—one full of pity, one flaring with anger. One desperate to return to Ryder, one dreading the next time I would see him.

"I must wake Mr. Carbreigh and his crew," Father said quietly, "tell them to be on alert." He glanced across the entrance hall at the morning room, where everyone was gathering. "I'll be back soon."

Then he left, sweeping out the front doors with a snap of his coat.

The ruckus had woken some servants—Lilianne, Gemma's maid, and my own, Hetty, and two wide-eyed kitchen maids—but Gilroy ushered them away, his stern voice brooking no argument. I hurried past them into the morning room and shut the door behind me.

Talan lay on a broad table someone had dragged into the room's center—Madam Moreen's nurse, probably. Bili was also her son, a strapping young man with quick hands and an iron stomach whom Madam Moreen had trained at her knee since he was a child. He was brisk and efficient, though not as impressive as Madam Moreen herself. She was a ballast of a woman, slender but solid, with smooth brown skin like polished oak and eyes hard and clear as cut glass. She'd been with my family for as long as I could remember, and I'd never been so glad to see as her as I was in that moment.

She glanced up at me, frowning. Her pressed white nightgown was already splattered with Talan's blood. "Good, you can help hold him, my lady. I'll have to cut away the infected flesh before we can sew him up."

I obeyed at once, my stomach turning as Talan's body came into view. He'd been stripped of his clothes, though Madam Moreen had thrown a sheet over his lower half—a sheet that was already soaked through with blood. The wounds were worse than I had thought: huge gashes across his chest and stomach, some running ragged down his sides. Something had torn into him, leaving him in ribbons. And even worse, the edges of the wounds were a sick purple-green color, like a bruise—and the color was growing, spreading. *The infected flesh*, Madam Moreen had said. My gorge rose. Infected with *what*?

"It's all right, my darling," Gemma was saying, her voice remarkably calm, though I saw the fear on her face, how her eyes glittered with tears. She held on to his left arm, her grip firm. "Madam Moreen is the best healer in Gallinor, better even than the queen's healers. She'll have you fixed up before morning. And I'm here, I'm right here beside you, and I love you, Talan. Do you hear me? I love you."

He looked up at her in obvious agony, his breath labored. "Gemma," he choked out. His eyelids began to flutter closed. "Gemma?"

"I'm here, my love, I'm right here." Gemma looked up frantically. "Madam?"

"He's lost a lot of blood, my lady. He's bound to fade in and out. Bili, are you ready?"

Her son took a slender knife from the array of tools laid out neatly on a nearby divan. He opened a vial full of acrid-smelling liquid and doused the blade with it. A smell like burning filled the air. I knew what that meant; the knife had been cleaned. Now Madam Moreen could start cutting.

"My lady?" she said, with a sharp glance at me. "His right arm, please. He'll fight us."

I obeyed at once, grasping Talan's upper right arm and holding on tight, hoping my grip wasn't adding to his pain.

As if sensing my reluctance, Madam Moreen said, "Don't worry about hurting him. The important thing is to get the poison out."

At once, I recalled the queen's ball. Whatever was in Talan, it looked far worse than the venom that had hurt me that night, and there was certainly far more of it. My chest ached with pity, with horror, and without even thinking, I began to sing a lilting tune, one of the thousand lullabies that lived in my mind's catalog of music. *In war, there is no room for grief or terror*, Ankaret had told me. I thought of running at her through the trees at Ravenswood, dodging her fire, singing my battle chant as I thought one thing again and again, my music focusing the word into a blade: *Stop*.

My eyes burned to remember it. Not long after that, the precious new world I'd been building with Ryder had shattered under the weight of his confession and my own frantic, spitting anger. And there in the morning room, with a song in my voice and terror lodged in my throat and my heart breaking, it seemed impossible that I could rebuild it.

Then Madam Moreen began to cut, carving away dark ribbons of infected flesh. They wriggled grotesquely, as if they were alive, as if they contained some burrowing, wicked thing. She dropped them on rags held out by Bili. He hurried to the roaring fire and tossed the dark bundles into the flames. Horrible shrieks rang out from the hearth as they burned.

I fought hard not to be sick and breathed through the putrid stench filling the air, forcing myself to keep singing. I kept the notes round and sweet, the words lilting, thinking of spring rain and solid mountains, clasped hands and cool breezes. Tender things, strong things, images of healing and resilience and a refusal to break. I tried to sing each image into the notes and shape the music around every phrase as if they were spoken commands—firm but gentle, and unflagging. To focus in such a ceaseless way made my whole body ache with effort. Sweat dripped down my back, and my tired mind obeyed with increasing reluctance.

You must practice this. Ankaret's words returned, a faint whisper in my mind. *You have let it sit idle for too long. She had to remind you.*

Tears ran down my cheeks unchecked. It was an assault—the heat, the agony in Talan's cries, the memory of my fourteen-year-old self sitting down happily to perform her first public concert, knowing nothing of the violent scene her music would soon unleash. The humiliation of knowing I'd bared myself to Ryder only hours before, the shame crawling through me to remember how cruelly I'd spoken to him. The desperate hope that he did love me, that he would still love me, even after I'd accused him of such terrible things—all of these horrible thoughts sat like boulders in my chest. Would I lose Ryder now? Should I want to?

I wiped my face, set my jaw, and concentrated on my breathing. *In war, there is no room for grief or terror.* I reset my grip on Talan's arm, glanced up at Gemma's stricken face. I kept singing.

With my song in the air, Talan's screams softened, and the strain on his face became a little less pronounced, but he still writhed, his entire body fighting to get away from Madam Moreen's flashing silver knife. I looked over at her and saw the sweat dripping down her forehead as she worked. The fire in the hearth was huge, its heat oppressive, but I was glad for it.

At last she cut away the final bit of infected flesh, and Bili tossed it with disgust into the fire. An hour had passed, maybe two. I had lost all sense of time.

"You can ease up on him a bit," Madam Moreen instructed us. Her son wiped her brow with a clean cloth. "He won't have the energy to keep fighting us now. But my lady, if you wouldn't mind continuing to sing?" She gave me a grim smile. "I find it relaxes me."

So I did, disappearing into the song's simple cadence as Madam Moreen and Bili worked with their vials and salves, their bandages, their needles. While Talan moaned in quiet agony, they washed out all his wounds and packed them with medicines, wrapped him tightly in bandages. When they finished, they bundled every bloody cloth into a clean sheet, then another one, then tied it all up tight. Only then did I allow myself to stop singing. I sat heavily in the first chair I could find.

"Take those out to the refuse pile and burn them all," Madam Moreen told her son. "Every last shred of them."

Bili nodded gravely and hurried through the open door. Father stood there, having just come in from the entrance hall. He stopped for a moment—appalled by the smell, no doubt—and then recovered himself and came inside, with Ryder right on his heels.

As exhausted as I was, the sight of him still managed to shock me. He wore traveling clothes in his typical black and midnight blue—coat, trousers, tall boots—and he had his crossbow, and knives at his belt. His dark hair was pulled back into a tight knot; his eyes were sharp, lupine. He was ready to fight.

Only when our eyes met did his fearsome expression falter. I couldn't read the emotion I saw there. Regret? Apology? Defiance? I went around the table to Gemma and helped her sit. She was trembling, ashen, her hands red with Talan's blood.

"Can someone bring water?" I asked sharply. And of course Ryder was the one to do it, offering a full glass before I'd even finished the question. I glanced up at him with a prickly glare, took the glass from him, and looked away. I helped Gemma drink, my heart pounding. My two selves began warring once again. One angry, one aching. One resolute in her rage, the other longing to go to him.

"Carbreigh and his crew are on alert, patrolling the grounds," Father said, "and I fetched Lord Bask because I thought he should be here to hear whatever information Talan has brought us. And because"—he looked at me cautiously, a little hopeful—"I thought his presence might be reassuring."

I didn't know how to respond to that, didn't know how I felt about it. Their clothes were dry; they must have come back to Ivyhill using not our greenway but the Basks', which meant that Ryder had decided to trust my father with its location. Did he hope that would impress me? Soften me? And then there was my infuriating father, fumbling to do what he thought might make me happy. He wasn't wrong, not entirely, but what did he expect me to say? Thank you? Now everything is healed between us?

Even though part of me longed to say just that, I fought against the instinct. A single clumsy kindness wasn't enough to warrant forgiveness, no matter how desperately I yearned for such peace.

"We must move quickly," Ryder said, breaking the awkward silence. "If Talan can tell us how he found Moonhollow—"

"Absolutely not," Madam Moreen said firmly. "He needs to rest and remain under my close observation. I'm not accustomed to treating demons. His body may react adversely to the medicine, especially if he experiences undue stress. And besides all that, I don't even know what attacked him."

"It's all right," Talan whispered. He shifted on the table, his eyelids fluttering open. "I can talk. Ryder's right. It's important. And Madam Moreen should stay. She should hear...what got me..."

Gemma went to him at once. "Darling, you don't have to—"

"You know that I do." He smiled weakly up at her. "My fierce wildcat. Don't worry. All of this looks worse than it is."

Not one of us believed that, but Gemma didn't argue. She bent to kiss his forehead, smoothing back his damp hair. "Fine." Then she looked up at Father and Ryder, her blue eyes blazing. "But the moment you start to push him too hard, I'll put an end to this."

"And I'll help," Madam Moreen added irritably.

"I was caught in a storm past the Spine of Caiathos, near Marrowgate," Talan began, his voice faint but steady. "I was chasing a rumor I'd heard of a great fire—maybe a Mistfire—that had run wild in the woods there, and a mighty elemental who had managed to stop it. I'd wondered if..." He paused, glanced at me, at Ryder. I suspected what he wanted to say—that he had wondered if this mighty elemental, talented enough to extinguish a Mistfire, could have been yet another god reborn. Caiathos himself, perhaps, living in a human body just as Kerezen now lived in Philippa's.

"Well," Talan continued, "the storm came quickly, as storms sometimes do, and this one was particularly fierce. I lost my way in the wind and the dark, and then thought I saw a path. A glimmer of moonlight like a road through the forest."

He glanced over at his raven, who sat with regal indignation on a cushioned perch in the corner of the room, his broken wing bound. He let out a single cross chirp.

"Ianto tried to stop me," Talan continued with a fond smile. "He tugged at my hair and sleeves, flew right at my face, but the moonlight road was calling me. It grew brighter and brighter, such a welcome sight in that howling storm. I had to follow it. Of course, I see now that it was pulling at me with some sort of magical lure. It *wanted* me to follow it, and I couldn't resist. And suddenly I was there, like when you see something out of the corner of your eye—you're sure of it—and then you turn, and immediately the thing is gone. That's how quick it was for me, only when I turned to find the shape flickering at the edge of my vision, it didn't disappear. It became...a city."

He paused, recovering his breath. Gemma took his hand in hers. "Talan, please, it's all right," she said. "You can rest. We can talk about this later."

"No, no. I'm fine." He took a deep breath and continued. "There were gardens hanging from towering trellises. A sprawling city—or so it seemed at first. With each step I took, my perception of its size changed; it was as grand as the capital, then a mere bustling village. I did at least have enough sense to take on a disguise and decided I would explore and observe for as long as it seemed safe to do so. The sky was full of stars, the moon brilliant and huge. And there was a palace...a palace on the horizon, and then suddenly I was on its steps, and then the next moment it was far away again, like the distant shadow of a mountain. Then Ianto...he felt something. I don't know what it was, but suddenly he stopped trying to fight me, and off he went like a shot. I followed him. I thought..."

He shifted, wincing, to look at Ryder. "I thought maybe he'd sensed Alastrina. One of your ravens, raised by the two of you... Your wilding magic runs thick in his veins. It's possible, isn't it?"

Ryder nodded once but said nothing. I wondered if anyone else could see past his rigid posture and stern glare to the terrified hope shining in his eyes. I clasped my hands in my lap and stared at my fingers. I would not go to him. I would *not*.

"I followed him through...gods, I can't even describe it. A city of white stone, all of it gleaming in the moonlight as if lit from within. Great houses with no doors or windows, just breezeways and promenades open to the night air. Music everywhere, the streets running gold with honey and jewels, or maybe it was...I don't know, maybe it was blood. The place kept shifting, you see. Whenever I looked at it just right, the surface of it flickered and changed, then snapped back to itself. Everyone dancing...grand theaters full of roaring creatures... humans fighting each other in pits..."

His eyes drifted shut, his face contorting in pain.

Yvaine's words whispered ominously through my mind. *Moon by day, fire by night. Come and dance. Don't try to fight. The beauty of shadows, the garish sunlight. Spin for the watchers, their revels so bright.*

"What creatures did you see?" Father demanded. "Olden creatures? And humans were their prisoners?"

Talan nodded weakly. "Yes, so it seemed, and then...they found me. A clan of them. Old family friends."

His voice went dark there at the end.

"A clan of demons?" Gemma whispered.

"They sniffed me out. I don't know how. They set chimaera on me—three of them, leaping down from the rooftops. They shouted awful things at me, curses that lashed at my skin like whips. *Human-fucker*, they said. *Traitor to the blood.*"

Father looked away, his hands in angry fists. I didn't dare look at Gemma.

"Ianto came back to me, helped guide me to the moonlight road. He wasn't alone." Talan's voice came weaker now, his words less clear.

He was fighting hard to stay awake, to tell us everything he could. "There were others—birds, creatures, forest beasts. They fought off the chimaera. They...they were helping me. Showing me the way out. The demons—gods, they were beautiful, shining like waves, all of them sleek as cats. They shot the creatures who were helping me. They fell around me, and I tripped over them. Someone must have been helping them help me. I can't reason how else it could have happened. Some wilder instructing them to lead me out of there..."

Talan wet his dry lips. The room was deathly quiet; even the fire in the hearth had begun to die.

"But one of the chimaera got me before I found the road. I couldn't disguise myself anymore. The demons pursuing me must have been working some kind of magic to stop me from doing so. I couldn't even see the beast's face, what aspects it wore. Its claws tore me open and knocked Ianto flat. There was venom in its claws, and teeth. The pain was..." He shuddered. "Lightning in my veins. I think one of the demons' arrows caught it then, by mistake. Sending chimaera after me wasn't enough for them, apparently. They wanted to make certain I was dead. The beast reared back, roaring. If that hadn't happened, I think it might have killed me. The moonlight road wasn't far. I could see it shimmering at the edge of my vision. I scooped up Ianto and crawled toward it. I crawled and crawled, and then...I was here."

"Here," Ryder repeated tensely. "You mean where Farrin found you, in the hedge maze?"

Talan nodded, squeezing his eyes shut.

I went cold with fear. "But how did the road know to bring you here?"

He shook his head wearily, no longer able to speak.

"Such a powerful construction of magic as the road he described might have been able to read his thoughts," Father suggested, "at least enough to take him where he wanted to go."

"Maybe it was curious to see where that would be," Gemma said quietly. "A demon trespasser someone clearly wanted to help? The road—or whoever made it—might have wanted to know more about that."

Father burst into action. "Gilroy?" he shouted.

A moment later, our butler entered the room. In his sleeping cap and dressing gown, he looked too dear, too vulnerable. Everything suddenly felt that way, as if the whole façade of the house had been torn down to reveal the fragile people cowering within.

If Gilroy was surprised by the state of the room, he betrayed nothing. "Yes, my lord?" he said smoothly.

"Wake everyone and arm them," Father said. "Carbreigh's crew is already patrolling the grounds, but I need the household on alert as well. Organize shifts, post staff at every window and door. I trust your and Mrs. Seffwyck's judgment. I'll be leaving soon for Fairhaven and will come find you before I depart, give you further instructions."

Gilroy's eyes did widen a bit at that, but he paused for only an instant before replying, "Yes, my lord," and hurrying out of the room.

"Fairhaven?" I asked.

Father nodded. "The Royal Conclave needs to know what's happened, as does the queen. They'll want to know everything about Moonhollow and ready the Upper and Lower Armies to invade. It will take time to put together such regiments, with everyone scattered in the wake of the abductions. Farrin," he added, "you'll go to Rosewarren, request aid from the Warden. The Roses should be prepared to join forces with the armies. We'll coordinate from those locations. No doubt the Warden has means to communicate with the queen directly from the priory."

I opened my mouth to protest—this was happening too quickly, too rashly. An *invasion*?—but Father cut me off before I could speak.

"I know this seems extreme," he said, "but we have to act now, before we lose our chance. Talan," he continued, "tell me more about where precisely you were when you first saw the moonlight road. What were you thinking about at that exact moment? What was the temperature of the air? Were there any notable landmarks? Had you been in the proximity of any particular magic just prior to finding the road?"

Talan cracked open his eyes, his face horribly pale. "I smelled... fire and flowers. I smelled rain. There was cinnamon on my tongue. The sea roared and roared."

"So you were near a coastline? But you said you were near Marrowgate." Father looked impatiently at Madam Moreen. "Is he delirious?"

Madam Moreen raised her eyebrows. "Of course he is, my lord. He's just had a pound of poisoned skin cut off of him and has lost gods know how much blood."

"I'll send for Illaria," Gemma said quickly. "Talan's delirious, but he's also a demon. His mind is strong. Some of this might actually be valuable information, and if anyone can decipher gibberish about scents and flavors, it's her."

Father looked unhappy but didn't push Talan further. He looked up at me. "You'll go to Rosewarren?"

"And tell them what?" I said. "You speak of an invasion, but we don't know yet where to send anyone."

"Tell them to be ready. Mobilize their soldiers, bring them back from their assignments. It'll take time to rally our forces, and hopefully by then Talan will be well enough to tell us where to send them."

Their soldiers. As if the Order of the Rose didn't include his daughter in its ranks. But I couldn't argue with him. These were Father's strengths—his battle prowess, his strategic mind, his ability to act quickly. And he was right. The country was already wounded, its people frightened and grieving and scattered. Gathering forces strong enough to invade such a place as Moonhollow, a secret city hidden somewhere in the Old Country, would take time—and with every passing moment, things could change. The moonlight road could vanish, denying us access forever, or worse, Kilraith could come sweeping down it with an army of his own at his back.

I hurried up to my rooms and dressed quickly and warmly, gave a disgruntled Osmund a kiss, secured Ankaret's feather in my bodice, and raced back downstairs. Ryder was waiting for me at the doors, armed and ready. I drew myself up as tall as I could, kept my expression flat. *Am I that obvious?* I'd asked him the first time we'd sparred. *To me you are*, he had answered.

"I suppose you want to come with me," I said, sweeping past him without a second glance. My arm brushed against his as I crossed the threshold; I fought hard against the urge to close the distance between us.

He followed me, looming and quiet. "I'd like to, if you'll allow it. If I sit still and wait, I'll go mad." He was quiet for a moment, then said, "Do you think it could have been Trina? Could she have wilded those animals to help Talan?"

The guarded hope in his voice threatened to crack me open. I braced myself against the feeling, and my voice came out sharp and mean. "How am I supposed to know that?"

He didn't chastise me for the unkindness. Instead he said softly, "I'm so sorry, Farrin. I know you don't have to accept this, but I'll say it nonetheless—I've broken your trust. And I promise you, with everything I have in me, everything I am, that I love you not for your music but for your courage, your strength, for how fiercely you care for everyone around you."

His gruff voice wavered, breaking my heart anew, and yet I said nothing. What was there to say? Everything was still too recent, too overwhelming—our naked bodies moving together in that quiet, cozy room; the shock of understanding who he really was, what he'd done. My cheeks burned, thinking of all the years I'd wondered about the shining boy, even *pined* after him. It was a mystery I'd thought I would never solve, and all the while Ryder had known the truth. And gods, how would I ever forget the devastated expression on his face as I shouted at him in the Ravenswood trees? As a boy, he'd risked everything to save me, and I'd returned that kindness by spitting all my thorns at him. So he had saved me, and hadn't told me. So he had loved my music for years, and through it, had fallen in love with me. Were these really such terrible things? In his place, would I not have done and felt the same?

Exhaustion fell over me like a shroud. Everything had been easier before I'd known him, when I'd been alone, enduring all my worst moods without inflicting them on anyone else. Ryder certainly didn't deserve them. When we got to Rosewarren, I'd have to rest, at least for an hour or two. My mind was fuzzy, my thoughts scattered. Maybe sleep would scrub away at least some of this awful ache.

"After I left, what did Ankaret do?" I managed to say. We were nearly at the hedge maze, the greenway to Rosewarren churning silently within.

"She left not long after you did," he replied. "She told me..." He hesitated. "She told me she was sorry."

"I'm not. I'm glad she told me the truth. I'm glad someone did. Now I know the real face of things." Even I didn't believe myself; the sound of my voice was brittle and tired in the quiet night air.

I plunged into the hedge maze, my side aching. I was walking too fast; my legs were shaky. But I liked the force of my heels digging into the ground and my fists punching the air, propelling me forward. I followed the maze's winding path, ducked under the arbor heavy with vines. There was a slight dip in the hedge, where a familiar, eager magic pulled at me. To anyone else, it would have looked like just another stretch of immaculately groomed bushes. I stepped into the greenway without looking back. Ryder would follow, or he wouldn't. What did I care? My mission was the same either way.

But I knew right away that something was wrong. I'd used this greenway to travel to Rosewarren many times. It was a fluid, easy passage, like floating on my back down a lazy river, and in only eight seconds, it always deposited me gently on the grounds of Rosewarren, behind the veil of chiming snow-blossoms.

This time, however, the passage was sharp, jolting, and all too brief. A blink, a heartbeat, and it threw me out. I landed roughly and banged my knee. Ryder came out just after me, hitting the ground with a slightly pained grunt.

We were in a tangled, brambly thicket. I winced at the prick of thorns and gingerly peeked through the branches. What I saw wasn't Rosewarren; it was the nearby town of Derryndell, mere miles from Ivyhill. The night was quiet, the town asleep, but a few windows glowed with soft yellow light. Overhead, thunder rumbled. A flash of lightning illuminated a black line of storm clouds stretching across the sky to the east.

"I don't understand," I whispered.

"Maybe Talan brought some foul magic back from Moonhollow," Ryder said, "or Mhorghast, or whatever the godsdamned place is called. It could have infected the greenway."

"Or whatever sickness plagues the Middlemist—and Yvaine—has begun degrading other magical structures."

He grunted. "A comforting thought. How far are we from Ivyhill?"

"Five miles or so."

"We should start back before the storm gets worse. The greenway could work just fine next time, and it's the quickest way to Rosewarren. Maybe this is only a momentary aberration."

But I was only half listening, distracted by the line of dark clouds leading east—almost like a black road, or a shadowed forest path. I shivered at the sight of it, my heart racing. It was as if some switch had been flipped deep inside me, shifting the mechanism of my body from one state of being to another—watchfulness to eagerness, caution to easy courage.

"*All the storms that now live are his,*" I said. "That's what Ankaret said. *Follow them to the place where they are born, and you will find his city.*" I turned back to look at Ryder, beaming. "If we follow this storm, we'll find the moonlight road. I'm sure of it."

"And do what when we find it?" His eyes gleamed in the storm's strange light. "We can't go traipsing into an enemy city by ourselves."

"No, of course not, but we can test the theory and determine whether or not this is a reliable way to find the road. If it appears, we'll take note of where we were, how we found it, the state of the storm. We'll bring that information to Rosewarren and send it to the capital."

Ryder said nothing, glaring out at the dark landscape.

"I know you want to," I told him. "You're worried about Alastrina. If she did help Talan escape, she could be punished for it. Don't you want to do whatever you can to help her?"

It was a cruel thing to say, but at that moment I would have said anything to make him agree with me. I wasn't tired anymore; I felt no despair or anger. Instead I felt *ready*, like a hook in my heart was tugging me out of a mire toward fresh air.

I saw the moment the feeling took hold of him too—his angry brow smoothed out and his tense posture relaxed. A twinge of warning tickled the back of my throat, but I had no Ianto to try and stop me, no Osmund or Una or Freyda with their clear animal minds, so I ignored it.

"All right," Ryder said, giving me a hard little smile. "Let's try it."

I grinned up at him and took his hand, tugging him out of the thicket and into the open air. The wind hit us like a wall, knocking the breath out of me; cold, hard sheets of rain pelted us, soaking us through in seconds. But I hardly noticed any of that as we trudged across the sodden fields of Derryndell, keeping the line of storms in our sights. We were on a path I had never traveled before, and instead of feeling frightened, I felt giddy, triumphant. At the other end we would find Gareth, and Alastrina, and all the others who'd been taken. They'd been waiting for us; they would be overjoyed. I could see Gareth's smiling face, Alastrina's exasperated smirk. *Took you long enough.*

My teeth started chattering, my body responding to the storm even though my mind couldn't be bothered to. Soon I lost sight of Derryndell, the trees and the fields and the sky and its clouds all melding into one massive dark shape. I laughed through the awful cold, spun around to smile up at Ryder—and then I saw it, a glimmer in the corner of my eye.

I froze, afraid to blink, afraid to move. If I so much as breathed, I might lose it.

But Ryder had seen it too, and after a moment he seized my hand and ran toward it, laughing, as carefree and silly as a boy. My whole heart ached with love for him; was this what he could have been, had he grown up in a different house with a different father? Was this what *I* could have been? An untroubled girl so happy she could skip through even the fiercest storms and not be afraid?

The glimmer grew brighter and became a shimmering swath of moonlight rippling across the ground. It was the most beautiful thing I'd ever seen; tears pricked my eyes as I took my first steps along it. A soft warmth bloomed through my body. I was skipping across a sparkling lake; I was lighter even than the birds. The whole world was silver and soft, and Ryder's strong, steady hand was around mine. I'd never been happier.

Then came another flicker of movement at the corner of my

eye—this one darker, the dart of a shadow. It pricked the bubble of my happiness, and in that brief instant of clarity, I dug in my heels and pulled Ryder to a stop.

At once the world shifted, as if it had been tilted on its side and was now righting itself. The path of light under our feet faded, leaving us standing in an ordinary field under an extraordinary sky, with a huge, brilliant moon and more stars than I'd ever seen. Underneath it all stood a small but grand city, and gardens, and a palace, all twinkling with as many lights as the sky above held. The air was full of music—pipes and drums and fiddles—and distant singing, distant screams. Some of delight, some of pain.

It was like being dashed with ice-cold water. *Gareth. Alastrina.* I froze, Ryder's hand gripped in mine, both our palms clammy with sweat. Only then did we understand what we had done, what had been done *to* us.

Like Talan, we had taken the moonlight road—or it had taken *us.* We had found the city of Moonhollow.

The voice of Nerys the harpy hissed through my mind, correcting me.

Mhorghast.

CHAPTER 23

T error stole my breath. If I hadn't stopped us, we might have skipped right on into the city, ripe for the taking.

Immediately I looked behind us for the moonlight road but saw only a quiet forest where there had clearly been some kind of revel. Plates and cups lay scattered across the ground amid discarded clothes and empty shoes. Strings of lights were draped between the branches overhead, magicked to glow pink and violet in their paper cups. The road was gone, and the sky was clear, each twinkling star crystalline. My stomach sank. How were we supposed to find the road home if there were no storms here to guide us toward it? Talan had found it, but he might not have without the help of those beasts and birds, wilded by his mysterious benefactor.

No, by Alastrina. I told myself that three times, saying her name clearly in my mind. Alastrina had helped him. Even if it wasn't true, the thought was a comfort.

"Farrin…" Ryder's voice was low and awed, tense with warning. "It's happened again. You look…"

When I met his gaze, I could see that he wanted to avert his eyes, to shield them as if from a bright light. But he made himself look at me, even gave me a small smile. *It's all right*, his expression seemed to say. His gaze was soft. *We'll figure this out.*

A laughable sentiment—there was no guarantee of anything here except danger—but I clung to it nevertheless and looked down at myself, holding my breath. Ryder was right. I had changed. My skin glowed from within as if I'd swallowed a star. I touched my hair, which I'd tied back in a hasty braid, eager to get the greasy strands out of my face; I sorely needed a bath. But here, my hair was clean and thick, still bound in its braid but now soft and silken. I pulled the braid around to look at it, and my breath caught to see its lustrous sheen. Kerrish, Gemma's stylist, would have demanded to know whom I'd hired to achieve such an impressive effect. It was as though candlelight had been combed through the strands, leaving each tress shimmering and golden.

In Edyn, I'd felt tired, worn out, full of heartache and uncertainty. But here—in the city of Mhorghast, hidden somewhere in the Old Country—I felt reborn. All the pain in my heart remained, but my body felt renewed and rested. I could have run ten miles. I could have outrun Ryder.

I smiled a little to think of it, but then a jubilant whoop from somewhere not too distant sent me crashing back to myself. Ryder grabbed his crossbow, nocked an arrow. I whirled, a song in my throat. But we were safe. Whoever or whatever had yelled was elsewhere. We hadn't yet been spotted.

"What do we do?" Ryder muttered, his crossbow still held at the ready. "The road is gone. Are we stuck here?"

I shook my head, refusing to entertain such a terrible thought. "Talan wasn't. He found the road back. We can too."

"Preferably without being spotted by demons and chimaera first," he said drily. "But we don't have Talan's power of disguise."

"No," I agreed, "but we have mine."

The thought had dropped into my mind with perfect clarity. I could sing a firebird quiet, sing a demon down from his pain, sing an audience into a lustful frenzy. So I could do this; I could weave a disguise around us using only the power of my voice. *Farrin of the gods.*

The memory of Ankaret's voice gave me courage, and I began to sing quietly, a mere thread of sound under my breath. The tune was new to me, and yet it poured out as if I'd been practicing it for years. It was as swift and relentless as a swollen river. I fought hard to keep my voice low and not let myself be carried away on my power's eager current. I felt the danger of it keenly, as if I were dragging my finger along the edge of a knife. Any sudden movement might cut me open. For a moment, Philippa's face came to me on a thin undertow of fear. *You should have stayed with me,* she said. *What you carry is dangerous, and only I can help you understand it.*

Ryder shifted uneasily beside me. "You'll draw someone to us. They'll come after such a song, desperate to know who it belongs to."

I saw the tears in his eyes before he could wipe them away. My heart ached for both of us. Yesterday, I might have reached out to comfort him. Today, I kept a wary distance. I envied the old Farrin, the one who didn't know what I now did.

I looked out at the glittering city, trying to shove that ache down as deep as I could and think only of the task before me. "As long as I think of discretion," I explained, "distraction, deception, the song will provide for us what I command it to."

I didn't tell him that this was a hopeful guess, that I was only just beginning to learn how to direct my music with such singular purpose and didn't know the full reach of it—or its limits.

Ryder let out a thoughtful grunt. "Is that what you did before, when we fought Kilraith? Is that how it works here in the Old Country?"

That's how it could work anywhere, came the thought. It was my own, and yet it carried the flavor of Philippa's voice.

"I wasn't so deliberate about it when we fought Kilraith," I answered, thinking back. "That was instinct and fear. But now I understand better how it works. At least, I think I do." I felt the urge to look over at him but resisted it. "Do you trust me?"

The question tasted sour on my tongue.

"With my life," he answered gravely. He hefted his crossbow back into position, then went still. "I've an idea. There's a bird over there, a sparrow. Will you sing while I try to wild it? If it doesn't interfere with your magic, maybe I can work under the cloak of your power and ask it how to get out without being detected by...whoever or whatever is here."

It was a sound enough idea, but watching the sparrow hop innocently about left me cold. "How are we to know that whatever animals you find are actually what they appear to be? Their true forms could be disguised, or they could be under an enemy wilder's control."

Ryder knelt, holding out his hand to the sparrow. "After so many years of wilding near the Mistlands, I know when something is what it appears to be and when it isn't. I wouldn't try wilding an Olden creature, not under these circumstances. This little fellow is simply a sparrow."

Still skeptical, I nevertheless quietly resumed singing. If this worked, if we could move safely through this place under the veil of my song while Ryder wilded information out of the local fauna, we would be safe for as long as my voice held out. Maybe we could even find a few prisoners to bring home with us.

I tried not to think of Gareth's smiling face, his glasses that always seemed to need a good cleaning, his ridiculous messy hair. Instead I focused on my song and watched Ryder murmur his wilding magic. The sparrow came to him immediately. It hopped onto his palm, fluffed up its feathers in obvious happiness, chirping quietly.

Ryder stroked its chest, frowning. "He's from Edyn. He doesn't belong here. Must have slipped through the cracks somehow."

I fell quiet. "Or else he was brought here against his will."

"I don't sense any other animals nearby. When I wilded him, did you feel any sort of interference with your song?"

"Not for even a moment."

Ryder shot me a wry smile. "Perhaps it was foolish of me to imagine that my magic could do anything to unbalance yours."

He said it playfully, without ire or envy, but I saw the guarded look in his eyes, and the words sat uncomfortably on my skin. *Demigods is the word.* What would that mean for us, if we made it out of here? A creature who belonged in both worlds, or neither of them, and a human—Anointed and skilled though he was—who belonged solidly in the world of Edyn.

I pushed the thoughts aside. He'd kept the truth from me, but I was a wreck of a woman who insisted on thinking the worst of someone who loved me. That was the true chasm between us.

"Come on, then," I said, turning away with an ache in my chest. "If there aren't any other animals nearby, we'll have to find some."

At first Ryder and I tried to skirt the borders of Mhorghast and remain somewhat hidden in the forest, but at every turn, the trees rearranged themselves and the ground before us shifted directions, making us stumble, and suddenly the city was right ahead of us once more, as surely as if someone had picked us up and put us right where we didn't want to go. Mhorghast was pulling at us, and no matter what we tried, we couldn't resist it.

Grimly we surrendered to whatever magic lived here and entered the city proper. My skin prickled, a warning of danger that I desperately wished I could heed. Just as Talan had said, it was impossible to comprehend the true size of Mhorghast. The hope that my demigod blood would allow me a truer vision of the place vanished immediately. One moment, we walked through a grand city of glittering houses draped in fog, every eave trimmed with lights, every avenue paved with gilded stones. The next, we were in a cozy village with thatched-roof houses—humble but pretty—and tidy gardens bursting with flowers, and cobblestone paths illuminated by iron gas lamps. Then a blink, a breath, and the splendid city returned.

And always in the distance was the palace—Kilraith's palace, I assumed, hardly daring to look at it. Sometimes it looked like what I guessed was its true form—a palace agleam, grand and domed and turreted. Sometimes it was a mountain on the horizon, or a foothill blanketed with woodlands. But even as its shape shifted, its size remained the same. Mountain, woodlands, palace with a thousand twinkling eyes—it was always there. Looming. Waiting.

My throat was dry, my entire body hot with nerves. The streets felt hot and crowded, and they buzzed with noise, but the air was strange, shimmery, and whenever I tried to peer through the hazy chaos at a shape that looked like it could be a person, it disappeared. Instead I tried to focus on the air in my lungs, the notes of my song rich and full in my throat, the road in front of me. The ground was real, physical, whether it was gilded stone or pocked cobbles. Whatever it was, it was solid beneath my feet. I was alive, I was moving. I still had my body and my breath.

I let my vision blur to soften the disorienting effect of the shifting stones and flitting gray shapes around me. I heard Ryder breathing next to me and clung to the reassuring sound of his footsteps. The low murmur of his voice as he worked his wilding magic acted as a familiar undercurrent to my song. Birds darted here and there, brighter and more numerous the deeper we traveled into the city—a sparrow, a jay, a finch—as unnoticed and ordinary as they were back in Edyn. But every now and then, a brilliant jewel tone shimmered, or an unusually long tail flapped past me like a hissing ribbon. The murky shapes around me began to resolve and become distinct, as if my eyes were slowly becoming used to a new kind of sight. With each step, the shimmering haze that clouded the streets faded, allowing me a better view of the world around me. I saw a white lizard with two heads, each sporting two gorgeous aquamarine eyes. I saw a sleek golden cat bright as coins, a looming black hound with a sharp red gaze, even a pearlescent flash I thought might have been the horn of a unicorn, though it was there and gone too fast for me to be sure. These creatures Ryder did not touch and guided me to avoid as well.

The others, though—the sparrows, the gray squirrels, the harmless garden snakes—he spoke to in so many bestial tongues I couldn't tell one from the next. Quiet, fluid, his words were a melody in their own right, and the beasts answered back in hisses, quiet trills, soft chatter.

But watching him was a distraction I couldn't afford. I kept my eyes straight ahead and my voice steady, determined not to falter even as the labyrinth of Mhorghast became terribly clear to me. It felt wrong to ever again call it Moonhollow, as lovely and aptly moonlit as it was. Mhorghast—the deep vowels, the harsh consonants—seemed much more fitting a name. For no matter how pretty the lights on all sides and the stars above, no matter how grand and soaring the towers of each building we passed, everything about this place was deeply wrong. Every street, every building housed a party, some wild revel: dancing and feasting, or a contest of some sort—races, wrestling matches, games with hoops and balls and flung axes.

And everywhere I looked, I saw Olden beings, as if all the tales I'd ever been told, all Gareth's lectures I'd patiently sat through, had suddenly come garishly to life. No one seemed to notice us, and no traps magicked to catch trespassers sprang up to snare us, so it appeared my song was working, but the impossible horror of it all nearly stole my voice from me. There were pale vampyrs in rich brocade coats, their eyes black and glittering. Hulking wolfmen skittered up the walls, water nymphs and wood nymphs held court at the edge of a lake rippling with fountains, and furiants—who could move objects using only their minds—tossed doors and tables and trees at one another as lightning crackled up their arms.

Seeing such extraordinary beings on their own would have been surreal enough, but they weren't alone.

There were humans too. Humans everywhere. Humans in chains, humans in cages. Ankaret's words took on new, sinister life. *Taken humans are there in chains and cages, on tables and stages.*

And she was right. At first it was as though my mind couldn't understand what my eyes were seeing, and then, as I found my courage and looked harder, I saw the truth. Those axes were being thrown at humans forced to dodge them. The water nymphs and wood nymphs were fighting each other, some sort of playful war game, with their elements as ammunition and pet humans on chains as the targets. The wolfmen chased frantic humans, limping and in rags, across the gleaming rooftops. They were entertainment, I realized, my bile rising. They were *prey*.

A vampyr sprawled luxuriously across a claw-foot couch on a breezy veranda. I watched in horror as she lured close a man who was absolutely goggle-eyed for her, unaware that others around him were pointing and laughing, for he was wearing a ridiculous costume: too-big shoes, a too-tight velvet suit, his limbs heavy with jewels wrapped so tightly that they were cutting into his flesh. As he approached, leaning in for a kiss, the vampyr—who I realized with a shock of horror held a knife—opened his throat with one quick flick of her wrist. Blood came pouring out of him in sheets. She held him to her until her goblet was full, then let his body fall and took a long drink.

All around her, an audience cackled—other vampyrs, tittering light-nymphs with glowing teeth and hair, a huge muscled man gobbling down fistfuls of wriggling raw fish. He had sleek blue skin, sea-foam hair, and a long beard tangled with weeds. A titan, I thought, hot-cold with terror. A titan of the sea, who'd decided to take solid form and join in the fun.

Worst of all, there were *other humans* among the giddy onlookers—some in finery, some in rags, some gaunt, some well fed. Their eyes were wide and white, all of them laughing and smiling as the dead man's blood pooled at their feet.

I nearly got sick watching them. I felt like I was quickly losing my wits. I had known, of course, that Olden beings existed. They populated our lore and decorated our storybooks. There were whole courses about them at the university, and my own sister patrolled one of the boundaries between their world and ours. But to see them in reality, to see so many of them here together, populating a city that, if Ankaret and Nerys could be believed, existed solely to imprison and torment humans…

I faltered in my song; for the space of a breath, the notes broke.

An eerie, cold feeling swept across us A dark hound lounging at the feet of the feasting vampyr raised its head. The wind whispered with a sly voice, and the sea titan stopped eating, scaly wads of fish flesh clutched in his giant hands.

"Farrin, keep singing," Ryder said tensely. He touched my lower back, making me jump. I recovered myself, my heart pounding, and continued my song. After a few seconds, the eerie feeling faded, the sea titan resumed eating, and the hound lowered its head. My own spun with wild relief.

"I know it's terrible," Ryder murmured, "but you're doing wonderfully. Please keep going. I…" His voice cracked a little, and I looked over at him in alarm, but he wasn't hurt. He was *fuming*, his jaw tight and his eyes blazing. An impudent little jay perched on his shoulder, chirping quietly into his ear.

I didn't dare stop my song to ask even a single question. Instead I touched his arm, trying to ignore the nightmarish sounds from the veranda.

"Alastrina is nearby," Ryder explained. "Three different birds have told me so. She's…" He shook his head roughly. "Their words are disjointed, slow, like they're drunk. They say she's…*fighting*? They say there's a hole in the ground not far from here."

He glanced at me, saw the question on my face. "They've said nothing about the moonlight road," he said grimly. "I've asked in five different languages, and each one confuses them. They think I'm talking about the moon or the stars or the road we're walking on now."

My heart sank. An arrow whizzed past us, so fast and close that Ryder had to duck. I shrank against his side, and he held me there, his arm like iron around me.

"Can we go to her?" he said, very low, his voice thick. "If there's even a chance we can find her in all of this, take her home with us…"

I found his hand, squeezed it, and tried not to cry when he whispered his thanks and bent to kiss my brow. But my tears were perilously close, tingling behind my nose and eyes; it was this awful place, the smell of it, the beautiful rot of it. We waded through ankle-deep water, warm and clear as the Citadel baths. Huge white blossoms floated atop it, pushed along by some magical current, and fireflies bobbed lazily from bloom to bloom. Exquisite. Breathtaking.

And yet from everywhere came the sounds of tortured screams, frantic music, rapturous moans. I gripped Ryder's hand hard as we followed his birds upstream, trying not to imagine the monstrous things that were being done in every house we passed. Shapes undulated against windows framed by gauzy curtains; bodies floated lazily in courtyard pools—alive? Dead? I couldn't tell, didn't try to find out.

The image of the humans back on the veranda had lodged itself in me. How ecstatically they had celebrated the execution of one of their own. It didn't make sense to me. Either their happiness was a lie, and they smiled and laughed only because, that time, the doomed person hadn't been them. Or perhaps they were not themselves at all.

There were any number of Olden beings who carried the power of Jaetris, god of the mind. My own mind frantically ran through a list, the echo of Gareth's voice eagerly whispering each word. There were readers, who could study and influence others' thoughts; figments, who could trick others into believing illusions; furiants, who could manipulate objects with their minds; and dreamwalkers, who could enter someone's mind, and even travel from person to person, using dreams as their conduits.

And then there were others, like the greater demons—like Talan—who were descendants of Jaetris and Zelphenia, goddess of the unknowable. These greater demons could not only create disguises but also read, possess, and even alter the minds of their victims.

And beyond that, there was Kilraith, whoever he was, *whatever* he was. How far did his powers extend? How much could he control?

"There she is," Ryder murmured, wresting me from my frantic recitation. He pulled me to a stop, and when I followed his horrified gaze, all hope drained from my body.

We stood at the edge of a huge sunken arena—*a hole in the ground*, the birds had called it—and at the bottom, on the hard-packed black earth, stood Alastrina.

A chimaera faced her—huge, quick, and clever, with the head of a mountain cat, giant bony pincers, and a dozen scuttling legs. It scrambled toward Alastrina and lunged for her with one of its claws. She rolled at the last moment, and the pincer stabbed the ground, cracking it open. Steam escaped, blasting the chimaera in the face. It reared back, shrieking, and Alastrina took advantage of its confusion to dart under its body toward a crude spear lying on the far side of the arena.

The crowd gathered in the surrounding seats—hundreds of people, Olden and human alike—roared their approval at her maneuver. They pumped their fists, threw coins and flowers and silk ribbons. Clearly they adored her, and it was easy to see why. She was fearless, nearly as fast as the chimaera, and when she flung the spear, it landed true, piercing the creature's exposed soft belly. Bright green blood spurted across the arena, splattering the crowd.

But they didn't care about the mess, or its boiling, sour stench. They were on the edge of their seats; the chimaera wasn't yet done fighting. The spear stuck out of its belly, and it trailed a thick swath of green blood wherever it went, but that was no deterrent. It reared around just as Alastrina threw another spear and knocked it from the air with one of its pincers. It advanced on her fast, crossing the arena in mere seconds. She shouted at it, some ferocious growling command in a bestial tongue, but whatever she'd said only made the chimaera falter for an instant. It stumbled, shrieking with anger, and reared up once again to strike—but that brief distraction was enough. Alastrina grabbed its right pincer with one hand, a broken spear clutched in her other hand. She dangled twelve feet in the air, barely managing to hang on as the chimaera snapped its jaws, trying to snatch her legs—but its last confused effort wasn't enough. With a triumphant scream, Alastrina thrust her spear right into its exposed throat.

Its death was quick—a waterfall of green blood, a stumble left, then right, and then it crashed to the ground, releasing Alastrina to roll out from under its tumbling bulk. It did not move again.

The crowd's applause was thunderous. They surged to their feet, shouting two unfamiliar words over and over again. I couldn't interpret them, nor could Ryder, judging by his frown. He glared down into the arena as two hulking figures in armor ushered Alastrina away. They clapped her in chains but didn't drag her through the door in the arena's far wall. No, she walked there herself, her head held high. I thought I saw her flash a grin up at the bellowing crowd.

I licked my dry lips and kept singing—no matter what, I couldn't stop singing—but my legs were shaking with fear, and when Ryder pulled me away from the arena, his grip strong on my elbow, I was glad for it. I wasn't sure I could have moved on my own.

"We have to find her," he said, his voice thin with anger, and then he murmured something to our jay friend, who had not stopped flitting back and forth over our heads. The jay gave a raucous cry—an answer to Ryder's question?—and sped away.

As the arena's crowd emptied into the streets, we followed the jay, dodging rivers of beasts, beings, humans, flares of fire and lightning. A laughing swirl of air nearly knocked us both off our feet. I thought it might be one of the four Winds, or perhaps one of their squalling children.

If I hadn't been so frightened, so absolutely petrified of what might happen should my voice give out or should something hit me and knock me out, I would have laughed. I would have sat down right there in the road and laughed until I cried. It was absurd, what we were doing and where we were. Some strange flickering city where the sun never shone, tucked away somewhere in the Old Country and only accessible by a road paved with moonlight? My thoughts became frantic, started spinning into one another. Why had we let the road coax us here? Why hadn't we been stronger?

Ryder pulled me around the corner of a huge canvas tent. Bright banners hung from its peaks, fluttering in the breeze. A small golden craft sped through the air over our heads, trailing glittering dust in its wake. I stared after it, dazed, my voice continuing its song automatically, as if I were a machine, a golden craft myself.

Ryder shook me hard enough to break my stare. "Farrin? Farrin, look at me. Don't stop singing, but look at me."

I obeyed slowly, gazing at him through a shimmer of tears. When I sang, I tasted salt. Every time I breathed, I smelled another new, terrible thing—a putrid yellow stench that reminded me of Talan's dead skin. A floral perfume so sweet I had to fight not to follow it, find its source, and claim it for myself.

Ryder's expression softened. He gathered me to him and held me against his chest. I clung to him. I sang and sang; I feared I would have to sing forever. The jay hopped frantically on his shoulder, letting out angry, piercing cries. I hoped my song was enough to hide it too, or someone might notice a bird losing its mind for no apparent reason. Though did there have to be a reason in such a place?

"I know," Ryder muttered angrily into my hair. "It's awful here. Evil is too mild a word. Even the air feels malevolent. But you're doing so well, Farrin. You're so good, so brave and strong. Can you keep on for a little while longer?" He tightened his hold on me. "I have to see her, even if it's only for a moment. And the jay says she's near. Maybe we can free her, or…"

There was a question in his voice, one he didn't dare put to words. *Can we? Will you help me?*

I squeezed my eyes shut against the burning air and nodded against his chest. Of course I would. We could certainly at least try.

Ryder gave my temple a fierce kiss. Then he pulled me forward, following the jay's darting path through a small village of opulent tents and glittering pebbled paths. A child in silken robes glided between the tents with jeweled amulets on gold chains draped over her arms. A rather peckish-looking vampyr sold fine crystal goblets and brocaded cloaks while gazing longingly after every passing warm body. At the mouth of a black tent spangled with tiny diamonds like stars sat a creature I could not name. She was pale and faceless—a woman on her upper half, a glistening worm on the bottom. When we passed her tent, she said nothing, but she spread her arms wide. I heard the chime of distant bells and tasted honey on my tongue.

Ryder's grip was painful, but I squeezed back just as hard, and after what felt like hours of winding through this awful clanging maze, we reached a shimmering, sky-blue tent. Ryder whispered hoarsely, "I think this is it. He says it's clear. Sing hard, love."

I obeyed, marveling at the unwavering cascade of my voice. I'd never sung for this long without rest, without even a moment's pause, and yet my throat felt as smooth and supple as if I were lounging in the Green Ballroom at home and trying out some new aria, completely at my leisure.

Ryder held the jay close to his chest, whispering something to it. It went very still and quiet. Its beady black eyes sparkled with eerie intelligence. Then it flew off into the night.

Ryder lifted his crossbow. "Stay close," he whispered, "and ready your knife." I grabbed the obsidian-handled dagger from my boot and nodded up at him. He took a breath and ducked into the tent. I kept as close to him as I could. My heart pounded so hard I worried it might disrupt my song. My hand that gripped the knife was slick with cold sweat.

The inside of the tent was dim and quiet. The sudden change disoriented me, and I stumbled a little, right into Ryder's back.

"Who the fuck are you?" spat a sharp, familiar voice.

It was Alastrina. She sat at a large table laden with food, a roasted chicken leg in her hands and her lips smeared with grease. She wore a vest and trousers, just as she had in the arena, and her bare feet were splattered with mud and blood. Scars striped her face and arms, and though she clearly didn't want for food, she looked newly gaunt— her cheekbones sharp, shadows in the hollows under her eyes. Her wrists were still bound in chains, though fortunately her guards were nowhere to be found.

But when I stopped singing my melody of disguise, I could see at once that she didn't recognize our true faces. My stomach sank to my toes. Her eyes were wide and white—sharp, aware, but glazed—and she was glaring at Ryder as if he were not her brother but an enemy.

She shot to her feet, spat out her food, and opened her mouth to shout something. She was fast, but Ryder was faster. He grabbed her, spun her around, clapped his hand over her mouth. He looked at me, desperate—she was strong, and she was fighting him. She bit down on his finger, hard, and kicked over her chair, sending her drink clattering. Someone would hear us, someone would come—

Unless I sang a different song. A song of reason, of clarity.

I shifted on a heel-turn of sound, my power knowing what I meant even if I couldn't fully articulate it in my own mind. The melody I'd been singing for an age changed at once to something sweeter, calmer, in a major key instead of a minor. Into each note, I sang every clear thought I could think of, every open feeling I'd ever known—hope, contentment, assured industry. I imagined a dew-drop, a winter lake, a cleansing rain, the ping of a silver fork against a crystal glass.

The effect was immediate. Alastrina calmed in Ryder's arms, and her glazed eyes cleared to their familiar sharp blue. She let out a gasping sob against Ryder's palm, and when he released her, she turned and threw herself against him, clutching his jacket—the best embrace she could manage with her hands bound.

"Ryder, oh gods, I'm sorry, I..." She leaned back and punched his arm. "How are you here, and *why*, you unforgivable idiot? You should never have come. Don't you understand?"

I took a step forward, infusing my song with a note of urgency. I didn't dare stop, but I needed them to understand the danger we were in, now that we'd lost our disguise. *Make it fast*, I thought into every light-footed note.

"We'll tell you everything later," Ryder said quickly. "Right now, we've got to get out of here. How do we find the moonlight road?"

Alastrina frowned. "The what?"

I pushed on past my dismay. I could not allow my song to waver a second time.

"It's how we got here," he said, "and how we can get out. Have you never seen it?"

Alastrina blew out a sharp, sad laugh. "I've seen this tent, and I've seen the arena. That's about it. Luthaes keeps me on a short leash. If there's a way out, I've not found it. Others, though…" She hesitated, shaking her head a little. Her eyes clouded, then cleared.

I dared to sing slightly louder, my body breaking out into a cold sweat. Whatever had hold of Alastrina wasn't giving her up without a fight.

"Wait." Alastrina glared at Ryder, then at me. "Did you come alone? Just the two of you?"

Ryder glanced at me, uneasy. "Yes. We didn't plan to, but the road—"

"And you're going to rescue me and leave everyone else?" Alastrina stepped back from him. Her eyes glistened with angry tears. "You can't. You fools, if you were going to come you should've brought an *army*, one strong enough to raze this place to the ground."

Before either of us could respond to that, the tent flap flew open and a gleaming figure strode in. His beauty nearly knocked me flat. His skin was a burnished copper, his hair a long white cloud of braids that seemed to dance like cottonwood seeds in his wake. His eyes were a bright turquoise, his pointed ears glittered with bloodred jewels and silver chains, and his gauzy robes were filmy as clouds, the same perfect sky blue as the tent.

My blood ran cold, and my song at last fell silent. I'd never seen one in the flesh, but I knew at once what he must be: one of the fae.

"And here's our gorgeous champion," he said. His voice was light and silver, like water rushing over stones. But then he saw us and froze, and those cheerful bright eyes turned dark with fury.

"What is this?" he purred, a slow smile curling across his face. "I don't believe I gave you permission to entertain guests, my pet."

The fae snapped his fingers, and an instant later the two armored guards from the arena burst into the tent, their swords flashing. But just then came a clamor of noise from behind us—shrieks, caws, feline yowls. The fae's eyes widened; even the guards faltered. I whirled to see a whole herd of beasts stampeding into the tent, our jay friend leading the way—at least two dozen birds, a handful of raptors, a sleek panther wearing a jeweled collar, a white stallion with its silver reins trailing.

"Farrin!" Ryder bellowed, running toward me. He dragged a stunned Alastrina behind him. I noticed with dismay that without my song to help clear her mind, her eyes had begun to cloud over again. But now was not the time for a song of clarity. I heard the desperation in Ryder's voice: *Hide us!*

Together we ran from the tent, and I began singing the melody from before, the one that had cloaked us. Note for note, phrase for phrase, the song poured out smoothly, as if my frantic running body were one creature and my serene voice quite another. The song carved a path for us through the crowds, and though I could see people turning all around us, exclaiming and curious, their eyes slid right past us, and we ran on—until, suddenly, Alastrina changed. She jerked on Ryder's arm, wrenched herself free of him, and kicked his legs out from under him. He fell hard, hit his face and elbow. Alastrina pounced on him, started pounding him with her bound fists, and in my shock I stopped singing for only an instant—but it was enough. I felt eyes cut toward us from all sides, heard hisses and gasps, roars of anger. An arrow flew past us, then another; the second one grazed my arm.

I cried out in pain but somehow managed to hold on to the threads of my song—no longer the song of distraction but the song of clarity. I stopped long enough to scream, "Alastrina, *stop!*"

That seemed to jolt her, as did my song, each note shaky but clear. She staggered back from Ryder, looking at her fists and then at him in horror. Her eyes were free of fog. Ryder reached up and yanked her down just before a spinning ax went flying through the air where she'd been standing.

"Whatever's in you," he shouted at her, "you need to fight it! Farrin can't hide us if she's busy holding you together!"

Alastrina looked at me, then spun around and shouted something I didn't understand—another bestial language, each word sharp as a knife. I hoped she was shouting for help, calling out to any beasts she could find. I huddled on the ground, shifting back to the song of distraction. But it was too late to hide; everyone knew we were here. Cascades of colors and shapes streamed toward us from all sides. Ryder jumped to his feet to shield me, desperately firing arrows from his crossbow. But he quickly used them up, and whatever Alastrina was shouting wasn't enough. I saw no animals running to our rescue, no jay wings cutting through the air.

I closed my eyes, pouring every bit of strength I still had into my song. Maybe I could change it yet again, sing a song not of simple distraction but of *defense.* Or maybe I could somehow hold all three songs in my head at once and infuse my voice with three instructions— distraction, defense, clarity. But as soon as I tried to make that shift, a wave of sickness rushed up my body. I fell to my hands and knees, fighting not to retch. What I was trying to do couldn't be done—not by me, at least, or perhaps simply not *yet.*

Then, all at once, everything around us disappeared: our glittering attackers, the flowering streets of Mhorghast, the great shadowed palace looming over it all. The world turned bright and white and cold, so brilliant and overwhelming that it sucked the breath right out of me, and my song died in my throat. The air shimmered, holding me still, humming its own eerie melody. I couldn't move; I could hardly *think*.

Suddenly I felt a hand on my arm—not Ryder's hand but someone else's. The grip was strong and cold, the skin hard and smooth as polished stone. I squinted up into the glare and saw a face that was both strange and familiar to me—Philippa, golden-eyed, sharp-toothed, resplendent in platinum armor. She wore a necklace of gilded bones around her pale swan's neck, and her long, loam-dark hair glittered with dozens of topaz jewels.

The sight of her turned me as cold as her grip on my arm. Any sliver of doubt that remained inside me regarding the truth of her claims shriveled up and blew away like ash on the wind. This was not simply Philippa. This was Kerezen, goddess of the senses and the body. Kerezen, reborn.

Somehow I found enough of a voice to rasp their names. "Ryder. Alastrina."

"Of course I have them," Philippa responded, her voice booming and bold as brass. It rang through my every bone, made my teeth chatter. "But I can bring no more with us. What a fool you were to come here. My brave little bird."

A memory fell softly into my mind. *Your music, little bird, will give the gods new life.*

Then she bent to kiss my forehead. I expected a frigid touch, but in fact her lips were scorching and turned me limp and pliant in her arms. The white world grew whiter still, and all sound fell away, including my own pounding heartbeat. Then I knew nothing more.

CHAPTER 24

Angry voices woke me, all of them muffled, garbled, as if I were underwater listening to the world above spin on without me. I came to slowly, struggling to find my fingers, my toes, my limbs. I listened for my pulse, heard the in and out of my breath. I ached, and my mouth was parched, but I was alive.

When I cracked open my eyes at last, I saw a ceiling overhead—elaborate white molding, a painted pastoral scene, Ivyhill's ever-present glossy green vines. Vines my mother had made.

Mother. Philippa.

Kerezen.

Suddenly, everything I'd seen in Mhorghast came rushing back to me in a torrent of fear. I bolted upright and immediately regretted it; a sharp pain stabbed my temples, the worst headache I'd ever felt. For an instant, my vision went black, then returned fuzzily, a shimmering aura softening every edge and brightening every color. I caught my breath and realized I was on a couch in the morning room, with Gemma beside me. Across the plush green-and-ivory rug was another couch, on which Talan reclined, looking wan and sweaty but at least a little healthier than when I'd last seen him.

"Ryder?" I croaked, struggling to look around the room. Even with Gemma's help, the effort was monumental. "Alastrina?"

"They're both here and alive," Gemma said quietly. My bleary vision made her glow like some dream creature. Her golden hair cascaded over her shoulder, bound with a silk ribbon; her dressing gown fell around her in emerald velvet folds. I gaped at her, marveling. I gripped her hand hard and leaned gratefully into her slim, sturdy form.

"Madam Moreen's tending to Ryder over there," Gemma continued, nodding at the corner of the room. "You suffered an arrow graze. Him, a few lacerations. Nothing too severe, thankfully."

I shifted a little to look, and when I saw him, alive and whole, glowering up at Madam Moreen as she bandaged his left arm, relief swept through me and tears pricked my tired eyes. Ryder met my gaze from across the room. His whole self lit up when he saw me, his scowl softening to that tender expression I now knew so well—his face open and dear, the years falling away from his face so that he looked more the young man he actually was, and less the angry son forged in our fathers' fires.

But then a shadow fell over his face, and he looked quickly away, frowning at the floor.

My heart twisted. How marvelous it was, how frighteningly precious, to be able to read another person's face so well. He thought I was still angry with him, and of course I *was*, but... Gods, we were alive. At that moment, nothing else mattered. If I'd been able to stand, I would have thrown all my hurt and wounded pride out the window and run to him.

"And Alastrina..." Gemma's voice trailed off.

Alarmed, I looked back at her. My vision was beginning to clear, and with it came a sort of creeping dread. "What is it? Is she hurt?"

"Not any worse than you and Ryder, at least not physically. But she hasn't said a word, and only Illaria could get her calm enough for

Madam Moreen to tend to her wounds. She wouldn't even calm for Ryder—"

"Whoever you are—*whatever* you are—if you have the power to heal them all, as you say you do, then do it at once, right this instant, or leave!"

Father's voice rang with fury, drawing my attention across the room to where he stood in the doorway wearing his travel cloak, boots, and riding gloves. He had said he would go to the capital to alert Yvaine and her councilors of what had happened; someone must have ridden after him and brought him back. Behind him in the entrance hall, armed and ready, hovered six of our house guards and our groundskeeper, Mr. Carbreigh, with his apprentices—all of them elementals with as much talent for combat using natural magicks as for crafting a topiary with simple shears.

And facing Father, I realized, my stomach leaden, was Philippa.

Her face was hard, and her green dress and gray coat were as simple as they'd been at Wardwell. And though the splendor she'd worn around her like a gleaming cloak when she'd come for us in Mhorghast was gone—that shining armor, her hair full of jewels—it still burned my eyes to look at her, as if some remnant of that godly glory still clung to her.

"I told you, I can't," she said, her voice flat and clean as a fresh blade. "I've already risked too much by going to Mhorghast and rescuing them. Even in the brief instant I was there, I'm certain they sensed my presence and knew me for what I was."

"*Who* knew?" I asked, pushing myself up onto my forearms.

She glanced over at me, her expression unreadable. "Everyone. Even the simplest of creatures there—your bird friends from Edyn—sensed it, even if they didn't understand it. But those who *did* understand…"

She fell silent. My whole body turned cold. "Kilraith," I whispered.

"He Who Is All, they call him," she muttered in agreement. "Though I don't know why. I sensed so many things in the moments I was there. So much agony, so much blood lust..."

Father was practically trembling with rage by the door. "As I said," he ground out, "if you don't intend to heal them, then—"

"You think I don't *want* to heal them?" Philippa snapped. She glared back at him, her dark eyes flashing gold. "My own daughter, her lover, her friends? Gideon, I *told* you: We are being watched. All of *Edyn* is being watched. A god wandered into their midst and then was gone. They'll sniff me out like a hound on a blood trail. Even my presence here is dangerous; the world will start responding to me as anything would to its creator, and people will begin to notice. And intentionally working magic would without question bring the wrath of Mhorghast down on Ivyhill. You are woefully unprepared for such an assault."

They stared each other down, Father and Philippa, before Father relented at last and sank into a nearby chair, his head in his hands. He didn't say anything more. My heart ached for him; I could only imagine what he was thinking, how it hurt him to see Philippa. His beloved wife had returned—not a trick this time, not Alastrina donning a cruel glamour, but perhaps something even worse. The wife he'd lost had come back and was no longer entirely herself. She was something more, something unignorably mighty. The whole room vibrated with her presence, as if some great drum were sounding in Ivyhill's basement, its rumbles traveling up the walls.

Desperate to break the silence, I somehow found my voice. "You said you sensed many things while you were there. What were they? Is it information we can use? Weaknesses in Mhorghast's perimeter, the city's population, Kilraith's location—"

A dark curl of laughter sounded from behind me, but when I sat up to find it, my heart pounding with sudden fear, I saw only Alastrina.

She was curled up in a chair by the window, her arms bandaged and her feet bare. My breath caught in my throat. She had looked gaunt in Mhorghast but still vital enough. Now she looked skeletal—her eyes haunted and red-rimmed, her scarred face draped in harsh shadows.

"You won't be able to find him," she whispered. "No one ever has. You think you're the first to try and crack the shell?"

She stared at us for a moment, her eyes glittering with tears, and then looked away, back out the window. Gemma's friend Illaria, who was also one of our closest neighbors, sat tensely on a nearby bench. She wore her long black hair neatly tied back from her lovely brown face, and a belt of herb sachets and stoppered essences strapped to her waist. Gemma had said she would send for her to help Talan decipher the scents he remembered from when he found the moonlight road, but now it seemed she had another task. Alastrina gripped her hand tightly, as if Illaria's presence were the only thing keeping her from being pulled back through the night to Mhorghast.

I shot Gemma a look, remembering her words from months ago. *I may have to play matchmaker with those two.*

But Gemma just shook her head at me, looking as bemused as I felt. I desperately wanted to ask Alastrina what she meant—*You think you're the first to try and crack the shell?*—but I stayed quiet, chewing my lip. She was in no state for questions.

"There were thousands of beings there," Philippa said quietly, as if she hadn't heard Alastrina. "Perhaps three thousand in total, most of them Olden. Most of them willing, but not all. And of the humans…" Philippa's voice darkened. "Most of them were unwilling, but not all. There were many deals being struck, many bargains being made. For wealth, for power, for flesh."

"And Kilraith?" Ryder asked from his corner. Madam Moreen had finished tying off his bandages, and he stood up, bristling with anger. "Did you sense him among all those thousands?"

Philippa's brow furrowed. She tapped her pipe against her teeth. "I sensed...a presence, certainly. A tremendous will. And it was familiar, which surprised me. This Kilraith...I do not know the name, nor have I met him, whatever he is. And yet..." Her expression grew more troubled, as if she were recalling a nasty memory. "And yet I know what I felt when I came to save you, my dear." She glanced at me, her gaze a bit absent. "I felt a great power in that place, stretching into every corner. Like ward magic, in a way, only much stronger. And..." She went to the fire and lit her pipe, puffed on it in contemplation. "So *familiar*. Like seeing a face across a crowded room, and you *know* that face somehow, or at least you recognize shades of it. But you can't put a name to it, can't remember where you first saw it. A kindred feeling."

"Kindred?" Talan turned toward her, his damp hair clinging to his forehead. "Do you think what you felt could have been the presence of another god?"

Philippa looked at him in astonishment. "Gorgeous demon. I'll attribute that question to your tremendous loss of blood. Another god? Absolutely not. I would have known one of my own brothers or sisters immediately, without question. Would you have caught my Gemma's perfume on the air and questioned that it belonged to her? Or would you know immediately, right down to your bones, the scent of your mate?"

Father shot to his feet. "All right, enough of this," he spat. "You are no *god*. You are either Philippa Ashbourne, with her mind scrambled by some nefarious magic, or you're a piece of nefarious magic yourself—a figment, or some glamoured impostor sent to confuse and distract us. Carbreigh! Captain Nomi!" he barked over his shoulder. "Confine this creature to the basement before she can say another word."

"Why, Gideon Ashbourne," Philippa cooed, still puffing thoughtfully on her pipe. "The mighty Anointed sentinel who boasts about his strength from coast to coast now sends his loyal house soldiers to fight *for* him? Are you sure you're not the impostor, darling?"

It happened quickly. Father's face twisted with rage. He lunged at her, his sentinel power booming out of him and rippling across the room like a hot ocean, stealing my breath and tipping every piece of furniture onto its side.

But Philippa didn't move, didn't even blink. With a breath, she grew taller, fiercer, the shape of her expanding to fill the room. Shadows shivered around her fingers as if they'd been drawn out of every nook and cranny to worship her. The fire in the hearth vanished; all the flickering candles in the room went out. The only light was Philippa—her eyes like torches, her skin like the sunset sky. Again I saw the faint glitter of jewels in her hair and the shimmer of mail across her bodice. Father came at her, but all his mighty strength was nothing. A flick of her hand, and he was down, sprawled on the floor with a huge gash carved across his chest. Blood spilled out of it, staining his clothes, the carpet, his skin. He gaped down at himself, gasping for air.

I tried to move but couldn't; Philippa's power pinned me to my seat. Instead I watched, tears streaming down my face from her unearthly incandescence, as she knelt at Father's side. She watched him for a moment, something like sadness in her eyes, and then she drew her hand up his body, and he was well again. No gash, no blood. Only a rip in his coat where the wound had once been.

The fire roared back to life; the candles reclaimed their nervous light. The shadows returned to their corners, scurrying away like spiders. And Philippa was simply a woman in a green dress, crouching beside a speechless man who looked like he'd just learned that the sky was in fact the ocean, that up was down.

"So you see now," Philippa said at last, "that I am what I claim to be. My story is a long one, and I won't tell it all again right now. It's far more important to tend to our wounded—which I suppose I should do momentarily," she added, with an irritable look at my father. "Now that I've already had to use some of my power to demonstrate your foolishness, I might as well fix everyone up. So, for now, suffice it to say, I am here and I am real. I am your wife, the mother of your children, and I am also a god. This is no trick. And I don't think you want to see what will happen if you or any of your staff tries to confine me again."

She rose and settled wearily into a chair by the fire. The sadness in her expression was quiet, resolute, and though her face was ageless, her eyes held lifetimes. I shivered as I contemplated an eerie question: Someday, if I lived to see it, would my own eyes look like that? A god's eyes trapped in a human's face?

"Now," she said, looking around at everyone, "while my power works to heal your wounds—it will be slower than I'd like, so as to hopefully not attract too much undue attention—let's all of us talk. We have an invasion to plan."

That startled me. Somewhere in the dregs of my exhaustion, I found a shred of my old anger, and it gave me the strength to speak. "I thought you were content to stay forever at Wardwell. You're a mere shadow of your former self, you said. You fear Kilraith will want to use you."

Her eyes cut quickly to mine. "And so I am, and so he most likely will. But I have had to show myself already, haven't I, in order to rescue you and your lover from your own lunacy? First you two, then your father and his temper. A moonlight road." She said the words scornfully, glanced at Ryder with an impatient curl of her lips. "I would have thought a daughter of mine and a man impressive enough to be her chosen mate would be able to resist the lure of a mere pretty trick of light."

Ryder drew himself up, as if to defend our honor, but Philippa waved him silent. "To Wardwell I will return, hopefully before the enemy comes sniffing around to find me. There I will hide myself away for everyone's sake. But first, since my cover has been so spectacularly blown, I'll help you. Someone take notes. My penmanship remains atrocious."

The comment was a stab to my heart. She had indeed always had sloppy penmanship, the sort of careless loopy lettering that as a child obsessed with neatness, I'd both abhorred and quietly admired. I glanced at Father. Ashen with shock, he had dragged himself back into his chair and now sat there in silence, his shoulders slumped, his whole posture defeated. Mr. Carbreigh and his crew, and the house guards, milled about uncertainly in the entrance hall.

Somehow I found the strength to rise. It was not a new thing, forcing myself into action to keep the house running when my father found himself unable to do so. I sent the guards away with instructions: continue patrolling the house and grounds; run drills using their elemental magic; reinforce the doors and windows; assign a partner to every staff member so no one ever walked alone.

Then I limped back to the couch and opened a drawer in the table beside it. A notebook lay within, along with a selection of pens. I opened the notebook to a blank page. When I looked up at Philippa, she was watching me fondly, a softness in her face that reminded me more of the mother I'd lost and less of the god who'd just saved my life.

I hardened myself against the pain screwing itself into my chest. "Well?" I said briskly. "I'm ready. Someone start talking."

Hours later, I staggered upstairs in a bleary-eyed daze, wincing with every step. Philippa had sworn I would wake in the morning feeling like nothing had happened, and I suppose I believed her, but my head was full, and my hand ached from writing, and my heart felt too heavy to carry. *War. Invasion.* The words sat strangely in my mind, tilting my whole world out of alignment. Armies would be gathered—both the Upper, with all their Anointed and low magicks, and the Lower, whose soldiers possessed no magic and instead fought with conventional weapons. We would send for reinforcements from the other continents, Aidurra and Vauzanne. Troops needed to be sent to every village, to reinforce their borders and teach the citizens what to look out for, what to guard against. They would have to lock themselves inside during storms, ignore glimmers of light, never walk alone, and carry tokens of reality and reminders of danger wherever they went—pieces of home, paintings of loved ones, locks of hair, handwritten notes. Anything that might jog them back to themselves and break them free of Mhorghast's hungry hold. Gemma had suggested hiring a crew of artisans to make more of the wooden tokens that poor Phaidra had given us before going to the Old Country—shapes that were dear to the owners, all of them carved from Edynic trees. They would serve as physical anchors to help people remember their homes—where they came from, where they belonged.

And then there was the Warden.

As I limped down the hallway of our family's wing, I imagined with dread what the Warden would think of this. We would need to delay the draft yet again and ask her to send the armies any Roses she could spare. I could predict the response we'd get. *And what do you think will happen if I send Roses to you and leave the Mist unguarded? Don't you think that's exactly what this Kilraith wants?*

And it was quite possible she would be correct to fear such a thing. The more I thought about it, the faster my thoughts scattered and spiraled. Could we trust anything we'd seen in Mhorghast? Or was all of it—the arena, the gilded streets, the looming palace—an illusion constructed to divert our attention from what really mattered? Philippa didn't think so; she insisted that even such an elaborate illusion as that would be no match for her godly senses.

"The same godly senses that you yourself compared to a child learning how to walk?" I had snapped at her, finally pushed past the edge of my patience by all the suggestions being thrown at me, the many tasks and questions I'd scribbled in my notebook.

Philippa had looked at me evenly through the veil of her damned pipe smoke. "A god learning how to walk is still a god, and more powerful than any Anointed human. Do not worry, angry daughter of mine. When I say that I would be able to sniff out a lie, I speak the truth. You can trust me."

Trust. Another word that sat askew inside of me. *Trust* a mother who had left us without explanation. *Trust* a god who had, along with her kindred, created a curse as reckless and dangerous as the *ytheliad*.

Trust a woman who had happily spent years locked away from all memories of the life she'd left behind.

Trust a man whose greatest crime was saving my life and being afraid to tell me about—perhaps in part because he feared I'd react exactly as I had.

I sat in my room, Osmund purring obliviously in my lap, and pored over my notes. A hundred new things to do, a thousand messages to write. Supplies to gather, weapons to stockpile. The egg, the key, the goblet, the black lake under a full moon, the Three-Eyed Crown.

Those five things I'd written at the very end of my notes, each object underlined. I hadn't mentioned them to Philippa, nor had anyone else. I'd been afraid to. Even looking at the words felt dangerous, as if rearranging the letters in a certain way would reveal some awful piece of spellwork that would activate upon being discovered. A silly fear; I scolded myself for it. Was I holding back information from her as some sort of petty revenge? *You left us when we were children, so I won't tell you about the strange images Gareth and Heldine deciphered from the Three-Eyed Crown's shadows. How do you like that?*

I laughed to myself, leaned back against my pillows, closed my eyes, and stroked the soft fur between Osmund's ears. Philippa was staying the night to help Carbreigh reinforce the grounds. She would leave for Wardwell in the morning. I would tell her then, at breakfast. *An egg, a key, a goblet, a black lake under a full moon.* What did it mean? Were they anchors? Were they clues? Were they nothing?

The words cycled through my mind, making my heart ache. With my free hand, I held my notebook to my chest and pressed it hard against my skin, as if that would do something to soothe my aching heart. Because of course thinking about the crown made me think of Gareth. *Gareth.* Tears burned behind my closed eyelids as my mind summoned the image of his smiling, bespectacled face, his messy hair, his rumpled tie. I imagined him surrounded by books, chewing on a pen until it stained his lip. I refused to think of him in Mhorghast, enduring whatever cruelties might be done to him there—if he was still alive, that is.

I bit my lips raw, thinking the words over and over: *Gareth is alive. Gareth is alive.* I would absolutely *not* think of how I wished we'd managed to save him and not Alastrina. She'd been there for longer than he had; it was only fair. But then, Alastrina had been well taken care of—pet of a fae, a popular attraction. A warrior, a wilder. What creatures of Mhorghast would value Gareth's sage mind?

I fell into a troubled sleep sitting slumped against my pillows, and when I jolted upright, my windows were soft with dawn and my skin was cold with fear. I lay there for a moment, my heart racing. Osmund was cleaning himself contentedly on the hearthrug. I heard no sounds of battle from downstairs, no cries of anger. And yet I couldn't ignore the panic twisting in my stomach. Something was wrong.

I hadn't ever changed into my nightclothes and raced downstairs in the ragged gown I'd worn to Mhorghast, just as Gilroy came into the entrance hall with the morning post. Ryder was behind him, tramping in through the front doors wearing dirty boots and smelling of horses.

"Ah, Lady Farrin," said Gilroy genially, as if we hadn't all stayed up half the night planning for war. "A letter has arrived for you from Fairhaven bearing the seal of the queen."

And there was the reason for my dread. I knew it the moment he lifted the envelope into the air, the moment I saw the distinctive purple wax seal. I didn't even thank him, just ripped the envelope from his hand and tore it open. I quickly read the hastily scrawled letter five times, my heart sinking so fast I felt dizzy.

Finally I looked up, tears in my eyes, and found Ryder standing tensely by the doors. He was focused entirely on me, his expression grim, as if he knew what I had to say before I even uttered the words.

"Yvaine is dying," I choked out. "She's bedridden, hardly talking, not eating. I'm to come at once to say…" I shook my head, unable to finish the awful sentence. "They think she may have only days left to live."

I crumpled the letter in my fists, as if that could somehow render false the news it carried. As if pain and heartbreak could be banished with a flick of my demigod wrist.

I tried to anchor myself with the steady blue steel of Ryder's gaze. There were so many things to say, and I couldn't find the words for any of them. My heart still twinged with hurt and disbelief. This was a man for whom I'd bared my entire self—body and heart and mind. That he hadn't told me what he'd done until Ankaret urged the truth out of him still ate at me, but what felt even worse was remembering the unfair accusation I'd leveled at him. *You love my power*, I'd told him. *Not me*. All the extraordinary kindnesses he had shown me, and in my anger the only response I had found was cruelty. Remembering how I'd lashed out, how the words I'd spat under those dark northern trees had seemed for a moment to strike all the light from his eyes, made it painful to look at him.

And yet I wanted no one else with me but him. Not for this, not for anything.

"Will you come with me to see her?" I asked him, tears hot at the back of my throat.

His grave expression softened. "I would go with you anywhere."

CHAPTER 25

W hen we arrived at the palace, two royal guards were waiting for us in the queen's tower. One of them was Captain Vara, the guard's golden-sashed commander.

"Ah, Lady Farrin," she said, striding forward. "Lord Ryder. She's been expecting you."

That surprised me, though perhaps it shouldn't have. "She's been expecting both of us?"

"Well." Captain Vara cleared her throat. "I suppose I should say, she expected you would bring Lord Ryder, my lady. This way, please."

I hesitated. Captain Vara was startlingly calm, even pleasant—not at all what I'd expected. In fact, nothing here was as I'd expected. Besides the protesters gathered at the gates and the general unrest in the air since the second wave of abductions, the mood of the palace itself was almost serene. No one was running through the marbled hallways bemoaning the tragedy of losing their queen.

I glanced up at Ryder, who was glaring around the corridor with a furrowed brow, like an angry watchdog determined to sniff out an intruder. His hand hovered at the small of my back; I was glad for it, and for the knives hidden up our sleeves and in our boots, the dagger tucked into his jacket, and Ankaret's feather tucked into mine. I held a song at the ready in my throat. This practice of preparing a melody with intent—like Ryder nocking one of his arrows, ready for battle—was easier each time I tried it. *You must practice this*, Ankaret had told me. *You have let it sit idle for too long. She had to remind you.* And remind me she had, with her fire and her lightning eyes. The memory of her unreadable face of flames was a strange comfort.

We followed Captain Vara through the tower's winding hallways until I suddenly realized where she was taking us—a winter garden in a small atrium tucked into one of the queen's receiving rooms. I knew it well.

At the room's entrance, Captain Vara stepped aside and gestured solemnly at the atrium's lush greenery. "Don't worry, my lady, we'll stay on this side and guard the passage."

"What is the meaning of all this?" Ryder growled under his breath. "Where is the queen?"

"She's at the Green House," I murmured, starting to put together the pieces of this bizarre puzzle. "My family's cottage on the edge of town. This is a greenway that leads to it."

"Her Majesty enjoys spending mornings at the Green House, my lady," Captain Vara offered. "She thinks it a peaceful place."

I sensed Ryder's surprise, though he bit his tongue and kept quiet. I slipped past the captain into the atrium and let the greenway's magic carry me gently through its passage. This greening magic was particularly fine; the crossing was quick and soft. Two seconds later, I stood in the gardens of the Green House, sheltered from the morning sun by a canopy of golden flowers. All around us, tall autumn grasses, white with puffy fronds, whispered in the wind.

Ryder was right behind me, and he stayed close as we crossed the quiet lawn. The house stood unlocked; no ward magic rippled at our passage, and the dining room doors had been thrown open to receive the morning air.

"There you are!" Yvaine burst through the doors and hurried across the veranda to embrace me. She wore a diaphanous gown of brilliant purple chiffon, the bodice spangled with diamonds, the iridescent sleeves trailing the ground. Her hair was loose, unornamented, her arms thin but fierce around my neck, but when she pulled back to look at me, I saw the gray under her eyes, the gray of her cheeks. Even the pink scar on her forehead had changed and now shimmered silver.

But she was alive, and for a moment all I could do was exist in the wash of my relief. I drew her back to me and put my hands on the silken down of her hair. I felt the wild pounding of her heart against mine and blinked back tears, trying to find my voice. She was alive, she was alive.

"What's happening here?" Ryder muttered behind me. "Farrin received a note that you were dying, bedridden, that you had only days left in this world. And yet here you are, looking more or less as you always have."

Yvaine looked up at him, her eyes sparkling. "Oh, Ryder. I do love your bluntness. No, I'm not dying. At least, not today. And I'm certainly not bedridden. I just...I wanted you to come quickly, both of you, and I knew that would do it. I wasn't sure where you'd be—these days, it's far too exhausting to use my power to locate anyone—so I sent one note to Ivyhill and another to Ravenswood. Hopefully no one in your family will open it in your stead, Ryder, and fly into a panic."

I stared at her, horrified. "And would you blame them for that? A message from the capital telling them their queen lies near death?" I stepped back from her, detaching myself from her embrace. "You sent *me* into a panic. I thought..." I struggled to collect myself. "Why didn't you just send for me as you normally would? Of course I would have come to you."

For an instant, Yvaine looked crestfallen. Then she lifted her chin. "The last time we saw each other, I attacked you. I was badly hurt. I wasn't myself. I wasn't sure that you *would* come unless I resorted to drastic measures. I thought you might be afraid of me after what happened."

"Honestly, I'm more afraid of you now," Ryder said drily. "That you would think it reasonable to lie about your own death speaks to its own kind of unsoundness."

Yvaine shot him a look, started to respond, then stopped. She let her thin shoulders fall. "You're right, of course. I'm sorry. I truly am. It's just…" She ran a hand through her hair, her fingers trembling. "Things are so strange now. Even stranger after I healed from my burns, as if parts of me were seared away and never quite came back. Some moments I feel wholly myself. Other moments are entirely lost to me, or else some mad idea comes into my head that I think is brilliant but is in fact reckless or nonsensical. Thirsk has been hovering over my shoulder like a fussy mother. He wouldn't have let me send such a message to you, of course. I managed it while he was sleeping. I exhaust him. I exhaust myself."

The bleak tone of her voice frightened me. I reached for her. "Never mind how you did it. *Why* did you send for us? Do you need help? Do you have news?"

She took my hand. "I need company," she said simply. "People I like, people I trust. People who aren't fretting old men or hard old women. Will you both sit with me and eat?"

❖

The day passed strangely, Yvaine flitting about the house like a nervous hostess. She stuffed us with food and drink, all of it fine and delicious, cooked by her own hands using ingredients from the royal kitchens. Over all the years of her life, she'd become a splendid chef.

She fed us puff pastries stuffed with goat cheese, bright green sprigs of parsley, and thinly sliced ham; roasted chicken garnished with dates and orange zest and served on a bed of crisp shaved greens, the meat so tender it seemed to melt in my mouth; a chocolate cake drizzled with raspberry syrup and dusted with icing sugar. Divine, all of it.

She bade me play the piano, which I did, haltingly and then with relief, for while my hands danced over the keys and my feet worked the pedals, I didn't have to look at her, didn't have to hear her shrill voice going on and on about meaningless palace gossip, the new gown her stylist was working on for the annual winter solstice gala, the renovations being done on the palace's north wing. It was all idle chatter, and whenever Ryder or I tried to bring up the abductions, the draft in the Senate, what we'd seen in Mhorghast, the impending invasion, she silenced us with a look, a word, a tap of her fork against her crystal goblet of sparkling lemonade. They were only little pings of magic butting against us, but she was High Queen Yvaine Ballantere of Edyn, and even little pings of her magic were enough to reshape our words and make us forget what we meant to say.

In the late afternoon, Ryder went upstairs to rest, claiming aches from his healing wounds. Our gazes locked for an instant before he left me. I had no doubt his body was indeed demanding a rest, but I couldn't imagine he would actually relent to one.

His absence did the trick; a few minutes after he went up, Yvaine paused her chatter to listen for him. Everything was quiet save for the breeze outside and the wind chimes Gemma had helped Philippa hang in the gardens when she was small.

Satisfied, Yvaine sank back onto the couch and closed her eyes. "Finally, some quiet."

My eyebrows shot up. "You're the one who's been talking without pause ever since we arrived."

After a moment, she opened her eyes to look at me. "I'm sorry I kept silencing you. All anyone ever talks to me about is how horrible everything is—the people taken, the Middlemist deteriorating, how everyone is afraid. And they're not wrong to do so. But I'm tired, Farrin." She drew in a shaky breath and gave me a thin smile. It was as if some dam within herself had been opened. She curled into the sofa cushions, drew her knees up to her chest. No pretense, no false bright smiles for the benefit of Ryder or her advisers. No, this was simply Yvaine, weary and too thin, drowning in her dress.

"And I wanted a day with my friend is all," she said quietly. "A day—a single day—of only good things and nothing bad. Before everything changes. Because it will, don't you agree? I taste it with every breath I take. Every time I move through the castle, I feel like my next step will send me plummeting over the edge of a cliff into a raging sea. I hear it rumbling always, in the air and even in the ground. Even now, with the sinkhole closed and my palace intact. All those storms in my skies, churning and growing, more and more every day."

There were so many things to address in what she'd said that I hardly knew where to begin. The exhaustion in her voice terrified me, as did the sight of her curled up on the couch. She looked alarmingly vulnerable, not a queen chosen to rule the world but instead a young woman who could easily be snapped in two by any number of monsters, man and beast alike.

"I do feel that," I answered truthfully. "And I think we'd be better prepared for that change, when it comes, if you'd let me talk to you about some things that have happened."

She closed her eyes, her mouth thinning. "Please don't. I don't want to use my power to quiet you again, but I will if you force my hand. I just want to talk about ordinary things, earthly things. Nothing Olden, nothing violent."

"But you yourself are Olden," I pointed out.

As am I, I wanted to say. A confession hovered on the tip of my tongue. I wondered if Yvaine remembered anything of that awful day in the dining room when she'd attacked me. *What do you know about demigods?* I'd shouted at her, the question pulled out of me by the seeking tongues of her chaotic magic.

But there was nothing in her eyes now except for a fond softness. She rested her cheek on her knees and smiled at me. "When I'm with you, though, I'm not Olden or mighty, not a queen chosen by gods. I'm just...whatever I was before they plucked me from whatever field or town or valley I lived in. I'm just a person when I'm with you. Just a friend talking to a friend."

I let out a frustrated breath, determined not to be charmed by the simple candor of her words. "And what about after today? When you go back to the palace to resume your duties, what will you do then? Will you let me come with you? Will you listen when I tell you what needs to be said?"

"Of course."

"People are *dying*, Yvaine," I continued sharply. "I've been there. I've seen it. They're being preyed on by a monster and his followers, forced to entertain and fight and seduce, doing things they would never do if they were in their right minds, and..."

I trailed off, shaking my head. The nerves that had been bubbling inside me for the entire strange day spilled over at last. I looked out at the garden, tears blurring my vision and turning everything into a shimmering wash of gold and green.

"Gareth's there somewhere," I whispered. "And countless others who are dear to their own families and friends. And you call me here, *trick* me here, to lead Ryder and me through some strange song and dance, and then go on and on about how nice it feels to spend time with me, as if there's nothing else happening in the world, as if it's only you and me, friends idling away an afternoon."

I looked back at her, gratified to see her expression of quiet shame.

I fought the instinct to comfort her or apologize. She was my friend, but in that moment she deserved neither thing.

Finally, something in her seemed to give way. She nodded, her mouth thin, and sat up straighter, legs crossed neatly on the cushion.

"You're right, of course," she said quietly. She gave me a small smile. "You're always right, and I seldom am these days, it seems." Her gaze turned distant. "It's selfish of me, isn't it, to want escape and distraction, when so many are hurting?"

"It's more complicated than that," I said, but she shook her head.

"Not for me it isn't. Not for the queen of Edyn." She sighed a little, looking at me with quiet resolve. "I'll return to the palace, let you have some peace this afternoon, and if you'll join me there for dinner tonight, both of you, we can discuss everything you've seen. Privately, or with the Royal Conclave, if you wish. But first..." She folded her hands in her lap. "Can we talk for only a few minutes? We've not talked in so long, you and me. I know so little of what's happened to you in recent months."

Then she glanced upstairs, the tiniest bit coy. "Tell me about Ryder. Is he as handsome in bed as he is outside of it?"

The abrupt change of subject made me laugh in surprise. "He...I..."

"Does it embarrass you to talk about it?"

"No, it's not... I mean, yes, I suppose, a little."

"You don't have to answer, then, if it's a private thing. It's only that..." Yvaine sat very still for a moment, then looked away with a rueful sigh. "You're going to think this is silly."

"I'm too curious to think it silly," I replied.

That amused her. She brightened, then almost as quickly grew quiet again, subdued. She picked at the sofa's embroidery.

"I was in love once," she said softly. "It was a very long time ago, I think, years and years before any of you were born. I think this is true, anyway. Lately, these peculiar memories have been floating to the surface of my thoughts. Memories that are clearly mine, and yet they're strange to me, unfamiliar, but dear at the same time." She looked up at me. "Does that make sense?"

It didn't, but I hated to discourage her. "I think so."

"I know it sounds ludicrous—memories that aren't mine and yet are? But whatever they are, I know what they're telling me, and what they say is that once, long ago, I was in love. I can feel it right here." She touched her throat, her chest, then her belly. "And here too. I feel the rightness of these ancient echoes. I was in love, and what I can remember of it warms me, makes me feel less…extraordinary. Love—that's a thing everyone understands. And I'm a thing no one understands, not fully. Do you see what I mean?"

Her eyes were beginning to fill with tears, a sight that broke my heart. She looked so lonesome there amidst the cushions, so small and tired. When I offered my handkerchief, she took it without a word and held it bunched in her lap.

After a moment, she cleared her throat. "So I thought that if you could tell me a little about you and Ryder, about what it feels like to you, to be in love, I thought…" She shrugged helplessly. "Maybe it would help me remember more of what I'm trying to remember. Maybe there's something in this memory struggling to surface within me. An explanation for everything—my sickness, the Mist's sickness, the abductions, the sinkhole. Everything. Is that mad?" She held a silent plea in her eyes. "Is it mad to think that understanding love might explain so many terrible things?"

"No," I whispered. I knew for certain that was the right answer, though I couldn't have explained why. "No, I think love lies at the root of most things, both good and evil. And if you think it will help you…"

"It might." She smiled a little, her hope painful to look at. "Do you think it might?"

"It's certainly worth a try." I drew in a breath carefully, held it around the feeling of Ryder in my heart. "To warn you, I'm not good at talking about these things."

"Shocking information, since I'm only meeting you for the first time today."

I made a face at her, trying not to smile. "I suppose I'll start by telling you about the night of the fire."

"At Ivyhill?" She looked surprised. "When you were small?"

I nodded. "I've told you about the boy who saved me that night. But what I haven't told you—what I've only just learned myself—is that the boy was Ryder."

I watched Yvaine closely. Would she remember what she'd told me, reassuring me that Ryder couldn't *possibly* be the shining boy?

But the only thing I saw on her face was rapt, astonished interest. "Extraordinary," she whispered. She found a pillow and held it to her stomach like a girl at a party, then waved at me in encouragement. "Go on, darling. How did you find this out?"

My heart sank. It was clear she remembered nothing of what she'd told me that day, and the horrible thought came to me that, given her sickness, and the fire that had burned her, it was impossible to know how fractured her mind was or wasn't. What pieces of her had been seared away? What precious memories had been lost?

My despair came on so fast that I nearly stopped my story then and there. But Yvaine looked so eager, so happy to listen to me, that I somehow found my voice, and once I started the story in earnest, I found I was glad to tell it. I'd been bursting to show someone the wound of Ryder's lie of omission, which had felt to me like nothing short of betrayal; how fresh and mean that felt, how mean *I'd* been in my anger and shock. How even though my rational mind insisted it wasn't true, I was terrified that whatever he felt for me couldn't be trusted—that he loved a power, not a person. And how impossible it felt to reconcile all of this with the sheer breathless truth of how much I loved him.

I stared at my hands. For a moment, I couldn't speak; if I did, I would start crying, and the thought of that was too exhausting to contemplate. Then Yvaine put her hand on my arm—the lightest touch, warm and unwavering—and so steadied, I found the strength to continue.

◆◇◆

When I woke, it was to a world of confusion.

I didn't remember falling asleep, or taking off my shoes and curling up on the sofa beneath a blanket. The last thing I recalled was talking to Yvaine about Ryder—his strength, his tongue, his hands, the surprising gentleness of him, the endearing gruffness of him, how safe I felt in his arms, and how when I was with him, I felt utterly seen, utterly cherished. I remembered Yvaine hanging on my every word as if I were a master storyteller, gasping and laughing, and looking suitably impressed—and delightfully scandalized—in all the right places. Her sympathy was a balm, her attention addictive.

But now the room was black, and my body was prickling, drenched in a cold sweat. The wind outside was roaring. It had blown back all the doors and pinned them to the walls.

I bolted upright and nearly ran upstairs for Ryder, but then my foggy mind understood what it was seeing. A storm had come as I slept, and now it stretched across the sky on dark wings.

I hurried outside for a better look, and my heart stuttered when I saw the vastness of it. The Green House was situated on a hill along the capital's perimeter, a normally lovely vantage point that was now horrific. Towering clouds, black with tinges of purple and green, loomed over the city, spitting sheets of driving rain and torrents of hailstones. The wind howled, churning like some great herd of beasts stampeding across a plain. The clouds blocked all daylight, making it impossible to tell how much time had passed since I'd fallen asleep, but I could still see everything as clear as day, for the air crackled with lightning. Bolts lashed out of the clouds, a whole bright forest taking fiery root among the city's sparkling towers and winding streets. The thunder was deafening, immediate. I watched the destruction in horror. Lightning tore through the streets, knocking down buildings and carving the university's lush green parks into canyons. This was not ordinary lightning; these bolts were weapons, unleashed with intent.

And then, in the midst of the clouds, a shape unfurled—a great bird, wings spreading wide as if to envelop the entire city, with flashing eyes and a gaping chasm of a beak that roared wind and fire. It shifted as it flew across the sky, breaking apart and reforming. It was a bird, then a thunderhead, then a monstrous chimaera with reaching human arms and a long serpent's body.

My blood ran cold as I stared down the hill at its grotesque hugeness, the unthinkable horror of it. Ankaret's words rang in my mind, clear as bells. *They call him storm, they call him He Who Is All, they call him...*

Kilraith.

The storm reared up high and then dove into the streets, flooding them with darkness. I couldn't hear anything over the fury of the rain and thunder, but I could imagine the screams underneath it from the people now trapped in their houses, pinned beneath rubble.

I didn't go back for Ryder. What could a wilder do, even an Anointed one, against such a thing as this? He would see it well enough for himself if he hadn't already, and I didn't want him to try and stop me.

I ran out of the garden and down the hill, each step a fight against the confused maelstrom of wind whipping the air into a frenzy. My body screamed in protest, still tender from the trip to Mhorghast, but I ran as hard as I could until my cramping side forced me to stop. I bent over, hands on my knees, and caught my breath at the edge of one of the university parks. Massive trees lay uprooted, scattered across the ravaged grounds. I climbed on top of one, perched unsteadily on its charred trunk, and began to sing.

In Mhorghast, I'd thought of deception, clarity, defense. I'd held each concept in my thoughts, three stones in the ceaseless river of my voice, my breath, my power. And now I did the same, this time thinking only one simple command, as I'd done in the forest that day when I'd run at Ankaret: *stop*.

What would happen, I didn't know. Was the storm truly Kilraith, or was it simply a magical tool he was controlling? Either way, if the awful thing yielded to my voice, what then?

But these questions were useless, mere distractions. I focused hard on my voice, calling my power to rise within me. At first, even my voice was no match for such a fury. The wind swallowed my every note. The ground shook as if from distant explosions, nearly knocking me off my precarious perch. I thought of pulling Ankaret's feather from my dress and using it to summon her at last. But I had only one feather and a whole war stretching before me. First I would try singing.

Somehow I managed to remain standing, to draw deeper breaths. I lifted my face to the black sky and sang from every part of me—the soles of my feet, my clammy palms, my shaking knees.

The storm's attention turned to me with a shift in the air and a sudden rush of heat. I cracked open my eyes, the wind knife-sharp on my cheeks, and saw darkness bearing down on me like a black wave rising out of the sea—relentless, cresting, threatening to break. Something whipped out of the churning sky—a tendril of shadow frosted with rain—and slammed into my stomach, knocking me to the ground. The blow disrupted my song; I huddled in the mud, my head reeling. Darkness slithered across the ground like snakes, wound around my torso, and lifted me up into the air.

I choked in the storm's cold grip, managing only a thin thread of song, a mere unsteady hum. The storm brought me up to its bright unblinking eyes—each as large as a door, rimmed with ribbons of lightning—and inspected me. And then, the storm smiled, a bright arc of lightning so piercing it felt like a blade carving into my skin.

Suddenly I was back in that awful house by the sea called Farther, fighting to sing as Gemma tore the Three-Eyed Crown from Talan's head. It was the same feeling crowding at my fingers, nipping at my throat. The same angry, hungry violence. But this time, I faced it alone. I had no Gemma or Mara, no Ryder or Alastrina.

Stop. I held the thought frantically in the crumbling grip of my mind and drew another ragged breath, but when I sang, I couldn't hear my own voice. Thunder boomed in my ears, lightning crackling all around me. There was a distant rumble of low laughter, and within the laughter, something like a voice, calm as a storm's eye. *Why, hello again.* The words rang in my head, more a feeling than anything. *I know you.*

I didn't want to let in the word, but it flooded my thoughts anyway: *Kilraith.*

The pierce of his smile deepened, peeling me open. A horrible pressure was tightening around my body. My ribs would crack; they would puncture my lungs. The realization came to me in a desperate burst of panic, just as it had in that long-ago house of smoke. I was going to die.

Then, a streak of brilliant light shot through the storm, sending darkness flying like shattered glass. Kilraith lost his grip on me, and I fell, gasping, expecting the end. I was too high in the air; the impact would crack open my skull. But something caught me: a softness, bright and warm. Dazed, I found myself in one piece, once again on my hands and knees in the mud. I looked up, squinting at the dazzling radiance of whatever now stood between Kilraith and me. Inside my soaked bodice, pressed against my skin, Ankaret's feather bloomed to life, warming me.

For it was she, towering over me with wings of her own—a bright pillar of light and feathers and fire. A low moan shook the air, a sound of despair. *No*, came an agonized plea. It was Kilraith, I thought, the thunderous boom of his voice vibrating against my skin. *Wait, beloved*—

But if it was Ankaret he pleaded with, she did not listen. She rushed at him with beating wings, her every feather outlined with blazing gold. She drove him up into the sky as if he were a mere piece of rubble being swept along by the tide. The immensity of him shrank, no longer mighty, a weak cyclone of shadows. The sky cleared, twinkling with stars. Dazed, I watched as she rammed into him again and again above the city's scattered fires. Time moved both slowly and quickly; I felt as if I were watching an eerie dream unfold.

As Kilraith trembled before her—a mere blot on the sky now, faint tendrils of darkness reaching up through the blaze as if to entreat her, placate her—Ankaret reared up. Her wings spanned the entire breadth of the ruined parks, the white clusters of university buildings. She dove, engulfing him. A churning current of fire and shadow rushed over the city and outward in all directions, as if someone had dropped an impossible stone into an impossible sea. A great heat blew past me; I curled into myself, hiding my face as best I could. A thick blanket of silence fell and then was gone. In its wake, I heard distant screaming, desperate wails, urgent shouts.

I dared to lift my head and look around.

Kilraith was gone, as was Ankaret. The sky was clear, the air calm.

I pushed myself to my feet and staggered toward the university, not really understanding where I was going or what I was doing. I felt only the urge to see, to understand. I pressed my palm against my bodice and nearly cried with relief to feel the warmth of Ankaret's feather. I took it as a sign that wherever she was, whatever she'd done, she was still alive.

But then I came to one of the cobblestone university courtyards, where on any other day you would see students gathered around their books or bustling to their next classes, professors arguing spiritedly over their lunches. On this night, it was chaos. A great furrow had been carved into the ground, and people were rushing everywhere, ashen, sobbing, holding each other. I hovered at the courtyard's edge and watched them, my skin icy with dread. I heard their whispers, caught pieces of their desperate conversations. *Gone. Disappeared. Shadows.*

Taken.

For a moment, I couldn't move. I kept listening, as if to convince myself that what I was hearing wasn't real, that all these panicking people were wrong, that I was in fact still asleep in the Green House.

Someone across the courtyard, hidden from me by the rubble and the frantic crowd, howled out their grief. The sound shocked me into action. I spun around and left them all, hurrying back to the Green House as fast as I could. I couldn't run, could hardly walk. I was bruised, wobbly-kneed, lightheaded. But the fear flooding me was stronger, and by the time I reached the Green House, I hardly even noticed that I had a body. I was pure terror, pure pounding heart and cold sweat. I dragged myself upstairs and burst into the parlor, Ryder's name hoarse in my throat.

But the room was empty. His boots stood at attention, untouched on the carpet.

Ryder was gone.

CHAPTER 26

I took the garden's greenway back to the palace and ran out of the atrium and into the queen's tower. Captain Vara, of course, wasn't there, nor were her fellow soldiers. They had more important things to worry about at the moment.

I tried not to look out the windows as I rushed through the tower, searching for Yvaine. Outside was ruin and smoke, a ravaged city. When Ankaret had engulfed Kilraith and driven him away, she had also put out the fires started by his lightning. But every glance outside showed me toppled buildings, dark swaths of destruction carved through the streets like new roads.

By the time I found Yvaine, my heart was pounding so hard that I felt sick. She was hurrying down one of the great corridors outside her tower with a huddle of her advisers around her and a passel of guards around them, all bustling to the palace proper. This was the state I had expected the Citadel to be in when Ryder and I had arrived that morning—absolute chaos, servants scrambling, the city guard lieutenants shouting orders at their squadrons. The air was thick with confused terror.

I pushed through it all, keeping the queen's entourage in my sights. "Yvaine," I cried out, so relieved that she was alive that I forgot all decorum.

She stopped at the sound of my voice and came to me at once, waving aside her tutting advisers and frowning guards. I saw Captain Vara among them; she calmed her charges, bade them lower their weapons. I shot her a grateful look as I rushed toward Yvaine. How useful it would be, came the distracted thought, to be able to send a feeling toward a person, as Talan could do.

But I was only me, human and limping, my throat raw from smoke and song. The best I could do was hold Yvaine tightly to me and try not to cry into her hair.

"What's happened?" she said, her voice cool and unafraid. She wore a structured gown of charcoal gray, the iridescent fabric flashing purple in the light. Her abundant white hair was pulled back into a neat bun. Gone was my friend asking about love in the Green House. In her place stood the high queen of Edyn.

"Ryder's gone," I rasped, my throat burning. I realized as I said it how foolish I sounded—the queen's friend, crying to her about her lost love while an entire city smoldered. But Ryder wasn't just anyone; Yvaine had said so herself weeks ago. The six of us—Ryder, Gemma, Talan, Mara, Gareth, and I—we were important. Among Yvaine's many gifts was one of seeing, of prophecy, and she had seen that much. We all had roles to play in what was to come.

I refused to consider that whatever Yvaine had seen was just another oddity her tired mind had conjured, some symptom of the Middlemist's illness that couldn't be trusted. If it meant nothing, then Ryder was simply gone, like so many others.

But I couldn't believe that was true. Kilraith had held me in his shadowy grip; I'd stared into the lightning of his eyes. *I know you,* he'd said.

"It was Kilraith," I told her, keenly aware of the attention I was drawing to us—the staring servants, the annoyed Thirsk. "That storm was him, or some form of him. I used my power against him—I sang, tried to make him stop. But he was too strong, or maybe I should've tried a different command, I don't know." I sounded crazed, but I needed to tell her. "Whatever I did, it was enough to attract his attention. He grabbed me, he was going to kill me. He *knew* me. I think he remembered me from when we fought him to free Talan. And then... she came. Ankaret."

Yvaine's brow furrowed. She was listening hard. "Ankaret?" Then understanding illuminated her face. "The firebird? We saw her from here."

"Yes, that's her. She's...I don't know what she is or where she came from, but she's a friend, and she fought him. She saved me. I came to tell you that. Whatever she is, we can trust her. If and when she comes back, don't be afraid of her." I hesitated, considered telling her about the feather, and decided against it. Tears pricked my eyes; I couldn't stop seeing Ryder's boots in my mind. "How many more people have been taken?" I whispered.

Yvaine's expression was grim. "So far, a dozen from here in the Citadel, but I'm sure we'll soon hear reports of more. Lady Goff is one of them."

I glanced past her at the waiting circle of advisers. A chill raced through me when I saw them—Thirsk, Bethan, Jarvis. Three of the queen's closest advisers, her councilors, her confidantes. And now one of them was gone, presumably in Kilraith's grasp.

"What can I do?" I dragged my gaze back to her. "Tell me what I can do to help you. I can take Goff's place, or sing comfort to the wounded while the healers tend to them—"

"The best thing you can do is return to Ivyhill," Yvaine said, "and open your doors to anyone who might need sanctuary. There are many frightened people out there, and your family will be a comfort to them."

She glanced around at the panicked servants rushing past, the battalions of soldiers and teams of robed elementals and beguilers, all hurrying out into the city with their weapons at the ready, roaring wakes of magic trailing after them. Her gold and violet eyes flashed with anger. She looked invigorated, mighty, more herself than she had in months. Even the scar on her forehead looked healthier, its normal rosy pink. I allowed myself a brief moment of gladness at the sight.

"Will you send for me if I can be of help here?" I asked her.

She softened, squeezing my hands in hers. "I always will. And don't fear for Ryder," she added with a gentle smile. "He's stubborn and strong, just like you are. In that way, and in many others, you're perfectly suited to each other. Take comfort in that. Won't you, darling?"

I nodded miserably, attempting a brave smile of my own. Then Yvaine released my hands and hurried back to her entourage. Thirsk shot me a final exasperated look and bustled after her. I let the palace's chaos rush past me and watched Yvaine glide swiftly away down the grand corridor. Her distant head gleamed silver in the warm torchlight glinting off the walls. Something nagged at me as I watched her go, a feeling I couldn't name that kept me rooted to the polished marble floor.

A harried-looking healer's apprentice with an armful of supplies jostled me as she ran past, shaking me from my daze. I turned and left for home.

→◇→

Under a canopy of cheerful distant stars, I trudged across Ivyhill's great lawn from the greenway that connected our land to the capital. I made my way up the front steps, feeling utterly wrung out, every breath catching in my throat like silk on thorns. *Ryder.* I held his name on my tongue, in the cradle of my lungs. *Ryder, don't be afraid. I love you. I'll find you. I love you.*

Sick with worry, body and heart aching, I stepped through the front doors of Ivyhill and almost ran right into Gilroy.

"Gilroy, good." I took hold of his sleeve, so thankful he hadn't been taken that the tears I'd successfully stifled threatened to return. I blinked them back hard and walked with him toward the dining room. "We'll need to send messages to Derryndell, Tullacross, Summer's Amble," I told him. Giving instructions was a relief. Never mind godly power and giant malevolent storms; this I knew how to tackle.

"The capital has been attacked," I continued, "and people were abducted from the Citadel. It's possible many others around the country have been taken, too, and that there have been other attacks. We'll open up Ivyhill to anyone who needs shelter or medical attention, or to anyone who would simply feel safer here on the grounds. We'll need to be organized about it. We don't want a mad rush. Tell Madam Moreen and Bili to convert the Blue Ballroom into an infirmary, and have Mrs. Seffwyck lay out beds and supplies in the Green Ballroom and make up all the spare rooms we have. Mr. Carbreigh and his crew will need to constantly patrol the estate's perimeter, reinforce the wards without rest. Tell him he may recruit any of the tenant farmers and their hands to help. They'll be happy to, they're always asking to study under him—"

I broke off, realizing suddenly that Gilroy was tottering after me in a daze, a piece of paper in his hand. His face was ashen, his forehead covered in a sheen of sweat. Instantly I was on alert, fear prickling my skin.

"Gilroy? What is it?" I took the paper from him. It was fine as silk in my hands, thin, shimmering silver. Gorgeous lettering swooped across the page.

"A man brought it to me," Gilroy said wonderingly. A small smile played at his lips, as if he were recalling some forgotten joy. "A smiling man with a voice like summer. He told me it was important. He told me to bring it to the master of the house. But Lord Gideon is busy with the others, my lady. So I've been waiting for him. I've been waiting at the doors."

I guided Gilroy to a chair at the side of the entrance hall and helped him sit. Absently he touched a white-gloved hand to his temple. "A beautiful man," he murmured, "in a long fine coat."

Shakily I held the paper up to the light and forced myself to read it.

To the most esteemed daughters of the House of Ashbourne—

You are warmly invited to what is sure to be the season's most spectacular event: a weekend revel held in glorification of He Who Is All, in celebration of his vision for the new world. Dress is formal. Bring any guests you desire. But do not be late. When the road comes, you will take it. To ignore it or delay your crossing would be unwise.

The invitation had no signature, but of course I knew very well who had written it. I folded the paper into crisp thirds, stuffed it into my pocket, and knelt before Gilroy.

"You said Lord Gideon is busy with the others," I said, my voice coming out much steadier than I felt. "What does that mean? Where is he?"

"You don't understand!" cried a voice from somewhere deeper in the house—a woman, each word rough with agony. "He'll find us!"

I left Gilroy sitting bleary-eyed in his chair and raced through the corridors, following the shouts to a terrible scene in one of the northern receiving rooms. Alastrina cowered in the corner, ripped bandages trailing off of her, a crazed look of grief in her eyes. Illaria stood between her and Madam Moreen, her hands up and her expression stern.

"You're frightening her," Illaria said firmly. "It's the smell of the tonics. They remind her of that place."

Madam Moreen looked to be at the end of her patience. "I understand, my lady, truly, but I can't help the smell of my tonics, and since she won't use any more of her magic," she added crossly, throwing a glare toward Philippa, who sat near the hearth, "if Lady Alastrina keeps opening up her wounds, they'll never heal, and they'll get infected. The tonics will help prevent that."

Past them, Talan sat in a chair with a fresh wound on his arm. One of his own bandages had been ripped open and hung off him in tatters. Gemma was hurrying to him with a fresh bandage, a cloth, a basin of water. Father was prowling back and forth behind them like an angry tiger, and Philippa—Philippa was still and quiet, a stricken expression on her face. She held her pipe in midair, as if she'd been interrupted just before taking a puff from it.

The look on her face chilled me. I tore my gaze away from her and went to Father.

"What's going on here?" I demanded.

"Is the queen alive?" he asked tightly. I'd left him a note telling him where I'd gone.

"She is. It was a misunderstanding." I avoided his keen gaze, took in the scene around us. "But this is... What's *happening*?"

Talan looked up wryly from Gemma's ministrations. "Alastrina fears I am not who I claim to be."

"She was quiet, calm, wouldn't talk to anyone but Illaria and occasionally Madam Moreen," Gemma said. Though her movements were brisk and assured, her voice trembled. "About two hours ago, she lost her senses, started wrecking the furniture and pulling pictures from the walls. Screaming about a storm, though there's not a cloud in the sky. We managed to sedate her, but a few minutes ago she rushed at Talan, screaming about Kilraith, and—"

Gemma waved her hand irritably through the air. Then she looked up at me and went very still. "What is it? What's happened?"

"A storm." Philippa rose quietly from her chair, staring at me. "There was a storm, wasn't there?"

"Kilraith attacked the capital. I don't know why, but Ankaret stopped him." I hesitated, realizing that neither Ryder nor I had told any of them about her. "The firebird," I explained quickly. "The creature I saw at Ravenswood. She fought him, vanquished him." The invitation sat like a weight in my pocket. "But not forever, it seems."

"She?" Father looked at me quizzically. "How do you know this creature's name?"

In a rush, I told them everything, and when I had finished, both Gemma and Father looked furious. Philippa stared hard at the hearth, as if within its flames burned a message only she could see.

"You and Ryder kept all of this from us?" Gemma shook her head in disbelief. "This could have been helpful to know, Farrin."

"I don't see how anything would be different now if I'd told you," I shot back, though guilt burned hot in my stomach. I couldn't say for sure that this was true. "We thought the fewer people knew about her, the safer it was for everyone, including her."

"This creature could be an informant of Kilraith's," Father pressed. "She could have been spying on you all this time, bringing information back to him."

"She's a *friend*. She fought Kilraith and drove him away from the capital."

"Which only just happened, and even that we can't rightly interpret," Father pointed out. "These are Olden creatures. We can't trust them, no matter what pledges of friendship they offer."

"Certainly that's true of Kilraith, but not Ankaret." The desire to sit down on the floor and never get up was overwhelming. In my exhaustion, I was starting to disbelieve my own self, and as my doubt crept in, so did my grief.

Right at that moment, Talan hissed out a breath. "Ryder," he murmured. He looked up at me sadly. The warmth of his concern brushed against me, unasked for but welcome, and as soft as the flutter of a butterfly's wing.

I nodded, realizing with a jolt of unreasonable self-loathing that I'd forgotten to bring home his boots.

"He was taken," I said thickly. "Many were from the castle as well, and I assume from everywhere else." I glanced at Father. "Have any of our people disappeared?"

He frowned, as if the question were an irritant. "No, and I suppose we have her to thank for that?"

Her. I looked past him to Philippa, who still stared at the empty hearth. "Is that true?" I asked her. "Is your presence protecting us? Have you decided to stay and help us after all?"

It was as if she hadn't heard me. "Ankaret," she murmured, tracing her finger across the mantel. "What a strange name. Familiar, as if from a dream."

"What does that mean? You know the word? You've heard it before?"

From behind me came a crash of glass. I whirled to see Madam Moreen squatting down to clean up a shattered vial. The burning medicinal scent of the spilled tonic wafted up from the carpet, and a bright magenta stain dripped slowly down the wallpaper.

Alastrina stared at the mess, medicine splattered across her front. She looked imploringly at Illaria, who grabbed a cloth and started to clean her cheeks. I almost looked away—the expression on Alastrina's tearstained face was terrible, desolate, so unlike the imperious woman

I'd always known that it frightened me. But then a memory flew forward from the tumult of my mind. Alastrina, before Ryder and I had left for the capital and we'd all been gathered in the morning room, had laughed quietly to herself and said, *You won't be able to find him. No one ever has. You think you're the first to try and crack the shell?*

Crack the shell.

A goblet, a key, a black lake under a full moon.

An *egg*.

The revelation hit me like a shock of cold water.

"Alastrina, when we came back from Mhorghast, you said something I think is important," I said, struggling to keep my voice calm. "'You won't be able to find him. No one ever has. You think you're the first to try and crack the shell?' Do you remember saying that?"

She glared up at me through greasy locks of black hair, her fingers digging into Illaria's arm. "Ashbourne, you're talking gibberish."

I tried again. "'You won't be able find him,'" I said calmly. "'No one ever has. You think you're the first to try and crack the shell?'"

This time, the words seemed to ring a bell inside her. Her eyes widened; she went very still. "Crack the shell," she whispered.

My heart pounded. "Yes, exactly. Is it the shell of an egg, Alastrina? Is that what you meant?"

She held her head in her hands. Her breathing started coming quickly. "An egg. Crack the shell."

I thought back to the cryptic information Ankaret had given Ryder and me. I found the words at once; they were not easy to forget.

"Mhorghast is a city and a palace," I said. "Isn't it, Alastrina? And gardens that stretch for miles, all of it ruled by a great storm. Where is this egg kept? What does it do? Do you know?"

Alastrina stared at me, her pale face turning ashen. She licked her dry lips.

I pressed on. Maybe, if I kept reciting Ankaret's words, they would spark something in Alastrina, give her strength, or at least lucidity. "'The storm lives in the walls, and sometimes in the sky.'"

"In the walls," Alastrina whispered. And then her face crumpled. "In the *walls*!"

"Farrin, please, no more," Illaria said tightly, but I couldn't stop now, not with that look of recognition dawning in Alastrina's eyes. *Ryder's* eyes—that same piercing, unflinching blue.

I swallowed my heartache and remembered how Alastrina's gaze had clouded over in Mhorghast. Some power there had muddled her, turning her against her own brother.

I flung the words at her. "'The storm lives in the walls, and sometimes in the sky. The storm is not like others. It has a will—'"

"I feel it again," Philippa said, interrupting me. She sank down onto the carpet, peering curiously at Alastrina. "I can see it on your face, my girl—the same presence I felt when I was there. A face across a crowded room, a shade of memory. A trace of it lingers in you."

She reached out to touch Alastrina, who tried to scramble away in a panic—but then Philippa touched her cheek, and though it was nothing more than a light brush of her fingertips, it held Alastrina in place as surely as an unbreakable chain.

In an instant, the room seemed to expand, as if to accommodate Philippa's power. Goose bumps erupted all over me; behind me, Madam Moreen let out a soft cry of dismay.

A breath, a frozen instant, and then Philippa's face went slack with horror. She released Alastrina, staggered to her feet, stumbled toward a chair. She sat down hard, missed the chair's edge, and fell gracelessly to the floor.

"No," she breathed, her voice a mere rasp. "It's not possible."

Alastrina collapsed against Illaria, her breathing shallow and quick. "It's not possible," she whispered, echoing Philippa's words.

"It *can't* be," they cried in unison.

Not once since we'd met Philippa at Wardwell had she shown any sign of shame, apology, or fear. But now she seemed to shrink into herself. Her eyes flickered blue and gold, and her image rippled before me—fading, then returning, like a flame sputtering in the wind and threatening to go out.

Anger shot through me. I hurried to Philippa and grabbed her arms. "No, don't you *dare* leave us yet. What did you see? Tell me, quickly and plainly."

Philippa's expression was wretched with agony, tears streaming down her face. I hated the sight of her, how pathetic and vulnerable and *human* she looked, how much like the mother I remembered. With all her calm coldness gone, she seemed not mighty but haggard.

"My brother is alive," she said hoarsely. "He's alive, and he's in chains. He has him." She wrapped her hands around my arms, drawing me closer to her. "Kilraith *has him.*"

Gemma came to us and sank down slowly beside me. Her face was white, and her hands were bare; the glittering scar Kilraith had marked her with grinned up at me. "Your brother," she said quietly. "You mean another god. Caiathos?"

I went cold. I heard Talan mutter an angry, horrified curse. Suddenly the particular madness of Mhorghast made sense to me— Alastrina's clouded eyes, the humans who laughed when the vampyr slew her victim. Ankaret herself had told us the answer, hidden in the folds of her many riddles. *They are not themselves. They are made to do things they don't want to do.*

"No," I said quietly. "Not the god of the earth." I met Philippa's eyes. "Jaetris. God of the mind. Father of readers, furiants, figments, sages." My heart twinged, thinking of Gareth. I glanced back at Talan. "Father of the greater demons."

Talan's gaze was hard and dark. "And Kilraith is using him as a weapon, a tool to draw people to Mhorghast and hold them there."

"And to torture them." I closed my eyes, my gorge rising as I thought of Ryder in that place, of Gareth, of the horrors that now lived in Alastrina's mind.

"I don't understand," Father said faintly, still standing behind Talan's chair. He gripped the back of it hard. "How can a creature—any creature—control a god?"

I saw the answer in the sadness and sudden, wide-eyed fear on Philippa's face.

"Because he's newly reborn," I said, echoing her words from Wardwell. "A mere shadow of what he once was."

Philippa nodded. Her gaze shifted as I watched her, from the watery blue eyes of a human woman to a god's frantic flickering gold. "But even a god reborn is still a god." She looked to Father. I thought I saw a flash of regret on her face. "Think of what I did to you, how quickly I opened you up and made you bleed."

Father was grim. "And if you didn't have control of your power, if someone else was using it? You'd be a murderous puppet with a monster pulling your strings."

"And the egg must be an anchor of the *ytheliad* curse," Gemma added. She looked to Talan, a softness in her eyes. "He's using it to control Jaetris like he used the crown to control Talan."

"It would give him strength and mobility," Talan agreed quietly. His brow glittered with its own swirl of lines and thumbprint scars, partners to those on Gemma's hand. "Allow him to use his influence—and that of Jaetris—in both realms."

"And plant visions in people's heads," I whispered, thinking of Mara's story—the woman driven mad by the images in her mind, the woman who'd attacked her brother. "Making them sick, driving them to him."

"Some he abducts himself," Father added, "or else he sends that shadow magic to do it for him. An army of figments, maybe? Quick, skilled at deception." Father's hands were in fists. "It's a strange strat-egy. Untidy. Chaotic."

Philippa hid her face in her hands. "Chaos is just what he wants."

"Chaos is just what he wants," Alastrina whispered, leaning against Illaria and staring at the floor.

"Chaos," Talan agreed darkly, "and entertainment. That's always been a part of it. He's playing a game. Whatever ends he's aiming for—whatever dark plots he's engineered throughout the realms using me and the others before me, now using Jaetris and the captive humans he's making certain the effort is fun. He has all the cards, and he's enjoying it."

"And look at this." I reached in my pocket for the invitation. "He's not even hiding himself away anymore. He wants us to go to him."

As soon as I withdrew the shimmering piece of paper, the world went deathly silent—the house, my heartbeat, my breathing—except for a high, faint whine in the distance.

Philippa reared back from me, her mouth open in a silent scream. Our gazes locked, and when her body started to flicker again, fading in and out of existence, I dropped the paper and grabbed on to her bare wrist.

She sucked in a breath and held me to her for a brief moment. The world's silence roared in my ears.

"I have to go," she told me—jewels in her hair, bones for armor, eyes of liquid gold. "If I stay, he'll find me. Burn that thing immedi-ately. It isn't what it seems." Her arms came around me again, then let me go. "I'm sorry, my little bird. It's to protect you. What I do is always to protect you."

Then the world went white, and when it faded, when sound returned, all of us were gasping for breath on the floor, and Philippa was gone.

Tears burning in my eyes, anger sour at the back of my throat, I grabbed the invitation from where it lay on the floor and crushed the delicate paper between my palms. A hiss wafted up from it, as if it were a living thing I'd stomped flat. Alastrina clapped her hands over her ears with a soft cry of despair. I ran for the hearth; Father was already there, lighting the wood. He'd heard Philippa's words, or else he simply sensed the wrongness of this thing in my hands and knew it must be destroyed. Either way, I was grateful. I tossed the wad of paper into the tiny fresh flames, watched it light up and blacken. A wheezing sound puffed up from it as it burned. It was laughing at us; Kilraith was laughing at us.

I watched the fire grow and snap until the paper was ashes in its teeth, swearing to myself all the while that he would not be laughing for long.

CHAPTER 27

Father went to Rosewarren to bring back Mara, for which I was immensely glad. The last thing I wanted to do at that moment was argue with the Warden. I couldn't even imagine how I would explain the impossible danger of what we must do.

When at last Gemma and Mara and I were alone in my rooms, I realized with a quiet thrum of shock that this was the first time Mara had been back to Ivyhill since she was ten years old, the day the Warden had taken her away.

She sat rigidly in one of the chairs by my hearth, Osmund purring in her lap and Una lying contentedly upon her boots. She rested her hands lightly on Osmund's head and back, not petting him, not even moving. I couldn't read her face, stoic and stony as it was, but when I tried to imagine what she might be thinking, how it must feel to sit in that chair in a house she knew and yet did not, my heart filled with sadness so fresh and sharp that it hurt to breathe.

But there wasn't time for sadness. Gemma and I told her what had happened. I recited to her what the invitation had said, hating the feel of the words on my tongue. Una gave a low whine from her position on Mara's feet.

It was the best thing I could have done. A threat, a mission, planning how best to accomplish it: this was Mara's life. She listened hard, and when we'd finished, she said, "'Bring any guests you desire.'" She looked wryly at me. "A pity we don't yet have the armies ready to deploy. What a sight they would make, marching in after us. Guests indeed."

"Who *will* we bring?" Gemma asked. "Talan will insist on going, and so will Father."

"Even in his current state, yes, Talan must come." Mara frowned. "I hate to put him anywhere near Kilraith, but of course his past experience with him could be an asset."

"And perhaps having another sentinel to help us is an advantage we can't ignore."

"As long as Father can keep his temper in check," I said, "or at least directed at the right people. That's the thing that worries me most of all. This is Kilraith we're talking about. He already had a talent for mind games." I shivered a little, remembering the house of horrors we'd navigated by the Far Sea, all the cruel things those walls had whispered. "And now his arsenal includes Jaetris, god of the mind. Father has not been well, and his moods have been unpredictable. Fertile ground for Kilraith to play with, I'd say."

"But Philippa said there are three thousand souls in Mhorghast," Mara pointed out. "In my estimation, we need Father. We *need* an army."

"Alastrina certainly thought so," I said, remembering her dismay when she had realized Ryder and I had come to Mhorghast alone.

"Could you convince the Warden to send at least your own unit down here to join us?" Gemma asked.

Mara shook her head grimly. "Father barely managed to convince her to let me go, and I think he did so only because she's too exhausted to fight yet another battle. If we go back and ask for more, she might forget how tired she is and become angry. At most, I could perhaps persuade her to send Nesset."

Gemma's face brightened at the mention of her resurrected Vilia friend. "She did say in her last letter that she's now been on, what, twenty missions with the Roses?"

Mara nodded with a fond little smile. "Her body's held up well, even in the thick of the Mist. If she's not careful, the Warden might officially induct her into the Order."

Finally I voiced a thought that had been turning slowly in my mind since I'd first read Kilraith's invitation. "Maybe we're thinking about this all wrong—as a battle, not a game. He'll expect us to come ready for a fight." I looked at Mara. "What if we did the opposite?"

She frowned. "You mean surrender immediately?"

But Gemma seemed to catch on, her eyes sparkling. "You mean arrive not with our swords drawn but with our dancing shoes on. A celebration, the invitation said. A glorification."

"So we celebrate," I said. "We dance and enjoy the party, entertain the revelers. Kilraith has invited us into his city. He's even going to send the road for us, if that letter can be believed, and I think it can. Based on how strange Gilroy was acting, Kilraith delivered his invitation in person. If he wanted to kill us, he would have done it already. Talan said he likes games. I think he's curious about us. I think he wants to show off what he can do and see how we respond."

Mara looked at me thoughtfully. "An experiment."

"Something like that. We'll bring Talan. He won't expect that, not when Talan's been constantly on the move specifically to elude him. We'll join in the fun. He won't expect that either."

"Surprise will be our weapon," Mara agreed. "Defiance of expectations."

"He might think we'll come with an army at our backs," Gemma said, "or bring no one at all so as not to endanger anyone else's lives."

"How noble of us," Mara said drily.

"And so we'll do neither of those things," I said. "No army, and we won't go alone either. A single companion each?"

"Like proper, polite guests," Gemma said, amused.

"Nesset, Talan." Mara looked at me. "Father?"

I sighed. It was the right thing to do, and yet the thought of Father at my side during such a mission left me uneasy. "I suppose. If we can't have an army, at least we'll have him."

Mara looked at me keenly. "Do you really believe what you said earlier? That his temper could be a liability?"

"To be perfectly honest, when it comes to Father these days, I don't know what to think. He's at his best when he's fighting." I smiled sadly. "Maybe this will give him the outlet he's been craving since we all stopped trying to kill each other."

Another silence fell. The name *Bask* hung in the air, and suddenly I found it hard to swallow past the dull pain in my throat. *Ryder.* I closed my eyes. *Ryder, hold on. Gareth, stay strong. We're coming.*

After a moment, Gemma asked, "Do you think Kilraith knew Mother was here when he sent that invitation?"

"If he didn't before, he does now," Mara said. "That invitation was a spy. Hopefully Wardwell's magic remains strong enough to hide her."

"He may have realized *Kerezen* was here," I mused, "but not who she is besides that."

"In other words, he may not realize who *we* are," Gemma added. "*What* we are. Though he may suspect, or at least wonder."

"Hence the invitation," Mara said, nodding. "He wants to observe us, test us, show us he's not afraid. We beat him once. Can we do it again, now that he has a god to use as a weapon? What's the limit of our strength?" She began to pet Osmund at last. "Once he has his answer, he may strike to kill."

"Or he'll tell Jaetris to do it," Gemma said darkly. "Maneuver him into our minds and make *us* do the killing for him. Just as he did to Talan."

"So we'll keep surprising him," I said. "We'll keep him guessing, entertained, distracted."

"And while he's distracted, we'll find the egg."

"If the egg in fact exists," Mara pointed out, "and if its function is what we think it is."

"I choose to believe it does," Gemma said, "and that our suspicions are correct. It makes too much sense not to. So we'll destroy it, break his hold on Jaetris and thereby his hold on everyone else."

Mara made a thoughtful noise. "It'll be a shame not to be able to study the egg as we've done with the crown."

"But anything that's been used to control a god…" I said.

"Exactly," Gemma agreed. "It *must* be destroyed. Hopefully we'll be able to gather any information we need by questioning the freed prisoners."

Right away, I thought of the harpy, Nerys, and the ruthlessness on Mara's face as she'd interrogated her. An awkward silence fell.

Mara met each of our gazes evenly. "You're thinking of Nerys. She's still alive, you know, kept under tight guard. It's a drain on our resources, and the Warden wants to execute her, but I won't allow it."

I bit my tongue, thinking that Mara had allowed quite enough to happen to Nerys. I lightly touched the pocket of my dress, inside which Ankaret's feather rested. I hadn't used it that day to help Nerys, and I'd regretted it ever since.

Mara considered Osmund's silky ears, petting each one with reverent care. Whatever she felt about Nerys, she kept it well hidden. "'A storm that sometimes lives in the walls,'" she murmured. "And he took the form of a bird while attacking the capital?"

"Among other things, yes," I answered.

"Hmm. Where do birds keep their eggs?"

"In their nests," Gemma answered, frowning. Then her face lit up. "The palace in Mhorghast. He's hidden it there, and part of him lives in the walls, guarding it."

"It's only *possible* that it's there," Mara said. "We can't know that for sure. And we don't know where in the palace it would be. It seems a good place to start, at least, but it will be well guarded."

"Jaetris could be there too," I guessed. "All Kilraith's most valuable treasures, tucked away where he goes home to roost."

"He'll do everything in his power to stop us before we get that far," Gemma said. "And he'll want to separate us. The last time we faced him, all of us together, we bested him."

Barely, I thought, with a frisson of fear that I pushed past with no small effort. "So we'll not let each other out of our sights," I said. "That way, if someone starts to stray, the others can reel them back in."

"Which may be difficult. He may want to play a game, but he's not a fool. He's dealt in lies and cruelties for longer than any of us have been alive. The stories Talan has told me…" Gemma shuddered. "At his core, he's impatient, capricious."

"And boastful," Mara added. "Everything you've told us of Mhorghast, Farrin, screams of decadence and swagger. In such pride lies the potential for great error."

"Then we'll take advantage of that," I said. "Entertain him so completely that he won't notice how close we are until it's too late."

Gemma looked doubtful. "How are we supposed to do that?"

"I have some ideas," Mara mused, her gaze distant.

I took a breath, then withdrew Ankaret's feather from my dress and held it gingerly in my palms. It was the strangest thing I owned, and perhaps our greatest advantage. I could no longer keep it for myself. I remembered how Kilraith had pleaded with Ankaret as they had battled above the capital. *Beloved*, he'd called her.

I looked up at my sisters, who stared at the feather in wonder. "So do I," I said.

◆◇◆

Two days later, the moonlight road came without warning.

We were all in the dining room, dressed and ready, existing in a sort of tense daze. The table was scattered with daggers and small pistols from Father's collection of Lower Army gear—weapons we could easily hide in our boots and under our coats to maintain the appearance of revelry rather than combat. We had no way of knowing when Kilraith would send for us, or if he would even send for us at all. My mind raced with doubts. What if this entire thing was a trick? The road would never come, and while we were here waiting for it, something terrible would happen elsewhere. We were fools to enter Mhorghast without an army, without even a proper arsenal of weapons. Weeks ago, Gemma had described her panic to me, how episodes of it could render her numb with dread or frantic with fear. I thought I was beginning to understand what that felt like.

I sparred with Mara, desperate to calm my nerves. Nesset sat nearby, appraising us with narrowed eyes. The Warden had allowed her to leave Rosewarren after all. "A little too hastily," Nesset had commented wryly. "She doesn't care if I come back, but she's more than happy for me to look after her favorite."

She'd said it without any real feeling other than amusement, and ever since she had hovered around Mara with the air of a fussy nanny, hardly leaving her side. I was glad for her looming presence. She was tall and muscular and fearsome, her gnarled flower-woven skin as rough and gray as it had been when I'd first met her. She wore a plain dress with a bodice of tough leather, and her eyes darted everywhere—calculating, eager. Ready to fight.

Glad as I was of her presence, I tried not to look at her as she watched me. I knew I was clumsy, that next to Mara I looked like a tottering kitten, especially with my fiddle strapped to my back. But I would have it with me in Mhorghast, and I needed the practice.

Talan sat with Father, both of them poring over the map of Mhorghast I'd drawn. We had studied it for nearly two days straight, and the longer everyone looked at it, the more nervous I became. What if I had misremembered something? What if the layout of the place had changed entirely and all our studying was for naught? I wished I'd been able to consult with Alastrina, but since Philippa's departure, she'd fallen insensate, not responding to my singing, not speaking even to Illaria, who sat tirelessly with her upstairs. Gemma fussed around everyone, adjusting our fine dresses and suits and honing the minor glamours she'd put on our faces and hair. Every now and then, she sat to catch her breath, looking a little pale, and in those moments, no matter where she was, Talan found her at once and held her, murmuring to her until she'd regained her strength.

Watching them was a dual torment. I was worried for them both. Thanks to Talan's demon blood, Madam Moreen's excellent care, and Philippa's careful, quiet power, he had healed quickly from his wounds. But for all his bravery, asking him to go to Mhorghast felt like asking a boy to return to a nightmare from which he'd only just awoken. And then there was Gemma. In Kilraith's house of horrors at the Far Sea, she'd been extraordinary, pushing past her pain to fight as fiercely as any Rose. Even at the Citadel, without the Old Country enhancing her power, she'd torn trees from the grounds when Yvaine had attacked me, commanding their sprawling roots with ease. But I knew my sister. She was expert at hiding her hurts, and none of us knew what Mhorghast, what Kilraith, would demand of her, or of any of us.

Worst of all was the agony of seeing Gemma and Talan together—how sweetly they touched each other, how they huddled together as if they existed in a world that belonged to them alone. How easily Talan could make Gemma smile and ease her pain. How soft his eyes were when he looked at her.

Not so long ago, I'd known what that felt like. I'd known passion, tenderness, devotion, and then I'd pushed it away. My reason for doing so seemed even more foolish now, with Ryder gone. If I had known what would soon happen to him, I would have forgiven him at once, maybe even forgiven myself. I would have held him to me and never let him go, not until the turning of the world forced us apart. And now he was gone, and though I tried for fierce hope, it kept slipping from me, dislodged by horrible images. Ryder afraid and in chains; Ryder with his throat slit; Ryder with white eyes that didn't know me.

Distracted, I didn't see Mara's staff coming at me. It clipped my leg and sent me stumbling to the floor.

Nesset clucked her tongue. "Good thing you fell on your knees and not on your back. That fiddle's far too fragile for battle, and you're such a slight thing, and too slow. You don't need any extraneous weight dragging you down."

I glared at her as Mara helped me up. I heard the judgment in her voice and her true criticism—not unkind, simply assessing. *I* was too fragile for battle, she meant. Yet another doubt slithered into my mind to join the countless others.

"I don't know, Nesset," Mara said briskly, readying her staff. "Cira's fifteen and thin as a reed, and she's knocked you on your ass more than a few times. I'd think you'd know better by now than to judge every fighter's abilities by the same measure. And I think you'll be glad to have Farrin's fiddle with you, before the end. Not every weapon looks like yours."

Mara shot me a small smile, and I returned it, raising my staff once more. I thought of Ryder's steadiness, the solid bulk of him a ballast against the world, and tried to find some of that steadiness within my own teetering nerves. Ryder would want that for me; he'd want me to be sharp and alert. He would believe me capable of it. I took a step toward Mara, gripping my staff hard with both hands.

But before I could let it fly, Talan spoke softly from the table. "Wait," he said. He stood, an odd expression on his face. He looked to Gemma, then took a breath. He looked remarkably unafraid. "It's here."

And it was, the shimmering length of the moonlight road unfurling down the front steps of Ivyhill like a silver banner. We loaded ourselves with weapons and went to it in silence. The household had been prepared for the lure of this eerie, gleaming path. Carbreigh and his crew of elementals, as well as our house guards, sternly held back the other servants and the few refugees from neighboring towns whom we'd welcomed into the house after the most recent wave of abductions. There were only six of them so far, but the lostness on their faces, the grief and fear they dragged through Ivyhill like stones, told me more would come. Whatever was happening, whatever Kilraith had planned, was only just beginning.

Nesset went first, followed by Mara. Talan took Gemma's hand and followed. Unease coiled tightly inside me as I watched their shapes glimmer, fold in on themselves, and disappear. I felt none of the giddiness that had come with my first sighting of the road. It was simply there before me, a beam of light, waiting. No tricks, no coy glimmers at the corner of my eye. It had been sent with clear intent.

Father stepped up beside me. He was brimming with energy, the air around him snapping hot with sentinel power. It was a reassuring sight—the familiar neat cut of his beard, his flinty brown eyes, the grim set of his jaw; he was a soldier, and I was glad to have him with us—but when our gazes locked, a whole current of unsaid things passed between us, memories that hurt me to think of, even if I only looked at them sidelong. My wrists twinged with phantom pain, and the tender parts of my heart that had only just begun to heal with the balm of Ryder's love ached anew. They remembered, and they always would, every fit of temper, every drunken stupor. Every blurry month of grief when Gemma and I hadn't had a father, only a distant, brooding man stuck in the mire of his own sorrow and anger, forgetting he had daughters at all.

If we made it through this, would I somehow find the courage to tell him this? To confess how he'd hurt me, to tell him how close he was to losing me? Looking at him, I thought of Alaster Bask in his cold black house, little Ryder and Alastrina hiding in the cupboards. My eyes burned with tears I couldn't afford.

"What is it, Farrin?" Father asked. The promise of conflict had brought him a clarity that had been all too rare in recent months. His voice was full of concern, and his gaze was bright and sharp. There were lines around his eyes, and I noticed for the first time that his golden-brown hair was beginning to gray at the temples. If anyone tried to hurt me, he would fight them to his death.

There was a lump in my throat—a knot of love, fierce and frustrated and tender. I gave my father a small smile. "Nothing," I said. "I'm ready."

Then I took a breath and stepped onto the moonlight road, expecting to find what I had seen before: a glittering city, gardens, a palace. Houses full of music and dancing; Olden creatures everywhere, both gorgeous and grotesque.

But the passage was swift, uneventful, and all that awaited us on the other side was a great dark expanse with seemingly no end. The ground was neatly cobbled, each stone glimmering with faint white light. Overhead shone the eternal moon. And beneath it stood three distinct shapes. Two of them I recognized. One was Talan's house by the Far Sea. One was Ivyhill, its turreted silhouette unmistakable.

The third thing I'd never seen, but I felt a chill of recognition nonetheless. It was a black lake, huge and calm, the moon reflecting off its surface like light on glass. The *full* moon.

A goblet, a key, an egg. A black lake under a full moon.

The others stood nearby in their finery, all of them frozen like I was. My sisters were breathtaking, each line of their bodies gilded from the inside out. Their hair was thick and streaming, streaked with starlight. Specks of gold made their eyes shine, and the air around them rippled softly, as if they moved through shallow water so clear it was impossible to see. Their gowns shone of moonlit silk, each pleat and fold casting soft starbursts of light across the road.

Seeing them, seeing *me*, Father took a stunned step back.

"Gods, it's true," he whispered.

"I don't understand," Gemma said unsteadily. "This is Mhorghast?"

They were all waiting for me to say something; I'd been here before, I'd drawn the map. But my shock at seeing Mhorghast so changed left me speechless. Everything I'd told them had been rendered useless the moment we arrived.

"Someone's here," Talan breathed. In the Olden air, he stood taller, his dramatic beauty startling. "Can't you hear them?"

And suddenly, hardly daring to breathe, I could—faint whispers, a distant chorus of voices. I closed my eyes, straining to listen. Laughter, music, drums. A tambourine?

"It's a trick," Nesset growled. With her hard gray fingers, she pried loose a stone from the cobbled road and tossed it, fuming. A wave of laughter, whisper-soft, cascaded over us in response.

I remembered how the shape and breadth of Mhorghast had shifted when Ryder and I had last been here—how the towering palace had been itself one moment and the next a mountain had stood in its place—and struggled against my rising terror for composure. "It *is* a trick. The city changed often when we were here. The shape and substance of the road, the size of the city, the placement of things. They shifted without warning."

"Perhaps the whole thing is an illusion," Father said, glaring around. "Not a true city at all, just a construction of magic."

"Magic bolstered by Jaetris, no doubt," Gemma whispered. She looked back at me. "We thought ourselves so clever, coming here dressed to celebrate, not to fight. But this is..." She gestured miserably at Talan's house. "This is another kind of game entirely."

"A game," Talan suggested, his voice hard and angry, "or a show."

My heart racing, I began to hum under my breath. As I did, I concentrated on the sensation of Ankaret's feather against my skin and thought one word: *truth*. I infused every crystalline note with it, and as I sang, vague shapes shimmered into being. Each one was brief, disappearing as soon as I looked directly at it. But I saw enough. We were being watched by thousands of staring eyes situated hundreds of feet above us. It was like Alastrina's arena, I realized with a cold twist of fear. We were on some grand stage for the entertainment of the entire city. I saw only fuzzy shapes, blurs of color, but I could guess who was there—every smiling vampyr I'd seen in Mhorghast, every glittering nymph, every desperate human. Somewhere in the crowd was Luthaes, Alastrina's dazzling fae keeper with the burnished copper skin.

I stopped singing, my mouth suddenly dry. "They're all watching us," I whispered. "Thousands of them, seated above us."

"Waiting for us to do *what*?" Nesset snapped. "Dance for them? Play your fiddle?"

"No," Mara said quietly. She was staring at the lake, breathing hard. Seldom had I seen my warrior sister afraid, but the look on her face now was one of abject terror. "No, not again. No. *No*."

A glint of light caught my eye, drawing my attention back to the silhouette of Ivyhill. My heart sank as I saw flames shooting out of a first-floor window. At the same moment, the windows of Talan's house lit up all at once, and a bonfire sprang to life on the shore of the lake—an odd one with an eerie, still light that was hard to look away from and seemed somehow to smile.

I turned to Mara, a question on my lips, but she was drifting away from us toward the lake, her gait stiff and strained. A faint path of moonlight unfurled at her feet.

"Nesset," she said tightly. "Do you feel that?"

"Yes," said the Vilia, her voice suddenly small. "What is that?"

I felt it too, my legs suddenly carrying me forward without my permission, some invisible force—an unignorable compulsion—crackling impatiently at the backs of my thighs.

"Father, dig in your heels," I told him, taking the fiddle from my back. He obeyed, the stubborn force of his sentinel power rooting him in place—for now. "Hold on to my waist," I said. "Keep me here for just a moment longer." He obeyed, and I cradled the fiddle under my chin and began to play.

Wait, I thought, drawing the bow across the strings with ease. *Hold.* A mule refusing to move. Beautiful Jet, back home at Ivyhill, snapping at anyone who dared come close with a lead rope. A mountain, a wall of stone. My fingers knew what to do, even as they shook with terror. A lilting waltz, popular at weddings. Easy, cheerful.

"Everyone listen to me," I called out. "Listen to the music and remember yourselves, no matter what he shows you. We've done this before. We've faced Kilraith, we've seen through his deceptions, and we survived. We can do it again."

It was a desperate guess at what Kilraith intended. He liked games, and Jaetris was the master of illusions. What better way to torment us than to separate us and force us to relive our worst nightmares? A grand game for the spectators, and for Kilraith most of all. I watched helplessly as they staggered away from me—Gemma and

Talan toward his lonesome seaside house, Mara and Nesset toward the lake. Warring noises pulled at me from both directions. From the house on the Far Sea came a crash of waves; from the lake, pounding drums. On the lake's distant shores, I saw dark flittering shapes. As afraid as I was, I still felt a twinge of curiosity. What was Mara seeing? What memory had Kilraith conjured for her?

In the distance, Ivyhill's fire was growing fast. Father blew out a furious breath. I could feel him fighting to hold on to me, fighting the force that commanded us to move.

"You've done this before!" I called out once more. "You can do it again. Trust yourselves, not him!"

A low rumble grew all around me, like the climb of a cresting wave. Its roar swallowed my voice. Ivyhill's flames spilled orange and gold across the world. Father let out a pained grunt and released me. The fiddle and bow flew out of my hands and disappeared, and the world raced forward beneath me. I had to run to keep from falling, but I couldn't run fast enough, and soon the ground reared up beneath me, bucking me off my feet. I flew forward into a yawning black void.

CHAPTER 28

Then, all at once, I stopped hard, as if I'd been flung into a wall. I swayed, my head ringing, and groped through the thick darkness for something to grab on to. I felt the heat first, then heard the roar of the flames. For a moment I just stood there, knees wobbling, trying to understand how what I saw was possible.

It was a place I would've known anywhere—my old music room on the second floor of Ivyhill. And underneath the piano, curled up in a pile of quilts, was a sleeping girl. She was eleven years old, with golden-brown hair like her father's and a black kitten on the pillow beside her. The air was hot and the windows glowed orange. Fingers of smoke crawled under the door.

I watched Osmund wake up and start hissing, the hair on his spine standing up in fear. My blood roared in my ears. I felt as if I were floating, a particle of dust caught on the wind and watching the world from a great distance.

"What in the name of the gods?" Father whispered. His face was slack with horror. "What is this? Farrin, is this the night…"

He couldn't even finish the sentence. He started to go to her, to the child—to *me*—but I clutched his arm and held him back. I sang quietly, a wordless melody. *Calm*, I thought, though I felt anything but calm. My tears blurred the room. I had to keep breathing, I told myself. Without breath, there would be no song, and with no song, I would surely lose my mind, or else lose my father to whatever trick was unfolding before us.

My song soothed Father enough to keep him where he stood beside me, though he was desperate, practically pawing at the floor. "Farrin!" he called out over and over, his voice cracking. But the girl didn't wake, not until it was time for her to. I saw her shift and open her eyes, saw her fingers press against her thigh one at a time: *Farrin. Mara. Gemma. Gideon. Philippa.*

No, I wanted to tell her. No, it's not a nightmare. You're awake. Run. *Run.* I stopped singing and tried to scream at her. But my voice caught in my throat, and a pressure clamped over my mouth, silencing me.

Anger roiled in me, steadying me. I resumed my song, and the pressure yielded. So, I could sing—Kilraith, it seemed, couldn't tamp down my power—but I couldn't otherwise interfere. I would have to stand back and watch.

Fine, I thought. *Fine.* I gritted my teeth and watched myself choke and cough, then scramble for the door with Osmund clinging to my chest. My heart broke to see her, this girl—nightgown sweeping the floor, hair in a messy braid. She threw a desperately sad look at her towering shelves of music before bursting out into the hallway. I ached for her, and I envied her. What a terrible night, but at least she didn't know how many more terrible nights were to come, how eventually she would look back at even the days just after the fire with perverse nostalgia.

I followed her through the house in a daze, remembering every step as she took them. There, the long corridor that led to the art gallery. No, that way was fire. There, the collapsing stairs, the smoky hallway. The girl staggered, clutching the kitten she'd tucked under her nightgown.

"Farrin!" Father roared. He clawed futilely at the air between us. "*Farrin*, over here! I'm here, darling!"

But he hadn't been there that night, and he wasn't now. He was already safely outside with the others—Gemma, Mara, Mother, the staff. The thought came to me, for the first time in my life, that perhaps that had been the point. The fire had been engineered to burn down the house, yes, but maybe also to take me with it. A sick feeling rose inside me as I watched my younger self crawl desperately toward the parlor wall and its window. Yes, I could see things clearly. Alaster Bask would have noticed Ryder's fascination with me and seen the danger in it. He would not have been satisfied with simply destroying our house and our things; he would also have wanted to kill the Ashbourne girl who'd somehow ensnared his son and planted ideas of peace in his head.

Suddenly Ryder appeared—his younger self, the shining boy—as if I'd summoned him with my thoughts. Masked and gangly, bony elbows and knees, dark hair slick on his neck. Around him hummed a dazzling aura—Lady Enid's work, I now knew. A spell to persuade me to trust him. My heart leaped.

"Who is that?" Father looked at me in astonishment, then back at Ryder. "The shining boy? He's real?"

"It was Ryder," I said thickly, watching him pull the girl up from the floor and press a damp cloth over her nose and mouth. "He saved me."

They ran through the house hand in hand, dodging flames and falling debris, and I glided after them in amazement, unable to tear my eyes from them even to ensure that Father was still with me, though every now and then I heard his hoarse cries of dismay, the choke of furious sobs. Being here, I realized, was more of a torment for him than it was for me. A savage gladness swept through me. It was his war, after all, that had nearly killed me; his and Alaster's, and all their foolish fathers'. None of them, even with all their Anointed might and power, had been strong enough in heart or mind to resist Kilraith's machinations. It was only right that Father should be forced to watch.

Then I nearly fell. *She* nearly fell, the child Farrin, her skin glistening with soot and sweat. But Ryder caught her, caught *me*, and lifted me into his arms and ran with me. My heart twisted; I knew so well, now, how it felt to be held by him, and my body ached with yearning for the Ryder I knew, the man I hoped with all my might was still alive. I watched our child selves, tears in my eyes. I was small, but he was only a boy. He labored a bit under my weight and let out a terrible hacking cough. I knew what happened next. Eagerly I followed them outside, waiting for the fresh air, the damp cool grass, the waxing moon. Ryder's hand on my cheek. *Star of my life.*

He ran with me into one of the receiving rooms on the house's northern side and reached for the door. I held my breath, and he flung it open. But on the other side was not the veranda that should have been there, nor the moonlit grounds beyond. Instead a wall of pale brick blocked the exit.

Ryder froze, blinking, then turned back and looked at me. He ripped off his mask, and I wanted to cry. There he was—a beardless boy with messy dark hair and fierce blue eyes.

"How do we get out?" he shouted at me. He staggered over, my unconscious child self still in his arms. "What's happened to the doors?"

I flushed hot-cold with dread. Again there was the feeling of being outside of myself, watching the world below from a great distance.

"But that didn't happen," Father said dully, his expression blank with shock. He pointed at the brick wall. "The night of the fire, you escaped. You both escaped."

My growing panic made me livid. I wanted to kick him. "Take her," I told him, gesturing at my younger self. "Give him a rest."

But Ryder backed away from us, turning away slightly as if to protect his burden. His scowl was fearsome, furious. He looked at me with new suspicion.

"Who are you?" he demanded.

I bent down to look him in the eyes. "We're friends. You can trust us. We want to help you get out." An idea came to me. "We're a new sort of ward magic, spelled to activate in times of disaster and keep the family safe. You want to get out, don't you?" I glanced at my younger self's soot-stained face; I heard her labored breathing. "You want to save her?"

Ryder looked closely at me. I thought I saw recognition flash in his eyes. "Yes. All right." He shifted my body into Father's arms. I couldn't look at my father, couldn't bear the devastation on his face. He cradled the girl's body to him as if it were the most precious thing in the world.

I grappled for what was left of my courage. "Quickly, now. We'll try the other doors." But I knew even as I ran for them what we would find, and indeed, past each door stood a solid brick wall. At every window, I tore away the burning drapes, but that only revealed more walls of brick. We were trapped.

I stood before the last of them on the first floor, clenched my fists, planted my feet firmly, and started to sing. *Fall*, I commanded. I imagined a tower of children's blocks collapsing, a felled tree crashing to the ground with a groan. I thought of my own bed, how marvelous it felt to plop down on it at the end of a long day. Surrender. Capitulation. Relief.

"Farrin," Father said warningly. I glanced back at him and saw the flames leaping closer. Soon we would lose the ability to go back upstairs. My mind raced. What was Kilraith trying to prove?

I tried singing down the wall for a moment longer, and just as I saw the stones begin to tremble, my younger self screamed. I whirled to see her awake and clinging to Father, her eyes wide with horror.

"Papa!" she cried. Her voice was hoarse, terrible. "Where do we go?"

He held her to him, looking desperately at me as a huge slab of ceiling caved in. Ryder grabbed my hand and yanked me forward out of its path.

"This way," I said breathlessly, and then I raced toward the entrance hall. It was a pit of smoke and fire; through the mess, I saw one of the great staircases still standing. I scrambled up it, fear bolting through me like lightning. The others followed me, Father's boots heavy on each step. My mind spun with panic. Where to go? This was some sort of game. I didn't think Kilraith would have created this whole thing just to kill us. No, that would come later; this was a torment. A display of his power, of Jaetris's power.

On the second floor, I ran for the closest door—one of the guest bedrooms—and threw it open, remembering the hysterical logic of my child self. Try every room, every window. A courtyard, a balcony, *anywhere* there was fresh air.

But on the other side of the door was not a bedroom. It wasn't even Ivyhill. It was the Green House. It was Mother's parlor. And there was my younger self, a little older now. Twelve years old and stone-faced, glassy-eyed. Osmund on her lap, she stared out the windows at the gardens beyond, where Gemma wandered in her nightgown, bawling piteously.

My stomach dropped. I knew this night. In truth, it could have been any number of nights after Mother left, all of them bleak and endless. Father had deposited us at the palace and gone to the city to drown his feelings in drink, in rich food, in anonymous arms he would soon forget. In defiance of his instructions, I'd taken Gemma to the Green House. There we would stay until he finally regained enough of his senses to come find us. There we would stay, I remembered thinking, until Mother returned.

As I stared at twelve-year-old Farrin—her rigid posture, the stubborn set of her jaw—I felt unspeakably sad. I remembered that feeling. The determination not to cry. The loneliness opening like an abyss under my feet. Every shadow was a monster, every small sound a leaping hope.

As if responding to the frantic thrum of my thoughts, the scene before me began to change. The shadows *were* monsters, suddenly, toothy and reaching. The proportions of the furniture became grotesque, surreal, looming. My mouth went dry as I watched the shadows wrap around young Farrin. She didn't move; she just sat there in silent acceptance. And then the floor dropped out from under my feet, and I was falling. An abyss indeed. Utter blackness, the air so stifling I couldn't breathe, my pounding heart threatening to crack me open. I tried to look for Father and Ryder, for the soot-stained Farrin, but the force of my fall had me tight in its grip.

I squeezed my eyes shut and forced out a quiet song. *Real*, I thought shakily. I pictured the ground solid beneath me, the impossible hugeness of the northern mountains, the warm weight of Ryder's body. Safety. Shelter.

Abruptly I juddered to a halt, and when I opened my eyes, gasping, swaying a bit on my feet, I was in one of the second-floor guest rooms at Ivyhill, staring at bricked-up windows and a burning bed.

Father was pulling at me, desperate, as my younger self screamed in his arms. Ryder was stamping furiously at the burning carpet.

"What are you doing?" Father cried. "This is not the way out!"

I turned to stare at him. "Did you not see the Green House? Didn't you fall?"

"What? No!" His grip was iron. "Move, Farrin!"

I did, staggering out into the hallway after him just as the bedroom floor collapsed. The door slammed shut on my heels.

Ryder glared at me. "You're not doing a very good job of helping us. Do you know the way or don't you?"

I ran clumsily down the hall after Father. For a moment I locked eyes with my younger self, and her mouth curled into a sly smile. "Oh dear," she said quietly, looking around us at the burning house. "What a shame."

Kilraith.

I set my jaw and moved past them, ignoring the feeling of the little girl's eyes boring into my back. The next door led to another bedroom. I had no choice. The air was cloying, darkening. I threw open the door.

And there was Gareth's bedroom at his family home in Big Deep. And there we both were, young and naked and embarrassed, awkwardly detaching from each other amid damp, tangled sheets as the sunset poured through his windows.

Numb with shock, I watched myself totter out of bed and toward his bathing room. I remembered with breathtaking clarity the slight sting between my legs, and the nervous curiosity I'd felt upon noticing the spot of blood on the bed.

But then Gareth swung his legs over to sit on the edge of the bed and watch me leave. There was a terrible expression on his face, one of disgust and disappointment. He assessed my body coldly; his lip curled. He scrubbed his hands on the sheets and then stood and tore them off his bed in a fury.

I watched him in horror. No. That wasn't what had happened. I had cleaned myself in the bathing room and then come back to bed, and Gareth had been standing there waiting for me, flushed and bashful, dressed in his rumpled clothes. He had held out his arms to me. "Please hug me," he'd said, "and tell me you still love me." And I had, and I did.

But this Gareth before me looked nothing like mine, until

suddenly he did. My younger self came out of the bathing room, and he stood, flushed and bashful, holding out his arms. "Please hug me," I heard him say, and I watched fifteen-year-old Farrin laugh through her confused tears and lean into his embrace, a warm hug of relief that I remembered well. But now it seemed different. Gareth's shoulders were tense and square. He held me gingerly. Reluctantly?

Slowly I stepped back from them, tears burning behind my eyes. Was *that* what he'd done while I was in the bathing room? Wiped himself clean of me, scorning me, *despising* me? And then he'd schooled his features to look like the friend I knew and pretended away his true feelings?

I staggered out of the room, blindly pushing Father and Ryder out ahead of me. I yanked the door shut and leaned on it, my throat aching with trapped sobs.

"Did you see any of that?" I asked hoarsely.

Ryder was bewildered, exasperated. "See *what*?"

Father, I thought, was beginning to understand. "It was only one of the guest bedrooms to us," he said. "With bricked-up windows like all the others."

I was relieved, of course. I wanted neither of them to see Gareth or me in such a state.

"It's a game," I breathed. "We'll have to go through every room to find the way out, and each one of them will hurt me."

"Hurt you how?" Father demanded. He looked ready to tear down the house with his bare hands.

I shook my head. I couldn't bear the thought of describing anything I'd seen. I pushed past Father with a choked laugh, cursing our ancestors for building such a stupidly grand house—two hundred and fifty rooms. If we ever got home, I decided, I would seriously consider hiring an elemental with a talent for stonework to remake the whole thing.

The next room was one of the guest parlors. I grabbed the brass knob and threw the door open, secretly hoping it would knock flat some smirking past version of myself who stood on the other side, waiting for me.

But I had no such luck. On the other side of the door was a stage I knew well, a stage built specifically for me in the town of Derryndell. My parents had decided that for my first public performance, a smaller location would be ideal, instead of the crowded capital or one of the bustling coastal cities. But hundreds of people had come anyway, from all over the continent. They'd heard of the Ashbourne girl with the voice sweeter than an Olden siren, with fingers more dexterous than any of the great master pianists.

I stood frozen at the threshold, watching my fourteen-year-old self sit down at the piano—my own piano, my lovely cherrywood girl. I saw that Farrin take a deep breath and square her young shoulders, and panic bolted through me like a spooked horse, just as fresh and terrible as it had been that day.

"No, wait!" I cried, rushing across the stage. I tried pulling her from the piano bench, and when that didn't work, I tried pushing her, ramming against her side. It did nothing. She began to play; her small fingers danced across the keys with precision, grace, confidence. I could feel her little heart pounding, the delight and nerves bubbling inside her. Her first performance outside of Ivyhill, and there were so many prestigious figures in the audience—the queen's court composers, members of the royal orchestra, soloists and singers and revered instructors from as far as Aidurra and Vauzanne.

And then, only a few minutes into her performance, it happened. The listening crowd grew restless. They whispered, they sighed, they burst into euphoric laughter. I couldn't stop myself from watching them as they rose from their seats and surged toward the stage—a whole wave of them, confused and blubbering, reaching for the girl at the piano. She didn't notice them at first, content in the cocoon of her power.

I screamed at them and threw myself in front of her. But they raced past me, through me, and lunged at her, at her instrument. They pawed at her and pleaded with her. Old men and young men, women and grandmothers and children, all of them desperate, adoring, insatiable. They would tear her apart if it meant keeping a piece of that music with them forever.

It happened so quickly and was such a shock that our house guard didn't respond right away. Father was the first one to reach her, Gareth just behind him. Gareth swept her away, sheltering her against his body, and Father pounded twenty people flat before the guards were able to push through the teeming masses and join him. A hundred brawls broke out; the music hadn't driven *everyone* mad with ardent devotion. Some desperately fought for order. Soon the stage was swarmed, and I watched in horror as those grasping hands began to tear bits of flesh from Father's body, from Gareth's, from mine. My admirers trapped us in the wings, and their cries were fervent, wet prayers.

I backed away, tripping over my own feet. I stumbled into Father and turned to hide my face in his sleeve. *No*, I thought frantically. *Real.* I gasped out a fragment of song, fighting hard to steady it.

Father held me with his free arm. Little Farrin, in his other arm, was crying.

"What do you see?" I whispered.

"A guest parlor," Father answered. "What do *you* see?"

I looked up at him, and I thought he might have seen the answer in my eyes. Surely he remembered that day as vividly as I did.

His face was a stony mask, but his eyes burned. "Shut the door," he barked at Ryder, and the boy obeyed, closing the bricked-up room away from us.

In the next room, what awaited us stopped me cold and tore an angry sob from my throat. It was a pleasant spring day at Ivyhill, full of birdsong and tender blooms, and all of us stood at the house's open doors, watching the Warden take Mara away. Gemma wailed, Mother cried behind her hand, and so desperately sad, so shocked, that she couldn't find her tears. I remembered that feeling of the world closing in on me, could feel it tightening my throat even now. And then there was Father, trying in vain to comfort us all. "It's an honor," he told us, standing tall, dry-eyed. "The Warden thinks she will pass the trials more quickly than any Rose before her." But he couldn't fool me even then. I heard that gruff note in his voice and saw the hard set of his mouth.

I stared after the departing carriage, watching in horror as the Warden crawled out the window, spiderlike, and crouched on the roof. Our eyes met across the growing distance between us. She smiled and stood, and then the severe dark shape of her bloomed into a winged shadow with round yellow eyes, stern and staring. She was no longer the Warden, but instead an owl with gleaming talons and a shrieking cry, looming with huge dark wings over the carriage that took my sister away from me.

I turned away furiously, snapped the door closed, and sang the cheeriest tune I could think of. *No*, I thought. *You won't beat me. That isn't real. This isn't real.* I would *not* be trapped in a maze of my own home. It was *my* home, *our* home, not his.

I thought I heard a curl of laughter at the back of my mind. I wasn't convinced by my own trembling bravado, and neither was he.

On we went through the house, each room a nightmare of memory. In another bedroom, the artificer worked to stifle Gemma's power—power that I now knew had been unstable because it came from a woman with an awakening god living inside her. Mara and I were in my bedroom, holding on to each other tightly as Gemma's screams rang through the house. Father had wanted to send us away while it happened, but Mother had begged him not to. If she had to sit and watch one daughter be cut open, he would not deprive her of knowing that her other daughters were safe and unhurt and right upstairs. Young Farrin's and Mara's bodies began to peel open before my eyes, as if the artificer's knives of magic were carving into them too. I turned away from their screams and shut the door behind me.

The art gallery, my father's study, every guest room, every parlor. Myself at every age, at every moment of humiliation. Every day of anguish I'd ever known unfurled before me, each one wounding me anew. I pushed my power to its limits, singing desperately through each plunge of dread and embarrassment. *Real*, I thought. *Truth. Clarity.* Midmorning sunlight burning away a damp fog. A single drop of clear water clinging to a trembling leaf. My piano's keys under my fingers, Osmund pressing his silken head against my neck before settling down beside me to sleep. Gemma's summer-blue eyes. Mara's warm hand, worn and rough from her years of service.

And then, without warning, came Ryder.

I stumbled into the room in a state of numb terror, my song pouring automatically from my tired lungs. Then I saw what awaited me and my voice died in my throat.

It was the little room in Ryder's stable—*his* room, his haven. There were my clothes hanging to dry; there was the glowing stove, the little bed. And there I was, naked, my back to Ryder as he assessed me with cold appraising eyes. Every lump on my body, every dip and imperfection—he saw them all, and so did I.

I couldn't breathe, couldn't move. I watched myself step away, shivering, and reach for Ryder's clothes that lay abandoned on the floor.

"I can't," I told him, my voice small and frightened.

He caught my wrist and pulled me back against him. He kicked the clothes away, then shoved me toward the wall, where a mirror stood. A distant part of me knew such a mirror didn't actually exist in that room, and yet as I stared at it, I believed it. Ryder made me look at it, holding my face hard in his hands. I struggled, I kicked him. He pulled back my arms and held them, grinned meanly at me in the mirror.

"Farrin in the forest light," he said mockingly. "Cold and strange. Doesn't even know how to fuck herself properly. And you thought I found you beautiful. *You.*" He laughed. "Lucky for you that you were born into an Anointed family. Without that power you have, you'd be nothing. No one in their right mind would want *this.*"

I felt I was going to be sick. I wrenched myself free and ducked away from his reaching arms, away from the mortifying sight of my body in the mirror. I stumbled out of the room and slammed the door shut behind me. I couldn't sing, couldn't breathe. I ignored Father calling after me, young Ryder's bewildered questions, the gleeful laughter of the little girl in Father's arms. I found the last door in the hallway—the door to my own bedroom.

I sagged against it, pressing my hands flat to the wood. The air was scorching, my sweat-drenched hair was plastered to my neck, and my fine dress of blue silk had turned black and clinging. I hummed through my tears, pushing aside the horrible image of Ryder leering cruelly at me in the mirror. *Real,* I thought. I scrabbled through my mind and poured every true memory of him, of us, into my song. Ryder teaching me how to fight. Ryder holding me after I'd sung the Devenmere chimaera into submission, the shelter of his strength. His hands on my skin, his kisses in my hair, his hard, hot weight pinning me to the bed in the Citadel, in the Torch and Thorn, in his cozy stable room. His voice breaking on my name as he moved in me, tender, slow. His words falling on me like soft rain. *To love you, Farrin. All I want is to love you.*

I pushed open the door to my room and saw the moonlit grounds of Ivyhill stretching out before me. The air was cool and fresh. I gulped it down as little Farrin gleefully ran past me, pulling young Ryder after her. They turned back and waved at me. "Come on, hurry!" Ryder cried. "This is the way out!"

And I very nearly did. The breeze was delicious, and my skin crawled from everything the house had done to me. I wanted to walk away from it and never look back. But when I turned back to find Father, I saw him standing not far from me, wrapped in chains of shadow. There was a shadowed clamped over his mouth, and another wrapped around his throat. For a frozen second, his terrified eyes found mine. Then the shadows yanked him away from me, pulling him back into the flames as if he were a mere cloth doll. The speed with which they took him was brutal. His neck bent horribly.

"Hurry up!" young Farrin called. I looked back once to see her standing in the safe moonlit night, her face sparkling with happiness, Ryder now grown and standing tall beside her. And this was not the cruel Ryder from the house's nightmares; it was *my* Ryder, his eyes soft.

He held out his hand to me, a smile on his face. "Come here, love," he said. "It's time to go."

But I couldn't. I *couldn't*. I turned back into the flames and ran after my father, a scream stuck in my throat. I tore through the burning hallways, shielding my eyes against the glare. I would not leave him as Philippa had left me, as *he* had left Gemma and me on all those long, lonely nights of grief. As often as I'd wished that same pain on him, prayed viciously that he would someday feel it and understand, I couldn't abandon him to it now. No, that pain, that legacy of hatred and war, cowardice and abandonment—it ended here. It ended with me.

Suddenly, the house and all its fire disappeared into blackness, and I stood in a field strewn with ashes. It was Ivyhill, now in ruins, the estate utterly devastated. Not even my piano had survived. There was only rubble and embers, and in the midst of it stood a grinning man made of shadows. He held a golden bow, its arrow trained on another man who sat bound on an opulent gilded throne. This man was ancient—white beard to his knees, his brown skin ashen and wrinkled. His eyes were sad, coated with yellow film.

"Jaetris" came a whisper beside me.

I turned and nearly fell with relief. There were Mara and Nesset, and on the other side of me, Gemma and Talan. All of them were haggard, the echoes of terrible things on their faces and in their eyes, my sisters' shimmering gowns torn and mud spattered. But whatever they had seen, whatever nightmares Kilraith had thrown at them, they had pushed through, as I had. They were alive.

Nesset gaped at the old man on the throne. "It can't be," she whispered.

But I agreed with Mara. The man on the throne was indeed Jaetris, god of the mind. My heart, my bones, my very breath knew it as soon as I looked at him. He appeared to me, in all his rheumy disarray, with the same kind of bright clarity that Philippa had when she'd rescued Ryder, Alastrina, and me from Mhorghast. The ragged breaths he took made the ground tremble under my feet; the air pulled tight around us with each inhalation, each sputtering, pained gasp.

And Kilraith had an arrow pointed right at his heart.

Shapes shimmered all around us, and suddenly Jaetris wasn't alone. Columns of shadow alit from the sky, curling like smug smiles against the ruined ground. And out of each of them tumbled a man bound with invisible chains that held him frozen, powerless. Their unblinking eyes stared at me, and for a moment I could only stare back at them, dread pounding a wicked rhythm against my ribs.

Gareth, thin and dressed in shabby finery, quite obviously ill, a pallid sheen to his skin.

Father, still covered in soot from the fire.

Ryder, raging in furious silence against the power that held him. His eyes found mine, bright and angry, that brilliant blue I knew and loved.

Fight, they told me. *No matter what he does to us, you must fight him.*

And in that moment when our gazes locked, the certainty of violence thick in the air around us, the memory of young Ryder fresh in my mind—precious boy, so brave and unafraid in that house full of smoke—I knew. I knew it in my deepest core. It didn't matter if it was my song that had first drawn him to me. It didn't matter if my power was the thing that had allowed something like love to begin unfurling in his heart.

What mattered was what that love had become, what we had shared—every touch of his hands, every moment of sameness, of *rightness*, that had passed between us. Two tired, angry hearts finding solace in each other. I could not doubt the truth of that. He had pressed it into me with his every kiss, his every caress, with every utterance of my name.

For one exquisite moment, that conviction was my entire world, Ryder's blazing expression the only thing I could see. He would forgive me; he would help me learn to forgive myself. In that instant, I felt stronger and more at peace than I ever had.

Then the columns of darkness whirling behind each of the captive men took on the same shape as the grinning shadowed figure who leered beside Jaetris with his arrow. I returned to myself, to my racing heart and the dangerous, terrible present.

Before me stood four Kilraiths, three bound men, and one bound god.

"Such a fine, brave display," said the four Kilraiths, their voices a perfect scornful chorus. "But now the game is nearly over, and it's time for you to make the final move, little bird. Which arrow shall I let fly?"

I felt the bloom of Mara's and Gemma's power on either side of me—one quick and nimble as twining vines, the other solid and bright as steel. They had to be as tired as I was, and yet they still found some strength inside themselves. They were ready to fight, and so was I.

I didn't dare glance at Talan. If I saw how tired he was, how completely it had taxed his demonic power to distract Kilraith from our final deadly secret all this time, I would lose my nerve.

"Come, now, we're waiting," Kilraith crooned. Above us, all around us, hissed a sea of excited whispers. "Which one will it be? The god, the friend, the father, or the lover? Quickly, or I'll kill all of them. You know I will. Five seconds. Four. Three. Two…"

I moved faster than I ever had, humming the opening notes of a rondo to spur me on. From the ruined mess of my gown I withdrew the blazing feather—untouched, unhurt, bright as the sun—and held it high.

I stopped singing only long enough to draw a breath and cry out her name.

"Ankaret!"

CHAPTER 29

At first I was afraid she wouldn't come. In a single instant of icy fear, I thought a hundred things: the feather was a lie, Ankaret's strange friendship was a lie, I was foolish to have trusted her. I was wrong about what I'd seen at the capital. She hadn't beaten Kilraith; he had beaten her, and now she was dead.

But then there was a distant boom like a far-off explosion, and the ground began to shake. Kilraith—all four of him—shifted forms. He was a great bird of storms and shadows with eyes like lightning; he was a roaring column of darkness; he was a whirling fist of night sky; he was a bear chimaera with a crescent-moon smile. And then he was a man—tall and bare-armed, as Talan had described his appearance on the night they'd first met. He wore a fine vest and trousers, gloves and gauntlets, and an onyx diadem in his long white hair.

I froze. This was the form he came back to most often amid all the flickering others, this tall, finely built man with skin as white as his hair, angry eyes of violet and gold, and, on his forehead, a bright starburst scar.

I didn't have time to work through my shock, for suddenly she was there, streaking down out of the sky in a cascade of fire. *Ankaret.*

Kilraith roared with fury and rose to meet her, his voice warping as he shifted between his many shuddering forms. The elegant body of the white-haired man stretched and darkened, becoming the massive winged creature I'd seen at the capital. He shot up into the air and crashed into Ankaret. Their eyes flickered—eyes of lightning, eyes of blue fire. The tremendous impact knocked us all off our feet.

A distant wave of terrified cries rose up underneath the cacophony of their fight—all Mhorghast's spectators, still distant, now screaming. The shapes of their assembled crowds flickered in and out of sight at the corners of my eyes. The illusion that hid them was buckling.

"Gemma!" I cried. "Mara!"

I ran for Jaetris and heard my sisters, Talan, and Nesset close behind me. I sang as I ran, still the cheerful rondo, my steps as light as each twirling note. *Distract him*, I thought, charging my song with the command. *Hide us*. A song of deception, a plea for protection. *Ankaret*. I laced her name into the notes of an upward bend in the melody, as light and brilliant as her fiery feet upon the ground.

Ryder, Gareth, and Father still lay bound, their bodies frozen in agony. It killed me to run past them, to leave them to whatever torment Kilraith had devised for them, but our time was short. I didn't know how long Ankaret would be able to hold off Kilraith; every second seemed to race faster than the one before it.

We reached Jaetris on his throne. When his tired gold eyes slid over to look at me, I felt the instinctual urge to kneel before him in reverence. But instead I steeled myself against the might of him and stood fast. Even bound and at Kilraith's mercy as he was, his presence made my skin buzz.

"Talan, Nesset, keep watch," Gemma said sharply. "Anyone or anything who comes near—"

"I'll make them think they're skipping through a meadow without a care in the world," Talan replied pleasantly. "Nudge them right past us."

"And I'll tear out their throats with my teeth," Nesset spat. She crouched, lithe and battle-ready, and then a wave of warmth rippled through the air as Talan called upon his demonic power. Right before my eyes, he shifted into a horned chimaera, scaly, cat-faced, prowling. I thought of what he'd told us about the many forms Kilraith had forced him to take while he was bound to him, how his cruel parents had transformed into the shapes of whatever had most terrified their victims. The greater demons were beings of deception and illusion, descendants of Jaetris and Zelphenia—god of the mind, goddess of the unknowable.

I turned back to Jaetris, who watched Talan with bland interest. Beyond and above him, the sky rippled. I tried not to think about how many Olden beings were lurking just past the range of our vision, ready to strike.

"Jaetris, god of the mind," I said, "where is the egg that binds you to the creature Kilraith?"

He didn't answer. He stared with bleary eyes at the warring shapes of Kilraith and Ankaret in the sky.

I shot Mara a silent plea. She was the one used to prying information out of people.

Grim-faced, she approached him. "Jaetris, tell us where it is," she commanded. "We can destroy it. We can free you."

That got his attention. Slowly he looked up at her and let out a thin, wheezing laugh.

"You?" He took in all three of us—our shining skin, our lustrous hair, the gold flecks in our eyes. Unimpressed, he chewed on his cracked lip and let his eyes drift closed. "Leave me," he moaned.

Gemma tried next. She knelt before him and placed a hand on each of his. "Uncle," she said softly. "Hear me. Hear us. Come out of the place where he's put you." Her fingers glowed a faint blue white as she gently probed him with her power, just as she'd done to pull the Three-Eyed Crown out of Talan. The scars on her hand lit up like stars.

Shadows shifted across Jaetris's gnarled face. Tiny green vines sprouted at his heels and climbed up curiously to show him their budding faces.

He sneered down at Gemma. "How dare you," he gasped. *"Uncle?"* Then, trembling violently with the effort, he knocked her back with a sharp jut of his chin. She flew several feet before slamming into the ground. Talan slunk over to her at once and nudged her upright with his massive horned head.

That display of power had taxed Jaetris. He slumped back against his throne, even thinner and grayer, as if entire layers of his being had been scraped away by that single swipe. I looked back over my shoulder and saw the brilliant twist of Ankaret spiraling up into the air, Kilraith racing after her in a torrent of black clouds.

An impatient burst of inspiration exploded through me, as quick and hot as Ankaret's own fire. I grabbed the obsidian-handled dagger from my boot and sliced open my arm. The pain was instant, searing, and for a moment I crouched over the wound, gasping first in shock, then in relieved wonder. My wild guess had been correct.

The blood dripping down my arm was bright red swirled with gold—a human's blood and the blood of a god, awakened by Mhorghast's Olden air.

Mara cursed and grabbed for me, but then she saw the sheen of my blood and stopped, staring. I pushed past her, blinking back tears, and slashed open Jaetris's own arm. His wrinkled skin opened like paper, and out of the thin wound trickled blood so brilliantly gold that it hurt my eyes.

He stared stupidly down at the gash, then blew out a short angry breath. I thrust my own arm at him, showing him the red-gold blood staining my skin.

"You see?" I said angrily. "Uncle indeed. I'm no mere scrabbling human deluding herself with heroic ideas. Your sister's blood runs in our veins."

The words were like an incantation. Above, the sky cracked open like thunder. The air shifted violently, cold and angry, and without even turning around I knew that Kilraith was flying toward us. I heard Ankaret's distant scream. A shock wave of heat rushed past us, nearly knocking me off my feet.

Jaetris was staring at me. Awareness flashed in his gold eyes.

Behind me, Talan growled a warning.

"Whatever you're doing to do, Ashbourne, do it fast," Nesset barked.

"We can *help* you," I insisted desperately, fighting not to look back over my shoulder. "If you only tell us where it is, we can destroy it." I bit back my many teeming doubts. *Maybe* we could destroy it. But it would do no good to admit to him, or to myself, how desperate a hope that was.

A shell of air pulled tight around Jaetris and me. He closed his eyes, his mouth twisting, and then there was a popping snap, deep in my ears. I tottered as if punched, dizzy, but his wizened old hands held me firm. There was a new steadiness in his golden eyes.

"You will have to kill me to get it, child," he said, his voice thin but firm. "This body must be destroyed. Do not fear. I am more than this form and will come back, though I cannot say when or how. Do you understand?"

No, I wanted to tell him. *No, I understand none of this.* I was operating on instinct alone, and I felt lightheaded from the loss of blood, but I lied and gasped out, "Yes. I understand."

"Good. Now, this will hurt. You will live, but you will need much rest afterward. With this body gone, someone needs to know what I know, or else the knowledge will be lost, and I may not remember it all when I return." He pulled me close. "You must live, daughter of Kerezen. Live, and leave this place. Destroy the anchor. Take my knowledge and run."

Then he pressed his bleeding arm to mine and grabbed the back of my head, holding me steady. A searing pain rushed into me where our wounds met, and his fingers were like scorching needles piercing my skull. But as soon as I opened my mouth to scream, the pain was gone, and when I opened my eyes, I found myself standing on a vast northern plain.

Images rushed at me too quickly to decipher. I saw five great stars joining together as one over the snowy landscape. A white explosion, too loud and impossible to be heard by anyone but the gods. It bloomed in silence and tore across the world, and when it cleared, the stars were gone, and the snowy plain was a charred ruin of ice and ash.

My heart thundered wildly. I knew in my bones what I had just seen—the Unmaking, the day on which the gods had died and separated the world of Edyn from the Old Country. The destroyed landscape stretching to the horizon in front of me was part of the brutal Unmade Lands in the farthest north, an unpredictable glacial country where no one dared live.

More images came, flying at me like arrows. Each one stole my breath. From the ruin of the unmade gods careened two gleaming silver comets. They arced over the Unmade Lands in opposite directions and disappeared over the horizon. Somehow I was able to follow them with my mind, both at once. One crashed into the sea south of Aidurra, carving a great canyon into the ocean floor before coming to rest far inside the earth. The crash extinguished its light; it was now a mere shadow, indistinguishable from the cold darkness, seething miserably inside the deepest rock the god Caiathos had ever created. It would take some time for the creature to claw its way back to the living world. For now, it raged unheard in the frigid depths of the ocean, where there was no other life. And there it stayed for an age, buried and alone.

The other comet had a softer time of things. It tumbled into the Bay of the Gods on the southwestern coast of Gallinor, and when it hit the water, it didn't sink or float. It skimmed across the surface like a skipped stone, like glimmering sunlight, and when it came to rest on the shore, it was a twisting, pale thing, a mere wisp of cloud. It pulled itself weakly into a seaside cave, where it became a white flame, shivering in the dark. As it rested in the cavern, the bruised power of all five gods churning in its deepest heart, it discovered it could grow wings, that it could shift and snap like fire, that it could grow monstrously huge if it wanted. It crawled deeper into the cave and discovered a vast network of caverns. Alone, content, it soared over underground lakes, dropping cinders into the black water.

Ankaret.

Her name burned in my mouth, an ember I couldn't swallow.

And I watched her, Ankaret, as she discovered how to take other forms too—a sleek speckled seal, a cool breeze with no body that whistled through the caves. Her favorite form was that of a young woman, for in the reflection of a dark underground lake, illuminated by her inner light, she could admire the woman's long hair of sea foam, her delicate bones, the pink starburst scar on her forehead.

And then, on a summer morning bright as diamonds, Ankaret awoke as the woman she had come to adore, remembering nothing else. She was alone in a cave; she was frightened, desperate for sunlight. She walked on shaky legs into the city of Fairhaven. The people who lived there knew at once who she was, *what* she was. Before she even opened her mouth, they fell prostrate at her feet, weeping with thanks and praise, for the gods were dead and they were afraid.

She knelt before them and gently raised each of their anguished faces to the sky.

"You need be afraid no longer," she told them, her voice spilling across the land like the dawn. And they named her high queen, and when they asked for her name, she told them what it was, though she couldn't remember who had named her or what her life had been before she crawled out of the seaside caverns. She had forgotten the name Ankaret, had forgotten falling to the ground as a comet, a remnant of the gods' Unmaking. And she had no memory of the other comet—the other god relic, her other half—who stewed in deep darkness on the other side of the world.

"I am Yvaine Ballantere," she told them simply, a name she pulled from her newborn heart and knew to be true. "And the gods have chosen me to protect you."

I would have crashed to my knees then if Jaetris had let me, but he didn't. He stood beside me, bearded and old but hale, his eyes glinting.

"We're running out of time," he said. The burning pressure on my head and arm heightened.

The images that came at me were like illustrations on the pages of a book being flipped too fast for any human mind to absorb. Shadows and storms, lightning and fire. The Crescent of Storms in Vauzanne. The Knotwood in Aidurra.

The Middlemist, and the glittering streets of Mhorghast.

"You understand now, I trust," said Jaetris tightly. His face was calm but his eyes were desperate.

Impossibly, I did. The information now crammed into my mind was a mess of colors and feelings, but somewhere in that jumble gleamed a polished stone of truth.

"Hide it," Jaetris breathed, a note of pity in his voice. "Protect it."

His body was fading, flickering. I grabbed for his arm. "Wait, please! How do I do that?"

But before he could answer, he was gone, sunken back into the depths of the *ytheliad* curse that bound him to Kilraith's will. That he'd been able to fight the curse for long enough to share with me what he had... I shuddered, imagining the agony of it. I held his face in my hands and searched for any lingering glimmer of godly gold, but staring back at me were two ordinary eyes, blank and understanding nothing—the gaze of the horribly unlucky human who'd been born with a god inside him. Imagining my mother in his place—all of Kerezen's godly power bound to Kilraith while trapped inside the body of the innocent human Philippa Wren—I felt choked with sadness; all of this was so horribly unfair. What was this man's name? What had his life been before the god in him awakened?

Then a great force threw me back from the throne, and I landed flat on my back. I gasped, seeing stars, and Ryder came into view. His skin was ashen, and his shoulder was bleeding, but his eyes were clear and strong.

"Is it really you?" I said hoarsely. I realized that I was crying. My head hurt so terribly I was convinced it would split open. A shimmering white aura suffused my vision, turning everything dreamy and glittering.

Ryder helped me rise. "Yes, love," he told me. "It's me, and I've got you." His hands were warm and familiar. I clung to them, gasping, and leaned hard into the warm mountain of his body.

"We have to kill Jaetris," I said.

He stared at me. "What?"

"Not *him*. Just this body." With Ryder's help, I staggered toward Gemma and Mara. "The egg... He said we had to kill this body he's in to get at it. It must be destroyed." I couldn't stop crying, everything I'd seen beating on the inside of my skull with iron fists. "He'll come back, he said, and I believe him."

Grim and pale, my sisters joined me at the throne. Dimly, as if from a great distance, I realized what was happening all around us.

Kilraith's illusion had crumbled, and now all of Mhorghast was emptying out of the giant arena above us. Father was free and on his feet, a blur of speed. He was fighting a clutch of gray stone-nymphs with white eyes and boulder fists, and past him raced Nesset. With a fierce cry, she jumped onto the back of a fae with skin that gleamed like green jewels. She plucked a long red thorn from the knot of flowers sewing up her cheek and stabbed the fae in the throat. Talan, still in his beastly disguise, tackled a chimaera with plates of bone jutting out of its back. He swiped black claws across its face and sent it tumbling.

"Gareth," I croaked. "Where's Gareth?"

"He's unconscious but alive," Ryder replied shortly. "I won't let anyone touch him."

I had no idea how he could promise me such a thing, but I chose to believe him and turned to my sisters, heart in my throat, pain smashing my temples like battering rams. Two words darted like panicked birds through my mind: *Ankaret. Yvaine. Ankaret. Yvaine.*

They were the same. They were the same, and she hadn't told me. Why hadn't she *told* me?

"Do we have to kill him in a particular way?" Mara was asking.

I could only stand there, trying desperately to think and blinking back hot, overwhelmed tears. I didn't how to answer her. From behind us came a scream I thought might belong to Father.

Suddenly Jaetris lurched forward on his throne chest-first, as if someone had thrust a spear into his ribs and yanked him toward them. He let out an agonized scream, horrible, like metal scraping against metal. A cold force pulled at my back as if trying to drag me away along with him. Mara grabbed on to him, her arms glinting like swords. Caught between her sentinel strength and Kilraith's furious, ravenous will, the gilded throne twisted wildly in place, its back legs tearing divots into the ground. Gemma let out a triumphant cry, and suddenly black roots limned with silver burst out of the ground where the throne's legs had cracked it open. I felt a burst of hope. She had found, in all of this illusory chaos, a piece of nature. A fierce, proud love blazed up inside me as I thought yet again of young Philippa Wren, born with simple botanical magic that she would someday pass on to her youngest daughter, not knowing that her body housed a sleeping god.

Gemma flung the roots around Jaetris and his throne, helping Mara hold him in place, and I started singing an aria from the final act of one of my favorite operas—the heroine, triumphant, feels the sunlight on her skin for the first time after years of unjust imprisonment. *Strong*, I thought, staring at Jaetris, at the throne, at my brave, bright-eyed sisters. *Hold*.

Once my grip on the song was sure, I looked back over my shoulder and saw Kilraith coming at us. His grasping shadowed hands were huge as trees. His mouth yawned wide. He was storm and lightning, he was shadow, he was a monster. He was a vestige of the gods—lonely, vengeful, burning with hate. His wings blacked out the world. Through the dark haze of his attack, I saw Ryder kneeling over Gareth's body, shouting desperately at a swarm of birds swirling in the air near him—hawks, starlings, Olden birds with silver eyes and brilliant plumage. He'd wilded them from somewhere, I supposed from the chaotic streets of Mhorghast. They gathered into a mass like a fist and flew at Kilraith—huge, fearless—but as soon as they hit the crackling mass of his fury, they disappeared, burned to ash in an instant.

I closed my eyes, a sick peace falling over me. I didn't know what had happened to Ankaret—to *Yvaine*—but I knew I was going to die. We were all going to die.

Then a roar of heat shot down from the sky, and when I opened my eyes, tears streaming down my face from the sudden blaze, I saw Ankaret standing before us—a solid tower of fire with one snapping wing outstretched, holding back the tide of Kilraith's wrath. The relief of seeing her gave me new strength, and yet the despair of knowing what she really was—*who* she was—nearly felled me. I thought her name desperately, the most earnest prayer I'd uttered in years. *Yvaine, Yvaine. Why didn't you tell me?*

"Gemma!" I spoke quickly, afraid what would happen if I stopped singing for too long. "Like before, with the crown!"

Gemma's face was hard, her eyes glittering. She had torn the crown from Talan's body; she could tear the egg from Jaetris's. I hoped, I *had* to hope.

She placed her hands flat on Jaetris's chest, seeking, and when her fingers began to glow, she choked a little, her stony expression faltering with horror.

"It's inside his heart," she cried. "It's hidden deep, underneath a whole lattice of glamours, but I can see it. I feel it!"

"Get it out!" I cried. "Now, hurry!"

Gemma set her jaw. She pulled a knife from her boot, hesitated only a moment, then drew it fast across Jaetris's throat. Within moments he was dead, and my baby sister was soaked with his golden blood, and shaking horribly, but at least now Jaetris—and the body he'd lived in—would feel no pain.

"Hold him, Mara!" Gemma cried, tossing away the knife.

Mara obeyed, her whole body beginning to coruscate as if she were a river shimmering beneath the sun. With a great cry, she tore one of her arms from around Jaetris and flung it out like a whip, knocking away with a boom of power a whole swarm of attackers that, in my panic, I hadn't noticed were almost upon us.

Gemma screamed, and I looked back in terror to see her glowing hands pinned to Jaetris's chest. His flesh and bone were opening at her touch, peeling outward like bloody petals. The protections Kilraith had glamoured into Jaetris's body were fiercer than those with which he'd bound Talan to his crown. Sweat poured down Gemma's body, her slim frame straining with the effort. New roots sprang up out of the earth at her command and dove into the bloody cavity of Jaetris's chest to help her. Her power crackled furiously; brilliant bolts of light burst from her fingers and shot into Kilraith's seething darkness. I was reminded of the two comets I'd seen in Jaetris's vision. So much new knowledge bubbled inside me, and if I looked too hard at it, I'd lose my nerve, my song, my self.

Instead I closed my eyes and kept singing that same soaring aria. *Hold strong.* But my mind careened between so many fears and feelings, so many worries for all my loved ones around me, that I could feel the song's focus start to split in different directions. At first, I choked on the feeling. It was as if all the power inside me was at war with itself, each branch of my music fighting for supremacy. I felt stretched thin, pounded flat. My whole body ached from the strain of forcing out my confused song.

But out of this chaos rose a memory, like a single blossom that had been plucked from a meadow bright with color. A humble gift for me alone. It was Philippa's voice from her quiet kitchen at Wardwell. *You are the daughters of Kerezen and therefore demigods of the body, of the senses. Fighting and creating glamours and making music—these things you can already do. But there is more buried in your power, and I can help you find it.*

It was like receiving permission I didn't know I was asking for. My eyes snapped open, a strange calm flooding through me. The last time we were in Mhorghast, I'd tried this very thing—holding multiple songs in my heart and mind and voice all at once. It hadn't worked; I'd been overcome, my body unable to withstand the disarray of confused magic. But now, a certainty rose in me like the sun. What I had tried before was possible. It was necessary. Maybe it was desperation that urged me to try, or perhaps it was simply the presence of Gemma and Mara fighting so close to me. My precious, brave sisters. I watched them and drew a fresh breath, no longer afraid to attempt this mad thing. Five songs at once was what I needed. And I could do it. I could sing them all and hold them fast. I could trust my power; I could trust myself.

Hold strong, to give Gemma and Mara endurance. *Protection*, to keep the others safe: Ryder, Gareth, Father, Talan, Nesset, all fighting bravely, lost somewhere in the flame and shadows. *Release*, to coax Jaetris's battered body to release the treasure it held. *Confusion*, to divert and deflect the swarming Olden attackers. *Love*, for Ankaret, for Yvaine.

My voice split open into five parts, as if my single song were the work of an entire chorus. Each shining branch of it connected me to my purpose, my dearest ones. Gemma and Mara—*hold strong*. Ryder, Gareth, Father, Talan, Nesset—*protection*.

Tears streamed down my face. Slowly I stood, allowing my column of breath a clearer passage. I watched Jaetris's body unfold. *Release*, I sang to it, to the memory of the man it had been. *Be at peace. Give us the egg, and all your suffering will not be in vain.*

Past the body roiled a dark sea of enemies. The citizens of Mhorghast—some Olden, some human—fought for Kilraith, fought each other. *Confusion.* I glared at them with unfocused eyes, directing my song to wash over them like a tidal wave. Brutal. Relentless. Driving. Unfeeling. An arm of nature sweeping coldly over them, leaving ruin in its wake.

I didn't dare turn to look at Ankaret, but I could feel the heat of her—a bloom of warmth that should have burned me, should have flayed me to my bones, but didn't. I heard Kilraith's distant roars and imagined what she looked like just behind me. An impossible creature, all fire and feathers and light, holding back the tide of death for us. Shielding us.

Love. This branch of my song called out to her, tender, seeking.

I felt the moment when the soaring notes reached her; I felt her take them into herself and receive them as an audience might, with wonderment, with delight.

A horrible cracking sound met my ears; Jaetris's body was a mess of shattered bones and ruined flesh. The roots that held him to his throne dripped gold with his blood. Mara released the throne and sped off into the shadows with a fierce warrior cry. Now she could properly fight, as she was no doubt desperate to.

Gemma, shaking, turned to me. She held in her bloody hands a large gleaming egg—a cousin of the Three-Eyed Crown, with the same metal body and elaborate carvings, rimmed with round-cut topaz jewels.

"Farrin?" Her voice was in shreds, her face gray. "Can you?"

I ended the part of my song that had been for Jaetris and began a new one to replace it: *destroy*. It was like holding in my mind a jewel with five facets, constantly aware of every sharp turn, every gleaming surface, the size and weight of the jewel, how to direct and refract its light. And all the while, I stood on a stone in the middle of a rushing river, struggling to keep my balance.

The egg began to glow in Gemma's hands. She cried out in pain and set it quickly on the ground at her feet, then cradled her hands against her stomach. One of my feet lost its purchase on the slick rock of my mind. The jewel of my song flew out of my hands and into the roaring water.

I fell to my knees beside the egg and reached desperately for it, choking on the dregs of the song I'd lost. My throat was raw, my lungs burning. I dragged the egg toward me and curled my body around it.

And then, suddenly, there was a snap of roaring fire behind me, a fresh rush of heat, and a single steady flame came into view. My vision was blurry. At first she was only a column of white fire stepping out of Ankaret's larger inferno. Then she knelt before me, and I saw her clearly—Yvaine, her hair glinting with feathers and fire, her eyes bright as gold and violet stars.

"I know how to destroy it," she told me. She held out one small white hand covered in a thousand glinting sparks. White and gold feathers encased her slender arm.

Despite her remarkable appearance and sheer spectacular impossibility of everything that was happening, her voice was so familiar, so her own, that I started to cry. "Yvaine, I saw… Jaetris showed me…" I couldn't finish, overwhelmed by the pounding pain in my head. I didn't yet know how to explain what I'd seen—the comet plunging into the dark sea, the other coming to Gallinor and becoming a human. A queen.

Yvaine's face flickered with brilliant light. Diamond tears gathered at her lashes. "I know," she said softly. She touched my throat, and the pain there eased. "I'm sorry I didn't tell you. For a long time, I hardly knew myself. I've been awakening slowly, you see, for a very long time. Ankaret has, I mean. My first true heart. I didn't understand what was happening until after he attacked Fairhaven. Farrin, I'm so sorry."

Then she leaned close to me, touched my cheek, kissed my forehead. She held me to her for a moment, her eyes closed, and then said, "We're running out of time. Can I have it, Farrin?" She drew in a shaky breath. "I can't hold him off for much longer. I know how to destroy it. I promise you."

I shook my head, sobbing, understanding that something terrible was about to happen. "No. *Please*."

But I held out the egg to her nonetheless, hating the rough carved feel of it in my palms. It was heavy, slick with Jaetris's blood. Yvaine took it from me, and it immediately lit up in her hands, too bright to look at. My arm flew up instinctively to shield my eyes, and by the time I managed to look up again, she was gone, stepping back into the enormous wave of Ankaret's fire.

Beyond that shield of light, Kilraith raged. His anger was like mountains crashing down. "Ankaret, look at me!" he howled. "Don't you understand me? I know you do! It's what they deserve! Don't do this! *Look at me!*"

In the visions Jaetris had gifted me—an entire history of an entire world—one particular story flickered brightly, one among millions. I held my breath and let the current of memory sweep over me. Two beings—confused and chaotic and bright as comets, created by irresponsible gods in a thoughtless dying instant—had fallen to the earth from their birthplace in the ravaged skies. In the few blazing seconds it had taken to fall, they had known each other, and loved each other, as fiercely as anyone ever had. And then they had crashed to the ground—the unfeeling ground of a nascent human world—and been separated.

I was in love once, Yvaine had told me in the Green House, her gaze distant and sad. *It was a very long time ago, I think, years and years before any of you were born.*

I couldn't believe it. I didn't want to. Kilraith and Ankaret. Kilraith and *Yvaine*. And yet I could not shake myself free of that truth; it was too real, too huge. It clung to me like a bramble and always would.

Kilraith's furious roars pulled me back to the warring waves of flame and shadow crashing into each other above my head. Despite all his raging thunder, Ankaret's fire was unwavering, unfading. The tiny white form inside that blistering inferno—the form that wore Yvaine's dear face, the face of my impossible friend—turned back once and found me shivering on the ground, miserable in my shock and fear. Somewhere in the brilliant glare, I thought I saw her smile.

"Come and find me," she said gently. The world was crashing apart around us, and yet her words were clear as rain.

Then she turned away from me and disappeared completely into Ankaret's flames. The wave of her fire surged hard against Kilraith.

Light and darkness crashed together like stars colliding—blinding, booming—and then, all at once, Ankaret disappeared. Her blazing light shrank and coalesced into a single glowing shape: Yvaine, alone, unprotected, her shield of fire gone. Serene in a cloak of white-gold feathers, the egg a glowing star in her hands. Kilraith was already diving for her, raising one huge shadowed wing to swipe. He was expecting Ankaret, a firebird as monstrous as his own storming self. And he couldn't stop in time; he was too large, too fast. I heard his cry of horror the instant before he crashed into her, but it was too late. Yvaine was ashes, and so was the egg. White as snow, they were a flurry in the air, and then they were gone.

Kilraith fell from the sky, the vast might of his shadow self collapsing. When the darkness cleared, his human form knelt at its epicenter—pale as Yvaine had been, tall and beautiful, shadows clinging to him like shredded skin. He clutched ashes in his hands and howled out his grief. The sound was like a roaring wind ready to carve the world to pieces.

I watched him in disbelief, and through my tears, I choked out a small song of hope. *Are you there?* But nothing answered. The notes skipped weakly across the ashen ruin before me and quickly sputtered out. I tried again, and again, vaguely noticing the world shifting and turning all around me. A distant part of my mind understood that Mhorghast was collapsing, folding in on itself. Erratic, short-lived moonlight roads shot out in all directions. The city was shrinking, brought to ruin by the grief of its creator, and soon it would crush me.

I closed my eyes, too tired to move, too heartbroken to run. *Let it crush me*, I thought. *Let me die as she did.*

But Ryder wouldn't allow death to claim me. He came out of the shadows and helped me to my feet, everyone else just behind him—Gemma and Talan, Mara and Nesset. Father had Gareth slung over his shoulder. Ryder lifted me into his arms, shouted something to the others, but my shock was too complete to understand him. I pressed my face against his chest and hummed my song into the folds of his coat. *Are you there?* It was the most desperate prayer I'd ever known. *Yvaine. Are you there?*

No answer came to me. I knew it wouldn't. Past my closed lids shone the glow of fractured moonlight. I clung to Ryder and let him carry me home.

CHAPTER 30

Somewhere on the moonlight road that brought us back to Ivyhill, I gave in to the pain that had been battering my head since Jaetris had planted his visions in me. I slipped into blackness, and when I next awoke, I was in my bed in my room, my body aching, Osmund curled up in a tight ball against my side.

Immediately the loss of Yvaine rose up inside me, a pain in my throat that made it hard to swallow. Everything made it hard to swallow; my throat was raw, and each breath was fire. Suddenly I wanted to be rid of all the blankets on me. I tried to sit up and free myself. My movement disturbed Osmund; he jumped down onto the carpet with a disgruntled meow. The sound ripped something open inside me, and I let out a choked sob.

All of this brought Ryder in from the bathing room. He was drying his face with a towel, which he dropped to the floor when he saw me. He paused at the foot of the bed, then started to come around and reach for me, then stopped. His expression was grave, his eyes soft. There were fresh cuts on his cheeks and neck and arms, but they were healing nicely. A drop of water clung to his beard, just to the left of his mouth.

"We've been watching over you in shifts," he said at last, his voice rough. "You've been falling in and out of consciousness for three days. Madam Moreen didn't know what to do for you." He cleared his throat and rested his hands carefully on my polished footboard. He considered me for a moment longer before lowering his gaze to his fingers.

"Shall I get one of your sisters?" he said quietly. "Do you want me to leave?"

His voice was gentle. He looked unbearably dear standing there, big and brawny and quiet, very still, as if he'd entered a temple to pray, and in the lines of his face I could see the echo of the boy he'd once been, the boy who'd run through fire for me. The boy who had saved me. I began to cry then, truly cry. The weight of everything that had happened pressed against my chest.

I held out my arms to him. "Please don't go," I whispered. "Please, Ryder, come here."

He did at once, crawling into the bed beside me. He wrapped me up in his arms and in the blankets, in the cocoon of his fierce love. I touched his face, his beard, and cried against his chest. He held me to him, his hands warm on my back.

"Farrin, love," he said hoarsely. "I'm so sorry."

For a moment, I considered trying my song once more. I felt it building inside me, stubbornly hopeful: *Are you there?* But I decided that if I asked again and still heard that awful silence, the lack of Yvaine in the world, I wouldn't survive it.

Instead I held on to Ryder and cried until I couldn't anymore. My exhaustion was mighty, my headache constant. Ryder rubbed slow circles between my shoulder blades. The rhythm of his touch helped me find sleep.

◆◇◆

Two days later, I sat on a sofa in the morning room, searching for courage.

It helped to have Ryder beside me, and to know that everyone in this room loved me: Gemma and Mara, Father, Talan. I tried not to think about Gareth lying silently upstairs. He ate and drank obediently, but he hadn't spoken since returning from Mhorghast, not even angry or confused words like Alastrina's. He'd been utterly silent, his eyes glassy and distant. When he'd first seen me, a look of relief had passed quickly across his face, but still he had said nothing. He just lay on his bed in one of our guest rooms and slept, or else stared at the ceiling.

It was the sight of him more than anything that had gotten me downstairs. I was wobbly on Ryder's arm, brilliant flares of pain still pulsing in my head, but I'd done it, and Gemma had fed me breakfast tenderly, fussily, as if she were bottle-feeding a kitten—never mind that after the onslaught of magic in Mhorghast, she could barely hold herself upright without Talan's help. And now, with my belly full and my chest in knots, I would tell them all what I had seen.

"What I saw is difficult to understand," I said first. "Jaetris didn't explain any of it for me. I've had to interpret it on my own, and I think I've done it right, but we will need to study it further. Gareth..." I swallowed. "Gareth, when he's well, will be useful in that regard."

They said nothing, waiting patiently for me to find my words. I kept my eyes trained on the designs in the plush carpet under my feet. They were vines, of course, an elaborate swirl of greenery dotted with pale flowers that mirrored my mother's handiwork on the ceiling. The thought sent a pang of longing through me, which I furiously dismissed. I didn't miss her or want her, certainly not in any sort of maternal capacity. She hadn't been there to see what I had seen, to watch Yvaine die right before her eyes. She didn't deserve my company; she hadn't for years, and the fact of her godliness changed nothing.

To get her out of my mind, I started to speak.

"On the day of the Unmaking," I said, "when the gods came together to create Edyn and then died, two pieces of their joined magic flew out from the cataclysm in opposite directions. Each piece contained the remains of the gods, a remnant of each of their five powers. One of these entities crashed into the sea south of Aidurra and was lost to the depths for…" I shook my head. "I don't know how long he lived there. But that being became Kilraith. And the other…"

I paused, struggling for composure. Ryder put his hand on the cushion beside me, palm up, and I grabbed it and held on until I caught my breath.

"The other fell into the Bay of the Gods and became Ankaret, otherwise known by the name she took in her human form, Yvaine Ballantere. What she truly was and where she came from, she didn't know. She only knew that she wanted to protect Edyn—I don't know why, perhaps some lingering instinct of the gods—and so she assumed that the gods had chosen her for that task. She came to Fairhaven, and they saw her power and believed her. Legends grew up around her. She became the high queen of Edyn."

I drew in a shaky breath. "She didn't understand what she truly was until very recently. That was the reason for her strange behavior, I think—her lost memories and declining health. Perhaps it began when Philippa started becoming aware of herself, or when Kilraith found Jaetris and bound him. I can't be certain. But I think she rediscovered Ankaret unintentionally, and that whatever power brought her back to that form—her true, original form—was beyond her control. Until…" I stopped, swallowing hard. "Until I called her to me. Until Mhorghast."

"Perhaps," Talan suggested thoughtfully, "an instinct awoke in her that sensed the growing danger of Kilraith, prompting her to take the form of the creature who could most effectively protect us."

I nodded, grateful to have heard a voice other than my own. "That's what I suspect as well. And then…" I paused, closing my eyes, thinking back over the images I'd seen in Jaetris's visions. I'd spent the last few days sorting through them, trying to organize them in a way that made sense, but already they were beginning to fade. A protective measure, I assumed; Jaetris wouldn't have wanted such a story to live inside me forever. I was only a demigod, after all, and even Jaetris himself had fallen prey to Kilraith.

"Kilraith wants to destroy them," I whispered. "All the gods. He found a way to wake them—I don't know how—and now he wants to kill them truly, as they didn't succeed in doing themselves on the day of the Unmaking. He hates them for his own creation, for the years of agony he endured alone in the ocean, for the conflict of five gods living forever inside him. He has never been able to make peace with this confusion of power, as Yvaine did. Perhaps he carries more of their darker, baser instincts than she does, or maybe everything he suffered is what corrupted him. Whatever the reason for his nature, it's one of anger, vengeance, and hatred. He wants to tear down all boundaries between Edyn and the Old Country—the Middlemist, the Knotwood, the Crescent of Storms. It wasn't Yvaine's declining health sickening the Middlemist; it's been him all along, though I don't know how, and neither did Jaetris. What I do know is that Kilraith believes the separation of humans from Oldens to be subjugation. An unfair restriction on those in the Old Country made only for the sake of humans, whom he believes to be inferior and undeserving of the gods' affection. He believes we are the reason for all the pain he's endured. And once Edyn is destroyed…"

I opened my eyes. Tears streamed silently down my cheeks. "Then I think he will destroy himself. His life has been a torment, too many clashing powers trapped in one form. He blames the gods for the aberration he is. In his eyes, they are irresponsible, careless, cruel. And he loves only one thing: his equal and his opposite."

This time, when I tried to say her name, I found that I couldn't.

Mara, leaning against the far wall, said it for me. "He loved Yvaine. Ankaret."

"*Loves*," I corrected her, looking up fiercely. "I don't believe she's dead, at least not truly. Maybe she's dead in the sense that we can't perceive her, but she's not dead altogether, not destroyed." I bit my lip, realizing how desperate I sounded. "'Come and find me.' She said that to me, right before the end. 'Come and find me.' Jaetris said he would come back in a different body. I believe him. Why would Yvaine have said such a thing unless she intended to return as well?"

This was the thing I'd been telling myself since awakening and realizing she was gone: that she *wasn't* truly gone, that this was all part of something grand and godly that we couldn't yet understand.

Talan leaned forward heavily, elbows on his knees, and considered his hands. Gemma and Mara avoided looking at me altogether. Only Father, frowning thoughtfully, seemed willing to entertain the thought that I wasn't just mad with grief and grasping for any comfort, no matter how outlandish.

"I suppose it's possible," he said. "Many things have happened of late that I would have deemed unthinkable not long ago. Your mother returning and being a god. All of you being…"

He couldn't bring himself to say the word. He blew out an incredulous laugh and scrubbed a hand over his face. He looked old and tired, and yet somehow more himself than he'd been in years, and when I thought of Kilraith's arrow trained on him in Mhorghast, how close I'd come to losing him—losing all of them—I almost couldn't bear to look at him.

"*Mother*," Gemma said thickly. The disgust in her voice surprised me. "Part of me really believed, right until the end, that she would come to our aid in Mhorghast, that we wouldn't have to do all of that alone." She shook her head and looked imploringly at Mara, at me.

"Do you think she really is doing the right thing, the wise thing, by continuing to hide at Wardwell? Or is she simply—"

"A coward?" Mara finished. I couldn't read her expression; I could see only how tired she looked, and heartbreakingly awkward, sitting there among all Ivyhill's finery in her drab Rose garb. How brave she was. How brave we all were.

"It doesn't matter if she's a coward or not," I said, realizing only as I said it that it was true, and that I could know this harsh truth, say it out loud, and still keep breathing, keep fighting. "We'll drive ourselves mad trying to determine what's going on in her head. What matters is that we can't depend on her to help us reliably. She'll come when she wants to, maybe." I shrugged, feeling a little lightheaded with surprise, with relief, at my own matter-of-fact attitude. "We're on our own, and we have been for a long time. Nothing has changed. Being angry with her is a waste of emotion."

The room rang with quiet shock. It was as if a great weight had been lifted from my shoulders. Philippa had broken my heart as a child, but when I'd spoken of her just then, it had been with a sort of coldness, a detached clarity. I didn't know what that meant, couldn't untangle my motives—and I certainly didn't dare look at my father to gauge what he thought of my little speech. But I did nudge my foot ever so slightly against Ryder's, and when I felt him return the gesture, I realized that at least one thing I'd said simply wasn't true.

I was not on my own, not anymore.

Gemma spoke next, briskly, brightly, as if she could lift the mood in the room simply by willing it. "Well, I suppose what we have to do, then, with or without Mother's help, is find and destroy the other anchors of the *ytheliad*, which are presumably giving Kilraith the power to move between realms with ease and gather followers."

"And we must find the other gods before Kilraith does," Ryder said darkly. "Or else destroy him before he can find them."

"But how do you destroy such a creature?" Mara mused. "A being who was created by the gods and contains enough of each of their power that he can control them?" She crossed her arms over her chest, looking grim. "Either he's truly that powerful on his own, or he's using something that is. A tool. A weapon. Is it the *ytheliad* anchors, or something else?"

Silence fell, perhaps the heaviest I'd ever experienced. These questions were impossible to answer.

We tossed ideas between us all through the afternoon until Ryder took my cup from me and told me softly that I was falling asleep sitting up. Gemma sent down to the kitchens for supper, but I was too tired to eat and too heartsick to remain conscious. I touched Ryder's arm and leaned into him. "Will you come with me upstairs?" I whispered. I looked up at him, fresh tears building behind my eyes. I couldn't seem to stop crying, and if I was going to cry, I wanted to be with him and him alone.

"Of course," he said, kissing my hair. Then he helped me rise, and we were slowly crossing the entrance hall when Gilroy stopped us, grave and gray, his voice hushed. The whole house was hushed, despite the number of people in it; we were now sheltering dozens of citizens from nearby towns, and more were coming every day. Word had gotten out that the queen was dead. The air was thick with dread and sadness, and Ivyhill's rooms were full of new beds. I felt guilty for leaving the care of all those people to the staff, but I didn't think I was strong enough to shoulder their grief in addition to my own. Not yet.

"Pardon me, my lady," Gilroy said, "but a messenger from the palace just arrived with this note for you. It seems to be from Lord Thirsk."

Ah, Thirsk. I had wondered when I would hear from him. I took the letter from Gilroy and thanked him, and only when Ryder and I

reached the privacy of my rooms did I dare open it with shaking fingers and read it.

I looked up at Ryder, who waited tensely in the middle of the
room. His worried frown was comically at odds with the purring
Osmund, who lounged contentedly in his arms.

"What is it?" he asked.

"It seems," I said quietly, "that the queen has named me in her
will."

At sunset the next night, I stood at the windows of my bedroom in the
Green House, looking out over the capital city. From there, it looked
almost peaceful: a quiet sea of flickering lights, and rooftops gleaming
red and orange, pink and violet and gold. Ankaret's colors. Yvaine's
colors.

But I had just been in the city, and I knew the true state of the
people living in those shimmering streets. They were absolutely terrified. Their queen was dead. Something existed in the world that was
strong enough to kill a queen chosen by the gods to protect them. A
few of those imprisoned in Mhorghast had resurfaced—I didn't know
how; perhaps some last effort of Jaetris before his death—but many
others had still not been found, and I feared never would be. And
soon enough, the people of Edyn would know the rest of it—that
the gods were reawakening, that they were being hunted, that the
thing hunting them was also trying to tear down their last protections
against the Old Country. The Middlemist, the Crescent of Storms,
and the Knotwood were all in danger. Now that I had briefed the
Royal Conclave on what had happened, they would brief the Senate,
and truth would flood across the world. The armies would train and
disperse, and the Senate would issue its draft to bring a slew of new
initiates to the Order of the Rose.

Our world would be at war with the gods' own angry son—our brother, in a way, as Gemma had pointed out with dark humor.

And yet, as I stood at the windows that night, watching the sunset splash its colors across the city's towers and parks and the placid water in the bay beyond, all I could think of was the simple fact that I missed my friend. I missed Yvaine.

"Farrin?" Ryder came down the stairs, his voice hoarse with sleep. He hadn't been allowed to accompany me to the reading of the queen's will, and though I'd planned to give him a full report, that idea suddenly seemed almost too sad to contemplate.

Instead, I said it quietly, as quick as I could. "She gave me all her belongings. Everything, Ryder. The Citadel. The royal archives. Everything, to do with as I will."

His frown deepened at this extraordinary statement, and he let out a soft, frustrated grunt. "That seems like far too much to place on your shoulders."

I smiled at him, gently teasing, "Are you calling me weak, Ryder Bask? And if you are, isn't a student's skill—or lack thereof—due to the quality of her teacher?"

He came to me and took my hands, his frown softening into a sweet smile I was beginning to realize he showed to no one else.

"My brave Farrin," he said. "In fact, you're the strongest person I've ever known. But love, the responsibility of that—"

"Is something I don't want to think about just now," I said, "though I do have a few ideas." I rubbed his fingers softly. "I'd like to convert some of the palace into additional hospitals, temporary housing and schools, anything to help people in the coming months."

He made a low sound of approval. "A fine idea. It will be needed."

"And I'd like to evacuate as many northerners south as we can."

That surprised him, and pleased him. He kissed my hands, his eyes shining. "The Warden won't like that."

"No, she won't," I said sharply, and left it at that. I stood with him in blessed silence for a moment, then took a deep breath and let it out slowly. "Are you frightened? Of what's to come, I mean?"

"Of course," he answered at once. "Anyone who isn't is a fool, and I don't care to associate with fools." Gently he turned up my chin so our eyes met. "But I also have hope. And I think you do too. I see you try to hide it, but I know your face. I know you." He touched my cheek with the backs of his fingers. "Farrin in the sunlight. Star of my life."

"I've been wanting to ask you what that means," I said softly. "I've never heard the phrase before, not until you."

"It's a northern term of endearment. Star of my life: a fixed beacon, a guiding light. Beloved, and always there, day or night, but brightest when all around it is dark." He shrugged, looking a little uncomfortable. "Flowery, I know. But I've always liked the sound of it. I always hoped…" His mouth twisted. Now he looked deeply embarrassed. "That is, I always thought it would be rather nice to have someone I loved enough to say that to."

I was crying again. I gestured helplessly at myself with a rueful smile. "Now you've done it. And I'd only just managed to stop."

He took my face in his hands, his touch as gentle as anything I'd ever felt. "Is it wrong of me," he said quietly, "to be honored by those tears? That you would show them to me? That you love me that much?"

"Love you? Oh, so you think…you…" I put my hands on his chest, then shook my head in exasperation. "Ryder, I was going to say something clever, but I've lost all capacity for cleverness. Please." I looked up at him. "Take me to bed. I want to see you. I want to be with you, now, right now, on the eve of war. I don't want to think about anything else but that. Is that selfish?"

"Yes," he said, "and beautifully so."

Then he lifted me into his arms, and I wondered if I would ever stop being delighted at how easily he could carry me. I laughed through my tears and wound my arms around his neck. Allowing myself this happiness felt revolutionary. War would come, but tonight, in this house that had seen so much sadness, there would be only this: only the two of us and the silk of my bed. Our hands joined, my legs hooked around his as he moved in me, his voice rough and tender around the shape of my name. The violet gold of sunset paid silent tribute to Yvaine as it danced across our skin. We were alive, and we were together. I buried my face in his neck and held on tight, pressing all of myself against him—my body, my heart, every song my power carried. We were alive, and I would cherish every moment of it.

War would come, but not tonight.

ACKNOWLEDGMENTS

Each of the Ashbourne sisters is dear to me for different reasons. Gemma, I love for her earnest and unabashed passion. Mara, I love for her resilience and courage. And writing Farrin made me fall in love with how devoted she is to those she loves, even when they enrage her, or sadden her, or hurt her. Crafting the story of her and Ryder—two angry souls finally finding peace in each other—was so special to me, and I couldn't have done it without the support of many, many people.

As ever, I'd like to first thank my agent, Victoria Marini, and my editor, Annie Berger, both of whom are two of the most brilliant, most supportive women I know. I could not do what I do without their guidance and belief.

I'd also like to thank the incredible crew at Sourcebooks, who continue to embrace me and my work with enthusiasm and kindness. Special thanks go to Pamela Jaffee, Alyssa Garcia, Jocelyn Travis, Katie Stutz, Madison Nankervis, Siena Koncsol, Ashlyn Keil, Gabbi Calabrese, Emily Luedloff, Stephanie Beard, Ellie Tiemens, Sophie Kossakowski, Mattea Barnes, Megan Donnelly, Rachel Gilmer, Susie Benton, Todd Stocke, and Dominique Raccah.

I must also thank the amazing Stephanie Gafron, associate art director extraordinaire, and artist Nekro for creating this book's truly spectacular cover. And, of course, thank you to my intrepid copy editor, Alison Cherry, whose sharp, thorough work elevates my own.

One of the loveliest things about being an author is becoming friends with other authors, and I'd like to thank a few in particular who have welcomed me so kindly into the romance space—Piper J. Drake, Maxym Martineau, Jeneane O'Riley, Laura Thalassa, Leia Stone, Scarlett St. Clair, B. Celeste, and Danielle Jensen. I'd also like to thank one of my newest and dearest author friends, Kate Dramis, who has held my hand through many an anxiety spiral and who is, it must be said, 100% That Bitch.

And to my friends and family—of whom there are far too many to name—thank you for being my dearest ones, for tirelessly cheering me on, and for being my biggest fans. And last of all, but most certainly not least, thank you to my partner, Ken. I love you with my whole heart.

ABOUT THE AUTHOR

Claire Legrand used to be a musician until she realized she couldn't stop thinking about the stories in her head. Now she is the *New York Times* bestselling author of several novels, including *A Crown of Ivy and Glass*, the Empirium Trilogy, the Edgar Award–nominated *Some Kind of Happiness*, the Bram Stoker Award–nominated *Sawkill Girls*, and *The Cavendish Home for Boys and Girls*.

claire-legrand.com
Instagram: @clairelegrandbooks